EXTRAORDINARY PRAISE FOR SARA BLAEDEL
AND HER ACCLAIMED NOVELS

THE DAUGHTER

"Compelling and unique, THE DAUGHTER delves into a dark and fascinating world rarely explored in suspense fiction. Sara Blaedel knows how to reel in her readers and keep them utterly transfixed."

—Tess Gerritsen, *New York Times* bestselling author
of *I Know a Secret*

"The Danish crime novelist takes a trip Stateside in this exhilaratingly morbid tale of a forty-year-old Copenhagen widow who travels to Wisconsin to run her dead father's funeral home—and is forced to confront the enemies he left behind."

—Oprah.com

"Ilka is a complex and interesting character."

—*RT Book Reviews*

"A great start for mystery lovers looking to dip a toe into international intrigue."

—*Library Journal*

ACCLAIM FOR THE LOUISE RICK SERIES

"Blaedel is one of the best I've come across."

—Michael Connelly

"Crime-writer superstar Sara Blaedel's great skill is in weaving a heartbreaking social history into an edge-of-your-chair thriller while at the same time creating a detective who's as emotionally rich and real as a close friend."

—Oprah.com

"She's a remarkable crime writer who time and again delivers a solid, engaging story that any reader in the world can enjoy."

—Karin Slaughter

"One can count on emotional engagement, spine-tingling suspense, and taut storytelling from Sara Blaedel. Her smart and sensitive character, investigator Louise Rick, will leave readers enthralled and entertained."

—Sandra Brown

"I loved spending time with the tough, smart, and all-too-human heroine Louise Rick—and I can't wait to see her again."

—Lisa Unger

"If you like crime fiction that is genuinely scary, then Sara Blaedel should be the next writer you read."

—Mark Billingham

THE STOLEN ANGEL

"Blaedel keeps everything well-oiled and moving with nary a squeak as she leads the reader through the book to a series of startling and satisfying conclusions."

—BookReporter.com

"This book really takes you on quite a ride. It's dark and twisted, and I was floored when I realized just who the crazy sociopath was behind the evil acts...I never saw that coming! I have to say that one of my favorite aspects of this series is the character development we get. This is an addicting, thrilling read. I was glued to the pages, wondering just what was going to happen next and if Louise and her team were going to figure it all out before it was too late. The mix of police procedural and compelling characters really makes this book (and series!) one you don't want to miss."

—Always with a Book

THE RUNNING GIRL

"Sara Blaedel is amazing. She is in no particular hurry to get things moving in the first part of THE RUNNING GIRL as she begins to set things up, but as secrets and schemes unravel, you will find that you simply cannot read fast enough."

—BookReporter.com

"I found myself completely captivated by this book. There are quite a few twists and turns here and it really does keep you on your toes as you race to the conclusion of this book. I found myself completely engaged and loved that the writing is so vivid and descriptive—it was like I was right there in Copenhagen myself!"

—Always with a Book

THE LOST WOMAN

"Leads to...that gray territory where compassion can become a crime and kindness can lead to cold-blooded murder."
—*New York Times Book Review*

"Blaedel solidifies once more why her novels are as much finely drawn character studies as tightly plotted procedurals, always landing with a punch to the gut and the heart."
—*Library Journal* (starred review)

"Long-held secrets and surprising connections rock Inspector Louise Rick's world in Blaedel's latest crime thriller. Confused and hurt, Louise persists in investigating a complex murder despite the mounting personal ramifications. The limits of loyalty and trust, and the complexities of grief, are central to this taut thriller's resolution. A rich cast of supporting characters balances the bleakness of the crimes."
—*RT Book Reviews* (4 stars)

"Sara Blaedel is a literary force of nature...Blaedel strikes a fine and delicate balance between the personal and the professional in THE LOST WOMAN, as she has done with the other books in this wonderful series...Those who can't get enough of finely tuned mysteries...will find this book and this author particularly riveting."

—BookReporter.com

"Blaedel, Denmark's most popular author, is known for her dark mysteries, and she examines the controversial social issue at the heart of this novel, but ends on a surprisingly light note. Another winner from Blaedel."

—*Booklist*

"Engrossing."

—*Toronto Star*

THE KILLING FOREST

"Another suspenseful, skillfully wrought entry from Denmark's Queen of Crime."

—*Booklist*

"Engrossing...Blaedel nicely balances the twisted relationships of the cult members with the true friendships of Louise, Camilla, and their circle."

—*Publishers Weekly*

"Blaedel delivers another thrilling novel...Twists and turns will have readers on the edge of their seats waiting to see what happens next."

—*RT Book Reviews*

"Will push you to the edge of your seat, [then] knock you right off… A smashing success."

—BookReporter.com

"Blaedel excels at portraying the darkest side of Denmark."

—*Library Journal*

THE FORGOTTEN GIRLS
WINNER OF THE 2015
RT REVIEWER'S CHOICE AWARD

"Crackling with suspense, atmosphere, and drama, THE FORGOTTEN GIRLS is simply stellar crime fiction."

—Lisa Unger

"Chilling… [a] swiftly moving plot and engaging core characters."

—*Publishers Weekly*

"This is a standout book that will only solidify the author's well-respected standing in crime fiction. Blaedel drops clues that will leave readers guessing right up to the reveal. Each new lead opens an array of possibilities, and putting the book down became a feat this reviewer was unable to achieve. Based on the history of treating the disabled, the story is both horrifying and all-too-real. Even the villains have nuanced and sympathetic motives."

—*RT Times* Top Pick, Reviewer's Choice Award Winner

"Already an international bestseller, this outing by Denmark's Queen of Crime offers trademark Scandinavian crime fiction with a tough detective and a very grim mystery. Blaedel is incredibly talented at keeping one reading...Recommend to fans of Camilla Läckberg and Liza Marklund."

—*Library Journal*

"THE FORGOTTEN GIRLS has it all. At its heart, it is a puzzling, intricate mystery whose solution packs a horrific double-punch...Once you start, you will have no choice but to finish it."

—BookReporter.com

"Tautly suspenseful and sociologically fascinating, THE FORGOTTEN GIRLS demonstrates yet again that the finest contemporary suspense fiction emanates from Europe's snowbound north."

—BookPage

"Sara Blaedel's THE FORGOTTEN GIRLS is an emotionally complex police-procedural thriller set in Denmark. With a gripping premise, fast-paced narrative and well-developed characters, THE FORGOTTEN GIRLS is an incredible read."

—FreshFiction.com

"Tightly knit."

—*Kirkus Reviews*

"THE FORGOTTEN GIRLS is without a doubt the best the author has delivered so far...strikingly well done...The chances are good that THE FORGOTTEN GIRLS will become your favorite crime novel for a long time to come."

—*Børsen* (Denmark)

"[THE FORGOTTEN GIRLS] is gripping when it depicts some horrific crimes...[An] uncompromising realism...distinguishes this novel at its best."

—*Washington Post*

THE
DAUGHTER

BOOKS BY
SARA BLAEDEL

THE
DAUGHTER

SARA
BLAEDEL

Translated by Mark Kline
Previously published as *The Undertaker's Daughter*

GRAND CENTRAL
PUBLISHING

New York Boston

The Daughter copyright © 2018 by Sara Blaedel; translated by Mark Kline; translation copyright © 2018 by Sara Blaedel
The Night Women copyright © 2018 by Sara Blaedel; translated by Erik J. Macki and Tara F. Chace; translation © 2012 by Sara Blaedel
Excerpt from *Her Father's Secret* copyright © 2019 by Sara Blaedel; translated by Mark Kline; translation copyright © 2017 by Sara Blaedel

Grand Central Publishing
Hachette Book Group
1290 Avenue of the Americas, New York, NY 10104
grandcentralpublishing.com
twitter.com/grandcentralpub

Originally published in Denmark as *Bedemandens datter* in June 2016
First North American edition published as *The Undertaker's Daughter* in hardcover and ebook in February 2018
First compilation edition: August 2018
First mass market edition: April 2019

Grand Central Publishing is a division of Hachette Book Group, Inc. The Grand Central Publishing name and logo is a trademark of Hachette Book Group, Inc.

The publisher is not responsible for websites (or their content) that are not owned by the publisher.

The Hachette Speakers Bureau provides a wide range of authors for speaking events. To find out more, go to hachettespeakersbureau.com or call (866) 376-6591.

ISBNs: 978-1-5387-6026-0 (mass market), 978-1-4555-4109-6 (ebook)

Printed in the United States of America

OPM

10 9 8 7 6 5 4 3 2 1

To Victoria

THE
DAUGHTER

1

"What do you mean you shouldn't have told me? You should have told me thirty-three years ago."

"What difference would it have made anyway?" Ilka's mother demanded. "You were seven years old. You wouldn't have understood about a liar and a cheat running away with all his winnings; running out on his responsibilities, on his wife and little daughter. He hit the jackpot, Ilka, and then he hit the road. And left me—no, he left *us* with a funeral home too deep in the red to get rid of. And an enormous amount of debt. That he betrayed me is one thing, but abandoning his child?"

Ilka stood at the window, her back to the comfy living room, which was overflowing with books and baskets of yarn. She looked out over the trees in the park across the way. For a moment, the treetops seemed like dizzying black storm waves.

Her mother sat in the glossy Børge Mogensen easy chair in the corner, though now she was worked up from her rant, and her knitting needles clattered twice as fast. Ilka turned to her. "Okay," she said, trying not to sound shrill. "Maybe you're right. Maybe I wouldn't have understood about all that. But you didn't think I was too young to understand that my father was a coward, the way he suddenly left us, and that he didn't love us anymore. That he was an incredible asshole you'd never take back if he ever showed up on our doorstep, begging for forgiveness. As I recall, you had no trouble talking about that, over and over and over."

"Stop it." Her mother had been a grade school teacher for twenty-six years, and now she sounded like one. "But does it make any difference? Think of all the letters you've written him over the years. How often have you reached out to him, asked to see him? Or at least have some form of contact." She sat up and laid her knitting on the small table beside the chair. "He never answered you; he never tried to see you. How long did you save your confirmation money so you could fly over and visit him?"

Ilka knew better than her mother how many letters she had written over the years. What her mother wasn't aware of was that she had kept writing to him, even as an adult. Not as often, but at least a Christmas card and a note on his birthday. Every single year. Which had felt like sending letters into outer space. Yet she'd never stopped.

"You should have told me about the money," Ilka said, unwilling to let it go, even though her mother had a point. Would it really have made a difference? "Why are you telling me now? After all these years. And right when I'm about to leave."

Her mother had called just before eight. Ilka had still been in bed, reading the morning paper on her iPad. "Come over, right now," she'd said. There was something they had to talk about.

Now her mother leaned forward and folded her hands in her lap, her face showing the betrayal and desperation she'd endured. She'd kept her wounds under wraps for half her life, but it was obvious they had never fully healed. "It scares me, you going over there. Your father was a gambler. He bet more money than he had, and the racetrack was a part of our lives for the entire time he lived here. For better and worse. I knew about his habit when we fell in love, but then it got out of control. And almost ruined us several times. In the end, it did ruin us."

"And then he won almost a million kroner and just disappeared." Ilka lifted an eyebrow.

"Well, we do know he went to America." Her mother nodded. "Presumably, he continued gambling over there. And we never heard from him again. That is, until now, of course."

Ilka shook her head. "Right, now that he's dead."

"What I'm trying to say is that we don't know what he's left behind. He could be up to his neck in debt. You're a school photographer, not a millionaire. If you go over there, they might hold you responsible for his debts. And who knows? Maybe they wouldn't allow you to come home. Your father had a dark side he couldn't control. I'll rip his dead body limb from limb if he pulls you down with him, all these years after turning his back on us."

With that, her mother stood and walked down the long hall into the kitchen. Ilka heard muffled voices, and then Hanne appeared in the doorway. "Would you like us to drive you to the airport?" Hanne leaned against the doorframe as Ilka's mother reappeared with a tray of bakery rolls, which she set down on the coffee table.

"No, that's okay," Ilka said.

"How long do you plan on staying?" Hanne asked, moving to the sofa. Ilka's mother curled up in the corner of the sofa, covered herself with a blanket, and put her stockinged feet up on Hanne's lap.

When her mother began living with Hanne fourteen years ago, the last trace of her bitterness finally seemed to evaporate. Now, though, Ilka realized it had only gone into hibernation.

For the first four years after Ilka's father left, her mother had been stuck with Paul Jensen's Funeral Home and its two employees, who cheated her whenever they could get away with it. Throughout Ilka's childhood, her mother had complained constantly about the burden he had dumped on her. Ilka hadn't known until now that her father had also left a sizable gambling debt behind. Apparently, her mother had wanted to spare her, at least to some degree. And, of course, her mother was right. Her father *was* a coward and a selfish jerk. Yet Ilka had never completely accepted his abandonment of her. He had left behind a short letter saying he would come back for them as soon as everything was taken care of, and that an opportunity had come up. In Chicago.

Several years later, after complete silence on his part, he wanted a divorce. And that was the last they'd heard from him. When Ilka was a teenager, she found his address—or at least, an address where he had once lived. She'd kept it all these years in a small red treasure chest in her room.

"Surely it won't take more than a few days," Ilka said. "I'm planning to be back by the weekend. I'm booked up at work, but I found someone to fill in for me the first two days. It would be a great help if you two could keep trying to get hold of Niels from North Sealand Photography. He's in Stockholm, but he's supposed to be back tomorrow. I'm hoping he can cover for me the rest of the week. All the shoots are in and around Copenhagen."

"What exactly are you hoping to accomplish over there?" Hanne asked.

"Well, they say I'm in his will and that I have to be there in person to prove I'm Paul Jensen's daughter."

"I just don't understand why this can't be done by e-mail or fax," her mother said. "You can send them your birth certificate and your passport, or whatever it is they need."

"It seems that copies aren't good enough. If I don't go over there, I'd have to go to an American tax office in Europe, and I think the nearest one is in London. But this way, they'll let me go through his personal things and take what I want. Artie Sorvino from Jensen Funeral Home in Racine has offered to cover my travel expenses if I go now, so they can get started with closing his estate."

Ilka stood in the middle of the living room, too anxious and restless to sit down.

"Racine?" Hanne asked. "Where's that?" She picked up her steaming cup and blew on it.

"A bit north of Chicago. In Wisconsin. I'll be picked up at the airport, and it doesn't look like it'll take long to drive there. Racine is supposedly the city in the United States with the largest community of Danish descendants. A lot of Danes immigrated to the region, so it makes sense that's where he settled."

"He has a hell of a lot of nerve." Her mother's lips barely moved. "He doesn't write so much as a birthday card to you all these years, and now suddenly you have to fly over there and clean up another one of his messes."

"Karin," Hanne said, her voice gentle. "Of course Ilka should go over and sort through her father's things. If you get the opportunity for closure on such an important part of your life's story, you should grab it."

Her mother shook her head. Without looking at Ilka, she said, "I have a bad feeling about this. Isn't it odd that he stayed in the undertaker business even though he managed to ruin his first shot at it?"

Ilka walked out into the hall and let the two women bicker about the unfairness of it all. How Paul's daughter had tried to reach out to her father all her life, and it was only now that he was gone that he was finally reaching out to her.

2

The first thing Ilka noticed was his Hawaiian shirt and longish brown hair, which was combed back and held in place by sunglasses that would look at home on a surfer. He stood out among the other drivers at Arrivals in O'Hare International Airport who were holding name cards and facing the scattered clumps of exhausted people pulling suitcases out of Customs.

Written on his card was "Ilka Nichols Jensen." Somehow, she managed to walk all the way up to him and stop before he realized she'd found him.

They looked each other over for a moment. He was in his early forties, maybe, she thought. So, her father, who had turned seventy-two in early January, had a younger partner.

She couldn't read his face, but it might have surprised him that the undertaker's daughter was a beanpole: six feet tall without a hint of a feminine form. He scanned her up and down, gaze settling on her hair, which had never been an attention-getter. Straight, flat, and mousy.

He smiled warmly and held out his hand. "Nice to meet you. Welcome to Chicago."

It's going to be a hell of a long trip, Ilka thought, before shaking his hand and saying hello. "Thank you. Nice to meet you, too."

He offered to carry her suitcase. It was small, a carry-on, but she gladly handed it over to him. Then he offered her a bottle of water. The car was close by, he said, only a short walk.

Although she was used to being taller than most people, she always felt a bit shy when male strangers had to look up to make eye contact. She was nearly a head taller than Artie Sorvino, but he seemed almost impressed as he grinned up at her while they walked.

Her body ached; she hadn't slept much during the long flight. Since she'd left her apartment in Copenhagen, her nerves had been tingling with excitement. And worry, too. Things had almost gone wrong right off the bat at the Copenhagen airport, because she hadn't taken into account the long line at Passport Control. There had still been two people in front of her when she'd been called to her waiting flight. Then the arrival in the US, a hell that the chatty man next to her on the plane had prepared her for. He had missed God knew how many connecting flights at O'Hare because the immigration line had taken several hours to go through. It turned out to be not quite as bad as all that. She had been guided to a machine that requested her fingerprints, passport, and picture. All this information was scanned and saved. Then Ilka had been sent on to the next line, where a surly passport official wanted to know what her business was in the country. She began to sweat but then pulled herself together and explained that she was simply visiting family, which in a way was true. He stamped her passport, and moments later she was standing beside the man wearing the colorful, festive shirt.

"Is this your first trip to the US?" Artie asked now, as they approached the enormous parking lot.

She smiled. "No, I've traveled here a few times. To Miami and New York."

Why had she said that? She'd never been in this part of the world before, but what the hell. It didn't matter. Unless he kept up the conversation. And Miami. Where had that come from?

"Really?" Artie told her he had lived in Key West for many years. Then his father got sick, and Artie, the only other surviving member of the family, moved back to Racine to take care of him. "I hope you made it down to the Keys while you were in Florida."

Ilka shook her head and explained that she unfortunately hadn't had time.

"I had a gallery down there," Artie said. He'd gone to the California School of the Arts in San Francisco and had made his living as an artist.

Ilka listened politely and nodded. In the parking lot, she caught sight of a gigantic black Cadillac with closed white curtains in back, which stood first in the row of parked cars. He'd driven there in the hearse.

"Hope you don't mind." He nodded at the hearse as he opened the rear door and placed her suitcase on the casket table used for rolling coffins in and out of the vehicle.

"No, it's fine." She walked around to the front passenger door. Fine, as long as she wasn't the one being rolled into the back. She felt slightly dizzy, as if she were still up in the air, but was buoyed by the nervous excitement of traveling and the anticipation of what awaited her.

The thought that her father was at the end of her journey bothered her, yet it was something she'd fantasized about nearly her entire life. But would she be able to piece together the life he'd lived without her? And was she even interested in knowing about it? What if she didn't like what she learned?

She shook her head for a moment. These thoughts had been swirling in her head since Artie's first phone call. Her mother thought she shouldn't get involved. At all. But Ilka disagreed. If her father had left anything behind, she wanted to see it. She wanted to uncover whatever she could find, to see if any of it made sense.

"How did he die?" she asked as Artie maneuvered the long hearse out of the parking lot and in between two orange signs warning about roadwork and a detour.

"Just a sec," he muttered, and he swore at the sign before deciding to skirt the roadwork and get back to the road heading north.

For a while they drove in silence; then he explained that one morning her father had simply not woken up. "He was supposed to drive a corpse to Iowa, one of our neighboring states, but he didn't show up. He just died in his sleep. Totally peacefully. He might not even have known it was over."

Ilka watched the Chicago suburbs drifting by along the long, straight bypass, the rows of anonymous stores and cheap restaurants. It seemed so overwhelming, so strange, so different. Most buildings were painted in shades of beige and brown, and enormous billboards stood everywhere, screaming messages about everything from missing children to ultracheap fast food and vanilla coffee for less than a dollar at Dunkin' Donuts.

She turned to Artie. "Was he sick?" The bump on Artie's nose—had it been broken?—made it appear too big for the rest of his face: high cheekbones, slightly squinty eyes, beard stubble definitely due to a relaxed attitude toward shaving, rather than wanting to be in style.

"Not that I know of, no. But there could have been things Paul didn't tell me about, for sure."

His tone told her it wouldn't have been the first secret Paul had kept from him.

"The doctor said his heart just stopped," he continued. "Nothing dramatic happened."

"Did he have a family?" She looked out the side window. The old hearse rode well. Heavy, huge, swaying lightly. A tall pickup drove up beside them; a man with a full beard looked down and nodded at her. She looked away quickly. She didn't care for any sympathetic looks, though he, of course, couldn't know the curtained-off back of the hearse was empty.

"He was married, you know," Artie said. Immediately Ilka sensed he didn't like being the one to fill her in on her father's private affairs. She nodded to herself; of course he didn't. What did she expect?

"And he had two daughters. That was it, apart from Mary Ann's family, but I don't know them. How much do you know about them?"

He knew very well that Ilka hadn't had any contact with her father since he'd left Denmark. Or at least she assumed he knew. "Why has the family not signed what should be signed, so you can finish with his…estate?" She set the empty water bottle on the floor.

"They did sign their part of it. But that's not enough, because you're in the will, too. First the IRS—that's our tax agency—must determine if he owes the government, and you must give them permission to investigate. If you don't sign, they'll freeze all the assets in the estate until everything is cleared up."

Ilka's shoulders slumped at the word "assets." One thing that had kept her awake during the flight was her mother's concern about her being stuck with a debt she could never pay. Maybe she would be detained; maybe she would even be thrown in jail.

"What are his daughters like?" she asked after they had driven for a while in silence.

For a few moments, he kept his eyes on the road; then he glanced at her and shrugged. "They're nice enough, but I don't really know them. It's been a long time since I've seen them. Truth is, I don't think either of them was thrilled about your father's business."

After another silence, Ilka said, "You should have called me when he died. I wish I had been at his funeral."

Was that really true? Did she truly wish that? The last funeral she'd been to was her husband's. He had collapsed from heart failure three years ago, at the age of fifty-two. She didn't like death, didn't like loss. But she'd already lost her father many years ago, so what difference would it have made watching him being lowered into the ground?

"At that time, I didn't know about you," Artie said. "Your name first came up when your father's lawyer mentioned you."

"Where is he buried?"

He stared straight ahead. Again, it was obvious he didn't enjoy talking about her father's private life. Finally, he said, "Mary Ann decided to keep the urn with his ashes at home. A private ceremony was held in the living room when the crematorium delivered the urn, and now it's on the shelf above the fireplace."

After a pause, he said, "You speak English well. Funny accent."

Ilka explained distractedly that she had traveled in Australia for a year after high school.

The billboards along the freeway here advertised hotels,

motels, and drive-ins for the most part. She wondered how there could be enough people to keep all these businesses going, given the countless offers from the clusters of signs on both sides of the road. "What about his new family? Surely they knew he had a daughter in Denmark?" She turned back to him.

"Nope!" He shook his head as he flipped the turn signal.

"He never told them he left his wife and seven-year-old daughter?" She wasn't all that surprised.

Artie didn't answer. *Okay*, Ilka thought. *That takes care of that.*

"I wonder what they think about me coming here."

He shrugged. "I don't really know, but they're not going to lose anything. His wife has an inheritance from her wealthy parents, so she's taken care of. The same goes for the daughters. And none of them had ever shown any interest in the funeral home."

And what about their father? Ilka thought. *Were they uninterested in him, too?* But that was none of her business. She didn't know them, knew nothing about their relationships with one another. And for that matter, she knew nothing about her father. Maybe his new family had asked about his life in Denmark, and maybe he'd given them a line of bullshit. But what the hell, he was thirty-nine when he left. Anyone could figure out he'd had a life before packing his weekend bag and emigrating.

Both sides of the freeway were green now. The landscape was starting to remind her of late summer in Denmark, with its green fields, patches of forest, flat land, large barns with the characteristic bowed roofs, and livestock. With a few exceptions, she felt like she could have been driving down the E45, the road between Copenhagen and Ålborg.

"Do you mind if I turn on the radio?" Artie asked.

She shook her head; it was a relief to have the awkward silence between them broken. And yet, before his hand reached the radio, she blurted out, "What was he like?"

He dropped his hand and smiled at her. "Your father was a decent guy, a really decent guy. In a lot of ways," he added, disarmingly, "he was someone you could count on, and in other ways he was very much his own man. I always enjoyed working with him, but he was also my friend. People liked him; he was interested in their lives. That's also why he was so good at talking to those who had just lost someone. He was empathetic. It feels empty, him not being around any longer."

Ilka had to concentrate to follow along. Despite her year in Australia, it was difficult when people spoke English rapidly. "Was he also a good father?"

Artie turned thoughtfully and looked out his side window. "I really can't say. I didn't know him when the girls were small." He kept glancing at the four lanes to their left. "But if you're asking me if your father was a family man, my answer is, yes and no. He was very much in touch with his family, but he probably put more of himself into Jensen Funeral Home."

"How long did you know him?"

She watched him calculate. "I moved back in 1998. We ran into each other at a local saloon, this place called Oh Dennis!, and we started talking. The victim of a traffic accident had just come in to the funeral home. The family wanted to put the young woman in an open coffin, but nobody would have wanted to see her face. So I offered to help. It's the kind of stuff I'm good at. Creating, shaping. Your father did the embalming, but I reconstructed her face. Her mother supplied us with a photo, and I did a sculpture.

And I managed to make the woman look like herself, even though there wasn't much to work with. Later your father offered me a job, and I grabbed the chance. There's not much work for an artist in Racine, so reconstructions of the deceased was as good as anything."

He turned off the freeway. "Later I got a degree, because you have to have a license to work in the undertaker business."

They reached Racine Street and waited to make a left turn. They had driven the last several miles in silence. The streets were deserted, the shops closed. It was getting dark, and Ilka realized she was at the point where exhaustion and jet lag trumped the hunger gnawing inside her. They drove by an empty square and a nearly deserted saloon. Oh Dennis!, the place where Artie had met her father. She spotted the lake at the end of the broad streets to the right, and that was it. The town was dead. Abandoned, closed. She was surprised there were no people or life.

"We've booked a room for you at the Harbourwalk Hotel. Tomorrow we can sit down and go through your father's papers. Then you can start looking through his things."

Ilka nodded. All she wanted right now was a warm bath and a bed.

"Sorry, we have no reservations for Miss Jensen. And none for the Jensen Funeral Home, either. We don't have a single room available."

The receptionist drawled apology after apology. It sounded to Ilka as if she had too much saliva in her mouth.

Ilka sat in a plush armchair in the lobby as Artie asked if the room was reserved in his name. "Or try Sister Eileen O'Connor," he suggested.

The receptionist apologized again as her long fingernails

danced over the computer keyboard. The sound was unnaturally loud, a bit like Ilka's mother's knitting needles tapping against each other.

Ilka shut down. She could sit there and sleep; it made absolutely no difference to her. Back in Denmark, it was five in the morning, and she hadn't slept in twenty-two hours.

"I'm sorry," Artie said. "You're more than welcome to stay at my place. I can sleep on the sofa. Or we can fix up a place for you to sleep at the office, and we'll find another hotel in the morning."

Ilka sat up in the armchair. "What's that sound?"

Artie looked bewildered. "What do you mean?"

"It's like a phone ringing in the next room."

He listened for a moment before shrugging. "I can't hear anything."

The sound came every ten seconds. It was as if something were hidden behind the reception desk or farther down the hotel foyer. Ilka shook her head and looked at him. "You don't need to sleep on the sofa. I can sleep somewhere at the office."

She needed to be alone, and the thought of a strange man's bedroom didn't appeal to her.

"That's fine." He grabbed her small suitcase. "It's only five minutes away, and I know we can find some food for you, too."

The black hearse was parked just outside the main entrance of the hotel, but that clearly wasn't bothering anyone. Though the hotel was apparently fully booked, Ilka hadn't seen a single person since they'd arrived.

Night had fallen, and her eyelids closed as soon as she settled into the car. She jumped when Artie opened the door

and poked her with his finger. She hadn't even realized they
had arrived. They were parked in a large, empty lot. The
white building was an enormous box with several attic windows reflecting the moonlight back into the thick darkness.
Tall trees with enormous crowns hovered over Ilka when
she got out of the car.

They reached the door, beside which was a sign: JENSEN
FUNERAL HOME. WELCOME. Pillars stood all the way across
the broad porch, with well-tended flower beds in front of it,
but the darkness covered everything else.

Artie led her inside the high-ceilinged hallway and
turned the light on. He pointed to a stairway at the other end.
Ilka's feet sank deep in the carpet; it smelled dusty, with a
hint of plastic and instant coffee.

"Would you like something to drink? Are you hungry? I
can make a sandwich."

"No, thank you." She just wanted him to leave.

He led her up the stairs, and when they reached a small
landing, he pointed at a door. "Your father had a room in
there, and I think we can find some sheets. We have a cot
we can fold out and make up for you."

Ilka held her hand up. "If there is a bed in my father's
room, I can just sleep in it." She nodded when he asked if
she was sure. "What time do you want to meet tomorrow?"

"How about eight thirty? We can have breakfast
together."

She had no idea what time it was, but as long as she got
some sleep, she guessed she'd be fine. She nodded.

Ilka stayed outside on the landing while Artie opened
the door to her father's room and turned on the light. She
watched him walk over to a dresser and pull out the bottom
drawer. He grabbed some sheets and a towel and tossed
them on the bed; then he waved her in.

18 SARA BLAEDEL

The room's walls were slanted. An old white bureau stood at the end of the room, and under the window, which must have been one of those she'd noticed from the parking lot, was a desk with drawers on both sides. The bed was just inside the room and to the left. There was also a small coffee table and, at the end of the bed, a narrow built-in closet.

A dark jacket and a tie lay draped over the back of the desk chair. The desk was covered with piles of paper; a briefcase leaned against the closet. But there was nothing but sheets on the bed.

"I'll find a comforter and a pillow," Artie said, accidentally grazing her as he walked by.

Ilka stepped into the room. A room lived in, yet abandoned. A feeling suddenly stirred inside her, and she froze. He was here. The smell. A heavy yet pleasant odor she recognized from somewhere deep inside. She'd had no idea this memory existed. She closed her eyes and let her mind drift back to when she was very young, the feeling of being held. Tobacco. Sundays in the car, driving out to Bellevue. Feeling secure, knowing someone close was taking care of her. Lifting her up on a lap. Making her laugh. The sound of hooves pounding the ground, horses at a racetrack. Her father's concentration as he chain-smoked, captivated by the race. His laughter.

She sat down on the bed, not hearing what Artie said when he laid the comforter and pillow beside her, then walked out and closed the door.

Her father had been tall; at least that's how she remembered him. She could see to the end of the world when she sat on his shoulders. They did fun things together. He took her to an amusement park and bought her ice cream while he tried out the slot machines, to see

if they were any good. Her mother didn't always know
when they went there. He also took her out to a centuries-
old amusement park in the forest north of Copenhagen.
They stopped at Peter Liep's, and she drank soda while
he drank beer. They sat outside and watched the riders
pass by, smelling horseshit and sweat when the thirsty
riders dismounted and draped the reins over the hitch-
ing post. He had loved horses. On the other hand, she
couldn't remember the times—the many times, according
to her mother—when he didn't come home early enough
to stick his head in her room and say good night. Not
having enough money for food because he had gambled
his wages away at the track was something else she didn't
recall—but her mother did.

Ilka opened her eyes. Her exhaustion was gone, but
she still felt dizzy. She walked over to the desk and
reached for a photo in a wide mahogany frame. A trotter,
its mane flying out to both sides at the finishing line. In
another photo, a trotter covered by a red victory blanket
stood beside a sulky driver holding a trophy high above
his head, smiling for the camera. There were several more
horse photos, and a ticket to Lunden hung from a window
hasp. She grabbed it. Paul Jensen. Charlottenlund Derby
1982. The year he left them.

Ilka didn't realize at the time that he had left. All she
knew was that one morning he wasn't there, and her mother
was crying but wouldn't tell her why. When she arrived
home from school that afternoon, her mother was still crying. And as she remembered it, her mother didn't stop
crying for a long time.

She had been with her father at that derby in 1982. She
picked up a photo leaning against the windowsill, then sat
down on the bed. "Ilka and Peter Kjærsgaard" was writ-

ten on the back of the photo. Ilka had been five years old when her father took her to the derby for the first time. Back then, her mother had gone along. She vaguely remembered going to the track and meeting the famous jockey, but suddenly the odors and sounds were crystal clear. She closed her eyes.

"You can give them one if you want," the man had said as he handed her a bucket filled with carrots, many more than her mother had in bags back in their kitchen. The bucket was heavy, but Ilka wanted to show them how big she was, so she hooked the handle with her arm and walked over to one of the stalls.

She smiled proudly at a red-shirted sulky driver passing by as he was fastening his helmet. The track was crowded, but during the races, few people were allowed in the barn. They were, though. She and her father.

She pulled her hand back, frightened, when the horse in the stall whinnied and pulled against the chain. It snorted and pounded its hoof on the floor. The horse was so tall. Carefully she held the carrot out in the palm of her hand, as her father had taught her to do. The horse snatched the sweet treat, gently tickling her.

Her father stood with a group of men at the end of the row of stalls. They laughed loudly, slapping one another's shoulders. A few of them drank beer from bottles. Ilka sat down on a bale of hay. Her father had promised her a horse when she was a bit older. One of the grooms came over and asked if she would like a ride behind the barn; he was going to walk one of the horses to warm it up. She wanted to, if her father would let her. He did.

"Look at me, Daddy!" Ilka cried. "Look at me." The horse had stopped, clearly preferring to eat grass rather than walk. She kicked gently to get it going, but her legs were too short to do any good.

Her father pulled himself away from the other men and stood at the barn entrance. He waved, and Ilka sat up proudly. The groom asked if he should let go of the reins so she could ride by herself, and though she didn't really love the idea, she nodded. But when he dropped the reins and she turned around to show her father how brave she was, he was back inside with the others.

Ilka stood up and put the photo back. She could almost smell the tar used by the racetrack farrier on horse hooves. She used to sit behind a pane of glass with her mother and follow the races, while her father stood over at the finish line. But then her mother stopped going along.

She picked up another photo from the windowsill. She was standing on a bale of hay, toasting with a sulky driver. Fragments of memories flooded back as she studied herself in the photo. Her father speaking excitedly with the driver, his expression as the horses were hitched to the sulkies. And the way he said, "We-e-e-ell, shall we...?" right before a race. Then he would hold his hand out, and they would walk down to the track.

She wondered why she could remember these things, when she had forgotten most of what had happened back then.

There was also a photo of two small girls on the desk. She knew these were her younger half sisters, who were smiling broadly at the photographer. Suddenly, deep inside her chest, she felt a sharp twinge—but why? After setting the photo back down, she realized it wasn't from never having met her half sisters. No. It was pure jealousy. They had grown up with her father, while she had been abandoned.

Ilka threw herself down on the bed and pulled the comforter over her, without even bothering to put the sheets on. She lay curled up, staring into space.

3

At some point, Ilka must have fallen asleep, because she gave a start when someone knocked on the door. She recognized Artie's voice.

"Morning in there. Are you awake?"

She sat up, confused. She had been up once in the night to look for a bathroom. The building seemed strangely hushed, as if it were packed in cotton. She'd opened a few doors and finally found a bathroom with shiny tiles and a low bathtub. The toilet had a soft cover on its seat, like the one in her grandmother's flat in Bagsværd. On her way back, she had grabbed her father's jacket, carried it to the bed, and buried her nose in it. Now it lay halfway on the floor.

"Give me half an hour," she said. She hugged the jacket, savoring the odor that had brought her childhood memories to the surface from the moment she'd walked into the room.

Now that it was light outside, the room seemed bigger. Last night she hadn't noticed the storage boxes lining the wall behind both sides of the desk. Clean shirts in clear plastic sacks hung from the hook behind the door.

"Okay, but have a look at these IRS forms," he said, sliding a folder under the door. "And sign on the last page when you've read them. We'll take off whenever you're ready."

Ilka didn't answer. She pulled her knees up to her chest and lay curled up. Without moving. Being shut up inside a room with her father's belongings was enough to make her feel she'd reunited with a part of herself. The big black hole inside her, the one that had appeared every time she sent a letter despite knowing she'd get no answer, was slowly filling up with something she'd failed to find herself.

She had lived about a sixth of her life with her father. *When do we become truly conscious of the people around us?* she wondered. She had just turned forty, and he had deserted them when she was seven. This room here was filled with everything he had left behind, all her memories of him. All the odors and sensations that had made her miss him.

Artie knocked on the door again. She had no idea how long she'd been lying on the bed.

"Ready?" he called out.

"No," she yelled back. She couldn't. She needed to just stay and take in everything here, so it wouldn't disappear again.

"Have you read it?"

"I signed it!"

"Would you rather stay here? Do you want me to go alone?"

"Yes, please."

Silence. She couldn't tell if he was still outside.

"Okay," he finally said. "I'll come back after breakfast." He sounded annoyed. "I'll leave the phone here with you."

Ilka listened to him walk down the stairs. After she'd walked over to the door and signed her name, she hadn't moved a muscle. She hadn't opened any drawers or closets.

She'd brought along a bag of chips, but they were all gone. And she didn't feel like going downstairs for something to drink. Instead, she gave way to exhaustion. The stream of thoughts, the fragments of memories in her head, had slowly settled into a tempo she could follow.

Her father had written her into his will. He had declared her to be his biological daughter. But evidently, he'd never mentioned her to his new family, or to the people closest to him in his new life. Of course, he hadn't been obligated to mention her, she thought. But if her name hadn't come up in his will, they could have liquidated his business without anyone knowing about an adult daughter in Denmark.

The telephone outside the door rang, but she ignored it. What had this Artie guy imagined she should do if the telephone rang? Did he think she would answer it? And say what?

At first, she'd wondered why her father had named her in his will. But after having spent the last twelve hours enveloped in memories of him, she had realized that no matter what had happened in his life, a part of him had still been her father.

She cried, then felt herself dozing off.

Someone knocked on the door. "Not today," she yelled, before Artie could even speak a word. She turned her back to the room, her face to the wall. She closed her eyes until the footsteps disappeared down the stairs.

The telephone rang again, but she didn't react.

Slowly it had all come back. After her father had disappeared, her mother had two jobs: the funeral home business and her teaching. It wasn't long after summer vacation, and school had just begun. Ilka thought he had left in September. A month before she turned eight. Her mother taught Danish and arts and crafts to students in several grades. When she wasn't at school, she was at the funeral home on Brønshøj Square. Also on weekends, picking up flowers and ordering coffins. Working in the office, keeping the books when she wasn't filling out forms.

Ilka had gone along with her to various embassies whenever a mortuary passport was needed to bring a corpse home from outside the country, or when a person died in Denmark and was to be buried elsewhere. It had been fascinating, though frightening. But she had never fully understood how hard her mother worked. Finally, when Ilka was twelve, her mother managed to sell the business and get back her life.

After her father left, they were unable to afford the single-story house Ilka had been born in. They moved into a small apartment on Frederikssundsvej in Copenhagen. Her mother had never been shy about blaming her father for their economic woes, but she'd always said they would be okay. After she sold the funeral home, their situation had improved; Ilka saw it mostly from the color in her mother's cheeks, a more relaxed expression on her face. Also, she was more likely to let Ilka invite friends home for dinner. When she started eighth grade, they moved to Østerbro, a better district in the city, but she stayed in her school in Brønshøj and took the bus.

"You *were* an asshole," she muttered, her face still to the wall. "What you did was just completely inexcusable."

The telephone outside the door finally gave up. She heard soft steps out on the stairs. She sighed. They had paid her airfare; there were limits to what she could get away with. But today was out of the question. And that telephone was their business.

Someone knocked again at the door. This time it

sounded different. They knocked again. "Hello." A female voice. The woman called her name and knocked one more time, gently but insistently.

Ilka rose from the bed. She shook her hair and slipped it behind her ears and smoothed her T-shirt. She walked over and opened the door. She couldn't hide her startled expression at the sight of a woman dressed in gray, her hair covered by a veil of the same color. Her broad, demure skirt reached below the knees. Her eyes seemed far too big for her small face and delicate features.

"Who are you?"

"My name is Sister Eileen O'Connor, and you have a meeting in ten minutes."

The woman was already about to turn and walk back down the steps, when Ilka finally got hold of herself. "I have a meeting?"

"Yes, the business is yours now." Ilka heard patience as well as suppressed annoyance in the nun's voice. "Artie has left for the day and has informed me that you have taken over."

"*My* business?" Ilka ran her hand through her hair. A bad habit of hers, when she didn't know what to do with her hands.

"You did read the papers Artie left for you? It's my understanding that you signed them, so you're surely aware of what you have inherited."

"I signed to say I'm his daughter," Ilka said. More than anything, she just wanted to close the door and make everything go away.

"If you had read what was written," the sister said, a bit sharply, "you would know that your father has left the business to you. And by your signature, you have acknowledged your identity and therefore your inheritance."

Ilka was speechless. While she gawked, the sister added, "The Norton family lost their grandmother last night. It wasn't unexpected, but several of them are taking it hard. I've made coffee for four." She stared at Ilka's T-shirt and bare legs. "And it's our custom to receive relatives in attire that is a bit more respectful."

A tiny smile played on her narrow lips, so fleeting that Ilka was in doubt as to whether it had actually appeared. "I can't talk to a family that just lost someone," she protested. "I don't know what to say. I've never—I'm sorry, you have to talk to them."

Sister Eileen stood for a moment before speaking. "Unfortunately, I can't. I don't have the authority to perform such duties. I do the office work, open mail, and laminate the photos of the deceased onto death notices for relatives to use as bookmarks. But you will do fine. Your father was always good at such conversations. All you have to do is allow the family to talk. Listen and find out what's important to them; that's the most vital thing for people who come to us. And these people have a contract for a prepaid ceremony. The contract explains everything they have paid for. Mrs. Norton has been making funeral payments her whole life, so everything should be smooth sailing."

The nun walked soundlessly down the stairs. Ilka stood in the doorway, staring at where she had vanished. Had she seriously inherited a funeral home? In the US? How had her life taken such an unexpected turn? What the hell had her father been thinking?

She pulled herself together. She had seven minutes before the Nortons arrived. "Respectful" attire, the sister had said. Did she even have something like that in her suitcase? She hadn't opened it yet.

But she couldn't do this. They couldn't make her talk

to total strangers who had just lost a relative. Then she remembered she hadn't known the undertaker who helped her when Erik died either. But he had been a salvation to her. A person who had taken care of everything in a professional manner and arranged things precisely as she believed her husband would have wanted. The funeral home, the flowers—yellow tulips. The hymns. It was also the undertaker who had said she would regret it if she didn't hire an organist to play during the funeral. Because even though it might seem odd, the mere sound of it helped relieve the somber atmosphere. She had chosen the cheapest coffin, as the undertaker had suggested, seeing that Erik had wanted to be cremated. Many minor decisions had been made for her; that had been an enormous relief. And the funeral had gone exactly the way she'd wanted. Plus, the undertaker had helped reserve a room at the restaurant where they gathered after the ceremony. But those types of details were apparently already taken care of here. It seemed all she had to do was meet with them. She walked over to her suitcase.

Ilka dumped everything out onto the bed and pulled a light blouse and dark pants out of the pile, along with her toiletry bag and underwear. Halfway down the stairs, she remembered she needed shoes. She went back up again. All she had was sneakers.

The family was three adult children—a daughter and two sons—and a grandchild. The two men seemed essentially composed, while the woman and the boy were crying. The woman's face was stiff and pale, as if every ounce of blood had drained out of her. Her young son stared down at his hands, looking withdrawn and gloomy.

"Our mother paid for everything in advance," one son said when Ilka walked in. They sat in the arrangement room's comfortable armchairs, around a heavy mahogany table. Dusty paintings in elegant gilded frames hung from the dark green walls. Ilka guessed the paintings were inspired by Lake Michigan. She had no idea what to do with the grieving family, nor what was expected of her.

The son farthest from the door asked, "How does the condolences and tributes page on your website work? Is it like anyone can go in and write on it, or can it only be seen if you have the password? We want everybody to be able to put up a picture of our mother and write about their good times with her."

Ilka nodded to him and walked over to shake his hand. "We will make the page so it's exactly how you want it." Then she repeated their names: Steve—the one farthest from the door—Joe, Helen, and the grandson, Pete. At least she thought that was right, though she wasn't sure because he had mumbled his name.

"And we talked it over and decided we want charms," Helen said. "We'd all like one. But I can't see in the papers whether they're paid for or not, because if not we need to know how much they cost."

Ilka had no idea what charms were, but she'd noticed the green form that had been laid on the table for her, and a folder entitled "Norton," written by hand. The thought struck her that the handwriting must be her father's.

"Service Details" was written on the front of the form. Ilka sat down and reached for the notebook on the table. It had a big red heart on the cover, along with "Helping Hands for Healing Hearts."

She surmised the notebook was probably meant for the relatives. Quickly, she slid it over the table to them; then she opened a drawer and found a sheet of paper. "I'm very sorry," she said. It was difficult for her not to look at the grandson, who appeared crushed. "About your loss. As I understand, everything is already decided. But I wasn't here when things were planned. Maybe we can go through everything together and figure out exactly how you want it done."

What in the world is going on? she thought as she sat there blabbering away at this grieving family, as if she'd been doing it all her life!

"Our mother liked Mr. Jensen a lot," Steve said. "He took charge of the funeral arrangements when our father died, and we'd like things done the same way."

Ilka nodded.

"But not the coffin," Joe said. "We want one that's more upscale, more feminine."

"Is it possible to see the charms?" Helen asked, still tearful. "And we also need to print a death notice, right?"

"Can you arrange it so her dogs can sit up by the coffin during the service?" Steve asked. He looked at Ilka as if this were the most important of all the issues. "That won't be a problem, will it?"

"No, not a problem," she answered quickly, as the questions rained down on her.

"How many people can fit in there? And can we all sit together?"

"The room can hold a lot of people," she said, feeling now as if she'd been fed to the lions. "We can squeeze the chairs together; we can get a lot of people in there. And of course you can sit together."

Ilka had absolutely no idea what room they were talking about. But there had been about twenty people attending her husband's service, and they hadn't even filled a corner of the chapel in Bispebjerg.

"How many do you think are coming?" she asked, just to be on the safe side.

"Probably somewhere between a hundred and a hundred and fifty," Joe guessed. "That's how many showed up at Dad's service. But it could be more this time, so it's good to be prepared. She was very active after her retirement. And the choir would like to sing."

Ilka nodded mechanically and forced a smile. She had heard that it's impossible to vomit while you're smiling, something about reflexes. Not that she was about to vomit; there was nothing inside her to come out. But her insides contracted as if something in there was getting out of control. "How did Mrs. Norton die?" She leaned back in her chair.

She felt their eyes on her, and for a moment everyone was quiet. The adults looked at her as if the question weren't her business. And maybe it was irrelevant for the planning, she thought. But after Erik died, in a way it had been a big relief to talk about him, how she had come home and found him on the kitchen floor. Putting it into words made it all seem more real, like it actually had happened. And it had helped her through the days after his death, which otherwise were foggy.

Helen sat up and looked over at her son, who was still staring at his hands. "Pete's the one who found her. We bought groceries for his grandma three times a week and drove them over to her after school. And there she was, out in the yard. Just lying there."

Now Ilka regretted having asked.

From underneath the hair hanging over his forehead, with his head bowed, the boy scowled at his mother. "Grandma was out cutting flowers to put in vases, and she fell," he muttered.

"There was a lot of blood," his mother said, nodding.

"But the guy who picked her up promised we wouldn't be able to see it when she's in her coffin," Steve said. He looked at Ilka, as if he wanted this confirmed.

Quickly she answered, "No, you won't. She'll look fine. Did she like flowers?"

Helen smiled and nodded. "She lived and breathed for her garden. She loved her flower beds."

"Then maybe it's a good idea to use flowers from her garden to decorate the coffin," Ilka suggested.

Steve sat up. "Decorate the coffin? It's going to be open."

"But it's a good idea," Helen said. "We'll decorate the chapel with flowers from the garden. We can go over and pick them together. It's a beautiful way to say good-bye to the garden she loved, too."

"But if we use hers, will we get the money back we already paid for flowers?" Joe asked.

Ilka nodded. "Yes, of course." Surely it wasn't a question of all that much money.

"Oh God!" Helen said. "I almost forgot to give you this." Out of her bag she pulled a large folder that said "Family Record Guide" and handed it over to Ilka. "It's already filled out."

In many ways, it reminded Ilka of the diaries she'd kept in school. First a page with personal information. The full name of the deceased, the parents' names. Whether she was married, divorced, single, or a widow. Education and job positions. Then a page with familial relations, and on the opposite page there was room to write about the deceased's life and memories. There were sections for writing about a first home, about becoming a parent, about becoming a grandparent. And then a section that caught Ilka's attention, because it had to be of some use. Favorites: colors, flowers, season, songs, poems, books. And on and on it went. Family traditions. Funny memories, role models, hobbies, special talents. Mrs. Norton had filled it all out very thoroughly.

Ilka closed the folder and asked how they would describe their mother and grandmother.

"She was very sociable," Joe said. "Also after Dad died. She was involved in all sorts of things; she was very active in the seniors' club in West Racine."

"And family meant a lot to her," Helen said. She'd stopped crying without Ilka noticing. "She was always the one who made sure we all got together, at least twice a year."

Ilka let them speak, as long as they stayed away from talking about charms and choosing coffins. She had no idea how to wind up the conversation, but she kept listening as they nearly all talked at once, to make sure that everything about the deceased came out. Even gloomy Pete added that his grandmother made the world's best pecan pie.

"And she had the best Southern recipe for macaroni and cheese," he added. The others laughed.

Ilka thought again about Erik. After his funeral, their apartment had felt empty and abandoned. A silence hung that had nothing to do with being alone. It took a few weeks for her to realize the silence was in herself. There was no one to talk to, so everything was spoken inside her head. And at the same time, she felt as if she were in a bubble no sound could penetrate. That had been one of the most difficult things to get used to. Slowly things got better, and at last—she couldn't say precisely when—the silence connected with her loss disappeared.

Meanwhile, she'd had the business to run. What a circus. They'd started working together almost from the time they'd first met. He was the photographer, though occasionally she went out with him to help set up the equipment and direct the students. Otherwise, she was mostly responsible for the office work. But she had done a job or two by herself when they were especially busy; she'd seen how he worked. There was nothing mysterious about it. Classes were lined up with the tallest students in back, and the most attractive were placed in the middle so the focus would be on them. The individual portraits were mostly about adjusting the height of the seat and taking enough pictures to ensure that one of them was good enough. But when Erik suddenly wasn't there, with a full schedule of jobs still booked, she had taken over, without giving it much thought. She did know the school secretaries, and they knew her, so that eased the transition.

"Do we really have to buy a coffin, when Mom is just going to be burned?" Steve said, interrupting her thoughts. "Can't we just borrow one? She won't be lying in there very long."

Shit. Ilka had blanked out for a moment. Where the hell was Artie? Did they have coffins they loaned out? She had to say something. "It would have to be one that's been used."

"We're not putting Mom in a coffin where other dead people have been!" Helen was indignant, while a hint of a smile appeared on her son's face.

Ilka jumped in. "Unfortunately, we can only loan out used coffins." She hoped that would put a lid on this idea.

"We can't do that. Can we?" Helen said to her two brothers. "On the other hand, if we borrow a coffin, we might be able to afford charms instead."

Ilka didn't have the foggiest idea if her suggestion was even possible. But if this really was her business, she could decide, now, couldn't she?

"We *would* save forty-five hundred dollars," Joe said.

Forty-five hundred dollars for a coffin! This could turn out to be disastrous if it ended with them losing money from her ignorant promise.

"Oh, at least. Dad's coffin cost seven thousand dollars."

What is this? Ilka thought. *Are coffins here decorated in gold leaf?*

"But Grandma already paid for her funeral," the grandson said. "You can't save on something she's already paid for. You're not going to get her money back, right?" Finally, he looked up.

"We'll figure this out," Ilka said.

The boy looked over at his mother and began crying.

"Oh, honey!" Helen said.

"You're all talking about this like it isn't even Grandma; like it's someone else who's dead," he said, angry now.

He turned to Ilka. "Like it's all about money, and just getting it over with." He jumped up so fast he knocked his chair over; then he ran out the door.

His mother sent her brothers an apologetic look; they both shook their heads. She turned to Ilka and asked if it were possible for them to return tomorrow. "By then we'll have this business about the coffin sorted out. We also have to order a life board. I brought along some photos of Mom."

Standing now, Ilka told them it was of course fine to come back tomorrow. She knew one thing for certain: Artie was going to meet with them, whether he liked it or not. She grabbed the photos Helen was holding out.

"They're from when she was born, when she graduated from school, when she married Dad, and from their anniversary the year before he died."

"Super," Ilka said. She had no idea what these photos would be used for.

The three siblings stood up and headed for the door. "When would you like to meet?" Ilka asked. They agreed on noon.

Joe stopped and looked up at her. "But can the memorial service be held on Friday?"

"We can talk about that later," Ilka replied at once. She needed time to find out what to do with 150 people and a place for the dogs close to the coffin.

After they left, Ilka walked back to the desk and sank down in the chair. She hadn't even offered them coffee, she realized.

She buried her face in her hands and sat for a moment. She had inherited a funeral home in Racine. And if she were to believe the nun in the reception area laminating death notices, she had accepted the inheritance.

She heard a knock on the doortrame. Sister Eileen stuck her head in the room. Ilka nodded, and the nun walked over and laid a slip of paper on the table. On it was an address.

"We have a pickup."

Ilka stared at the paper. How was this possible? It wasn't just charms, life boards, and a forty-five-hundred-dollar coffin. Now they wanted her to pick up a body, too. She exhaled and stood up.

4

Ilka walked out into the high-ceilinged hall and glanced around. The two glass showcases against the wall looked like they came from a jewelry store. One of them held small, elaborately carved wooden boxes and something that resembled the mantel clock over the fireplace at her grandmother's place in Bagsværd. She walked out to the reception area to find Sister Eileen and talk her way out of the pickup.

"No one else can drive," Sister Eileen said without looking up. She was sorting through the day's mail, slitting envelopes open and laying them on a pile without looking inside. "But maybe you don't have a driver's license?"

"I have one, yes," Ilka said, before realizing she should have said no.

"Good. The keys are in the car. Here's the morgue's address. You need to make sure you bring along gloves and masks. It sounds like he's been mangled badly." She pointed at a door at the end of the hall. "You have to walk by the preparation room to get to the garage. Gloves, masks, and body bags are on the top shelf. And take a look at the coffins in storage; see if there are any unvarnished coffins. Apparently, the deceased was a homeless person; it's possible that no one will cover the expenses. But you'll have to take that up with Artie."

Ilka had stopped listening. She had to call Artie and talk him into coming. She lifted her phone out of her pocket and noted a backlog of messages from her mother; the phone had been on mute.

"Niels will do jobs tomorrow and Friday, but can't next week. You have four jobs Monday when you get home."

"The code to get into the garage is six-seven-eight-nine," the nun said, adding that Ilka would need help to pick up the deceased. "It takes two."

"I'll figure it out," Ilka said, looking for Artie's phone number in her address book.

"By the way, someone sent you a bouquet," Sister Eileen said as Ilka walked out. "I put it in Mr. Jensen's office."

Ilka turned in surprise. "Who's it from?"

"There's a card." The nun looked up suddenly now, as if she'd finally noticed Ilka. "You look like your father. You have the same nose. And chin." She smiled. "Please let me know if there's anything I can do for you."

Something in the sister's voice gave Ilka the impression she had been close to her father: her familiar tone. Ilka was puzzled for a moment; then she smiled and thanked the nun.

She returned to the room to change into a pair of jeans and a long-sleeved T-shirt. The wrapped bouquet stood on the small coffee table beside the bed. Written on the card: "We look forward to closing the deal with you." It was signed by Golden Slumbers Funeral Home.

She stared at the card for a moment before sticking it back in the flamboyant purple and white flowers. She went upstairs and grabbed her fleece jacket from the pile of clothes on the bed. She would have to ask Artie what the hell this was all about.

It was one thing to put her to the test. See what she was made of. Have a little laugh at her expense. Fine. And if they were going to get involved with another business in town, honestly, she was more than fine with that. She might even avoid having to figure out how to dismantle her father's business. But she was getting annoyed at how it was happening drip by drip. Why couldn't they just sit down and talk about things? Hatch a plan and divvy up what needed to be done. She punched in the code to the garage. Then it hit her: She was the one who had yelled no, every time Artie had knocked on the door trying to talk with her. She was also the one who had signed the IRS document without reading it.

"Just get this over with," she muttered to herself. She froze when she stepped into the garage.

The space was as large as what she'd seen of the funeral home's first floor. Right inside stood an open coffin. Glossy black, with large gilded handles. It looked to her like something for a head of state, or at least someone who didn't want their final journey to go unnoticed. The coffin had a white satin lining, with a pillow featuring embroidered initials, and it was open in a way that gave Ilka the impression that a person had just sat up, climbed out, and walked off. A coffin that looked a bit less pretentious stood up against a wall, but what she couldn't tear her eyes from was the refrigerator at the far end of the garage. Not exactly like what she'd seen in large restaurant kitchens and institutions, but something along those lines. Unburnished steel, about six feet wide and not as tall as a normal refrigerator, with three drawers. A few rugs and a box had been tossed on top. The whole garage seemed a bit messy.

Ilka knew she shouldn't do it, but her feet were already on the way. When she opened the top drawer, the cold reached out and zapped her. But the tray was empty. She needed to open the next drawer only a crack to see the bluish foot on the steel tray inside. She shivered, closed the drawer, and looked out the window, checking the view—the same as from the room where she'd slept. In other words, her lodgings were above the funeral home's morgue.

She was being silly; she understood that. And yet she was caught in a mood that made her stare momentarily at the drawers of rust-free steel. The boy's grandmother lay inside. The smell— It was true, the air smelled like death. And cold. And like something that had been disinfected. Mostly it smelled cold to Ilka, even though she couldn't put her finger on what that meant.

Thoughts roiled in her head, but she knew she was only stalling. She had an address and a body waiting for her, and she needed to figure out how to go about picking it up. She'd called Artie a few times, but he hadn't answered. At last she pulled herself together and walked over to the hearse, which was parked just inside.

A wheeled stretcher, like the ones used in ambulances, stood against the opposite wall. Under the stretcher were blankets lined with thick plastic and straps to fasten down a corpse. There was also a low cart, something that looked like a forklift. She didn't need anyone to explain it was for transporting coffins.

Ilka was unsure whether she was supposed to take along an unvarnished wooden coffin, or if she should just see if there were any left. To start with, she needed to find where the coffins were stored. She pressed the button to open the door to the funeral home's spacious backyard.

An addition to the house stood next to the parking lot. An overhang under which a vehicle could be backed connected the garage and the addition. FLOWERS was written on the door beside the garage. Ilka walked by a large Dumpster with a biohazard sticker, and over by the next door she noticed a small sign: STORAGE.

Ilka walked in. The room seemed cramped. She turned the light on; she was right, the room was filled from floor to ceiling. In the back, two coffins had been stood up, one a light metallic blue, the other in imitation oak. She recognized the American coffins from films, yet these seemed to her even bigger and more pretentious. She also spotted one that was simple and unfinished—surely the one the nun had been talking about. It looked like a coffin from an old Western, rough wood, no carving or decoration whatsoever.

She ran into Sister Eileen on her way back to the garage.

"You haven't left yet?" the nun asked. It sounded like an accusation.

"I need to talk to Artie before I leave." She looked for plastic gloves and masks on the shelves. She'd called him several times now, but he hadn't answered. She tried again, but no luck. "Unless," she added, "you can come along and help me."

Immediately the sister shook her head. "I can't, and calling him will do you no good. He's gone fishing; he always leaves his phone—"

"I've decided I'm going to help until we figure out what to do with the business." She spoke sharply—*too* sharply, she thought. "And if I have to bring in a corpse, I will drive the hearse. But I'm not going alone."

The nun handed her a note. "Pick him up on the way. Drive as far as you can down the last road. The last stretch before the lake is a bit steep."

Ilka looked at the note and shook her head. Sister Eileen had planned on having her pick Artie up the entire time; she'd been testing her. Ilka was about to say something, but she realized it wasn't the right time for a show of authority. In fact, right now she had little authority to show. How had it suddenly become her job to pick up a dead person? She hadn't even eaten since her flight, apart from the chips she'd wolfed down during the night.

She took the note. "I'll find him. Do I need documents or something to pick up the deceased?"

Suddenly memories from before her father had abandoned them popped up, of him saying, "I have a pickup." She had misunderstood and asked if he'd forgotten some thing, but then he explained it was called a pickup when he had to go someplace—a nursing home, for example—to put a dead person in a coffin and drive them to the funeral home. He also explained to her that you didn't call a dead person a corpse. You always called the dead person "the deceased." It was all about respect for the person. She had even gone along on pickups, but she'd never been allowed to go inside. She'd sat out in the hearse and waited until he came out with the coffin and rolled it into the back. And by then, the lid of the coffin had been screwed down.

"You won't need any documentation when Artie is with you. They know him." The sharpness in Sister Eileen's voice had disappeared. "This is a very simple pickup; you can handle it easily. But remember to take a stretcher to wheel the deceased on. And bring along some extra plastic. It sounds like it might be a mess."

Ilka nodded and smiled, reminding herself that it would soon be over.

5

Ilka settled in behind the wheel of the hearse and adjusted the mirrors; she quickly checked out the instrument panel. She wasn't used to an automatic, so the car jerked when she braked at first. Tense now, she looked in the side mirror; this boat seemed twice as long as the station wagon she drove back home. The engine growled as she slowly backed out of the garage. She realized that a sensor would warn her if she was about to back into something. It actually did feel as if she were navigating a large boat instead of driving a car. The axles creaked noisily.

Was the rear door completely shut? She'd tried to fit the stretcher to the tracks, but it hadn't seemed to sit exactly right, or maybe the wheels underneath hadn't been pushed up well enough. Finally, she had shoved it in and slammed the door shut as best she could. Hopefully it was heavy enough that it wouldn't spring open while she was driving.

She turned around in the parking lot behind the funeral home, then punched in the address on the GPS. It wouldn't take more than ten minutes to drive to where she hoped Artie was still fishing, she saw. It was just outside town.

She drove down the broad residential street. It was deserted, but she noticed a school across the way from the funeral home. A group of kids were laughing as they hung over a fence and tossed their school bags down on the ground.

The houses in the area all looked the same. Front porches and lawns open to the street, hedges to the sides. The Stars and Stripes swayed over several of the porch railings, and every house had the classic American mailbox in front. Ilka followed the directions given by the GPS, turning from one street to the next. She passed a supermarket with its doors open, though there seemed to be no one inside, no cars parked outside. She'd just turned onto the main street when her phone rang.

"He can't take care of your jobs on Friday after all," her mother said, after asking how things were going. "Can you make it home by then?"

Ilka assured her that everything was going fine. She sensed that her mother held back from asking more. "I don't think I can be back that soon. But I'll probably leave on Friday. Otherwise this weekend. Call West District School Photography. They usually have trainees; maybe we can borrow one. If we can't, call back." The GPS said to turn and drive over a small canal that looked like it ran far into the city. She seemed to be in an old industrial area, long since abandoned, though ships still lined the wharf.

And though stores were open, the downtown streets were also empty. The town simply seemed deserted. As if it once had been alive but now was gasping for breath, about to give up the ghost. Ilka reminded herself it was early September. Maybe there had been tourists all summer; the atmosphere might have been different earlier. But when she drove up a hill and shortly after found herself leaving town, she doubted there had been much life here. Ever.

Everything around her was green. Horses grazed in large

pastures on the left, and on the right, toward Lake Michigan, she glimpsed houses built on the cliff facing the lake. She slowed and tried to look down, but her view was blocked by high fences and hedges.

Quite the place—nice! she thought. She drove by a white-washed lighthouse. For a moment, she was tempted to drive down there, but the GPS said she would reach her destination in two minutes. She drove on until it told her to turn right.

The road was winding and quite steep. Ilka drove so slowly that a person could easily have walked beside her. The vehicle swayed and floated its way down to a fence with an open gate; she wasn't at all sure she could make it through. Slowly she coaxed the big Cadillac forward, and only one side mirror scraped as she slipped between the gateposts. She stopped at a cliff, where a small path led to the water. She slammed the door hard, hoping Artie would hear and not be too surprised when she appeared.

She started down the path, and within short order, a breathtakingly magnificent sight spread out before her. Had she not known better, she would have thought Lake Michigan was an ocean; the calm waters looked boundless. So beautiful and peaceful. It smelled of freshwater, and despite the mirror surface on the lake, a light breeze was blowing.

"Two men drowned down there last week."

The voice from behind almost scared her to death. Artie. She tried to hide her embarrassment.

Two fishing rods were clamped under his arm, and he was carrying a lidded white plastic bucket. He didn't seem at all surprised to see her; maybe Sister Eileen had had better luck getting through to him. He waved his bucket and said there would be fish on the grill if she wanted to stay and eat.

Ilka shook her head and handed him the keys to the hearse. She didn't at all care to listen to him talk about food. She was so hungry she could almost eat the fish in the bucket raw. "We have to work. A dead man at the morgue is waiting to be picked up. I brought along gloves, masks, and extra plastic, because they say he's in bad shape."

Artie broke out into a broad smile at the sight of the hearse parked with its front grille just above the cliff. He shook his head at her, his grin still smeared all over his face. "You think we can get it back up?"

She didn't bat an eye. "Of course. If it can get down, it can get back up. Okay?"

He opened the rear door and stood for a moment looking at the stretcher. Then he placed the bucket with the fish beside it.

"You're bringing the fish?" She couldn't believe it, but Artie didn't answer.

"Let's go." He got in behind the wheel and backed the hearse up slowly.

They reached the gate without speaking. "Yes, thank you very much, the meeting with the Nortons went well," Ilka said. Artie backed the hearse between the posts. "They would like to hold a funeral service on Friday. Can they? You don't need to answer right now, because you'll be talking to them tomorrow."

He stared straight into the side mirror. "You talked to them?"

"They showed up, and you weren't there. Someone had to do it."

Obviously, he was thoroughly amused by the situation he'd put her in. "Friday is out. Maybe Saturday. How'd it go otherwise?"

"It went fine." She explained that the family wanted to do the flowers themselves. "The deceased loved her garden, and they all believed it would be a beautiful thing if the flowers came from there."

"Joanne won't be happy about that," Artie said without looking at her.

"Joanne?"

"The flower shop that usually delivers for the big funeral services. I'm assuming the family wants everything as magnificent and successful as when Mr. Norton passed away."

"I don't know anything about that. But anyway, they want to do the flowers. The deceased is to be cremated, and they want to buy some charms. What are they?"

Artie looked over at her. "A charm is a piece of jewelry that can hold some of the ashes of a deceased. They can hang from a bracelet or a necklace. Don't you have them in Denmark? They're really popular over here."

Back in town now, he drove down the main street in the opposite direction from where they'd arrived the evening before.

"They expect between one hundred and one hundred fifty people," Ilka continued. "And they want to borrow a coffin for the funeral service."

"Borrow a coffin?" He almost lost his grip on the wheel. Ilka ignored him.

"And I promised that everyone can log on the memorial page we're setting up for them. I don't know how it works with passwords, but they want everyone to have access."

Artie ignored her right back. "We don't loan out coffins. They'll have to buy one."

"She will only be inside one for a few hours. There's no reason to pay forty-five hundred dollars when she'll be burned up anyway."

She felt his eyes on her. Then he shook his head, but not in respect, not like the way he had when he saw she'd driven the hearse down to the cliff. "The coffin's already paid for. We don't make refunds on anything prepaid that the deceased requested."

"After the funeral service we can move Mrs. Norton over to one of the cheap wooden coffins. They can pay for that."

He shook his head again; she knew what he was going to say wouldn't be nice, and she cut him off. "Before my father moved over here, he owned a funeral home in Denmark that he left to my mother. One of the ways her employees cheated her was, after a funeral they took off the coffin lids and reused them. They bought coffins without lids and sold them for full price."

Ilka remembered how it had driven her mother crazy, but there was nothing she could do about it. Without the two undertakers, she couldn't run the business, and without running the business, she couldn't sell it.

"Sometimes they even took the body out of the coffin after the services and put it in a box they made out of this, whatever it's called, cheap wood stuff, and then they drove it to the place where people are burned."

This was one of the many stories her mother had told in the years after selling the funeral home.

"We loan out coffins," she declared. Artie had handed the reins of the conversation over to her. She owned the business; she made the decisions. "About money, we'll figure something out. Like I said, they want to buy some charms, so we have to take care of that. We agreed that you will talk about that with them tomorrow."

His expression was closed up now, the smile that cast nets of wrinkles from the corners of his eyes long gone. "Okay. Now's the time for you to learn what's going on with your dad's business. It was all in the letter I gave you, but I guess you haven't read it."

A message beeped in, and she grabbed her phone. She didn't want to hear what Artie Sorvino had to say.

She nodded. "I know that I've inherited the business."

"This came out after he died," he began, again without looking at her. "At the same time we found out about you." He paused for a moment, as if weighing his words.

"I don't know anything about the business's books. Never have; that was your dad's department. I guess I might as well tell you straight out that he owes a hell of a lot of money. And when you say we can just lend them a coffin, so they can save money, I say, sure! That's a hell of a good idea! Let's just make the debt bigger. Listen, we can't afford to lose the income from selling coffins. And we can't afford higher prices from the crematorium because we change things around so they can't send the coffins to a scrap-metal dealer to earn a little bit extra. The books are in bad shape; the business is about to be turned over to the creditors. I've managed to buy a little time with the IRS; I told them I had to bring you over from Denmark. It wasn't easy to delay them, but now we have until Friday afternoon before they come in and shut us down. And that means," he added, his tone hinting that there was more to come, "it's too late to save anything. After Friday, you will not have access to your father's private belongings. It's all going to be seized until the government makes sure it has enough assets to cover what it's owed. Then a long process is going to start; it's something neither one of us wants to go through. And it's probably not going to end before we have one foot in the grave. So right now, every single hour that goes by without us fighting to save your father's business is a complete waste of time."

"But you went fishing and forced that meeting on me, instead of staying and telling me how things were," she muttered.

He nodded. "I had to find a way to get you out of that room. We don't have time for you to lie in there and whine. We've got until Friday to put our rescue plan into action. You need to understand that this isn't only going to hurt you. It's our skins, too, if your dad's business closes down this way. But I didn't think you'd go through with the meeting. And I really didn't think you'd put your signature on something without reading it, either."

He might as well have slapped her, several times.

"What about my father's new family? You say they live in a big house in West Racine. It must be worth something too."

The crow's-feet spreading out from the corners of his eyes returned for a moment. Single strands of his long hair, which was combed back over his head, drooped down alongside his face. "What Paul and Mary Ann had together is her own property. You won't get anything there. Whether it was her who saw it could end up bad, or your dad who wanted to protect her and the girls, I don't know. But the debt is in his business, so if the IRS needs to seize assets any other place, to cover the losses in the funeral home, the first place they'll go to is your property."

She heard her mother's voice in the back of her head: *If you go over there, you risk being liable for something you can't get out of. And they might even arrest you.*

Artie glanced at her. "Do you own anything?"

She shook her head. "I don't have anything valuable, and no, I don't own anything."

"Probably the first thing the tax authorities will do is investigate your financial situation in Denmark. But we do have an offer that can save everything your dad built up."

"But there must be money coming in, too," she said, ignoring her knifelike pangs of hunger. "Because it looks like you're busy enough. And with those prices! It's not exactly cheap to die here."

They were outside the city again, driving down a long, straight stretch of highway with nothing but an occasional house and a few large barns. "I can't say what he spent his money on, but he milked the business dry; no doubt about that." Artie spoke with a seriousness that made it absolutely clear to Ilka: Her situation right now was desperate.

She took a deep breath. *Story of my life*, she thought. She tried, really tried to get a grip on her life, and yet it always ended up with other people or circumstances controlling her.

"Tell me about this offer. It wouldn't be coming from a place called Golden Slumbers Funeral Home, would it?"

Artie looked surprised. He nodded. "Yeah, the Oldham family runs the biggest undertaker business in the entire region. They have their own crematorium and can hold funeral services for over a thousand people. They can put up as many as sixty people when relatives show up from out of town. And they want to take over your dad's business. To stop the IRS from freezing the assets, we must pay sixty thousand dollars before banks close on Friday. And that's just a sort of deposit. We don't have the money, but the Oldhams are willing to pay it if we sign a statement that we're in the process of transferring the business to them."

"It sounds like you've already talked with them."

"Your dad started the negotiations before he died." It seemed like Artie understood just how lousy the situation felt to Ilka, being dragged into the middle of a deal already taking place.

"What do they want?" Ilka tried to ignore her hunger and jet lag, to keep her head clear, because she had a bad feeling about this.

"They'll take over the order book and all the debt in the

business. That means you won't be involved financially in the settlement with the IRS or with any of the other creditors. You would still be able to take any of your dad's personal belongings you want."

"What does it mean—they'll take over the order book?"

They drove into a parking lot behind a long gray building. Artie nodded to a security guard and showed his ID, and they parked near a gateway leading to a ramp. "It means they'll take over all the funerals paid for in advance. A lot of people begin making payments for their funerals when they're young, so their relatives don't have to borrow money to bury them. Like you said, it's very expensive to die in this country."

"So the Golden Slumbers people take over the funerals already paid for? And my father already spent that money?"

"No. That money can't be touched; it's in a special account."

"But what do they get by taking over the business?"

"They also get a list of people who have signed up for a funeral but haven't paid yet. Because of the expense, some people take out funeral insurance and pay on it their entire lives, and the insurance covers the funerals when they die."

Ilka nodded. "Okay, so that's what they're going after."

"If you'd bothered to read what I gave you, you'd know your dad's will says that Sister Eileen and I have the preemptive rights, the right to buy, if you decide to sell the business."

"Okay," she said, without understanding what would be left to buy.

While they were sitting in the parking lot, another hearse had driven up to the gateway. Two people had gone into the morgue, but they must have returned without Ilka noticing them, because the hearse drove off.

"I'd like to buy the house, if we manage to get out of this situation. But that won't happen unless we avoid everything being frozen and then getting dragged into bankruptcy."

"The house isn't part of the deal with the Oldhams?"

Artie shook his head. "All they want is the actual business. I'll buy the house from you, so at least you get something out of coming all this way."

Ilka was certain the deal with the Oldhams was to their advantage, but she didn't care, as long as she avoided being held inside the US with an enormous debt. "Let's get this deal going."

He nodded and asked if she was ready to go inside.

6

Artie handed Ilka a mask and a pair of white latex gloves, then walked behind the hearse and opened the rear door to pull out the stretcher. He shoved the bucket of fish to the side.

"Have you ever been in a morgue before?"

Ilka shook her head. She had been to the Forensic Institute in Copenhagen to see her husband one last time after his autopsy, and it had been horrible. She wasn't sure why, whether it had been because no one had been careful enough to conceal the Y-incision in his body, or if it was more because he'd been lying there grayish and cold, and it all had happened too fast for her to realize he was truly gone. The autopsy had been unavoidable, because his death had come out of the blue. No illness, no sign that the end was in sight. Suddenly he was just lying there.

"Okay then, I'll see if there's someone inside who can help lift, but I might need some help out here."

She nodded and followed him down the long hallway with frosted glass panes in the doors.

"Wait here," Artie said. A double door opened automatically and closed behind him as he walked around a corner.

Ilka leaned against the wall. She was dizzy and weak

from hunger. She should call her lawyer and get her opinion on this deal with Golden Slumbers. The time difference between Racine and Denmark, however, was seven hours; she would have left work long ago. Ilka tried anyway, and to her surprise she got an answer.

"Hello!" her lawyer repeated. She had worked for Erik long before Ilka had met him, and after his death, Ilka had kept her. The phone connection was breaking up on every third word because of the thick morgue walls, so Ilka walked back outside. The piercing voice of the lawyer came through again, loud and clear.

"No, I don't know if there's a mortgage on the house," Ilka said after she explained her situation.

"Do not sign anything before I've read it," the lawyer warned her. "Send it over right away."

"I've already signed something."

The wind was warm, but Ilka was freezing, and she gave a start when she heard a long, mournful scream behind her. The morgue door was open; a woman was being helped down the ramp by two uniformed police officers. She wore a light summer jacket and walked bent over with both hands clutched to her chest, as if she were afraid her heart was about to fall out. The sounds she made were those of an animal. Between her screams rising and falling in waves, she sobbed desperately, sobs that cut into the place where Ilka had stowed away her own sorrow.

"What in the world is going on? Are you there?" the lawyer asked, but before Ilka could answer, Artie walked out the door, pushing the stretcher. He was still wearing the mask and gloves, but now he also had on a disposable lab coat with rust-red stains from dried blood.

"I have to run," Ilka said. She hung up and hurried down the ramp.

"Someone beat him to death," Artie said after they had rolled the stretcher to the hearse. "He might as well have been hit by a train."

Ilka nodded at the police car. She was still shaken by the anguished screaming, though the woman had stopped and now was sobbing deeply. "Is that a relative?" she asked after the police car drove off.

Artie shook his head and nodded toward the morgue. "She's the mother of a little girl in there who drowned earlier today on a class trip. They just got hold of her; she works at the pharmacy in Racine, but today is her day off. She was in Chicago visiting her mother. The lake is a big part of people's lives here, but it's dangerous. It looks peaceful enough, but it's cold and it's deep, and it's windy once you get away from land. It takes a seaworthy boat to sail out there."

Ilka watched the police car drive off. "Is he from town too?" She glanced at the stretcher, which Artie was sliding into the hearse.

He shrugged. "Looks like he's been living on the street; he only had a few clothes in a bag. The police are trying to locate his relatives. A security guard found him behind one of the empty factories at the edge of town, lying in the grass. The police report says he died at the crime scene; maybe he'd been sleeping there and someone attacked him."

He shrugged again and closed the back door. "Usually the funeral homes in town take turns handling the homeless. Sometimes we get a small fee from the state, but it hardly covers the cremation, not to mention the cost of a coffin."

"So it's not something you're crazy about doing," she said.

He shook his head. "When you become an undertaker you take this oath, that everyone has the right to a dignified departure from this world. And that includes the people who can't pay. But you're right; we don't fight over these jobs. Like I said, we take turns."

They pulled out of the parking space. Ilka's phone rang. "No one can do your jobs," her mother said. She sounded tired and irritable. "I've tried everyone, but now I would really like to go to bed."

"Shit! Would you please try again tomorrow? I'm sitting in a hearse; we've just picked up a homeless person in a morgue. I'm tired and I'm hungry and really, I don't know what to do—"

"Don't worry," her mother said, her own warm voice on the edge of breaking from anxiety. "We'll find a solution."

"Thanks, Mom," Ilka said, quickly adding, "Say hi to Hanne."

Ilka hung up before her mother could say anything more. She sank in her seat and sighed deeply.

Artie glanced over at her. "Problems?"

Ilka shrugged and stared out the window, letting him know she didn't want to involve him in something he wouldn't understand anyway.

"Is it okay with you if we stop to get something to eat?" Artie asked when they reached the town square. He parked the hearse across from Oh Dennis!, the saloon where Artie had met her father, Ilka remembered.

"Yes, it's very okay." As she stepped out of the car, she glimpsed the body behind the curtains in back, packed under a blanket and strapped in place. Before shutting her door, she said, "Shouldn't we deliver him first?"

"It'll only take a minute," he said. "They have the best chicken wings in town, and the ribs are good too. What would you like?"

"Chicken wings and ribs; that's fine. Anything."

Loud music was playing when they walked in, and sports channels blazed out from two televisions on both sides of the bar, just under the ceiling. Artie obviously knew the young woman behind the counter, who was juggling several enormous glasses. The diner smelled greasy and a bit sour, the floor felt sticky, but Ilka couldn't care less. All she wanted was something to eat. Two older men sat across from each other in a corner, their eyes glued to the two televisions. One of them had hair combed forward from the back of his head.

She heard Artie order at the counter, and she shook her head when he turned to her and asked if she wanted a beer. She went to look for the bathrooms. On her way to the door at the back of the diner, she stopped and put a few coins in one of the slot machines hanging on the wall. One-armed bandits, her father had called them. Nothing happened, and she put a few more quarters in. Ten quarters tumbled out. The machine's reels clicked every time they came to a stop. Artie and the woman were talking and laughing together. A couple came in and sat down by the window.

Ilka won five more quarters and fed them back into the machine; then she went into the bathroom. Their food was ready when she came out. Artie had drunk his beer and packed the food into two large paper sacks. Ilka nodded at the waitress and followed him to the car. The odor from the paper sacks seemed out of place in the hearse.

"There're also curly fries and sliders," he said. He handed her the bags, which felt heavy enough to feed an army. "I'll probably be working late this evening."

He explained he was repairing a face that had been caved in on one side. "He lived in senior housing, and he fell against the edge of a table and hit his temple. It keeps collapsing. The family is coming tomorrow, before I drive him over to the church, so I've got to get going on the makeup and then dress him. They just sent me the clothes. His grown-up daughter wanted to choose them, and she just got in from Minneapolis this afternoon."

Artie backed the hearse under the carport next to the house; then he punched the code to the door. Ilka grabbed the sacks of food, and after getting out she remembered the bucket of fish in back. She didn't want to look in there.

Artie pulled the stretcher out of the hearse. He'd obviously had much practice locking the wheels down and pushing it into the passageway. Ilka followed. The pungent odor of formaldehyde rammed into her. The first time she'd held her breath and rushed through so fast that she had barely registered it; now it seemed to cling to her skin, the inside of her nose, her eyes. She eyed the sacks and retreated a few steps to keep them away from the odor while she waited for Artie.

A cat meowed, then sauntered over and rubbed against her leg. It had white markings on its chest and down over its stomach; otherwise it was coal black. A second later it was on its way into one of the sacks. Ilka lifted it up and set it down off to the side. She was ready to eat straight from the sacks herself if Artie didn't hurry up. She heard him open the refrigerator in the garage and glimpsed him setting the fish bucket in the bottom. After locking the garage behind him, he walked into the preparation room and turned on the powerful fan; a glaring light streamed down from the ceiling.

"This'll only take a sec," he said.

Ilka noticed a long steel table over by the wall, where in place of the countertop was a grating over a drain in the floor. In the middle of the room, another table stood under a large, broad operating room lamp.

He walked back and stood in the hallway, as if he didn't notice the stink. "What do you want to drink? Beer, water, iced tea?"

"Water is fine." She followed him into the office and started emptying the sacks. Two small mountains of meat soon lay on the table. Ilka suppressed any thoughts of death and formaldehyde and dove into the food.

"Why in the world do you want this house?" she asked after wolfing down five enormous chicken wings and noting that even though the doors to the hallway were closed, a whiff of death and formaldehyde still hung around. *Who would want a house that had been a funeral home?* she wondered. She looked around.

Shelves of urns lined the walls, and a poster demonstrated how a large machine could thaw the ground if a coffin had to be lowered in the winter.

He laid his spareribs down and wiped his hands on a napkin; then he looked at her. "When your dad was alive, he did the talking with the relatives. I did it occasionally, after he was gone. But for the most part it was his job. I took care of the deceased. We did the pickups together."

She started eating again while he spoke. "And when we get out of this mess, hopefully, I'm going to start working for the Oldhams. But as a freelancer, so I can help the other undertakers around here, too. That way I'll only be doing the embalming, reconstructions, preparation, makeup. I'll make sure the deceased look the way they'd want to be remembered."

Ilka nodded. She wasn't all that surprised to hear he already had a deal in place. But if he wanted to take over the house and had arranged things to his advantage, that was fine with her too. "And Sister Eileen, what about her? Is she also an employee? And what does she actually do?" Her mouth was half-full of coleslaw.

Artie smiled briefly. "She's from a parish west of here. A lot of nuns work voluntarily in different places, in daycare centers, schools, nursing homes, funeral homes. Some nuns are supported by the parish; other places pay for their services. That's the way it is here. Your dad always took good care of Sister Eileen. She lends a hand; she gives our clients a sense of peace. It's her calling to help wherever she can, wherever she sees it's needed. She wants to work where it's cooler than down south. The heat bothers her."

Ilka was getting full now, and it was hard to ignore the stink of death in her nose. They could have it all, lock, stock, and barrel, as far as she was concerned. Really.

"I just don't want to get dragged out of bed in the middle of the night anymore, when someone dies. And I don't want to scrape people up off the highway, either. You know what? Crushed bones feel like jelly when you lift them over into a coffin. And I won't have to pick up anyone dead so long that their skin slips off like overcooked chicken. I just want to do the creative work; it's what I'm best at."

Ilka nodded. She was finished eating now, and an image of the chickens she cooked for soup was not something she wanted stuck in her head. She always covered chicken bones on her plate with a napkin; it was instinct. "So you want to keep the house as your workshop." That made sense.

"I can take on customers from the entire area. When a funeral director gets severe accident victim cases they can't do anything with, they can send them to me. Just like we pay the Oldhams for using their crematorium."

Artie stood and began picking things up. There was still

food left in the sacks. When he walked into the preparation room, she went to look for the cat. It was right outside, and it made plenty of noise when Ilka opened the door. She squatted down and gave it some chicken; then she stroked its back. She turned around and jumped at the sight of Sister Eileen in front of her.

"I made the reservation at the hotel. I'm very sorry about the misunderstanding, but now it's taken care of. Your room is ready, and you can use your father's car." She held out a set of keys. "You won't have to pay for your stay at the hotel, of course."

Who will? Ilka wondered. Artie walked out pushing a stretcher holding the old man who had fallen. Music from the room streamed out: "California Girls." The Beach Boys. He hummed along as he slipped his arms into a long white lab coat and covered his loud shirt. She couldn't care less if they turned her father's funeral home into a beauty salon for the dead. She just wanted out. Now that she'd eaten, her exhaustion returned.

"But I don't mind staying here," she said. "In fact I'd rather sleep in my father's room. I go to bed early anyway." She walked over to Artie's door to say she was on her way up. She'd stopped holding her hand over her mouth, but the embalming fluids still seemed to line her throat, all the way down.

He promised to gather up all the papers dealing with her inheritance and the upcoming sale, so she could mail them back to her lawyer. Then he walked inside and closed the door.

"I've already moved your belongings," Sister Eileen said, behind her now. "Everything's ready, and your father's car is outside, parked in the large space." She pointed down at the asphalt behind the trees.

"You've already been up and packed my things?" Ilka asked.

"Yes, everything's at the hotel, but I didn't unpack for you. I thought you'd rather do it yourself."

Ilka could see the pile of clothes on the bed, the empty potato chip bag. What else had been lying there? "I'd rather stay here." She tried to smile. "I also have to go through my father's things and decide what to take home with me."

"We can do that together. Do you know where the hotel is?"

Ilka's head began to spin. She needed to lie down, be alone.

"When you pull out, just drive straight ahead and then to the right," Sister Eileen explained, but before she could continue, Ilka raised her hand.

"I'm staying here. I'll pick my things up at the hotel, and please make sure I'm not locked out when I return."

The nun stood for a moment, looking like a child who had just been bawled out, but then she nodded. "Of course. You're quite welcome to stay. I just thought it wouldn't be nice for you sleeping upstairs while Artie works. We've all gotten used to that, also to the smell. But you are more than welcome if it doesn't bother you."

7

"No," Ilka told the receptionist. "I won't be needing the room. I'm just here to pick my things up."

"But we can't cancel a reservation when the room has already been occupied," he argued. He was so big that Ilka couldn't see the chair he was sitting in. His arms filled the sleeves of his blazer, and when he moved them, she smelled stale sweat and something else she couldn't put a finger on.

"Yesterday you didn't have a room, even though we'd reserved one, so doesn't this even things up?" Ilka didn't care if it cost her a night's fee, or rather, if it cost Artie and Sister Eileen.

There was a small coffee bar across from the reception desk. Unmanned. Ilka could stand a cup of coffee, and she looked around for someone to serve her while the receptionist conferred with a coworker. Several minutes passed, and she couldn't hear anything from the back room, only the insistent whining sound she'd heard the day before, like a telephone ringing somewhere.

At last she gave up and walked through the hotel lobby. The nun had given her the room card along with the car keys. When Ilka walked past a wide ice machine, the humming drowned out the monotone whining sound for a moment. The room smelled of cigarettes when she walked in; she was glad to know the embalming fluids hadn't ruined her sense of smell. Sweat and smoke apparently trumped the scents in a morgue.

Her suitcase lay on the bed beside her neatly folded coat.

The reception desk was still empty when she returned. She laid the room card on the desk, walked outside, and threw her suitcase into her father's silver-gray Chevrolet. She got in behind the wheel and sat for a moment with her eyes closed. Again, she felt as if he were with her, though not because she recognized anything in the car. It was more a presence.

Inside the pocket on the door was a package of gum, an empty water bottle, a Post-it with an address, and a receipt from a parking machine. Ilka leaned over and opened the glove compartment. A pile of papers lay under the car manual, and she glanced at them. A questionnaire from a car wash—how was the service? A reminder from the dentist; a chimney sweep was coming. Things that come in the mail, but nothing about him. She stuffed the papers back in, but then she had second thoughts.

She brought out the reminder from the dentist and punched into the GPS the address it had been sent to. It would take ten minutes to reach the destination, she was told.

Ilka headed toward the harbor. A large, open area behind the hotel looked like a construction site that had been deserted for years, from the way the weeds and small trees had taken over. The windows of enormous warehouses closer to the city were boarded up, but a new park had been built in the southern part of the harbor area. It would have looked nice had there been people around. Someone here must have been ambitious, had wanted to accomplish something, she thought, but likely had failed. For a moment, the sense of emptiness and abandonment overwhelmed her. She looked at the GPS. Who knew what she'd find at that little black-and-white marker?

The residential street looked like the ones she'd driven around on earlier. But behind the house where her father had lived with his new family, the ground sloped down to a river with large trees leaning out over the banks. It wasn't hard to see that this was one of the town's better neighborhoods. Ilka approached the house slowly. She took in everything around her, tried to imagine how it had been for him to come home to the life being lived here. It was far from Brønshøj Square, in every way.

She parked in front of the large, square, white wooden house with a porch extending all the way across the front. It took her a moment to notice someone on the porch, a woman in a wheelchair moving toward the front door. The small, frail woman's light hair was pinned up on her head. Her father's wife; Ilka was sure of it. The front door opened, and a blond woman appeared carrying a tray. The two women spoke; then the younger woman looked over toward the car. She took the tray back into the house. The woman in the wheelchair stayed outside, but she didn't look Ilka's way.

Suddenly Ilka realized she was clenching the wheel. The engine was still running, and the car jerked when she stepped on the gas and drove away. Obviously, they had recognized the Chevy.

She reached the end of the street before noticing it was blocked, leaving her no choice but to turn around and drive back. This time she drove past the house without slowing. Out of the corner of her eye, she saw the other woman in the doorway, this time without the tray.

8

Ilka blinked as the bright sun shone directly in her eyes. Mentally, she felt dead tired, and she was thirsty. Annoyed by the sunlight, she turned her head to the side. After her little excursion to her father's house, she had tiptoed up to his room and closed and locked the door. She'd sat on the bed for a while before pulling out the drawers in his desk one by one, first carefully, then with greater impatience. She wanted answers. She felt his presence strongly, all the time, not only there in the room but when driving his car. At his enormous box of a house, with the charming front porch and the lawn that looked as if it had been trimmed with nail scissors, she hadn't sensed him at all.

She curled up. Later she realized she had fallen asleep with her clothes on. Her pants pinched her waist. She raised herself onto her elbows and noticed that the pile of letters she'd found in her father's desk drawer the evening before was about to fall behind the bed.

Some of the letters she'd found were hers, the ones she'd sent him over the years, bound by a wide rubber band and stuffed in the top drawer. The envelopes had been cut open, the letters unfolded. And read. She could see that from the dog-eared corners and creases. She felt a lump in her throat when she found them, and when she read the last one, the one in which she had written about Erik's death, she began sobbing. The letter was stained; it had been read more than once; that much was certain. But it wasn't that pile she had knocked over in her sleep. Another, smaller pack of letters had been stored in the desk, letters he had written to her. Her name was on the envelopes, but they had never been stamped and sent.

There were birthday cards and Christmas cards, and a photo of a little pony had been enclosed in the first letter. A date had been written in the right-hand upper corner—April 1983, six months after he'd left Denmark.

"See who's here waiting for you, you'll be the finest little horse and rider." The photo had been taken in front of a large racetrack, and her father posed beside the pony. There wasn't a word in the letter about him leaving for good. It was only a happy note from a father to his little daughter.

Almost eight months passed before he had written again. On December 2, 1983, he was looking forward to showing her how Americans decorated for Christmas. "They don't hold back," he wrote. "Wait until you see the elf arrangement in one of the fancy department stores in Chicago, and they also put caramel in the hot chocolate. I'm looking forward to seeing you again, Trotter, the pony is doing fine."

Trotter. She'd forgotten that name. His little trotting horse. Images began popping up. Lost memories, pulled up from out of the deep. Summer evenings at Havnsie Lake, where they ate fried eel, her father's favorite food, at the inn. One of his friends from the racetrack had owned a summerhouse down there, and occasionally they had borrowed it. They had eaten outside in the small yard. She'd been given extra scalloped potatoes, which she mashed.

She could almost physically recall what it had been like, walking down to the harbor to look at all the boats. The smell of tarred bulwarks, the sound of the water lapping against the railing. She'd held her father's hand while carrying an ice cream cone, her mother smiling from under her broad summer hat.

After the first few years, the letters became less frequent.

"My big girl," one of them said. "I think about you. And I think about how your mother is doing. Nothing went like I expected it to, we know that now. I have so often thought about the direction your life has taken. Do you have children? Have you found a good husband?"

There were fourteen letters in the pile. The last one had been written four years ago. Of course, that wasn't many over a thirty-three-year period, yet she was shaken. Why had he never sent them?

She heard a faint knock on the door. Sister Eileen called out.

"Just a moment," Ilka called. Quickly she gathered up her father's letters and put them back in the drawer; then she walked over and opened the door.

The gray-clad nun stood holding a breakfast tray. Tea, toast, jam, and a glass of juice. "I am so very sorry about the inconvenience you had yesterday, having to fetch your things at the hotel. I hadn't understood that you preferred to stay here."

Ilka stepped aside. "It wasn't a problem. Please don't worry." The sister walked in and set the tray down.

Ilka needed a shower, and she still had to unpack her suitcase properly. Even though it wouldn't affect her appearance much, given how little she'd brought along to wear.

"I only thought that you might have felt uncomfortable

sleeping in your father's bed." Sister Eileen glanced over at the bed.

"I'm okay with that; it's no problem for me being here."

The nun wouldn't leave it alone. "Some people would probably not like it. We don't know exactly how long he lay there before he was found."

Now Ilka looked over at the bed. "You mean this is where he died?" For some reason, she had assumed it had happened at his home.

"Yes, this is where he departed this life."

Ilka stood for a moment, not knowing what to say, and Sister Eileen misinterpreted her silence. "Of course I changed the bedclothes immediately."

"Wasn't my father living with his family?" Ilka asked, ignoring this bed business. She told the sister about driving by his house and seeing the two women on the porch, one in a wheelchair, the other younger.

"Your father and Mary Ann were involved in a serious traffic accident eighteen years ago. She was injured worse than he was, she never walked again, but he was also affected by it." She stepped over to the window. "He was driving the car."

Ilka had unconsciously moved away from the bed. Yet she didn't feel uncomfortable knowing he had died there. It was more as if she were standing in a very private space, very intense, which her father filled even more now.

"It was probably Leslie you saw on the porch; she's their oldest daughter. She stayed home to take care of her mother, even though Amber also has been living there since your father died. But make no mistake, he lived there, even though he often spent the night here. I believe he did so mostly out of consideration to his wife and daughter, so they wouldn't be woken when he was dragged out of bed."

Ilka nodded. That made sense. She set down the glass of orange juice she'd been drinking. "It's very sweet of you, but you don't have to take care of my breakfast. I don't want anyone to be bothered because I'd rather stay here. It's no problem for me to use the kitchen."

"It's no bother whatsoever," the nun said. "I'm happy to help. The business is yours now, so if there's anything I can do, please let me know."

She stood with her hands clasped in front of her.

Ilka nodded. True, the business was hers now, as if for one happy moment she could have forgotten.

She poured herself a cup of tea and walked over to the window. A woman was sitting on a bench by the parking lot, staring up at the room, or so it seemed. Hadn't she been sitting there yesterday, too, when Ilka came home? Ilka leaned forward and studied her. "Do you know that woman on the bench down there?"

Sister Eileen shrugged. "Don't worry about her," she said, without even glancing outside. "Two men are waiting for you downstairs."

Ilka looked at her in surprise. "Who?"

"Policemen. They would like to talk to you." The nun grabbed the empty juice glass and headed for the door.

Ilka set her teacup down and checked the clothes she'd slept in. "Police! How long have they been waiting?"

"They arrived when I was about to come up with the tea. Go ahead and eat your breakfast; it won't hurt them to wait. They could have called and let us know they were coming."

Ilka promised to be ready in ten minutes. An idea suddenly came to her. "I'd like to give away all my father's clothes to your parish, if you think they could use them. I could also take them there."

Sister Eileen looked a bit confused for a second. "That's

very thoughtful of you." She added that she could have them sent; Ilka wouldn't have to bother. "If you'll just sort them, so we can put them in plastic sacks. Thank you so much. I'm certain people will be very pleased."

After the sister closed the door, Ilka gobbled down the two pieces of toast and found her toiletry bag. Ten minutes later, she stepped into the arrangement room where she'd sat with the Norton family the day before. "Can I help you?" She looked at the two police officers.

All sorts of thoughts had rushed through her head while she'd taken a lightning-quick shower and put on clean clothes. She still hadn't sent the papers to her lawyer, so if the visit had anything to do with legal matters, she was very much on her own. Which she was anyway, no matter what the reason for their visit, she thought, as she studied the two uniformed men who had stood when she came in.

One of them was an older man with a thick, full beard; the other looked to be in his early thirties. He had strong features and broad shoulders. Ilka noticed the brown cardboard box on the floor beside them.

"Morning, ma'am!" the older officer said. He stuck his hand out and introduced himself as Officer Stan Thomas. He was trying—and failing—to hide how astonished he was by Ilka's appearance. No doubt he wasn't expecting a tall beanpole of a woman with wet hair, wearing jeans and sneakers.

Ilka held the hand of the younger policeman longer than necessary, mostly to see how he reacted. It didn't seem to bother him; on the contrary, he smiled. "Officer Jack Doonan."

"Sorry if we're interrupting anything," the other officer said.

Ilka was still looking at the younger man's prominent

chin and the line leading up to his cheekbone. His face was like something out of the comics, where masculine men looked as if they had been carved from granite. *He's on the list,* she decided, even though he wasn't exactly her type. The list of possible decent screws in Racine, which had only one name: his.

"You're not interrupting anything." She wrenched her eyes away. They weren't here just to chat. Should she offer them something? Should she be a bit more aloof before she found out what was up? Would it be better to ask them to come back when Artie was around? He had messaged her once last night; he wasn't coming in until the meeting with the Norton family. He'd worked until two in the morning and wanted to sleep in.

She cleared her throat when they sat down. "I'm sorry, would you repeat that?"

The officer nodded seriously. "We think we know who he is." He leaned forward, as if he thought she might not understand English so well. "Is it Denmark, where you come from?"

Ilka nodded. "You think you know who *who* is?" She was confused, and now she was the one who leaned forward.

"At least we have a very strong suspicion of who he could be."

"He," she said, impatient now. "Who do you mean?"

"The man you picked up at the morgue yesterday."

"Okay!" Her shoulders slumped. "And now you need to see him again?"

The younger officer shook his head, and he pointed down at the box to say something, but his partner beat him to it. "I would like to have a look at him, in fact." He nodded. "We believe it's a guy from here in town. He disappeared twelve years ago, but I knew him back when he was a boy. And I know his mother. His dental records are arriving later today, but we're still waiting to hear from his former doctor. So, our identification isn't confirmed yet, which is why we haven't contacted his relatives."

"You're very welcome to go out and look at him," Ilka said, well knowing she would have to pull out all three of the refrigerator drawers, because she didn't know where Artie had put him.

"There was a bag close to where he was assaulted, and our techs found his fingerprints on it," said Officer Doonan, the younger of the two. "We brought along his belongings."

Ilka nodded hesitantly and remembered what Artie had said about the expense of taking in deceased homeless. Maybe that problem was solved? "I'll make sure his belongings are taken care of." She tried to remember the code for the garage. "Why did he disappear?"

The officers followed her past the preparation room. They kept discreetly in the background when she punched the code in to unlock the door. The black coffin was gone. In its place was the plainer one that had been standing up against the wall, trimmed and ready to go. Suddenly Ilka realized there must be another room where the deceased were placed after being embalmed and laid into a coffin. She thought about the door between the preparation room and the door out to the garage.

"Mike Gilbert was a seventeen-year-old boy back then, or maybe he'd just turned eighteen," Officer Thomas said. "The way I remember it, he and Ashley had been going together a few months when it happened."

"Ashley?" Ilka held the door for them.

"A girl from here in town. She was a year ahead of him in school, a real head-turner. And Mike wasn't anything special." The way he said this made Ilka think he'd turned his head for a look at her a few times himself.

"The afternoon it happened, they'd planned to meet after school down at the lake, at the south end of town. It was freezing. I couldn't understand what they were doing down there."

They reached the refrigerator.

"Later we found out they met there when they wanted to be sure they were alone. Mike had a little sister, so it was their hideout, guess you could say. There's a little fishing cabin up on the cliff by the lake; they had blankets and a few sleeping bags stowed away there. Afterward Mike admitted they'd smoked pot and had sex; then he'd left a few hours later for work. She was found on the shore, at the bottom of the cliff. But he claims she was still alive when he left her, still in the cabin."

"Did you think he pushed her?"

Officer Thomas shook his head. "First we thought she'd slipped on the ice. Some places around here it's hard to see in the winter where Lake Michigan ends and the beach begins. Unfortunately, there are way too many serious accidents on the lake, and not only in winter. But the dirt on her clothes indicated she fell from above, even though there's heavy underbrush along the cliff up by the cabin. You don't just step off into empty space there. And the next day, like we said, Mike came into the station and admitted he and Ashley had been at the cabin. He insisted she was alive when he left, and her phone was in her pants pocket; we could see she'd sent a message to her father at four thirty. That gave Mike an alibi, because he showed up at work at four, and his boss and others at the shop confirmed he'd been there all the time. He was our main suspect, though, but we never managed to charge him. And then suddenly one day he was gone. We haven't seen him since, and that sort of supported what we all thought we knew. That he'd done it. But what happened, and how he managed to slip out of town, I don't know. He just disappeared, and that's one way to admit you're guilty."

Now the younger officer asked, "But you didn't have any leads when he disappeared?"

Officer Thomas shook his head. "Not even one. He left his phone in his room, but we put a wiretap on his mother's phone just in case he called home anyway. No luck. He didn't make any cash withdrawals, and his mother says he couldn't have had more than ten or fifteen dollars on him when he left. We started thinking he was dead too. In a lot of ways, it resembles a case from 1988, where a young man from Milwaukee disappeared the same way. Though he wasn't suspected of murder. He was going to visit a friend but never showed up. The police thought he'd run into a serial killer who later was sentenced for killing several young men in Wisconsin."

"But now you believe Mike Gilbert came back?" Ilka pulled out the top drawer—old Mrs. Norton. Gilbert was in the middle drawer, and Ilka stepped back to give the two officers room.

Officer Thomas's face changed expression when he pulled the steel tray out to view the battered corpse. Artie hadn't worked on the deceased, since there was no money for embalming or reconstructing the battered face, and the body was still covered with blood and dirt from where he was found.

The policeman stepped back. "If we hadn't identified him from fingerprints, it would've been nearly impossible."

The young man had a full beard and head of hair; splotches of dried blood clung to his head. His face was puffed up badly, and both eyes were swollen shut. It was indeed difficult to recognize a face so badly beaten as this one.

Why am I staring down at this? Ilka thought. The officer shook his head and pushed the tray back in again. She hadn't intended to look. And it did her no good to see someone in such bad shape. Thirty years old, and beaten to death.

Shit! she said to herself. Not so much because the dead young man lying below her bedroom had probably murdered a girl, but while alive he had possibly been on the run most of his adult life, and now he lay in her funeral home, a shattered wreck that no one wanted anything to do with. Even if she had to pay Artie herself, she decided that at the very least he would be washed off before being interred. She followed the two officers back.

"I'll give the box of his things to Artie Sorvino," she said.

"Thanks," Officer Thomas said. "And, of course, you'll hear from us when we get a definite identification; his family will have to cover the expenses. Though I just heard his sister is sick; they think it's cancer, so if the family doesn't have good health insurance, don't expect to get much out of them."

Ilka nodded, but she already knew she didn't have the heart to squeeze money out of a mother who had lost her son many years ago, a son who'd finally returned, only to be killed.

Artie walked in the door and stopped when he saw the two officers. He glanced over at Ilka.

"I let them look at the man we picked up from the morgue," she said. "They think they know who he is."

"Yeah?" Artie said. Ilka thought he looked relieved that the policemen weren't there regarding the funeral home's demise.

"We have a good idea," Officer Thomas said, "but it hasn't been officially confirmed."

"Mike Gilbert," the younger officer said, as if the entire town should know who that was.

"Really? I didn't see that coming." He pulled the refrigerator drawer out and studied the body for a moment before closing it again. "It can't be his face you recognized."

9

"Do you know anything about what happened to him?" Ilka asked when the policemen left. She followed Artie out into the kitchen.

"I know his mother." He grabbed a few plates out of a cupboard. "She never got over it. I didn't know him or the girl, either, but they were the talk of the town."

Ilka shook her head when he asked if she had eaten. He handed her some silverware, and she asked if he was ready to talk to the Norton family.

"I already talked to them. I stopped by on the way; they were all at the mother's house. The funeral service will be on Saturday. They're keeping the coffin, as was agreed with the deceased, and they're also going to buy four charms and a silver chain; I've billed them for that. But we kept the agreement on the flowers from the mother's garden."

Ilka nodded. She thought about a waiter she once knew. He'd taken pride in his ability to convince guests who ordered meatballs to drink an expensive burgundy. It was all in the way you sell, he'd said. And she'd had to agree. Though it said more about him than about the customers at his restaurant.

After Artie finished bragging about his sale, he said the

Golden Slumbers Funeral Home had invited them over, so Ilka would have the chance to meet the new owners before starting in on the transfer of ownership. "We can grab a bite to eat before we go; I started the grill." He nodded toward the back before walking into the garage for the white bucket of fish. "They need to be eaten today."

Ilka nodded. Not because she was particularly wild about eating the fish he'd put in the back of the hearse, but she could see in Artie's look that he was testing her again.

Why in hell is there a grill in a funeral home? she asked herself, though she kept her face blank.

"What would you like to drink?" Artie walked over to the refrigerator. "I'm having a beer."

His words were innocent enough, but something in his tone and, again, the look in his eye annoyed her. "I don't drink alcohol."

"Not at all? Never a beer, never a glass of wine?" He eyed her. "You have a drinking problem?"

She tilted her head and gazed at him. Whenever she turned down an offer of alcohol, the obligatory question followed: Why? She weighed which version would be best to throw at him. "I don't have a problem with alcohol. It's just I don't like it."

She read his eyes; he seemed to accept her explanation and presumably categorized her as a bore. "So you don't smoke, either?" he asked later, when he returned with the grilled fish.

Ilka shook her head and found a root beer in the back of the refrigerator.

She held her plate out, and he gave her two delicious-looking pieces of fish, which he offered to fillet. She squeezed lemon juice over them. "There's bread in the kitchen too," he said.

"Do you ever miss your gallery and your life in Florida?" she asked.

He slid some fish onto his own plate. "I do, yes." He spooned up some coleslaw and dumped it over his fish; then he passed it over to her. "I miss the life, sitting in the sun and watching people on Duval Street while I work. It's a little hard to do that here."

Ilka asked if he ever painted or sculpted anymore.

"I do wood carving. You'll see that if you ever stop by my place."

"But don't you miss people coming into your gallery and getting excited about what you've created?" She remembered how proud Erik had been when people praised his photographic portraits at the few exhibitions he'd held.

He chewed without looking at her. "It's more that I miss talking to people, like when they stopped by to see Artie the Artist."

She almost laughed but stopped herself when she saw he was serious.

"I miss all the variety, the diversity, the tolerance. You probably won't be here long enough to see how people in this town all think the same way. How little anyone stands out, how much gets left unsaid, because no one thinks it's worth making someone mad. I miss the crazy guy with the big hat who got drunk and sang on the way home from Sloppy Joe's bar. I miss the tourists kissing on the beach at sundown. Keith telling crazy stories he made up about Hemingway. Bald-faced lies. All the pleasuremongers and street artists. And the women. You meet the best women in Key West. And then of course I miss the climate," he added. "It's cold as a well-digger's ass up here, most of the time. And everybody talks about the weather, *all* the time."

"We do that in Denmark, too. In many ways, we're lucky to live where the weather is always changing. At least it gives people something to talk about."

He smiled and took the last bite of his fish. Ilka looked him over for a moment. It was easy to imagine Artie the Artist on a porch, wearing his Hawaiian shirt, listening to the Beach Boys. In fact, it was harder to picture this gaudy undertaker behind a closed door with the big fan roaring.

"And I miss the food," he added.

"Why didn't you go back?" She drank the rest of her root beer, which tasted like bubblegum in a bottle.

Artie checked his watch before standing and picking up their plates. He nodded toward the preparation room. "If I weren't here, who would make sure they look decent?"

"There must be others who could. Surely you don't need an art education to learn how to embalm."

"Anyone can do the embalming, but not many people can re-create a face and bring it back to life."

Ilka didn't ask, but then she didn't need to. It wasn't hard to see that the appreciation of a deceased's relatives was much deeper and more meaningful than remarks from happy tourists strolling by Artie the Artist on the main street of Key West.

He carried the plates into the small kitchen and returned. "Ready to go?"

She nodded; then she asked if Sister Eileen ever ate with him.

"Once in a while. Mostly she eats lunch by herself at her place."

His black pickup was parked just outside the door. Artie pointed to the end of the addition that held the coffin storage room. "She has a little apartment; she likes to go over there on breaks. I don't know how it is in Denmark, but here, she's not on salary. She's a volunteer, and she receives donations for the work she does. She gives most of the money to the church. Occasionally your dad put on small charity auctions; the profit was donated to her parish. She liked your dad a lot, and he understood how important it was to her to be useful. But nuns aren't allowed to take salaried jobs. I haven't said anything to her yet, but if I take over, she can stay with me."

Ilka got into the passenger side of the pickup.

"Even though there probably won't be much to do at first. All this business with laminating and bookmarks and folders, I won't need that. But she'll still talk to people and greet them, and a lot of them like how the church is represented here, sort of."

They drove past several small bars and restaurants she hadn't noticed before. On the sidewalk in front of a big Harley-Davidson dealership, enormous bikes were lined up in an impressive row. But it still seemed like no one was home in Racine. Artie hung a right on the coast road, and after a few hundred yards he turned in. They drove past an impressive building and farther on to a large parking lot that spread out on both sides of the road; Ilka thought it was the city hall until she noticed the sign with cursive script—GOLDEN SLUMBERS FUNERAL HOME. Behind the parking lot, Lake Michigan was completely calm, and the American flag on the enormous flagpole barely moved. The flagpole was fenced in on a small plot of grass in the middle of the parking lot.

Artie led her to a back door with EMPLOYEES ONLY written on it. A tall body-builder type in his early thirties stood outside nearby, smoking a cigarette. His face had delicate features, and he nodded when they approached and told them to go on in. Ilka couldn't help looking closely. His dark eyes were so deep set that his forehead cast a shadow over his irises. Otherwise he was handsome enough.

"What are we actually going to talk about in here?" she whispered. She looked around. "I haven't heard from my lawyer yet. I don't dare sign anything that has to do with the deal, not before she contacts me."

They walked down a long, high-ceilinged passageway with big windows on both sides that reminded Ilka of the party tents rented out in Denmark, except the passageway was wood. A red deep-pile runner lay on the floor, and small decorative gold rosettes lined the walls. Three short steps at the end led up to the building itself. Red rugs also covered the floors inside, and behind a massive mahogany desk sat a nun who looked like Sister Eileen's twin. She stood and smiled when they approached; then she asked them to follow her. She wore the same type of shoes as Sister Eileen, beige and soft, almost indistinguishable from her tightly woven skin-toned nylons.

"We're just here to say hello; they want to meet you," Artie said. She felt his hand on her back, as if he were leading her on a dance floor.

"They're waiting for you. Please go on in!"

Ilka hadn't thought much about what to expect, but she froze when she walked into the enormous high-paneled room with heavy draperies and an oval conference table, high-gloss finish, made from the same massive mahogany as the desk outside.

At one end of the table sat a plump but elegant elderly woman wearing a dark blue suit, her hair piled on top of her head. A man sat at the other end. Ilka guessed he was in his early sixties. His hair was neatly cut and almost white, and he wore a vest under a dark blue suit with a muted tie. A small, neatly folded handkerchief stuck up out of his suit

pocket. A thin woman a few years younger than Ilka sat between the two. Carlotta was arrogant and snobbish; Artie
had told her before they walked in. That sounded accurate to
Ilka, the way the woman watched her as she walked around
the table shaking hands. Beside her sat her older brother,
David, a stocky man with acne scars. He stared down at a
stack of papers. The third brother, Jesse, was still outside
smoking. All three of Phyllis's children had deep-set eyes
that gave their faces an oddly anonymous look.

Artie had explained that Phyllis Oldham inherited the
funeral home from her husband, Douglas. He had run the
business with his brother, Howard, the English-gentleman
type at the end of the table.

Mrs. Oldham stood up and warmly welcomed Paul
Jensen's Danish daughter to Racine. Her large ice-blue eyes
sparkled. The children must have gotten their eyes from
their father, Ilka thought, which a glance at their uncle confirmed.

"Have you been to the museum? There's a great deal
about the Danish immigrants who came to Racine in the late
1800s. Two-thirds of the townspeople at the time were once
from Denmark, did you know that? You'll meet many of
their descendants out in West Racine." She added that some
of them still spoke Danish.

"Coffee will be served in a moment," Howard said, "and
we also have kringles. After all, you Danes did bring the
kringle to our town." *You Danes*—it was almost as if Ilka
personally had introduced the pastry to Racine.

"We have three Danish bakers famous for their kringles.
Thanks to them, Racine is known as Kringle Town." He
laughed. "President Obama even visited one of our bakers
in 2010 to try out a kringle before a meeting."

The sister knocked on the door and came in with a large

white cardboard box containing an oval kringle with icing. "A black currant kringle." She set it on the table and then handed out cups to everyone.

Ilka bit into what they proudly called the "famous Danish kringle." Unlike the kringles in Copenhagen bakeries, it was as heavy as a rum ball. There was nothing light, airy, and sugary about the clump of dough with thick icing, so sweet that her teeth screamed. Everyone else seemed happy with it, though; Artie had already gobbled his up before coffee was poured.

"We were very fond of Paul," Mrs. Oldham said after everyone had been served. "He was a good and loyal colleague, though we of course were competitors. But we always chose to think of ourselves as colleagues; that's a much better way to do business in a small town like Racine. We were all very sad when we heard he passed away."

The door behind them opened, and Jesse, the son who had been standing outside smoking, walked in. He sat down beside his mother and helped himself to a piece of the kringle.

None of the children had spoken; it was easy to decode the hierarchy at Golden Slumbers.

"We were also very sorry to hear about the difficulties your father fell into before his death," Mrs. Oldham continued. "And as we told Artie, we would like to help you out of this unfortunate situation."

Ilka said nothing, though it annoyed her that the family matriarch made it sound as if they only wanted to bail an old friend out of trouble. To top it off, an old *dead* friend. As if they were forking over sixty thousand dollars only as a personal favor.

"Fortunately we're also able to act quickly. Tomorrow is the IRS deadline, isn't that right?"

Artie nodded.

"What exactly happens with this type of business deal?" Ilka asked. "As I understand, it's not the physical assets of my father's business you're buying, only...the business part."

Phyllis and Howard Oldham both nodded. "Business activities, yes."

"And now you'll be dealing with the tax authorities?" she added.

They nodded again. The three siblings sitting in silence like stone statues were getting on Ilka's nerves. Apparently, they were following the conversation; each sat with a pen and sheet of paper, onto which they occasionally scribbled something.

"We are completely okay with that," Howard said. "The first thing to take care of is the sixty thousand dollars to be paid tomorrow. After that, the final amount will be settled, presumably within the next...maybe six months."

"But you can take over all the business activities immediately?" Ilka asked. She was thinking of the man they had just picked up at the morgue. It would certainly be nice to avoid the expenses connected with him, especially now that it looked like his family wouldn't be able to pay for his burial.

Howard nodded. "Of course that's contingent on you signing the sales agreement; that has to be done by noon tomorrow at the latest to avoid having the IRS freeze all the assets. But if everything goes smoothly, we'll be ready to take over by this weekend. We'll be able to handle the current clients you have and all those who might come in."

He pointed at the sons. "Jesse handles the pickups in our business; his older brother and I do the embalming; while Phyllis and Carlotta handle all contact with the relatives, all sales and marketing and printed material."

"But we'd like to show you around," Mrs. Oldham said. "You haven't even seen what we have to offer." She pointed at her eldest son and asked him to take Miss Nichols around. "Have a look across the street, too."

He looked terrified; his mother might as well have grabbed a belt and whipped him. He uttered a weak excuse about having to go downstairs, something about a coffin that needed to be sent to the crematorium before three.

Mrs. Oldham's eyes lingered on him for a moment. Then she straightened up, smiled at Ilka, and told her she would be very pleased to take over. She immediately stood and strode toward the door. "Follow me; I'll show you our business."

Ilka was already impressed when they reached the second floor, where a large display room was practically decorated with coffins. As if it were a safari hunter's trophy room, they had hung the ends of coffins in perfectly spaced rows on all the walls. Coffins of all colors, coffins with carvings and without any decoration. Varnished and unvarnished. It was like stepping into a luxury catalog; nothing was ordinary. Urns of gold and glazed clay, large centerpieces to be decorated with photos and placed on coffins. There was even an example of how it would look if an enlarged photo of the deceased covered the entire coffin lid. Overwhelming, and way too much. Nothing could be further from the more Spartan Danish mentality concerning funeral and burial ceremonies.

After Erik died, Ilka didn't get out of her pajamas for three days. The funeral director had come to their house and showed her a folder. Photos of various coffins that looked absolutely nothing like what hung from the walls here. Ilka had also chosen the chapel from pictures he brought out. Also, the decoration for the coffin, though she changed her mind later. Erik's coffin had been covered with yellow tulips, a flower he had loved.

They walked back downstairs. Phyllis Oldham was agile and a fast talker. Ilka noticed the same stink of formaldehyde as in their funeral home, not only in the hallway but all over the first floor. Heavy paintings in gaudy frames hung from the walls. It was all overwhelming, yet it also projected authority, proof that the Oldham family was successful and had been for many years. One wall was devoted to pictures of the family over four generations; *it probably goes even further back*, Ilka thought. She followed Mrs. Oldham across the street to an even larger building.

"These rooms are for larger funeral arrangements we can't handle across the street." She nodded at the building they'd just left. "We also have live music here. We've had gospel choirs as well as string orchestras."

They walked into a large, high-ceilinged hall with seats and a stage at the end, like a theater. It was beautiful. And it could hold almost one thousand people, Mrs. Oldham said. "We rent this out for weddings when there are no funeral arrangements. The acoustics in here are so good that we've also put on a few concerts open to the public."

Ilka smiled. She wondered how her father had made any sort of a living, having to compete with Golden Slumbers.

Mrs. Oldham smiled back at Ilka. "There will always be a need for funeral homes." She turned off the lights in the large crystal chandelier, and they headed back to the office across the street. "It's a bit like hairdressers and lawyers."

She walked faster now, though it seemed wrong somehow, moving so fast through a funeral home. Ilka could barely keep up.

"As I said, David takes care of preparation. We have an elevator, so the deceased comes directly up to Reception from the parking lot. We have two large cold rooms in there, and out back the florist has her own room. When they come to decorate, they can just walk in. They can also decorate out here when necessary. And we have our own crematorium; it's on the outskirts of town."

Earlier, Ilka had thought that the crematorium might be at the rear of the building, that they burned the deceased in the middle of town, which made her uneasy. But Artie had explained there were small apartments in back that they rented to relatives arriving from out of town.

"All of our marketing material is upstairs," Mrs. Oldham said. "We send representatives to all the senior citizen fairs, and we visit nursing homes to speak with the elderly. Carlotta has begun arranging home parties; they've been an enormous success. It's like Tupperware parties, where female friends and families get together and hear about all our offers. Jewelry for ashes has become incredibly popular."

Ilka gawked, though she said nothing.

"We have to protect our interests. Paul would have said the same. Now that people can order coffins on the Internet, we have to emphasize service and extras."

"Time to go," Artie said when they returned to the arrangement room, where Ilka had laid her jacket. The kringle box was empty, and it appeared he'd had the pleasure of the snobbish daughter's company the entire time Ilka had been gone.

"You're welcome to walk through the garage," Mrs. Oldham suggested after they said their good-byes and thanked her for the pastry.

Artie nodded, but instead he led her out the way they had come. "She just wants you to see their two new hearses and the escort cars to lead them." He held the door for her.

10

Ilka had just sat down in her father's office chair to take a look at his will and the legal papers on the transfer of activities when her phone beeped: an e-mail from her lawyer in Denmark. The attorney was furious that right off the bat, Ilka had signed papers confirming she was Paul Jensen's daughter. Now Ilka was stuck with the consequences. This wasn't good. On the other hand, it was unavoidable, because, quite likely, their relationship would have been confirmed anyway. And presumably Ilka had a way out of the hopeless situation she'd put herself in.

"Just don't count on any financial windfall. You'll be lucky to get out of this without losing anything. If you enter into a transfer agreement with Golden Slumbers Funeral Home, it looks like they can take over your debt. Both to the IRS and the other creditors. But it's important to pay the sixty thousand dollars tomorrow, to prevent the governmental wheels from starting to turn. Otherwise you risk them making a claim on your assets in Denmark."

Ilka was about to write back that she had just visited the Oldhams, that everything was ready to be signed, when Sister Eileen appeared in the doorway and asked her to come.

"Can it wait a moment?" Ilka glanced at her father's will with a mixture of fear, excitement, and anxiety; she had decided to put off looking at it until last.

The nun shook her head. "No, unfortunately. You should come right now. There's someone you need to talk to."

"Can't Artic handle it?"

Sister Eileen shook her head again and began walking back to the reception area. Ilka followed her. She noticed the woman from a distance, sitting on one of the high-backed chairs along the wall. Her hair was in a loose ponytail, and she wore an oversized cardigan, a white blouse, and a pair of dark pants. It was her shoes, however, that revealed she'd left home in a hurry. Red Crocs with splotches of paint and blades of grass clinging to them.

Ilka looked in puzzlement at Sister Eileen, who said, "The police sent her here."

The woman walked over to them. "I want to see him." She took both of Ilka's hands in her own and looked pleadingly at her. "I have to see him."

Her face was pale, her lips pressed together to keep from sobbing, but tears appeared anyway when she began talking and slowly shaking her head. "It can't be true," she murmured.

"Go get Artie," Ilka said, sending Sister Eileen off with a gentle but firm shove.

"Let's go in here, into the arrangement room, shall we?" she said to the woman—Mike Gilbert's mother, Ilka was sure. They had just sat down when Artie walked in, but she stood and walked to him.

"Oh, Shelby!" He put his arm around her.

"You never met Mike, but I've got to know if it's my son they found," she said. Artie murmured something soothing; Ilka couldn't hear what. Obviously, they knew each other well. "The police say they're sure. Fingerprints and dental records match."

She looked exhausted, but she settled down as Artie spoke to her. Her head and shoulders sank, and suddenly her clothes looked much too big, as if she had shrunk. Tears dripped onto the floor, and Artie held her. Ilka left the room, but she heard him say the woman couldn't see her son.

"What do you mean?" she sobbed. "You don't have the right to stop me."

Artie spoke calmly. "I can't show him to you the way he is now. That wouldn't be good for anyone, least of all you. Give me a little time, and I'll get him ready. Come in tomorrow afternoon; then you can see him."

She pulled herself together and nodded. For a moment, she stared straight ahead; then she lifted her shoulders. Artie offered her a chair.

Ilka went out into the tiny kitchen, found some cups, and filled a carafe. She dumped some small wrapped chocolates into a bowl, then brought it all in and set it on the table and went back for a few bottles of water. She wasn't used to serving in this sort of situation, but she used what they had. Quickly she moved everything around on the table to make it look appealing, but it wasn't her strong suit; she realized that. Finally, she gave up and left everything alone.

Shelby Gilbert sat down. Pale, stone-faced, weeping. And so small and alone in her sorrow, Ilka thought.

"Do you have a photo of Mike?" Artie asked. He pulled a chair over and sat beside her.

Shelby didn't react, so he repeated his question and added, "I'll do everything I possibly can to make your son look like himself. But I need to see how he looked before he disappeared."

"But I can't afford it," she sobbed, gasping for breath.

"First I thought I'd have to sell the house, now that Emma is sick, so I could pay for her treatment. Then Mike wrote that he was coming home to help us. But now he's dead, and I can't afford to pay for his funeral."

That surprised Artie. "You've been in contact with him?"

Ilka offered her a cup of coffee in the pause that followed. Shelby nodded, then lifted a Kleenex out of the box and dried her cheeks. "I knew all the time he was out there. And I knew he would get in touch when he was ready. And he did; three years ago, he sent me a post office box address I could write to. We were careful; we only wrote a few letters a year. We were scared the police would come for him if they knew where he was. It's hard when you've been made the scapegoat. But then I wrote to him when his sister got the diagnosis. I just thought he should have the opportunity to say good-bye to her, if it came to that."

She began crying again, and Ilka felt her eyes growing damp as well at the thought of Shelby Gilbert's son lying in there. No one had been given the chance to say good-bye to him.

"We'll find a way," Artie said. "Don't be thinking about the money. But help me with the photo, so I can re-create his face. Unfortunately, there's been a lot of damage."

"Is it that bad? How bad?" Shelby looked straight into Artie's eyes. "What did they do to him?"

Artie ignored her question. "I won't be finished this weekend, but tomorrow I'll let you see him. And next week he'll be ready so you can say your good-byes. Do you want a funeral service?"

Shelby shook her head. "We just want to say good-bye, real quiet. It'll only be Emma and me, and of course I'll let their father know. He can come if he wants."

Artie nodded and suggested that Ilka and Shelby talk

some more about the interment. Or the inurnment, if she chose to have him cremated. He motioned for Ilka to follow him outside; then he closed the door behind them. "This is going to be on us, but try to keep the expenses down." He left, and shortly after she heard the fan start and the garage door open.

Keep the expenses down. Great idea, but how? How could she save money in this crazy undertaking business? She shook her head and walked back inside.

A pale Shelby Gilbert sat in the arrangement room, staring off into space. She'd stopped crying, but the corners of her mouth were quivering. Ilka handed her a cup of coffee. She set it down without drinking.

"She was no good," she said, her voice low now. "I warned him, told him she was a devilish girl; you can just tell, the kind of girl she was. She had him wrapped around her little finger, talked him into skipping school. And he admitted to smoking pot; he'd never done anything like that before. But he wouldn't listen; he was in love. And now they're both dead. So young."

Ilka sat down beside her in the chair Artie had pulled out. "But he came back," she said. She asked if he had seen his sister after he had returned.

"No. I didn't know he was back in town. The plan was that he would go to Milwaukee and I would meet him there. He wanted to visit Emma; she's in All Saints Hospital here in Racine, but I was scared that people would recognize him if he showed up here."

Her mouth began quivering again; her voice sounded brittle. "He didn't do it. You know that, right?" she asked, even though she had to be aware that Ilka couldn't know what had happened back then. "He wasn't the one who killed her. They used him as a scapegoat and ran him out of town. The town he was born and raised in. Jesus!"

She hid her face in her hands for a moment; then she straightened up and reached for Ilka's hand. "I can't pay for a big expensive funeral. I can't even pay the bills for my daughter's treatments. Our health insurance has turned us down because she has a brain tumor; they don't cover it when there's too big a risk to operate. But when I get the house sold, I hope there'll be enough money to cover your expenses with Mike."

She looked down at her hands. "I've already taken out a bank loan to cover Emma's first round of chemotherapy, so I'm not sure I can borrow any more. But the house should be easy to sell if I price it low enough."

Her tears began falling again. "I just want to see him one last time, so much," she murmured.

Ilka stroked her hand. "It sounds like you and Artie have already made a deal, and if you don't mind a plain coffin, I know we can work something out." She thought of the unvarnished wooden coffin they had decided to give to the homeless man, who as it turned out wasn't actually homeless.

"We'll need some clothes for him," Ilka said, and she asked if there was anything special Shelby wanted him to wear.

"I don't know if he can fit into anything he left behind. I haven't seen how much he's grown."

Ilka smiled at her. "Go home and have a look. Otherwise we'll find something. It was just if there was something you preferred."

They were standing up now, and Ilka noticed that the coffee had been left untouched again. Maybe she was doing something wrong during these conversations?

11

After her meeting with Shelby Gilbert, Ilka had gone up to her room and stuffed most of her father's clothes in some large grocery bags she'd found in the kitchen. Sister Eileen could send them to her parish. She'd placed a note on the nun's desk in the reception area, informing her that she could have the sacks of clothes in the hall. Later she dropped by the taco shop two blocks from the funeral home and grabbed a bite to eat. Then she shopped at the supermarket and picked up water, crackers, and a bag of chips. And some bread she could toast the next morning. She surveyed the refrigerator; the bread Artie had mentioned was more cardboard than bread. On the way to the checkout, Ilka had dropped two cream sodas in her cart.

Now everything was lined up on the desk, and she was reading the will from the very beginning.

"I bequeath everything I own except my funeral home business to my wife, Mary Ann Jensen, and my two daughters, Leslie Ann Jensen and Amber Ann Jensen. That includes the money deposited in my private accounts and the contents of the bank box in Mid-America Bank, 21075 Swenson Dr., Suite 100,

Milwaukee, Wisconsin. Everything is to be divided equally among the three, as my wife is wealthy. In addition, the house is in her name, and she has purchased most of the contents of the house. I bequeath Jensen Funeral Home to my daughter from my first marriage, Ilka Nichols Jensen. The business is to be transferred directly to her, and she is to be the sole owner of the business. If, however, she wishes to sell the funeral home business, Artie Sorvino and Sister Eileen O'Connor are to have first right of refusal before it is put on the market, at a price set by a person knowledgeable of the funeral home business."

Ilka was interrupted by her phone. Most likely not her mother, she thought; it was the middle of the night back home in Denmark, and hopefully she was sound asleep.

"Can you do a pickup?" Artie asked. Music was playing in the background.

"Not just now. I'm about to eat," she muttered. "And I'm reading through my father's papers." Also, she had an offer on Tinder. Some guy a few blocks away had invited her to meet him at a bar. "You'll have to take it yourself."

"You can be here in fifteen minutes; I'll be ready," he said, ignoring her objections. "Bring along plastic and the light stretcher. It's up on the second floor."

He hung up. A moment later, he'd messaged her his address.

It's a quick pickup. You'll be back in an hour.

She sighed and gathered the papers, laid them on the desk, and grabbed her fleece jacket from the bed.

She recognized the lighthouse as she drove the twisting road north along Lake Michigan, but the GPS told her to continue past it before turning right. The road down wasn't quite as steep as when she had picked up Artie and his fish. Houses lined both sides of the small side street. Nothing big; more like summerhouses, with short driveways. At the end of the street, she reached a turnaround and a small path that led to the last house, which faced the lake. The surface of the water looked like quicksilver, an artificial gray metallic sheen.

Ilka was about to shut the engine off when a young, light-haired woman came prancing out of the house; her hair was a mess, and her jacket sat crooked, as if it were a bathrobe. She waved at Ilka energetically, a sign that she was satisfied now, that it was okay with her for Artie to go to work.

Who the hell does he think he is? Ilka slammed the door of the hearse extra hard. He ordered her around to give himself time to finish screwing. Before she reached the path, Artie came walking toward her. He looked like he was about to invite her in for a tour, and she promptly turned on her heel and strode back to the car. "We'd better get going."

"It's probably best that you drive," he said, and headed for the passenger side.

She was about to protest, but then she dropped it. It would be asking too much of him to be on standby 24/7 for pickups. On the other hand, she felt it was tactless of him to get drunk and screw someone while she was going through her father's will.

"I was in the middle of an important telephone call," she said, after they were inside the hearse. "You maybe don't know this, but I have a business to run in Denmark and I can't just drop everything because you want a night off."

He ignored her complaint. "Isn't it nighttime in Denmark? There's seven hours' time difference, if I remember right."

"We have early meetings. I thought you put off the pickup until tomorrow."

He nodded. "This is a new one. An older man. He's been dead quite a while, maybe a week, maybe longer. He lived alone with his dog. The police think the dog tried to wake him up; it nearly licked his cheek off. The people in the apartment below found him. The dog's dead too; we'll take it along, now that the police are finished."

The hearse swayed and the shocks creaked when Ilka sped up on the steep gravel road. She liked the personality of the hearse, a bit grouchy but with a strong will. The lake looked like an enormous gray river in the broad side mirror, a river that disappeared when she cautiously turned onto the highway.

"We're taking a dog along?" she said, suspicious now. "Can't the people living below bury it?"

"The dog was all he had. It's part of the deal." Artie leaned his head against the window while she drove. "We'll put it in the coffin before we go to the crematorium; they won't even know it's there. It's only right that the two of them leave this world together."

She turned to him "Are you drunk, or what?"

He shook his head. "I'm fine, I just need to…"

She shook her head too; then she turned on the radio and twisted the worn, leather-covered button. She found a station playing an old Paul Simon song.

The police car pulled out just as they arrived. A light on the top floor was still on, and from the side window she saw a couple walk out on the front steps as she turned into the driveway. Artie had told her to back into the parking space so they wouldn't have to carry the deceased so far. Meanwhile he'd dozed off, and she elbowed him after she had parked in front of the main building. "We're here." She stared at him in annoyance.

Darkness shielded them, allowing them to work without interference from neighbors and passersby. Ilka was fine with that; she wasn't sure what she'd see up on the second floor, and she didn't know how she would react. There was that business about the cheek, too.

The couple standing in the doorway shook their hands. "We've been gone all week; that's why we didn't notice Ed hadn't been down with his dog," the woman explained apologetically as they walked up the steps. Her husband opened the door to the small hallway and told them Ed was in the living room.

The police had been thoughtful enough to leave several windows open, but the stink was nauseating anyway. Ilka discreetly pulled the hood on her jacket around and covered her mouth and nose.

"We've always looked out for each other; we'd never have let him lie here like this," the woman continued. "You hear so much about lonely people dying alone. But we got along really well. And we kept an eye on each other."

Her voice was wispy and anguished, as if she expected someone would blame her for not discovering the man living above them had been dead so long.

"But you're the ones who found him," Ilka said. "You haven't done anything wrong. Lots of people don't have good neighbors who look out for each other. Of course you should be able to travel. No one could know this would happen."

Ilka had no idea where all these words were coming from. Just as she didn't know if she was trying to comfort them or if she was stalling to avoid going into the living room.

She felt a cold wind blowing from in there, and she

remembered to breathe in through her mouth, as Artie had recommended. He'd already brought the stretcher in, and now he handed her a pair of gloves.

"What about a mask?" she whispered before entering the room.

He shook his head and explained that masks were necessary only when there was a threat of infection. And when dealing with the homeless, because you could never know what they might have.

"This guy here is okay. It's not a pretty sight, but there's no danger of catching something."

Ilka pulled on her gloves and followed him. She noticed the bulky furniture and heavy picture frames, big pillows on the sofa, wide armchairs. Everything was nice, attractive. Ed McKenna was on the floor by the open bedroom door, lying on his side with his arms folded. His dog lay curled up beside him.

Ilka froze. Seeing them lying there felt like a punch to the gut. Loneliness and solidarity. Together they had left the world behind. She felt Artie's eyes on her, aware that he was giving her a minute. The sight must also have hit him hard.

She nodded and joined him as he squatted down to turn McKenna over. Standing over the body, Ilka realized her anxiety had disappeared. Sure, it stank in there, and he was bloated, his skin was gray, but she'd thought it would be worse.

They carried the stretcher over and pulled the wheels up so it lay on the floor beside him. "You take hold of his legs; I'll grab his shoulders," Artie said. He was on his knees, ready to go.

Ilka leaned down and gripped the back of his knees.

"Get a good hold on him; he'll be middle-heavy when we lift him," Artie said. He counted to three. "Kneel down and lift with your legs. Tighten your stomach muscles; careful with your back."

Ilka concentrated on lifting and moving him slowly, not looking at him until he was on the stretcher. The skin on the left side of his face was missing. The exposed muscle was dark, but in one spot his cheekbone was visible.

"Might be insects," Artie said as they strapped the body down. "We'll come back for the dog."

Ilka nodded. She felt so sad it had taken so long to discover Ed McKenna was dead. That no one had missed him. Except his dog. They carried him slowly down the steps, Artie in front, Ilka leaning over a bit to level out the stretcher. The couple had returned to their apartment, but now they came out. "What about everything up there?" the man asked.

Artie shrugged and said they would have to contact the police, to hear if he had any relatives.

"He does; Ed has a daughter," the woman said from behind her husband.

"But you haven't contacted her?"

The couple looked at each other before shaking their heads. "Matter of fact, we haven't. We should have, of course we should, but coming home and finding him like this, it shocked us. We called the police at once."

"We don't have her number, either," the man added. "She lives somewhere over in upstate New York, but I don't know where."

"Most likely the police have found her; she's probably on her way. Or she'll show up in the morning." Artie was reassuring them; Ilka was very surprised he'd shaken off the drinking and sex and was acting as if he'd just been sitting around, waiting to be called to take care of Ed McKenna. "We'll also speak with his family. They may want him buried closer to them."

He pushed the stretcher into the car and told Ilka to get in, that he would get the dog.

She nodded. Though it hadn't been as bad as she had feared, she was relieved to not have to go back up there. She watched him come down with the dog, which he'd packed in a sheet. He slammed the rear door.

"Okay, we'll drive back and get him and the dog taken care of, and then I'd appreciate you driving me home. You mind if I roll down the window and smoke a cigarette?"

She shook her head and held her fingers out toward him in a V.

He looked questioningly at her; then he tapped an extra cigarette out of the pack. They smoked in silence as Ilka drove back to the funeral home. After she tossed the butt out the window, she held her hand out, asking for another.

She couldn't stop thinking about McKenna and the dog. The loneliness. She chain-smoked three of Artie's cigarettes before reaching the funeral home.

12

Ilka dropped Artie off and finally arrived home just before midnight.

She left the engine running as she got out and punched in the code to open the garage door. The cat appeared and snaked around her legs as she walked back. Gently she pushed the cat away, got in behind the wheel, and maneuvered the big, klutzy vehicle into the garage. The cat was right there when she shut off the engine and stepped out.

"Okay, okay," she muttered as she closed the garage door and yawned. She called the cat to follow her through the garage and into the passageway. Then she went into the kitchen for the rest of the grilled fish.

She made small talk to herself as she walked; she knew she would fall asleep if she didn't keep moving. Mumbling helped her cope with the deep stillness of the funeral home. And the darkness.

She laid the fish on a small plate and opened the door to the carport just outside. "Dinnertime, kitty," she called. The cat hopped up on its hind legs before she could set the plate down. "You're a hungry little thing, aren't you?"

She shook her head at herself and let the cat do what cats do. She walked upstairs. The sacks full of her father's clothes and shoes were gone; Sister Eileen must have taken them. Ilka liked the idea of his clothes having a new life somewhere else, worn by people unaware that the dark suits had been a funeral home director's uniform.

The burritos on the desk were still unopened, but she was too tired to care about food.

Ilka had also been too exhausted to pull the curtains before collapsing on the bed. It was still dark outside when she woke up. She lay there listening, disoriented and unsure of what had woken her. A thud from something falling. Or was it a door slammed shut? She concentrated as she lay staring up into the dark, trying to isolate the sound, but now everything was silent. She'd just closed her eyes when she heard it again. And again. Had she forgotten to close the door after feeding the cat?

Still half-asleep, she swung her legs out of bed, stuck her feet in her shoes, and wrapped a sweater around her shoulders.

She glanced at the clock: three thirty. She'd slept some, but not much. Out by the stairway, she fumbled for the light switch, then started down. Somewhere she heard an engine, or perhaps a transformer. The ceiling light hummed.

Halfway down, she stopped. She heard the noise again, and now she was sure a door had been slammed. Her footsteps were muffled by the thick dark blue carpet as she made her way through the office and past the kitchen. She took a deep breath and opened the door to the passageway.

The silence and darkness outside pressed in on her. The door leading to the carport was closed; she hadn't forgotten that one. Ilka walked over to the door to the cold room. Locked. She opened it slowly and turned on the light. The man and his dog still lay on the stretcher. She shivered. The two coffins were in the same place as the last time she'd

been there. Maybe she'd heard the ventilation system? It rattled slightly, the only noise in the room.

She shook her head at herself; then she walked over to
the garage and punched in the code. It was dark in there,
too. When she finally found the light switch, the fluores-
cents sputtered a few moments before showering the entire
garage in white.

Nothing. Refrigerator shut and garage door down.
Everything exactly the way it had been when she had parked
the hearse.

Don't be so stupid! she told herself. She was letting her
imagination run wild over the slightest noise—ridiculous!
As if she believed that the dead could rise and walk around.
And she'd never heard of anyone breaking into a funeral
home. What was there to steal? Formaldehyde and coffins.
Get a hold of yourself!

She switched the lights off and shut the door, checked
the garage doorknob an extra time to make sure it was
locked, then walked back upstairs. *Relax*, she told herself. In
two or three days, she'd be on her way back to Copenhagen.

She had no idea whether ten minutes or an hour had
gone by when she was awakened again. The noise was back,
and this time she was certain. She lay a few minutes before resolutely throwing off the comforter, pulling on a pair
of pants, and slipping her shoes on. She was determined
to shove out this final shred of the fear of darkness inside
her. At no time had she been bothered by sleeping over
a morgue. The dead would be the last to come up here
and haunt her. But rattling noises in dark, strange places
had never been her cup of tea. Usually she could control
her fear, but she was too exhausted to stop her imagination from running away with her. She tried to calm herself
while sneaking downstairs. What she really needed was a

decent meal, a good screwing, and a good night's sleep. Then she'd feel strong enough to handle these ghosts. She realized she'd stood up her Tinder date. She'd completely forgotten about him.

Down on the first floor, Ilka switched the passageway light on. She was determined to check every door. If she didn't get at least a few more hours' sleep, she would be too spaced-out to think clearly when signing the transfer agreement over at the Oldhams.

Door to the carport—locked. Preparation room—locked. Cold room—locked. Garage—locked. She punched in the code, turned on the light, and was on her way to the big garage door when she spotted him. In shock now, she saw the open middle drawer of the refrigerator, the empty steel tray pulled out. Mike Gilbert lay on the floor, twisted and battered. Dark splotches of blood on his face stood out as grotesque shadows. He lay on his back, his arms spread like someone being arrested and patted down, his legs splayed out crookedly.

Ilka's heart hammered as she stood frozen in the middle of the garage, staring at the dead man. Silence; that's all there was now, a deep silence. Except for the low hum from the ventilation fan. She had no idea what to do, and Artie wouldn't be coming in for several hours. Instinctively she backed up until she hit the wall. Her legs prickled; her arms felt weak. What in hell was going on?

A thought struck her: There might be someone there. Without budging an inch, she surveyed the entire garage; then she knelt down to look under the two trolleys. No one there. She was alone, she was sure. Almost sure, anyway. She struggled to think clearly; mostly she wanted to run up to her room and lock the door and wait for Artie. Her phone was in the room. Why hadn't she brought it along? *Idiot*, she muttered to herself. Then she realized she couldn't just leave the deceased lying there on the floor. It was undignified; it looked all wrong.

Slowly she approached him, but then she turned to get the stretcher over by the wall. She maneuvered it around the coffins, pushing it in front of her like a shield. Sweat ran down her back as she wrestled to put up the wheels. The noise she made was unnaturally loud. Should she call Artie? The police? Get Sister Eileen?

Her fingers had forgotten how to work together; she couldn't find the mechanism to release the wheels so she could lower the stretcher to the floor. Finally, though, she succeeded. Simply doing something helped her fight off panic. Without thinking, she leaned over to take hold of Mike Gilbert's torso.

She slipped her arms under his shoulders to get the best possible hold on him, but suddenly she pulled them back, an instinctive reaction. What was she doing? Could this be considered a crime scene? And it felt as if she'd grabbed a pile of wet sand. Scared now, she looked down at the man, but then she took hold again, squatted down, and slipped her arms underneath his body. She tried to lift him, but it was hopeless. Only now, sitting with her arms around the dead body, did she realize she might have been mistaken the first time she was down here.

But she had checked everywhere. Ilka was sure he hadn't been lying on the floor. She fought down her uncertainty. It must have happened after she'd gone back to bed.

She considered again whether to leave the body there until Artie came, let him decide what to do. Her palms were sweaty, the back of her T-shirt wet. Her eyes darted around the garage, into the nooks and crannies.

She gave it one more shot, but it was impossible to lift him by herself. Instead of going back to bed, though, she opened the garage door and walked over to the addition. It was much too quiet outside, in contrast to all the noise in her head. It felt all wrong. And then there was the mauled body on the floor a few yards away.

The darkness made it difficult to make out what was written on the doors, but the one down at the end seemed to be the main entrance. She pushed the doorbell hard, let go, pushed it again. And again, and again, until a light came on in a room facing the parking lot.

She retreated a few steps and waited until Sister Eileen came to the door in a nightgown.

"I'm sorry," Ilka began. Suddenly she realized she was standing there in a sleep shirt, her hair tangled up. "Something's happened in the garage. I need your help."

The nun frowned and shook her head. She pulled the door shut behind her, as if she was afraid Ilka might push past her and make an even bigger nuisance of herself.

"Someone has been in there. Someone pulled Mike Gilbert out of the refrigerator and left him on the floor."

"Wasn't the door locked?" the sister asked, as if that changed something about the fact that he was lying on the floor.

Ilka shrugged. "He's lying over there; you have to come help me. I can't pick him up by myself." She was tired, but this had to be done. Now.

Sister Eileen nodded and went back inside. A moment later she came out wearing her practical office shoes, with a long cardigan wrapped around her.

They walked back to the garage without speaking. The garage door was still open; the light inside fanned out into the yard.

"I don't like being woken up in the night," the nun finally said when they reached the garage.

"I don't either," Ilka replied shortly. She made a gesture,

signaling that she wanted Sister Eileen to grab his legs, while she would take his arms. "If we can lift him up on the stretcher, we'll find a way to get him over on the steel tray."

They counted to three and lifted. This time Ilka ignored the feel of the dead body.

After carrying him to the refrigerator, the nun asked, "Is he wet?" She pointed to the large wet blotch covering his battered chest. Ilka leaned over and felt his hair, which was wet and sticky. It gleamed in the glaring ceiling light. She pulled her hand away.

Gasoline, was her first thought. She straightened up and looked around. If someone had planned to cremate Mike Gilbert directly on the garage floor, the entire funeral home would probably have burned down. But she should have been able to smell gas right off when she'd leaned over and lifted. She crouched down again and sniffed; then she sat for a moment and gathered herself before standing up and drying her hands on her T-shirt. "Urine. Somebody pissed all over him."

Ilka studied the broken face for a moment, the entire right side caved in. Not that she was an expert on these things, but it looked like his cheekbone was crushed. There was a hollow under his eye, as if a bone was missing or had been pulverized just under the skin.

She looked away and closed her eyes. Hoped that Artie would show up early so he could make Mike Gilbert look presentable before his mother saw him. Otherwise there was a rough day ahead for Shelby. Ilka took a deep breath and nodded at Sister Eileen to help lift him onto the steel tray; then they pushed him back into the refrigerator.

After shutting the door, the nun shook her head in irritation and left without a word of good-bye.

"Okay, well, good night, then," Ilka said to the closed door.

13

It was a terrible night's sleep. Adrenaline surged through Ilka's body, and several times during the night she had convinced herself she was hearing sounds in the garage. Half-asleep, she heard the dead coming to life and walking around the building, pulling each other out of the refrigerator, drinking coffee in the kitchen. She hadn't dared go down, and anyway, she knew it was all in her head. In the moments she was wide awake, she'd pulled the comforter tightly to her and thought about how strange it was, being stuck in the middle of the daily life her father had led for so many years, so far away from her. All those years she had needed him in her own life.

It wasn't because she was any closer to understanding him after these few days in Racine. But his physical presence felt strong to her. She was surrounded by her father, his odor and belongings and the people he'd been with every day. Still, though, she hadn't learned more about him, nor did she have the faintest idea how abandoning them had left its mark on him.

He had asked for a divorce less than two years after he left. At that time her mother was still struggling to turn the funeral home into a profitable business that could be sold without too big a loss. Ilka hadn't been aware of her reaction to his request—Ilka hadn't even known about the divorce before it was final. One evening her mother came into her room while she was doing homework.

"Your father and I are divorced," was all she said. Ilka still remembered the first thing she thought: *He must have come home.* Which meant she could see him. But her mother explained that he was still in the US, that their lawyers handled everything.

She'd rested her hand on Ilka's shoulder. "It means he's decided to stay over there. Without us."

As she lay in bed and gazed around the small room, Ilka couldn't understand why her father had traded owning a Brønshøj funeral home in the red with owning a Racine funeral home in the red. Racine, a town with less life on a weekday than Brønshøj Square on a Sunday morning.

And yet she knew he must have had a reason. But had he just been looking for adventure? Or did he run away from something? She knew everything had been going downhill for him—her mother had told her that much—yet Ilka had always looked at it as him leaving the two of them. It was telling, though, that he'd started up a new funeral home. And he'd fled suddenly, without making any arrangements. Maybe his reason for leaving did have to do with the business he'd taken over from his own father. But then there were the horses, of course. Her mother thought he'd accumulated a debt he'd never be able to pay, so he took off.

She'd loved it when he took her out to the horses. Except for that one time they'd never told her mother about.

It had been a sunny day. She'd been standing behind the living room door while he spoke on the phone, too low for her to hear. But when he noticed her, he told her to go out to the car and wait for him. Ilka looked down at the red toes of her shoes, uneasy and a bit scared. Her father usually didn't sound like that.

She'd been looking forward to spending that day with him, but now she wished her mother was there too. He was acting strangely. As if he didn't want her to be there. She grabbed the car keys on the dresser and picked her sweater up off the floor.

She was hoping they'd go to the racetrack or out to Mogens's. They'd been there before. He had a lot of horses, and last time they were there he'd let her curry one.

"Where are we going?" Luckily he hadn't spoken on the phone very long. IIe was wearing his brown suede jacket. He lit a cigarette, but he remembered to roll the window down a bit so she wouldn't get carsick. For a few seconds, he sat as if he'd forgotten where they were going; then he flipped his cigarette out the window and into the hedge.

"We're headed out to run and shout." He laughed, and she laughed with him, though there was still something wrong.

They drove a long time before turning down a gravel road with tall old trees on both sides. They had counted the number of yellow cars on the way. She sat up to see if there were any horses, but the corrals were empty.

"Who lives here?" she asked, as they drove in and stopped at a courtyard. She didn't like visiting people she didn't know, and she felt a small knot in her stomach when a dog came running up to the car.

"I'll only be a minute. Just stay out here." He reached into the back seat and grabbed a Donald Duck comic book for her.

Her father wasn't afraid of dogs. Ilka watched him walk over to a barn door; no one had come out to greet him. Maybe no one had heard them coming? She didn't like this.

What should she say if someone came while he was gone? Before going inside the barn, he turned and waved at her.

The dog was gone. Ilka sat for a while; then she opened the car door and hopped down onto the courtyard's cobblestones. The air smelled sour, like it did when manure had been spread out on fields—she knew about that from summer vacations when they drove out into the country.

She walked over to the horse barn and opened the door a crack. Riding gear hung all around. She heard voices, and she slowly opened the door and walked inside. The barn smelled of oil, hay, and leather, odors she knew and liked from the racetrack barn. She called out for her father, but the barn was quiet. For a minute, she stood gathering up the courage to walk down the long row of stalls, which were empty. Someone was cleaning them, though; a wheelbarrow full of straw and horseshit was parked there. They must be out back. She called out again, louder this time.

"Daddy!" She froze at the sight of a man she'd never seen before. He was gripping her father, as if he were trying to lift him up, and speaking angrily to him, hissing in his face. She screamed, and the stranger whirled around. But she couldn't move. Not even when her father yelled at her, told her to go back to the car. He walked over and took her hand.

The stranger was still angry. "You'll hear from me!"

It was light outside when Ilka woke up. She must have fallen asleep again. It was a few minutes past eight, and when she walked downstairs, feeling a hundred years old, she heard Artie rummaging around in back. The preparation room had no windows, but the door stood open and the ventilation fan roared like a range hood set on high. She found him in the kitchenette, pouring Red Bull in his coffee. His eyes were tiny, and he'd tied his longish hair in a small bun on top of his head. Something the under-thirty generation would usually do, she'd thought.

He nodded good morning to her and pointed to a plate of doughnuts. "Have one," he said, his voice low; instinctively she understood he preferred a quiet morning. But today he was out of luck.

She grabbed the powdered milk for coffee and started in. "Have you seen the refrigerator?" She followed him out under the carport, where he sat down on the steps with his coffee, doughnut, and cigarette. He shook his head silently and began eating; a small fleck of icing stuck on his mustache. "No," he finally answered, after he'd finished chewing. "But I'll do Mike first. I don't have time to work miracles before Shelby comes, but I can do a cover-up, so she won't see what bad shape he's in."

Ilka sat down beside him. She felt responsible for someone getting into the garage while she was there. And she should have looked for an alarm to turn on. But Artie should have told her; it wasn't all her fault.

"Someone has been inside the garage," she said.

Artie listened without interrupting while she explained she had found Mike on the floor last night and had to wake Sister Eileen up to help get him back in the refrigerator. Cigarette smoke curled around his fingers as he ate the rest of his jelly doughnut and sipped his Red Bull coffee without reacting.

"Was he covered with urine when we picked him up at the morgue?" she asked.

Now he looked surprised. "What do you mean?"

"Did he smell like piss?"

He shook his head. "Not that I noticed. Does he now?"

Ilka nodded. "I think someone peed all over him while he was on the floor."

He knocked another cigarette out of the pack and offered one to her, but she waved the pack away. "That sounds bizarre," was all he said.

"You forgot to tell me if there's an alarm," she said, not the least bit bashful to give him some of the blame. But he didn't seem to hear her. He smoked a while without speaking; then he flipped the butt away and stood up.

"There was so much hate simmering in town after what happened. Everybody had an opinion, but most people seemed to think Mike was guilty. And the talk picked up when he left town. There was even a rumor that Ashley was doing it for money; then other people said no, she was doing it for free. The gossip turned vicious, and I know this sounds bad, but it was almost like people enjoyed it. It was like this smear campaign against Mike Gilbert energized the town; people started making up stories and juicing up the ones they'd heard. And now you tell me this. I can't say I'm surprised the hate's flared up again, if someone found out Mike was back."

He opened the door into the garage and walked over to the refrigerator. Ilka followed him. "But Shelby is convinced her son didn't kill the girl."

"Don't you suppose most mothers would feel that way, without conclusive evidence?" He opened the refrigerator to pull the steel tray out. "We'll have to call the police."

He'd already whipped his phone out.

"But his own mother didn't even know he was back."

"Someone must've seen him," Artie said, while waiting for someone to answer.

"Then the same 'someone' must know he's dead. Otherwise they wouldn't have come here."

Artie nodded and turned away after being transferred.

Ilka was sitting out on the steps when the police car turned in and parked. Artie had agreed that someone had soiled Mike Gilbert with urine during the night, but he thought it probably had been poured over him; there was far too much for a single urination.

She hadn't understood what difference it made, but Artie thought pissing on the body could be a spur-of-the-moment act, whereas dousing it with urine meant it was planned. An insult, sick. More emotional.

When she saw the two officers from the day before, she walked over to meet them. Officers Thomas and Doonan nodded to her and asked if there were surveillance cameras in the garage.

She hadn't even thought of that. Artie would have mentioned it if there were, surely, she thought. Then she remembered about the alarm, and she asked them to follow her.

"Do we have surveillance cameras out here?" she asked Artie. Odd, she thought, how natural it was to say "we" after only three days here. A few weeks ago, she hadn't even known the funeral home existed.

"We have some installed, yeah, but it's been a long time since they've been working. Paul had a contract with a security company, but I have the feeling he didn't renew it. So they're just hanging there now."

"What time did you come down here?" Officer Thomas asked Ilka. The two of them had walked outside the garage.

"The first or the second time?"

"When you heard the noise the first time. And you're sure there was nobody here?"

She shook her head. "I don't think so. But I'm not totally sure anymore. I checked the room with the coffins; there was nobody there. Unless someone was hiding in one of the two coffins. I didn't think about that. I didn't check if the preparation room was locked, either, but I know the door was closed."

"It's always locked," Artie said, walking outside.

"The first time I came down, I was thinking mostly about maybe there was an open door banging; I thought that was what woke me up. But it was only the small window I'd left open for the cat. That was at three thirty." She added that the door out to the carport had also been locked.

Artie had pulled Mike out of the refrigerator; his body lay on a stretcher, covered by a sheet.

"Don't touch anything," Officer Thomas said as the two policemen squeezed past the hearse.

They leaned over the body. She heard them mention the stink from the urine. "If there was any doubt before, it's pretty clear now it wasn't a random assault that cost him his life," Officer Doonan said. "Someone knows he came back."

Ilka heard the cat purr before it started rubbing her legs. She squatted down and petted it. Long, soothing strokes, as if she were trying to calm her own nerves.

"We didn't really believe it was random, either," the young officer continued. "Something like this seldom is." He explained that they were looking at the case again, rereading the witness statements. "But we're not so far along yet."

Ilka stood up. The policemen asked Artie again about the surveillance cameras and alarms. And how many garage entrances there were. She herded the cat into the house and was about to lure it out into the kitchen, when Sister Eileen appeared in the doorway and said there was a telephone call for her. "We usually don't allow pets inside the funeral home," she said as Ilka walked into her father's office.

14

A small click made Ilka think the call was from a foreign country, and instinctively she thought of her mother. But then a dark voice introduced himself in a broad American accent. She didn't catch his name, only that he was associated with another funeral home.

The largest funeral home chain in the country, she learned, after listening for a few moments to the words flowing into her ears like melted chocolate, warm and creamy. It took her a while, though, to get what had actually been said.

"Yes," she said, "I'm Paul Jensen's daughter, and I'm the owner of the business."

The stream of words continued, and she grew impatient; she felt she should get back to the policemen in the garage. And they might need her fingerprints. After all, she'd touched the stretcher.

"No, unfortunately," she answered, in an overly polite tone of voice, which she was getting sick and tired of using to keep things civilized. "I already have a plan for the future."

She listened again. "No, I'm not planning to keep it. I'm about to sell to another funeral home in town."

Now there was an unpleasant insistence to his voice, like when a telephone salesperson won't accept you're in the middle of a meal. Erik had come up with a way of ending a call from a telephone company or someone else who had gotten hold of his number. "I'm screwing someone right now," he would say, and usually that worked. But it was way too late now for that trick.

"Fine," she said, breaking him off. "Thank you very much. I understand you are quite interested in buying my father's business. But like I said, the deal is almost done, so unfortunately I'm not interested. But thank you for calling."

She said good-bye and hung up before his next gusher of words erupted.

She held the phone for a moment. She hadn't caught the name of the funeral home chain. Or maybe it was an organization of funeral home businesses? She wasn't sure. But they were big and they were national, the man had emphasized several times.

She went out to join the others in the garage. The cat was gone, the door to the garage was open, and the two policemen were walking around the refrigerator. The stretcher she had used the previous night lay in the middle of the floor, and the big garage door was also open. Ilka noticed the woman on the bench by the parking lot entrance again, looking down at her hands. Ilka couldn't see her face, but her hair was unmistakable.

Ilka studied her for a moment; then she heard Artie's voice. "Could you come inside?" He stepped out from the house; he must have gone in while she was in the office with the door closed. "Phyllis Oldham is here with the papers. They're ready for your signature."

Ilka nodded and followed him. She thought about telling

him about the phone call, but then Artie might think she'd begun calling around, putting feelers out. The truth was, she didn't know if she could get an offer from another funeral home better than the one she had.

"Dear!" Mrs. Oldham chirped, when Ilka stepped into the arrangement room. Papers had been spread out in front of an empty chair, and beside them lay a large fountain pen with the Golden Slumbers logo. "Howard and I thought it would be appropriate to celebrate by inviting you out this evening. We have a fine Italian restaurant here in town. What do you say?"

Ilka smiled at the irresistible cheerfulness radiating from the well-tailored suit. Being back in Denmark before Monday had just come a step closer.

"Thank you, that sounds wonderful." She sat down in front of the papers.

"I would suggest we begin with champagne and hors d'oeuvres at our home," the woman said. "And then we'll drive from there."

Ilka grabbed the pen and began scanning the pages in front of her. It was the same as what she'd read before. What her lawyer had approved.

She was about to sign, when Mrs. Oldham said, "It's so nice we can do business with you. It was more difficult with your father; he couldn't see this is to everyone's advantage."

Ilka looked up.

"Or perhaps he didn't want to see," she continued.

Suddenly Ilka felt cold, all over. She stared at the woman without seeing her. *What is she saying?* Ilka wondered. *He didn't want to sell?*

She noticed Artie looking away deliberately, though he tried to be casual about it. He didn't say a word.

"Please excuse me," Ilka said. She laid the pen down

slowly. "Take a cup of coffee. I'm sure we have some out in the kitchen; otherwise, Sister Eileen can quickly make some. This will only take a moment."

She stood and turned to Artie. "Would you please come with me?" She practically spoke through her teeth.

He looked annoyed as he reluctantly stood up and followed her. Out in the hallway, she noticed the police still walking around in the garage, so she pulled him into the office and closed the door. "Can you tell me what the hell she meant by that? He didn't want to sell? You told me this deal was being worked on before he died, but she says he was difficult. Will you explain that?"

Artie was sitting on the desk now. "This is a real good offer they're giving us. Golden Slumbers Funeral Home is the most distinguished funeral home in town, and like you've already seen, they run a big business, do a good job. Their financial situation is excellent, and they're willing to take over right now."

"But he didn't want to sell to them," Ilka said. "This is going a little too fast now. Did my father even really want to sell his business?"

Artie nodded. "We talked about it. Yes! We discussed it several times."

"It sounds to me like the Oldhams tried to talk him into it several times, but he refused."

"If we lose this deal, I can't help you," Artie said, serious now. "I've been down on my knees to get this offer done, and you're not going to get a better deal than what they're bringing to the table."

Oh, really! she was about to say, but then she remembered she didn't know who had called. Before she threw that in his face, she had to find them.

"So what are you planning on doing, huh?" Artie was

starting to sound angry. "Are you thinking about sticking around? Keep this sinking ship afloat long enough for us all to drown? Or do you have the money to pay your dad's debt? Because I can guarantee you're not going to sweet-talk the IRS into anything. That money must be paid tomorrow, or else they will show up and throw us out and put big locks on all the doors. Really, I don't think you understand how serious the situation is."

Ilka caught herself holding her breath. She was enraged, close to exploding right in his face; an angry heat spread out on her cheeks and throat. "I'll be back in five minutes," she said, and walked out to find Sister Eileen.

The nun was at her desk, leaning over a sheet of paper with no folders or bookmarks in sight. It looked like she was writing a good old-fashioned letter. Ilka recognized the funeral home logo on the paper.

The door was open, and she knocked on the doorframe. "May I have a moment?"

"Of course." Sister Eileen nodded and slipped the letter in a drawer. She hadn't talked about what had happened last night, so Ilka decided not to, either.

Ilka walked in and sat down across from the nun. "I need to ask you about something."

The sister nodded.

"Do you know if my father was against selling the business to the Oldham family? What I heard is that they tried to talk him into it many times, but he always refused."

If anyone had been on her father's side, Ilka felt, it would be Sister Eileen. They seemed to have been close, so surely she would have known what he'd wanted.

The nun folded her hands on the desk and leaned forward. "It would be wise to stick with Artie when it comes to business. He knows what he's doing, and he wants the best for us all." Then she leaned back, as if the final word had been spoken.

Ilka stood up and left. Frustrated, tired, and about to call home to ask her mother for advice, she grabbed Artie's cigarettes as she walked through the kitchen and out to the parking lot.

The police had finished in the garage; their car was gone. She lit a cigarette, and again she noticed the woman sitting on the bench. She strode over and joined her.

They sat for a while in silence while Ilka smoked. She finished off that cigarette and lit another; then she sank back. "I think you knew my father," she said, without looking at the woman. A few moments later, she added, "Do you think he wanted to sell his funeral home to Golden Slumbers?"

The woman didn't react at first, and Ilka thought the woman might not have understood what she was asking about. Then she slowly shook her head. "Never." Her voice was barely above a whisper. "He would never sell to them."

Then she stood up abruptly and left before Ilka could ask any more questions.

Ilka smoked one more cigarette while looking the building over. A gigantic house filled with life and death, and suddenly it was all hers. She stood and went back inside.

15

Ilka returned to the conference room, where Phyllis Oldham was standing by the window, speaking in a low voice with Artie. She heard them mention something about the harbor and charity, but they stopped talking when they saw her.

"I'm sorry," she said to them. Mrs. Oldham's forehead twitched; Artie slowly turned away from the window. "The deal is off. I appreciate the work you two have put into this, but I can't sign something my father opposed."

A voice in her head yelled at her: *You didn't even know him; what the hell are you doing?* They both looked at her in disapproval.

"I'm going up to pack and return to Denmark. The estate will be…how do you say, finished by an official. Then whatever happens will happen." She asked Artie to tell Sister Eileen to pack her things, thinking that if the IRS showed up and closed the funeral home, they might as well be prepared.

Before they could say a word, she left the room, ran up the steps, and slammed the door behind her. Her first thought was to call her lawyer.

For a moment, she closed her eyes and rested her head

against the doorframe. She didn't even know if there were executors to administer estates in the US, but she didn't want anything more to do with this. The moment she'd found out what was going on, she should have refused to get involved, should have said she knew nothing about the funeral home business. Or her father, for that matter. Her mother had, of course, been right; she shouldn't even have come here. But she'd never been much for doing the smart thing, she reminded herself. She'd tried. And now she was giving up. It was simply too much for her, inheriting a funeral home in Racine. And even more too much to manage it and make decisions that ran against her father's wishes.

She fished her phone out of her bag and called her mother.

"Hi," she said, trying to sound calm and composed. "It's going fine. I'm coming home now. I just need to find out if I can catch a plane today, or if I have to wait until tomorrow. I'll finish packing; then I'll leave for the airport. No, nothing's wrong. But you were right—I'm not going to get bogged down in all this. I'm having an executor take over. Yes! I'm sure. Everything is fine. And I'll take care of the photo shoots starting Monday; don't worry about finding someone else."

Ilka heard the relief in her mother's voice, now that she was coming home without anything catastrophic happening. Knowing that Ilka hadn't ended up in an American prison undoubtedly kept her mother from asking more questions. Ilka promised to call again when she knew her arrival time in Copenhagen. It felt great to hear her mother say she and Hanne would pick her up at the airport.

She sat on the bed and glanced around the room. Less than two hours remained until the IRS deadline, and she hadn't even begun looking through her father's closets and all the boxes pushed up against the wall. Someone showing up and putting big locks on all the doors sounded like an exaggeration, but you never knew. When her hairdresser went bankrupt several years ago, all the employees in the chain's other shops had been ordered to close and leave without taking so much as a hairpin with them.

She had to get her father's things out of the house, but all she had to pack with was her small suitcase. At first Ilka considered dragging all the boxes downstairs, but where would she put them? They would still be on the funeral home property out in the parking lot. She would have to sort things out lightning quick and do the best she could.

The clock was ticking, and she felt a bit desperate, but finally she pulled herself together and went downstairs to look for boxes or something to pack with. She hated the thought of running into Artie. That asshole had known all along that her father didn't want to sell to the Oldhams, and yet he worked his tail off to do just that. Presumably he'd thought he could push the transfer agreement through before she found out how her father had felt.

She hurried past the office and arrangement room without seeing anyone. Phyllis Oldham had left, but her heavy perfume—cinnamon and something that nauseated Ilka—still hung in the air. The door into the preparation room was closed, but she could hear the fan running. Quickly she punched in the code to the garage, and for a moment she stood and looked around. A low shelf filled with black file boxes ran along the entire wall behind the hearse. For a second she thought about emptying and using them, but they wouldn't be able to hold much. She checked the high shelf on the other wall. Coffin liners, blankets. Farther down the shelf stood boxes of masks and plastic gloves. On one of the lower shelves, she found a large box with body bags. Ilka grabbed two of them and ran back upstairs.

At ten thirty, she started pulling drawers out of her father's desk. She scooped up all the letters; the most important thing was to rescue his personal papers. Of course, there could be other things with sentimental value, but they would have to wait. She had to get hold of everything that might explain why he had abandoned her and her mother.

She ignored a stack of old order books in one of the drawers. There were also calendars marked with birthdays of people she'd never heard of. The next drawer: opened envelopes containing letters. All addressed to him, some with a feminine cursive script, others with heavy block letters. She stuck them in a body bag, to be read when she got home. Underneath was a folder with children's drawings by Leslie and Amber. She laid them aside. Her half sisters would probably be happy to have them, or at least to know their father had saved them. She would drive by and drop them off before flying back to Denmark.

The bottom drawer was filled with scattered bundles of old bills and receipts. Something for the IRS to play around with. *Leave them*, she told herself.

It didn't take her long to decide about the few clothes that hadn't been given to the sister's parish. While sorting through them, it had felt wrong to empty out the whole closet. She left the few suits and shirts there.

Someone knocked, and she turned around. "Yes!"

Artie carefully opened the door. "May I come in?"

Should she tell him to leave, or what? Finally, Ilka nodded.

He glanced around the room before stepping inside and sitting on the bed, next to a pile of her clothes.

"I want to apologize," he said, his tone signaling unconditional surrender. "I totally understand why you got angry. It did come out sounding all wrong. It's true, Paul had several run-ins with the Oldhams over the years, and of course I should have let you in on that. I just didn't feel we had time to go over what happened so long ago. Like I already told you, I didn't know the business was in such bad shape before your dad's lawyer contacted me. I didn't know he owed the IRS so much, and I didn't know we were so close to bankruptcy. You can take this however you want, but I think I panicked. I've always had a good working relationship with the people at Golden Slumbers, and Paul could be stubborn as a mule. So when I contacted them, I felt I was trying to move things along, not acting against his wishes."

He leaned forward with his hands folded. "Of course you're the one who decides what will happen, now that you've inherited the business. But if that money isn't paid before the deadline, I'm out of work and the sister has no place to live. Shouldn't we try to work together and see what we can come up with? And you know what? It wouldn't be like Paul to throw Sister Eileen out with two hours' warning."

"Just like it wouldn't be like my father to sell the business, and you knew that. But you let me believe it was something he started."

The slow anger building inside her was about to explode again, and she did nothing to hold it back. She glared at him. "I've had enough of being a naïve fool. You could have fucking explained how things were. We could have talked about it, but instead I'm running around picking up dead people and talking to other people who just lost a relative. What the hell are you two thinking? You didn't tell me anything, to make me feel we could solve everything together. Honestly, I think you'd rather have done it all without me. And that's okay, but then don't fucking get me involved."

Sweat ran down her back, a stream of rage. "Everything

just roars along over my head. And I won't be part of it. When I'm packed, I'm going to call my father's lawyer. He'll have to take over from now on."

"I have the sixty thousand dollars we need," Artie said, without a word about the shelling he'd just taken. "You can have the money as a down payment on the house."

Ilka shook her head. "Stick that money right up your ass. I'm going home to Denmark."

Artie stood up. "So what do you plan on doing with Mike Gilbert, Ed McKenna, Mrs. Norton? You want to cancel the old lady's funeral service tomorrow? Who's going to take care of Mike and Ed? What about all the relatives counting on us? And all the people we have deals with? Do we just say the hell with them? This doesn't just affect you, us. But if that's how you want it, great."

He walked out and slammed the door.

Ilka stared at the door, speechless. She hadn't given a single thought to the 150 people who had cared about old Mrs. Norton and were coming tomorrow to say good-bye to her. She recalled the grandchild crying as he stood up and accused them of being cold and unfeeling.

She felt dizzy when she closed her eyes for a moment. It was as if she'd been ambushed, as if the ground beneath her kept shifting; she couldn't find her feet. She looked all around at the terrible mess she'd made of the small room; then she decided to go down and find Artie.

He was sitting on the steps near the carport with a cigarette and a Red Bull. He didn't even look up when she sat down beside him.

"What do we need for the funeral service tomorrow?" She took the cigarette he shook out of his pack.

"So you want the money after all?"

She nodded. "I don't think Sister Eileen can pack in such a short time." It was a quarter past eleven.

He crushed his cigarette with the heel of his shoe. "If we do this, it'll be a new situation. Do we need to sit down and talk this through before we decide if it's the right thing to do?" Ilka didn't hear even the faintest hint of sarcasm in his voice. She shook her head.

"I need a time-out to get a good picture of the situation and to find out how much money my father owes."

She told him about the call from the funeral home chain. "Golden Slumbers isn't the only one interested."

Artie set his beer down. "When did they call?"

"This morning."

"Did you promise them anything? Did you set up a meeting?"

Ilka shook her head. "I told them we already had a deal. But we could contact them and hear their offer. I don't know who it was, but surely we can find them."

She could tell he wasn't happy about that, but he let it go. "I'd better get to the bank so we don't miss the deadline." He started over to his car.

"Okay, and I'll let the sister know she doesn't need to pack anyway."

Ilka watched him go. His reaction to the call from the funeral home chain puzzled her. Again, she had the feeling he was trying to steer things to his advantage instead of following the path her father had laid out. Or at least selling the business the way her father would have.

Ilka had just stood up when a police car turned in and parked. She glanced at her watch; Artie had left for the bank no more than ten minutes ago; they still had time, so it couldn't be someone telling her to leave. Then she recognized the two officers, Thomas and Doonan. She walked over to them.

"We need to talk," Officer Thomas said.

Ilka nodded and asked them to follow her, but he pointed across the street and explained that the school had a surveillance camera. "We've just checked the recording."

Ilka looked over at the school, right across from the entrance to the funeral home parking lot. The bench on which the mysterious woman had sat was beside the entrance. She spoke hesitantly, unsure of where they were going with this. "Okay."

"Last night at three twenty-two, Howard Oldham walked across the street to the back of your house," Officer Doonan said, as if he were reading from a report. "The recording doesn't show him leaving the property."

He paused for a moment, giving her time to grasp the situation. He smelled of aftershave, and she looked directly at him so long that he finally lowered his eyes. "We've tried to contact him, so far without any luck." He looked up at her again with a glint in his eye that she couldn't read. "So that's why we have to ask if you can tell us what Howard Oldham was doing here last night."

Ilka gave him a puzzled look before shaking her head. "If you think he was with me, you're wrong; he wasn't. I haven't seen him either."

Officer Thomas's hands were in the side pockets of his jacket, as if that helped him rest his sizable body. "You're sure about that?" He looked at her expectantly.

She stared back at him as if he was joking. True, she had a healthy and natural appetite for men, but Howard Oldham wasn't on her to-do list.

"If that's the case, it's going to be interesting to find out why he was on your property last night."

Once again she felt like she was on shaky ground, and she wished Artie was there. She simply nodded when he said they would know more when they had Howard Oldham's DNA and compared it to what was found in the garage.

"Do you think he might have killed Mike Gilbert?" she asked. In her mind's eye, she saw the well-dressed undertaker. The nice suit, tie, the folded handkerchief in his breast pocket.

"No comment on that," Doonan said, a bit sharply. "We're interested only in his possible connection to what happened in the garage."

Ilka nodded wearily. She couldn't imagine what could make that gentlemanly man break in and haul a dead man out of the refrigerator.

"I'll have to ask you not to tell anyone who we've seen on the recording," Officer Thomas said, his voice leaving no doubt that this was an order.

She nodded again, and soon the two policemen were driving away for the second time that morning. She watched them disappear, then went over to Sister Eileen's door.

"I don't have the strength to carry the furniture out," the pale, red-eyed woman said after letting Ilka inside. "That little bureau was my mother's; I would be terribly unhappy if I can't get it out before the deadline."

"You don't need to pack; we're staying. Artie and I have found a solution. The IRS is being paid now, and as soon as he comes back I want all three of us to meet in my father's office."

A large suitcase was standing in the living room, and two travel bags were almost full. A stack of newspapers lay on the table; the sister had been packing her porcelain. Ilka recognized two pairs of shoes on the floor, identical to the practical ones she wore, and a pair of Adidas, which was so far from the nun's usual style that Ilka thought she must have borrowed them.

"So shall I unpack?" She sounded confused. She looked over at the full suitcase.

Ilka nodded and tried to smile.

16

Ilka had set out the cups and filled a bowl with chocolates. The coffee was almost finished brewing out in the kitchen when Sister Eileen and Artie walked in.

"I paid, and I just got a receipt from the IRS that confirms it," he said. He collapsed onto a chair on the other side of the desk. "So this is when we breathe a sigh of relief."

Was it really so easy? Ilka wondered. Throw a little money at them and everyone was happy. For the moment, maybe.

She poured the coffee ceremoniously and pushed the chocolates over to them. She'd taken a notebook from the shelf, and now she pulled her father's oversize office chair closer to the desk. "I think it's time to review the situation." She considered thanking Artie officially, but honestly, she thought, she had done just as much to save the day by letting him pay the sixty thousand dollars. She concentrated on what they needed to discuss.

"We have Mrs. Norton's funeral service tomorrow. What do we need for that?" She looked across the desk.

"The coffin was supposed to come today, but I haven't checked to see if it's been delivered," Artie said.

"But she's already in a coffin," Ilka said. She was in the cold room beside Ed McKenna and the dog.

"She's not in the one we ordered. I had to lay her in another one until it came. I finished working on her; she's ready. I was thinking that later we could use the coffin for Mike Gilbert, so I used the cheapest one we have in storage. We need to move her over into the right coffin today, so it'll be ready tomorrow morning, in case the family shows up early to decorate."

"Did they arrange for music?" he asked Sister Eileen. She shook her head.

"I informed them that they can use CDs or connect to an iPhone over our sound system," she said. She added that a choir would be singing at the chapel.

"What should we do if the coffin doesn't arrive?" Ilka asked. "Do we have another one we can put her in?"

Artie shook his head. "They've paid for a glossy black coffin with glitter. If that's not what she's in, we'll have to give a refund. And anyway, it's too late to tell them we can't deliver, so that coffin has to come. It might be a good idea for you to call the supplier, if you don't already have a tracking number. Then we can follow it on the Net and see how far away it is."

Sister Eileen said nothing, even though she was the one who dealt with the suppliers.

"What about one of the coffins we have in storage?" Ilka suggested. "One is light blue; another is white. And we have that big black one that was in the garage. Is it in the storage room now?"

"We can't use that one; it was delivered by mistake and will be picked back up. It's way too expensive to keep."

Ilka didn't answer, but she wrote: "Find coffin."

"We're low on formaldehyde," Artie said.

"Let's finish this first," Ilka said. "What else do we need for tomorrow?"

"Flowers are to be delivered, and there will be catering," the nun said. "I've ordered both."

"But the Norton family is bringing the flowers," Ilka reminded her.

"There are always flowers in the chapel and out in the foyer during funeral services," the sister calmly answered. "Those are the flowers I ordered."

Ilka nodded and made a note of it.

Sister Eileen hadn't touched the coffee or the chocolates, and suddenly Ilka remembered that she usually drank tea. How could she have forgotten?

"I've spoken with Ed McKenna's daughter," the nun continued. "She's coming to see her father this weekend. It sounds like she wants to take him home to Albany, which means we'll need a zinc coffin."

Ilka lifted an eyebrow. "For the plane," Artie explained. "When the deceased are flown, they have to be in zinc coffins."

Ilka nodded thoughtfully when he added that there were many on domestic flights.

"The distances are too long to drive," he said. "But there are strict rules for transporting them, of course. The coffins have to be zinc lined and contain absorbent material. We use charcoal powder. And then there must be a pressure equalizer. And the deceased must be embalmed. And usually the coffin has to be wrapped so the other passengers can't see there's a dead body on board."

Suddenly he seemed to take her wanting to be fully informed very literally.

"If there isn't anything more, I'd like to unpack my things now," Sister Eileen said, a bit sharply. She stood without waiting for an answer.

Artie was also on his feet. He wanted to take care of Mike Gilbert so his mother could view him when she came.

"How much formaldehyde?" Ilka yelled after him.

For a moment, she sat alone, staring into space before slowly rising and walking over to find the file with the Nortons' funeral service notes. After laying it on the table, she walked out to the sister's desk in the reception area. A calendar lay open on the thick green desk mat; beside it lay a black leather-bound telephone book with JENSEN FUNERAL HOME printed on it.

Ilka found the order book in the top drawer. It wasn't difficult to locate the coffin supplier where most of the sister's orders were made. She cleared her throat and dialed, with the order number on Mrs. Norton's coffin in hand.

"Why do you say you can't deliver coffins to us?" she said, baffled by what she'd been told. "You just received our order. You could have said you don't want to do business with us anymore when we sent the order, to avoid this terrible situation we're in. The *family* is in. We're holding a funeral service tomorrow, and the relatives expect to see the deceased in the coffin they ordered. No, I will not listen! You listen. It's unprofessional and horrible, what you're doing. Maybe it's right that we've exceeded our credit and you've had to send several reminders. But as you might know, Paul Jensen is dead and I've taken over and I'm trying the best I can to finish the agreements the funeral home has made. Of course we will pay what we owe you, but you must deliver the coffin we need now. And I'd like to—"

Ilka didn't know when they'd hung up; all she knew was that she was listening to static. She looked up and saw Sister Eileen turn around in the doorway—hadn't she gone over to unpack? How long had she been listening? She didn't care for the nun observing her like that.

She found two more coffin suppliers in the order book

and made a call. "Yes, we're prepared to pay extra to have FedEx deliver it today."

Her tense shoulders relaxed, and she leaned back in her chair. The supplier asked for the name and address of their funeral home.

"Jensen Funeral Home," she began, but was interrupted before she could give their address.

"Unfortunately you what?" This time Ilka tried to control herself and sound friendly. "I can assure you we'll pay what we owe you. We're in the middle of a sort of generational change here; we're putting in new systems to stop this type of error."

Generational change my ass, she thought. She briefly debated with herself whether she should continue this way until she found a supplier who didn't already know them.

"Yes," she said, "please send a bill on what we owe. Have a nice day."

After trying two more suppliers, she gave up in anger. She went out and hammered on the preparation room door until some sort of electric machinery was shut off and Artie opened up.

She couldn't help noticing the naked body on the steel table by the wall. She stiffened for a moment, but then she pulled herself together and walked inside. "It can't be true that we owe money to every single coffin supplier in North America, can it? I can't buy a coffin anywhere."

Artie shut the door behind her. He walked over and turned down the Beach Boys; then he glanced at the steel table as if he should be protecting the body. He wore a green apron and an elastic band around his longish hair. He struggled to take off his mask, which was tangled up in his glasses.

"That sounds about right," he said, after the mask was

finally off. He stunk, and Ilka instinctively backed off a few steps. "You probably should've let the sister call around. She can usually finagle a coffin out of them, even though they've shut us off."

"You could have told me that. What do we do now?"

He shrugged. "You're the boss!" His eyes twinkled a bit.

Ilka stared at him in anger, then turned on her heel. She was determined to get hold of a coffin, even if she had to nail one together herself and paint it black and spread glitter over it.

"They sell coffins over at Costco," he yelled at her back. "The closest one is in Pleasant Prairie. Just follow Lake Michigan down to Kenosha. You'll hit Highway 50, and then it's straight west from there. Really, though, I doubt if you can get them to deliver today, in time for tomorrow morning."

She turned at the door, tired now. "And what's Costco?"

"It's a warehouse that sells just about everything, most of it in bulk. They're about to drive the coffin suppliers out of business anyway, with their prices. You just have to pay an annual membership fee to shop there."

"Fine." Ilka imagined people at the warehouse, shopping for giant packages of toilet paper, paper towels, and coffins.

17

She drove through a landscape of open fields, lakes, and lush forests. She was just as stubborn as she was mad; all she could see was the white stripes on the road and the notepad on Sister Eileen's desk where she had crossed off the names of coffin suppliers one by one as they rejected her. In fact, she was enraged at how they had treated her. At the very least they could have given her a chance to make things right. They'd regret turning her down!

She stomped on the brakes when a car passed and nearly swiped her bumper as they swerved back in the right lane. The hearse rocked heavily.

"*Røvhul!*" she yelled, as loud as she could. Asshole! Not that the driver heard her, or understood her even if he had. It just felt good. If she stayed in Racine long enough to arrange more funerals, none of those fucking suppliers would get so much as one single order from her.

"Maybe it's a real idea to go organic," she muttered to herself. Just like in Denmark, surely someone over here was making coffins out of recycled material or paper, in that ashes-to-ashes, dust-to-dust way in which coffins decomposed in a relatively short time. She'd be the first funeral director in town to think environmentally. That would get the Oldhams' attention.

Her thoughts were in a jumble as she pulled into an enormous, almost empty parking lot. She chose a space close to the main entrance. Banners announcing the weekly bargains hung from both sides of the sliding doors, and pallets with gallon jugs of laundry detergent and stacks of white plastic lawn chairs stood just inside. She stopped for a moment to get her bearings. The warehouse had an optician and a photo center with good offers on tripods for various cameras. Ilka walked over to ask a young man behind the vision center counter, which was crowded with glasses and offers on vision tests, but on the way, she noticed ends of coffins sticking out from a small niche in the wall.

Seven hundred ninety-nine dollars and ninety-nine cents. And the price was the same regardless of color—dusty rose, silver, or marine blue—but there were differences in how showy they were. Two of them boasted large rosettes in all the corners and a broad, gilded piece of trim—plastic, no doubt, Ilka thought. She looked at the price again. It was a hell of a lot cheaper than the ones from the suppliers—about a tenth of the price of some of them.

She walked over and read a sign on the wall between the models on display: ALL COFFINS HAVE THE SAME FUNCTION. THEY ARE THE FINAL RESTING PLACE FOR THOSE YOU HOLD DEAR. CHOOSING A COFFIN IS A VERY PERSONAL DECISION. FAMILIES SHOULD CHOOSE A COFFIN BASED ON THEIR OWN PREFERENCES AND THE PERSONALITY OF THEIR LOVED ONE. Beside the sign was a plastic holder with order forms.

That's certainly good to know, Ilka thought, shaking her head. None of the models came even close to being black. But they all had a two-piece lid for viewing, and apparently, a coffin liner, pillow, and blanket were included. So far, so good.

She pulled out an order form. To her relief, the coffins came in several colors, including gold. There was also one in black. She read the instructions:

1. Choose a coffin in our selection.
2. Fill out Costco's Purchase Order.
3. Take to the cashier for payment.
4. Delivery time: 48 hours.

"Shit," Ilka said. She stuck the order form in her pocket; then she set off to find someone to help her.

"No, not at all," she assured the elderly gray-haired employee. Frank had reluctantly agreed to check returns storage to see if a black coffin had been returned, and he had come back with a discouraged look on his face. "One small scratch on one side doesn't matter. But docs it have glitter? Okay, okay, that doesn't matter either. I'll take it without."

Ilka had gone through three employees before ending up with Frank, the returns manager. The first two she'd talked to had told her she couldn't get a black coffin delivered immediately; it was out of the question, even if they had them in stock. That's not how things worked. The coffin had to be ordered and would be delivered. And the third employee got so sick and tired of Ilka that she finally said the only chance Ilka had of leaving there with a coffin was if they happened to have one that had been returned. But it probably had been damaged during transport.

"Fine," Ilka had said. That's when Frank came into the picture. He refused outright to sell her a damaged coffin.

He wasn't going to risk her complaining afterward and him ending up with having to supply her with a replacement.

"That won't happen," she said, but he wouldn't budge. She persisted. He kept saying no. But finally, Ilka talked him into checking to see if there even *was* a black coffin in return storage.

"I'll pay you right now; I'll give up my right to return the product," she said.

"You can't get a truck to deliver it today anyway," he said.

"I can take it with me," she replied quickly, and before he could say more, she added, "This is my last chance, and I will be so very grateful to you. My father is dead, and I've come all the way from Denmark to bury him. Yes, Denmark. Yes, like kringles. I never have, no, not with cranberries. We don't have nearly as many kinds in Denmark; we just sprinkle them with powdered sugar and hazelnut flakes. No, at least *I* don't think they taste plain."

He kept on about the kringles for a while, but finally he asked why she didn't just wait until Monday, when a new coffin could be delivered.

"I have to leave Sunday. Monday morning my mother is having some very important tests taken at the hospital. She's a terminal cancer patient, and her medicine is making her dizzy and confused. I have to be there for her.

"The thing is," she added, again before he could butt in, "she's too sick to come over here and be at my father's funeral. It's so terribly sad; none of us could bear the thought that there wouldn't be any services for him because I couldn't get hold of a coffin."

At last, he gave in. But only if she could arrange for the transportation of the damaged coffin to wherever she wanted it dropped off.

"That's no problem," she said.

He looked at her quizzically for a moment, but then he nodded and checked his watch.

"Well then, let's go get this taken care of." He ushered her over toward customer service. Two of the employees Ilka had spoken with were standing by some tall shelving, eyeing them as Ilka strode along behind Frank. She already had a credit card out by the time they reached customer service. Frank gave a number to a coworker at the desk; then he handed Ilka two forms to fill out and sign: her membership application and the other acknowledging that she couldn't return the item she was buying.

She signed and stood for an ID photo for her membership card. Frank hadn't told the man behind the counter what he had sold her, she was sure of that, so she didn't say anything either, just took the receipt and her new card and then nodded when the man told her to have a nice day.

"Give me ten minutes. I'll go back in and get it ready for you to pick up," Frank said, adding that he would help her load it in her vehicle.

Ilka thanked him without commenting on what he said about helping. She walked back to the hearse. The parking lot was much fuller now, but according to her watch, she'd been in the warehouse for almost two hours.

There wasn't much room between two trucks unloading at the docks. She backed in, and just as she got out of the hearse, she saw Frank bringing the coffin over on a forklift. Ilka waved at him and asked if she should drive forward for better access to the rear door.

"Where the hell did that come from?" he said when he spotted the hearse.

"It's my father's; he was an undertaker. He went bankrupt just before he died."

She could hear how suspicious that sounded, so she opened the door at once, then tried to distract him. "I want you to know how incredibly grateful I am for your help and your understanding of my difficult situation. And I know my mother will be, too, knowing that my father got a dignified burial." She unlocked the wheels of the rollers to push it over to the coffin.

"Wait just a second here," Frank said, rubbing his full gray beard. "You're not thinking about using this coffin in a funeral home business, are you? And I end up getting complaints and demands for replacement because it's damaged?"

"No, this is for my personal use. My father will be driven to the crematorium in it tomorrow."

Frank helped her get the coffin on the rollers and shove it in the back of the hearse. She slammed the rear door shut.

"Which crematorium did you book?" he asked.

Ilka pulled a hundred-dollar bill out of her purse and handed it to him. "Thank you so much for your help. I can't tell you how important this is to me." She meant every word she said, but then he startled her when he stepped back abruptly.

"I can't take that sort of money," he whispered, as if he suddenly was afraid someone was listening.

"It's okay," Ilka quickly assured him. "It's a donation to the church you support."

"What the hell makes you think I support a church?" It was his turn to look startled.

"People with a heart like yours always support a church." She left it at that and thanked him again before he could say another word. He took the bill and watched her drive away.

18

Ilka had just parked the hearse in the garage when Sister Eileen came out to tell her that Shelby Gilbert was there with photos of her son.

"Can you give them to Artie?" Ilka asked, as she was about to unload the coffin.

"I think she needs to talk. Your father probably spent more time talking to people than anything. It's important for relatives to be able to talk about those they've lost. And you are like your father; you're good at that." Ilka wasn't one hundred percent sure the nun meant that last remark.

"Of course," she said. On the way into the house she glanced down at herself; her blouse and dark blue jeans would have to do. After all, they hadn't scheduled a meeting.

In the arrangement room, Mike's mother sat at the table with an open photo album beside her coffee cup. Ilka noticed the picture of her son, smiling broadly at the camera. "I just came from the police station. They say they'll find out who did it. But who does these kinds of things?"

She was hurting badly. Ilka walked over and gave her a hug before sitting down across from her and pouring herself a cup of coffee.

"How could anyone hate him so much? And after so

many years?" Shelby looked imploringly at Ilka, then shook her head. They sat for a moment in silence; then she twined her fingers together in her lap and fidgeted; it looked like she was working up the nerve to say something.

"I didn't tell the police everything. I didn't know if it could harm my son. But after what happened last night, I think I might have to."

Ilka scooted forward and laid her hands on the table. "What do you mean?"

Shelby squirmed in her chair. When she finally spoke, she stared at Ilka, her eyes radiating pain and something else Ilka couldn't put her finger on.

"My son was paid to leave town. I didn't know about it back then. I thought he left because he was ashamed. Everyone thought that. But someone gave him money. A lot of money. So he could start a new life. He told me that the last time I talked to him. He'd changed his name to Mike Miller."

She hid her face in her hands and breathed deeply to calm herself down. Ilka reached over the table, but Shelby didn't take her hand.

"I hate this town," she whispered, spitting each word out. "I regret every single day that I went out on the evening I met my kids' father. We were both going to Wisconsin Parkside. I hadn't noticed him before, but all of a sudden, he was standing there, and, well..."

A few moments later she explained she came from Chicago, where her parents and sister still lived. "But Tommy was from Racine, and when I got pregnant we bought the house here and had two kids. Emma was a year and a half when he took off. He ended up somewhere in Ohio."

She breathed deeply again. "When Mike left, I thought for a while he'd moved in with his dad. But when I finally got hold of Tommy's phone number and called, he said he hadn't heard from Mike. And Mike wasn't welcome, either, after what he'd done. It was in all the papers."

"But you stayed here after he left you?"

Shelby nodded. "I had the house. And where could I move to? Back home with my parents?" Her lips quivered, partly from bitterness. Ilka shook her head.

"And I couldn't move when Mike disappeared, either; he wouldn't know where to find us. I feel like I've been tied to this place."

They sat for a moment in silence. "Who paid your son to disappear?" Ilka asked. "Did he say?"

Mike's mother shook her head. "I don't know. But I've always been sure he didn't kill her. He was so happy. No matter what I thought about Ashley Simpson, she made my son happy. Besides his afternoon job at the shop, Mike worked three evenings a week, at this Italian restaurant down by the harbor that closed several years ago. When he came home the evening it happened, he was in a good mood; he acted completely normal. He might even have been in a better mood than usual. They'd given him permission to bring Ashley along to the restaurant's Thanksgiving dinner, and already he was talking about what he was going to wear, even though it wasn't for another week and a half."

She shook her head. "The next day he went to school, just like always. But he was home in less than an hour, down in the living room. White as a sheet. He couldn't tell me what happened. I'd just had a shower, and I was on my way out the door; I had to go to work. Back then I was working full-time sorting mail. I still work there."

By now the coffee was cold, and Ilka offered her another cup, but she declined.

"He broke down, completely. He insisted on going to the police, telling them he and Ashley had been together the day before. I tried to talk him out of it—what good would it do? But he wouldn't listen. He said someone pushed her, because she hadn't been out on the ice. She was up in the fisherman's cabin, where they'd been together. It wasn't any accident."

Shelby shook her head again, as if the rest of the story wasn't important. But she continued. "It was like the whole town decided it was him, even though everyone knew there were others besides Mike, then and before."

After waiting several moments, Ilka said, "What others?"

"Like they say, she got around." Shelby spoke quietly, as if she wasn't sure she should let Ilka in on the town's gossip back then. "There were stories about the men Ashley attracted. And it wasn't just teenagers. They say she went after older men, and men with money. And yet she wanted my Mike. I didn't understand what she was up to, but maybe she really did like him."

Ilka leaned a bit farther forward. "Are you saying she was doing it for money?"

Shelby straightened up, shocked now. "No, definitely not. I just think she liked the power she had over men who fell in love with her."

Jealousy, Ilka thought. If the young girl had been easy, it wouldn't have been the first time in history that a boyfriend or girlfriend lost their head.

"If you only knew how much hate there is in this town," Mike's mother said. She folded her hands in her lap again. When people heard that Mike had been the last one Ashley was with, they broke out all the windows in their house, she explained. "People threatened us; they wrote the most horrible things on the outside of our house. At first, Emma didn't dare go out alone. But after her brother left, things settled down, thank God. Like people were satisfied with running him out of town. We weren't welcome in our own church, either."

She held her head and breathed deeply, all the way down into her stomach. "I can't stand thinking about someone who hated my son so much, just walking around out there. How could anyone kill him? And last night, how could they..."

Ilka felt the woman's loneliness, an icy chill slinking across the table "How did Ashley's family react back then?"

"They were angry and heartbroken, of course. Her mother died a few years ago, but the police have talked to her father. He moved to a nearby town five or six years ago, when he and his wife divorced. She had a brother, but he left Racine a long time before this happened. The police officer said they're trying to find him."

Mike's mother stared blankly for a moment; then she laid her hand on the photo album. "Artie promised I could see my son. I brought along the pictures he asked for."

Ilka stood up. She was relieved the conversation was over, but Shelby's story also confused her. "I'll tell him you're ready."

The woman nodded, but she seemed uneasy. Her eyes darted toward the door, as if she didn't feel quite ready after all.

"Here, please, have one." Ilka slid the bowl of chocolates across the table. As if that helped. "He'll be here in a moment."

She hurried out the door. She felt like a coward.

19

Ilka kept knocking on the door of the preparation room until Artie finally came out. "I can't let anyone view Mike right now," he said. "He hasn't been embalmed, so he's in no shape for her to see."

"Then you'll have to go out and tell her. You had an agreement." Ilka wheeled and walked away, but she heard Artie follow. "She has the photos you asked for. How do you think she feels about going in there to look at him? She's pulled herself together to do it, and after what happened last night it's probably not easier for her."

"Okay, but—"

"If you want to send her home again, it's you who has to tell her."

"Give me a second here." He walked over and washed his hands; then he took off his apron.

Ilka's eyes widened. "Do you plan on talking to her wearing that?" She pointed at his Hawaiian shirt, the blazing colors, the parrots.

Artie ignored her and walked out, leaving her speechless.

Ilka stayed in the background as he gave Shelby a hug. "I'm so sorry about what happened last night," he said, his arm still around her shoulder. "Believe me, it hurts to see you put through this; it was totally disgusting. And I'm sorry that someone could break into our building. We've had some problems with our alarm system, but of course this kind of thing shouldn't be possible."

He apologized again. Ilka had the feeling it wasn't all about Paul's daughter screwing up by opening the window so the cat could come in. Something else was going on. Maybe he was afraid Shelby might sue them for not taking better care of her deceased son; if she did begin thinking that way, it could turn out to be horribly expensive for them. Ilka let Artie keep talking. But then she heard Shelby wave off his apologies.

"The person who dishonored Mike's body would have broken in even if you had bars on all the windows and doors. This happened because someone in this town still wants revenge."

"I know what I promised you," Artie said. He explained carefully that he couldn't let her see her son after all. "Everything's been delayed; we had to call the police after what happened last night."

"You can at least let me see his feet," she said. "That's enough. He has two toes on his left foot grown together. I know you all say it's my son in there, but I need to see it with my own eyes. I hope you understand."

Artie nodded. "Of course. Just give me a minute. If you two would just step in there, I'll bring him in."

He pointed at the large chapel used for funeral services. It looked like a lecture hall, with rows of chairs filling the room, though the first row was filled with plush sofas. The entire room was in beige, even the ceiling and the soft carpet. Muted and austere in a way that couldn't offend anyone or clash with any style or religious belief. The acoustics were good, thanks to a carpet so thick that you sank into it as you walked.

Ilka followed Mike's mother inside and turned on the light. The vases were empty, and the pleated floor-length curtains were closed behind the catafalque that supported the coffins. A lectern stood to the right of the catafalque, and loudspeakers on stands were spread around the room so everyone could hear relatives talk about the person they had lost.

Jensen Funeral Home went along with any kind of funeral service the relatives wanted, so long as it didn't involve alcohol or anything unseemly. According to Artie, one time there had been karaoke at the lectern, because it had been the great passion of the deceased. It had been nearly impossible to stop once it got going, because there was always one more person who wanted the microphone.

The door opened behind them, and Artie rolled the stretcher in. Mike was covered with a white sheet. The stretcher's wheels left tracks in the carpet. Ilka couldn't help but notice Shelby's expression tighten as he approached the catafalque. She stepped forward and laid a hand on the woman's back, then asked her if she was okay.

Shelby nodded. Her face was like stone, her fists clenched, but her eyes followed Artie as he parked the stretcher between the sofas and the catafalque.

He nodded and told her to take her time.

"I'm ready," she said, and she walked over and stood at the end where her son's feet stuck up.

Artie took hold of the sheet; then he waited until she gave him a small nod. He lifted the sheet, and Mike's feet and lower legs appeared.

It took her only a moment to confirm what she already knew. She turned and collapsed into Artie's arms.

Ilka had kept in the background, but now she stepped forward and pulled the sheet back over Mike's feet. She thought about pushing the stretcher out again, but she decided that Shelby should be allowed to leave the room before her son. When and only when she was ready to leave.

She went out into the hallway to give the mother time. Ilka needed time herself, to gather her thoughts. Though she tried not to worry too much about the problems with coffin suppliers, she wasn't used to giving in and letting herself be patronized. She took it personally that no one was willing to be helpful. On the other hand, she did have the coffin for tomorrow; she didn't need to worry about that. But it exasperated her that they had simply shut her off.

Stop it, she told herself. Artie and Shelby came out, and Artie asked if there was anything she wanted her son to have with him in the coffin.

"Think it over," he said as they stood in the doorway. "Don't go out and buy something. It's more like if there's anything at home that you know meant something to him. Or to you."

Shelby promised to think about it and let them know. "I couldn't bring myself to throw anything of his away after he left; it's all up in the attic, but I haven't looked at it since then. I'll come over tomorrow if I find anything."

"And if you don't have any clothes for him, we'll take care of it," Artie added quickly. He hugged her one last time.

She nodded and thanked them; then she glanced again at the open door to the room where the stretcher still stood before walking out.

20

Back in her father's room, Ilka checked her phone. She had two messages, both from her mother. The first one: *"Let us know when you land. Will pick you up at the airport."*

The next message was a bit more demanding: *"You have three jobs Monday, and the entire week is filled up. The first job is nine o'clock Monday morning at Linde School in Virum."*

Ilka plopped down on her father's bed and closed her eyes for a moment. Earlier that day, she had been more than ready to go home. Turn her back on everything and pick up where she had left off. If she had followed that plan, she might even have been sitting on a plane right now. But that was no longer an option.

Insulted? Vindictive? Enraged? Ilka wasn't sure how she felt. Maybe she was just offended on her father's behalf, but pride and vanity were involved, too. She was not going to take the coffin suppliers' rejections lying down. Yet she didn't feel at all like they had won the first battle. On the contrary. And it would suit her fine if they found out she could manage without them. Then there was Shelby. Ilka had to make sure she got to say good-bye to her son in a dignified manner. And finally, of course, there were all her father's things. And the two half sisters she'd found out about. She was anxious to meet them, and she had in fact expected they'd stop by to say hello, but maybe they thought she needed time to settle in. As if she'd had time for that.

She smiled and glanced around the room, which was a complete mess. Almost everything lay in piles, and the two body bags she had begun filling had to be emptied again. What would Erik say if he could see her now? "Pack your stuff and go home," or "Get everything under control and figure out what you want."

To try to get herself going, Ilka filled several supermarket plastic sacks with things she was sure would be thrown out. She went downstairs with one in each hand and walked out behind the house to the big Dumpsters. She opened the door and tossed the two sacks inside, but as she was about to slam the door shut, something caught her eye. A jacket sleeve stuck up between the bags over in the far corner of the Dumpster.

Ilka stood on tiptoe and leaned over to grab the corner of the topmost sack. To her surprise she saw the bags of her father's clothes she had packed for Sister Eileen to give to her parish, hidden under trash sacks. But the nun had said she would take the clothes to the parish herself, so...

Ilka stared at the sacks for a moment; then she leaned back and slammed the Dumpster door shut.

Back in the bedroom, she gathered up the drawings her half sisters had made for their father. She would drive out later and give them to the two women, use them as an excuse for showing up and introducing herself. She was nervous but curious—would she see any of herself in them? Or something of their common father?

"Couldn't leave after all," she wrote to her mother. "Something has come up I have to take care of. Could you handle my jobs? Get Hanne to help set them up."

Her mother had helped several times when Ilka had been on a tight schedule, so she knew the routine on photo shoots, how the school students were to be placed. Granted, she'd never actually taken the photos, but that was the easiest part. All she had to do was press the camera's button, Ilka had explained.

Before sending her message, she checked her watch. Her mother was probably asleep and wouldn't see this for another eight hours. Ilka would be asleep then, and her mother would realize it was too late to find someone to do the jobs. Ilka knew she was conscientious; she would step in when she saw there were no other options.

The sun was about to go down, and Ilka felt restless. With a hint of a smile on his lips, Artie had helped her unload the Costco coffin out of the hearse. He decided to cover the scratches with black shoe polish; he doubted the family would notice. Fortunately, the damaged side of the coffin would be turned away from everyone.

There wasn't anything more Ilka could do to prepare for the next day's service, and besides, she was hungry. And in need of company, of a normal conversation that didn't include coffins, dead people, and complicated inheritances. She rose from the bed and picked her sweater up off the floor; then she went back downstairs to ask Artie if he wanted to go to Oh Dennis! for a bite to eat.

The preparation room door was open a crack, but she couldn't hear the fan. The Beach Boys were, however, at top volume, with Artie humming along. She stepped inside. Mike lay on the table in the middle of the room. Artie was leaning over his face, concentrating on brushing another layer onto the crushed cheekbone. Then he studied the face below him before using his brush on the cheek again.

The easygoing California summer surfer music contrasted sharply with the strange sight before Ilka, but in a way, Artie's movements were so gentle that it didn't seem grotesque.

Ilka cleared her throat loudly so as not to scare him to death; then she asked if she could come in.

He glanced up and nodded a bit absentmindedly before focusing again on the face. Mike's body was still covered by the sheet; only the face was visible. He lifted a small putty knife out of a bottle of something that reminded Ilka of modeling wax. Then he pressed a small clump of the material into the part of the sunken cheek he'd been brushing and carefully smoothed it out. He leaned closer in and compared the damaged and undamaged cheekbones; then he added more wax and rounded it off to make them look identical.

Ilka was fascinated by his work. He concentrated on applying layer upon layer, and Mike's cheek and eye socket soon were as prominent as they had been before someone had destroyed them.

"Are you hungry?" she asked. "I can pick up something if you want to finish here."

He glanced up at her as if he'd forgotten she'd come in; then he shook his head. "I'm okay, but thanks."

He concentrated as if he were creating a work of art, and in a way, he was. Ilka noticed the cans of Red Bull lined up on the table by the wall. One of them was open; three others sat there waiting.

"Text me if you change your mind, or if you want a beer when you finish. I'm going out and see if anyone in this town has discovered it's Friday, the day before the weekend." She left him to his work.

The food wasn't exactly a gourmet delight, though there was lots of it. The spareribs that had filled Ilka's plate were gnawed to the bone, though, by the time the waitress returned to her table and asked if she wanted coffee and cheesecake. Ilka answered with a question of her own: Where do you go on a Friday evening if you're looking for some company?

Ilka nodded as the young woman told her to drive down the main street and cross the small canal; a little bit farther down, on the right side, was a bar with live music. If she liked that sort of thing.

"But there are other bars," the girl said. She pointed up the street, away from the square. "I think they have music there, too; I'm not sure."

Ilka paid her bill and decided to try the bar across the canal. If it wasn't her type of place, she could check out another bar on the way home.

21

At least there was live music. A group of men about her age was standing around when Ilka walked inside. So far, so good. She squeezed her way through.

It was only a little past nine, but most of the tables were already taken, and the dim bar with the low-hanging lamps was lively. The only other light was a grainy yellow glare from above the bottles behind the bar and a colored string of lights nailed up along the edge, like an elaborate drapery.

Some people were rolling dice, and at a table up next to the stage, a group of women sang loudly. Western hats and boots; the guy standing there with his guitar was going for it, Ilka thought, as she pulled out an empty bar stool and sat down. He sang well, and the vibes in the bar were good. She glanced around while waiting for the bartender in the plaid flannel shirt to notice her.

"Root beer," she said, when he came over.

The men behind her burst out laughing at something she didn't hear. They ordered more beer. More people came in; greetings were being yelled all around her. Everybody seemed to know one another, from the conversations going on. "How's Greg doing?" "Is your mother okay now?" "Did Jenny have her kid?" Where in the world were all these people in the daytime? Not on the street; that was for sure.

Applause, more music. Several people also said hi to Ilka as they walked by or came up to the bar to order.

"Are you new in town?" someone behind her suddenly asked. She turned and stared straight into the face of a guy at least ten years younger than her. Dark hair, blue eyes. Handsome.

She nodded when he asked if he could sit down, but she said no thanks when he offered to buy her a beer. Though every seat around her was taken, he pulled up another bar stool from somewhere. His name was Larry; he'd moved to town to work at Johnson Wax, whose headquarters were located here. He was born and raised in Chicago, had gone to college there also.

Ilka listened with half an ear, nodding occasionally while trying to place the scent he had on. Masculine and yet light. Nice. She didn't hear his question, which he repeated when she didn't answer.

"No, I'm just visiting," she said. She told him she was from Denmark and would be going back. Soon.

"So have you seen anything while you've been here? Sailing is good on Lake Michigan, and there are some beautiful lakes in the area. I'll show you around this weekend if you like."

Either he was terribly lonesome or he was trying to score. The latter was preferable. Ilka turned to get a better look at him. His hair hung just over his eyes, but not enough that it seemed deliberate. He just needed a haircut. A point in his favor. Dark blue long-sleeved T-shirt and jeans, no problems there.

"That sounds nice," she said, and she ordered a beer

for him while looking at her root beer, which she hadn't touched.

The cowboy singer was on break; they were playing Taylor Swift over the house speakers. The women up front sang along. The bar was full now, every table was taken, and crowds of people were standing behind them. Ilka pulled her chair closer to Larry, their legs slipped in between each other's.

"How long have you lived here?" she asked. Someone walked by and nudged her leg against his; she kept it there. She leaned forward slightly to hear him better.

"Two years." His cheek happened to brush against hers.

The singer was back onstage, and the music seemed louder than before.

"Let's go outside," she suggested. "I can't hear a thing in here."

He hesitated for a moment when they stood up, as if he'd lost his nerve when he saw she was taller than him. Quite a bit taller. But he grabbed his beer and followed her anyway.

While elbowing their way to the door, Ilka couldn't help wondering if anyone here had something to do with the writing on Shelby's house. This was a small town; somebody here must at least know something, she thought, though everyone seemed friendly and nice enough.

"Denmark, you said?" Larry asked, as they walked down toward the canal. There were a few small sheds on the wharf; motorboats filled one side. "Have you checked out any of the Danish bakeries here? My boss speaks a little Danish. Helmersen's his name; his wife runs one of the bakeries with her brothers. I think she works behind the counter; the brothers do the baking."

His arm was around her as they walked, and when they reached the first shed, Ilka turned and kissed him. She maneuvered him over to the other side of the shed, out of sight, and he put his arms around her.

He mumbled something about the Danish Vikings and how nice she was, but she shushed him. No more talk. He kissed her harder and got rougher with his hands, and before she managed to unbutton his pants, he took over. No more thoughts about the coffin suppliers, debt, the funeral service that still could turn into a nightmare if the family discovered she'd cheated them on the expensive prepaid coffin. No more funeral home business and old murder cases. No more photo shoots and responsibilities. She nipped at his earlobe and held on to him as all thoughts disappeared.

"Thanks," she said after it was over, as if they'd just wound up some business.

"My pleasure." He held her face and kissed her on the forehead. "You want to go back and have a beer?"

Ilka smiled and shook her head. "I've got to get home." She said she had to get up early the next morning.

He studied her for a moment. "Would you give me your phone number?" He smiled a bit awkwardly.

She shook her head as she straightened her clothes.

"So will I see you again before you leave?"

"Sorry, I don't think so," she said, then added that it had been nice.

She kissed him and laid her cheek against his, breathed in his scent. When they reached the street, she walked away, but she noticed him turning to look back a few times before going into the bar.

Ilka smiled as she drove back home. He couldn't be a day over thirty, and he had made her evening. For a moment, she wondered if it was dumb of her not to get his number, but no. Once was enough.

As she moved through the deserted town, she realized that for the first time since she'd arrived in Racine, her head wasn't buzzing in confusion and wrestling with decisions to be made.

22

Ilka woke up to someone knocking on her door. At first she was afraid she'd slept late, but then she saw it was only eight thirty. She'd set her alarm for nine.

"Okay," she yelled. "Just a second."

"We have a decision to make," Sister Eileen said from outside. "We have a problem."

Why doesn't that fucking surprise me? Ilka thought. She was pulling her pants on when the sister knocked again.

"*Jeg gider ikke flere problemer,*" she yelled. She didn't want any more problems. Several messages had come in from her mother, she saw. She tossed her phone onto the bed and opened the door. Sister Eileen was holding a sheet of paper, which she handed to her. "Joanne had agreed to bring the flowers at eight thirty, so I could decorate before the Nortons and the caterers arrive. But she brought this instead."

She nodded at the sheet of paper. "It's a final bill. She refuses to work for us anymore. She says she doesn't think we will pay her what we owe, so now it's over."

Ilka glanced at the statement. They owed more than twenty-eight hundred dollars.

"I've informed Artie about this, and he has promised to

take care of the flowers for today. He'll bring them with him when he arrives. But we still have a problem."

"Why is she stopping right now?" Ilka asked after checking the dates. Deliveries had been made up to last weekend; they had begun all the way back in June. They'd been receiving flowers on credit for more than three months, almost four. And it wasn't even close to the first of the month, so why deliver the bill now? Something must have happened.

The sister shrugged. "We've always had a fine working relationship with Joanne, even back when her sister ran the shop. They've delivered flowers for us for all the years I've been working here. Your father wouldn't dream of ordering from anywhere else."

Ilka was angry now, and she decided to go down later to confront them and hash out some sort of installment agreement. "And Artie knows what flowers we need? They're going to take care of the coffin decorations from her own garden; it's just the room that needs decorating."

The nun confirmed that Artie was aware of all this.

"Is there anything else to be delivered for the funeral service today?" Ilka asked. She was counting on the family arriving at eleven, and if there were any more unpleasant surprises in store, she wanted to be prepared.

"The food. But it's coming. I ordered hors d'oeuvres, and I called yesterday to make sure everything was going according to plan. And it was."

"And we can count on that?"

"I hope so." She turned and walked back down the stairs so quietly that Ilka wasn't sure her feet touched the steps.

Ilka took a quick shower, and when she returned to her room, she opened her father's closet to look over what was left inside. She hadn't had time to wash her clothes, and besides, nothing she'd brought was appropriate for the funeral service of an elderly lady.

She slipped a white shirt off a hanger and glanced over at the two dark jackets. One of them looked new. It fit her across the back, but the sleeves were too short. The same was true for the other jacket. Along with the shirt, she tossed one of them over on the bed and tried on the black gabardine pants, complete with pleats and tucked pockets—the uniform of a funeral director. Unlike the jacket, the pants were long enough; her father had been tall. With a belt, they were okay, though she wasn't going to get a lot of compliments on her great ass when she wore them. Considering the occasion, that was probably the last thing anyone would notice anyway.

Before going downstairs, she shook her head and ran her hands through her straight hair to make it look fuller. She'd forgotten her hair dryer, or rather, she hadn't even considered taking it along. A quick application of mascara, and that was that.

She turned on the standing lamps in the two rooms that made up the chapel; a folding door had been opened and now the room was twice as big as it had been the day before, when Shelby had been there. There was room for 175 people, but they were expecting between 100 and 150 to show up. The Nortons had ordered food for 160, just to be safe. Ilka was a bit nervous that the caterer might pull the same stunt as Joanne had. She was on her way to the office to call them and double-check when Artie showed up, struggling to get inside.

"Could you give me a hand here?" he asked.

"What the hell is this?" He was carrying a jumble of flowers and wide satin ribbons.

"Time to decorate," he said, nodding at the closed door to the chapel, where Sister Eileen had brought in more chairs for the service.

Ilka stared for a moment; then slowly she understood where the flowers had come from. This was the moment to decide whether it was better not to ask so later on she could deny any knowledge of it.

She opened the door for him, and Artie managed to get to the table and dump the flowers. He pulled a pair of scissors out of his back pocket and started clipping the silk ribbons tied around the bouquets, tossing the ribbons on the floor one after the other; then he cut the strings holding the flowers together until they were strewn all over the table.

"Nobody's going to miss them," he said, even though Ilka hadn't said a word. "They come from the common grave; there are so many that no one's going to notice."

Ilka shook her head and turned around. Sister Eileen walked in with a jug of water and started filling the vases. She didn't so much as lift an eyebrow, though she glanced at the flower table and announced tersely that she would begin decorating.

"Hello," a voice called from out in the hallway.

Ilka immediately kicked all the ribbons under the floor-length tablecloth; then she walked to the door, where she was met by a young man in a light blue shirt and black pants. The insignia embroidered onto his shirt pocket looked like a delivery boy holding a dish.

"Hello," she said, closing the door behind her.

"Where do I put the food?"

You actually showed up! she almost cried out. But instead she simply smiled and showed him out to the kitchen. When he saw the table she pointed at, he shook his head. "Usually we put food on long tables; are they ready?"

Ilka tried to think where the long tables might be, when Sister Eileen came out and took over.

"They're out in the front hall." She followed him out toward the stairway. "When we receive funeral guests, we take them directly in to the service, so it won't be open out here until the service is finished. That should give you enough time to set up."

Once again Ilka sensed the nun was deliberately not letting her in on procedures in the funeral home. As if she didn't think it was worth the effort. Or maybe she wanted Ilka to remain an outsider. She watched the sister show the boy exactly where she wanted the various dishes placed. But that wasn't what was gnawing at her.

Ilka had the feeling Sister Eileen was keeping something to herself. It was hard to put a finger on what it was. It just seemed that she kept Ilka at a distance most of the time. And then suddenly she could be pleasant and helpful.

For a moment, she thought about insisting on participating in the planning, to show she wouldn't be brushed aside, but then she looked at the clock. The funeral service would begin in less than half an hour, and the relatives were already getting things ready in the chapel.

Ilka stayed in the background while the family made the final preparations. She watched Helen arrange the pillows, shift the Kleenex boxes at the end of every row by a few inches, and light all the candles, even though sunlight streamed through the windows. She also took care of the flowers, while the two brothers stood with arms crossed, speaking softly to each other. Ilka tensed up when they started walking over to where their mother lay. She wished she were invisible.

She held her breath while the brothers approached the coffin. The upper half was open, and the elderly woman was visible from the waist up, her hands folded and her eyes closed. As usual with corpses, the skin on her face was smooth, almost like that of a little girl.

Ilka stared at the floor while they circled the coffin. After a few minutes, she looked up and breathed out through nearly closed lips. They hadn't noticed any scratches; the shoe polish had worked. The only thing bothering them was the missing easel for the life board they'd ordered.

She pretended not to have eavesdropped. First and foremost because she didn't know what a life board was, and therefore couldn't tell them where it and the easel could be. It dawned on her that it was something Mrs. Norton had told Ilka's father she wanted, back when she had preordered her funeral. When they had gone through all the details after the first meeting, the sister had been assigned to take care of it.

Knowing she would have to confront the nun about something that should have been taken care of felt great—but only for a few seconds. The sister appeared with the life board and easel. It was a long sheet of cardboard, the size of the mirror on the back of the closet door in her father's room, with photos of the deceased illustrating her life story. A black-and-white photo of a young Mrs. Norton with big curls and a sugary smile, then a grinning young college graduate wearing the coveted square graduate cap. Then a happy wedding photo. Then a large leap in years to an older lady smiling pleasantly at the camera. An entire life in four photos. It almost looked to Ilka like a poster for someone running for office, promising voters a long and prosperous life. Then a sharp odor of food interrupted her thoughts, and she turned to the door, where Mrs. Norton's grandchild walked in holding a full plate in each hand.

It wasn't until he pushed aside the box of Kleenex on the small table between the sofas that Ilka realized what she smelled: a combination of macaroni and cheese and pecan pie, a dessert his grandmother had loved to make. Still warm, Ilka discovered, when she walked over to the boy and asked if she could help.

"I want Grandma to have this in her coffin. Mom helped me, but she says it can't go in until the guests leave. But she'll forget it for sure; she's more worried about whether there's enough food for everybody."

"I'll make sure we remember," Ilka said. She was just beginning to enjoy how everything was going as it should, when she noticed the younger brother prowling around the back of the coffin, again with a critical eye. He stepped back and took a good look; then he walked around to the head of the coffin. Again he stepped back, as if the light wasn't exactly right where he was standing. He kept to the front of the podium; it couldn't be the scratches he was looking at, Ilka thought, as she listened distractedly to the grandson.

"The plates are ovenproof, but Mom says we don't need to tell the guy who's burning the coffin."

"Don't worry about that," Ilka murmured. Joe was at the back of the coffin again, and he called over his older brother. They began scowling in Ilka's direction. She couldn't hear what they were saying, but she was certain they were discussing how big a refund they should demand if they could prove the coffin was damaged or the wrong color.

"You're right; it's not the right coffin." The older brother spoke so loudly that Ilka couldn't help hearing. Ilka was beginning to catch on; the older brother was less conflict shy, while the younger brother was the brains of the outfit. They walked toward her.

"There's no glitter in the paint. It's glossy, but it doesn't glitter."

They spoke almost in unison, and Ilka reacted by taking a step back and bumping into Artie, who had parked himself behind her without her noticing.

"It doesn't, no," he said. "It's not exactly what your mother ordered, which isn't available anymore. This coffin, though, is a jet-black limousine. It's the replacement model, more exclusive, like the name suggests. That's also the reason it's much more expensive."

The older brother butted in. "We're not paying one penny more. You didn't warn us about any extra expenses. And we're not paying just because a model was discontinued. It's not our fault!"

"No, though a lot of people insure themselves against things like this, so they don't have to worry."

The brother was about to protest, but Artie beat him to it. "But of course you don't have to pay the difference." He laid a hand on Steve's shoulder, as if they were old friends. "It's part of our service. With us you don't have to worry about expensive insurance to guard against extra costs. And no one who preorders their burial in this funeral home will ever see us compromise on quality, even when prices go up. In fact, we try to give our customers more than what they pay for."

Ilka realized she'd been holding her breath again during this whole conversation. Not so much because of what Artie had been rattling on about, but because he spoke in an entirely different manner: Everything sounded so convincing. She hadn't known he had this in him. Impressed with how he had saved the day, she turned to him and nodded in acknowledgment before heading for the door. It felt like the room was closing in on her; she needed some air, but just as she reached the hallway, she was called back.

"Is there a hook for Mother's dogs, to hang the leashes on?" Helen had just finished placing flowers on the floor around the coffin.

"Not a real hook, no," Ilka said. "But I was thinking you would have the dogs with you in the first row, and you can fasten the leashes to the sofa's leg. Or will your mother's dogs be too close to the coffin that way?"

"Oh no!" Helen said. "We want the dogs up front. That's what Mom would have wanted."

"Fine, then we'll do it that way." Ilka was about to leave again when she ran into the choir, seven men and three women from the seniors' club, who wanted to know where to stand.

Suddenly Ilka realized she hadn't seen anything of Sister Eileen since she'd brought in the life board. And now, as guests were beginning to arrive, she was still nowhere in sight.

"Just a moment," Ilka said, walking away without answering them. The nun wasn't in the reception area or the front hall, where the food was set out.

On the way to the small kitchen Ilka glanced into the arrangement room and her father's office—empty. Back in the hallway now, she was heading for the garage when the door opened and Sister Eileen entered.

"The guests are arriving," Ilka said. She was annoyed; she hadn't yet asked about the clothes in the Dumpster, either. Couldn't bring herself to. She was afraid of being too pushy. Though it might just be a question of learning something about the way nuns like her live, Ilka thought. Maybe she'd been praying over in her apartment, or whatever the proper thing to do was. "I would appreciate it if you could go in and welcome them. The choir is here too. Could you show them where to go?" she added as she headed back to the chapel.

The people attending the service streamed in, and a low murmur slowly spread throughout the chapel. Ilka made her way into a corner behind the open folding doors. Artie was in the middle of the crowd; she sensed he was giving some final tips to the family, who had wanted to arrange the funeral service. He nodded when Steve signaled he was ready to start the music. The choir would sing after the two brothers each spoke about their mother.

Ilka noticed the grandson sitting on the plush sofa. One of his grandmother's dachshunds was on his lap; the other sat at his feet. The chapel was almost full; people were speaking in hushed tones. Most of them were older, but there were also many close to Helen's and her brothers' ages.

"Thanks," Ilka said, when Artie came over and stood beside her. Soft music poured out of the speakers, and the voices fell silent. For a moment, everyone listened to the music; then the two brothers stood and walked up to the podium to welcome everyone.

When one of the brothers began his speech, Ilka looked over at the table with the long tablecloth. One of the broad satin ribbons from the stolen flowers stuck out, a scarlet ribbon, and part of a woman's name—not the name of the deceased lying in the coffin—stood out in gold.

"Come on," Artie said, pulling her away. "They'll handle the rest themselves. And Sister Eileen will take care of the food; it's all been put out."

She followed him out back under the carport. He lit a cigarette and blew the smoke out slowly.

"I think Sister Eileen threw my father's clothes away

instead of giving them to her parish, like we talked about," Ilka said. She sat down on the steps.

He looked surprised. "Why would she do that?"

Ilka shrugged. "I don't understand it either. She even offered to take them herself, when I said I would deliver them."

He crushed out his cigarette, then walked over and threw the butt in the Dumpster. It was as if what she'd said didn't really interest him.

"And what got into you back there at the coffin?" she asked. "Have you been smoking weed or something?"

When he didn't answer, Ilka realized she'd put her finger on the real reason for his bravado in front of the Norton family. "Damn, Artie, what if they'd noticed it?" She was serious now.

"The only thing they noticed was the coffin model wasn't what they'd ordered."

Ilka nodded. After a few moments, she shrugged. "You handled that great. But what if someone had found out about the flowers? It would have ruined our image!"

He gazed at her a second longer than necessary before saying, "Sweetheart, we don't have an image. Not anymore!"

The choir began singing.

23

The coffee had just finished dripping through the filter, and Ilka had brought two cups out to the steps where Artie was smoking another cigarette, just as Shelby came marching across the parking lot. Her face was ashen, her lips pursed in anger. She carried a pair of pants and a shirt over her shoulder.

Ilka had hoped that Shelby wouldn't show up until the people attending the funeral service had left. It would have been best given the present situation—Artie wouldn't have been stoned any longer, hopefully—and Ilka needed a breather. The past days had simply been too much pressure.

"I'll kill him," Shelby said, when she reached them. She threw the clothes at Artie, who was on his feet now. "I'll wring his neck; I'll cut him up into pieces."

Ilka handed one cup of coffee to her, the other to Artie.

"Shelby, what happened?" Artie said, trying to placate her. He pushed his hair back so it wouldn't fall into the steaming cup of coffee.

"I'll tell you what happened!" she yelled as she looked for a place to sit.

Ilka took her elbow. "Come in; let's go sit down."

She gestured at Artie in no uncertain terms for him to follow.

"I just came from the police station," she said, after she and her coffee had been settled in the plush chair in the arrangement room. Ilka and Artie sat across from her.

"It's Howard Oldham! You already know he was on the tape of the school's surveillance camera that night; the police said so. And he admitted doing it, but you'll never guess what made him break in and do the horrible thing he did to my son."

She made it sound as if an undertaker from the town's leading funeral home breaking into a competitor's business, pulling a corpse out of the refrigerator, and urinating on it was a minor detail compared to what she was about to say.

Artie set his coffee down and hunched over a bit. He looked frozen. Through the thin walls they could hear singing from the funeral service.

Shelby looked back and forth between the two of them.

"No, you're right," Ilka said. "We'll never guess."

She didn't seem to have heard Ilka; she was too outraged to deal with what was about to burst from inside her. Her anger stood in total contrast to her small, delicate body. "He was wild about her. Howard Oldham claims that Ashley was his great love. The police told me he broke down; they had to postpone the questioning because he wasn't able to speak."

Tears appeared in her eyes. "He says my son stole her from him. That Mike ruined his life. Howard claims that if it hadn't been for Mike, he would have been engaged to her."

Artie was confused. "Are you saying he and Ashley had a relationship before she met your son? He must've been twice her age."

"It's not like that's never happened before," Ilka said.

She was thinking of the center of Copenhagen on Friday nights, where men in their forties and fifties puffed themselves up like roosters, drinking cocktails, with teenage girls all over them.

"I don't know if they actually had a relationship," Shelby said. "But he was courting her, per the police report. They let me see it down at the station. He must have thought their age difference wouldn't be important if he could just show her he was serious. Something must've gone on between them, anyway."

Artie began nodding, as if something was dawning on him. "Ashley Simpson's dad was a chauffeur for the Oldhams. Not for the funeral home, but the private chauffeur for Douglas Oldham, the old undertaker." He explained that Ashley had lived in the chauffeur's quarters with her brother and parents. "It's behind the Oldhams' house, farther out on the coast road. I remember hearing the old man couldn't keep his hands off the daughter. But I thought they meant Douglas Oldham. I only met him a few times. He killed himself a year after all this happened. Or maybe he just got sick? There were a lot of rumors flying around back then."

Shelby looked fragile and pale as she sat slumped over, staring down at the table seemingly without seeing the coffee or her folded hands in front of her. She shook her head weakly. "It never would have happened. What would she do with an old man? She was just a big kid. Even if Mike hadn't fallen in love with her, she wouldn't have hooked up with a man old enough to be her father. Would she?"

She looked up, confused and in despair.

"But was it Howard Oldham who paid your son to leave town?" Ilka asked. So it was jealousy, just as she had guessed.

"Paid?" Artie said, still looking at Shelby. "What's that about? Paid for what?"

She straightened up a bit. "My son was paid to leave town. He was given a lot of money to start a new life. A lot. Someone bought him."

Artie stared straight ahead in thought. "Which made it look like he ran away." He nodded.

"Like he was guilty." Shelby spit the words out. She drew herself up, tried to get a grip. "But the money didn't come from Howard. The Oldham family was questioned, because they knew Ashley and her father, and maybe they knew something, but Howard wasn't even in town back then. He was in Minneapolis, taking extra courses to add to his undertaker degree."

She paused a moment before explaining that it was his alibi, not being in Racine during the three weeks between Ashley's death and Mike's disappearance. "He didn't kill her, and he wasn't around when Mike was paid either."

"No one can be sure he wasn't home some of those days, can they?" Ilka said. "It was a long period. It almost sounds too good to be true, gone the entire three weeks. Very convenient."

"He was gone for four weeks, in fact," Shelby said.

Artie nodded at Ilka. "He fabricated the alibi, you're thinking."

"That's what I said too, down at the police station," Shelby said. "But they reopened the old case, and the alibi is good. He enrolled in the continuing education half a year before all this happened, and he had no absences from class. And besides, it's written in the witness statements that his reaction clearly showed he had no knowledge of what had happened. Back then, though, he didn't mention his relationship with Ashley. The police just found out about that."

They sat in silence as the magnitude of his confession sank in. A grown man, Ilka thought. How could he let himself break in and pull a body out of the refrigerator and piss in hate—over twelve years of hate—on it?

"And he wasn't the man who killed my son," she finally continued. "He also has an alibi for the evening that Mike came back."

"That's even more convenient." Artie sounded suspicious. He seemed to be completely sober now; his eyes were clear and focused, as was his anger.

"The police have arrested the two Oldham sons," she said. "They're suspected of doing the dirty work for their uncle. The officer couldn't tell me more, but obviously they deny having had any contact with Mike after he came back. But why would they admit it if they did?"

"*Hold da kæft!*" Ilka said. Unbelievable! She sat back in her chair. Everything began swirling in her head: names, dates, people she didn't know. None of it made sense to her. She needed to take a walk, be by herself for a while.

She turned and glanced across the parking lot. People who had attended the funeral service were beginning to drift outside in small, scattered groups, and she thought about Mrs. Norton's favorite dishes, which were to be placed inside the coffin before it was taken to the crematorium.

"Please excuse me," she said. She bumped into the table when she rose, spilling coffee. "There's something I have to take care of."

The grandson was standing alone by the coffin when Ilka walked in. She heard voices out in the front hall; a few people must still have been eating canapés.

Pete stood with his back to her. The two small, ovenproof dishes were still on the small table, and the two dachshunds were curled up, each at one end of the sofa. There was something comforting about the silence. Peaceful, Ilka thought.

He turned and watched her approach. "My uncle thinks it's stupid, about the food." He glanced over at the table. "Grandma doesn't know we're doing this."

Ilka smiled. "Don't you think she does?"

He wasn't sure if she was serious. "Isn't it a little bit yucky?"

"Well, yeah. It's a little bit yucky. But so what? No one will know, and if it feels right to you, I think she should take it along with her."

"Maybe we're not supposed to do it?"

"Maybe not, but we can just not ask anyone about it."

"But aren't you the one who decides?" He looked at her suspiciously.

Ilka nodded. "Yes, but you didn't ask me, either. You just said this is what you want to do. And rule number one is that the nearest relatives should decide how they want to send someone off. I think this is very thoughtful of you, to give your grandmother a few of her favorite dishes on her last journey. That's how they did it a very long time ago. They gave the dead something to eat for their journey."

Ilka should have stuck a bottle of red wine in Erik's coffin; she just hadn't thought of it.

She opened the bottom half of the lid and told him he could put the food down there, that no one would discover it.

As soon as the boy grabbed the two plates, the dachshunds jumped up and began barking, shrilly and very loudly. They wagged their tails and danced around Pete's legs. "I could just..." He nodded down at the dogs.

Ilka laughed. Not because she thought dachshunds were particularly lovable, but the glint in the grandson's eyes told her this wasn't the first time the two small, dark-brown wiener dogs had begged their way into his heart. He had already surrendered, and there was something proper, something touching, about him shifting his attention from death to what was still a part of life.

"What do you think your grandmother would do?" she asked, but he'd already set the goodies on the floor. Two minutes later they were licked so clean that you couldn't see the plates had been used.

"What's going to happen with the dogs?" Ilka asked as they walked out into the front hall. His mother was putting her coat on.

"They're going to stay with us."

Helen had red splotches on her cheeks. She smiled at her son. "It went so well." She shook Ilka's hand. "Everything was like Mother would have wanted. And there were no problems whatsoever. I am so grateful to you. Should we take the flowers with us, or will you take care of them?"

"If you don't want to take them with you, we'll make sure they are laid on the coffin after it's closed." Ilka spoke with such authority that she surprised even herself. It struck her again that only a few days ago, all she knew about the funeral home business was what she had picked up as a child, but now here she was, talking as if she were running everything. Which, in a way, she was. At least on paper.

She shook her head and watched Helen walk to the car with her arm around her son, the two dogs running at their feet.

24

Shelby had left by the time Ilka returned, so she kicked off her shoes, shrugged out of her father's stiff jacket, and hung it back in the closet along with the pants. She'd just pulled a sweater over her head when someone knocked on the door. At first, she thought about hiding somewhere, but they knocked again. When she opened the door, Sister Eileen was standing outside holding a small tray with tea and a bowl of cookies that had been left over from the funeral service.

"Something to eat and drink?" The nun held the tray out and looked at Ilka exactly the way her mother did whenever she thought her daughter was working too hard.

"Thank you." She was surprised, and suddenly she felt hungry.

"There's also a plate of canapés downstairs. I wrapped them up and put them in the refrigerator."

Ilka eyed Sister Eileen, who politely stood out in the hall. Nothing about her smile gave the impression she was holding anything back from Ilka. She looked friendly and considerate. Maybe Ilka was only imagining this mistrust.

She took the tray. "Thank you so much. I really am hungry, in fact."

Once again she considered asking about the clothes, but instead she pointed at the small pile of drawings beside the odd clay figure and homemade Father's Day card. "I've been thinking about driving out to my half sisters and giving those to them."

"That's very thoughtful of you," the nun said. She offered to find a bag for them.

"That's okay; there's not very much, only those things. Is there anything I can do to help downstairs before I go?"

Sister Eileen shook her head. She stood in the doorway, as if there was something else on her mind, but she didn't say anything. Ilka broke the awkward silence. "How did you end up in Racine, by the way? Was it because of your parish? You didn't grow up here, did you?"

She was just being friendly, making small talk so they could get to know each other better, but the nun's reaction was so dismissive that Ilka wondered if she had said something wrong.

"I've picked up downstairs, and the tables have been put away. I'm going to lock up and take the rest of the day off. If, that is, you don't need me for anything more."

She'd already turned to leave when Ilka quickly shook her head. "No, go ahead, take the day off. What time is Ed McKenna's daughter coming tomorrow?"

She answered from halfway down the stairs. "She won't be here until twelve; there aren't so many flights during the weekend."

"Fine. We can sleep a little longer." Ilka smiled at her back.

She had tied a wide green satin ribbon around the drawings and put them aside. While going through the drawers, she had also found some photos of her father with her half sisters. And a brown envelope with several letters from them addressed to him. It looked like they were written while he was traveling in California. Naturally she had read all of them; no one would mind, she thought. The letters were mostly about things like the rabbits doing well, their homework was hard. And their mother had been in the hospital, but they had visited her, and she had come home after a few days. Even though their father had been gone only three weeks, the girls had dutifully written him every other day.

Ilka folded the letters up again. Surely he had written back? Nothing they had written seemed like answers to any questions he might have asked. They were just small, childlike updates. She guessed that some of the drawings had been sent with the letters.

On the way to her father's family, she tried not to think too much about meeting them. She tried to convince herself there was no reason to be nervous. And she wasn't, not really. And yet. Should she have called, given them the chance to prepare for her?

She still hadn't heard from them. It struck her that they might be angry about her inheriting the funeral home business. They might feel she had taken something from them. But they could just come right out and say it. They could have it. Right now. Maybe that was why she was a bit nervous: They hadn't reacted.

She thought about the wheelchair. Possibly they assumed she would come to them. Maybe they couldn't understand why she hadn't already contacted them. But she was the stranger, the guest. She was the one to be welcomed.

Stop it, she told herself. Though it felt like an eternity, she hadn't even been in town for a week, and they'd had plenty to do after her father's death. Of course they had.

She drove under the viaduct, above which the wide free-

way ran north. She thought of something else: Her half
sisters must resemble her, surely? Did they share some of
the same features? She hoped for their sake they hadn't inherited her father's height like she had. It had been hard
to see the evening she'd caught a glimpse of Leslie on the
porch. From a distance, she'd looked very feminine. Not a
skyscraper, like the boys in Ilka's class at school had called
her, when they weren't asking if her parents had forgotten
the *B* when they named her—Bilka, the name of the Danish
hypermarket chain. All through the lower classes at school,
she was called Bilka. But that stopped one day when she
lost her temper and grabbed a chair and smashed it over
Jakob's head—he had been her worst tormentor. The chair
leg broke his nose, but otherwise nothing happened. After
that, no one had felt any need to comment on her name. Or
her height, for that matter.

Leslie and Amber were two common names; no one
would have teased the two girls. Her father must have turned
into a lightweight after coming over here. Or else he hadn't
seen the same strength in them that he'd claimed to have seen
in her as a newborn baby. That was his explanation when she
asked him about her ridiculous name. "You're a winner, Ilka,
and they'll find that out sooner or later. A person has the advantage when the odds are against them, when they're the
big surprise. When they're someone no one had seen coming, when they strike when it's least expected."

"Talk, talk, talk," Ilka muttered to herself. It annoyed her
that her nerves were getting the upper hand. And what the
hell for? She didn't need her father's new family. "I'll leave
if I don't like them," she told her windshield.

Massive treetops drooped over the street where Ilka turned
off a bit later. She was close now. A large American flag

hanging from the gable end of a corner house nearly touched the ground, and there was a round plastic swimming pool under a square parasol on the front lawn. Kids' bikes were parked near the gate, and plastic toys were scattered around, as if some game had suddenly been interrupted. She drove past slowly, her eyes glued to her father's house. Even at a distance she could see the porch was deserted, but the front door was open, though barely.

She took a deep breath as she parked at the curb and shut the engine off. She sat and stared at nothing, then grabbed the bundle of drawings and letters. The small clay figure was in her pocket.

Before she shut the car door, she saw Mary Ann in the doorway, coming through in her wheelchair. Ilka hesitated before walking up the flagstone sidewalk to the house. She smiled as her father's wife, a frail, light-haired woman, wheeled across the porch to meet her.

"Hello," Ilka said when she reached the steps. "I'm Paul's daughter from Denmark." She started up the steps.

"Yes, I figured that, when you drove by the other day," Mary Ann said. She backed her wheelchair away from the steps so Ilka could pass.

Ilka shook her hand and smiled, and immediately the two sisters appeared in the doorway behind their mother. "I'm Ilka. Ilka Jensen."

She walked over to say hello to the sisters, one of whom had stepped behind the door. There was something familiar about the dark-haired woman. After stepping closer, to Ilka's surprise she saw it was the woman from the bench by the funeral home parking lot.

How about that, she thought. Then the blond older sister, the one she'd seen on the porch the other day, asked if she could help her with something.

For a second, Ilka wasn't sure why she had come, but then she remembered the things she'd brought along. She smiled when she realized the older sister must not know who she was.

"I'm your half sister." She added that she had been looking forward to meeting them, that she hadn't even known she had sisters. "It's so nice to meet you."

The blond sister—Leslie, according to Sister Eileen—stood behind her mother's wheelchair, and when no one spoke, the moment became so awkward that Ilka began to regret she'd come.

"I brought this along," she said. She showed them the bundle of drawings and letters. "I found them up in our father's room."

The dark-haired sister—Amber, she must be—seemed uncomfortable; obviously, she hadn't wanted to reveal who she was. Apparently the two other women weren't supposed to know she and Ilka had met. Leslie reached for the drawings.

"Thank you very much. That's very thoughtful of you."

Ilka gave them to her; then she fished the small clay figure out of her pocket. "And I found this." She held it so it sat in the palm of her hand. Leslie took it, too.

"We don't have any of your things here," she said. Then she walked back toward the front door.

Ilka was about to follow her, when Mary Ann quickly stuck out her hand and thanked her for stopping by.

Ilka stood for a moment and looked the three of them over. Her half sisters didn't resemble her, apart from being tall, though not as lanky as Ilka. In fact, Amber's figure had more than average female curves, which made her height less obvious. Ilka took a final glance at the younger sister; she looked a bit like a clumsy ox, she thought, rather ungenerously. Then, taking the hint, she started down the steps, but quickly turned around. "Would you like to get together for a cup of coffee one of these days?"

"Unfortunately we won't have time before you go home," Leslie said. Amber still hadn't said a word.

"Thank you for stopping by," Mary Ann repeated. "It was interesting to meet you."

Ilka started for the car again. She felt their eyes on her back, and she turned around again. "You're very welcome to stop by the funeral home," she said, staring directly at Amber. "There might be some of your father's things you'd like to have."

None of them reacted to her invitation, and she decided to give up, yet she took a few steps back toward them. "By the way, are there any plans for when my father's urn is to be interred?" This time she looked at Mary Ann, who simply shook her head and answered, "No."

Ilka nodded quickly and walked back to the car. For a moment, she stared out the windshield; then she pulled herself together and started the car.

Twilight seemed to have fallen during her short visit with her father's new family. Shadows had lengthened; the evening sunlight hung low over the treetops. Ilka turned on the windshield wipers when it began sprinkling. She drove slowly to the end of the street and was about to turn, when a gray squirrel darted over a low wooden fence. Over by the gate, a woman whacked a doormat against the fence; then she tossed it down by the front door, walked inside, and shut the door. Neighbors, people who had known her father, Ilka thought. It was hard for her to imagine the man she had known and missed all these years, living his life here. In a residential district, so dull that it reminded her of a stage set, and with a family as stiff as starch. So different from her own mother.

They hadn't given her one single opening. Not one sign of any interest in getting to know her. Obviously, they wanted nothing to do with her.

Ilka tried to put herself in their shoes. The sisters had just lost their father, a man who had been with them all their lives, and of course they were mourning him. She could see that. And maybe they hadn't known about her, either. But their total lack of interest in digging just a bit deeper into his past surprised her. And admittedly she had hoped his new family could help shed some light on what had happened back then. Why he had chosen to settle down in Racine. She had so many questions.

Ilka made a U-turn, and when she drove by their house again, the porch was empty and the front door shut. Maybe they preferred to look on his life as having begun with them.

"Have a great life, assholes," she said. She noticed her hands gripping the wheel, so hard that her knuckles hurt.

I was the first, she thought. As if that were a victory in and of itself, being the first child he had created. On the other hand, she was the one he had left. And the one he had cut off all contact with.

Ilka drove blindly now, noticing nothing. The monotone voice of the GPS guided her as she relived the loneliness and abandonment she'd felt for long periods of her childhood after he left.

She noticed a gas station up ahead, and on impulse she signaled to turn in. A moment later she was facing a freckled guy with wild red hair and a cap with the bill turned backward. Cash or credit card? "Cash," she said. "And a pack of Marlboro's."

She tossed the sack filled with bottles on the front seat, pulled out her phone, and checked the address.

25

Ilka parked her father's car and walked down to the house. At first, she thought Artie wasn't home. She walked up the stone sidewalk and called out several times, but no one answered. The lake was over to her right; she could sense it. A pleasing smell of freshwater and earth.

She laid the sack of beer and root beer down on a table carved out of a tree stump; then she went up and knocked on the front door. After waiting several moments, she knocked again and called out his name. Finally, she walked around to the side of the house facing the lake. It looked a lot nicer than what she had expected, with an outdoor kitchen against the wall, a large stove with a log still glowing. To top it off, he had the largest gas grill Ilka had ever seen. And the wooden sculptures, some abstract, others animals, meticulously carved so even the slightest details were visible. Impressive! She walked over and admired the works.

"Sorry." Artie appeared around the corner, out of breath. "Must have left my phone in the car. You been calling a long time?"

He wore a heavy sweater, and the tails of his Hawaiian shirt hung down in front. Judging from his rubber boots, he'd been down at the lake. He carried a rolled-up fishing net under his arm, with a bag over his shoulder. He threw everything on the ground beside the end of the house.

"Where are we going?" He walked over and unlocked his door. Then he noticed the beer Ilka had laid on the table. "What's going on? Are we celebrating something?"

She shook her head and explained that she'd just visited Mary Ann and her daughters.

"Say no more!" He lifted his palm up; then he fished a cigarette out of his shirt pocket underneath the sweater. "They weren't all that friendly, am I right?"

She nodded. That was one way to put it.

"I guess I've already explained they're not really interested in the business. Truth is, I don't think I ever saw the girls with their dad at work. Mary Ann was there a few times, but only to pick him up when they were going somewhere. That was before the accident, of course; she doesn't drive anymore. But the girls. I always got the feeling they were ashamed of what Paul did for a living. It wasn't dignified enough for them."

While he spoke, Ilka walked over to him, put her arms around him, and leaned down to kiss him. Her lips were nearly touching his before he stopped talking. He tasted of lake water and something sweet he'd eaten. Hard candy, she guessed.

He was startled. "Are you sure about this?" he murmured, but he allowed himself to be backed up and led into the house. With her hand on his chest, she tried to steer him around even though she'd never been inside his house. She backed him through the kitchen with big windows facing the lake, then through the living room. She sensed more than noticed the sofa and dining room table. The small TV on a box in the corner, low priority. Paintings on the wall, antlers. She felt his breath against her neck as her heart hammered away. And she felt the freedom to loosen the knot of anger that had built up since she'd left Mary Ann's big white house.

Artie managed to open the door at the end of the living room. "Are we sure this is a good idea?" he said, his words streaming directly into her mouth.

Ilka kissed him harder and began unbuckling his pants with one hand, her other hand still around his neck. That seemed to wake him up. He ripped his sweater off and helped her loosen his belt.

She sat down on the bed and pulled him down to her. Then she noticed he was still wearing his rubber boots. Her greedy hands got rid of the Hawaiian shirt in short order, and they both smiled when Artie stood up and took his pants and boots off. The bun of hair on top of his head was coming undone; it looked like something exploding. Ilka didn't bother taking off the white shirt she'd been wearing since the funeral service. Her father's shirt. Though that detail was the last thing on her mind at that moment. She stared as Artie pulled his boxers off and fell back onto the bed, muttering, "Jesus Christ!"

He spoke directly into her ear, asked if Danish girls usually took whatever they needed, whenever they felt like it.

She leaned over and pulled her jeans off as she assured him that it was completely normal, that there was nothing more to it than that.

He could have thrown her out. He could have invited her for a drink afterward. Or asked why the hell she hadn't at least called before showing up. But Artie Sorvino simply followed her out onto the front porch after they'd taken a quick shower and wrapped themselves up in thick blankets he pulled out of a reed basket in the hallway. Ilka handed him a can of beer and opened one of her root beers; he tossed a few cushions on the porch chairs and grabbed the lighter in the kitchen.

The sun had set; the darkness hid Lake Michigan. The only part of the lake that reached them was the roar of the waves rolling in over the rocky shore. And the smell.

She sensed him looking at her. Sensed that he was unsure what she expected from him. If it was affection she wanted.

Ilka pointed to a chair on the other side of the table, hoping it was enough to make him understand that this wasn't anything more than what they'd already done.

"What is it about that family?" she asked, after they sat down. "It's like they don't want to have anything to do with my father. Has it always been like that?"

She pulled the blanket tighter around her, though she enjoyed being outside this late.

Artie lit a cigarette and pushed the pack over to her, but she let it lie. He shook his head. "That's not how I see them, but you're right that Paul kept his private life and the business separate. Very separate. It wasn't something I thought about so much. That's just how it was."

He hesitated a moment. "A lot of people have problems with this business. Several very nice female acquaintances jumped ship on me when I told them what I did for a living. It's almost like people think that death disappears if you ignore it. Or that you can keep it at a distance by not talking about it."

"But the business must have been a big part of his life."

He nodded. "I think they had an agreement. He wouldn't bring the dead home into his private life. And he kept his private life away from the dead. That's how I always saw it. And it probably wasn't a bad way to do it. A business like ours can dominate your life."

Ilka set her bottle down and pulled her legs up.

"You might not want to hear this, but your dad was very caring toward Mary Ann and the girls. I thought he overprotected them, but I never told him that. If anyone so much as mentioned something like that, he'd turn around and walk off."

She stared into the flame of the small square electric candle in the lantern. It flickered mechanically, as if an invisible wind blew inside the glass and shook the wick. She didn't want to hear any more. It might have been naïve of her to expect them to greet her with open arms. If they'd felt that way, they would already have visited her. She thought about Amber, who clearly hadn't told the others she had sat for hours on the bench in front of her father's business. Maybe she had hoped Ilka would invite her in or take her up to her father's room, which still held so much of him.

Artie interrupted her thoughts. "That name of yours—is that a usual name in Denmark?" He opened another beer.

Ilka shook her head. "I'd be surprised if there is one other person so unlucky. My father named me for the horse that won the Derby in 1947. Ilka Nichols only won once. It was the year my grandfather took my father to the track for the first time. He talked my mother into giving me this idiotic name because he said it was the symbol of a winner and... how do you say, someone not like other people. Someone who fought and did okay against the odds. But the name has been more like a curse, when I think about what the racetrack meant for my father's life."

She had the feeling Artie was about to protest but then changed his mind. They sat for a while in silence.

"He couldn't have been more wrong." Ilka spoke quietly as she pulled the blanket around her legs. "I've never really fought for anything. I can't remember ever deciding to point myself in one direction. My life has been all these coincidences. My high school grades were good enough to get me whatever education I wanted. I took a year off after high school, and then I started law school, but after six months I found out I had cancer; they took out my womb and ovaries. The tumor was ... bad; I didn't have a choice.

"I was sick for a long time; then when they finally said I was okay I celebrated by putting on my backpack and traveling. First stop Argentina. I worked with cattle; then I went to Australia. I was gone for a year and a half, and when I got home my mother had moved in with another woman. That surprised me, but it was good for her. Then I met Erik, so instead of going back to law school I started working for him. As a school photographer, can you believe that!"

Ilka took a drink of root beer. She'd been aware for a while that she was running off at the mouth, but she didn't care. She needed to talk, and he was a good listener. He opened another beer.

"Maybe it's true that everyone has a soul mate. Erik was mine. After losing my father, it felt like I finally came home. He was fifteen years older than me, and I thought we'd be together forever. I took over his business when he died. I never took any photography courses, but he taught me what I needed to know. And I'm happy."

She folded her hands. That last sentence sounded forced to her, but she meant it. She would never have chosen to be a school photographer, but now there wasn't anything else she would rather do.

"And now it's happened again," Artie said. "Now circumstances have made you a funeral home director."

Again, Ilka felt his eyes on her. She shook her head, though she wasn't sure he could see. "No. I could have chosen to stay home; I could have let my lawyer handle everything. I told my mother I had to be here personally, though it wasn't true. I'd needed to meet my father. Even though he wasn't around anymore, this was my last chance to get closer to him. Missing him has been way too big a part of my life. Maybe I didn't even know how much. And really, it's not that he wasn't around when I grew up; it's more that I never understood why he left."

Artie wouldn't let it go. "But now you *are* a director."

"Like hell I am. I'm just a daughter trying to sell her father's business so his reputation won't be damaged too much." She snorted. "All right, that's not exactly true. It's probably more that I'm trying to pick up the pieces of a life I never really understood."

Her phone rang several times before Artie suggested she answer.

"Aren't you asleep?" Ilka said when she heard her mother's voice. "Is something wrong?"

"What's going on over there? I have a bad feeling about this. I can't sleep. I'm worried."

"That's so nice of you, Mom." Instead of being annoyed, she suddenly felt warm inside. Her mother had been through a hell of a lot, too, when it came to Paul Jensen. "Everything's fine. I just need to take care of the last details before I can come home. And I would be very grateful if you'll do the jobs for me. Of course I'll pay you."

"Come on! Money doesn't matter; you know that, dear. I just don't like you being over there. I can feel it in my bones, all this worry, and I don't like it."

"Mom, really, there's nothing wrong. Everything's just taking longer than I expected. That happens a lot with estates." Ilka didn't mention that she was the one who'd messed up a transfer agreement at the last moment. "I have to know what's going on with the business before I can put it up for sale. By the way, I met my half sisters today," she added, hoping the abrupt change of subject would distract her mother. "It doesn't look like we're going to be great friends, but both Leslie and Amber have inherited Dad's height, and the youngest one has the same stringy Jensen hair. But honestly, it doesn't look all that good on her." As if it looked good on anyone! Ilka laughed to lighten the mood.

"Were they nice to you? What did they say?"

"Mom, I have to run—there's someone at the door. I'll call you tomorrow." She hung up, hoping her mother didn't hear her voice starting to thicken. She closed her eyes and sat for a moment, tried to swallow the lump in her throat.

"Are you okay?" Artie asked as she stuffed her phone back into her pocket.

"I'd better get back. Are you coming in tomorrow? McKenna's daughter is coming to view her father."

Ilka didn't know what Sundays were like in the funeral home business. Many people were protective of their days off, but she had the feeling Artie wasn't that way.

"See you tomorrow," he said, sitting expectantly as she stood up and grabbed her sweater off the chair. He had another think coming if he thought she was going to kiss him! She nodded shortly before walking to the car.

The drive home was strange. She felt loose after sleeping with Artie, sad after talking to her mother, and tense after meeting her father's new family. But most of all unsure of how things would turn out.

She drove into the parking lot and noticed a light in one of Sister Eileen's windows, while the rest of the funeral home was dark. She parked and got out. Stood for a moment, enjoying the mild late summer evening, though she still felt bad about being so short with her mother.

Why the hell did you even come here? she thought, scolding herself as she walked up the steps. She decided to spend Sunday going through the last drawers and boxes in her father's room. She would send the whole mess to Denmark by FedEx, so her mother could see what he had left behind.

On the way up, the thought struck Ilka that it might help her mother stifle some of her anger if she knew what had happened back then. Even though she had found Hanne and had gotten on with her life, it was obvious to everyone that being abandoned still plagued her.

She walked in, threw her bag on the floor, and turned the desk lamp on. Suddenly she heard breathing and something moving on the bed, and she whirled around.

Amber sat cross-legged on the bed; she hadn't even bothered to take her boots off. She leaned lazily up against the wall. Nothing about her hinted at how long she'd been waiting for Ilka to come back.

"Hi," Ilka said. She held on to the back of her father's chair, which she had grabbed in shock a moment before. Now she tried to act nonchalant, though her heart was in her throat.

"Don't come by the house again," her half sister said. Slowly she leaned forward and slid her legs off the side of the bed. "It's not good for Mom. It's not good for anything."

"How did you get in?" Ilka tried to calm her heartbeat; her temples were pounding like shutters in a hurricane.

"Dad gave me a key several years ago."

Ilka heard the provocation in her voice; she wanted to show she could come and go as she pleased. Apparently without Artie and Sister Eileen noticing. But why had she sat out on the bench when she could come inside?

Ilka walked over to the bed. She was so frightened, so

angry, that she had to fold her arms to keep from hitting her youngest half sister. "What is it I've done to all of you? If it's about this"—she held her arms out—"you can have it; I didn't ask for it, this business. Really, I'd rather go back to Denmark. You're more than welcome to take over, right now. In fact, I think it's totally unfair that I'm the one who has to put things right, to get out of this horrible situation our father put his employees in. And none of you even come by and offer to help. What's wrong with all of you? Don't you know how much money this place owes? What kind of daughters are you?"

Amber was standing now, and for a moment they stood face-to-face. But she shrugged. "I'm sorry it has to be this way."

Ilka listened to her footsteps fade down the stairs; then she threw herself on the bed.

What was it with these people? It was one thing if they didn't care for her, didn't accept their father having had a family before them. That she could handle. But not caring about what had been his daily life—that simply wasn't normal. It was almost as if they were afraid of something.

26

"Wake up! You've got to come downstairs," Artie said as he banged on the door.

Ilka lay still for a moment with her eyes closed. Fragments of his face close-up, the sense of freedom she had felt after their quickie, kept his voice and the sunlight through the curtains at a distance. She thought about Amber, about her father, everything she didn't know about him. She had sat up half the night, going through the storage boxes piled up against the wall. Racetrack results and old programs, with notes written in ornate script in the margins. Winning tickets and receipts from losses that had been added to expenses. There were lots of those.

She had found several pictures in the bottom of one of the boxes. Photos of her father with his parents, her grandparents. She had seen them only sporadically after he left, and finally not at all. Both had died before she was twenty. In several of the old photos, her father was with boys Ilka didn't recognize. Cousins, maybe? One box held old clippings from newspapers, again mostly having to do with racing. Which driver had switched stables. Who had new sponsors; trainers moving around. Some of them in a plastic folder were about a Danish trotter manager brought in to

Maywood Park racetrack, Melrose Park, Illinois, in 1982. In the article, the manager was proclaimed to be one of Scandinavia's most promising, with extensive experience and several Derby victories by drivers he represented under his belt. Ilka wondered about that. Her father had certainly not understated his accomplishments.

Her father. She had recognized him immediately from the grainy photo. Farther down in the article, she read that Paul Jensen was co-owner of the all-star team, that he had chipped in three hundred thousand dollars, the same as the other investors, but he was the only one involved in managing the stable. He looked exactly the way she remembered him: tall, with a tweed cap pulled down over his forehead. He smiled for the camera. A man of the world.

So. Her father had gotten a job over here. But three hundred thousand dollars! She couldn't imagine where he'd gotten hold of that kind of money, with the funeral home in the red when he left Denmark. He did have his winnings, but they didn't even come close to that amount. Her stomach sank.

Artie knocked again. "Shelby's here. It sounds like all hell is about to break loose. You've got to come down and talk to her."

Ilka reached for her watch; it was almost eleven. Quickly she swung her legs over the edge of the bed. "What's breaking loose?" She wrapped her father's striped robe around her and stumbled over to open the door.

"It's best to let her tell about it," he said, his voice serious. "She's just come from the police station."

Not a word about what had happened yesterday. Nothing in his expression, either. That was fine with her. "Give me two minutes."

She shut the door and pulled her clothes on. Before

rushing down, she hurriedly gathered up the clippings spread out over the floor and tossed them back in the box. She was getting used to people invading the room whenever they felt like it, but she didn't want anyone to see she'd been delving into her father's life.

Coffee! The smell hit her as she stepped into the arrangement room, and her stomach cramped from hunger. Shelby stood at the window, her back to the door, gazing out at the parking lot. She looked so tense that Ilka hesitated a moment before walking over and putting her arm around the woman's shoulder. "What's the matter?"

She turned to Ilka. She'd been sobbing, and her face was pale, on the edge of collapse. "It was Phyllis Oldham who paid my son," she whispered. "She gave him twenty thousand dollars to leave town, even though she knew he didn't kill Ashley Simpson."

The words came out of her mouth, but it was as if someone else were speaking them. Her expression was frozen.

Ilka held her close before leading her carefully over to an easy chair and pouring her a cup of coffee.

"The police came this morning and asked me to follow them to the station. They felt I had the right to know after everything we went through back then. The young officer asked if I had someone who could take me down there, but I don't. I thought about you and Artie, but it's Sunday, and I didn't want to bother you."

"You can call us, anytime," Ilka said. "But what happened?"

She sat as stiff as a board, her eyes unfocused as she spoke. "Last night Phyllis Oldham came to the police station after most of the policemen had gone home. She admitted she'd pressured Mike to take the blame, but he wouldn't do it. So instead she offered him money to leave town, to make it look like he did. I knew it wasn't him."

Her hands were clenched. "There wasn't any evidence, either. She's a witch, and this is only happening because both her sons have been arrested. If it hadn't been for them, she'd never have confessed."

Ilka poured herself a cup of coffee and grabbed a few small cookies from the bowl before leaning back in her chair. She was determined to let Shelby talk, even though she couldn't make sense of the woman's story.

"It's terrible you can get away with something like that, just because you have money," she wailed, her voice firmer now that she was worked up. "They destroyed my son's life. Our lives. And then when he comes home after so many years because his sister is dying, they kill him!"

Her pale cheeks reddened; tears streaked from her eyes.

Ilka reached across the table and held her arm, her fingers gently stroking the sleeve of her green blouse, buttoned at the wrist. "Who was Mike supposed to take the blame for?" she asked, her voice low. "Why did Phyllis Oldham try to make it look like it was your son?"

After a moment, Shelby looked up. "Because her husband killed Ashley." Her voice was so cold that Ilka pulled her hand back. "Phyllis told the police she saw him walking down from the fisherman's cabin when Ashley was killed."

Ilka pushed the box of Kleenex over to her and waited as she pulled a few out. She blew her nose and dried her eyes; then she cleared her throat. "Phyllis told the police it was a coincidence she saw him on the path from the cabin. She'd wondered about it; it's not a place he normally went to. Later, when she heard about Ashley, she put two and two together. But she didn't say anything."

"And now finally she tells this to the police?"

Shelby nodded and pursed her lips but quickly got hold

of herself again. "She's only doing it because she hopes to get her sons out of jail. By sacrificing her dead husband."

"And what do the police say about this coming out now?"

"Phyllis says she kept quiet because of her children, the funeral home business, and the family reputation. She made her choice, to be the silent wife. She did nothing. Except she likely drove him to his death, little by little."

"What do you mean?"

"Douglas Oldham hung himself in the embalming room." She paused for a moment to let her rage and despair die down. "The oldest son found him. I think the whole town knew he'd taken the easy way out. The story was that he suddenly felt sick and lost consciousness because of the dangerous chemicals. But everybody talked about a rope. It was rough on the sons."

"What about the daughter?" Ilka asked.

"Carlotta has always been a mama's girl, but of course it affected her too. After his death, it seemed like the boys sort of dropped out, and it wasn't long before they left to go to school. They didn't come back until they were grown and ready to enter the business."

"So all these years your son was gone, Phyllis Oldham knew her husband killed the young girl?"

"Yes." Shelby stared at the dark mahogany table and nodded, as if she was slowly becoming aware of the extent of the tragedy.

"Do the police say the Oldham sons are responsible for killing Mike?"

After a few moments, the woman shook her head. "But they don't need to. Isn't it obvious?"

Maybe, Ilka thought. *If they thought he had come back to expose the family . . .*

Her hunger was gone, replaced by an emptiness inside her. She thought about all the years the secret had hung around Racine like a dark cloud, casting its cold shadow, particularly on Mike's mother and sister.

Shelby stood up. A handful of balled-up Kleenex lay on the chair. While buttoning her coat, she turned to Ilka. "Phyllis claims she didn't know anything about Howard falling in love with the girl. Just like she didn't know her brother-in-law broke into your garage and desecrated my son's body."

She looked away. "What kind of people are they?"

She shook her head and left the room.

So. A young girl had turned the heads of two grown men. *Nothing new there*, Ilka thought.

Sister Eileen appeared in the doorway. "She'll be here in twenty minutes," she announced, adding that Ilka might want to change into something more respectable before Ed McKenna's daughter showed up to view her father.

The nun was right. She didn't look like someone who should be meeting a grieving daughter. But first, she needed some clarity about finding her father's clothes in the Dumpster. The whole thing was confusing, and Ilka just couldn't let it go.

"I keep meaning to ask you," Ilka started, turning to Sister Eileen. "Why were my father's things thrown into the Dumpster?"

A look of sheer surprise crossed over the nun's face as she stared, with seeming bewilderment, into Ilka's eyes. "What are you talking about?"

"I know; it was so strange. I saw them in there and couldn't figure out why you would have thrown them away."

"I most certainly didn't," Sister Eileen said assertively.

"You must be mistaken. I would never have done that. Never. Oh my goodness, no."

It was all so odd, but Ilka didn't want to cause any more upset or spark an argument. Apologizing for the mistake, she excused herself to change into something more appropriate, and headed upstairs.

Up in the room, still shaking her head, Ilka grabbed her father's black suit. Her uniform, she thought. Once again she felt homesick for her own bathroom and bathtub, her clothes, which might not have been the most fashionable, but at least they hadn't been bought for a man in his seventies.

27

Please, have a seat." At the doorway, Ilka gestured discreetly toward the oval table in the arrangement room. Lisa McKenna entered without a word, leaving in her wake a strong scent of lavender, which Ilka followed.

"This won't take long," Lisa said, her voice deep, almost masculine. That surprised Ilka; Ed McKenna's daughter was light in complexion and thin, her hair set up loosely in a very feminine look. "We haven't really seen much of each other the past several years."

"Of course," Ilka replied quickly. She wished Artie was there, but she knew he was busy reconstructing Mike Gilbert's face. He had told her what to focus on: coffee, kringle, and Kleenex. Sister Eileen would bring everything in, he'd said. And then just talk to her, or rather, let her talk. Anything she wanted to talk about. "And call me if she wants to know what it takes to prepare her father for transportation by air."

Ilka had asked if they should also show the dog. "Only if she asks," he'd said.

Ed McKenna was prepared for viewing, and he lay in the front part of the chapel, which had been curtained off so the room didn't seem so big. The two large altar candles, one on each side of the coffin, were lit. For a moment, Ilka considered mentioning that the dog had licked her father's cheek off before lying down to die beside him, but Artie had done a fantastic job of reconstruction, and she probably wouldn't even notice that part of his face was wax now. There wasn't any reason to let her in on this macabre detail.

"Coffee?" Ilka kept her voice down, thinking it would help the woman feel at home, cared for.

"No, thanks, but I'd like to use your bathroom before we go in."

The woman's voice surprised her again. "Of course. This way." She pointed and led her out into the front hall.

The daughter's hair was graying, and a fine net of wrinkles softened her face. In her fifties, Ilka guessed.

"I couldn't stand him," Lisa McKenna said when she returned from the bathroom. "If it was up to me, you could pour his ashes in a can and take it to the dump."

Ilka froze; so much for her plan of action. It looked like they wouldn't be needing the Kleenex.

"He was an egotistical, self-centered asshole. But for some strange reason my children want him to be brought home and buried in our cemetery."

Sister Eileen stood in the doorway. She must have heard what the daughter had just said, and Ilka was sure she spotted a glint in the nun's eye after the outburst that left the room silent. The daughter's anger was deep, savage; her attractive face had morphed into a grimace as she spat the words out.

Ilka had no idea what to say, but fortunately Artie stepped into the room and saved her. He wore a black coat with a white shirt attached over his Hawaiian shirt, though part of the turquoise collar stuck out at his neck.

Still unable to speak, Ilka walked over to the section of

the chapel being used as a reposing room and opened the door. "If you want to see him, it's this way."

The daughter glanced at her and, seemingly in spite of herself, walked over to the coffin.

"If you need to be alone, you can just come out whenever you're ready. Then we can take care of the practical details about transporting him."

Ilka was about to close the door, but the daughter said, "No, that's fine. I'll come with you now." She turned on her heel and followed Ilka out of the room. "What happened to Toodie?"

"The dog?"

The daughter nodded.

"It's being kept cold," Ilka said. "We didn't want to do anything before you arrived."

"May I see her?" The anger on her face was gone.

Artie stepped forward and said of course. If she could wait just a minute, he would bring the dog in.

"My father didn't care about us. About me or the kids. He was never there when we needed him. The past twenty years, we've only seen him the few times I came from Albany to beg for help. I've been alone with the kids since they were small, since their father... well. And Mom died before the kids were born."

She looked as if she'd made up her mind not to cry. "I gave him Toodie, and he loved her. I thought the company might mellow him out. Thought maybe we could have a connection that way. But he just didn't want anything to do with us. Maybe you think he was lonesome, but I can assure you, he chose to be lonesome. Nobody should feel sorry for him."

Artie came in one of the side doors, pushing a small cart in front of him. He looked like a hotel worker delivering room service. A white sheet covered a mound on the cart.

"Just a second." Lisa McKenna took a moment to gather herself. She looked like Ilka had expected she would when she went in to view her father. "Okay, I'm ready."

Artie lifted the sheet, and he and Ilka stepped back. Ilka looked questioningly at him.

"You poor little thing, were you all alone?" She spoke to the dog as if it still were alive. "Did she die of starvation?"

Ilka wasn't expecting that question. She looked at Artie, who was rocking on his heels. "I'm afraid so, yes," she said.

While the daughter continued talking to Toodie, Ilka couldn't help glancing at the coffin where Ed McKenna lay; he should be the one she was grieving over.

"I don't know what it would cost to have the dog embalmed," she said, after they returned to the arrangement room and coffee. "But my father had plenty of money, so I'm bringing her home and burying her in the yard."

After saying good-bye, Ilka stood in the reception area and watched her leave. In a way, she could relate. The difference was that Lisa McKenna had known where her father was. But the rejection must have felt the same.

28

The next morning, coffee, a soft-boiled egg, slices of bread, and a newspaper were lined up on the table in front of Ilka. A large photo of a young Mike Gilbert was plastered on the front page of the paper. The photo bore no resemblance to the ruined face Artie had spent all Sunday afternoon and evening on, shaping it to match the photo his mother had brought. By the time Ilka said good night and went up to her room, the face had been transformed from a bloody mass of broken bones and swelling into a sleeping man with slightly too prominent eyebrows and lips painted on, but it was still far from the big, smiling, happy teenager on the front page.

Ilka guessed it was a school photo. She would have arranged it similarly, but unlike the smiles of many of the students she had photographed over the years, Mike's smile reached all the way up into his eyes. It wasn't just a reaction to the photographer saying, "Smi-i-ile!"

The photo had probably been used often following Ashley's death. In the accompanying article, all the details of Mike's death were described, at least as well as the journalist could with the few facts that were known. Nobody had been found who had seen Mike Gilbert back in town;

that was clear. No one had any idea how long he'd been hanging around before being murdered. Judging from the reactions of the people on the street interviewed by the journalist, most were surprised that Mike would dare show his face in town again. The owner of the tobacco shop even believed that Mike Gilbert had tempted fate by returning to Racine. The short statements were accompanied by small head shots to prove the journalist had done some leg work before writing the article.

The long and short of it was that apparently no one saw him before he was killed. Which was why no one knew when he'd returned. The only new information in the article came from a former pathologist, who colorfully described how little it took to crush a skull, with the right weapon.

His guess was that Mike had been murdered with a baseball bat. "Incredible," Ilka muttered to herself. Then she skimmed a description of Ashley Simpson's death. The journalist had found an old school friend and asked her what she remembered from back then. The woman, who obviously hadn't been taking good care of herself, was photographed behind the warehouses where Mike's body had been found. She stood with folded arms and stared grumpily into the camera. In the article, she claimed Mike Gilbert had been cursed.

"Everyone around him dies," she was quoted as saying. Ashley, himself, and now his sister was dying, too.

"Idiot!" In her irritation, Ilka spilled coffee on the newspaper. Beside the article was a small box containing a short statement from the police. Two people detained for questioning that weekend had been released.

Poor Shelby, Ilka thought, sad and tired now as she glanced over the local announcements and sports section.

Soft rain fell from the gray Monday morning sky,

streaking the window and blocking the sunlight. But Ilka enjoyed the peace and quiet. For the first time since she'd been in Racine, her morning hadn't been disrupted, no one banging on her door to rouse her out of bed; that alone was enough to loosen her shoulders up, relieve her tension. She'd planned on spending the day going through her father's business papers. Yesterday she had found a cabinet filled with files, but it had seemed far too much to tackle. She'd also called her mother and explained why she had to stay in Racine. Everything was up in the air—finances, creditors. No one knew much about the orders that had come in. Or how many prepaid funerals the funeral home had. She'd realized these things made up the business's actual worth.

"I've got to take care of this. You know yourself how much work it takes to turn around a funeral home in debt."

The moment she said it, she knew how rotten it sounded to bring her mother's struggles into this. But at least it would help her mother understand why everything was taking so long. Ilka had begged her to take care of the photo shoots until she could find a solution. She still hoped Niels from North Sealand Photography could take the jobs. If he'd ever answer her.

Her confrontations with the suppliers who had bailed out on Jensen Funeral Home had pissed her off. It was okay for people to drop a customer when they got tired of unpaid bills. But she wasn't going to stand for suppliers not giving her a chance to right the ship. And she wouldn't accept that the problems could have been avoided if Sister Eileen had made the calls. They were damn well going to do business with her! She stood up to answer the phone out in the reception area.

"We've booked a business meeting today at twelve

thirty," said a man whose name Ilka didn't catch. "Two con-sultants will be there, and the meeting will last one hour, so please bring along the books for the last two years."

She set her coffee down. The carefree morning mood had evaporated the second she heard his brusque voice. At first, she wasn't sure that Artie had been able to hold the IRS off.

"Excuse me, who are you again?"

"We spoke last week. We informed you of our interest in taking over Jensen Funeral Home. And now I understand there are no longer any other transfer agreements standing in the way. We're prepared to reach an agreement quickly to take control of your family's business."

Ilka had pulled Sister Eileen's chair out and was sitting on its arm. She remembered the call, but back then the voice had been ingratiating and as smooth as melted chocolate. Now he sounded ice-cold and arrogant. "There is no 'your family.' It's 'my' business, and I've decided to run it my-self, so I'm not interested in your proposal. Jensen Funeral Home is not for sale. Thank you anyway."

She was shaken when she hung up. Not so much be-cause the call had sounded more like a demand than a polite business inquiry, but because something in the man's tone made her skin crawl.

Sitting briefly in thought, she shook her head. If she'd had any doubts about the wisdom of taking up the challenge and righting the ship, they were gone now. The decision had been made.

Something else stirred underneath her anger about the call. Sitting there at Sister Eileen's desk, she realized she'd just made the first clear decision of her career. It may have been spur of the moment; it was definitely a rash decision. And it was stubbornness, not ambition, that had motivated her to become a funeral home director. But she didn't give a damn, because she was going to show them.

The phone on the nun's desk rang again. Ilka stood up to return to her breakfast; if it was that man again, he would have to wait until the sister was back. But then she changed her mind and picked up. "This funeral home is not for sale, and it will not in the future be for sale either. And any business meeting has to be approved by me."

"Excuse me," a woman said warily. "Is this Ilka Jensen? I was referred to this number when I called her cell phone."

"Yes, this is Ilka."

The woman began speaking in Danish. "I'm calling from Linde School in Virum. We're very dissatisfied with the photographer you sent. It's disgraceful that the photographs are taking so long."

Ilka was startled. She'd never worked for that school before, and she had the feeling the school secretary was just warming up.

"The woman you sent only managed to get through two classes today. I've never seen anything like it. You can't expect students to have the patience to be steered around so much. This isn't about details and shadows; you should know that. We're talking about school photos here. And they missed far too many classes!"

Ilka tried to get a word in, but the woman ignored her. "This is about giving students a memory of their time in school, of their schoolmates throughout the years. We're not paying for all the extra time being used. Choosing you was obviously a mistake. And it's going to be difficult to give you a good review on Trustpilot."

Ilka finally broke in. "Yes, I would say it was a mistake

that I sent our prize-winning portrait photographer out to you. But I've heard that for years, parents with children attending your school have been complaining that the individual photos were taken like the students were on an assembly line. If your school administration doesn't appreciate higher-quality work, you shouldn't be using us. You should go back to the standard you're used to. I'm afraid we can't offer that." She could almost hear Erik cackling up on his cloud. "I think we should stop here. We don't serve clients who prefer discount work."

"But, you're not . . . you're not finished."

"No. It seems you weren't well enough prepared. I suggest you contact another school photographer. I will send out photo orders only to those students we photographed. Have a good day." She hung up.

Okay. One less client to hand over to North Sealand Photography. Her mother of course would want to take good pictures of every single child. She should have realized that. She could see it now: her conscientious mother using far too much time in placing the students properly, getting the light just right, adjusting the height of the chair so everything would be perfect.

She smiled. What a mess.

29

"Shall I order the zinc coffin for Ed McKenna, or will you?" Sister Eileen asked. She looked disapprovingly at Ilka, who was sitting in her chair.

The white band of her wimple sat tight around her forehead, hiding the short dark hair Ilka had noticed the night she roused the nun out of bed to help with Mike. She stood erect, with a closed, dismissive look of professionalism— *Get out*, it seemed to be saying to Ilka.

"We also need to make reservations on the plane for the coffin. The dog will need its own zinc coffin. It will be embalmed this morning. I can imagine it would fit in a child's coffin."

Ilka nodded. If this was how it was going to be between the two of them, then okay. She'd given up on trying to follow the shifts between the warmhearted sister who brought tea and cookies and the person in front of her now, the one trying to freeze Ilka out. But if Sister Eileen wasn't going to cooperate and accept she had a new boss, she'd have to go. Ilka didn't have the same devotion to nuns as her father.

"What about putting the dog into the coffin along with him? That way we'd save one coffin."

Stone-faced, the sister said, "You'll have to talk to Artie about that." She laid a pile of envelopes on the desk. "Bills."

Ilka looked them over; she should start handling the mail, if she was ever going to have a clear understanding of their situation.

Artie stepped into the reception area. "Let Sister Eileen order the zinc coffin so we don't risk having him stranded here."

Ilka had the feeling he'd been standing out in the hall, eavesdropping on them. And that the sister knew he was listening.

His long hair was now gathered in a bun on his neck, and the gaudy red shirt with the palms and surfers hung outside his pants. He walked over and set his glass of Red Bull and coffee on the desk; suddenly Ilka felt trapped between the two people who knew the daily routines of the funeral home and her own ignorance. Again, she sensed they had a secret agenda, while pretending to be going down with the ship.

She went into the arrangement room, where her breakfast lay untouched. Her coffee was cold. Artie appeared in the doorway after she sat down.

"What about the dog?" she asked. Without looking at him, she started in on her egg. "Can't we put it in his coffin?"

"Ed McKenna wasn't very tall; let's see if there's room for it at the foot end." He asked if she'd like fresh coffee, but he'd already picked up her cup and walked out to fill it. When he returned, he set a bag from the bakery in front of her.

Ilka surrendered and pushed her cold egg aside. She stuck her hand down in the sugary, oily brown paper, brought out a warm glazed doughnut, and laid it on her plate as she told him about the call from the funeral home chain.

"Damn!" Artie said. "Guess they didn't get the message. I thought I'd made myself clear yesterday."

"Yesterday?"

"Yeah, they called me and wanted to set up a meeting. I told them we weren't interested."

"And then they call again after that? Why didn't you say something? So I could have been ready for them."

"I didn't think they'd be so stubborn. American Funeral Group is always on the lookout for acquisitions. What did you tell them?"

"They definitely heard about the deal with Golden Slumbers failing, but I told them Jensen Funeral Home wasn't for sale, so there was no reason for a meeting. I think we three should sit down sometime today so I can tell you about my plans for the funeral home. When is a good time for you?"

Artie had been leaning up against the doorframe, his coffee in one hand and a doughnut in the other. Now he laid everything down and fished out a cigarette, which he lit on the way out the back door. "I'm going to start embalming Mike Gilbert now," he said over his shoulder. "Then I'm driving Mrs. Norton to the crematorium. But I'll have time when I get back."

Clearly he wasn't happy about it being *her* plans, not *their* plans. She walked back into the reception area and asked Sister Eileen if they could all meet that afternoon.

The sister nodded, friendly now, as if the little episode they'd just gone through had never happened. "I have an errand to do in town around noon. I should be back around two."

Ilka thanked her, but before she could leave, the nun added, "Would you please consider how much we can give to the fall church bazaar next month? Your father was known to be very generous with donations."

Ilka squelched her anger and studied Sister Eileen for a moment, wondering if she even realized that the business was almost completely underwater, gasping for air, that she should count herself lucky if she ended up keeping her job and room. Then Ilka reminded herself that even factoring in the generous donations, the sister probably was the least drain on the budget, given that she wasn't paid for her work. And besides, tongues in the community would start wagging if they were less generous to the church. Not a good signal to send if they wanted to give the impression that the business was stable and under control.

"We'll give the same as last year," Ilka decided, even though there wasn't much left in her private accounts. She asked how the sister wanted the money to be donated.

"Cash would be best. Two thousand dollars. It will be greatly appreciated. Shall I order the zinc coffin?"

Ilka was sitting at her father's desk with the mail when Artie knocked on the doorframe. "You want to come by for a beer tonight?"

Beer was the last thing he was interested in; she could hear that. She shook her head as she sorted out the advertisements and threw them in the wastebasket. He stared at her for a moment, then nodded and walked out.

It didn't take her long to go through the letters. She opened a yellow envelope from the local racetrack and pulled out a bill. It was time to renew her father's weekly racetrack ticket. Occasionally back home she bought a ticket herself; once she had even had a subscription. She could handle that if she stayed away from the racetrack and the smell of horses, the excitement as they neared the finish line. Ilka was about to wad the renewal up, but instead she stuck it in her pocket. She was almost finished going through the bills when Artie showed up in the doorway again. "You have a visitor," he said, his voice muffled by his mask. He was wearing his white coat, and he smelled of formaldehyde.

"If it's that man who wants to hold the business meeting, tell him no, he'll just have to leave."

"It's not him. It's some guy who wants to talk to you. You want me to send him in?"

She eyed him for a moment, unused to him playing the secretary and unsure who wanted to see her. But she nodded, and a moment later the guy from the bar appeared at the door. She ignored Artie's look. "Thanks," she said, and she gestured for him to leave.

"Hi," Larry said, a bit hesitantly. He glanced over his shoulder when Artie left. "You have a moment?"

"Not really," Ilka said, quickly covering up how flustered she was by his suddenly stopping by. Before she could find a way to get rid of him, he was standing by the desk.

"I was just thinking that maybe you'd like to go out to eat some evening? Or for a drink?"

Ilka was standing behind her chair now, as if that would stop Larry from reaching her. The rain had plastered his dark hair to his skull, and his blue Windbreaker clung to his chest, but there was a sparkle in his eye, something she couldn't totally resist. She had to stop herself. Immediately. That was the whole idea with casual relationships.

"I'm sorry." She started for the door to follow him out. "I'm just way too busy."

She could hear how lame that sounded, and she was being mean, too. But damn it, it was a one-night stand, with no obligations, nothing that committed her to having seconds.

He followed her reluctantly. "Can I call you?"

She shook her head. Out in the hallway she noticed Artie ducking back into the preparation room. Presumably he had been at the door, listening.

"How did you find me?" she asked as she opened the door to the parking lot.

"People are talking about you." She was relieved he didn't say anything about her rejection. "There aren't that many supertall foreign Viking women in town right now. And not so many of them who came to take over a funeral home."

She smiled at him. So, people in town knew who she was and what she was doing here.

The door to the preparation room was closed, and Ilka assumed Artie was at work inside. Out in the foyer, Sister Eileen was stuffing brochures in the holders beside the glass case displaying charms. The brochures contained information about the funeral home's services and gave the dates for the next senior citizen fair, where Jensen Funeral Home would be explaining about their offers and the advantages of making payments on a preordered funeral. Ilka would have to learn about all this, too, if she was going to try to lure more customers in.

Though she'd never done anything remotely like selling funeral home services, she already knew she was going to hate it. That and going around holding home parties, like Golden Slumbers did. The question was if she could afford not doing these things; the only way to turn the business around was to increase revenues.

Her mother and Hanne would be perfect for something like this. They would come off as trustworthy, and they were both good at talking to people. And her mother would throw herself into it body and soul, like when she started her online yarn business and the knitting courses she taught.

Unsure of what to do now, Ilka felt a bit useless. Artie was working, and the nun was taking care of her duties; she felt she should be the motivating force, the engine in her father's business, but the others had the fuel to make everything run. They knew the routines; they had the experience—they should be the ones trying to get the business back on track so it could be sold. So Artic could take over the house and start his own business.

Determined now, she walked over and knocked on the preparation room door. She had to knock again a few times before he unlocked it.

"Is there anything I can do to help?" She walked inside and looked around for a white coat. "It would be good for me to know how this is done, and I promise I won't get in the way—"

She looked down at the steel table. The exhaust fan hood loomed over Mike's body, which was covered by a white sheet from the waist down. It was so very different from seeing the bodies they had picked up. There was something clinically dead about this, yet it seemed almost intimate, vulnerable.

"Are you okay?" Artie joined her. She stood motionless, her eyes stuck on the exposed upper body like thin skin to a frozen iron pipe.

She knew bodies were pumped full of formaldehyde during the embalming; Artie had explained that. But she hadn't imagined a person could seem so lifeless.

He'd made an incision on each side of the throat. On one side the embalming fluid entered through a tube, while on the other side the body fluids drained out. A pump whirred, and at short intervals it emitted air. It sounded like sighing.

In her head, she heard Erik's calm voice, and she tried to imagine him explaining how to photograph the body in bright light: Use a filter and change the aperture. But she was still unable to move. She struggled to find a suitable expression, one that would look professional.

Artie was back at the table, but occasionally he glanced over his shoulder, as if making sure she was still standing.

"During the embalming, you remove the eyes," he explained, after she'd gotten a grip on herself and put on the white coat he'd handed her. She fumbled to put on the mask. "Eyes are too fragile to handle the process."

He turned and pointed at some small plastic boxes on the shelf beside the door. "We have fake eyes over there, but I don't put them in until I'm done. And it's only for cosmetic effect, the facial expression. The eye cavities have to be filled, because I close the eyes."

His deep voice was calm, something like her mother's in schoolteacher mode when she forgot that Ilka wasn't one of her students, not to mention an adult.

She nodded and watched. The skin over Mike's stomach was bumpy—the fluid had gathered in pockets—and Artie concentrated on smoothing the skin by stroking it carefully with the flat of his hand.

The odor in the room stung her sinuses when Ilka breathed through her nose. She opened her mouth and sucked in air through the mask, which hopefully filtered the poisonous particles. But the rough paper didn't stop the sensation of breathing in fumes from a putrefying body. She pressed her tongue up on the roof of her mouth to hold back her nausea.

Though slightly dizzy, Ilka stood beside Artie while he

finished up. She was determined to file away every single detail of his work so she would understand the process.

He turned off the pump and pulled out the thin tube. "You thinking about coming along to the crematorium to watch Mrs. Norton burn up?" He took the tube over to the sink, but he didn't shut off the exhaust fan. "Everything has to be rinsed and washed; otherwise, it's too dangerous to be in here."

"I'd like to go along to the crematorium, yes." He mumbled something behind his mask. "If you don't mind?"

She had the feeling her presence made him uncomfortable, prevented him from getting into his work as he normally did. He nodded and said she was welcome to come along; they could leave as soon as Mike had been laid in the coffin and wheeled into the cold room.

"It's too hot in here for him; he needs to be cool. I got a coffin ready out in the garage. You want to give me a hand with it?"

Ilka nodded and asked if she should keep the white coat and mask on.

"The mask doesn't matter; it's only for not breathing in too much poison. But keep the white coat on so you don't get your clothes dirty."

He went outside and opened the garage door. He'd already covered the bottom of the coffin with a white sheet. There was no embroidery or decoration, just a common white sheet and a small flat pillow up at the head. He tossed her a thin blanket in a plastic sack and asked her to unwrap it. Then he rolled the casket carriage over to the door. "You want to help me with the step here?"

She leaned over and grabbed a small handle on the front of the carriage. The coffin looked like the coffins common in Denmark, not like the ones she had seen since she'd arrived. Apparently, this was the discount model.

He parked the coffin in the hallway. "Normally I'd wheel the body out and lift it over, but since there's two of us, we can carry him out."

She nodded and tried to conceal her discomfort. Though it wasn't the first time she'd lifted a corpse, she wasn't really used to it. Though Mike Gilbert now looked more like a wax dummy than a real person. But she followed him, and when Artie told her to grab under his knees and lift while he lifted his upper body, she did so without batting an eye. A moment later the body was in the coffin, and she covered it with the blanket and swept the wrinkles out until it looked as smooth as a tablecloth.

"Do they want anything in the coffin with him?" Artie asked.

She shook her head. "Not that I know of, but maybe they'll bring something along at the viewing."

"When are they coming, do you know?"

"Five o'clock. His father is coming too; he's driving up here, so they couldn't make it earlier."

Artie nodded. "Do they need anything for the funeral service, or maybe that's been arranged already with the sister?"

"There won't be a service. They just want to sit with him and say good-bye."

"Okay. Make sure the stereo system is ready so there's music in the background. Otherwise it can be really hard for the relatives to take the silence."

Ilka nodded.

They rolled Mike's coffin in and parked him beside McKenna and his dog, who were to be flown out Wednesday or Thursday; the details weren't taken care of yet—they were waiting on the final papers.

"Ready?" Artie grabbed the casket carriage with Mrs. Norton's coffin. "I'll clean up when we get back."

Ilka wanted to take a quick shower, but Artie was already on his way to the hearse. He asked her to find Mrs. Norton's death certificate in the office while he loaded the coffin.

"And bring the urn with you," he said.

"Is there a specific urn, or should I just pick one out?"

Artie let go of the carriage, obviously annoyed. No, she couldn't just pick one out. "Which urn did they pay for? It's on the order sheet. That's not ready?"

She looked at him in confusion and asked if this was something she should have taken care of.

"It's something Paul always did, anyway."

Ilka was about to defend herself, but instead she straightened up. "Starting today, that will change. From now on, the person driving the body to the crematorium will also take care of the urn." She stared at him until he gave her a nod.

Ilka turned and left the room. She almost slammed the door, but she thought better of it. After a moment, she walked into the garage. Artie was over on the other side, opening the rear door of the hearse.

"I'm sorry," she said. "I'll go in and find the papers."

Artie turned to her. They stood for a moment, letting their anger seep away. Then he offered to help find the urn if she would look to see which model Mrs. Norton had ordered.

Now that they'd cleared the air, Ilka scolded herself. She was going to have to make this work.

In the office, she brought out the folder on Mrs. Norton's funeral. A clay urn had been ordered and paid for, nothing fancy. Just a common model to be put in the grave where her husband already lay.

Before going over to the storage room to find the urn, she noticed two men in dark suits about to get out of an expensive car. They walked across the parking lot toward the front entrance. She stepped back just inside the door, out of sight. There was something purposeful about them, the way they walked silently, straight to the door.

Curious now, also a bit nervous, she moved closer to the reception area. The doorbell rang, and Sister Eileen said something Ilka didn't pick up. A dark, masculine voice replied. She stayed in the foyer and listened. It seemed that the American Funeral Group hadn't accepted her refusal to meet with them. Or else they were extremely hard of hearing. Which she doubted. Either way, she was annoyed.

She walked up to them and introduced herself. "Like I already said earlier today, this business is not for sale." She didn't want to sound directly rude. Just almost.

Instead of backing off, however, one of the men simply walked farther inside and looked around, as if he'd been invited to take a tour of the house. It was a conscious provocation, obviously, and insolent, which worried Ilka. The sister sat behind her desk, her eyes lowered, while the other dark-suited man stood to the side like a silent threat.

"I want you to leave, now," Ilka said. She walked over and opened the door. As she held it open, she caught Sister Eileen's eye; she looked guarded, uncertain, sitting there slumped in her chair. Ilka briefly thought about getting Artie, but instead she again told them to leave.

"I don't think you know who you're dealing with," said the smaller of the two men, the stocky one standing beside the desk. His hands were stuck deep into his pockets, as they had been since the two men had walked in.

"Dealing with? I don't plan on dealing with anyone. I'm just telling you my father's funeral home business is not for sale. Not now, anyway. Which I told you on the phone this morning."

"But it'll be up for sale later?" he said.

Ilka immediately regretted her choice of words, but she was losing patience. "There's no reason for you to think that. Right now it's not for sale."

There was something in his eye that stopped her from being more forceful. *Don't burn your bridges*, a small voice in the back of her head was telling her; *these people could prove to be useful*. But they couldn't just barge in this way, and besides, it was none of their business whether or not the funeral home would be for sale in the future.

"We knew your father," the taller man said, walking over to her. "We also know about his problems. What I think is, you're making a big mistake, not listening to our organization's offer."

He was in her face now, inches away; they were the same height, and it felt as if his eyes were burning straight through her, which enraged her. She stared straight back at him. "Leave, now."

They stood there without moving; then he broke the tension by glancing over at his partner. They turned and walked out without closing the door.

After they drove off, Ilka slammed the door and glared at it. When she turned around, she saw the nun was pale and frightened. "Have they been here before?"

"They've never showed up in person. But American Funeral Group contacted Paul; they've been trying to monopolize the market here in Racine for some time. Several years ago, they took over a funeral home on the outskirts of town, an old family business. He should never have sold."

"Are they trying to control prices?" Ilka still felt uneasy. She would never claim they had threatened her, and perhaps she was just sensitive. But what that tall man had said about her father was about as close as he could come to a threat without being direct about it.

"Paul said they had a reputation for ruining undertakers who didn't go along with them. But he always managed to avoid them."

"But they contacted him?"

Sister Eileen nodded. She still looked pale. "They did, a few times. But Paul wasn't interested in being part of their chain, even though they offered to let him run the business. Changes would of course have been made; we would have had to follow their way of doing business. All their funeral homes are run the same way. But he would have kept his position as funeral director. Your father called it a monopoly, and he kept them at a distance."

Artie stood in the doorway now. He spoke quietly. "This is exactly what I wanted to keep you away from."

She turned to him. "What do you mean?"

"If we'd gone through with the deal I set up with Phyllis Oldham, they wouldn't have targeted us. Now we won't be able to shake them. American Funeral Group wants to take over everywhere. They undermine businesses, pressure people to sell. I've seen it before, and it's not pretty. They're brutal. They'll stop at nothing. If they can't scare us into selling, they'll make sure no one dares do business with us. They'll ruin us, take everything we have so we can't fight them. And they won't give up until we surrender or close down."

"They can't do that," Ilka said. "It's not like this is the Wild West."

"Oh no?" the sister muttered.

"Matter of fact, they can. They're financially powerful, and they've got connections in places that make us vulnerable. They can see to it that we can't renew our license. Or they can get the IRS to come in and check every last detail in our books. That would be trouble for anybody. They can invent problems for us we never even heard of."

Ilka listened without speaking as she tried to ignore the knot growing inside her, the one that made her bend over a few inches and fold her arms.

"Just look at Gregg, like Sister Eileen says. He was forced to sell his funeral home to them a few days before declaring personal bankruptcy. You've seen him around town; he usually hangs out on the square or in Oh Dennis!, when they let him in. He's a shadow of himself. The rest of him disappeared the day he turned over the keys to his funeral home. Drive by and you'll see how they've let the place go. Like, the flag outside the door is ripped; they've boarded the windows. The best thing they can do for the place is level it. American Funeral Group closed it right after they took over. They weren't one bit interested in running the business. All they wanted was one less funeral home. No one knows how they managed to ruin him, but it was a lesson for all of us."

Artic fished a cigarette out of his pocket. His voice was thin now. *He's under pressure*, Ilka thought. *And he feels bad. Maybe he's even scared.*

She watched him walk out of the foyer; then she turned to Sister Eileen. "I'm going along to the crematorium to see how everything is done. If we're not back before you leave, just lock up."

The nun forced a faint smile and nodded.

30

Artie had already driven the hearse out of the garage. He asked if Ilka had remembered the urn and papers.

"I've got it all right here." Carefully she laid the urn in the hearse. Mrs. Norton's death certificate was in her bag. She hoped Artie had calmed down.

"Ready?" He pointed to the coffin. "We're putting her in feet first."

Ilka looked up in surprise, and he smiled. "That way, if she wakes up and sits up in the coffin, she'll be able to see out the front windshield. Paul taught me that on our first trip together."

They grabbed the handles on each side of the coffin, lifted it over onto the small rollers in the back of the hearse, and carefully pushed it in.

Ilka noticed several rusty spots around the rear door as she closed it. In fact, a few places looked almost rusted away. Iron peeped through the uneven rusty brown splotches, which looked like scabs. She inspected the back; the rust was worst at the bottom of the door. But as long as it drove okay, she thought, it would do. At a distance, it looked decent enough. It wasn't something she had to take care of right now, and anyway, if the funeral home business was sold, it would probably end up at an auto salvage yard.

She got in. "Is it a long drive?"

Artie shook his head. "The crematorium is on the edge of town. Douglas Oldham was going to build onto Golden Slumbers, but Phyllis didn't want the soot from burning dead bodies bothering her when she was out on her terrace. Douglas promised there would be a particle filter and machinery installed to remove the mercury in the smoke, and he got permission from the city, but not his wife. So they built it at the end of a residential street where the Oldhams owned a big lot. Now the neighbors out there get to enjoy the crematorium's chimney."

"Why didn't they just build it outside of town?" Ilka fastened her seat belt as the hearse slowly swayed out of the parking lot. Their mood lightened as they chatted.

"Probably for practical reasons. So they wouldn't have to drive so far. And I think Douglas wanted to show everyone who's boss, after the county gave him permission to build within city limits. The people living there raised hell, of course, but that didn't change anything. You got the bucks, you can get it done. It was a great status symbol for his funeral home."

Ilka looked over at him; she didn't understand.

"A lot of people think funerals are cheaper if the funeral home has its own crematorium. That's not true, of course, but the Oldhams hoped it would bring in more customers."

Gray two-story buildings slid by. Failed businesses, abandoned industry, empty back lots with graffiti smeared on walls visible through mesh fences and open gates. Construction waste and trash had been bulldozed into large piles. It looked like no one had taken responsibility for cleaning up after everything had closed. So much of Racine was like a ghost town that Ilka could hardly imagine the lively trade center where many Danish immigrants had settled. And her father had been one of them, though he must have arrived at the end of Racine's glory days. *What the hell were you doing here?* she thought. She leaned her head against the window and watched it all pass by.

They crossed a four-lane bypass that led to the freeway, and after a church and a gas station, Artie signaled and turned off into a residential district with tall trees on both sides of the street. The hearse swayed.

They had ridden silently most of the way, but suddenly he asked, "So we're not going to see each other? Privately, I mean?"

That took Ilka by surprise. She glanced over at him and smiled. "Like you said, it's probably not so smart." She looked out at the front lawns with their low hedges and neat lawns.

"You didn't think it was so wrong the other day," Artie reminded her quickly.

"It's not at all that I think it's wrong. We're adults; we don't owe each other anything. I'm just not so good at planning. Anyway, not at this sort of thing."

"We don't have to plan anything," he said. "It was nice that you just showed up. But it might be even better if I was a little bit prepared."

"You mean so I don't walk in on you and your other women." She expected that would embarrass him, but he didn't react. Maybe he'd already forgotten the woman who had driven off the first evening Ilka came to get him. Then she thought about the guy at the bar who had showed up at the funeral home. She dropped it.

Artie hummed something she couldn't hear. At the end of the street, a low, square brick building with an enormous chimney came into sight. A small paved driveway to the left led around the building. CREMATORIUM was written in the same gold cursive script as on the sign at the Oldhams' funeral home. But there was nothing pretentious about anything else. The chimney rose above the treetops, pointing to the sky like a symbol of death.

Artie drove around the building and backed the hearse up to a green door. He'd just gotten out when an older man wearing a black shirt tucked into a pair of heavy canvas pants stepped outside. His Irish cap pulled down over his forehead shaded his eyes. Ilka sensed a problem, and sure enough, the man folded his arms and shook his head when Artie approached. For a moment, the two men stood talking, but before she could loosen her seat belt, Artie was back in the hearse. He slammed the door angrily and turned the key.

"This is fucking blackmail; I'll be damned if I'm going to stand for this."

They roared out of the driveway, as much as the hearse could be said to roar, and the chimney disappeared behind them as he floored it.

"Blackmail?" Ilka didn't understand.

They drove for a while in silence while he calmed down.

"He demanded cash before he would accept the body! And they're charging us thirty percent extra for being late on our payments." He was furious again. "If they think they can run us out of business because we backed out of the deal, they've got another think coming."

"Can they do this? I mean, I'm sure they can demand cash if we owe them. But can they add thirty percent? Isn't that a lot? Isn't it usually just a few percent for a late payment?"

Artie shrugged and stared straight ahead, though he kept his eye on the cars crossing the highway ahead. "In principle they can do whatever they want; they own the place. But we're not taking this lying down. I don't know if Paul had a special arrangement with them. It wouldn't surprise me if he'd been paying extra to keep the peace, since the Oldhams didn't try to cut prices and run him out of business. But if I know Golden Slumbers, they profited from it."

"Do we have to take Mrs. Norton back? Or are there other crematoriums we can just show up at?"

Artie nodded. "There's a private crematorium just outside of town; it's open twenty-four hours a day. We can drive up there, but it's expensive. And there's one down in Kenosha. They also burn pets; not all crematoriums do. Right now, they're closed, though. They're renovating the place."

Ilka thought of the crematorium at Bispebjerg Hospital back in Copenhagen. It was hard for her to understand that Americans could charge whatever they wanted, though she didn't know anything about it. It just seemed so improbable that there weren't regulations. But then, she didn't know if pets could be cremated in Denmark, or if cremations were done twenty-four hours a day. She'd never needed to know.

Artie had turned off, and now they were headed west, away from Lake Michigan, according to Ilka's sense of direction. Which wasn't particularly reliable. "We're not going north?"

Artie didn't answer, but soon, when the trees seemed to close in on the narrow road, he turned off again. They drove through hills with large, open fields, sectioned off into enormous squares. "First let's see if Dorothy has her oven up and running," he said.

He slowed down and turned off onto a winding gravel road leading to a farm nestled in the hills. Ilka couldn't spot a sign, which made her wonder, but she waited for Artie to say something.

"Here we are," was all he said.

Two long ells of a farmhouse lay at angles to each other. Potted plants stood in the windows of the one Ilka guessed was the living quarters. A building with an oddly shaped tall roof lay farther back. *The crematorium*, she thought, when she noticed the tall chimney at one end. A thin, almost invisible wisp of smoke rose out of it. There were no other cars in the parking lot, no signs indicating this was a crematorium. In contrast to the wooden and masonry houses in town, the buildings were made of red stone.

Artie punched the hearse's horn several times, and soon a middle-aged woman in coveralls, her medium-length gray hair held in a scarf, came out and stood on the front steps. When she saw the hearse, her face lit up in a big smile. She waved.

Artie jumped out of the car and walked over to her. She didn't look at all like someone who ran a crematorium, nor did the place even look like a crematorium to Ilka. Beside the building with the chimney, though, the ends of two coffins stuck out from under a tarp, with firewood stacked beside them. An ax stuck up out of a chopping block.

She looked back at the woman. Obviously, she and Artie knew each other well. Something in the way they faced each other told her they might have been lovers. Curious now, Ilka leaned forward for a better look. Suddenly the woman stared over at the hearse; her smile disappeared as she concentrated on what Artie was saying. They seemed to be negotiating.

Being ignored this way annoyed her. She got out of the car, walked over right past Artie, and introduced herself.

"She's from Denmark," Artie said. She waited for the woman to measure her up. Reluctantly she held a surprisingly big, strong, dry hand out to Ilka.

"Dorothy Cane."

When she stepped down to face her, Ilka was surprised to see they were the same height. They eyed each other for a moment before Artie broke in. "We can carry the coffin ourselves." He pointed out at the hearse.

"What is it?" Dorothy asked. "The cold room is shut off; I can't have anything sitting around here. And I'm busy."

"This is one of the quick ones," Artie said. "A small older lady."

She nodded. "Okay, then."

Artie smiled at her; then he got back into the hearse and slowly backed up toward the red building. He waved Ilka over to help him with the coffin.

"What about the money?" Dorothy said.

"We'll pay you right here and now," Ilka said. Not that she had any idea how much it would cost to burn Mrs. Norton, but the two thousand dollars she'd promised to Sister Eileen was in her pocket, and she wanted so badly to shut Dorothy Cane up. For some reason, the woman irritated her.

Ilka felt the woman's eyes on her as they lifted the coffin out. She straightened up and concentrated on gripping the two handles. It wasn't pretty, but they managed to keep the heavy coffin level so Mrs. Norton wasn't shaken too much on the way across the farm's parking lot.

Dorothy held a small gray gate open for them. "There's a catafalque over there by the wall. Go ahead and set the coffin on top of it."

She pointed at a long box the length of the coffin, equipped with two tracks to slide coffins in. With her foot, she unlocked the catafalque's wheels, and they pushed it into a room across the tiled hallway with two empty coffins, lids open. As if two people had just gotten up and walked away.

Ilka looked around. Whitewashed walls, clean reddish-brown floor tiles. The place was nice, not musty at all, and a bit cool, though there was a faint odor of an extinguished fire out in the hall. In here, though, where they left Mrs. Norton, she couldn't smell anything. Cool and dark; that was it.

"Cash would be fine," Dorothy said. "You want a look at the oven?"

She started down the hall before Ilka could answer. At the end, she opened a heavy double door. The noise was more pronounced than the heat when they walked into the room, which was open all the way up to the roof. An iron monster with glass doors stood in the middle in front of the brick chimney. Flames leapt up on one side. Underneath the glass doors was a broad trapdoor. The box the ashes fell into, Ilka guessed.

Artie and Dorothy stood behind her, their voices drowned out by the noise from the oven. She resisted the temptation to walk over and peek inside the glass doors, not knowing what she would see. An iron cupboard with doors and drawers stood against the far wall, with a few iron boxes on the floor in front of it, filled with something. Bolts, it looked like, only bigger than the ones in Ilka's toolbox back in Copenhagen. She walked over to check it out.

From behind, Dorothy said, "Hip operations and artificial knees, complicated broken bones. All the reserve parts from the dead end up here. I sell them; I get a good price for titanium. The former owner donated the money to the local athletic club. Nowadays it takes a long time to fill the box up."

"How long does a cremation take?" she asked, now that Dorothy had warmed a bit to her.

"Three, four hours. If it's a kid, it doesn't take quite so long. It's all a matter of size."

Interesting, Ilka thought. There was something in

Dorothy's eye, now that she was talking about her work. As if fire was a craft she could control. A passion she wanted to share. "How hot does it get in there?"

A long iron rod with a short, wide scraper on one end stood up against the wall. Dorothy walked over, opened the glass doors, and stuck the poker inside. She pushed around whatever was in there, and the flames leapt up again. "It can get hotter, but you cremate at between a thousand and twelve hundred degrees. It takes a while for the bodies to start burning, but when they start the heat is stable. It helps if the body is in a wooden coffin so the flames have something to work with."

Ilka nodded. Not that this interested her, but suddenly it felt important to break the ice, even though she had no plans to see this woman in coveralls again.

While they stood talking, she remembered the urn. She went out to the hearse to get it, and on the way, she heard Artie ask if it was okay to come by after supper. The woman nodded and suggested he bring along a bottle of wine.

It was quiet outside. A slight breeze whispered in the trees surrounding the farm buildings; on the steps stood several large, elegant glazed pots, blue, green, and yellow, that didn't at all match the tall woman in working clothes. Despite the circumstances, Ilka wasn't uncomfortable. The relationship between Artie and the woman did bug her a bit, which surprised her. She picked up the box containing the urn, walked back, laid it beside the coffin, then waited for Artie to say good-bye. On the way to the hearse, she noticed an old metal sign leaning against the end of the house by the covered coffins. CREMATORIUM.

She looked around for a moment, but other than the old sign, nothing pointed to this being an authorized crematorium.

"What *is* that place?" she said as they drove up the hill. She was still upset about being rejected at the Oldhams' crematorium, and she was tired of it all. All the enthusiasm she'd felt that morning, the determination to turn things around, had gradually slipped away without her realizing it. And now this. It felt like they'd been let in through the back door to get a body burned. A body they otherwise couldn't get rid of. "It can't be a legal crematorium, can it?"

Suddenly she felt old, older than these hills, and she shivered even though the sun was blazing. She couldn't take any more. Maybe it was the men from the American Funeral Group that morning, acting as if they already owned the business. That had seriously shaken her, surprisingly so, and as the hearse rattled down the gravel road, she couldn't see any use in staying to fight for the funeral home.

Artie forced the hearse up the last stretch of hill. "It is; it's actually legal. It's a closed crematorium, or not really all the way closed, of course; it's just that Dorothy doesn't run it as a crematorium anymore."

"Who is she?" She stared in the side mirror. At the bottom of the hill, the farmhouse, the red stone building, the tall chimney with wisps of smoke curling up out of it as if it were about to vanish from sight.

"Dorothy is a potter and artist. She bought the place five or six years ago to use the big ovens for her work."

"She burns clay in those ovens! *And* bodies?"

Artie sighed and ignored her outburst. "She fishes down at the lake occasionally. That's where I met her. She went to an art institute in Ohio where an old friend of mine in Key West went. Though they didn't know each other. When she told me where she'd moved to, we talked some about that, and she's helped us a few times with interments where there weren't any relatives."

"The homeless, you mean, who also deserve a decent burial," she said, repeating what she'd heard one of the first days she was in Racine.

"Your dad made a big deal about everyone being treated with dignity after their death, including people without much money. Not all funeral directors in town see it that way, but Paul did. So, Dorothy let us use her oven."

"But is she allowed to do this?"

"She's not allowed to do the burning herself; you're supposed to be a certified undertaker. But I am. All she has to do is renew her license every year; then it's a hundred percent legal."

"But Mrs. Norton has paid for her cremation."

He nodded. "And she will be cremated. We're paying Dorothy for helping us, of course. Just not as much as the Oldhams charge."

"And we get the same out of it?"

He nodded again. "We'll get her ashes in an urn. Any pieces of bone, silver fillings, and any screws she might have from operations are filtered out. And we'll get her teeth in a bag to give to the family. We put them in small boxes stamped with our logo and deliver them with the photos from the funeral service and our final bill."

"Did we take photos?"

He looked at her as if he didn't know what she meant, but then he nodded. "The sister always takes pictures of the coffin during the services. And then some mood photos. Pictures of the buffet and the flowers. And then she gathers up all the condolence cards. We take care of everything so the family doesn't have to worry about remembering. And when it's over, we give it all to the relatives."

Ilka wasn't aware of all that. "But surely someone knows about Dorothy Cane's little moonlighting business?"

"She doesn't do it that often. If someone brought it to the government's attention, she might have some problems. The IRS would probably be who's most interested; they might check to see if she's not reporting some income. I doubt she'd actually be in trouble. The crematorium meets the environmental standards, but of course the Oldhams might be pissed off if they found out about it. They'd make as much trouble for her as they could. But Dorothy isn't interested in competing with all the others. She's just making a few extra bucks so she can do her pottery thing."

"Does the government keep an eye on crematoriums?" Ilka said.

"Sure, of course. But every state has their own cremation laws, and like I said, Wisconsin requires a valid license, and cremations must be done by a certified undertaker. It's possible the oversight is stricter after what happened down in Georgia, but I doubt it."

"What was that about?"

"There was this guy who inherited a crematorium from his father in the mid-nineties, and five or six years later, bodies began showing up at the place. It was a major scandal. If I remember right, the first person to notice something was a driver delivering gas or oil to the crematorium. He said he saw body parts lying around, but nothing was done because the local sheriff thought it had to do with regulations, nothing criminal. The driver complained again, and the deputy sheriff went out there, but he didn't find anything."

"All they did was go out there and look? They didn't talk to the owner?"

Artie shook his head. "Guess not. Then the next year someone reported seeing body parts in the forest near the crematorium. This time the sheriff went out, but he didn't find anything either. Then finally two years after the first report, someone walking their dog stumbled onto some human bones in the forest, and the authorities moved in. They found fifty body parts spread around."

"That sounds insane."

"Yeah, it was unbelievable. They brought in a federal disaster team, and things really heated up. It was hard to identify the bodies; they were so decomposed. They found—I think it was three hundred thirty-four bodies on the property. Some of them were in the forest behind, some in sheds; there were bodies in coffins out in the yard. I think one body was even stuck halfway inside the oven. There were bodies everywhere. Some of them had been lying around for five years."

Artie shook his head. "The entire funeral home industry was in shock, of course, not to mention the relatives. Some of the deceased were in their Sunday clothes wearing jewelry, others in hospital clothes. The police found out that over twenty years, several thousand bodies had been sent there, the Tri-State Crematory. It was the only crematorium in the whole region. But all this happened after the son took over."

"How in the world could something like that happen?" Ilka realized she was sitting with her mouth open and fists clenched.

"I haven't followed the case since he was sentenced to twelve years in prison. But back then they called him the Mad Hatter; somehow he got poisoned and went crazy. Mercury poisoning can do that, make people insane and lazy, and mercury just so happens to be one of the dangers with cremation. The regulations are strict about filters, to avoid just that, mercury poisoning. Some people claim something went wrong when he left school to help his dad. They say he'd always been popular, a nice kid, but he didn't want to take over the crematorium, and something in his head just went 'click.' What do I know, though? He's the only one who does, but I don't think he ever spoke out."

"How did the relatives take it? It must have been horrible for them."

"Yeah, no shit. It really stirred people up. And it turned out he'd been filling urns with cement dust and giving them to the families. They had no idea about all this until the story hit."

"*Hold da kæft*," Ilka muttered. Incredible. She couldn't imagine anything like that happening in Denmark.

"It didn't exactly promote trust in the funeral home industry. Other things have happened, just not as big a tragedy. The authorities found eight bodies in the house of another licensed undertaker; the guy apparently was in trouble financially. Over three hundred bodies, though, that's a whole different level."

They were almost back in Racine. Neither of them spoke the rest of the way; Ilka couldn't shake the terrible feeling inside her, and she badly needed a cup of coffee and a sandwich.

31

The back door out to the parking lot was unlocked when they returned. Ilka ignored it; even before they'd left Dorothy Cane's crematorium, she'd been holding back the call of nature, and now she rushed through the foyer to the guest bathroom while Artie parked the hearse in the garage. She heard him call out for Sister Eileen; then he walked by the bathroom toward the reception area and called her name again.

Ilka came out of the bathroom and said, "Do you need help with something?"

"I asked Sister Eileen to clean up after the embalming, and she didn't put the key back."

"Where do you usually put it?"

"I told her to lay it on the desk in the office, but it's not there. Usually I keep it on me."

"I'll look on her desk," Ilka said, turning to go.

"I already checked; it's not there."

She walked back to the reception area anyway to see if she'd stuck the preparation room key in one of her drawers. "Is it on a key ring?" she yelled back.

"There's two keys, on a leather string with a ceramic amulet on the end of it. You can't miss it."

Ilka tugged on the drawers. Two of them were locked; the top one was open. Paper, stapler, tape, envelopes, but no keys. When she closed the drawer, she noticed the nun's bag beside the desk chair.

A small, dark gray woman's bag.

"I don't think she's left," Ilka said after she returned empty-handed. "Her bag is still here. And I told her to lock up if she left before we came back, and she didn't. She must be in her apartment."

Ilka walked up the stairs to her father's room to pack up all the folders containing the business's accounts. She'd planned on going through everything, but now she didn't feel like starting on anything that might help save the funeral home. It simply wasn't worth it any longer. What did she think she was proving? Other than that she wouldn't be scared off.

"She's not in her apartment," Artie yelled from the hallway. His voice was higher than usual, and she stopped on the stairs. He sounded worried. She turned and took the last steps down in one jump.

He grabbed the doorknob to the preparation room and shook it as he called the nun's name. He knocked, then slammed the palms of his hands against the door, as if he hoped it would cave in.

"Why do you think she's in there?" Ilka asked. What had gotten into him?

"I don't necessarily, but she might be; maybe she started feeling bad while she was cleaning up."

She heard the worry in his every word; she hadn't thought much about the relationship between her father's two employees, but clearly, Artie cared about her.

"Maybe she lost track of time and suddenly realized she had to go," Ilka said, wanting to reassure him. "And forgot about returning the key because she was in such a hurry."

"And forgot to lock the back door?" He didn't believe it. "Her apartment door wasn't locked, either, and her lunch was on the kitchen counter, half-eaten, and her tea was cold."

He knocked again.

"You're afraid she's locked herself in," Ilka said.

"It's dangerous in there when the exhaust fan isn't running. The fumes are poisonous."

"But surely she didn't stop in the middle of her lunch to come over and clean up. Don't you think she finished cleaning first?"

He banged on the door again and called her name. "You said her bag was in the reception area. Was her wallet there?"

"I didn't look for it," Ilka admitted. Artie said he would run home for his extra key.

The house was oddly quiet after he left. As if no sound could get in or out. She felt jittery, agitated, and the feeling spread throughout her body. Suddenly it was as if she were in a house of farewell, a house filled with loss and sorrow. Not a chilling feeling, but empty.

She went over to the preparation room and slumped to the floor beside the door. The stillness was intense; it spread under her skin like a gust of wind.

When Ilka heard Artie drive in, she opened the back door. Infected by his worry, she followed him to the preparation room and stood behind him as he unlocked the door and opened it.

The room had been cleaned. Every surface had been washed; water still stood on the floor here and there after the hosing down. But the sister wasn't there. The only thing that caught Ilka's eye was the thin gold chain Mike had worn around his neck, lying flat under the architect lamp on Artie's small worktable.

"If we're giving the chain to Shelby, I can put it in an envelope for her so it doesn't get lost."

Artie shook his head; then he walked over and picked it up. "I forgot to put it on him. I'll do it right now."

He looked around the room as if making sure the nun wasn't in one of the corners; then he turned off the light.

Ilka stayed while he walked over and punched in the code to unlock the cold room door. She was hungry. She could pick up some tacos over at the Mexican place. Or she could start packing the old accounts, like she'd planned on doing before, and lay aside everything she wanted to take home to Denmark. She was halfway up the stairs when she heard the scream.

Sister Eileen lay on the floor just inside the cold room. The temperature was in the thirties, to hinder the decomposition of bodies without freezing them.

The nun's body was limp; her head covering lay beside her. Artie quickly kneeled; then he told Ilka to hold the door so he could carry her out.

They took her into the office, which had a thick carpet. Artie spoke quietly to her, shaking her lightly. Finally, she opened her eyes, but she was so confused that Ilka couldn't understand a word she said. She was alive, though, and Ilka let out a sigh she'd been suppressing for several minutes, as if she'd been holding her breath.

Artie checked her pulse, and Ilka grabbed a thick blanket from a chair in the arrangement room. As she wrapped it around Sister Eileen, her hand grazed the nun's ice-cold skin. She closed her eyes again, but her eyelids were quivering in fright. "I'm calling an ambulance," Ilka said after she'd tucked the blanket around the sister's feet.

"Let's see if she comes out of it first," Artie said. Carefully he lifted her head and stuck a pillow underneath. Her short dark hair, damp from the cold, clung to her forehead. He rubbed her arms.

"She's not really conscious. It's like she's in and out. I'm calling." Her hand was on the phone to call 911.

"Wait!" Artie ordered. "She'll make it. It's not life threatening until the body is under seventy-nine degrees; that's when you need special treatment to survive. The important thing is to warm the body carefully."

"I'm not taking responsibility here; we're calling an ambulance. If you're afraid we don't have insurance to cover this, I'll pay for the hospital. She's not conscious. This is irresponsible."

She lifted the receiver, but before she could call, he shocked her by wrenching the phone out of her hand. "We're going to wait."

Sister Eileen stirred, and Ilka hesitated. "Okay. But being cooled down this way can kill you."

He nodded. "Go up and see if there's a hot water bottle or an electric blanket in your father's room, and fill the bathtub with hot water."

Artie kept rubbing the sister's arms, as Ilka remembered her mother doing when she'd been out sledding and came in freezing, her cheeks red and fingers tingling from the cold.

"Right now the important thing is to get her own heat regulation going," he explained when Ilka came down with a heavy electric blanket. "But we have to be careful. Her skin can be numb from being cooled down. Make sure the blanket isn't too hot."

She went out to fill the bathtub. When she came back the sister had lifted her arms, and she was moving her fingers one by one, as if she were making sure they were still there. She stared at a spot behind Artie's shoulder, her eyes fluttering as if she'd just woken up.

"How in the world did this happen?" Ilka asked. She squatted down and massaged the sister's feet. "It's way too unsafe if the door locks automatically when it shuts."

"It doesn't," Artie murmured. "The door only locks when you push the red symbol in on the doorknob outside."

"So what does that mean?"

He stared at her, his eyes doing the talking: The nun hadn't locked herself in the cold room.

"We need to call the police." She got up to call, but the sister spoke, asking her to come back.

Ilka sat down again beside her. "What happened?"

Sister Eileen tried to sit up using her elbows. Her body wasn't cooperating fully; her movements lagged behind. She groaned and lay back down, and Artie tucked the electric blanket around her.

"Did you see who it was?"

The sister shut her eyes again, but this time her voice was clear. "Forget about it. It was an accident, and everything's okay now."

"What are you talking about?" Ilka said. "You could have frozen to death in there if we hadn't found you."

"Let's just drop it." Artie stood up. "If Sister Eileen doesn't feel like being questioned by the police, she shouldn't have to. Right now, the most important thing is to warm her up."

He slid both arms under the nun and helped her sit up. "I'll walk her out to the bathtub; you can get everything ready for Shelby and her daughter. They're coming at five."

Ilka wasn't sure whether what had just happened was the last straw, or if she'd already made her decision after leaving the old crematorium. But instead of preparing for the two women's farewell to Mike Gilbert, she went into her father's office and plucked out of the wastebasket the transfer agreement Phyllis Oldham had brought.

She smoothed it out and dabbed at the oily spots that came from its lying in the trash. Luckily there were none on the back side where Phyllis Oldham's signature was written in steep, loopy handwriting. Ilka thought it almost looked like it had been written with a fountain pen. She reached for a cheap plastic pen with their logo on it and signed her name on the dotted line. The document now had both of their signatures.

"Are you sure?" Artie said from the doorway.

Ilka hadn't heard him. "Yes. I'll have to sell sooner or later anyway, and now I guess it's going to be sooner. I've had enough of the funeral home business."

The thought of driving around to schools in Copenhagen and photographing students was more attractive than ever to her.

"She's going to be all right," he assured her. "It will help when she gets into the warm water."

For a few moments, they looked at each other. Then she walked over to the desk for the keys to her father's car. She stuffed the transfer agreement in her bag and left the office.

32

Ilka drove into the enormous parking lot behind Golden Slumbers Funeral Home. The spaces closest to the building were taken, so she parked facing Lake Michigan. Across the street, a flag hung at half-mast over the door of a building, and she hesitated at the prospect of going in during a funeral service. But she got out anyway and headed for the employee entrance Artie had used on their previous visit.

She walked down the long hall decorated with family portraits. The soft, deep blue carpet engulfed her sneakers with each step, and the pungent odor of the embalming fluids was every bit as nasty as it had been the first time she'd been there.

She took the few steps up to the desk, where the nun wearing the same garment as Sister Eileen had greeted them the other day. Now the desk was cleared and the chair empty. She looked around, then walked on to the office. Just before reaching the door, she noticed someone with his back to her, looking out over the river. Ilka recognized the youngest son, Jesse. He didn't seem to remember her, because when he turned he simply smiled politely and said it was going to be a beautiful evening on Lake Michigan.

Ilka asked if he knew where she could find Phyllis.

Jesse pointed to his mother's office and walked up the steps.

The door was open, and she knocked on the doorframe. Phyllis was sitting behind an old mahogany desk. She gave a start when she saw Ilka. She must have been lost in thought.

"May I come in?" Ilka asked.

After a moment of silence, Ilka walked to the chair across the desk from Phyllis and laid her bag on the floor. "I'm sorry I behaved so badly earlier. Now that I've thought about it, I can see the right thing to do is sell the business to you."

She smiled apologetically and tried to show that she knew she had behaved childishly. But Phyllis Oldham sat staring straight ahead, stiff and unresponsive. Petrified. Had she heard Ilka?

Ilka fumbled around and finally brought out the transfer agreement she'd signed. She laid it on the desk; then she saw the woman was shaking her head.

Phyllis Oldham was dressed in an elegant blue suit with a blouse underneath buttoned up to her neck; a heavy gold cross rested on her breasts, and her slightly wavy hair was perfectly brushed. In short, she resembled herself. But when Ilka looked closely, she realized that in reality, nothing was the same. The pale woman seemed older than the last time she'd seen her, only a few days earlier. What really struck her, though, was Phyllis's stare—was she even aware Ilka was in the room?

"Phyllis," she said, but the woman didn't answer. It was almost as if she wasn't there. Had she gone into shock? Maybe that made sense, given that she'd just admitted to paying Mike Gilbert to leave town.

Ilka said her name again, and suddenly Phyllis looked

at her. She reached for the transfer agreement and tore it in half, and without a word she swiveled her chair and turned on the shredder under the window. Before Ilka could react, she'd stuffed the two halves of the agreement in the machine. A second later they were reduced to confetti.

Ilka watched silently as the agreement she'd just gathered the courage to sign disappeared into a wastebasket.

"My offer no longer stands," Phyllis said, her voice flat and a bit rough edged. "I've decided to sell the family business. From now on Golden Slumbers Funeral Home will be a part of American Funeral Group. It's best you go now."

Ilka opened her mouth, then closed it as what Phyllis Oldham had just said sank in. "But I don't understand—"

Phyllis waved her hand. "No questions. I'm not at liberty to speak about the deal, but you're welcome to contact the new owners."

Ilka simply stared at her, unable to move, while thoughts of her own situation and the future of her father's funeral home ran through her head, now that selling to the Oldhams was no longer possible.

"This is my last day at the office," Phyllis said. "I've been told that I mustn't remove anything, not even personal belongings. Not even the family portraits. No one coming in should suspect new ownership."

Ilka backed up toward the door. Suddenly the room felt claustrophobic, airless. Golden Slumbers had been the biggest funeral home in town, but it was nothing compared to the bulldozer forcing everyone else out of business.

"And saying you could take over my father's business at the end of the month won't change your mind?"

For a moment, Phyllis didn't seem to understand what she meant, but then she shook her head. "It's too late."

Ilka nodded.

"Fuck, fuck, fuck!" she yelled, on her way to the car. She kicked an empty cola can at a black Dodge parked in front of the building. Then she turned and took one last look at the funeral home. Things hadn't exactly become easier for her.

33

Back at her own funeral home, Ilka parked the car, shut off the engine, closed her eyes, and rested her head against the steering wheel. What she wanted most of all was to call her mother and ask her to come and help her out of the mess she'd gotten herself into.

She pressed her temples and tried to control her breathing. They were going to be crushed; she had no doubt about that. The smartest thing to do was to look for a new buyer before word got out that American Funeral Group had bought Golden Slumbers. Otherwise no one would dare take over a small operation like hers. And now that the funeral home chain owned a big funeral home in town, they probably weren't interested in hers. She just didn't understand why Phyllis Oldham had decided to sell when she so recently had planned on expanding.

As Ilka saw it, she had only one option left. Determined now, she jumped out of the car and trotted across the parking lot to find Artie. His car was still there; he couldn't have gone home, she thought. But the hearse was gone, and she found a note on the desk: "We've got a pickup. I'll try to be back before Shelby and the family arrive."

Ilka had forgotten all about them. It was almost four

thirty, and she hadn't opened up the chapel or prepared the music.

She rushed in and switched on the light. The room was cool; the curtains had been left closed. Ilka wasn't familiar with the stereo system, but she pressed the CD button. Soft Muzak streamed out of the hidden speakers. She found a box of matches and walked over to the candles to be placed around Mike Gilbert's open coffin. Even though the rear section was closed off, the room seemed much too big and impersonal. They should have a room even smaller, Ilka thought. Then she shook that idea off; it wasn't her problem, or at least it wouldn't be.

A car drove in. She went outside to give Artie a hand.

"That was quick," she said, as he got out of the hearse to open the garage door.

"It was just down at the nursing home. She died yesterday; it was expected. The family was there today to say their good-byes."

"When do we meet with them? Are they coming here, or do we go to them?"

"No meeting necessary. They've said their good-byes; they just want to know when to pick up the urn."

Ilka stared. "So we won't be involved? Except for the pickup?"

"And the cremation."

Here we go again, she thought. She started to walk over for the casket carriage, but Artie stopped her. "She's there on the stretcher; there's no coffin."

Ilka gave up and simply waited. "Is something wrong?" she asked. "Isn't this just something to get over with?"

Artie looked in the back of the hearse at the body covered by a white sheet. "Irene was only thirty-four years old. She was born with a mental handicap, and it's been years since she recognized her parents. She's been in the nursing home the last fourteen years. She was too much for the family to take care of at home."

"That's so terribly sad." She walked over to the hearse. "Shouldn't we put her in a coffin? We can't have her lying there like that."

Artie looked at her. "Incredible how much you remind me of your dad."

Ilka pointed over toward one of the coffins by the wall. "Can't we use one of those?"

"Yeah, why not? Irene might as well get some use out of it before the Oldhams take over and clean everything out."

Ilka stopped. It took a moment for him to realize something was wrong. "What?" asked Artie.

"The deal is off. Phyllis tore the transfer agreement up and shredded it."

Artie started laughing. "She'll come around; she's just trying to show you who's boss."

"No, she won't. She just sold Golden Slumbers to the American Funeral Group."

Though he was thirty feet away, she saw his face fall. "She didn't!"

Ilka nodded. "They're taking over immediately. We won't be selling. Unless we sell to them."

He swiped at his forehead, as if he needed to clear his mind. He shook a cigarette out of his pack and lit it, even though they were in the garage.

"Shelby's coming in ten minutes," he said. "You better go in and get ready for her. I'll get Mike's coffin. We'll take care of Irene later."

Ilka nodded and went back into the house. She unlocked the front door so the family didn't have to use the back entrance, as Shelby had been doing. A door slammed and something rolled across the floor; then she watched Artie maneuver the catafalque through the doorway. She went out to start the coffee, fill a bowl with chocolates, and find a new box of Kleenex.

The doorbell rang, and Ilka walked out to let them in. Shelby entered with her arm around her daughter, who was using a cane. She'd been allowed to leave All Saints Hospital to say good-bye to her brother. Emma was frail, almost translucent. She wore a black cape over her much-too-loose clothing and a scarf over her bald head. A gust of wind could almost scoop her up and carry her away. Ilka knew she was on her second round of chemotherapy; the tumor in her brain was still too big for an operation that Shelby wasn't even sure she could pay for. It seemed unbearable to Ilka, so different than in Denmark, where it wasn't a question of money, but of whether a treatment was good enough.

Shelby was also dressed in black. She seemed more poised than before. "The only one missing is Tommy," she said, with a long-suffering annoyance in her voice she surely wasn't aware of. "He's always late."

"Let's sit down while we wait," Ilka said. She picked up a small stack of laminated photos of Mike, on which the date of his birth and death were printed. Sister Eileen had been a bit unsure of whether or not it was appropriate, since this wasn't a real funeral service, but Ilka had thought it was a good idea, that the family would appreciate something to remember him by.

She had already given up trying to figure out whether or not something was appropriate; American burials were so different from the ones back in Denmark. Her main impression was that nothing could be too much over here when it came to commemorating deceased loved ones.

Inside the arrangement room, Shelby helped her daughter sit down in the armchair while Ilka brought in the coffee and chocolates, which she set on the table.

Ilka noticed something different about her. Something lighter, even though in a few moments she would be going in to say good-bye to her oldest child. Ilka smiled and looked away when Shelby met her eyes.

"Emma is a bit nervous about seeing her brother in there," she said, glancing affectionately at her daughter. "But I told her not to worry, because Artie Sorvino has taken good care of him."

"He does look very good," Ilka said. She asked Emma how she remembered her brother.

At first Mike's sister stared down at her hands. Should she not have been so direct? Ilka wondered. But then Emma looked up with a big smile on her face. "He always needed a haircut. And he wouldn't put on a shirt, even though Mom told him to. Isn't that right, Mom?"

She turned to Shelby, who nodded. "I'm sure it's true, even though I can't remember about the shirts." She smiled. "But I do remember he always got holes in the toes of his tennis shoes. They'd start fraying, and you knew it was just a matter of time before they'd fall apart." She shook her head at the memory.

"I always did like Ashley," Emma said after a few moments of silence. "She was always nice, and she asked me several times if I wanted to go down to the harbor when they went to look at the ships. Back when Mike hung out with Jesse and the other guys, I never got to go along."

Her mother tilted her head, as if she were surprised that her daughter had suddenly spoken about something that had happened years ago. "But you and your brother spent a lot of time together," she said.

Emma nodded. "Maybe it was mostly Jesse who didn't want me along."

"Were they together a lot back then?" Ilka asked. "I mean, Mike and Jesse Oldham?"

Shelby said the two boys had been in the same class, but it wasn't until they were fifteen or sixteen that the younger Oldham boy started acting friendly toward Mike.

"And it was only because Mike was the starting quarterback," Emma said. "Jesse wasn't any good at football, but he hung around, a real wannabe."

She snorted. "But when Mike started going out with Ashley, he stopped hanging around with Jesse."

"Yes," Shelby said. "And look where that got him."

Emma slumped in her chair. The film of old memories had stopped abruptly; reality had returned.

Shelby looked at her daughter, then turned to Ilka. "Phyllis Oldham came up to us at the hospital today." Her expression changed, and again it looked as if her sorrow had lightened, but there was anger, too, in the furrows around her mouth.

"She offered to pay for the rest of Emma's treatments. No matter how long it took, how many treatments were necessary. And if the doctors at some point think it's no longer too risky to operate, she'll pay for that too. She's even offered to have Emma moved to another hospital, if we can find one with better specialists."

Again, her daughter stared down at her hands, intertwined in her lap.

"I accepted her offer. Maybe I shouldn't have; she shouldn't be allowed to buy her way out of responsibility for what she did to Mike. Of course she shouldn't. But I said yes and thank you."

Mostly Ilka sensed some sort of embarrassment. As if

she was ashamed of having to accept the offer, though she surely wanted nothing to do with the Oldhams after what they had done to her son. "Of course you should let her pay. It's so wonderful for the both of you."

Shelby simply nodded, as if she was relieved to have said it. "We'll give him ten more minutes. This is so like him. He could just have said he didn't want to drive all the way over."

"You can't know; he might be parking outside right now," Emma said, looking at her mother.

The doorbell rang, and Ilka smiled.

"You stay right here; I'll go out and bring him in."

Ilka put on a professional smile as she walked through the foyer to greet Mike Gilbert's father, but she stopped at the sight of a woman with short blond hair holding the hands of two small children. She'd been sobbing, and she seemed utterly crushed and exhausted.

"Hello," Ilka said, feeling a bit awkward as she approached her. How was she going to deal with this right now, when Shelby and her daughter were about to enter the chapel?

She might want to talk to Artie about the woman he'd brought in, Ilka thought. She could be a relative who had changed her mind and wanted to view her anyway.

"May I help you?" It annoyed her that Sister Eileen wasn't there, even though it was totally unfair.

"We're here to see Mike Gilbert," the woman said. The two children looked as if they had just woken up. Shy and a bit frightened, they glanced around in confusion. The haggard woman's lips trembled. "We first heard what happened this morning, and we've been driving all day. Tommy called and told us you're holding a funeral service for him."

"Tommy?" Ilka tried to gather her thoughts.

"My father-in-law. I'm Mike's wife."

"Of course," Ilka said hurriedly, though she didn't know what was going on. "Come inside. Do you need anything?"

She looked down at the boy and girl. Two or three years old, she guessed. "The bathroom is right over there." She pointed it out. "Mike's mother and sister are here. Actually, we thought you were Tommy arriving." Ilka hoped that explained some of her confusion.

"It would be nice to use the bathroom." She began herding the children over.

"I'm hungry," the girl said, her voice thin and tired.

"So you didn't come with your father-in-law?" Ilka said. The boy whined about wanting to sleep.

"He's not coming," the woman said.

After the door closed behind them, Ilka thought about what to do. Shelby hadn't mentioned anything about grandchildren; Ilka doubted very much that she knew about her son's family.

She returned to the arrangement room, where the two women were whispering. They stopped and looked up when she walked in.

"It wasn't Tommy. It's three people who were very close to Mike. They only heard what happened to him this morning, and they're very shaken up. They've been driving all day, and I think you should all have a little time together before we go into the chapel."

A child yelled out in the foyer, "Thirsty, too!" It sounded as if she was about to cry.

Shelby sat up. Emma looked uneasy as she lifted her hand to her scarf. The woman appeared in the doorway carrying one child and holding the hand of the other.

No one spoke for a moment as the three mourners looked at each other. Then the woman stepped inside uncertainly, set the girl down, and ignored the small whimpers, which quieted when Ilka offered the children crackers in a bowl.

"I'm Kathy. I lived with Mike." She held her hand out to Shelby. "This is Ellen and Don. They're three years old."

Mike's mother shook her hand mechanically, but otherwise she looked completely paralyzed at the sight of the twins. Finally, she tore her eyes off them and turned to the woman, but Emma was already standing with tears running down her cheeks and arms spread, reaching toward Kathy.

Shelby stood up uncertainly, as if everything was going too fast, but then she hugged her daughter-in-law and squatted down in front of her grandchildren.

"There's soda and juice in the refrigerator," Ilka said. "And there's bread and stuff for sandwiches. And more crackers. You're welcome to it all, and please take your time. Just say when you're ready."

Ilka caught her breath for a moment before going in to Artie and telling him who'd just walked in instead of the father. "It's not okay at all that she drove this far with two small kids, right after hearing about her husband's death," she said. "The father-in-law surely could have driven them. Or she could have called. We could have waited until tomorrow."

Artie shrugged. "I'm guessing she wouldn't have waited until tomorrow anyway. It's normal for people to not believe a relative has suddenly died. They have to see with their own eyes."

"Of course. But his father apparently didn't need to see

his son. Or his daughter, for that matter. That's so damn tragic," she muttered. She nodded when Artie asked if she would give him a hand with Mike's coffin.

The candles were still flickering slightly when they opened the chapel door. Music streamed out from speakers on the wall.

Artie had covered the catafalque bearing the coffin with a black sheet. "You want it all the way up to the podium, or should we just roll it over to the wall so the room doesn't look so big? Seeing as there's only a few people here."

"Let's put it over against the wall. It'll be a bit cozier. And I'll move the candles over there. Leave some space between the coffin and the wall so they can stand around it."

Ilka had just moved the last floor candelabra when Shelby appeared and said they were ready.

"Lift the lid of the coffin," Artie said. "There's an arm that holds it in place when it's up." While Shelby and the family walked over to the coffin, he told her he was driving out to Dorothy's to cremate Mrs. Norton. "Just close it again when you're finished. I'll roll it back into the cold room when I get back."

"Can't I do that?" Then she remembered what had happened to Sister Eileen, and she gestured that she would leave it there until he returned. "Okay, we can do it then."

Shelby's arm was around Emma when they walked in. Kathy followed. The children must be right outside, Ilka noted. Shelby hesitated at her son's coffin; then she turned and reached for her daughter-in-law's hand. They waited while Ilka walked around to lift the coffin lid.

She moved a few feet to the side, the family stepped forward, and all four of them looked down—at an empty coffin.

For a moment, they all stared, as if they expected Mike to appear. Then the three women looked at Ilka.

"Oh my God!" Ilka apologized profusely, said it had to be a mistake. She rushed out of the room in a rage and found Artie outside walking toward the hearse, his back to her.

"What the hell were you thinking?" she yelled at him, striding over as if she were about to grab him by the collar and drag him back. "You put an empty coffin in there! How could you? How hard could it be? There were only three coffins, and he was the only one in a wooden coffin!"

Suddenly she realized what she'd just said. Mike Gilbert lay in the only wooden coffin they had. Artie hadn't made a mistake after all.

She stopped. "Shit," she muttered. Her legs were about to give out from under her. Quickly she explained what had happened, and they went back inside. Artie's hand rested on her back, as if he were nudging her along.

Ilka felt herself walking like a mechanical doll as she followed him into the cold room. Irene's blue coffin was just inside the door. Her hands were folded over a blanket, and a small flower stuck up from between her fingers. Artie must have plucked it out from among the bouquets in the foyer.

At the far wall stood the zinc coffin with Ed McKenna and his dog, to be flown to Albany. Ilka waited just inside the room while Artie unscrewed the coffin lid, which took some time. Even from a distance, she could make out the elderly man.

Without a word, Artie screwed the lid back on. Ilka pulled herself together, returned to the chapel, and asked Shelby to follow her into her father's office. They sat down across from each other.

"Something absolutely terrible has happened, and I

can't explain it." Ilka told her about finding the sister in the cold room earlier that day. "But I didn't think it could have anything to do with Mike."

Shelby listened silently; she looked as if she expected Ilka to make some sense out of all this, to help her understand why it had happened to her. She leaned forward. "Is Sister Eileen all right? Is she hurt?"

"She's okay. We found her in time. She was lying on the floor, with a weak pulse. She wasn't breathing well. Her voice was...blurry, and she wasn't making much sense. But at least she was conscious."

Artie appeared in the doorway. "The police are coming, but the dispatcher couldn't say exactly when they'll be here. There's a big accident outside town. They're still cleaning up."

Shelby asked if they could go home. "The children need to go to bed, and Kathy looks like she's about to collapse, the poor girl. I don't know what she knows about Mike's background, either, and what happened back then. She deserves to hear about that."

"Of course," Ilka said at once. "I'll call you as soon as we find something out."

She nodded, but before she stood up, she said, "Did you see how much they look like him? Both of them. It's like looking at Mike when he was three. And Kathy seems very nice, don't you think?"

Ilka nodded.

"They've known each other five years, but they weren't married. Her parents live in Oregon. I'll never forgive Tommy for not telling me about them. He knew, but he never visited them, even though he had their address. And he didn't come here to say good-bye, either. He's always been an asshole."

Ilka followed them outside. Shelby and Kathy each carried a child, while Emma opened the car doors for them. Her head felt frozen as she watched them drive away. Frozen, or emptied out and stuffed with cotton. Artie came over and stood behind her.

The red taillights disappeared in the dark, and she turned and accepted the cigarette he held out to her.

34

No," Ilka repeated, "we have no idea who broke in and locked Sister Eileen in our cold room. No sane person would do such a thing. She could have died if we hadn't found her."

"Can she describe the assailant?"

Artie shook his head. "Sister Eileen didn't see anything. Someone pulled a shroud over her head."

Ilka stopped listening. She sank into a funk; she'd given up trying to make sense of it all.

"But we know that Sister Eileen was locked in the room," Artie persisted. "And we know we didn't shut and lock the door from the outside, because we weren't here."

"Where were you?" Officer Thomas said. He pulled a notepad out of his pocket.

"At the crematorium."

"Which crematorium?"

The policeman looked up when Artie hesitated a beat. "Oldhams'," Artie said. "And then we drove to Kenosha to see if they could do it quicker, but it was closed. I'd forgotten about that. And then we came back."

"So you delivered a body to the Oldhams to be cremated?"

"Look, do you really think we locked Sister Eileen in? Shouldn't we be focusing a little bit on Mike Gilbert disappearing from his coffin? Christ, don't you think he and his family have suffered enough? If nothing else, take it seriously for Shelby's sake."

Officer Thomas grunted; then he straightened up, still holding his notepad. "What about the surveillance cameras? They must cover the back too; you should be able to see who comes in."

Ilka glanced over at Artie. He looked tired. "They still haven't been activated. But Sister Eileen was here. It was the middle of the day."

The officer leaned over the table, his stomach rolling over the edge. He also looked tired—exhausted, in fact. And sad. "I understand if you're thinking Howard Oldham might be on the warpath again. But it's not him. Right now, he's being operated on; the doctors are trying to save his life. He was involved in a serious traffic accident earlier today. For some reason, he lost control of his car out on the highway. He hit a truck head on. He'd been in Chicago, meeting with the family's lawyers. I don't know if you've heard, but he and Phyllis recently decided to sell their funeral home to the American Funeral Group, the big chain."

"We don't suspect Howard Oldham," Artie said, none too politely. "We're just asking you to help us find Mike Gilbert's body. It's been stolen, and we're just trying to file a report about it."

Officer Thomas looked away and nodded. "Agreed. Let's keep our focus here." He wiped his forehead and straightened up again. "When was the last time you saw him in the coffin?"

"Right before we drove to the crematorium. Just before noon. And we were back around two."

"So it's within that time frame?"

"Yes. At the same time that Sister Eileen was locked in the cold room."

"But that's where the coffin was, too. Is that correct?"

Artie and Ilka both nodded. Ilka knew it was going to be a long evening if everything had to be spelled out. Artie seemed to realize that, too, along with the policeman, who stuck the notepad back in his pocket and stared blankly for a moment before wiping his forehead again.

"Two people died in that accident." He sounded distant. "They'd been at the swimming pool. They rammed into the back of the truck that collided with Oldham."

Ilka shifted in her chair. She wasn't sure he'd even been listening closely to them; he might have been too much in his own world. She slumped when he started in again.

"Howard drove into the opposite lane on purpose. I'm sure of that. It was a straight stretch of road, no dangerous curves. Nothing blocking his sight. Witnesses said he'd been driving at a steady speed, and nobody noticed him swerving, or anything that might have meant he was feeling bad. Suddenly he just pulled into the other lane, and that was that."

No one said anything for a moment. Then Officer Thomas pushed his chair back. "It was my neighbor in the car behind the truck. A father and his five-year-old son. I'm sorry. It's just that some days on this job are better than others. How's Shelby taking it? Was her daughter there when you discovered Mike's body was missing?"

Suddenly the mood was personal, close. As if it had helped him to get that off his chest.

Ilka nodded. "And the daughter-in-law and Mike's two children. The only person not there was his father."

The policeman looked puzzled. "What? Mike had a family?"

"Yes, and I think it will help Shelby get through this. And, of course, knowing that Phyllis Oldham is going to pay all the bills for Emma's treatments."

Now it was Artie's turn to be startled. There simply hadn't been time to tell him before now.

"I'll get some men together and we'll get a search started immediately," he said, adding that he would keep them informed.

35

Artie left for Dorothy's old crematorium. Ilka hadn't noticed if he had brought a bottle of wine, but she didn't really care. She was up to her neck in shit, as she had put it earlier that evening, when she called home for moral support.

"Come home, then," her mother had said. She brushed aside what Ilka had told her about having to sell off the business first. "Why do you feel it's your responsibility? You'd be better off coming back and focusing on your own business before it goes down the drain. Honestly, these school secretaries aren't all that easy to please." Several times she had emphasized that Ilka didn't owe anything to anyone. Not to Artie or Sister Eileen or, especially, her father.

"If this Artie Sorvino guy is interested in the house, sell it to him. Let the business go. It sounds like that town has plenty of funeral homes. Surely people will find another place to go to."

She was right, of course. They would; no doubt about that.

"And then it's Sorvino who decides if the nun will stay or not. You don't have to get involved in that. And under no circumstances should you let anyone threaten you into doing anything."

This was Karin Jensen in a nutshell. Black or white. Ilka didn't care to explain that her staying to fight for her father's business had nothing to do with the American Funeral Group. Or with the business, not really. It was him, her father. She still had almost no idea of why he had abandoned them. Walking around the funeral home, she sometimes imagined she could feel his presence, but no more than that. She hadn't found out more about the life he'd led in Racine. Occasionally small fragments of his working life came out, but there was so very much she didn't know. All the things still in darkness, things that appeared only in short, unpleasant glimpses. The unpaid bills, what people talked about indirectly. They knew things about her father that Ilka didn't. Things he had done or messes he had gotten himself into. As if he had a shady side to him. Things they hinted at but never elaborated on.

She's right, Ilka told herself after she shut the door and started down the steps. Through the dormer window she had noticed Sister Eileen's light was out. Which wasn't so strange. She'd just gone through a terrible experience. Ilka had bought sandwiches for herself and Artie, and she'd taken one over, but the sister didn't want it. She lay in bed under a thick blanket, pale, still unable to remember what had happened, even right before the attack.

She hadn't seen anything; she hadn't heard anything; she hadn't noticed any smells, sounds, voices. Nothing. She didn't remember if there had been someone in the cold room with her, either. Suddenly the door had slammed behind her. She didn't answer when they asked if she had gone in there under her own power.

Something had scared Sister Eileen out of her wits, Ilka sensed, and she either couldn't or wouldn't remember what.

She stuck her hands in her pockets and strode down toward Oh Dennis!. The next day, she decided, she would hand everything over to Artie. Except the things from her father's room she was taking home with her. And he could do anything he wanted with it. He could get rid of the business and move into the house. He could set up a studio or get together with Dorothy and spin pottery with her and fire it in the crematory oven. Or he could doll up corpses to his heart's content. Ilka didn't give a damn.

She didn't even notice if there was anyone in the restaurant when she went up to the counter and asked for a hundred dollars' worth of coins. When the young guy asked if she wanted something to drink, she just shook her head, grabbed the coins, and walked to the one-armed bandit in back. She began stuffing the coins in the machine and soon disappeared into a world where nothing existed except the rush when she won.

Coin after coin fell in. Ilka didn't move her left hand from the buttons on the bottom controlling which wheel should spin and which should be held back. She kept the wheels going, following the Native Americans, tents, horses, fruit, and stars when they showed up on the line in the middle of the glass. Most of the time the combinations didn't pay out, but she was in a frenzy, caught up in surges of adrenaline.

A dark voice spoke next to her ear. "Would you like a beer?" Someone rubbed against her right arm resting on the machine just beside the coin slot. She smelled fresh air, light aftershave.

Without looking, Ilka shook her head.

"Wine, maybe?"

She shook her head again and noted that he didn't move.

Coins rattled into the cup when she won. He yelled out; then he said something—Ilka didn't know what. She concentrated on sticking the coins back into the machine, and she shut out every sound, every person, the sense of even being there, and focused on the line behind the glass. Finally, he gave up and walked away.

Maybe an hour or two went by, maybe only half an hour; Ilka had no idea. She walked up to the counter and laid another hundred-dollar bill in front of the bartender. This time he didn't ask if she wanted a drink; he brought the coins out to her and shoved them across the counter. They weighed a ton, but she hardly even noticed. Just returned to her machine.

The restaurant was almost empty now. An elderly couple sat by the window, and at the table in the rear next to the bathrooms sat a small man in a light blue windbreaker much too big for him. There were spareribs on his oval plate, French fries in a dish. Leftovers served by a cook who had taken pity on one of the town's losers.

Ilka didn't pay attention to these things either. She stared straight ahead and disappeared into her own world.

36

The next morning, Ilka had just made toast and a cup of coffee when her phone started ringing. Her head felt leaden, her soul numb; she'd given in to the thing that clouded her judgment and left her vulnerable, and she'd spent half the night cursing herself for it. What the hell had she been thinking? Now that she'd decided to throw in the towel and go home after her failed mission.

She'd put a sign in the front-door window. CLOSED. She hadn't talked to Artie since he'd driven out to Dorothy Cane's place the evening before. Maybe he was still out there, for all she knew. She didn't even know when she'd gotten home herself. The guy behind the bar had followed her, but all she remembered was that it had been a long night. For him. She'd paid him to let her sit glued to the one-armed bandit, and she'd spent her last cent. Had tried to talk him into letting her use her credit card, but he'd refused.

She recognized the number. Artie. "Yes?"

"We have to go out and get Mike Gilbert. I'll take a quick shower and I'll be there." He told her to find a roll of plastic and get the stretcher ready. The one they'd used to pick up Ed McKenna. "And we'll need a body bag."

"What happened? Where did they find him?"

"Up in the fishing cabin where Ashley died."

Ilka dropped her phone while pulling a sweater over her head. "Hello!" she yelled, to make sure he was still there. "Does Shelby know?"

"I don't know. All the police would say was that we should come get him."

Ilka rushed down the stairs and into the garage to look for the roll of plastic they'd taken when they picked Mike Gilbert up in the morgue. It was on a shelf beside boxes of masks and plastic gloves. She grabbed a handful of both, along with two disposable white coats

It was almost ten thirty when they drove out of the parking lot. Artie's hair smelled clean and lay plastered to his head. Ilka had never understood older men with long hair, but she was getting used to it. He hadn't said much since picking her up. He asked what she'd done last evening but didn't seem particularly interested when she told him she'd lain around reading. And she didn't ask about his night.

She had in fact planned to tell him right off about her decision to hand everything over to him. He could decide whether to continue her father's funeral home or close it and pursue his dream. The alternative was that she simply lock up and call it quits. She wanted to get it over with, but that moment, in the car, didn't seem like the right time.

From a distance, they could see all the police cars parked at the foot of the path leading up to the fishing cabin. The path where Phyllis Oldham had seen her husband when he shouldn't have been there.

An ambulance was parked a bit farther on. Artie slowed and stopped when a uniformed officer approached them. "Pull behind the ambulance," she said. "We're waiting for the techs to give the okay to remove the bodies."

"What's going on?" Artie asked. He undid his seat belt and leaned farther out the window. The tips of Ilka's fingers were cold. She wasn't sure she wanted to hear the answer to his question. She shouldn't even have come along, she thought. She wasn't trained to handle dead people, and today, feeling completely defenseless, she just wasn't up to it.

"Who's up there with him?" Artie yelled out when the female officer walked away. Ilka's stomach lurched.

The officer didn't answer, but she unfastened the barrier tape so they could drive the hearse in.

"Sorry, I can't tell you anything," she said as they drove by.

Artie followed orders and parked behind the ambulance. Officers Thomas and Doonan were coming down the path when they got out of the hearse. The two policemen spotted them and waved them over. "Bring the stretcher," Thomas said, his voice unusually deep. "You get to carry him down."

Closer now, Ilka saw that Doonan's eyes were red, and there were deep lines around his mouth, as if he had pulled a mask over his face to shield himself.

Thomas's emotions were more open; his round cheeks quivered when he shook his head. "This is about as tragic as it gets," he said, his voice almost a whisper. He looked so miserable that Ilka involuntarily reached out and squeezed his arm. "This is just so sad, so, so sad, and it makes no sense at all. You'd better go on up."

"Does Shelby know?" Artie asked again.

Thomas raised a hand to his forehead, and a few seconds later he began massaging his temple, as if he hoped everything would go away if he rubbed hard enough. "Not yet. This changes everything about what's happened. I guess I'll have to show her the letter; otherwise, she'll never understand."

He turned and walked back up. They followed, though Ilka lagged behind. The two men carried the stretcher, while she bore the body bag under her arm.

Lyme grass grew on both sides of the path; tangled wild roses stood out in windblown bushes. They followed the winding path, and finally Ilka caught sight of the cabin, a wooden shack with small windows. Fish traps and nets hung from the end of the structure; the wind and foam from the lake had weathered the unvarnished boards. The cabin looked like it had been built from driftwood.

She counted eight police officers before they reached the cabin. A technician squatted, packing up a camera.

"We've been waiting on that tech, but now it looks like he's finished," Thomas said, gesturing at the man. "The dogs found them a little past eight this morning. And nothing has been moved; they're lying just like they were when we came."

Again Artie asked what had happened as they walked to the door, which hung crookedly on two hinges. The police stood off to the side now, speaking quietly among themselves. None of them looked at the cabin when Thomas led them in.

Ilka couldn't stop from crying out when she saw the two men on the floor. Mike Gilbert had on the same clothes as when he'd been in the coffin. He looked like a wax figure as he lay with his head in Jesse Oldham's lap, his hands folded across his chest. The undertaker's son sat slumped in a corner, his hair hanging over his closed eyes, hands resting on Mike's shoulders.

"The letter was on the floor beside them," Thomas said, his voice breaking. He cleared his throat.

The policeman must have known the two men on the floor since they were in school, Ilka thought. His face was gray, and it was obviously difficult for him to look over there.

The cabin was otherwise completely empty; no furniture, nothing indicating it was used by some of the many sport fishermen along Lake Michigan. Jesse Oldham had placed himself and Mike so they faced the crooked door that opened to a magnificent view of the lake.

"The door was open when the dogs found them," the policeman said. "Must have been hard for Jesse to drag Mike up here, though he was a strong guy."

"But why?" Ilka asked, after they'd all stepped out of the cabin. The wind whipped her hair around in front of her face; all she could see was the image of the two men on the floor.

The stocky officer crossed his arms as if he were freezing, even though the sun bore down on them. He cleared his throat again and said that in the letter, Jesse Oldham admitted killing Ashley.

"But the way he tells it, it was a mistake; he didn't mean to kill her. He was jealous, and he snuck along behind when Mike came up here to meet her. He waited outside and saw them together. Then when Mike left to go to work, Jesse knocked and went in. They argued, he got mad, got upset, and he yelled at her, told her to stay away from Mike. He wrote that Ashley made fun of him, taunted him about falling in love with Mike. She told him, 'Do you really think he wants anything to do with a fag like you?' And he pushed her. And she fell."

"Oh God," Artie said.

"He wrote that he had been in love with Mike already back in school. At first he thought Mike was interested, too, but then Mike met Ashley. Jesse was the odd man out."

Before continuing, Thomas gestured for two broad-shouldered men with MEDICAL EXAMINER printed on the back of their coats to go on in.

"Forensics is finished. They're taking Jesse to the morgue. They'll do an autopsy today or tomorrow. Though I'm sure the cause of death is the pills he says he took from his mother's medicine cabinet. When they bring him out, you can go in and pick up Mike."

Suddenly Ilka was so dizzy that she wavered a bit before plopping down on the ground. Artie pulled out his cigarettes and looked at the officer, who simply nodded and held out his hand. They lit the cigarettes and sat down beside her.

"Jesse also wrote that he hadn't heard from Mike for almost eight years; then all of a sudden he shows up and wants to meet him. Jesse thought he'd come back to see him, but it turned out he was only interested in money. He wanted help to pay for his sister's treatment. That hurt Jesse."

Thomas snubbed out his cigarette. Then he explained that Jesse had also felt threatened. Not that Mike would reveal what happened back then, because he didn't know. But he did know the Oldhams had something to hide. And he was putting Jesse under pressure to help get the money. It wasn't until Mike told him about Kathy and the twins, though, that Jesse lost control and started beating him.

"The letter is pretty mushy," Thomas said. He didn't try to hide that he couldn't care less how a decent, sensible young guy could end up so bizarrely deranged.

Artie had been quiet, but now he said, "It's not really so strange for young kids to experiment with their sexuality. But in a little place like Racine, you don't do it in public."

Ilka could imagine that two schoolboys in love was something people whispered about here. Twelve years ago, people had probably not even talked about it.

"Jack drove over to inform Phyllis and the rest of the family. We finally managed to contact them right before we called you. They were at the hospital all morning. Howard Oldham died, about the time our dogs found these two."

Thomas shook his head and began rubbing his temples again. Artie was smoking another cigarette, sitting and staring out over the lake. The wind blew hard enough to flatten the small, stiff bushes, but they ignored it.

Ilka had seen Jesse Oldham only twice. During their first meeting with Golden Slumbers and then yesterday afternoon, when he was gazing at the river. She shivered when she remembered what he'd said about the lake. He had been handsome, not very tall, but muscular and friendly-looking. From now on, though, when she thought about him, no matter how hard she tried not to, she would see him sitting on the floor in the fishing cabin with Mike Gilbert's head resting on his lap.

"So it wasn't Douglas Oldham who killed the young girl," Artie said, stubbing out his cigarette. "Wonder if he'd still be alive if Phyllis had known he didn't have anything to do with it."

Officer Thomas struggled to stand up. "Yeah, like I said," he muttered. "This job, some days are just better than others."

37

Leaning against the back wall during Mike Gilbert's funeral service, Ilka realized why her father had stayed with the funeral home business all his life. And why working with the dead was more meaningful to Artie than what he had been doing in Key West.

She barely remembered carrying Mike's body down from the fishing cabin. She had been in shock from the sight of the two young men. When they got back, Artie immediately began reconstructing the parts of Mike's face damaged on the way up to the cabin. At one point, she opened the preparation room door and watched him leaning over Mike's face, fully focused. When she closed the door carefully, not wanting to disturb him, she heard what was missing—noise, specifically music. Not so much as one note of the Beach Boys was going to distract him.

The Racine Police Department had permitted the Gilbert family to hold the services already planned for the day after the tragedy. Ilka had the feeling that the quick release of the body was connected with Officer Thomas wanting to see the whole agonizing case put to rest; everyone, including local TV news journalists who were on the love tragedy like dogs on a bone, pointed out that the Racine Police Department hadn't investigated Ashley's death thoroughly enough back then.

Candles were lit in the tall candelabras up by the coffin. She didn't notice the music in the background, but it filled the room with an air of serenity. She'd asked Artie to lay Mike in the showy coffin taking up space in the garage. The coffin with the large golden handles and the shiny white satin liner looked like something for a head of state. It had been delivered by mistake, and someone might come to pick it up, but that wasn't her problem now. After all Mike Gilbert had been put through, he wasn't going to be sent out of her house in some shabby wooden coffin.

Artie had dressed him in a suit Kathy brought in. He threw the old clothes away.

Officer Thomas had stopped by Ilka's office earlier that day to tell her and Artie that the police considered the case closed. They had ransacked Jesse Oldham's apartment and found several letters Mike had written him after he left town. Jesse had placed the letters on his desk in his small office. They had also confiscated his laptop and cell phone.

"What about his mother?" Ilka had asked. She was surprised to hear that Phyllis had known about everything. The morning before he committed suicide, Jesse had told her he was the one who pushed Ashley and killed her. He had panicked and called his father, who then came to the fishing cabin. Douglas sent Jesse home and got rid of every trace of Jesse's presence. And Phyllis had seen him after he'd finished, when he was on the way down. By keeping silent all those years, she'd thought she was protecting her unfaithful husband, when in truth, he'd saved their son.

"I think she realized she'd been living a lie all these years," Thomas had said. "After Jesse confessed, she called in her son David and told him. Then they contacted the

American Funeral Group and initiated the sale. It's like she's given up. She's home. Staring off into space."

Ilka thought about Douglas's suicide and the accusations Phyllis had made against him. But in a way, Howard Oldham's story was even more heartbreaking to her, his suicide on the highway after discussing with his lawyer the sale of the funeral home that had been in the family for several generations. An era was definitively over.

"Why didn't Jesse just keep quiet?" Artie sat with his head in his hands. "He didn't need to admit he'd pushed the girl; he could have gotten away with it, easy."

Thomas thought that over for a while. "He wasn't a murderer," he finally said. "Being rejected was what broke him. It wasn't about getting away with it. I don't think he thought that way. He wrote at the end of the letter that they were leaving together. Neither one of them would be left alone again."

Artie had looked sullen. "Yeah. Two little kids and a woman get left behind instead."

Ilka closed her eyes and took in the deep sense of peace in the room. That morning, when she and Sister Eileen were preparing for the service, they had closed the back part of the chapel off and pushed the plush sofas closer to the coffin, to create a more intimate atmosphere.

Kathy had asked to say a few words up by the coffin, and without thinking Ilka had asked if she needed a microphone. Shelby had said a few of Emma's friends might show up too, also some of Mike's old school buddies who had stopped by the evening before. The news about Jesse Oldham had spread through town like wildfire, and most people now knew that Mike had been innocent.

Ilka was unaware of when those attending the services had begun streaming in. At first she thought it must be Emma's friends and Mike's classmates she was hearing. But suddenly someone came up and introduced herself as his grade school teacher. Then some of the people he'd worked with at the Italian restaurant on the harbor walked in, then some from the shop where he'd worked afternoons. Finally, Sister Eileen suggested they open the back part of the chapel so there would be room enough for everyone.

It also took a while before Shelby discovered what was happening behind her. She was sitting on the plush sofa, a grandchild on each side of her. When the twins came in the room and saw their father, they called out his name. And they cried when he didn't answer. Kathy hugged them for a long time, and finally they calmed down. Now they sat on the sofa, staring up at the glittering black coffin.

Finally, when Emma tapped her mother's shoulder and pointed, Shelby turned and saw the chapel was full. Ilka had already sent the sister out to call the town's Danish bakers, to hear if they had enough kringles for an emergency delivery. Artie was making coffee and setting out more cups.

A bewildered Shelby stood up and gazed at all the people. She began walking around, greeting everyone who had showed up to pay their respects to her son.

Ilka smiled at her. *How could the entire town so quickly find out the time of the funeral service?* she wondered. Apart from the family, only the police had known. Maybe this was Officer Thomas's way of apologizing to Mike. She was a bit upset that they weren't better prepared; there were no hors d'oeuvres or bouquets of flowers on the round table in the foyer. The fireplace in the chapel wasn't even lit.

Fortunately, the people attending didn't notice much other than the elegant coffin. After they greeted the family, they filed past the coffin and took their seats.

From the snatches of conversation Ilka overheard, it

seemed Artie had done well. She shut out all thoughts and enjoyed the peace in the room as the voices died down. It was like sitting in a church just before a pastor began the sermon. And it occurred to Ilka that she hadn't thought much about her father the past few days. Suddenly, though, he was here again, like an almost physical presence.

Quietly she stepped out into the hallway and closed the door behind her. Then she walked upstairs and lay down on the bed.

The mood of the funeral service had moved her deeply, and now she felt closer to her father than she had ever before. She tried to imagine the version of him she'd never known. And she realized it was too early for her to go home, with so many facts that didn't add up, so much left unsaid, so many things still a mystery to her.

Another letter had arrived, at the bottom of the pile of advertisements, bills, and an offer for washing windows. A white envelope with the same feminine handwriting as some of the letters her father had hidden in the desk drawer. Ilka hadn't read the older letters yet, but she had opened the new one after recognizing the handwriting.

"You have a week to pay, otherwise the truth will come out."

To be continued...

ACKNOWLEDGMENTS

The Daughter is a work of fiction. Some of the places in this book are real, and certain people have been sources of inspiration. But the story comes from my imagination.

The idea for the book came to me in 2013. My parents died within three days of each other, and six weeks later, my beloved Aunt Kirsten followed them. Throughout my entire life, these three people have been my closest family.

All three funerals were handled by the same undertaker. I'd known nothing about her or her funeral home before then, and it surprised me when a young, smiling, and very sweet woman stood at my door.

In the chaos of all my sorrow, I felt that she picked me up. She took care of everything in the most caring and professional manner. Even when I called three days after meeting her and asked her to delay my mother's funeral, because my father had also died. And after I hung up, after we had planned all the practical details for the funeral of both my parents, it was clear to me that my next main character would be an undertaker.

Therefore, a special thank-you goes out to Christina Gauguin from Elholm Funeral Home. First and foremost, because of the perfect farewells arranged for my parents and Aunt Kirsten. But also, because you, Lone, Marianne, and Victor kept your doors open to me, answered all my questions, and allowed me to take an apprenticeship in undertaking. You are the greatest inspiration for *The Daughter*.

I would also like to thank the Wilson Funeral Home and Ann Meredith from the Meredith Funeral Home, both in Racine, for allowing me to come in and ask my many questions. Thank you for showing me around and teaching me about an undertaking tradition very much unlike that in Denmark.

Thanks go out to Steen Holger Hansen, a forensic pathologist who throughout my writing career has taken time to explain how my fictional ideas would take place in the real world.

Thank you, Trine Busch. You were the first person I shared my new idea with, and you believed in it right from the start. Thanks for accompanying me to Racine and helping me find my bearings in this area so new to me.

My publisher, People's Press, also deserves my heartfelt thanks. You were immediately receptive to the idea of a new series. It's so enjoyable working with all of you. And thanks to Rasmus Funder, who once again succeeded in designing the perfect book cover.

Thank you, Ditte Degner, for continuing as my social media manager, even though as a law student you have more than enough on your plate. I simply would have hated to see you go. I appreciate you staying on the team.

My editor, Lisbeth Møller-Madsen, is my better half

when it comes to my books. We constantly remind each other that it must be fun, and I thank my lucky stars that it was this time, too. Dear Lisbeth, thank you so much for so quickly agreeing to take care of Ilka and my new world. Working with you has truly been a gift to me.

It's also been fun working with Malene Kirkegaard Nielsen from the Plot Workshop, who helped form the framework for my undertaker universe. You're the best sparring partner I could have asked for, Malene. Thank you.

Also, thanks to my fantastic PR agent, Elisa Lykke. You know me very well, and you have an incredibly sharp eye for knowing what's in my best interest. Thank you for your wholehearted support.

There are four people who mean so very, very much to me, not only because they ensure that my books are published throughout the world but also because they are always there for me, backing me up in every way. Thank you, Victoria Sanders, my wonderful agent, Bernadette Baker-Baughman, Chris Kepner, and Jessica Spivey from Victoria Sanders & Associates, for such a tremendous team effort.

Benee Knauer helped me greatly with research for this book. She answered tons of questions and dug things up every time there was something I couldn't find myself. Thank you for making Racine and my American world familiar to me.

A special thanks goes out to Karin Slaughter, for sharing a story with me when I told her about my new venture. I would never have come up with the story myself. Thank you for your ability to shake me up with bizarre stories from the real world. But most of all, thank you for being my friend.

My greatest thank-you goes out to my son, Adam. You were the first one to read the initial draft of *The Daughter*, and you told me at once to keep on working because you wanted to read more. You're the best.

And finally, to my fantastic readers and my followers on Facebook—thank you so very much! You are my greatest incentive. Thank you for always trusting me to come up with what you want to read. It means all the world to me.

—Sara Blaedel

THE
NIGHT
WOMEN

SARA
BLAEDEL

Translated by Erik J. Macki and Tara F. Chace

Previously published as *Farewell to Freedom*

GRAND CENTRAL
PUBLISHING

New York Boston

For Adam

Author's Note

For readers who have been following Louise's story all along, *The Night Women* takes us back to an earlier time in Louise's life, before the events of *The Forgotten Girls*. Louise is still a lowly homicide detective as well as a single woman living on her own, and she hasn't yet joined the Missing Persons Department of the Special Search Agency.

The Night Women was first published in English many years ago under the title *Farewell to Freedom*, though this new edition has been revised and updated.

To my readers new and old . . . I hope you enjoy it!

1

The woman was lying on her back, her arms out to her sides, her head tilted toward one shoulder. Her throat had been slashed in one long, straight slice, her blood saturating her blond hair, which spread in a sticky mass over the left side of her torso.

Assistant Detective Louise Rick straightened back up from her knees and took a deep breath. Did anyone ever get used to this? God, she hoped not.

Darkness lay heavily over Copenhagen's Meatpacking District, the vast industrial tract between the train station and the harbor, where the city's slaughterhouses and meatpackers had sold their wares for centuries. It was almost two in the morning, so Sunday had already given way to Monday. Damp April air lingered over the Vesterbro District just west of the inner city, although the previous evening's rain had subsided. The flashing lights and police barricade that had been erected out on Skelbækgade were keeping most people away, but a few curious bystanders chatted as they watched the officers work.

A lone drunk sat on the doorstep of Høker Café, seemingly oblivious to the large police presence. He sang and occasionally screamed out whenever someone drove by.

The girls who usually worked this street were nowhere in sight, likely having retreated to Sønder Boulevard or around the corner to Ingerslevsgade.

The bright glare of the large crime-scene spotlights created sharp contrasts of light and dark. One of the first things the team had done was to go over the surface of the body with tape to secure any fibers and loose hairs before swabbing for DNA with slightly moistened cotton swabs. Forensic pathologist Flemming Larsen turned to Louise and the chief of the Homicide Division, Hans Suhr.

"The incision is approximately twenty centimeters long, leaving a large, gaping wound across the entire throat. It's a deep cut with clean edges, which means the knife was drawn across the throat quickly, and only once."

Pulling off his rubber gloves and face mask, he nodded at the techs to signal that he was done so they could investigate the area around the murdered woman.

"There are no other signs of violence, so it happened fast. She didn't see it coming; there are no defensive wounds on her hands or arms. I would bet that it went down within the last three hours," he said.

"Do you have any clues as to who she might be?" Louise asked. They hadn't found any ID on the body.

"Well, don't you think we can assume we're dealing with a prostitute?" Flemming asked, his eyes resting on the victim's skimpy cotton skirt and tight top, before adding that he doubted she was Danish, given the poor state of her teeth.

"It's not a bad guess," Suhr agreed, taking a step back so that the techs could get by.

They moved the floodlight Flemming had been working under farther down the street so they could search the entire area for evidence.

Louise squatted down next to the woman again. The wound was high on her throat and went all the way around to her cervical vertebrae. It was difficult to make out the facial features in the dark, but she was obviously young—probably about twenty, Louise guessed.

She heard footsteps behind her, but before she could stand up, her colleague Michael Stig came to a stop right behind her and placed both hands on her shoulders as if for support. He leaned forward to inspect the body.

"Eastern European whore" was his swift assessment before removing his hands and allowing Louise to stand up again.

"What makes you so certain?" she asked, taking a step away from him to disrupt the physical intimacy he had forced upon her.

"Her makeup. They still do their faces the way Danish women did back in the eighties. The colors are too bright and there's too much of it. So, what do we know about her?" Stig asked, shoving his hands into the pockets of his baggy jeans.

Louise caught the scent of her newly washed hair and fresh deodorant. She had been asleep for less than an hour when Suhr had woken her with his call, and she had left her Frederiksberg apartment and made it to the murder scene within twenty minutes. After almost five years as a homicide detective, she had a speedy routine for nighttime calls like this one.

"Not a thing," she replied tersely. "The local precinct received an anonymous tip about a dead body on Kødboderne Street behind the Hotel and Restaurant Management School, and then the caller hung up."

"So the caller must have had pretty thorough knowledge of this less than savory section of Copenhagen," Stig concluded. "Like someone who's a regular in this part of town."

Louise raised one eyebrow, and he explained:

"Only people who know the Meatpacking District fairly well would use one of the specific street names: Kødboderne, Høkerboderne, and Slagterboderne."

I wonder why you're so familiar with the area, Louise thought as she turned to join the others. Her partner, Lars Jørgensen, was off with some of their colleagues from the local precinct knocking on the doors in the apartment buildings on Skelbækgade whose windows faced the Meatpacking District. Another team was dealing with the people on the street as well as in the buildings immediately surrounding the scene. Even though the call had gone to the main precinct, formerly known as Precinct 1 on Halmtorvet, the case had been quickly turned over to the Homicide Division at Police Headquarters. Suhr had decided to call some of his own people in so they could be in on the investigation right from the start, but he had spared Toft, who had spent the weekend out in Jutland celebrating his sister's silver wedding anniversary. The chief said he'd figured he ought to let Toft sleep in after all the glasses of port and hours of brass band music that such an event would have required.

"Nobody has anything to tell us," Jørgensen reported. "Either that or they don't dare open their mouths. And strangely, it seems like no one has been anywhere near Skelbækgade in the past twenty-four hours. Not even the people Mikkelsen saw here earlier with his own eyes." He shook his head and yawned.

Mikkelsen was the local officer from the Halmtorvet station who was most knowledgeable about what went on in the Istedgade neighborhood with its prostitutes, pushers, and drug addicts. He was a short, stocky man in his mid-fifties, and he'd spent almost all of his many years on the force working this area. He had served one three-year tour with the riot squad before putting in for a transfer and getting his old office back.

"What about that guy over on those steps?" Louise asked.

"He said he hasn't seen anything except for the bottom of the last bottle he downed," her partner replied, repeating the remark a moment later when the chief came over and asked the same question.

"OK, nobody wants to say anything, so it's business as usual around here," Suhr said as he waved for Stig to come over and join them. "There's nothing more we can do right now. Mikkelsen and his people will continue interviewing passersby, but I doubt we'll get anybody to talk tonight. If any of the regulars around here saw anything, we know from experience that it will take time for them to share. So let's all get some sleep. We'll pick this up again in the morning."

"What about Willumsen?" Louise asked as they headed toward their cars. It surprised her that she hadn't seen the detective superintendent here yet.

"I'll brief him first thing in the morning," said the homicide chief, giving her a wry smile. "It's better to let him get his beauty sleep."

Louise nodded. They all knew what Willumsen was like when he got up on the wrong side of the bed. He had a bad habit of infecting everyone else with his lousy mood.

When Louise Rick woke again after four hours of sleep, she had a sore throat and her whole body felt sluggish. She had gotten up several times in the night, the image of the dead woman implanted in her mind's eye. She wondered why she had been killed that way. The deep wound in her throat seemed so aggressive, but the killer had come up on her from behind, so the woman likely hadn't had a chance to fight back. Thoughts drifted through Louise's mind, coalescing into more visuals from the night's murder scene. Again and again, she saw the nighttime shadows on the low, white-brick façades of the Meatpacking District, where butchers and delicatessen wholesalers served customers in the daytime.

Louise went to the kitchen to put some water on to boil before she climbed into the shower. She stood under the hot spray for so long that the whole bathroom was filled with steam before she felt ready to get out. Afterward, she sank onto a kitchen chair with a cup of tea cradled in her hands.

Suhr had announced just before they'd parted that there would be a briefing on the case at nine o'clock. Things had finally settled down again in their department after the big reorganization that had sent powerful shock waves through Police Headquarters. They had closed down both Division A, which had been in charge of homicides, and Division C, which had handled burglary investigations. Now everything had been reshuffled, dividing lines had been erased, and some of the most senior detectives had been moved elsewhere. And there was no longer room for all the assistant detective superintendents who had previously acted as team leaders. Which was why Louise had lost Henny Heilmann. Henny had been offered a job as lead detective at HQ and was now up in radio dispatch, stuck directing squad cars. Louise knew it had taken Henny quite a while to see the upside to her transfer.

Louise went into the bedroom and pulled a heavy sweater out of her closet. She was tempted to take the bus from Gammel Kongevej, but at the last minute mustered the energy to ride her bike.

The traffic on the bike path was heavy, full of morning

commuters. Even so, she moved over into the passing lane as she crossed H. C. Ørstedsvej. Pedaling hard, she pulled her helmet down low to shield her eyes from the glaring spring sunshine that had suddenly appeared now that the rain clouds had drifted away.

"Just have the downtown precinct keep doing the interviews in the neighborhood, especially in the red-light areas that the johns frequent. It's likelier we'll get something out of a regular client who happened to know the victim than out of any of the hookers. Meanwhile, we'll focus on identifying the victim and processing the forensic evidence. You're probably not planning on allocating too many resources to this case, right?" Detective Superintendent Willumsen asked, shooting Suhr an inquisitive look.

The homicide chief seemed to deliberately pause before responding. Louise leaned her chair back against the wall. It had been a year since Suhr had appointed Willumsen lead detective for Louise's group. Willumsen was widely disliked for his arrogance and rudeness; he didn't give a damn about anything or anyone, and he made no distinction between superiors and colleagues. All the same, Louise was actually quite fond of him. Willumsen had taught her to just say "Yes," "No," or "Kiss my ass," to say things clearly without a lot of screwing around.

His other trademark line was "Is that understood, or not, or do you not give a shit about what I'm telling you?" He was also the one who had signed Louise up a few years back to train in hostage negotiations.

Suhr took a step back and propped his arm against the wall, as if gathering strength to reply.

"You have all the resources you need right now—all four of the detectives in your group: Rick and Jørgensen,

Toft and Stig. Plus the assistance we're already getting from Mikkelsen and his folks at Halmtorvet precinct." Suhr let his arm drop again after firing off this remark.

Willumsen lowered his eyes to focus on his right thumb-nail. He meticulously cleaned it with the tip of his pencil. Finally, he tossed the pencil aside and announced that he'd decided Toft and Stig would keep tabs on the forensic techs and keep everyone up-to-date on the latest evidence. They would also attend the victim's autopsy.

Then Willumsen's eyes shifted to Louise and her partner.

"I want the two of you to go down to see Mikkelsen and concentrate on the investigation in the neighborhood." With that, he wrapped up the meeting.

2

The alarm clock went off at six thirty. It had rained hard through the night and into the early morning hours, so Camilla Lind decided to skip her morning run, which was supposed to be the first stage of her new exercise regimen. Instead, she decided to walk over to the Frederiksberg public pool two blocks from her apartment. There, she would force herself to swim at least twenty laps and follow that up with some time in the sauna. Hopefully, that would work off the effects of her weekend with a few too many mojitos and far too little sleep. Her son had been at his father's from Thursday through Sunday, and from there he'd gone straight to the home of a classmate, where he was going to spend the night. On Monday morning, his class was taking a field trip to the Open Air Museum, and they were supposed to meet at Nørreport Station at ten. But his friend's father was a pastor and worked at home, and the man had assured Camilla that he'd be happy to see the boys off for the field trip. So at ten o'clock on this Monday morning she was going to attend the weekly editorial meeting for the *Morgenavisen* crime beat.

With great purpose, Camilla took out her swimsuit and a towel. She didn't go to the pool often, but she was determined to get some exercise today. It was pathetic how

many times she had resolved to start exercising more, only
to have her best intentions fizzle out, resulting in halfhearted
attempts at best. She always felt extremely guilty when ultimately forced to admit to herself that she just really didn't
want to do it.

The newspaper's crime desk was deserted when she unlocked the door to her office two hours later, her cheeks
flushed, ready to tackle the new week. Thirty laps and a
good sweat in the sauna had filled her with renewed energy.
She had an hour before their meeting started with no leads
on anything worth writing about. Out of the news loop, she
hadn't read a newspaper or watched any TV because of her
date Saturday with Kristian—who didn't mention until Sunday that he'd promised his girlfriend he'd pick her up at
the airport when she got back from her girls-only trip to
London.

Camilla had just happened to run into Kristian at
Magasin, the department store. They had gone to elemen-
tary school together, but she didn't recognize him when he
stopped her at the bottom of the escalator. It wasn't until
he rattled off a bunch of names of other classmates that it
dawned on her who he was, and it turned out he lived in
Frederiksberg, too. So she had accepted when he asked her
out to Belis Bar on Saturday night, and they ended up at her
place after a couple of strong drinks. She had been fine with
it the next morning when he said he had to take off.

Camilla booted up her computer and went out to put
on some coffee. At the same time, she gathered up the
pile of morning papers from the floor in front of the door
to the crime division's modest conference room. She had
time to leaf through them before the meeting started, and
she also logged in to the website for the Ritzau news

agency to see what sort of crime stories they were running from the weekend. A serious stabbing incident in Ålborg and a major car crash on the island of Fyn with three dead. She was jotting these down on her notepad when she heard the door open, and she nodded to the intern, who said hello.

She kept searching, quickly scanning the other papers' news services and checking Radio Denmark and TV2, but there wasn't much. The stories she did find weren't going to end up on the front page. Camilla reached for the phone as she glanced at the clock. It was already quarter past nine, and the editor in chief, Terkel Høyer, nodded to her as he walked by. Camilla closed the door to the conference room before placing a few calls to the major police departments to find out what they had in their blotters from the weekend.

"OK, what've we got?" Terkel began once Camilla and her colleague, Ole Kvist, were seated along with Jakob the intern. Jakob offered them the cinnamon rolls that he'd picked up. It was his last week on the job before he returned to the School of Media and Journalism to finish his degree.

Camilla looked down at the one story she hadn't crossed off her notepad yet; neither the stabbing nor the car crash had made the cut. Kvist leafed through the clippings in front of him. He made a habit of stopping by the news desk every Monday morning on his way up to their editorial offices on the second floor. Like most large news desks, they subscribed to all the smaller newspapers in Denmark, and Kvist quickly tossed any crime stories. He didn't actually evaluate which items were worth discussing until it was time for him to pitch his own stories. His stack of clippings always looked so impressive, even though only a couple of them would actually merit any follow-up; by the time they reached the crime pages of *Morgenavisen*, they were considered old news.

"There's a gang of art thieves at work in the Silkeborg area," Kvist said, reading the lede of the first clipping and glancing sideways at his boss, as if to make sure the man's interest was piqued, before continuing.

"Apparently, the thieves go straight for the expensive art on the wall, and this weekend they took a pricey Per Kirkeby painting and two other works by a Norwegian artist in the same price range from some mansion. The police estimate the mansion has several million kroners' worth of art in it. And they've had similar types of break-ins over the past couple of months."

The tone of his voice grew more eager as he worked up enthusiasm for the story. "I don't think that's really anything for us," Camilla ventured. "That story's already old news."

"It'd be worth doing if we could help them nail the gang by publicizing the case a lot more," Kvist pointed out, adding a pleading look to his face for their boss's benefit.

"Which newspaper did you get that from?" the editor in chief asked, reaching for the clipping.

"It's from central Jutland, so the story probably hasn't run in any of the bigger papers yet," Kvist replied, then proposed that he at least take time to make some calls about it.

Camilla broke off part of her cinnamon roll. There wouldn't be anything to that story until the police made some sort of breakthrough, but it wouldn't surprise her if Kvist got away with it anyway.

"It's right out where all those car dealers live, with a fabulous view over the Silkeborg lakes. They can all afford to have that kind of art on their walls," Kvist reminded them. "So it wouldn't be that hard for the thieves to figure out someone's home address, case the joint, and then make their move when the occupants go out for cocktails with their neighbors."

Camilla thought about the officers handling the case. Surely that scenario must have occurred to them, too.

"Well, look into it then," said Terkel, interrupting her thoughts. "Have you got anything else?"

Kvist shook his head, shoving the other clippings under the story that had been accepted. He glanced over at Camilla, who quickly wiped the crumbs from her mouth.

"Lind, what have you got?" Høyer asked.

"I've got a homicide. A young woman was found murdered in Vesterbro last night."

Høyer raised an eyebrow to show his interest.

"There's not much to tell you right now. An anonymous tip to the police. They found her down by Skelbækgade somewhere near the entrance to the Hotel and Restaurant Management School."

"So, it's a prostitute," Kvist said, leaning back.

Camilla ignored him. "The woman's throat was slit, and Suhr has a team on the case," she continued. "They haven't ID'd her yet. But they're willing to say, off the record, that they suspect she was from Eastern Europe."

"Yeah, well, plenty of them are these days," Kvist said. Then he cut her off, suggesting that he go to Silkeborg to talk to some of the victims who had had their expensive artwork stolen. "I'd really like to follow up on this story," he said.

Trying to hold her boss's attention, Camilla raised her voice. "She was no more than twenty."

The editor in chief sat in silence for a moment, nodding.

"Go ahead and write it up, Camilla, but keep it to two columns."

"It sounds like a really brutal killing," Camilla went on, frustrated that Høyer didn't think the story deserved more space. "It could be a big story, especially if we haven't got anything else."

"But we do have something else," Kvist interrupted from his other side of the table, and it looked as if Høyer agreed with him.

"I'll call the forensic pathologist who examined the body last night. If it was a professional hit—"

Camilla was interrupted by her cell phone ringing. She was just about to switch it off to continue her argument when she saw it was Markus calling. She pushed her chair back from the table, quietly answered, and told her son to make it quick. At the same time, she kept her eyes on Høyer, who was asking Lind to present his suggestions for the paper.

"What do you mean 'a baby'?" Camilla asked, speaking into her cell and asking her son to speak up a bit. "In the church? When you were on your way to Nørreport Station?"

Camilla could hear the irritation in her own voice. As her son's words continued to spill out, she took a deep breath and calmly asked him to repeat everything he'd just said, but this time a little slower. Even though she could hear Kvist pushing his art heist some more, she turned to face the wall so she could concentrate on what her son was saying. Only now did she notice the quaver in his voice and how upset he seemed amid all his disjointed sentences. She let him go on until he'd gotten everything out that he needed to say.

"I'll be right there," she said, ending the call.

The others at the conference table could see the change in Camilla and looked at her with obvious curiosity as she returned her attention to their editorial meeting.

"I've got to go. My son and his friend found an abandoned baby on the floor of Stenhøj Church."

3

Down on Gothersgade, Camilla waved her hand for a taxi. The first three were occupied and drove right past, so she started jogging along Rosenborg Castle Gardens toward Copenhagen's Nørreport Station, keeping her eye out for a cab.

"Stenhøj Allé," she said after a minivan with its taxi light on veered over to the curb to pick her up. The morning traffic had subsided as they headed out toward Frederiksberg, the well-to-do suburb of Copenhagen where she lived, but she thought they were still moving too slowly. She knew she ought to be using this time to put in a call with the Institute of Forensic Medicine and locate the forensic pathologist who had been out to Skelbækgade last night, but she couldn't concentrate with all the adrenaline that Markus's distress had triggered coursing through her veins. She pictured his cheerful face, his short, spiky hair that he styled every morning with gel and hair spray. He was quite grown up for an eleven-year-old, but still enough of a child to call his mother when something upset him.

She had her wallet in her lap as they reached the white Lutheran church with the red-tile roof.

The cabdriver flashed her a look of irritation in the

rearview mirror as she passed him her card. "You should have told me that you were going to pay with a credit card before we started."

"Look, do you want to get paid or not?" she asked, gathering up her handbag from the floor.

A moment later, she was out of the cab, making her way down the side of the church.

A police car drove past and turned into the parking lot next to the cemetery. Camilla followed the path to the back of the church and the courtyard in front of the parsonage. The pastor, Henrik Holm, greeted her in the doorway, holding a little bundle in his arms. Markus ran over to Camilla from the kitchen chair where he had been sitting, with his friend Jonas close on his heels. Jonas greeted her with that slightly hoarse voice of his that Markus thought was so cool.

The pastor tried to hush them as they both started talking at once, telling Louise that they had been on their way out that morning when they heard a baby crying. But their eager explanation was interrupted by the piercing chime of the doorbell. The boys raced excitedly out of the kitchen and through the rooms to the front door to let the police in.

"What exactly is going on?" Camilla asked hurriedly once she was alone with the pastor.

He sat down, rocking the bundle back and forth. "I sent the boys off just before nine thirty and was standing in the doorway watching them cross the courtyard. Suddenly they stopped and stood still for a moment, and then they started running toward the church. I went out to tell them they needed to get going or they'd be late for the field trip. And that's when they came rushing back, yelling something about a baby crying."

Camilla leaned in over the infant in the pastor's arms.

The tiny face was sleeping calmly, the thick, dark hair plastered to the baby's head.

"Is it a boy or a girl?" she asked.

"It's a baby girl," he replied, turning to look toward the living room as they heard footsteps crossing the parquet floor.

"Let me put some water on for coffee while you talk to the police," Camilla suggested, then greeted the two officers who came into the kitchen.

"Hello," the pastor said in a voice close to a whisper. "She just fell asleep, but otherwise she's been crying nonstop ever since the boys found her."

The officers nodded sympathetically, which signaled to Camilla they must have children of their own and knew firsthand how important it was to avoid waking her.

"Where did you find her?" one of the officers asked as he turned to look at Jonas and Markus, who suddenly seemed nervous and shy.

"By the front entrance to the church," they said, but when they didn't say anything else, the pastor took over.

"The boys were on their way to school when they heard her," he explained and then nodded to Camilla, who was gesturing at a kitchen cupboard as she searched for the coffee.

"She was lying on the stone floor just inside the door, wrapped in this." The pastor fingered the dark blue terry cloth towel that was wrapped around the infant's body.

The baby girl stirred uneasily as the officer began unwrapping the blue terry cloth bundle, but she didn't wake up.

"I think she's exhausted from all the crying," the pastor said. Then he explained that he'd finally gotten her to calm down when he remembered how, many years ago, he used to soothe Jonas by stroking his face in little circular motions.

"She's probably hungry. She calmed down when her nursing reflex kicked in, and she was sucking like crazy on my little finger until she fell asleep just now," he said, moving back a bit so that he could lay the baby on his lap as the officers moved in closer to get a good look at her.

Camilla went over and stood behind them to look, too.

A day old, at most, maybe even less. She looked like a newborn, and she was naked except for a long, bloody umbilical cord dangling from her body, which was smeared with amniotic fluid and blood.

"She certainly hasn't been cleaned up since she was born. It kind of looks like she was born under rough conditions, maybe even without the help of a midwife," one of the officers concluded as he studied the umbilical cord. "I suspect the cord was ripped in two—it looks frayed, so they didn't use a knife or scissors to separate her from her mother."

The officer looked at the pastor.

"Could she have been born inside the church?" he asked.

Pastor Holm shook his head but then shrugged. "I couldn't really say," he admitted. "There was no sign of anything like that, but I haven't inspected the rest of the church."

Camilla put the coffeepot and cups on the table, hesitating a bit when the officer asked whether she would hold the baby until the ambulance arrived.

Turning to Pastor Holm, the officer added, "It'll only be for a few minutes, and we'd like to take you and the boys over to the church so you can show us where you found her." The pastor wrapped the child back up in the towel before carefully picking her up and placing her in Camilla's arms.

As the kitchen door closed behind them, Camilla sat down on the bench against the wall. She didn't dare pour herself any coffee while she was holding the baby. Instead, she sat motionless, looking down at the little girl. Something hard to put into words was swelling up inside of her. The tiny newborn radiated such enormous vulnerability, Camilla recognized the same emotion swelling up in the two policemen.

With her free hand, she pulled her handbag closer and took out her cell phone. She turned on the camera function and managed to take a couple of pictures of the sleeping infant, but when she heard a knock on the door, she tossed the cell back in her bag and called out: "Come in." A moment later the EMTs were in the kitchen asking her if the baby was still asleep.

"We'll go get the portable bassinet," one of them said.

Camilla nodded and carefully stood up. While she waited for them to come back, she hugged the baby close, noticing how calm her breathing was. She stood still, letting the feeling of calm pervade her body until she heard footsteps crossing the courtyard, and Holm returned with one of the officers.

Through the window, she saw that Markus and Jonas had stopped next to the ambulance, watching with obvious interest as the back door was pulled open and the bassinet was brought out.

They retreated a bit as the EMTs came back inside, and Holm quickly cleared off one end of the kitchen table to set the bassinet there. It was the same kind that Camilla had had when Markus was a newborn, made of see-through plastic;

this one was lined with a thick white blanket and a clean towel.

"We're going to take her to Frederiksberg Hospital, and they'll feed her before she's examined and cleaned up," said the officer. "They'll take some blood samples so we can run a DNA test on her, and then they'll keep her under observation."

Out in the courtyard, the crime-scene techs had arrived, and the officer explained to the pastor that they would take the blue terry cloth towel to the forensics lab for further testing after they were done with their work inside and around the church.

The portable bassinet was ready, and Camilla took one last look at the tiny girl before handing her over. The moment she let her go, the baby started crying again. It was loud and heartrending. Her little face contorted, and she began waving her little fists in the air. The young medic stepped back in alarm and asked Camilla if she wouldn't mind placing the baby in the bassinet.

"I'm sure they'll take good care of her at the hospital," he added, his voice reassuring.

Camilla looked at her son and his friend as the paramedics carried the bassinet out to the ambulance. They stood there distressed, clearly upset by the child's piercing cries, and they watched until the ambulance pulled out into traffic.

Then they all sat down at the table. Camilla poured coffee into the mugs and served them, while the police asked the pastor and the boys to recount what had happened.

"None of you heard or saw anyone around the church this morning?" the officer began.

All three of them shook their heads.

He looked at the pastor. "What time did you come downstairs to the kitchen?"

"I got up at six forty-five and was here in the kitchen by seven to make breakfast and pack their lunches," Holm explained, nodding at the counter. "From the window, I can see right across to the church."

The officer nodded. He'd already been over to the window and noticed that there was a good view of the church and the entire courtyard.

"The boys said that the church door was slightly ajar when they heard the baby. Did you see whether it was open when you came down to the kitchen to make breakfast?"

Camilla kept listening as she took a carton of milk out of the refrigerator and set it on the table. She sent Høyer a quick text message to say that she was going to be a little longer, but that he would definitely be getting a story for the next day's paper. Then she sat down on the bench next to Markus and put her arm around his shoulder.

"I really couldn't say," Holm admitted. "I didn't notice."

"But you would have noticed if someone went inside?"

"I'm sure I would have, but I wasn't looking at the church the whole time. I had to get the boys up and fed before they left for their field trip."

The officer nodded and shrugged. "Well, I guess we don't have much to go on if you didn't notice anyone in the vicinity of the parsonage or the church," he said.

"What will you do to find the mother?" Camilla asked when the officer looked like he was about to get up from the table.

"Mainly, we'll hope she turns up on her own," he replied, once again picking up his coffee mug. "In most cases like this, the mother usually does show up. And all indications are that the child was meant to be found, since she was left here in the church. Otherwise she might have been left anywhere at all, or even been killed."

Camilla pulled Markus close as she felt his body tense.

"But won't you do anything to try to locate her?" exclaimed Holm.

"There's really not much we can do if she doesn't want to be found. But, of course, we'll go to the media and make an appeal for the mother to contact us. And we'll interview people here in the neighborhood to find out if anyone saw anything."

The officer sounded a bit tired, and he leaned back in his chair. "But if nothing comes of our efforts," he added, "the child will be put up for adoption. Until adoptive parents can be found for her, I assume that she'll be placed in an orphanage, presumably Skodsborg."

"Isn't someone going to take care of her?" asked Jonas, who had stood up as the officer was talking.

"They absolutely will. Some very nice ladies will take good care of her until she gets new parents."

"But there must be something else you can do. Maybe the towel could give you a lead," Camilla interjected, removing her arm from Markus's shoulder as he, too, stood up.

"We'll certainly do everything we can. But at least the baby's alive, and if the mother doesn't want her, it's probably best for the girl to be placed with some couple who really wants a child," said the officer. Then he asked the pastor for a phone number where he could be reached.

As the officer stood up to leave, he gave his business card to Holm and handed one to Camilla as well. She noted that his name was Officer Rasmus Hem, and she automatically nodded when he said that she was welcome to call him if her son happened to remember anything else. Standard procedure, she thought, sticking the card in her pocket.

The boys disappeared upstairs to Jonas's room. Camilla shifted her gaze away from the stairs and nodded to accept the pastor's offer of another cup of coffee. A pall had fallen over the kitchen, and the silence weighed heavily between them.

"What a mess," said Pastor Holm, sinking onto a chair by the table and reaching for the sugar.

Camilla tried to imagine what would drive a mother to abandon a newborn to an uncertain fate, but in all the scenarios and feelings she considered, she couldn't find a single credible explanation.

"Can you think of any pregnant women who have been here?" she asked instead. "I've been racking my brain like crazy, but the only pregnant woman who comes here on a regular basis is Mette, and she hasn't delivered yet."

He shook his head and glanced at the clock on the wall.

"I have to go write a column for the paper this week," he said, gazing out the window at the church. "But I don't suppose they'll be needing me for the next couple of hours."

Camilla shook her head and got up. It was almost eleven thirty, and she called Markus downstairs to tell him she was leaving.

"I've got to get back to the paper," she said, running her fingers through his hair, flattening out a couple of tufts that he immediately retousled so it stuck out all over the place.

She smiled at him and placed her hands on his shoulders as she looked into his eyes, trying to determine whether he was still upset. But she started to relax, realizing he was likely impatient for her to leave so he could go back up to Jonas.

"I'll call as soon as I can get away," she promised, giving him a kiss on the cheek and another on his forehead before he writhed out of her grasp. Shouting "Sure, fine," he disappeared up the stairs.

Camilla turned to face Pastor Holm and smiled. "Well, it looks like they've moved on," she said, and after thanking him for the coffee, she left.

4

"At this hour of the day, you won't find a single person on the street who might have seen anything," Mikkelsen informed Louise and Lars when they arrived at the local precinct. A clerk had shown them to Mikkelsen's office, which had a window overlooking Halmtorvet, Copenhagen's old Haymarket Square, which was now somewhat gentrified and lined with cafés and restaurants. The detective, who had gray hair and wore small horn-rimmed glasses, crossed his arms and glanced outside before telling them he'd already chatted up a few individuals last night who usually knew a thing or two about events in the area.

"Were they able to tell you anything?" Louise asked. She wondered whether Mikkelsen had even been home to sleep, having immediately noticed the utilitarian daybed pushed up against one wall of his office when she came in. Currently it was covered with piles of papers and folders, but underneath was a cotton blanket with a floral pattern.

He shook his head but shrugged at the same time, as if to say that it wasn't always easy to know how much weight to place on their statements.

"I showed the picture around," he said, pointing to the photograph taken the night before of the woman's face from the chin up. "Several people said they'd seen her, but they claimed not to know who she was. Or who she works for."

"And you're positive she's a prostitute?" Lars asked.

Mikkelsen reclined in his high-backed office chair, pausing for a moment with his hands clasped over his round belly.

"We might never get that fact confirmed a hundred percent," he said, fixing his gaze on the wall behind them. "But I think we can proceed based on that theory."

"A colleague claimed he could tell by looking at her teeth that she was from Eastern Europe. Does that sound right?" Louise asked, noticing at once how Mikkelsen's face tensed up and his expression darkened.

He leaned forward again, placed his hands on the desk, and said, "It's always nice to have colleagues who are smart enough to observe everything in a single glance, and who are ready to lump all the girls together. But it's not that simple. We're not dealing with brand-name goods here. We can't just assume that if they look a certain way, they must come from a specific region. These are human beings we're talking about, not some cultivar of a flower that you can look up."

His tone was acerbic. This was clearly a pet peeve of his that apparently came up a lot.

"So, what's your best guess?" asked Louise once he'd calmed down.

"She could very well be from Eastern Europe," Mikkelsen admitted, but then he smiled. "I'm not basing that just on her appearance. That's based on what happened to her and where she was found. Plus, I'd be more likely to know her a little if she were one of the Danish prostitutes. And lately I've also been getting the impression that things have been getting difficult in Eastern Europe for these girls, so more and more of them have been showing up in Denmark in the past couple of years. Some of them work for pimps, others work for themselves, but ultimately they all have to pay to use the street."

"Use the street?" Louise interrupted with a puzzled look. "What exactly does that mean?"

"Some of the nastier pimps think they're in charge of the street, and they make the girls pay between 300 and 500 kroner a day for permission to use it."

"How the hell can they do that? If anyone 'owns' Istedgade, surely it's not a bunch of foreign pimps," Lars exclaimed indignantly.

"Do the women get anything in return after they pay?" Louise asked, staring at a large city map hanging next to Mikkelsen's desk that showed the Vesterbro District. There were also some photos on the wall of Istedgade and its side streets from an era when the shop fronts looked completely different, Louise guessed from the fifties. In one of the pictures a police officer was riding a bicycle, and another showed three men raising bottles of beer at the photographer in a toast. All of the photos were in black and white.

Mikkelsen shrugged. "Sure, they promise them protection," he said with a nod as he scratched his unshaven cheeks.

Louise understood this to imply that the prostitutes couldn't really count on this protection.

"They believe it because they have no other choice. They're told that the pimps are in cahoots with the police, and that they have to pay if they don't want to be thrown out of the country."

"But don't the girls find the truth when they talk to each other?" Louise asked. Mikkelsen shook his head and pushed his black-framed glasses up onto his forehead.

There was something retro about their styling, but she was sure that he hadn't chosen them for fashion but because he'd actually owned them since the sixties.

"Keep in mind that many of the girls who end up here don't necessarily have the world's best education. Where they come from, bribes aren't uncommon to get the authorities to leave you alone. At the same time, these girls aren't used to having much of a say about anything. So, when someone who talks louder than they do, so to speak, explains that these are the rules, they fall in line accordingly."

"So who's controlling the girls this way?" Louise asked next.

"The crime bosses. The ones who work with the Nigerian prostitutes, the Roma, and the ones from Eastern Europe. There are girls walking around out there"—he tilted his head toward the window—"who have no idea how many months there are in a year, or how many hours in a day. Those kinds of girls aren't going to rebel against someone who gives them an order. They do whatever they're told.

"They're here for only one reason, and that's to make money," Mikkelsen continued. "Either for themselves or for the crime bosses who force them into prostitution. But whether they're here of their own free will or they've been forced into it, most of them dream of being able to put a little aside or to send money home to their families. When there's a middleman involved, there's not much money left over, so sometimes a few of them try to go it on their own."

"Do you think that's what happened here?" asked Louise, leaning forward a bit.

"It's possible," Mikkelsen said, nodding.

Louise sat in silence for a moment, lost in her own thoughts, trying to put together a scenario that would explain the killing.

"Well, should we head out and see if anyone has shown up who might recognize the woman?" Lars suggested, interrupting her thoughts.

Mikkelsen stood up. "Let's do that," he said. "But just think of it as getting some exercise, because I don't think our odds are all that good. If this is what I think, the girl didn't want to follow orders. So, the only motive for the murder is to send a signal or a warning to the other girls, to show them what happens if they don't obey and do what they're told. And those guys do their job so thoroughly that there won't be any evidence for us to find, not even if we roll out our entire technical arsenal."

Mikkelsen put on a black leather jacket, pulled a pack of cigarettes out of his desk drawer, and stuffed it in his inside pocket.

"And if anyone happens to be unlucky enough to have seen something, you can bet they're not going to feel like picking the perpetrators out of a lineup later on," he added.

"But it is still possible that the victim was Danish and that the perp was a john, don't you think?" Lars asked as they made their way downstairs.

"I doubt it." Mikkelsen's voice was quite firm. "If so, there would have been some indication of emotion. Not the kind of emotion that makes married people kill each other, but the more ambiguous kind that can pop up suddenly between a man and a prostitute: feelings of domination, rage, or possessiveness. We see it all the time when we pick up hookers who've been beaten. But there was no emotion in this case. She was slaughtered like an animal."

Out on Halmtorvet, Louise squinted in the bright sunlight as they started walking down Sønder Boulevard. There were fewer cars now that the street had been closed to through traffic, but there weren't many pedestrians or bikers out, either. Louise spotted a young drug addict leaning against the door in an entryway. The woman's purse had slipped out of her grasp and was lying on the sidewalk. Louise guessed she was in her midtwenties. She was wearing stylish clothes: tight jeans and a short, light-colored leather jacket. Her short brown hair was disheveled, and at the moment she seemed to be going through hell. Violent spasms appeared to be racking her body. She leaned her head against the rough bricks of the building and clung to the door, her fingers jabbing at the doorbells. She doubled over, gasping for air.

Mikkelsen went over to her and cautiously placed his hand on her shoulder. "What is it, Sanne? What's wrong?" he asked.

The woman didn't turn to look at him, instead raising her arm and trying to push him away. He pressed one of the doorbells, and a moment later the door buzzed. He gallantly held it open for her as she staggered unsteadily into the stairwell, fumbling along the wall with one hand. Then she disappeared from Louise's view. Mikkelsen had picked up her bag and hung the strap over the woman's shoulder before pulling the door closed.

Rejoining his colleagues, Mikkelsen made no comment about the incident and just kept walking.

"It's always deserted around here in the early afternoon. But in an hour or two the johns will start heading home from work, and then the girls will show up," he told them as he waved to a couple of middle-aged men sitting on a bench, each holding a beer. Louise fell in behind Jørgensen as a group of school kids passed them, taking up most of the sidewalk as they made their way toward DGI-byen, the enormous conference center complex that included a gym, spa, and restaurant.

Mikkelsen was headed for Skelbækgade, which felt different to Louise in the daytime.

There had been much more life on the street the night before than there was now.

"Let's just go over and ask Nesip what sort of rumors are going around," Mikkelsen said, sounding like a local. He motioned for them to follow as he went down four steps into a basement grocery store, calling out: "Hello, is the little shrimp working today?"

Louise saw a young immigrant boy behind the counter give him a high five over the candy bins and the neat stacks of morning newspapers.

"He's in back," the boy said in the thick, local neighborhood accent.

Mikkelsen led the way through the shop, and Louise noticed the boy following them with his eyes, curious looking. He didn't seem concerned about a group of police officers tromping through the place.

In the back room, Mikkelsen sat down next to a small man who was apparently the shop owner. The tea was sweet, and the music was so loud that Louise had a hard time following the conversation, but it seemed as if Mikkelsen were a friend of the house, and Louise and Lars were merely along for the ride.

Mikkelsen placed the photo of the dead woman on the table, and Louise didn't need to hear what they were saying to see that Nesip didn't know her. She leaned forward to listen as Mikkelsen tried to ferret out what people in the neighborhood had been saying, and whether there was anything the police hadn't caught wind of yet.

Occasionally the Turkish man would have a highly emotional outburst, his voice rising in passion and temporarily drowning out the Middle Eastern music as he expressed his great sorrow that the harsh reality of street life had claimed yet another soul.

Mikkelsen glanced over at them and winked as he paused in his questioning, until the shopkeeper had calmed down a bit.

Ten minutes later, they were back on the street. They hadn't learned anything new, and the sweet tea had left a cloying taste in their mouths.

"So he didn't know her name, but he saw her walk by a few times recently, although he couldn't say whether it was a week ago or a month ago."

They started walking back toward Halmtorvet. When Louise looked across the street, she suddenly grabbed Lars's arm—she had seen the same drunk who had been sitting on the steps outside the Høker Café when the body was found.

"Isn't that the guy?" she asked, pointing at the opposite sidewalk.

"It sure is, and it looks like he's finally on his feet," her partner said. He told Mikkelsen that the man was one of the first witnesses he'd talked to. "But the guy was so far gone he hadn't even noticed anything was happening."

"Oh, that's Kaj," Mikkelsen said. "He lost his grip on reality years ago. He does better when he keeps to his own world. He puts away a liter or more a day, but he wouldn't hurt a fly. Sometimes he even makes his sofa available if someone needs a place to stay."

The man was walking in their direction on the sidewalk on the other side of the street and stopped to lean against the wall of a building as he rummaged through his pants pocket. He finally pulled out a pack of cigarettes, and with great difficulty removed one from the pack and then found his lighter.

Louise watched him as he started staggering forward again.

"He was sitting right across from the place where the body was lying. He must have seen her," she said. Then she asked Mikkelsen if he'd consider having a word with the man. "Maybe he'd be more willing to recall something if you were the one who asked."

Mikkelsen stopped abruptly and glanced over at Kaj, but then he started walking again. "OK, I'll do it, but not here. I'd rather catch him at home. Kaj would catch hell if people think he might have seen something. People consider a guy like him worthless, and the ones we're dealing with wouldn't blink at shutting him up for good."

Kaj was almost directly across from them now. He crossed the street, heading for the basement grocery store. When he got close, he recognized Mikkelsen and raised his hand in greeting.

"*Ça va, monsieur?*" Mikkelsen asked, going over to shake his hand.

"*Très bien, mon ami. Très bien,*" Kaj slurred, a smile passing over his ravaged face. He let go of the officer's hand, pointed down at the store, and then raised his hand to his mouth as if he were tipping a bottle to his lips.

Mikkelsen smiled and gave him a slap on the back before Kaj headed down the basement steps.

"He's OK. He was the chef at the Plaza Hotel until his wife dumped him, and then his son was killed in a car accident, or maybe it happened the other way around. In any case, his whole world fell apart, and he said goodbye to his old life," Mikkelsen explained. "Let's take a stroll over to Istedgade. I want to show the photo to the folks at Club Intim. If this woman worked here in the neighborhood, she probably used their booths. Although I doubt the guys over there will feel particularly motivated to share, either."

Rounding the corner onto Istedgade, Louise smelled the spicy aroma of grilling shawarma, and her stomach instantly contracted with hunger. She found a piece of chewing gum in her pocket and hoped that it would tide her over until she could get back to the office and the box of crackers waiting in her desk drawer.

A group of men was standing in front of the homeless shelter in the spring sunshine, clutching their beer bottles and chatting. A big dog had stretched out lazily in the middle of the sidewalk so that people had to walk in a big circle around him. The street scene was a motley mixture, with everyone from bums and schoolchildren to the parents of toddlers who didn't bat an eye at the sex shops, maneuvering their strollers home around the African prostitutes who were strolling in small groups.

Club Intim was three steps below street level. The three officers edged their way single file past racks of porn DVDs in the crammed shop.

Louise could tell that the guy behind the counter recognized Mikkelsen, and it took him only a quick glance at Lars and her to make clear he knew they weren't new customers. On the contrary, they were the sort of people he wanted out of the shop as fast as possible.

Club Intim promoted itself as Denmark's leading porn theater, with four separate screens and signs advertising topless service and draft beer for 30 kroner. But only a certain clientele knew about the business transacted in the numerous private booths where prostitutes serviced their customers. The prostitutes paid 90 kroner per visit to rent a booth, and according to Mikkelsen, they could turn over three or four customers an hour.

Louise and her partner hung back as Mikkelsen stepped over to the counter to show the guy the photo of the murdered woman found on Skelbækgade. Louise perused the DVD titles. Bare breasts and spread legs—the packaging was basically the same on all of them.

Two men in their early twenties came out of the back room, which Louise later learned was a bar. Topless and bottomless, as Mikkelsen described it. She stepped aside to let the men pass. They gave her a knowing smile, and she made sure she had a response ready if they tried to proposition her. But just then a middle-aged man in a work jacket and white mason's cap came barging out of the other corridor where the theaters and sex booths were. He was clearly in a hurry, and on his way to the door he happened to bump into one of the younger guys, pushing him into a rack. A couple of DVDs fell to the floor. Without even pausing, the man rushed up the three steps to the street, but before he got any farther, the young guys were on him. A punch slammed the middle-aged man into the shop's front window with a loud bang.

Louise was up the stairs by the time he had taken the second blow, and she grabbed hold of the assailant. With a quick twist, she had his arm pinned behind his back and her police badge out before Lars had even reached the entrance.

"All right, that's enough," she said, nodding at the older man to let him know he could go. She was just about to ask the young guys their names when a loud scream was heard through the open door. Lars quickly turned back, and

Louise let go of the man's arm to follow Lars as he ran back into the shop and down the corridor with the booths, toward the direction of the screams. Mikkelsen had remained inside while his colleagues dealt with the young men, but now he followed them into the corridor.

Inside the hallway, Lars stopped abruptly. Louise ran into him with such force that he lost his balance and fell against the wall.

The African girl was naked. Small and slender, with her feet dangling thirty centimeters off the floor, she hung from a row of coat pegs on the wall with her arms stretched through the coat hangers like a female version of Jesus on the cross. Her head hung limply to one side, her eyes were closed, and a thin stream of blood trickled down her cheek from a cut over her left eyebrow.

The screams stopped, replaced by faint sobs coming from a blond girl standing in the doorway next to the coat pegs. She was wearing black lace underwear and she rocked from side to side as she wept.

Mikkelsen and Lars lifted the girl down from the coat pegs. Her legs trembled, but she was conscious. Louise took a blanket that someone handed her from a door that opened but then quickly closed again. Then she helped the girl sit down on the bed in a little booth that stank of sweat, semen, and poor ventilation.

"Do you speak Danish?" Louise asked, wrapping the blanket around the girl's shoulders.

The African girl shook her head listlessly as she reached for a paper towel that she tore off a roll on a small table. The cut over her eye was bleeding heavily now, and she dabbed at her cheek first, then pressed the paper towel to her eyebrow to stop the bleeding. She looked like she'd taken more blows than the one that had split open her brow, but she looked away every time Louise tried to talk. Finally, Louise got up and left the woman alone to collect herself.

Mikkelsen was with the blonde who had summoned them with her screams. He knew her. The girl's name was Anita, and the needle tracks on her arms were so visible that it was obvious she had been using for a long time. Her sobs subsided, and she blew her nose loudly on the tissue Mikkelsen handed to her.

"I heard him hitting her, but I had to finish with my customer before I could see if she was all right," Anita said with a hacking cough. "And there she was, hanging there. Not making a sound. I thought she was fucking dead."

"Did you see who did it?" asked Mikkelsen. Anita shook her head.

"Was he middle-aged and a bit heavyset, in a white mason's cap?" Louise asked, jumping into the conversation.

Anita looked at her and then shook her head again.

"No, that was the guy with me," she replied. "He took off when his wife sent him a text message reminding him to buy some milk on the way home."

She gave a hollow laugh as she turned around and started getting dressed with the door still open.

"He gave me an extra hundred," she said, pulling her blouse over her head. "I'm sure he heard the guy punching her too. He probably thought the big tip would get him out of any obligation to find out if she was all right."

"It happened before we got there," Mikkelsen said once they were again standing outside on Istedgade. "So it's impossible to know who did that to her."

Louise refrained from pointing out he hadn't asked the African girl to produce any ID. They had walked the woman over to the Nest—a shelter for prostitutes where they could rest, take a shower, and get a hot meal—so she could recover. The volunteers would also be able to find her a doctor if she needed to have the cut over her eyebrow stitched up. "Some johns think they can get away with damn near anything just because they shell out 300 kroner for a lay," Mikkelsen said after they dropped off the battered girl. "If the man can't get it up, then it's the girl's fault, and she has to be punished for failing to deliver."

He shook his head and they began walking back toward Halmtorvet, which was where they'd decided to start searching for witnesses who might have seen the murder victim in the area or noticed anything unusual around Skelbækgade the previous night.

5

On her way back to the *Morgenavisen* building, Camilla called her editor to expand on the brief text message she'd sent earlier. She promised there was enough material on the abandoned-baby story for it to carry the next day's front page, what with the pastor and the two boys' statements, and she told him she also wanted to go ahead with the story on the murdered prostitute in the Meatpacking District.

"I wonder why the baby was left in that church," Høyer said fifteen minutes later as he sat down on the extra chair in Camilla's office. "You would assume it was someone from the area, someone who was already familiar with the church, wouldn't you?"

Camilla shrugged and said the pastor hadn't been able to think of anyone who was pregnant and due around this time who was associated with the church in any way.

"The police are questioning people in the neighborhood, but neither Pastor Holm nor the boys saw anyone. I'm waiting to hear back from the hospital to find out what they have to say about the time of birth or any other details about the birth. Personally, I'm guessing the baby wasn't more than a few hours old. The techs are investigating whether the woman gave birth in the church or if she maybe just left the baby there."

"You should head out there and find out what people in the area have to say. I think there's a day care or a nursery school a little farther down the road. We should do the rounds. Also, talk to a couple of pregnant women who are due to give birth soon. See what they have to say about someone abandoning a baby right after birth."

Camilla could tell that he was looking for the right way to put it before he added that, of course, they should also take advantage of the fact that they had a sort of inside scoop.

"We ought to be way ahead of everyone else when we run the story tomorrow," he said, standing up.

Camilla nodded. Of course he would see it that way. For her part, she wasn't sure how she felt about having her own son suddenly in the public eye like this, but of course at the same time she could see that it would be hypocritical to insist that he be kept out of it since she spent most of her time trying to get eyewitnesses to talk.

"I'll start with writing about how they found her, and then we'll see what the police have to say about the towel she was wrapped in."

After Høyer left, Camilla took out her cell phone and looked at the pictures she'd managed to snap of the newborn. She hadn't told anyone she had them, nor was she planning to. She could still feel the baby's tiny body against her chest and was trying to remember what the mood in the pastor's kitchen had been like when she arrived. Markus described how the baby cried and cried, and Pastor Holm had said the cries went straight to his heart.

Well, she couldn't have been crying like that all night, Camilla thought as she browsed through the pictures she'd taken. Such a tiny baby wouldn't have the energy for that.

She hung up and then dialed Rasmus Hem at the Bellahøj precinct, whom she had met at the pastor's residence that morning.

"Have you determined the time of birth?" Camilla asked immediately after explaining that she was Markus's mother and they had met each other that morning.

"I don't recall your mentioning you were a reporter," he said frostily.

"Well, I really didn't think it was the right time to get into that. The only reason I was at the pastor's residence this morning was because my son was upset about what he had just seen. If I had been planning to exploit the situation, I would have been pressing you for details this morning. I held that little girl in my arms and I would really like to help reunite her with her mother."

The officer sighed and grumbled a little before finally continuing.

"As I believe I also told you this morning, I have no idea if being reunited with a mother who abandoned her would be the best thing for her. Perhaps it would be better for the baby to be adopted as soon as possible, so she can get a fresh start on life," he said. After a brief pause he added that that last part was off the record.

"Of course," Camilla said. For a second she agreed with him, but then she admitted to herself that despite a rough start, she still thought it was best for a child to be with the woman who gave birth to her. After all, she thought, the child should have a sense of being rooted in her identity later in life.

Officer Hem hissed tersely. "Most women can give birth to a child, but that is absolutely not the same thing as knowing how to be a mother."

Camilla didn't touch that, but she did jot the expression down in her notebook.

Instead, she repeated her question about the time of birth, and she wasn't surprised when he said the doctors estimated late last night or early that same morning.

"Did it happen in the church?"

"Too soon to say."

"Do you have anything on the towel?" she continued.

"Afraid not. It's from one of the big national chain stores, Føtex, we think. They sell hundreds of them every year, so it'll be impossible to find the buyer."

"But you are going to have it analyzed to possibly ID the mother?"

"Of course, but obviously the technicians need a little time, and then they'll have to run whatever DNA they find on it. We won't get the results back until next week at the earliest."

"How is she doing?" Camilla finally asked.

The officer's voice perked up. "I just came from over there, and she's spending most of her time sleeping like most newborns, so I'm guessing she's doing quite well." He added that the little girl had gotten something to eat and been cleaned up.

Camilla thanked him and gave him her number, even though she didn't expect he would call if anything new turned up on the case. She would follow up on it later, and in the meantime she would try to find out what they'd learned about the murder on Skelbækgade.

She called the chief of homicide at Police Headquarters, who impatiently referred her to Willumsen, but so far that was still a dead end. Willumsen and Camilla had butted heads on several occasions in the past. The first time was when a coworker of hers at the paper had been murdered because of a drug story the coworker was working on. It hadn't improved Camilla and Willumsen's relationship, either, when she quoted Willumsen in an article and made prominent mention that his title had recently changed from "detective superintendent" to the lesser-sounding "police superintendent" as a part of the police reorganization.

So now she sat here with her hand on the receiver, wondering whom she could call instead of Willumsen. She decided to start with Louise to find out who else had been assigned to the case.

Camilla and Louise had known each other since high school in Roskilde, and even though they were quite different in many ways, they had become best friends over the years. She dialed Louise's personal cell number.

"Actually, I'm on that case," Louise said.

Camilla could hear traffic noise in the background. "Am I bothering you? You sound like you're outside."

"It's fine. I'm on Sønder Boulevard. We're trying to find out who the girl was. I'll just step into a doorway so I can hear you better."

"Is there anything new? Have you found out where she was from?"

"No," Louise replied. "Apparently, no one saw anything."

"What happened out there in the Meatpacking District?"

Camilla realized Louise was stalling to avoid giving privileged information to the press, so she tried reassuring Louise that she was of course aware that the lead case investigator should actually be the source for all the information about the case, and it worked.

"Her throat was slit in the middle of the night," Louise continued, "but you won't get much further on the story right now. We're going to spend the rest of the day and evening canvassing for witnesses, and obviously, we're hoping that someone can help us ID her. I'm under the impression Willumsen is planning on releasing a picture of the victim sometime tomorrow, but you'll have to talk to him about that."

Camilla nodded at the phone, knowing she would have to accept going through official channels if she wanted more information, so she changed topics and told Louise about the abandoned baby that Markus and his friend had found.

"I think what shook Markus the most was that a mother just abandoned a newborn baby like that, leaving her lying there all alone. If they hadn't found her, she could have died."

"It must have been a terrible experience for him," Louise said, suddenly warm again, and concerned. She asked how Markus was doing now.

Although Louise didn't have any children of her own— and had maintained for years that one could easily have a happy and meaningful life without them—she was very close to Camilla's son. Sometimes Camilla even felt a little excluded when Markus and Louise were together.

"I think he's all right, but I suspect it'll stick with him for a while."

"Is there anything I can do?" Louise said, full of concern.

Camilla said he was still over at his friend's house.

"Then I'll call him tomorrow and tell him he's welcome to call me if there's anything I can do. Also, I'll try and see if I can find out how the baby girl is doing. Another division would be handling that case, so I haven't even heard about it—and clearly we have plenty of our own cases to keep us busy."

6

"Homicide Division, Louise Rick speaking."
She stifled a yawn. She and Lars had been out until one the night before, working with Mikkelsen and a couple of his people. As darkness had slowly fallen over the city, they had made contact with every living thing in the vicinity of the murder that could crawl or walk.

"This is the duty desk. Are you working on that murder down in the Meatpacking District?"

"Yeah, me and several other detectives," Louise said, leaning back in her chair.

"There's a man down here who'd like to talk to you. He says he has information that might pertain to the murder."

Louise was on her feet before she'd hung up the phone. The new security procedures at Copenhagen Police Head-quarters meant that no one was allowed to walk around freely in the building without identification. They were so strict about it that even the chief superintendent had been asked to show ID, because the desk clerk didn't recognize him—or maybe he did recognize him but didn't think he should be given any special treatment.

She took the stairs down and then a shortcut through the memorial garden for fallen officers before crossing the round courtyard in front of the building.

The man who was waiting for her had his hands in his pockets. She quickly estimated him to be somewhere in his midthirties. He was leaning against the wall, but when he saw her approaching, he started over to meet her. He had his red visitor's badge clipped to the pocket of his light blue, short-sleeved shirt under his leather jacket. His dark hair was neatly combed back.

Louise noted that his eyes wandered a bit as she approached. She introduced herself, and they walked back across the courtyard.

"You had something you wanted to tell me?" she prompted.

He nodded in silence. Only now did it occur to her that she wasn't sure he spoke Danish, but when she asked he smiled.

"Some," he said. He had a definite accent, but they wouldn't need an interpreter.

Lars had been out making a fresh pot of coffee when the front desk called, and so he cocked his head with a puzzled look when they came into the office and Louise asked the visitor to take a seat.

"Would you like a cup of coffee?" she offered, gesturing to the coffeepot. "Or some water?"

The man politely declined both.

Louise briefly explained to her partner that their visitor was here because he might have information about the woman in the Meatpacking District.

Lars eyed the man with curiosity. "Sounds good." He turned and looked back at Louise. "Would you like some privacy?"

She shook her head. It was fine if he stayed.

"Then I'll take notes," he offered and turned to his computer screen.

To put it mildly, Willumsen had not been particularly thrilled with the lack of progress in the case at the morning briefing. Louise had caught Lars's eyes during Willumsen's rant, and she could tell Lars agreed with her. Willumsen could shout and scream. They'd figured out a long time ago why his cases always got off to such a good start. It was quite simply because he selfishly dragged detectives in from the other groups without asking for permission, so his team had triple the usual manpower or more for the first few days. In this case, however, he had not commandeered people, which was obviously a sign that a prostitute's murder didn't rank very high on his priority list.

She put aside her thoughts of Willumsen and looked at her visitor, who was sitting with his hands folded in his lap.

"Let's start by getting your name and address," Louise said. She was eager to find out what had brought him in. You didn't get many freebies in cases like these, and so far, they hadn't had a single one.

"Miloš Vituk," he said and then helped Lars with the spelling. He said he was thirty-six and Serbian, but he'd been living in Denmark since 1995, when he had come to get away from the civil war.

Lars's coffee got cold while his fingers were busy pecking on his keyboard. Once the formalities were taken care of, he and Louise waited for the visitor to start, listening patiently as he cleared his throat a couple of times before he spoke.

"In the beginning of January, I was stopped on the street by a young woman when I came out of a shop down on Halmtorvet. She was very unhappy, crying, and said she was scared and needed help."

"Did you know her or had you ever seen her before?" Louise asked, raising an eyebrow.

After a moment's hesitation, he shrugged his shoulders. "I may have seen her a time or two, but I didn't know her name and I didn't know where she was from."

Louise nodded and asked him to continue.

"She seemed really shaken. She didn't speak any Danish, and I had a hard time understanding her English, but I said we could go get something warm to drink. She was shivering and definitely wasn't wearing enough clothing for how cold it was. But she didn't want to do that. She was very afraid. She kept looking around the whole time."

He spoke quickly, concentrating, clearly trying to remember all the details.

"She wanted me to drive her somewhere where they couldn't keep their eye on her." Louise refrained from interrupting, but jotted "who?" on her notepad.

"My car was parked on Valdemarsgade, so we drove out toward the Fishmarket, down that street that runs over the Sjælland Bridge and out to that big parking lot at Bella Center. The whole way there she just sat there crying."

"Did she tell you what she wanted?" Louise asked after the man stopped talking.

"Yes, she said she was being forced to work as a prostitute and was desperate to buy her way out so she could go home."

"What was her name?"

"Pavlína Branková. She was twenty-two and came from Ústí nad Labem in the Czech Republic. She said she was working as a prostitute against her will. They forced her with violence and threats, and she showed me some of the marks on her upper arms and the back of her neck from their beatings."

Louise wrote "they" this time.

"And now she's been murdered," Lars stated, pushing his cup of cold coffee away. Miloš Vituk quickly shook his head.

"No, God almighty!" he exclaimed and held up his hands as if to ward off bad news. So, Louise asked him to explain what the connection was between Pavlína and the crime on Skelbækgade. Instead of answering, he started explaining the rest of what she'd told him out in the Bella Center parking lot.

"Pavlína never knew her parents; she grew up in an orphanage with her sister who's two years younger. When she turned sixteen, she was too old to stay in the orphanage and she's been on the streets since then. Her sister followed her two years later, and they got by on their own until Pavlína was forced into the back seat of a car late one night and brought to Copenhagen."

"Who forced her?" Lars interrupted, trying to get a sense of whom Miloš was accusing of kidnapping the woman.

"Arian and Hamdi, both Albanians," Miloš Vituk said curtly. He explained that there had been two other girls from the Czech Republic in the car to Copenhagen, but Pavlína hadn't known either of them before.

"The man in the front seat didn't want them talking to each other. She doesn't remember much from the ride, but that's probably because they were drugged most of the way."

Now Louise was starting to wonder what Miloš's role in this story was, since he'd decided to go to the police. So she asked if he was still in touch with Pavlína.

He nodded and then stopped to think for a moment, as if considering how much he ought to tell her.

"I met her a few times," he said, and added that was only

when she'd been able to slip away without being discovered. "She was under surveillance most of the time, at the hotel where they put her up with another girl and whenever the girls were sent out onto the street. I said I wanted to help her, but didn't know what I should do. She said that she was under a lot of pressure because she couldn't earn as much as they demanded. She was paying for her room and board and for permission to use the street. At that point, she was about to collapse under the pressure, and I got the sense that that was her handlers' intention, to push her to the limit, to a point where she no longer had the energy to put up any resistance. One night I met her in front of Café Yrsa. In tears, she begged me to help her find the money to pay her way free, and she promised to pay it all back."

There was a pause that made the mood in the office feel somber, and each of them sat quietly until Louise broke the silence.

"Do you have any sense of why she stopped you that first time on the street?"

Miloš Vituk shook his head slightly, as if that question had been bothering him for a while.

"Maybe there just wasn't anyone else around right then as she was reaching the breaking point," he finally said, clearing his throat so his voice sounded more solid. "I don't believe in coincidences. People usually meet each other for a reason. That's also why I wanted to help her."

Louise studied him for a moment. He seemed a little naïve, she thought, but at least he was being honest.

"I told her to find out how much they wanted to let her go, so we met again a few days later. They were demanding 50,000 kroner to release her. I didn't have that much, but I agreed to meet them at a bar on Victoriagade and we negotiated that I could have her for 15,000 kroner."

"That's a fair amount of money considering that you didn't know much about her and only had her word that she'd pay you back," Louise interjected.

At the same time, it was a shockingly small amount to pay for a woman, but Mikkelsen had told them the night before that you could buy a foreign woman for 1,000 euros.

That was less than Louise paid for her mortgage every month.

Miloš nodded and shrugged. "I was starting to grow fond of her," he admitted. "So I paid the money and she moved into my apartment with me."

"Is she still working as a prostitute?" Louise wanted to know.

He shook his head vehemently and said they were dating now. "She wanted to go back to the Czech Republic and find her little sister and tell her about me. Everything happened so quickly the night she was abducted. Her sister didn't even know where she was," he reminded them. He then explained that Pavlína had taken a bus to Prague on March 10, and from there she had continued by train to Ústí nad Labem.

"And?" Louise prompted, waiting for Miloš to continue. "Weren't you worried that you would never see her again? After you'd paid all that money?"

He smiled and shook his head. "We talked to each other every day. But two weeks ago, she called me one night crying and yelling that they'd found her. One of Arian's contacts was following her, and she didn't dare go outside. She was afraid that they might take her sister this time if they saw the two of them together. She wanted me to come and get her."

Miloš Vituk seemed to deflate a little, preoccupied by his own account, and then he was overcome with a rage that made his voice rise.

"Last week, she disappeared from my apartment. I'd been out the whole day," he said. His voice suddenly sounded tired, and he took a deep breath before continuing. "When I got home, she was gone. Then later that night I got a brief call from her. She was sobbing and asked me to pay 80,000 kroner. She said they were going to send her back out onto the streets again to earn the money if she couldn't come up with it and they threatened to cut her throat if she tried to run away."

Finally, Louise thought, an indication of how this related to the case, just as she had been starting to think they would never get there. But considering that they didn't have any other leads and still had nothing else to go on, she realized that Miloš Vituk was currently the best chance they had at solving the case.

Lars asked Miloš what had happened after he'd left Pavlína in his apartment. Louise could picture the whole thing as Miloš explained how they'd tricked the young woman into opening the door and then forced her to go down to the Albanian club on Saxogade, where they locked her up in a little room in back after punching her several times.

"After I explained that I didn't have that much money, I spent the next few nights driving around looking for her. I thought that if I found her maybe we could talk our way out of the situation. The third night I spotted her down in front of the conference center, but at first, she refused to even talk to me. They'd told her that I refused to help her again and that I was responsible for her being sent back out onto the street."

"As far as I know, slavery was abolished two hundred years ago," Lars interjected drily into the conversation.

Miloš shrugged.

"Some people say there have never been as many slaves as there are today," Louise said. She then asked Miloš if he had heard from the two Albanians again.

"They ambushed me down on Istedgade later that same night. They knew I'd talked to her, and now they were demanding 100,000 kroner, but in return they promised that that would be their last demand for her. But they keep women like slaves, abuse them, and extort money from anyone who tries to help them, so I don't believe them," he concluded.

Well, you're certainly wise not to, Louise thought. She sat for a moment letting the story sink in. It wasn't news to her that women were being bought and sold in Copenhagen, but realistically speaking, you couldn't do as much about it as you might think because the few cases they'd seen had been hard to clear up. The women were typically in Denmark only for the three months they were legally allowed to stay without a residence permit, and then they were off again, usually shipped on to some other country. And Louise had no doubt that most of the girls had been coerced into saying they were doing it voluntarily.

"I had just been in touch with someone who was going to help me get the money, so I said I would pay, but then this morning they sent me a message that the price had gone up to 120,000 kroner because it had taken me so long to show any interest."

"Does this have anything to do with the woman we found on Skelbækgade?" Louise asked, eyeing him earnestly.

He hesitated a bit before responding that, of course, he couldn't say for sure, but the threats the Albanians had made regarding Pavlína sounded the same as what had happened to the victim.

"And now you're asking us to catch these two men, Arian and Hamdi?" Lars concluded.

Miloš nodded and looked uncertain for the first time, as if he'd just sicced some pit bulls on a couple of little boys.

"How do we find them?" Louise asked. "And what are you planning to do?"

"I'm not sure—you might be able to find them at the club on Saxogade. I guess for me, I've decided to trust that they'll let her go this time, so I'll pay what they're asking," he said. "But I've told them that she has to be there when I get there, otherwise I won't pay. And I have to get her before they can have the money."

"When?" Lars asked.

"Tonight at six p.m.," he replied.

"What do the two Albanians look like?" Louise asked.

"Arian has shoulder-length hair"—Miloš gestured with his hands—"and he wears glasses. Hamdi has short hair and is short and thin."

A slight smile crossed Lars's lips as he jotted down the descriptions. Half the people they encountered on Istedgade would match that description.

"We're going to have to talk to Pavlína as well and find out if she knows anything about the woman who was killed. We'll need her help if we're going to try to put a stop to those two and their trade in Czech women," Louise said.

"Of course," Miloš said, "but I think she'd prefer to be free to come in on her own."

"We could meet in the parking lot at Bella Center, where the two of you went that time, if that would make her feel safer," Lars suggested.

Miloš nodded and promised to get back to them once he'd paid the money and she was hopefully back home again.

He didn't say anything as Louise escorted him back downstairs, but when they parted he thanked her for taking on the case and helping him so the Albanians couldn't continue with their outrageous extortion.

Willumsen was standing in their office when she got back upstairs. Lars had filled him in about their visitor and was just explaining how the Albanians had kidnapped Pavlína and sent her back out onto the street after Miloš paid for her freedom.

"Shouldn't we move in as he hands over the money?" Louise asked, eyeing Willumsen.

Toft stopped on his way down the hall and leaned against the doorframe to listen in.

He had one of those plastic nicotine inhalers in his mouth that he always used, a sorry substitute for the cigarettes he used to smoke until the total ban on indoor smoking went into effect at Police HQ. In the beginning, Louise had thought they were to help him quit smoking, but as time went by she realized her colleague had simply replaced his cigarettes with the nicotine from the Nicorette product so he wouldn't have to keep running outside every time he wanted to smoke.

Willumsen stroked his chin, clearly lost in thought.

"So he thinks the two Albanians might have some connection to the woman we found? I don't think there's enough here for us to get involved yet," Willumsen opined. "Instead let's try to figure out what's going on and how big a network we're talking about. Try to get a sense for the organization the Albanians are part of so we're sure we wrap up the whole syndicate when we do strike."

"Where was the girl living until the Serb bought her and she moved in with him?" Toft asked, stuffing his hands into the angled front pockets of his corduroy pants and looking at Louise.

"At one of the cheap hotels on one of the side streets coming off Istedgade," she replied.

"Maybe we should do a round of the hotels in the area with a picture of our murdered woman and find out if anyone knew her," Toft suggested.

Willumsen nodded to him. "Do that. If that doesn't give us any leads, we'll go back again after Rick and Lars have talked to the Czech woman. Surely she can show us where she was staying," he added.

"If she can recognize it. You hear about how these women are kept on such a short leash they never see anything other than the inside of the room they're kept locked in and the stretch of street where they earn the money," Toft interjected.

"We could also take a little look at the Albanian club," Lars suggested, but Willumsen waved Lars off the idea.

"For now, let's focus our attention on the Skelbækgade woman," he decided. "Once we get through with that, you can look into this other situation."

He lowered his hand again.

"I'm not ruling out a possible connection between the two. But I want to know who the dead woman is first, and until we have a name we're not going to get very far."

Willumsen adjourned the meeting and quickly departed.

7

Camilla had spent most of the day following up on her story about the baby abandoned in the church, even though she didn't make it into her office until after eleven.

Markus had woken up several times with terrifying nightmares about her abandoning him and never coming back, and Camilla had no idea what time he had stumbled into her room with his blanket under his arm, sobbing. He lay down beside her, and she stroked his hair until he settled down again.

"If we'd left for school earlier, we might have seen the mother," Markus said while they were eating breakfast. "And then we could have stopped it from happening."

Camilla had tried to explain to him that there were many reasons why a mother might choose to leave her child.

"Maybe she did it for the sake of the child, because she knew she would never be able to give the little girl the life she thought the child ought to have. And that she would be better off if she were adopted by someone else."

Camilla could see from Markus's expression that he didn't understand how it could be better for the little girl to wind up with strangers instead of her actual mother.

"You do know that it's very hard for a grown-up to be accepted as a foster parent, let alone an adoptive parent, don't you?" Camilla asked him. "You have to be preapproved so everyone is sure that you're suited to taking care of a child. And that you'll make sure the child has a loving, secure place to grow up in. It's a big responsibility. Maybe this was the best thing that could happen to that little girl if her own mother couldn't handle that responsibility."

Camilla hoped she sounded convincing enough to put the worst of her son's fears to rest.

They sat at the breakfast table for a long time. Finally, she got up and cleared away the Nutella and cardamom rolls and put the butter back in the fridge. Then she called the pastor to ask if he and Jonas wanted to come over for dinner so the boys could talk a little more about what they'd been through. She explained that the previous day's experiences had made quite an impression on Markus, and it turned out that Pastor Holm had decided to keep Jonas home from school for the same reason. He invited Camilla and Markus to come over to his place for dinner. When he said that Markus was welcome to come over right away if he wanted, Camilla decided to let her son play hooky along with his buddy.

They biked over to the pastor's residence together. Camilla put Markus's laptop with *World of Warcraft* in the basket on the front of her bike and followed him on the bike path. When they reached the church, she walked out back to the attached pastor's residence with Markus and knocked twice with the heavy door knocker before kissing him on both cheeks and promising that she would try to finish work at a reasonable hour. She smiled at Markus's friend when he yanked open the door and dragged Markus inside so they could start playing. She could see the pastor sitting at his computer in the living room and waved to him before shutting the door again and pushing her bike back down the drive to head to *Morgenavisen*.

When she called Frederiksberg Hospital, Camilla learned that the baby girl was still in the hospital; the doctor thought the infant would be there for a week or two longer until she was sent on to Skodsborg Orphanage.

"Unless the mother turns up before then," he added.

Then she called the social services office and spoke to a woman who was also really hoping the mother would come forward. She made it clear that they would be lenient on a woman who had left her child that way. She didn't need to be afraid of prosecution, because what was important now was looking toward the future, and they would offer her whatever help she might need.

When she finally got hold of the right social worker who could tell her how the system worked, Camilla asked, "If the mother comes forward now, will she be allowed to take the child home with her?"

"No," Tanya Jensen replied without hesitation. "First there will be a period for the two of them to get to know each other, and the child will remain with the orphanage during that time. Obviously, we must be convinced the mother can take care of the little girl now."

"And what if she can't?"

"Well, then we absolutely couldn't allow her to take the child home," she replied after a moment's contemplation.

Camilla wondered how they evaluated that. The story of a mentally disabled woman who received assistance from the Danish government to be artificially inseminated only to have the same government authorities turn right around and take her child away the minute it was born was still fresh in her mind. Who decided who was suitable, and what was the decision based on?

Camilla took a deep breath and decided not to ask that question.

"Let's say the mother doesn't show up," she said instead. "Then the child will be put up for adoption. When will that happen?"

Camilla had the sense that Tanya Jensen suddenly became a little less forthcoming. "Hard to say. The biological mother should always have the chance to change her mind. She may be suffering from postpartum depression, and she may need a while to come out of that."

Camilla interrupted her. "Well, surely there must be a limit to how long the little girl has to wait in limbo to see if her mother is going to change her mind?"

"Of course. We're not talking about limbo, as you call it. There's always a waiting period for any adoption, even ones that have been planned for the whole pregnancy, and that's true in this case, too."

"How long is it?" Camilla wanted to know.

"We figure it will take a couple of months before the child can be placed into her new family," the social worker explained.

After that, Camilla talked to a psychologist who strongly rejected the notion that a child who had been abandoned by its mother would suffer any permanent sense of loss.

"Of course, a newborn is affected when something is missing—eye contact, for example," Camilla wrote and further quoted the psychologist: "This is why it is essential for other people to start caring for an abandoned child quickly. But the most important thing is for the child to establish fundamental, basic trust either in her biological parents or in other people. The vast majority of children, four-fifths, will do well so long as that trust is there early on. The last fifth will have some problems, and a very small number will suffer serious harm. In those cases, a good outcome will depend on finding a family that can create a secure enough environment for the child."

Camilla's own writing suddenly struck her as too impersonal. She pictured the little girl in her mind. What about that last fifth? Oh, she wished she knew if the baby would end up in that group; she thought she would end the article with the psychologist's statement that there was really only one researcher out there who claimed people could recall their own births—so this little girl's loss should by no means cause irreparable harm.

Earlier she had stopped by the church with the paper's photographer in tow and watched police using tracking dogs in the area. But when she called Rasmus Hem about the dogs, he said the police still didn't have anything to go on.

Once Camilla finished her article and submitted it to her editor, she packed up her bag. She checked with the police to see if there was any news in the search for the mother. She had also been trying to get in touch with the coroner who'd been out to the Meatpacking District Sunday night. In sheer irritation at the lack of interest her proposal had aroused at the editorial meeting, she was going to pick the case of the murdered woman back up and pursue it until she had enough material to run the story by her boss again. Kvist was staying in a hotel out in Silkeborg and had an interview lined up with one of the well-to-do married couples the art-theft ring had targeted.

"Detective Larsen still isn't in, and to be quite honest, I don't think he will be in today. He gave a lecture at National Hospital today and then went straight home from there, I believe," said the receptionist at the pathology lab, where Camilla had given one last try before she headed home. "He'll be off for the rest of the week."

"Could you give me his cell number so I can contact him?" Camilla asked.

"Unfortunately, I can't give that to you," the woman said.

Camilla tried again. "Well, could I have you call him and leave a message to contact me?"

Sometimes that worked. Other times it annoyed people that she was assuming they had time to waste helping her.

"I can't promise I can get hold of him, but I'd be happy to leave a message," the woman agreed, and Camilla thanked her profusely.

8

Camilla had offered to pick up some dinner and bring it over to the pastor's residence, but Henrik Holm wouldn't hear of it. Instead, she brought a few bottles of soda in her bike basket.

"The boys are up in Jonas's room. They have a visitor," Henrik told her with a grin as she walked in and set her basket on the kitchen table.

She looked at him in surprise. He was standing at the stove stirring a pot that smelled of chicken and spices. She asked who the guest was.

"A good friend of yours, I understood. Markus asked very politely if it would be OK if she came over to talk to Jonas and him."

The pastor smiled when he saw Camilla's face stiffen.

"It's not a journalist," he reassured her quickly. "And your son seemed very happy to see her."

She relaxed and went upstairs to see if it was who she suspected.

Louise was sitting on the thick cushions on the floor with one boy on either side, and when Camilla stuck her head in, Louise was explaining what the police usually did about abandoned babies.

Louise flashed a smile at Camilla and then continued explaining the procedure, how the police would search for the mother in hospitals.

"We go through lists of women who are due to give birth around that time. Using the lists, we contact those women. Some of them have already had their babies and are busy taking care of them, while others are still walking around with their big bellies, looking forward to the birth."

Markus was holding Louise's hand as she spoke, and Jonas's eyes didn't leave her face.

"And then once in a while we find a woman who no longer has a big belly and who isn't busy with a new baby—and those are the mothers we're interested in, of course," Louise said. "But there can be lots of reasons why they don't have the child. Usually it's because the baby died before the birth or maybe right afterward."

Both boys' eyes were wide and they seemed to be holding their breath.

Typical Louise, Camilla thought with a little smile. She was not dumbing it down for the kids. She was telling it like it is. And it usually turned out that was actually what they liked best, even though the reality sometimes shocked them.

She went back down to the kitchen to help with dinner, and before she quite realized it she was telling the pastor about the previous night.

"I wasn't prepared for the fact that it had made such a strong impression on Markus," she admitted, then offered to set the table.

"Jonas woke up, too, and came into my room. I suppose an experience like that will affect them for a while," he said, then added that Louise was welcome to stay for dinner if she wanted. "There's plenty of food."

Camilla smiled at him and explained that she and Louise had known each other since high school in Roskilde.

"She works in homicide with the Copenhagen PD, and she's also Markus's godmother. Maybe I should have thought of it myself, asking her to come over and have a chat with them. But it's good that they figure these things out on their own without my help."

As Camilla set out the plates, she admitted that the event had also affected her more than she would have thought. "I keep feeling that tiny little body against me."

The pastor poured wine and lit the candles. Then he gestured to the bench, and they sat across from each other and waited for the rice to finish cooking.

"Little kids who are suddenly left without parents always make a big impression," he said. "They're so tremendously vulnerable."

He explained that many years before he had worked in a refugee camp in Bosnia.

"I had just become a pastor and really wanted to make a difference somewhere before I found a permanent parish position. My wife and I went and worked at the camp for two years, and it's never quite left me. Especially the children who'd lost their families in the war."

Camilla didn't have any trouble picturing him in a place like that, but this was the first time he'd mentioned his wife.

"My wife died when Jonas was four," Henrik continued, interrupting her train of thought. "She was born with a rare blood disease, which in the best-case scenario she might have lived her whole life with. But she wasn't that lucky."

The timer went off for the rice and Henrik got up.

Camilla watched him. He seemed as though he'd put the worst of it behind him. She felt safe in his company as she took the pot he passed across the table to her and he called the boys down.

Louise was in the lead when they came downstairs.

"We set a place for you," Henrik said, gesturing to the table. Louise smiled at Jonas when he invited her to sit next to him.

"That's so nice of you," she said, "but I have to get home. I haven't gotten much sleep the last couple of nights, so I'm planning to turn in early tonight."

Both boys stood in the kitchen doorway waving as she left.

"She's supercool," Jonas said, clearly filled with admiration as he moved over to the table. "She knew all about how the police work and what they do when they find a little baby that's been abandoned like that. Plus, she was really nice."

Camilla could tell how proud her son was that Louise had made such a good impression on his buddy.

"Maybe we should watch the news?" Jonas suggested, looking at his dad. "Maybe there's some news about the baby."

Camilla got the sense that Henrik was about to say no, but instead he shrugged his shoulders and then asked her if she minded.

Jonas took that as a yes and turned on the TV that was mounted on the wall. It showed commercials at first, but then the news came on, leading with the abandoned-baby story for the second day in a row. The first image shown was of the blue towel; the police deputy superintendent was holding it up as he explained that the baby had been wrapped in a towel just like it when she was found at Stenhøj Church.

The news crew had done their job well—they had taken plenty of footage of the pastor's residence and street while the CSI techs were working at the church the day before.

"As we indicated yesterday, the towel is sold at Føtex, so we have little expectation of identifying the mother that way," the superintendent said, answering the reporter's question with a discouraged smile, before he changed topics and turned serious again.

Camilla watched her son dish chicken and rice onto his plate, his eyes glued to the screen, hanging on every word as the deputy superintendent explained that they had been assuming the baby was born inside the church itself, because they believed it was a relatively short time between the birth and the baby's discovery. But without technical evidence to support this theory, they couldn't be sure, so the police were eager to hear from any witnesses who had seen or heard anything around Stenhøj Church in the early-morning hours that day.

"Well, they didn't say anything about that when I talked to them this afternoon!" Camilla exclaimed in irritation.

"Aren't they going to show a picture of the baby?" Jonas asked, looking at his dad. "So her parents can see how cute she is?"

A second later, a large picture filled the screen. Sound asleep, she was lying on a white pillow with all her dark hair surrounding her tiny head like a wreath.

Camilla felt her eyes mist over and hurriedly looked away when the cameraman zoomed out a little so the viewers could see that the girl was lying in the arms of a nurse who was saying the abandoned baby was doing well but missed her mother.

Camilla was annoyed the police hadn't told her that they were going to run the baby's picture on the news. Now she was going to have to go back to the paper and make sure they had a picture from the hospital to print alongside her article in the next day's paper. And she was also going to have to rework the article to mention the police now thought the baby might not have been born in the church where she was found. If Camilla didn't get these latest developments in, she would be way behind the other press coverage when the paper hit the streets.

Just then, the doorbell rang.

"Oh yeah," Henrik said, standing up. "I should have anticipated visitors what with the church on the news and all."

He went to answer the door, and a second later he came back with a tall young woman who wore her dark hair in a pageboy cut and a lot of mascara around her eyes. She was pale and she seemed a little nervous.

She was in her late twenties, Camilla guessed. She started to clear the table while the boys got up, thanked the pastor for the meal, put their plates in the sink, and disappeared back upstairs to their computer game.

She heard Henrik invite the woman inside and then ask what he could do for her. Camilla was assuming the visit had to do with Baby Girl, as the press had started calling the abandoned newborn, but the woman had come looking for work, obviously under the impression the pastor was looking for a housekeeper.

"No," Henrik said in English, "there must be a misunderstanding." He held out his hands apologetically. "I don't know who gave you that impression. But I will be happy to let you know if I hear of someone looking for one," he offered.

The woman quickly shook her head and explained she had been referred to him by a friend of her family.

She pulled out a slip of paper that, sure enough, had Henrik Holm's name and address printed neatly on it.

The pastor sat down with the slip of paper in his hand. It didn't say anything else, and the woman didn't have the name of the friend who had sent her to him.

"I don't know who gave you my name, and I'm very sorry not to be able to help. It's just my son and me living here, and I can manage the housekeeping on my own. But please give me your phone number. If you stop by again next week, I'll ask around to see if I know anyone who's looking for help with their housework."

She shook her head again and looked disappointed as he stood up to show her out. Meanwhile, Camilla called Markus to say she had to go back to the office.

"He's welcome to spend the night," Henrik offered when he returned from the door. "You can just swing by and drop off his backpack before school tomorrow."

He thanked her for loading and starting the dishwasher and apologized for leaving the cleanup to her.

"Do people often stop by the way that woman did?" Camilla asked, nodding at the front door.

"No, not often," Henrik said, explaining that the people who did stop by usually needed to talk and didn't have any-one else to talk to. Sometimes someone would spend a night or two if they didn't have anywhere else to go, such as a husband or wife going through a divorce, or people who were grieving.

Camilla looked at him and felt a flicker of admiration. She had a hard time finding the energy for that sort of thing herself.

"But this is the first time since I've been here that some-one has come thinking I needed a housekeeper," he said with a smile.

Markus kissed his mother good-bye, and Jonas hollered a hoarse "Bye" down the stairs.

"The hoarseness is chronic," Henrik explained with a smile. "In the beginning, we thought he would just get over it and then when it didn't go away, we assumed it was asthma, but he doesn't have any trouble breathing. It turned out to be a condition called multiple laryngeal papillomas, which are little bumps on his vocal cords." He added that you could have them removed with a laser if you didn't want to wait until puberty, when they would probably disappear on their own.

"No, well, then I don't suppose there's any reason to do it if they're not bothering him," Camilla protested.

Once Markus had planted yet another kiss on her cheek and she was in the kitchen doorway with her jacket on, she thanked Henrik for letting Markus spend the night.

"If anything at all comes up, just call," she told Henrik. Her son had assured her that he was totally cool with spending the night, even though he'd had a rough time the night before. "Markus says he's put the whole thing behind him."

"I'll keep an eye on him," the pastor promised. He pointed out that his bedroom was right next to Jonas's. Then Henrik held the door for her and waved as she left.

9

"Miloš just got Pavlína released," Lars said, as Louise stepped into their office on Wednesday morning, carrying the basket from the front of her bike.

She stopped abruptly in the doorway. Her thoughts had been somewhere else entirely. She had just managed to catch Markus on his cell phone while he and Jonas were on their way to school. She asked if they'd slept well, and both boys had assured her they were doing fine and that they had put their fears behind them. That had made her smile, but now she stared at her partner in surprise.

"Did you talk to him?" she asked.

Lars shook his head and explained that he'd just been out to the witness's address and found Miloš had been about to leave.

"He went into Spunk, a bar down on Istedgade, and it didn't take long before he came out again with a girl on his arm. Then they went back to his apartment."

Louise watched him for a second from her desk chair before she said anything. "Why didn't you say you were going to drive over there? I would've come with you."

"Yeah, well, I wasn't planning on it. It just hit me as I was sitting in the car about to head home," Lars said in his own defense. "If I'd planned on going, of course I would have told you."

"And then what?" Louise asked.

"Then? Then nothing. I drove home once they'd gone in the front door. But it is totally repugnant that you can just go out and buy a woman like that."

Louise agreed with him wholeheartedly and looked up at the clock. They had an office lunch every Wednesday, and it was their team's turn to provide the food this week, so she'd stopped by Hauen Bakery on her way in and filled her bike basket with Danish bread and rolls.

"We'd better go put some coffee on," she said, getting up.

"Done," Lars said. "I also tidied up the kitchen and emptied the dishwasher."

Louise sat down again. "What the hell's up with you? Is something wrong at home?" she asked. Not that Lars usually shirked his share of kitchen duty, but they usually did the less than appealing cleanup together. Each team was responsible for making sure the lunchroom was clean and for running the dishwasher during their assigned week.

"It's nothing serious," Lars said. "I just needed a little space from home." He got up and retrieved the bread from her bike basket.

"Let's go in and hear what they have to say."

Louise got up and followed him, deciding not to pry any further into his home life for now. She was all too familiar with that feeling, and she respected him for taking the space he needed for himself.

"I understand there's news in the Skelbækgade case," Suhr began once everyone had helped themselves to bread and their coffee cups were full.

He looked at Louise and Lars, who both nodded and explained that they had received a visit from Miloš Vituk. Lars added that afterward he had driven by the witness's address and followed him and seen that he had a girl with him.

Louise saw Willumsen furrow his brow, and it looked like he was going to say something, but Suhr beat him to it.

"Interesting," Suhr said. "We'll have to run a check on the two Albanians. But maybe that's already been initiated?"

Willumsen shook his head and confessed that he had decided they should observe for a little longer before they put anything bigger in motion, but in light of what Lars had seen, there was probable cause to believe there was something to the Serb's story.

"Let's identify the two people we're talking about— Arian and Hamdi—with their full names so we can get a court order and set up a wiretap," Willumsen said. He asked Toft and Michael Stig to take care of that.

Suhr nodded and pulled a hand through his short gray hair. He turned to Louise and Lars and asked if they thought they needed a court order for Miloš Vituk also, or if they believed his story.

"We probably ought to, since he intentionally caused trouble for the two Albanians by putting them in our crosshairs," Louise admitted with a nod. "But it seemed more like he came in because he was starting to fear that they were just going to keep raising their extortion price."

"First of all, we have to determine if any laws have actually been broken," Willumsen said. "We all know how hard it can be to figure out if something is common procuring or if it is in fact a case of trafficking in women. Meanwhile, if the two Albanians might be connected to the murder in some way, then we're interested in them."

His eyes wandered around the table and stopped on Stig, who signaled that he wanted to say something.

"Then we have to keep the pressure on that whole scene and try to get someone to start to move," Stig suggested.

Louise followed him with her eyes as he tipped forward in his chair and started rapidly tapping his pen against the table, filling the room with loud clicking sounds. It was a bad habit he had that had bugged Louise for years. Now she looked away, forcing herself to ignore the pen.

"And they say," Stig continued, pausing for dramatic effect, "that the girls, the Eastern European ones, have to pay about 400 kroner a day. Someone cons them into thinking they own the street and the girls have to pay to work there."

He leaned back and tossed his pen onto the table.

Louise sighed, glad that Mikkelsen wasn't here to hear him. That would have sent his blood pressure through the roof.

"We should keep that in the backs of our minds," Stig added, looking from Willumsen to Suhr. "Because if the same men are working with the trafficked girls, we ought to be able to spot them by keeping an eye on the money when it's handed over. There must be a discernable pattern."

Louise couldn't hold her tongue any longer. "It is absolutely true that someone has made a sham business of extorting money from the people on the bottom of the food chain on the street, but there are also quite a few Danish prostitutes who've figured out that there's money to be earned that way, so they are also demanding money from some of their fellow prostitutes. It's turned into a regular business practice. Everyone's cashing in on it in their struggles to make money," she said, her eye trained on Stig's pen, which was about to roll off the edge of the table.

Stig flashed her an irritated look. He squinted his eyes a little and was about to respond, but Willumsen beat him to it and assigned the next task to Stig with a subtle gesture of his index finger.

"That is exactly what I want you to check out. Set up surveillance on the area and keep an eye on the girls. Don't do anything. Just find out if there's a pattern."

Louise glanced away to avoid the look she was sure Stig was giving her. What Willumsen was asking of him was going to require some real legwork, but she didn't feel sorry for him. He'd brought it on himself.

After the meeting, they milled about in the hallway for a bit outside Louise and Lars's office. "Do we know anything about the two Albanian men yet?" Toft asked, looking at Louise and her partner. They both shook their heads.

"I'd be surprised if Mikkelsen couldn't tell us who they are," Toft said, offering to call his old friend. He and Mikkelsen had been partners for the brief period Mikkelsen worked as a plainclothes officer keeping an eye out for disorderly conduct.

"I'd really like to have a chat with Pavlína," Louise said, looking at Lars, who concurred.

Willumsen nodded and said, "Do that as quickly as possible. It'll be interesting to hear her version."

"I'll contact Miloš Vituk and set up a meeting." Louise nodded. "And then I was thinking that we ought to do a round of all the brothels and massage parlors in the neighborhood and see if the woman might have worked in any of them."

Willumsen nodded at the latter suggestion before turning back to Stig.

"We can certainly start putting pressure on the street scene, as you suggested," Willumsen said, "but make sure it's not too obvious, because then our folks will be way too easy to spot later if we seriously need to keep an eye on them."

He looked around at everyone again to make sure they understood he was serious. The bottom line, really, was that they wouldn't have an unlimited amount of manpower to call on if there happened to be a major break in the case.

10

Camilla felt sad and empty inside as she set her bag of beer bottles on the counter. She pulled one leg up under her, removed the first lid, and took a swig out of the bottle. Markus had gone to his dad's house after school and was going to be with him for the weekend; it was his grandmother's birthday, and the whole family was staying at an inn. Camilla was planning to spend the rest of the day and evening enjoying all the beer she could drink while she sniffed around Skelbækgade and Halmtorvet, and took a stroll up Istedgade. She changed from her skirt and high heels into jeans and rain boots. She wasn't planning for this to be an investigative reporting trip. She was just curious to see what Copenhagen's prostitution scene looked like at the street level.

She had had yet another run-in with her editor. It had all started when Terkel Høyer arrived that morning and slammed his office door behind him. A minute later the phone on Camilla's desk rang.

He was yelling when he told her that the free alternative paper had run a big interview with a woman—featuring her name and picture—who had come forward to say she had seen a young mother outside the church with a bundle in her arms. The woman also claimed she saw her open the door to the church and after a moment come back out empty-handed, then disappear down Stenhøj Allé.

Høyer lowered his voice a little and asked her to come to his office.

It turned out the article, which continued inside the paper, described what the mother looked like in detail, with long blond hair pulled back into a ponytail. Not very old, maybe just a teenager. No, she hadn't been with anyone, and she had gone quickly into the church and quickly come back out. And no, the woman didn't think she'd seen her before. So it couldn't be someone who lived on the street, because she thought she'd recognize most of the women who lived along this section of the wide suburban avenue in Frederiksberg, actually a separate city surrounded by Copenhagen on all sides. The witness stated that she even knew "the ones in the large mansion on the corner at the end of the street. Well, don't know them socially, that is," she was quoted as saying, "just what they looked like."

Camilla threw the newspaper onto Høyer's desk after skimming the story and beat him to it by asking why they hadn't scooped the story.

"Don't you wonder why she chose to take such an important witness statement to a free paper instead of telling the police what she saw?"

Høyer twitched in his chair and spluttered angrily into her face that he couldn't be bothered to wonder about things like that, because that wasn't what sold real newspapers like theirs. She turned her back to him and returned to her office.

First, she called the Bellahøj precinct to find out if they knew about this witness and ask why they hadn't mentioned it to her the day before when she last spoke to them. The officer on duty claimed he hadn't heard about any new witnesses. Then she called her own source, Rasmus

Hem, whom she'd met at the pastor's residence when the baby was found. The officer sounded sincere when he vehemently insisted he had never heard of the woman who'd given her statement in the free paper. He flatly denied it was because they hadn't been persistent enough looking for witnesses.

"But we did bring her in for questioning this morning," he added begrudgingly.

Camilla decided to head over to the precinct to hear the woman's explanation firsthand and—as she had to admit—to steer clear of Høyer, who was still pissed off. Before she could leave the building, however, Camilla's morning got even worse when the paper's longtime photo editor suddenly appeared in her office doorway. He asked her how the hell a journalism student from one of the smallest papers in the country had scooped them on this angle while Camilla kept claiming there was no new information to run about the case.

Holck, as he was called, said she should know this was exactly the type of case that appealed to their readers: Children and dogs! That's what sells papers! And then he took a few steps into her office, glaring at her the whole time, saying he was starting to doubt she could handle the story professionally since her own son was involved.

What a day it had been. Camilla drank half of her beer in one gulp. It had been a long time since she'd sat on a bench drinking beer out of a bottle—and maybe it was a mistake, she thought as she emptied it. But there was something that felt liberating and reckless about sitting out here alone without having to be accountable to anyone.

She had lost it with Holck, yelling at him that first of all, it most certainly was not a journalism student but an extremely well-paid, established journalist that the free paper had hired from Denmark's premier newspaper, *Berlingske*; and second of all, she was way fucking closer to the story than any of these other reporters, because she had held that little baby in her arms. She was not done making her point when Holck walked right over to her, leaned in over her desk, picked up her cell phone, and pointed to its camera lens.

"Well, if you think you're such a great damn journalist, then why didn't you so much as snap one single measly picture of Baby Girl with your handy-dandy little phone?"

She hadn't been able to stop herself before she snatched the phone out of his hand and showed him the picture. He accused her of being disloyal to the paper, possessing poor judgment, and being incompetent—which was when she stormed out.

But before she made it out of the building, she called Høyer and told him it was true. Then she recused herself and said she couldn't cover the story since Markus was one of the witnesses. She said good-bye before he could respond, but could just hear Holck starting to rant in the background as she hung up.

Camilla jumped slightly as a man sat down on the other side of the bench.

After she had stormed out, she ended up heading out to the Bellahøj precinct anyway and had waited for three hours until she learned that there wasn't anything to the woman's statement. Then Officer Hem invited her to coffee. He seemed tired as he explained that a reporter had rung the witness's doorbell right after the nine o'clock news on TV. The witness had let the reporter in, a charming, attractive man who seemed polite and interested. And without really knowing what had happened, the witness told him she'd seen a young woman with the bundle in her arms. The reporter had seemed so disappointed the first time when she said she hadn't seen anything. And then he took her out for a stroll past the church and then one word had just sort of followed another.

"Are you sure she's telling the truth now?" Camilla asked Hem.

Hem nodded, adding they knew the mother had not opened the church door as the witness claimed, because the CSI techs had dusted the handle thoroughly for prints, and there were no fingerprints or even smudged prints from someone wearing gloves—which meant someone had gone out of their way to remove them.

Camilla had the feeling that the man sitting at the other end of her bench was watching her, and for a second she felt the unease of trespassing into a world where she didn't belong. But what the fuck. She had as much right as anyone to sit here on a public bench drinking a beer, even if this wasn't her neighborhood.

When she turned to look at him, she realized he wasn't looking at her but at her bag of beer bottles. She smiled and offered him one.

"Thanks," he said, taking it. They sat together in silence watching the traffic and passersby.

"That guy there is the Meat Meister," the man said, raising his beer in the air in salute as a large Jaguar drove past them out of the Meatpacking District. The car returned his salute with a quick honk.

The Jaguar was certainly opulent compared to the man beside her in his gabardine pants, which must have been fashionable at some point in the distant past, but now they were threadbare. His shirt collar curled up through his worn blue sweater, and he seemed generally old-fashioned and unkempt.

Camilla turned toward him in curiosity. "How do you know the guy in the Jag?" she asked, pulling two more beers out of the bag.

He gallantly offered to open them and stuck the lids in his pocket instead of tossing them on the ground as so many before them had obviously done.

"I used to be one of his biggest customers. He was new back then and a little too expensive, but his product was better than anything else that was out there. So, I had faith in him, and that laid the foundation for the business that has made him rich."

Suddenly, Camilla thought back to the drug kingpin with whom she herself had crossed paths—Klaus West trafficked a drug known on the streets as "green dust." He might also have been driving around in a Jaguar if he hadn't wound up behind bars.

"Nice car," Camilla said, watching it as it disappeared.

The man was lost in thought for a bit, but then he finished his beer and mumbled, "That was some fucking good meat that one time. We drove a van with forty servings of tournedos Rossini with foie gras, truffles, and everything else down to the French Riviera for a big fête for Roger Vergé himself. Oh, the Moulin de Mougins!"

Suddenly the man turned to look at Camilla and his eyes seemed present again. "What a chef," he said, waiting to see if she had any idea who he was talking about.

"I'm talking about Paul Bocuse, the Troigros brothers, they were all there. But that night the Danish Gastronomic Academy was honoring Roger Vergé because his new cookbook had just been released in Danish translation. They even awarded him some sort of honorary degree."

The man reached over and pulled another beer out of Camilla's bag. Again, she could see that his mind was lost in the past.

"Monsieur Vergé came down to the kitchen afterward and admitted that he'd never had such good meat before."

He drank a practiced swig of his beer.

"There's a picture of the two of us together," he remembered, smiling.

Out of the corner of her eye, Camilla spotted two men talking to a young woman. She was fairly sure one of the men was Detective Michael Stig from Louise's division, and she recognized two more police officers standing a little farther over toward Halmtorvet.

The man next to her kept talking and drank more of her beer while she kept her eyes trained on the street. She could see a fair number of people from her vantage point on Sønder Boulevard, with practically the whole Meatpacking District in front of her, and she had a good view up Skelbækgade. Istedgade ran parallel behind her and Halmtorvet was to her left.

A car stopped and quickly picked up a girl before disappearing again. Camilla didn't stop watching until she noticed that the man next to her was holding out his hand.

"I'm Kaj," he said, introducing himself, his hand wrapping around hers in a firm handshake.

"Camilla," she said with a sigh. When he asked what she did, she replied, "I'm a reporter, and right now I'm so sick of it that I just might start making food or selling meat and getting rich myself."

Kaj pulled out another beer. This time he passed it over to Camilla without taking one for himself.

"That's not something you just do," he said with a sudden seriousness, turning toward her. "That's something you need a knack for. Like anything else you want to be good at. You need a knack for it, and skill. And then you need to put your heart into it. There are far too many young chefs who think it's just a matter of getting your name out there."

He made a face and Camilla couldn't help but smile.

"They make a little bit of food and then they do all they can to become famous and then they make a little more food while they wallow in their fame. I mean, look at someone like Erwin Lauterbach—that's a totally different story. He made a hell of a lot of good food and became known for that and then he continued to make a lot of fucking good food and now he is respected for that. That's how it should be. And just because those young chefs talk up a storm and attract a bunch of attention, they'll never be the next Søren Gericke. There's only one of him. And you should have seen him back in his glory days," Kaj said, his thoughts slipping back in time. "They'll never even measure up to his sock suspenders. Not even if they're on the morning talk shows every other day."

Camilla grinned and gave in. Here she'd been thinking the rest of the day would be full of prostitutes and pickpockets, but instead she'd gotten a regular rundown on major contemporary French and Danish chefs.

The bag had run out of beer, and Camilla asked if Kaj would stick around if she went and bought them another round.

"With the greatest of pleasure," he called to her as she got up and walked over to a basement grocery store.

She noticed a Citroën C3 stopped and was waiting to turn off Absalonsgade onto Skelbækgade. She recognized the prostitute in the passenger's seat from before, and when the driver turned his head, she made brief eye contact with Holck, the photo editor at the paper who had laid into her at work earlier. He quickly glanced

away and zipped across Sønder Boulevard between a
truck and a bus.

It took Camilla a moment to process what she'd just
seen.

"You'll never guess," she said when she returned to the
bench with a full bag and reported what and whom she'd
just seen.

"Yes, well, everyone comes here. You're a reporter—it
shouldn't surprise you. We regularly have the pleasure of
high-level media people and then there are the politicians.
Everyone needs to let off some steam," Kaj pointed out.

Now Holck was not exactly all that high-level, but given
the situation she was way too distracted to ask Kaj who else
he'd seen.

"What the hell?" she snapped. "He has a wife, children,
grandchildren, and I don't even know what all else!"

Kaj grinned, revealing his darkened teeth.

Day had faded into evening, but Stig was still on the
street talking to the girls as they showed up for work one
by one. Camilla didn't see the other pair of officers who
had been there before, but as she scanned the area for them,
her eyes settled on a head of long, curly dark hair that was
pulled into a loose ponytail. The person was standing farther up toward Halmtorvet with her back to Camilla.

Camilla had consumed too many beers to want Louise
to run into her here, sitting on a park bench next to an aging
alcoholic, who she otherwise had to admit was remarkably
good company. As a couple of large clouds slid in front of
the low evening sun and she felt the first drops start to fall
heavily, she got up.

"Come on," Camilla said. "Let's go to the pub instead of
sitting here and getting cold."

At first, Kaj tried to get her to sit back down, pointing to the bag, which wasn't empty yet, but Camilla remained standing.

"You can take those home," she suggested. When he still seemed reluctant, she added that it'd be her treat, of course.

Stig had vanished by the time they started walking up Skelbækgade. When Kaj pointed at Høker Café, she followed him.

Camilla went up to the bar to order. Kaj changed to a double whisky, but remained in the background until she passed the glass to him. They looked around for an empty table and found a spot by the window. They were right across from the gate at the entrance into the Meatpacking District and the Hotel and Restaurant Management School.

11

Louise stopped. She spotted Kaj standing up from a bench farther down the street and walking away, followed by a blond woman in loose jeans, who was carrying a plastic grocery bag. Louise watched them stagger through the Meatpacking District.

"Hey, do you know if Mikkelsen ever talked to Kaj?" Louise asked, walking over to Lars, who shrugged and said he hadn't spoken with Mikkelsen since they'd seen him last. "Toft might have talked to Kaj, instead. Otherwise we'll have to remind Mikkelsen to make sure he follows through on that," Louise said, as they walked back toward their unmarked car parked around the corner.

They had fifteen minutes until their meeting with Miloš Vituk and Pavlína at Bella Center. They'd just finished a lengthy tour of the neighborhood's brothels, with some of their colleagues from downtown, following Mikkelsen's meticulous notes. Some of the brothels were not that easy to find, and the police were not particularly welcome at many of them, either, but the brothel operators eased up when they realized the police wanted only to see if anyone recognized the still-unidentified dead woman.

Their Czech interpreter was waiting for them on the

corner of Sommerstedgade. She apologized for not having been able to meet them sooner.

"I was in court all day," she explained. "Then I had to make dinner for my kids at home before I could come back out again."

"No problem," Lars said, unlocking the car.

Once again, Louise sensed that Lars didn't mind in the least spending his evening at work. Not that she had anyone sitting at home waiting impatiently for her, either. She hadn't since Peter left her three years ago, precisely because he had gotten tired of sitting around waiting. And to tell the truth, Louise thought it had been very much for the best.

The rain hammered on the roof and windshield of the car as they drove toward Bella Center. Earlier in the month they had had a long spell of sunshine and warm weather, lulling Copenhageners into feeling summer had come to stay, but now the weather was constantly changing. As they drove over the Sjælland Bridge, a flash of lightning tore across the night sky, and the subsequent clap of thunder was so powerful that it shook the car for a moment.

The rain picked up, battering them. Lars slowed down and turned the windshield wipers up as fast as they would go.

"They're not going to come in this weather," Louise said, as they crawled along through the dense blanket of rain.

"It'll stop. It's just a front coming through," her partner replied calmly, sounding just like her father had whenever she didn't want to go outside as a kid because it was raining. "Of course they'll come. After all, they're the ones who want to be able to move around on the street without having people extort huge sums of money from them."

And Lars was right. When they turned off Center Boulevard, the rain stopped as suddenly as it had started. Lars turned off the windshield wipers, and Louise spotted a lone red car in parking lot P7.

"Where did you tell them we'd meet?" Lars asked.

"I think that's them," Louise replied, and he drove over and parked.

Pavlína Branková was short and slender. From a distance, she looked more like a high school student than an adult, but as Louise got closer she could tell that the woman must be in her early twenties. Her thick bangs ended in a sharp edge just above her dark eyebrows. Her hair was black and smooth and hung down just past her shoulders.

Her handshake was limp and her eyes hesitant, but she nodded when she was asked to follow them over to the benches along the side of the parking lot.

"Let's just begin with your name and date of birth," Louise told the female interpreter. She opened the trunk of the car to see if there was anything in there she could spread out on the bench so they wouldn't get wet when they sat down. Luckily there were a few wadded-up plastic bags.

Louise sat down across from Pavlína; the interpreter sat down next to the Czech woman and started talking. At first Pavlína's answers were very curt, but gradually the conversation began to flow more smoothly.

Miloš Vituk jumped in several times, and Louise sensed Pavlína was keeping her eye on him whenever she said anything, so she suggested that Lars take Miloš back to the car. Maybe the witness would speak more freely if there were only women involved. Miloš's presence was obviously making Pavlína clam up.

Once they were alone, at Louise's instruction, the interpreter began to probe in greater depth, asking Pavlína to talk about what she had been through since she had been stopped on the street back home in the Czech Republic, stuffed into a car, and brought to Denmark.

"Had you seen the driver before?" the interpreter asked.

Pavlína shook her head and said that she had been with a guy she knew from the street scene back home. She didn't know him well, but they'd been out a few times even though he wasn't part of the clique she normally hung out with. He turned up every now and then, and that last time he invited her to a party in an abandoned train station building.

"He brought drinks and cigarettes," Pavlína said as if to explain herself. Then she added that it had been so cold outside and her sister was with friends, so she'd gone with him.

On the way there, he had grabbed her shoulders as a dark car pulled over to the curb, and before she knew how it happened, she was suddenly sitting next to a foreign girl in the back seat of a car speeding away through the evening rush hour.

It took some doing for the interpreter to get the rest of the story out of her.

Pavlína didn't remember crossing into Germany or Denmark and said she must have slept a lot of the way. She sounded upset and watched the interpreter intently with each sentence that was said.

"At one point, another girl joined them in the car," the

interpreter said, turning to Louise. "She says she's sure they drugged them with the drink they offered because she has only a foggy memory of the whole trip and had no idea where she was when they arrived—not even what country she was in. They put the girls up in a hotel where they were greeted by two men, who later turned out to be Arian and Hamdi."

"The rooms were small and dark, and the bathroom was down the hall," Pavlína said through the interpreter, explaining she had shared a room with one of the girls from the car.

She started crying as she recounted how Arian had raped her after Hamdi took the other girl out of the room. Afterward, the men switched places, and they sat her on a chair outside the door while Arian kept an eye on her.

The next morning the two men came back and took the women out on the town to buy new clothes and makeup. They were very generous. But then that same night, they sent the girls out onto the street, ordering them to earn back all the money the trip, the clothes, and the hotel had cost.

Pavlína stared urgently at the interpreter while she spoke, and then the interpreter told Louise that Pavlína had never worked as a prostitute before and had asked the two men several times that first week for permission to return home to her sister, who didn't know where she was and was all by herself now.

"First, they threatened to cut her face if she refused," the interpreter translated, "and when she persisted, they threatened to cut her sister. After that, she didn't dare disobey.

"They demanded she pay 3,000 kroner a day. Some days she wasn't able to earn that much and then she would have to pay extra the next day and even more the day after if she were still behind. There were days when she did up to twenty tricks or more in a day to pay off her debt."

Pavlína had stopped crying, but there was an absent look in her eyes as she mentioned eight girls who gave money to the Albanians.

Louise quickly began calculating how much money the girls had been bringing in each week. Pavlína answered the interpreter's question by saying that they were forced to work six days a week. Louise closed her eyes and did the math. With eight girls that must have been about 144,000 kroner a week.

"There's a lot of turnover among the girls. Most of them only stay for the three months they're legally allowed to remain in Denmark as tourists. If they want to be here longer than that, they have to apply for a residence permit, which they won't get," the interpreter said, as Pavlína confirmed what Miloš Vituk had already explained.

"Several of the girls have been here multiple times," she added through the interpreter. "Some are sent home for a while, but then are brought back the following year. Some of the girls are also sent on to Norway or Sweden. If they move around from country to country, it's hard to keep track of them."

"That's what the Roma are known for doing," Louise said. She asked if Pavlína was sure the men were Albanian and not Roma, because the Roma were well known in Denmark for their brutal human trafficking and successful methods at evading detection: They were called "shepherds" for a reason. They moved their girls around Europe as if they were livestock, cleverly directing them from meadow to meadow to avoid attention from the various governments or police.

"What if the girls earned more than 3,000 kroner in one day? What would happen to the extra money?" Louise asked and watched the interpreter while she waited for the question to be translated.

"They got to keep that. That was the carrot," the interpreter reported after having passed the question on. "But that very rarely happened."

"Ask her if she could have gone home if she had enough money for the ticket," Louise asked, but the girl shook her head once she understood the question. "No, once you're with them you can say farewell to freedom. There's no way out again."

Louise nodded sympathetically and pondered it all for a moment before changing the topic. "I understand from Miloš that at one point you were forced out of his apartment and taken to a club on Saxogade."

Pavlína listened carefully to the interpreter, who then let her talk for a long time before she started translating. Louise couldn't tell from Pavlína's voice whether she was angry or afraid.

"She was raped again while she was locked in a small room in the back of the club. Someone hit her because she said they couldn't force her back out onto the street now that they had their money."

Pavlína's voice had become high-pitched and frenzied.

"They taunted Miloš, saying he couldn't look after me properly. Just look how easy it was for them to come and take me. They thought it would be better for me to stay and work for them because then I would have security."

That last part made Louise shake her head.

"Ask her if she knows the girl we found on Skelbækgade," Louise said, looking at the interpreter.

There was a longer pause during which a string of re-actions flickered like a slide show over the woman's face in rapid succession. Finally, Pavlína nodded and looked down at her hands.

"She was one of the girls who was in the car," she said quietly, but quickly added that it wasn't the girl she'd shared a room with.

Louise tried to catch the young woman's eye. She could have chosen to ask this right off the bat, but she'd thought it better to wait until they were done so it didn't get in the way of the woman's own story.

"Do you know what her name was, or where in the Czech Republic she was picked up?"

Pavlína said she didn't know anything other than that her name was Iveta—or at least, that was what she'd said her name was. Pavlína estimated they were the same age, but she didn't know where Iveta was from.

"Ask if she knows who murdered her, if she knows why Iveta was killed."

Louise followed along intently as her questions were translated and tried to discern some of the answers.

"She thinks Iveta fell victim to the threats the men were always making if the girls didn't obey," the interpreter said. "Once they arrived at the hotel, Iveta had begged incessantly to go home again because her mother was seriously ill and needed her. She wanted to go home and earn money so she could help her mother."

The interpreter added that unlike Pavlína, the murdered girl had worked as a prostitute back home, as well.

"But she found out that either she had to raise the money to buy her way out of the debt she was already in or she would have to find someone else to pay for her. A few days before she died, she received a message that her mother was in the hospital and in a final attempt to get permission to go home, she went to see Arian and told him that she was pregnant and couldn't work anymore because it hurt."

Pavlína started crying again. This time it took a long time before she was ready to continue.

"That was just something she said," the interpreter continued once Pavlína started talking again, "because she hoped that they would take pity on her. The next day she disappeared and Pavlína didn't see her again until Miloš showed her Iveta's picture in the paper, where it said she was dead. He had also asked if it were someone Pavlína knew. But she was afraid, so she just shook her head."

A heavy silence lay over them until Louise got up and thanked Pavlína for telling her story.

They walked back over to Lars and Miloš, who were sitting in the police car waiting. As soon as he saw them, the Serb leaped out of the car's front seat and rushed over to meet Pavlína with his arms outstretched. He put them around her shoulders and pulled her into an embrace.

"The girls have to show up at the main train station every morning and pay the two Albanians. They do that at the entrance onto Istedgade," Louise said when she reached her partner.

Lars walked the couple steps over to Miloš and thanked him for arranging the meeting with Pavlína.

"We promise we'll keep an eye on those two," Lars said. He explained that the police needed evidence to support Pavlína's story before they could do any more.

Before they parted, Louise requested that the interpreter ask if Pavlína would stop by the pathology lab and identify the dead woman, because no one had confirmed her identity yet.

"We'll also make sure to issue the Czech police a request to locate her ailing mother so she can be notified of her daughter's death," Louise said, shaking the hand Pavlína held out to her.

12

The waitress had just come and set another double in front of Kaj when Camilla's cell phone rang. It was almost ten p.m. and she didn't recognize the number on the display.

"Yes?" she said, holding a hand over her other ear to help her hear better. She pulled her chair back a little and sank further into the corner, trying to shield herself from the jukebox music.

Flemming Larsen, the pathologist, began by apologizing for calling so late.

"But to be honest, I forgot I had the message in my pocket and didn't happen to think of it until now," he admitted.

"That's perfectly OK," Camilla said. "I'm in a pub in Vesterbro and may have had a little too much to drink…so maybe we'd better talk tomorrow. But there's still one thing I want to ask."

Flemming laughed and apologized again for interrupting her evening.

"I was trying to get hold of you because I wanted to do a piece on the murder that happened just across from where I'm sitting. But I'm having a hard time getting my boss to bite. He doesn't think we have enough to go on. All we have is that the victim is presumed to be a foreign prostitute. Do you have any more information on what happened to her?"

Camilla nodded across the table in response to the waitress's question of whether she wanted another round. Meanwhile the pathologist hesitated a little on the other end of the line.

"It was a straightforward, execution-style killing," Flemming finally said, then made it clear that this information was off the record. "It was on the quite-brutal end of the scale—she never had a chance to defend herself," he went on. "During the autopsy, I identified a number of lesions on her body from blows, which she appears to have sustained before death. So this wasn't the first time someone had been after her."

"That sounds atrocious," Camilla said, her adrenaline surging through all the alcohol.

"I think there's every reason for you to follow up on this story," Flemming said.

Camilla totally agreed; she was determined to tackle the story whether Høyer wanted to run it or not. But it wasn't that easy, of course, she thought. Especially not since Holck was obviously more intimately acquainted with Copenhagen's prostitution scene than she had previously realized.

"There are so many prostitutes who are abused and raped. No group of people is more vulnerable to violent assaults than they are. We treat them when they take refuge at the Nest, where they are routinely sent to the Center for Victims of Sexual Assault at the hospital."

Camilla had the sense that Flemming had more to say on this topic, but she was starting to zone out, so she suggested that she call him back so they could have this conversation when she had her notepad and was some-where quieter.

"Sure, just give me a call," Flemming said and gave her his cell number, which she quickly wrote down on the back of a receipt.

Camilla pulled her chair back over to the table and took a sip of her beer while Kaj started telling her a story about another great French chef from the past, Auguste Escoffier, who had once been a visiting chef at Copenhagen's luxury Hôtel d'Angleterre.

"When he wanted to finish his menu off with poires belle Hélène, he got so angry he almost left the country," Kaj said, and a merry glint entered his bleary eyes.

"Why?" Camilla asked. She was eager to move on from thinking about the girl who'd had her throat slit across the street.

"Because they wanted to top it with whipped cream!"

Camilla had no idea what Kaj was talking about, so he had to explain that it was a deadly sin to put whipped cream on top of a dessert that consisted of vanilla ice cream, poached pears, and high-quality melted chocolate.

"Whipped cream!" Kaj scoffed indignantly. "That's something cooks do when they don't know any better and can't be bothered to listen. But this was his dessert. He created it, and they wanted to pull it down to a more plebeian level, which is how so many people have served it since."

His words dripped with derision.

Camilla smiled at him, thinking she would have loved to eat in this man's restaurant.

Sadly, she had met him twenty years too late.

They sat in silence for a bit while an old Johnny Cash number played from the jukebox in the background:

"Because you're mine, I walk the line," Kaj sang along in a deep voice when they got to the chorus. His tired eyes had come to rest on the window and the doorway across the street.

Camilla realized that she wasn't angry at her boss anymore, and that she'd had her fill of beer.

"I saw her," Kaj said suddenly, turning his head to Camilla as the song finished.

"The murdered woman?" Camilla asked after a pause and then followed his gaze out the window to the doorway across the street.

Kaj nodded.

"Did you tell the police?"

He shook his head and said he didn't have any plans to, either.

"Yes, but it's important," Camilla began, and he interrupted her by reaching a hand across the table and taking hers so she stopped talking.

"That's not always how it works in the real world," he said, pulling his hand back again. "I really want to be able to come and go here in my own neighborhood without being afraid. Even though our local beat cop, Mikkelsen, is nice enough, eventually they'll ask me to testify in court, and that's not going to end well for me."

"No, now listen here," Camilla blurted out, suddenly ordering another round. "You can't just not go to the cops. That woman was executed. Her throat was slashed."

Kaj sat there eyeing her. His face was lined with deep wrinkles, his hair gray, but she guessed he couldn't be older than his midfifties. His eyes were dark and held the experiences of a long, hard life, which made her feel like a naïve schoolgirl.

"All right," she said. "I don't know shit about that. I only know that no one is willing to talk in this case. All I know is that she was really young and now she's dead. It's just completely...unbearable!"

Camilla knew she sounded ridiculous, but she'd meant it. In her beer-induced stupor, she really wished she could have saved the girl, but it was too late. She also wanted to save Kaj, and the killers shouldn't get away with what they'd done, either.

Kaj didn't say anything, so Camilla spoke again. "What did you see?"

He studied her for a minute, and she sensed the alcohol hadn't had anywhere near the effect on him as it had on her. But, of course, he was also probably more used to these quantities.

"I really want to tell you what I saw, and you should also feel free to write about it if you want. But you have to guarantee me that you won't reveal me as your source."

"Goes without saying," Camilla exclaimed. Then she went over to the bar for a mineral water and some paper from the waitress's notepad.

"I knew her personally—the girl who was murdered. Her name was Iveta, and she has a little daughter who lives with the grandmother back in the Czech Republic. Sometimes I helped Iveta send money home to them. I could tell she was having some problems, but she wouldn't tell me what was going on because she didn't want me to get messed up in something. She had gotten word her mother was sick, and the last time I talked to her she was quite worried about her daughter and really wanted to go home."

Camilla took her notes in tiny letters so she'd have room for the whole story on the small pieces of paper.

"Sunday night, I saw her turning onto Skelbækgade off

Dybbøls Bridge. She was walking down the opposite side of
the street from me. She spotted me and started waving when
she answered her cell—I was close enough to hear the ring-
tone. I was sitting outside drinking a beer and relaxing right
over there on the steps." He nodded toward the front door
of the bar that opened onto the street. "At first I thought she
was going to come over to me. Instead, she stepped into that
gate over there." He pointed toward the entry into the Meatpacking District. "So I assumed the phone call was from a
john who was en route. It took only about five minutes before a car stopped and a man got out of the back seat and
followed her inside. But a few minutes later he came back
out and jumped into the car, which sped away."

Camilla flipped the paper over and started writing on the
back.

"I realized something was wrong, and I went over there
as soon as they were gone. But when I saw her I knew there
was nothing I could do. I called the police from that pay
phone in back." He tilted his head toward the back of the
bar, where there was a phone mounted on the wall.

"Did you see what make or model the car was?"

He nodded and said it was a dark Audi A4, and he was
also sure that the driver was the Albanian Iveta worked for.

"You have to talk to the police," Camilla said. "They'll
put you into witness protection and take good care of you."

"Yeah, yeah. They promise so much." He shook his
head. "I've done what I need to do for Iveta and her little
girl. It's up to you now whether this information makes it
any further," he said and emptied his glass.

Camilla nodded.

"But I have no idea where you heard all that from. If
anyone should happen to ask," he emphasized again.

"No, of course not," Camilla said and got up to go pay

the tab. It was time for her to go home. Even though she'd already decided her boss could go fuck himself, Kaj's account had pushed her spat with her boss aside. Considering the eyewitness report she was going to write up for the next day's edition, she would serve the story to her editor on a silver platter first thing when he showed up for work.

"Are you going to stay for a bit?" she asked when she returned to the table.

"*Oui, encore une minute, madame,*" Kaj replied in his Danish-accented French and nodded.

Camilla added 200 kroner to the tab and told the waitstaff it was for Kaj, in case he wanted another round.

13

It took Louise a long time to return his call, but when she found another message on her answering machine after returning from Bella Center, she finally sat down on the sofa and dialed Mik Rasmussen's home number.

"A foreign prostitute was murdered," she said apologetically, then felt guilty for making an excuse for not calling sooner. "We've been looking for witnesses the last several nights and are still hoping to find someone who saw something."

They had been dating since the fall. The relationship had started when Louise was on a case in Holbæk while assigned to the Danish National Police Mobile Task Force.

She and Mik were partners on that case, and Louise had fallen in love and let herself be whisked off her feet and into Mik's world—with his idyllic farmhouse and his passion for sea kayaking. They'd also taken a dreamy vacation to Växjö in Sweden, where they kayaked on lakes and rivers, gathered mushrooms, cooked over a campfire, and had sex under the open sky. And for a while she thought a long-distance relationship was the ideal answer for her, with Mik in Holbæk and her in Copenhagen. Things had been wonderful at Christmas when they went shopping together along Strøget, Copenhagen's downtown pedestrian shopping street. Hand in hand, they sipped warm mulled wine. But with the distance, they hadn't ended up seeing each other quite as often since then.

"Do you want to come up for the weekend?" Mik asked without commenting on her case. "A few of us from the club are going to take the kayaks out along Cape Tuse on Saturday. We're going to bring food and set up camp when we feel like it."

"I'm going to be working. Unfortunately," Louise added as she suddenly realized just how much she wanted to see him, with his gangly limbs and crooked front teeth. "But maybe we could take a trip when this case is over?"

He laughed into the phone. "Don't you think there'll be a new case then?"

"Oh, stop," she cried, hoping he could hear that she was smiling. "If you start driving now you could actually be here in Frederiksberg within the hour."

"Deal," he quickly replied, snatching the invitation. "You put the coffee on and I'll bring the rest. I just have to take the dogs for a quick walk before I leave."

He hung up. Irish coffee had been a staple of theirs ever since their night together sitting on a bench enjoying the view from his farm. He had just happened to offer her one after they'd finished their beer. Now it was "their" drink, and they had since explored the difference between whiskey with an *e*—which is Irish and not quite as smoky—and whisky with no *e*—also known as Scotch and totally out of place in an Irish coffee.

She smiled and pulled her legs up onto the sofa. She was far too tired to skip a night's sleep. On the other hand, a good, thorough roll in the hay would surely reinvigorate her and give her more energy than eight hours of deep sleep.

14

(Thursday)

Camilla was sitting at her computer when her boss walked into the office at nine thirty. His blond hair was still wet from his shower, and she guessed he'd run his standard fifteen kilometers before coming in. Her own head felt heavy, and the light from her screen glared in her eyes. She would have just stayed home if she hadn't stormed out of the office so dramatically the day before and if she hadn't been so eager to serve up Kaj's eyewitness statement for her boss along with his morning coffee.

He stopped in her doorway and watched her collect the pages of her article. "What's going on with you?" His tone was caring, and he sounded concerned. "You look sick."

She nodded and was surprised that he didn't start by commenting on their argument.

Maybe they were starting to butt heads often enough that he no longer noticed.

"Yeah, I'm going to go home in a bit," Camilla said with a nod before holding out the printed pages to him. "I've been looking into that murdered Czech girl on

Skelbækgade. She was evidently snuffed by her own pimp, and I have something here you should read."

Høyer stepped into her office and walked over to her desk to take the papers from her.

"The police don't have any witnesses or leads yet," Camilla continued. "But this is a person who knew the woman. He saw her go through the gate into the Meatpacking District off Skelbækgade, and he also saw the guy who followed her in shortly after."

Høyer stood there for a second just looking at her before reaching for the article. He was about to say something, but she cut him off.

"You should consider me out sick today. Which in practical terms means I'm not here and I'm not turning anything in for the paper. But if you want to print this article—and will respect the fact that I want to keep my source 100 percent confidential—then you can blow this story wide open, because this witness hasn't talked to any other members of the press besides me. And you can also be sure that this isn't just something he made up," she said, knowing that Kaj hadn't told anyone else.

Høyer sat across from her and skimmed over the two pages she'd handed him.

"But you also need to understand that I'm going to contact the police and pass on the information contained in this article," Camilla said.

Her editor set the pages down and leaned back resting on the arms of the chair. "Well, I should say so. How sure are you that this witness is telling the truth?"

"As sure as I am that it's a travesty to put whipped cream on top of authentic poires belle Hélène," she replied, enjoying the confusion in Høyer's eyes.

"Well, all right. I'll look at it. Kvist's report from Silkeborg won't be ready to run until tomorrow, anyway."

Fatigue suddenly washed over Camilla.

"Let me tell you one more thing," she said, mustering her courage. "Human trafficking is one of the most lucrative crimes out there. And here you are with a hard-on over some rich people's paintings worth a lousy couple million."

She stood up.

"I'm going to go home and nurse my cold," she said. "Call me if you decide to run it."

Camilla's voice was calm and she managed to keep her irritation under wraps. "But first I'm going to go hand over the witness statement to the police. I'll get them to sit on the new information and keep it from the rest of the press until tomorrow, then you can have the scoop if you decide to run it. But I can't ask them to withhold it any longer than that."

She ran into Holck in the hallway. She was wearing her sunglasses, but pushed them up onto her head as he approached her. He averted his gaze and before he had quite reached her and would be forced to look her in the eye, he turned and vanished into an empty office. But even that was enough for Camilla. She now knew that seeing him with a prostitute the day before would add a whole new dimension to their already tense relationship—meaning he wouldn't be able to walk all over her the way he wanted to anymore.

Camilla biked a printout of her article over to Copenhagen Police Headquarters. She parked outside the building, called Louise, and asked for five minutes. She had to wait for a bit at access control before the guard had time for her, and when she said that she was there to see Assistant Detective Louise Rick, he gave her a blank look.

"Where does this person work?" the guard asked.

Camilla explained that Louise had worked in Unit A before the re-org, and the guard flipped in confusion through a binder and asked Camilla for an office number, which of course Camilla couldn't remember. Finally, Camilla gave up on waiting and called Louise herself and asked her to come down and escort her up.

Her hangover was becoming more and more obtrusive, and Camilla guessed that the only reason she had been able to get up that morning and write her article was that, in all probability, she hadn't actually been sober yet. She had filled herself with black coffee before sitting down at her keyboard to write, and once done, she'd read her piece through several times to be sure it didn't ramble too much. But with the article written and her mission almost complete, she realized she was about to lose all her steam as her head started to throb.

15

Louise gave Camilla a quick hug, and when they got up to Louise's office, she grabbed the thermos on the desk and went off to the kitchen to fill it up.

"You look a little ragged around the edges," Louise commented when she returned.

Camilla nodded and smiled. "Not that you look all that chipper yourself," she retorted. "But you're right. I had a couple of beers last night. Mmm, or maybe seven...which is actually why I'm here."

Louise sat down, full of curiosity, and watched as Camilla pulled a few sheets of paper out of her purse.

"I ran into a man who was practically a witness to the murder in the Meatpacking District. He knew the murdered woman a little and saw her walk onto Skelbækgade right before she received a call on her cell phone. When she was done with the conversation, she went through the gate in front of the Hotel and Restaurant Management School, and immediately after that a dark Audi A4 pulled up, then a man got out and followed her in."

Lars Jørgensen had been sitting at his desk talking on his phone when they entered the office. Now he hung up and listened. He knew Camilla well and had worked with her several times on cases she had covered.

"A moment later the man came back out again and jumped into the car, which sped off."

Camilla took off her jacket.

"Is this a witness we can talk to?" Lars asked from his desk, which faced Louise's.

Camilla shook her head. "No. You have to use me for this witness statement."

Louise had suspected as much when Camilla had started telling the story.

"Before you continue, I just want to see if we can't get the rest of the group in here. I know that Mikkelsen is here today talking with Toft and Stig. We ID'd the woman yesterday, and they're informing the Czech police so they can locate her family and make sure they're notified," Louise said. Then she turned to Lars and asked, "Will you find Willumsen and the rest and ask them to come in here?"

Camilla stood up when everyone else walked in a few moments later. Louise introduced her to Mikkelsen. Camilla already knew everyone else.

"What's so important?" Willumsen asked brusquely as he entered the doorway and looked around at his investigative team. His eyes came to rest on Camilla and he took another step forward.

"God, are we here because of some reporter?"

Camilla stood up again and only then did Louise notice that the hair in her friend's ponytail seemed unwashed. And, she was barely wearing any makeup, which was quite unusual for Camilla. She must have hurried out the door faster than she usually did. Not that Louise was one to talk, because she looked the same way after a night with only a couple hours of sleep and countless cups of coffee with whiskey and whipped cream. But it was sort of more normal for her; she didn't always manage to do that thorough of a job with her makeup or tame her wild, dark hair. It just wasn't a burning issue for her.

"No, it's only a humble journalist here to provide law enforcement with some important information," Camilla responded, flashing Willumsen her sweetest smile.

Louise leaned back a little with her coffee mug in her hands, ceding control to the others.

Willumsen nodded a couple of times, looking around for a place to sit down. Stig was standing in the doorway with his pen in his hand, and only grudgingly did he give his place to Suhr when his superior asked him to make a little room.

Camilla repeated what she had already told Louise and Lars.

"That sounds like the two Albanians," said Mikkelsen, who had his leather jacket over his shoulder and his glasses up on top of his head. "And Arian drives a new Audi A4."

"Arian is also the name Pavlína knows him by," Louise added, saying that before Pavlína had ID'd Iveta in the morgue, she told them Iveta had a mother back home she was sending money to. "But she didn't say anything about a child."

Camilla shrugged and could only pass on what Kaj had told her.

"We must be able to trace the call she received," Lars suggested and was countered by Suhr, who shook his head.

"She didn't have a cell phone on her when CSI went over the body."

"Then it must have been removed," Lars concluded, and no one objected.

"Can we use this for anything?" Willumsen wanted to know.

"Of course, damn it," Mikkelsen exclaimed. "You can't

expect to get much more than this." He turned to Camilla. "But are you sure your source isn't someone we could talk to? He can remain anonymous and we can do the questioning off the books so he won't risk being called in later as a witness."

Willumsen was about to protest but was interrupted by Toft, who reminded them that the source's statements meshed well with Pavlína's.

"So now there's an extra reason for us to keep a sharp eye on those two Albanians."

Superintendent Willumsen stood there for a moment with his arms crossed, nodding thoughtfully, but as he was about to leave the office Camilla stopped him with her hand.

"In exchange for this, you must promise me you'll hold off until tomorrow telling any other reporters about what my source said, unless I call and tell you otherwise this afternoon," she asked, giving Willumsen a pleading look. His skepticism softened more when Suhr sent him a just-say-yes look.

"All right, we'll leave it at that. We really appreciate your going to the trouble to come to us with your information so we don't have to read it in the paper tomorrow," he said, sounding satisfied, before turning his attention to the others.

"Locate that Audi and then we can put a tail on it," he ordered to no one in particular. "And install a tracker once it's found." That was for Toft. "Spend today and tomorrow tracking down any witness statements to support Ms. Lind's anonymous source, and find out who those Albanians are and what they do. Once we have an idea about that, you can go to the main railway station and see whether girls really do meet there daily to settle their accounts with their pimps."

Then he gave Camilla a nod and left the office, while Homicide Chief Suhr took the time to thank her properly.

Stig lingered after the others left.

"Funny, I thought for a second I had seen you down on Sønder Boulevard last night," he said, his eyes running down Camilla's Malene Birger designer dress and high-heeled shoes. "But it must've just been someone who looked like you, because this lady was sitting on a bench drinking beer with an old alcoholic."

Camilla smiled at him, saying that sounded pleasant enough, but she'd taken her son to his break-dancing class.

Louise knew that was a lie. Markus had had break dancing on Monday—and that had been his last class. And then Louise recalled the same woman Lars was talking about. She wouldn't be surprised if Stig had seen correctly. Louise walked her friend back to the main entrance, and when Camilla said she was going home to bed, Louise gave her a hug.

"I'm going to do the same just as soon as I can," Louise said, waving after her.

16

On Saturday morning, Camilla was in her jogging clothes and on the way out the door when her phone rang. For a second, she considered ignoring it. She and Louise had a brunch date, and she was determined to get her run in beforehand.

Her story had filled the entire front page and two pages inside the paper the day before. The intern's last assignment before he went back to school was to put together a fact box on prostitutes murdered in the last few years in Vesterbro and also in the rest of the country. There were several brutal killings in Ringsted and Ålborg. Not that they seemed connected; it was mostly just evidence of the brutal violence that these marginalized women were subjected to, an angle Camilla was perfectly satisfied with.

"I'm going to have to cancel," Louise said after Camilla walked back into the living room and picked up after all. "There's been another murder."

Camilla could hear people talking in the background and a car driving by. "Where are you?" she asked.

"I'm standing down on Sønder Boulevard. The victim is in the courtyard in one of the buildings off the street."

"Is it a prostitute?" Camilla asked, already fearing a recurrence.

"No." The answer seemed calming in a way. "It's one of the drunks," Louise continued. "Mikkelsen ID'd him before I got on scene. It was pretty brutal, not something you want the families who have a view into the courtyard seeing."

Camilla sank down on her sofa's armrest. "Is it Kaj?" she asked softly, feeling an iron fist clench in her stomach.

"How the hell do you know him?" Louise asked, surprised.

"I just know him," Camilla responded tersely. "I'm coming down there."

"I don't think that's wise. They won't let you see him."

"God damn it! I don't want to see him, either. But don't you get it? He was the one who told me about Iveta and the Audi. How the hell did they find out it was him?"

Camilla's voice broke as the iron fist grew bigger and was now so large that she had a hard time getting up off the sofa arm. Suddenly she started shivering as the room seemed to contract around the sofa.

"Ah," Louise said. "Well then, you'd better come. We've cordoned off the courtyard and our cars are parked out front, so it ought to be easy for you to find us."

Camilla saw the investigators from far away, as well as the ring of curious bystanders gathered on the sidewalk outside. As she moved closer, she could hear people discussing and speculating about what had happened. She recognized a couple from the pub and the guy from the grocery shop on the corner.

Louise was standing by one of the blue vans talking to Niels Frandsen, the head of the Forensics Department. The barrier tape was strung across the entrance to the courtyard.

"He's still in there," Louise said, after Camilla parked her bicycle and greeted Frandsen, "so we'll stay out here."

An ambulance with tinted windows came around the corner. Louise took Camilla by the elbow and pulled her to the side a bit.

"Flemming just finished examining the site and doing the preliminary postmortem exam," she said. "They're getting ready to move the body."

"It's been a long time since we've seen anything this bad," Frandsen admitted when he heard that Camilla knew the deceased. "We speculate he was knocked down here in the archway before being pulled into the courtyard."

The ambulance stopped and Frandsen walked over and undid the police tape on one side so it could drive in.

He followed it over to talk to a couple of his people. Their faces were strained, and they were talking together quietly as they passed by. Behind them came the homicide chief followed by Willumsen.

Camilla confirmed that Kaj had been the source for her story and vigorously shook her head when asked who could have known that.

"What happened to him?" she whispered to Louise once they were alone. She noticed her heart racing while the rest of her body felt completely stiff.

She could tell that Louise didn't know how to respond.

Just then the pathologist ducked under the police tape and Camilla took her eyes off the gurney, which had just been pulled out of the ambulance.

"It's nasty," Flemming confirmed with a grim look. "Not something I've seen before."

"What happened to him?" Camilla repeated, now with a shrill desperation in her voice that she couldn't suppress.

Flemming and Louise exchanged a quick glance.

"The killers stretched out his four limbs and tied each

between four benches. Then, they gave him a variation on the 'Colombian necktie,'" Flemming said, watching her.

"And what's that?" Camilla asked, uncomprehending and not sure she really wanted to understand.

"The Colombian necktie is something the Mafia does to people who rat to the police," Louise explained, taking hold of Camilla as she began to sway.

"Normally what you see is the throat slit ear to ear and the tongue pulled through the gash. But in this case, his throat was cut vertically and his tongue stuck to the roof of his mouth with a knife inserted through the incision."

"So, this variant could be called a Balkan necktie," Camilla said, thinking about the two Albanians and leaning against the wall for support.

Louise had just suggested Camilla go back home when Suhr emerged from the courtyard, putting his arm around Camilla's shoulder when he reached her.

"I would really like to have you take a look at his face before the ambulance takes him away," the homicide chief requested. "We need to know for sure that we're talking about the same man who was your source."

Camilla nodded mutely and followed him under the police tape.

"Everything here will make sense if it is him," Willumsen said once they were in the courtyard.

Make sense, Camilla thought, spotting the body of the former chef ahead of her. Now the iron fist was so enormous it pushed its way up into her throat and obstructed her breathing. She could inhale only in brief gasps.

"We'll show you only the top of his face," Suhr said reassuringly when Camilla's footsteps started to stiffen in reluctance.

There were a fair number of people in the courtyard. The first person Camilla recognized was Mikkelsen, who was sitting slumped over on a bench, his face ashen, his eyes staring vacantly at the asphalt. Above him, a green tarp had been stretched out as a shelter to keep people in the building above from seeing the body. The CSI techs had made a white outline on the ground underneath the tarp to show where the body was found. Kaj was on a gurney now, the ropes with which he had been bound to the benches still dangling off the sides. The four benches had been pulled together from the courtyard's two seating areas and arranged like the vanes of a windmill, jutting outward from the spot where the body was left. His arms and legs had been fully stretched out at right angles from his torso, so he looked like a capital H on its side.

Camilla forced herself to look at Kaj's body on the gurney. It had been zipped inside a white body bag. The homicide chief now cautiously pulled the zipper down a little.

She recognized Kaj just from his hair and the deep wrinkles on his face, and she cried as she nodded in confirmation. Suhr didn't unzip the body bag any farther than the mouth so Camilla couldn't see the deep incisions that ran from the Adam's apple, where the knife had entered, down to his chest where it had been stopped by the breastbone. The homicide chief held her by the elbow, supporting her when she turned and started to walk away.

"I suggest that we drive over to HQ and have a chat," he said, as they started to make their way out to the sidewalk back out on the street.

Camilla heard the rear doors of the ambulance close, and leaned against the wall as it pulled away, heading toward National Hospital, where the pathology lab was.

Flemming squeezed her arm as he walked by, and Louise said they were ready to go.

Toft, Mikkelsen, and Stig stayed behind with Willumsen while Lars and Louise went with Suhr and Camilla.

"I just don't get it. How could it end like that?" Camilla asked, as Louise opened the back door of the car and helped her in. "No one could have known he was the one who told me what happened."

Camilla leaned her head against Louise's shoulder and kept her eyes closed for the short drive in to Police Headquarters. Camilla was reliving glimpses of the afternoon and evening she had spent with Kaj, thinking about her article as well. She'd gone through it several times—including after she was sure she was totally sober again. But there was nothing in it, nothing that could identify him in any way. She didn't get it.

But she had no doubt it was her fault he had been murdered so viciously and left in plain view in his own courtyard. Humiliated and chastised.

17

They were sitting in Louise and Lars's office. Suhr had brought in an extra chair and Camilla had downed two cups of black coffee before she suddenly leaped up and raced down the hall to the bathroom with her hand over her mouth.

A copy of the paper with her article was sitting out when she came back and they agreed that nothing in the story could have identified Kaj Antonsen as her source.

"The only thing I can see right off the bat that might have helped someone figure it out is the picture of you in your byline," Louise said, pointing to the small photo of Camilla that appeared next to her name under the title of the article.

Suhr reached for the paper as Louise pointed this out.

"If someone recognized you after seeing you with Kaj the day before the article ran, then they could have guessed your source," Louise explained, watching Camilla struggle with more nausea on realizing that she'd so carefully obscured anything that would point to Kaj while ignoring the possibility her own identity might give him away.

Suhr nodded. "It certainly could have happened that

way," he agreed. Then he asked Camilla where she and Kaj
had talked and who might have seen them together.

"Everyone," Camilla replied honestly. "Obviously, I had
no idea it would turn into a story like this. I was only there
to get a little feel for the neighborhood. I'm not really that
familiar with Istedgade and that area. I also didn't know
how visible the prostitutes were in the street scene. I was
interested in the case of the murdered prostitute, but then I
met Kaj and we got to talking, had a few beers together, and
lost track of time."

Louise wrote as Camilla talked.

"Afterward, we went over to the pub, Høker Café, and
we were there for a few hours while he filled me in on
how a proper poires belle Hélène should be made—without
whipped cream, of course," she added, unable to hold back
the tears.

There was a knock on the office door. Toft apologized for
the interruption, and then stepped in along with a tech.

"We found the Audi late yesterday afternoon," he told
Suhr. "And last night, I installed a tracker on it. It's parked
out in Valby, and we just went and checked if it had been
anywhere near Sønder Boulevard and the courtyard where
the body was found. But it's still in the same location and
hasn't been driven."

Louise learned that they had obtained a four-week wiretap warrant, and with the electronic chip Toft had mounted
on the car they could now follow the dark Audi A4 via a
screen in the surveillance room.

"One of the boys is monitoring it in there, so we'll know
the second he puts the key in the ignition. And we're working on getting an interpreter to help with the wiretap," Toft
said, mostly to Suhr. "I hope it's Igli. He does Albanian,

Serbo-Croatian, Slovak, and Czech. He's going to call in around lunchtime and let us know if he's in. I just talked to him, but he was at some little league soccer game out in Hvidovre, and his son had just scored a goal. He had to go home and look at his calendar before he could make any promises."

Suhr nodded, satisfied. Igli was one of their best interpreters when it came to cases that involved people from the Balkans. He used to be a police officer in the former Yugoslavia, and the Homicide Division often benefited from his experience now whenever he worked with them on a case. Suhr asked Lars and Louise to go through Camilla's account, from when she met Kaj to when they parted ways. Especially whether she had noticed anyone keeping an eye on them.

Louise promised they would let him know.

"I can't bear it," Camilla exclaimed after Suhr left. "It just occurred to me now that I put a couple hundred extra kroner on our tab for Kaj to use when I paid at the pub and then they had my name on the receipt for that. I just didn't even think about it. I wanted to do something nice for him, as a kind of thank-you for the story. Plus, I'd had a few too many beers to be thinking about things on that level."

Camilla hid her face in her hands, and Louise thought Mikkelsen must have had his reasons for not wanting to talk to Kaj until he could go visit him at his home, where no one could see them. But she didn't say anything, just put her hand on Camilla's shoulder while Lars called Mikkelsen and told him about the 200 kroner and the debit card receipt. When he hung up, Lars said someone would go talk to the waitress so they could find out if anyone had asked to see the receipt after Camilla had left.

"So Michael Stig did see you out there that night," Lars said, and Camilla nodded dully.

"I just feel so awful about it," Camilla said Sunday evening when they were sitting on Louise's sofa, a bottle of red wine between them. "It feels every bit as bad as if I'd murdered him with my own hands. Anyway, it's my fault he's not alive anymore and that they killed him in that gruesome way."

Louise listened and let her friend talk. At first, she'd tried to contradict her and assuage her guilt a little, but Camilla had told her to stop that.

"There's no getting around it. I have to own up to what I did."

"Yeah, but for Pete's sake, you were just doing your job. Neither you nor Kaj for that matter could have predicted that your conversation could have led to this."

"I mean, he was talking to me to protect himself," Camilla reminded herself. "Otherwise he could have just gone to you guys. If he'd done that he might still be alive."

Louise filled her glass but held back on Camilla's.

"You were protecting him," Louise said and got up to light a few candles in the living room. She went over to the stereo and put Big Fat Snake on repeat before sinking back down onto the sofa. "But you didn't need to go in to the paper today and write that article about your own role in the killing. Why are you putting all the blame on yourself? And so publicly?"

Camilla looked at her, her eyes unflinching as if Louise were the edge of a cliff between her and the abyss.

"There's no doubt what triggered everything yesterday," Camilla said plainly. "It's horrific every way you look at it, but I have to stand by it. And the readers deserve to know the kind of ruthless sickos we're dealing with here. Besides, I've seen way too many reporters stick their tails between their legs and refuse to take responsibility when they push their sources over the edge by leaking information and digging up dirt. I mean, you can't sink any lower than that."

They stopped by Camilla's place and packed her a bag of clothes and toiletries to take to Louise's apartment; contrary to expectations, Camilla didn't protest.

"I told the paper I wanted to take a leave of absence," Camilla said suddenly with her toothbrush in her hand after Louise had made up the guest room. "And if they don't give it to me, I'm going to quit. But I think I'm going to quit anyway," she added after a moment's thought.

Louise nodded. She had spoken with Camilla's boss herself. He was deeply concerned about one of his top reporters and told Louise he was prepared to support her. In the end, he was the one who'd run her byline photo with the article without thinking about it.

"I'd really like your permission to call a crisis psychologist I know at National Hospital," Louise said from the guest room doorway once Camilla was tucked into bed. "His name's Jakobsen. He's really good. And there's no point in your beating yourself up with all this guilt. There's really a risk all this will overwhelm you."

Louise expected a bunch of protests, so when they didn't come, she could almost hear her preplanned, must-convince-Camilla speech crash and burn.

"That's probably a good idea," Camilla said, turning off the light.

18

I'm guessing they wanted to secure his tongue so he couldn't scream," Flemming Larsen said as he and Louise sat in his office on the Monday morning following the autopsy. "Given the configuration of the courtyard, the killer or killers were probably standing in the archway waiting for him. They grabbed him from behind and plunged the knife under his chin so it attached his tongue to his palate. That silenced him while they dragged him into the courtyard and splayed him out between the four benches."

"Which is why no one heard anything."

Louise took one of the two sodas Flemming had brought up to his office from the vending machine. She was heartened that he, too, valued their friendship enough to take a little extra time to discuss the autopsy with her.

Her mind filled with images of the courtyard off Sønder Boulevard. There had been a number of bikes along the wall of the building in front of the garbage cans. So someone could easily have entered the courtyard while the murder was taking place, she thought, picturing the location of Kaj's body.

"I wonder how long it took for him to die," she said,

looking over at Flemming, who was almost done with his Fanta.

"We know he was still alive when he was tied to the benches. You yourself saw that his hands were dark and filled with blood," Flemming said, then added that they were also a little swollen. "That tells us there was still circulation in his body."

Louise nodded as he spoke, peering down at the crime-scene photos showing enlargements of the details on the hands and throat.

"He has red foam around his mouth," Flemming explained. "Which means he started aspirating his own blood. The blood that goes down the trachea froths up as the victim breathes rapidly out of fear. I'm certain he lived for a while before he asphyxiated."

Louise closed her eyes for a moment, acknowledging the shiver of horror that traveled through her body.

"In other words, he choked on his own blood," she said, opening her eyes again.

The gravity of the situation had drawn a deep wrinkle across the tall pathologist's forehead. He nodded, a thoughtful expression on his face.

"As long as his tongue was stuck, he couldn't swallow. After that, it looks like they turned the knife around and pulled it, creating a long incision which sliced open his throat and trachea longitudinally all the way down to his breastbone, where the incision fades away on the left side of the anterior thorax."

Louise couldn't hide the shudder that coursed through her. She knew Flemming well enough to tell that he, too, was profoundly affected by the depravity of this murder.

"They knew exactly what they wanted to do with this execution," she said, blocking out the light and sounds for a second while the pieces of this portrait of bestiality fell completely into place.

"To show everyone in that world that you keep your mouth shut if you see something," Flemming said, finishing her idea.

Their eyes met.

"And all the same, they took the time to tie him up and do the job thoroughly, before leaving him there in the courtyard. Which shows that whoever did this couldn't have cared less if anyone happened to walk into the courtyard and catch him in the act," Flemming concluded.

Louise got up and stuck the crime-scene techs' pictures back into the bag. Flemming came over and put his arms around her shoulders, looking into her eyes the whole time. "Are you OK?" he asked her.

Louise sighed and shrugged. "Mostly it's Camilla who's not OK," she responded. "I just really want to find out who's evil enough to subject a harmless elderly man to this. I mean, here's the evidence of how pointlessly brutal Eastern European crime gangs are—and apparently, we've got them right here in Copenhagen now, too."

"Yeah, you have to admit these people are more ruthless than the criminals we're used to," Flemming admitted, pulling Louise into a quick hug as they reached the elevator.

"Take care of yourself," he told her, as the elevator door opened in front of them.

Louise gave his hand a squeeze and thanked him for the soda, before stepping in and pressing the lobby button to return to Police Headquarters and her Monday briefing, which had been pushed back until after the autopsy.

❧

"This morning our interpreter, Igli, intercepted information that Arian is going to go pick someone up at the airport this afternoon," Willumsen reported once everyone was gathered around the circular conference table in Suhr's office. "It's Starling flight NB564 scheduled to arrive from Prague at 1:55 p.m. And I want all four of you out there. We're going to get to the fucking bottom of what's going on now. Before they slaughter anyone else."

Toft nodded. "Do you want us to follow his car out there? Or not make contact until the arrivals hall?" he asked, looking from Willumsen to Suhr.

"You two go wait at the airport," Willumsen responded, pointing to Toft and Stig. "Rick and Lars will tail them out there. But stay well back; don't let them see you."

"We're just going to be watching," Suhr added.

The group's collective mood had been tense ever since Kaj Antonsen's murder. Everyone had realized that they were going up against people who did not value human life in the slightest, and it was still rare to encounter this type of criminal in Denmark, even in the capital.

"Get out there and get into position. It's less than two hours until the plane lands, and I don't want you running through the airport at the last minute," Willumsen commanded. "From now on we're going to be right on their asses."

Then, as if he realized he was sending mixed signals, he started up again. This time, he spoke plainly, making clear that everything should take place without their being detected.

"And when you leave the airport, Toft and Stig will come back here and focus on the wiretap, and Rick and Jørgensen will stay on the two Albanians so we know where they go. Then everyone come back here. We have to find out what they're up to before we can plan our next move."

Louise and Lars were parked at opposite ends of the underground parking lot when Arian and his passenger drove their Audi down to P6 under Terminal 3.

They walked over to the elevator slowly, but there was a crowd of people with suitcases waiting to go up, so Louise pulled her partner over to the stairs instead. Up in the arrivals hall, they quickly spotted Toft and Stig, one of them with a newspaper, the other with a cup of coffee, expectantly eyeing the passengers as they emerged through customs. Louise nodded at the elevator and walked over to the arrivals screen, where she confirmed that the flight from Prague had just landed, five minutes ahead of schedule.

The two Albanians emerged from the elevator. Checking on the arrival status, they went to stand by the opening where the travelers came out.

"Do we guess the short-haired one is Hamdi? He matches the description Pavlína gave, and there is certainly no doubt that the driver is identical to the owner of the car," Louise told her partner, who nodded without taking his eyes off Arian, who had shoulder-length, slicked-back hair and glasses.

After waiting ten minutes with only a trickle of people clearing customs, a large group of travelers pulling suitcases appeared. Hamdi held up a white sign, but Louise couldn't see what it said from where she was standing. Stig walked right in front of her then, heading for a trash can to throw away his empty coffee cup.

Louise watched him.

"Ilana," he said on his way back past them as he returned from the trash can.

None of the new arrivals reacted to the sign, nor any from the next group, who came streaming out of customs and spread out in all directions. Louise walked over to the arrivals screen and saw that the baggage had already been assigned to a carousel. Which meant that the passengers could be out at any point. When she turned around to walk back over to her partner, she stopped and suddenly took a step to the left to avoid a column.

All the way over along the opposite wall she had caught a glimpse of bangs that had been cut just over the eyebrows. It was Pavlína, and Miloš Vituk was next to her. Both of them had their eyes trained on the two Albanians, who were steadily watching the stream of emerging travelers.

Louise walked back over to Lars and nodded in their direction. "Did you see when they arrived?"

He shook his head. "But they obviously aren't particularly eager to be seen," he remarked, returning his focus once again to the arriving passengers.

Louise agreed with him and followed along curiously as Pavlína suddenly took a few steps toward a young woman with long blond hair, who was carrying a big bag over her shoulder. The woman was almost all the way to the door and out to where the cabs were before Pavlína and Miloš made their presence known. After the two women greeted each other, Miloš gallantly offered to carry her bag, and they quickly walked toward the entrance to the train station underneath the arrivals hall.

"Who was that?" Lars asked after the three of them disappeared down the stairs to platforms 3 and 4.

"Maybe her sister," Louise suggested, shrugging her shoulders. She then added that of course it could also have been a friend coming to visit.

The two Albanians hadn't seemed to notice the other reunion, and were still standing there scanning the stream of people coming out of customs. The little luggage icon wasn't flashing on the screen anymore, which meant that all the bags had been picked up.

After ten minutes, they saw Arian take out his cell, and a moment later he stepped back from the crowd and spoke, gesticulating vigorously with his free arm. He walked over to the window that looked out over the luggage return carousels and scanned the area, but then came back and said something to Hamdi. It wasn't hard to tell from their body language that they were impatient and that something hadn't gone according to plan. They were pacing back and forth in front of the exit from customs.

Twenty minutes later, Arian made another call.

"I'm going to go over to the police service desk," Louise said. "From there, I can call Documentation and find out if there were any problems with the flight arriving from Prague. You hold the fort here, OK?"

Louise walked over to the office, which was in the corridor between arrivals and departures. She had a hard time imagining that the Documentation Group with the Danish National Police would be interested in an arrival from the Czech Republic, since anyone traveling between European Union member states that were covered by the Schengen Agreement could just walk right through without showing a passport—obviously, though, security might have flagged the flight, in which case passengers would have to show their passports.

Maybe they had detained Ilana for something like that.

Louise greeted a young officer and showed her police badge before asking if he could put her in touch with a person from Documentation and whoever was currently in charge of Concourse C, where the flight had been directed, to see if the flight had had any security flags.

"Ask him if they detained anyone, and to check and see if there was a passenger with the first name 'Ilana' on the flight manifest for Starling NB564 from Prague."

Louise waited patiently while he checked on this. Documentation didn't have anything. It took a little longer to access the flight manifest, but when the officer on duty called him back five minutes later, he was able to report that an Ilana Procházková was on the manifest but that she had never checked in.

Louise thanked him for his help. It wasn't hard to see that the young officer was intrigued, but he refrained from asking what was wrong when she didn't volunteer anything.

"Let's see what happens," Lars said when Louise returned. "I'm sure they'll give up at some point and drive back into town. At least now we've put faces to the two names," he said, trying to look at the bright side of a trip that hadn't turned up anything useful.

Louise nodded and glanced over at the men, wondering which one had done the knife work in the Meatpacking District. Since Arian owned the car and apparently also did the driving, she guessed it was Hamdi who had jumped out of the back seat.

The two Albanians gave up an hour later and drove back to Copenhagen. The whole way back in from Kastrup Airport, Louise and Lars took turns tailing the dark Audi with their two colleagues.

"Remember to maintain eye contact if he looks at you,"

Lars warned when they pulled right up next to the car at a stop light in Amager at one point.

Louise nodded. She knew looking away was an easy way to tip people off. They made room for Toft and Stig as they passed Hotel Scandinavia, and they agreed that their colleagues would turn off at Police HQ while they followed the Audi for the rest of the trip.

They continued along Tietgensgade behind Central Station with the sun glaring on the windshield, then drove down past the conference center.

There was a lot of traffic. It was a quarter after five, and the cars were inching along over Halmtorvet. If they lost the Audi, they could fall back on the electronic chip Toft had mounted underneath it, but they wanted to be able to follow them in person to see where they went after they parked.

With two cars between, they continued down past the Meatpacking District. Traffic was much less heavy here, and when they turned up Saxogade, Louise started to relax.

"They're going to the club," she said and started looking for a parking spot. They'd had the Albanian club under surveillance since Pavlína told them about it, but they hadn't seen any sign of Arian or Hamdi going there. The Audi parked two buildings farther up the street.

"Let me out," Louise said quickly. "I'll stay here while you find a parking spot."

She hopped out of the car just outside the club and busied herself by rooting around in her bag while she watched the two Albanians approaching her.

They were talking and didn't look her way. All the same, she pulled back in against the wall of the building and turned her face away. Arian sounded angry, as if it were

Hamdi's fault the girl hadn't shown up. They took the four steps down into the basement club in two bounds and disappeared through the door.

In the brief instant the door was open, Louise saw that there were a fair number of people inside. She smelled smoke and heard conversations. She stood a bit waiting for Lars, who'd found a spot not too far away.

They stepped into a doorway with a good view of the entrance to the basement club, but Louise realized the view was just as good from inside the club. So, every time the club door opened, they were sure to back farther into the shadow of their doorway.

"They've made us," Louise confirmed after she noticed a head pop up over the side of the stairwell to look in their direction. "Let's move over to the other side of the street."

Three older men deep in conversation walked down the sidewalk and went down the stairs into the club side by side.

"I wonder what they do down there?" Louise said, considering the basement windows covered with faded yellowish curtains.

"Play cards, talk, smoke," Lars said.

Louise smiled. "Sounds like just the place for you," she said.

Lars nodded. "Doesn't sound so bad to me. Nice to have a place to hang out," he said. "A woman-free zone with a bar and gambling."

"They're playing for money?"

Her partner started laughing. "What, did you think they were playing Go Fish? I'm betting that sometimes they play for quite a bit, but they're clever enough to use all kinds of codes so there'll never be money there in the clubs if the police stop by."

He shook his head. "But that's true of all clubs, not just the Albanian one," he hastened to add. "It's like that in most of the expat clubs we've raided."

"Damn," Louise exclaimed. "And here I thought they were drinking sweet tea and chatting about old friends and memories. In reality it's organized gambling with a bar."

Two hours had elapsed without any sign of Arian or Hamdi. At a little past six, they agreed to return to HQ, where Willumsen was still waiting for them.

They found him in his office, collecting all the information that was still coming in about Kaj Antonsen's murder. A large team from the downtown precinct was working on questioning the residents of the buildings surrounding the courtyard, and the first reports from the crime-scene techs had just been turned in. He stood up and cleared the meeting table while Louise went to get Toft and his partner.

"There's no doubt that those two were up to something that didn't work out for them," Toft stated. "We traced the calls made from Arian's cell phone during the time we were at the airport and they all went to a foreign number, which we weren't able to identify. But the country code was the Czech Republic, so I think we could assume that he was trying to get hold of the Czech contact who was supposed to see the girl off."

Willumsen nodded. "That's a good guess, anyway," he said, eyeing Toft and Stig. "I suggest you do another round at the hotels off Istedgade this evening and see if anyone knows the two Albanians, but stay on top of what Igli gets out of the wiretap so we make sure we're keeping up with them."

They both nodded, and Willumsen glanced quickly at Louise and Lars.

"You two are going to Istedgade," he ordered. "Get the rundown on the scene so we have some idea how many Eastern European prostitutes are working out there these days."

He asked Lars to set up one of the department's small video cameras in his backpack. "Stroll around and listen to the solicitations you get from the hookers. Keep the camera hidden, obviously, but make sure the lens is unimpeded when the girls talk to you."

Once Lars nodded that he understood, Willumsen added he could get someone to help him set it up in his backpack if he had any trouble.

"I'm sure I can figure it out on my own," Lars was quick to say. Louise knew he hated going to the techies for help, because they tended to scoff anytime there was something the "desk officers" couldn't handle.

Willumsen had already moved on to Louise.

"You keep an eye on the girls who use the rooms in that porn theater for their customers. We need to identify all those using the booths and, by elimination, the ones who are working for the Albanians. As of now, we still don't know if the Albanians' girls operate off the street or through a brothel—where they'll be harder to keep an eye on."

"They're working off the street," Louise said, reminding him what Pavlína had told them. "But, I'd still like to take a closer look at Club Intim and see whether Arian and Hamdi turn up."

Willumsen seemed to ignore her correction; he plowed ahead undeterred.

"First thing tomorrow, you guys are going to head over to Central Station. We're going to verify whether the girls meet there every morning to settle their tabs," he said, still to Louise and her partner.

"If what Pavlína claims is true, then there's definitely a pattern to it," Louise said.

"Exactly," Willumsen said. He added that Mikkelsen had put a few extra uniforms on the streets to keep a lookout for meetings of prostitutes and their potential pimps.

Earlier at the airport, Louise heard that Suhr had asked the downtown precinct for assistance detecting any pattern to identify locations on the Albanians' "route"—what Arian had called a few specific places in the neighborhood in one of the conversations Igli had translated. Mikkelsen had confirmed that the route included at least Istedgade, the streets around Halmtorvet, Sønder Boulevard, and Skelbækgade.

"How about if I start out at Arian's address early to-morrow morning?" Lars suggested. "Then I'll be on him as soon as he leaves his apartment, and Louise can head straight to Central Station and be ready if anyone shows up."

Willumsen nodded and looked at the time before getting up and retrieving his jacket from the coat hook on the back of the door.

"Let me know if anything interesting turns up," he said, closing his briefcase after he put his jacket on. "I'll see you two in here early tomorrow," he said to Toft and Stig. "You should also keep up-to-date on how far the CSI techs have gotten with the evidence from the murder site."

As the four detectives stood up, the chief was already on his way down the hall with a farewell wave.

Stig and Toft offered Louise a ride to Halmtorvet.

"Great," she said, popping back into her office where her partner was setting up his video camera in a backpack.

"Let's meet at Central Station later, OK?" she asked Lars.

19

In the pastor's kitchen, Camilla watched him operate the espresso machine. She was sitting on the bench at the table in an oversize T-shirt and a pair of faded jeans, with no makeup.

"I'm sure they'll find the people who did it," Jonas promised in his gravelly voice after he came into the kitchen to say hi to Markus and his mother. "Detective Louise told us that."

Camilla smiled at Jonas, tenderly running her hand over his hair while he kept his dark, serious eyes trained on her. She knew that Louise was still in touch with the two boys, and she was just as happy to have her friend handle that area of conversation. At the moment, she had her hands full just keeping herself above water.

"Louise also told us to take care of you because you're so sad about the murder," her son's best friend continued, which made Camilla choke up. Otherwise, she had mostly finished crying by this point. She felt a little more relaxed after talking to the psychologist at National Hospital and hearing she'd been granted the leave she had requested at work.

"Thanks," she said, giving the hand Jonas had placed on

her shoulder a little squeeze, before the boy disappeared up-stairs with Markus.

Høyer had given her a month off when they'd met at the paper earlier. He served her coffee as they sat on the sofas in the visitors' interview room and emphasized the leave was just long enough for her to get back up on her feet.

Camilla had sat across from him, staring as he spoke—it wasn't what she wanted. "The leave should be for an un-specified length of time," she said. "And if I'm not back in three months, I will totally understand if you hire someone else."

She had already heard he'd pulled someone off the news desk to replace her while she was away, and there would be a new intern starting next week as well.

Høyer had stood up and stepped over to the window with his back to her for several minutes before finally turning around and giving her a look she had trouble interpreting. It was a confusing combination of concern, helplessness, and burgeoning irritation. In the end he gave in, dropping his head in exasperation. But he wanted her permission to call her while she was on leave to check up on her.

She hugged him before leaving, because she was brim-ming over with relief.

"I read about Kaj Antonsen in the paper yesterday," Henrik said, setting a cup of espresso in front of her. "*Morgenavisen* wrote that you were seeking his next of kin, but from today's article I take it no one has come forward yet. Did you get hold of his ex, the one who left him when their son died?"

Camilla nodded. "But she didn't want anything to do

with him—as far as she was concerned, he had died years ago—when she lost her son. She said he doesn't have any family but made it abundantly clear she wanted nothing to do with the funeral, so I thought I'd take care of it myself."

The pastor sat down across from her. "You don't need to do that," he said. "If there isn't any next of kin, then the Danish government will take care of it."

Camilla shook her head and said that she didn't want that. Kaj should have a proper funeral.

"Which is why I wanted to ask if we could hold it here at your church."

"Certainly," he said warmly but with a look that meant he wondered if she was sure she'd thought her decision through.

Camilla knew she was going against the sad contemporary trend in Denmark where the next of kin try to get out of arranging funerals for family members to avoid the bill. But she'd thought a great deal about Kaj, and even though they had known each other for only a few hours, she knew she wasn't doing it merely out of compassion. It was also to ease her own conscience.

"What do you think about a funeral service, and then afterward we can inter his urn in the unmarked graves?" Pastor Henrik suggested.

Camilla shrugged. She hadn't made any decisions on the details and was happy to go along with whatever the pastor recommended, as long as Kaj got a proper sendoff. She didn't think a proper sendoff would fix anything, really— but it just felt right.

Her eyes drifted over to the TV, which was on but muted. The evening news was in the middle of its report on Baby Girl, who had been brought to Skodsborg Orphanage. It had been a week since the boys had found her, and the mother still hadn't come forward. That meant the baby would probably be put up for adoption. In other words, Skodsborg was just a layover on the little girl's journey.

One week, Camilla thought. The abandoned baby felt like the distant past already.

She wished she could forget everything that had happened since she was found.

"Can we play Johnny Cash in church?" she asked, turning from the TV to the pastor and gulping the rest of her espresso.

He smiled and said that since no one else was helping plan the service, there was no one to object to that.

Camilla felt herself grinning; it was totally liberating to feel something other than the hurt of the past two and a half days.

"There will be a ton of flowers," she said. "But I don't think we need to do any singing."

She sat for a moment, staring off into space.

"I guess I didn't know him," she said. "Maybe it's too much stuff." There was a little pause.

"I don't know if I'm going to go back to writing," she said softly, leaving the topic of the funeral for a bit. "Before all this, I felt like writing had a kind of legitimacy and gave meaning to the things I did. But it's pretty darn hard to see it that way now. No news story justifies what happened to Kaj."

She could see the pastor weighing what he wanted to say next, but she just wasn't up to listening to anyone else encouraging her to stop feeling guilty. So she was glad for the interruption when the kitchen door knocker made three loud clunks.

Camilla glanced up at the clock over the sink. Nine fifteen. The boys were still up in Jonas's room watching a movie or playing computer games. Markus had insisted that it wasn't too late for him, even though, at this rate, they might not be home until ten.

There was a young foreign woman standing outside, the same one who had been by the day the boys found the little girl inside the entrance to the church. The last time she came she'd rung the bell at the front door of the pastor's residence. Now she was standing at the back door, holding out a slip of paper to Pastor Holm.

He glanced at it and shrugged.

"I don't understand," he said, and invited her in.

It was a warm spring evening outside, and yet a cold draft rushed through the kitchen. Henrik pointed to the coffee cups, but the woman stood just inside the door and politely declined.

Camilla didn't remember the woman being so tall, and this time she had a more insistent look, which was trained on the pastor. Then Camilla remembered that Henrik had asked the woman to come back again after a week.

He apologized and explained that unfortunately he hadn't been able to find her any work, but offered to keep an eye out and let her know if anything turned up.

The woman shook her head vigorously and pointed at the slip of paper.

He studied it again, before passing it to Camilla and asking if she could make out any of what it said.

Daj ovoj devojci posao u tvojoj kući, i tvoj
dug je plaćen.

Camilla shook her head. She couldn't make sense of
even a single word.

"Looks like Croatian; if it were Serbian it'd be in
Cyrillic," Henrik said. "It's going to take me some time to
translate it. Luckily, I have a dictionary from my time in
Bosnia."

He started explaining to the woman again that he
couldn't help her right now. "Give me your number, and I'll
call you if anything comes up," he said.

She shook her head and kept pointing at the slip of
paper.

Finally, the pastor asked her to wait a moment. He
turned on the light in the living room next to the bookshelf
and he returned a moment later with a worn dictionary and
a pair of reading glasses.

Slowly, word by word, he translated the first sentence:

"Give this girl a job in your home, and your debt is
paid," he read after writing the words down on the back of
a shopping list. He started on the next sentence, but after a
couple of words he pushed the paper away and apologetically shook his head, once again explaining to her that he
didn't need any help with his housework, he preferred to do
it himself.

He watched her reluctantly leave the kitchen and start
down the back steps. "What else did it say?" Camilla asked
once he was seated at the table again. Henrik emptied his

little coffee cup and pulled the piece of paper over to him, scanning the tall, thin letters.

"It says: 'Greetings from a friend.' But, of course, that could be anyone who knew I used to work down there."

Camilla asked what it had been like working in Srebrenica.

"Awful and wonderful," he said, smiling at her. "Some of the worst things I've ever experienced, but also some of the most life-affirming. Once you got used to the darkness, the food, and the mud, you started to see the people. Although it took me quite a while to get to know the people, because they were hiding under so many layers of pain and displacement. It was hard to say who they were—or who they had been."

Camilla nodded. His words had struck a chord, reminding her of something she'd experienced in the spring of 1998. The year after she had Markus, the *Roskilde Dagblad* had sent her to Kosovo to write a story about a young Danish woman from Lejre who was cleaning up land mines. After the young woman took Camilla and her photographer out into the minefield, they spent that evening in a bar where the woman introduced them to a young man Camilla guessed she was interested in, although she never actually admitted as much.

The young man told them a little about his story, which began four years earlier when he returned home one day to find his family's house ablaze. After neighbors helped put out the fire, they found his father and two brothers on the floor of the kitchen, each shot in the back of the head, and his mother and two little sisters were down in the basement. The basement door had been locked from outside.

The pastor nodded as she shared her story.

"We'll never fully understand the kind of trauma something like that marks a person with," he said. "I have a lot of good memories, too. Of really bonding with people, and helping people create new lives, even though their minds and bodies bore the scars. Small Muslim children would come in by night, rescued from Serbian areas where their families had been exterminated—but inexplicably the children had escaped."

Henrik paused, lost in thought, and Camilla watched the subtle expressions flicker across his face as he relived the memories.

"One Serb came by several times, always after dark, after most people were in bed."

The pastor absentmindedly tore the shopping list into small strips, his eyes following the motions of his fingers.

"He knew no one would take care of a Muslim baby in a Serbian zone, so he brought the baby to us at great peril to himself should anyone have caught him."

Henrik looked up.

"So, there were inspirational stories, too," he added, pushing aside the memories as he brushed the little pieces of ripped paper into a small pile. "But it was definitely an experience I'll always remember. Even though I see a very intimate side of people and their lives in my everyday work here, my time in Srebrenica left an indelible impression on me."

"Didn't it help, doing the work with your wife? A shared experience?"

Henrik nodded. "Definitely. And we had Jonas while we were there," he said, trying to brighten his voice and discard the gloominess.

Now it was Camilla's turn to nod.

"But then Alice died, and Jonas and I were on our own. I may have been a bit naïve, but I tried to create a home life for my son and me where our relationship is as close as possible—so he won't suffer so much from growing up without his mother. Of course, I know that I can never make up for her," he said with a wry little laugh and then a moment of silence before he spoke again.

"Neither my wife nor I had any family left, so it's just Jonas and me." He hesitated a little before continuing. "I suppose that's also why the idea of a housekeeper seems so alien to me. There's no room for a stranger in the life Jonas and I have together."

Camilla understood what he meant. But at the same time, she felt sorry for him, because it would probably prevent him from ever falling in love again.

"Do you think the service could be Thursday or Friday? Or should we wait until the weekend?" she asked, turning the conversation back to Kaj's funeral.

"That depends on when the police will release the body," Henrik responded.

Camilla ran her hand over her hair, resting her face in her hands for a second. "Right," she said. "We'll have to wait and see what they say."

"Can we have some ice cream?"

The boys startled her, suddenly rushing into the kitchen.

She watched Henrik ruffle his son's hair as he nodded at the freezer. She warned Markus that they ought to be getting home.

"We can leave as soon as we're done with the ice cream," he said, and she nodded obligingly. She held out her cup when Henrik offered her more coffee, knowing it would keep her up all night. At least that way the thoughts and guilt that had kept her on the brink of sleep for the past two nights wouldn't haunt her tonight.

"Call me after you talk to the police. Do you have my cell number?" Henrik asked.

She reached for the scraps of the shopping list and wrote his number down on a free corner, thanking him for the coffee and especially the conversation.

20

"Suck and fuck, 500 kroner!"

Lars played the recording back for Louise on the video camera's tiny screen.

It was ten fifteen, and Mikkelsen had just called Louise's cell to let her know he was on his way over as well.

Lars explained that he began his tour by walking down Istedgade. He continued onto the surrounding streets and headed over on Skelbækgade, where he'd gone up to Dybbølsbro Station and back, before calling Louise and telling her he was ready to meet up at Central Station.

She grabbed another chair and pulled it over to their high table outside the only snack kiosk still open that late, just as Mikkelsen walked up with his hands in his pockets and his leather jacket open, revealing a bright red shirt that lit up the sleepy train station.

Mikkelsen laughed when he listened to the recording. "How could you resist such an appealing offer?"

Lars blushed, and Louise smiled.

"Nah, but a guy who works with my wife did walk by while I was talking to one of the women—so there may be some conversation over the watercooler at my wife's company tomorrow," Lars said, not looking particularly worried.

"What was he doing in that neighborhood?"

Louise briefly considered the possibility that Lars's wife might think her husband had been seeking comfort from a prostitute because they were having trouble at home.

"Oh, he had just come out of one of the restaurants."

She nodded. She, too, had been struck by the strange mix of crowds created as Copenhagen's red-light district had turned trendy in recent years, and there were a number of destination restaurants and cafés there now that drew in a whole new clientele compared to the people on the margins of life who lived there.

"How many of the women do you think were Czech?" Mikkelsen asked.

"A good number," Lars replied. He paused a moment, then admitted that he had a hard time telling exactly which country the Eastern European women were from.

"You can tell which ones are from Africa just by looking at them, and you can hear which ones are from Denmark by listening to them. But I really couldn't tell you if a woman was from the Czech Republic, Slovakia, Poland, or Romania, for that matter. Maybe Igli can help us narrow it down if he looks at the tapes?"

Mikkelsen nodded and said he got the impression a lot of them were Czech, actually. "Although we have taken a bunch of Czech women into custody lately in raids, and then they stay scarce on the street for a while after that. Of course, they come pouring right back in again soon enough."

Lars grabbed one of the kiosk's limited, laminated menus and decided on two Danish-style hot dogs. Mikkelsen got a Polish sausage in a bun, while Louise opted for the croque monsieur. After they paid, Louise told them that an elderly lady who lived on Istedgade across from

Club Intim had been nice enough to let her sit in her living room for the last two hours of her stakeout on the club.

"I also saw Arian in the dark Audi. He drove up a little after eight and parked farther down the street," Louise reported. "And Hamdi was working. He walked up and down the stretch of sidewalk in front of Club Intim with an armful of dark red roses that he was trying to sell to passing drivers. He apparently supplements his income that way."

She looked at Mikkelsen to see if this were something he was aware of. Her colleague ran a hand over his stubble, a smile lighting up his face.

"Well, you may be giving him a bit too much credit," he said and then grew serious again. "The roses are just an excuse. When he walks around like that, he's really just keeping his eye on the women. If he doesn't think they're doing enough, he goes after them."

One of Louise's eyebrows shot up as she nodded thoughtfully. Of course, she thought, suddenly remembering an old case from Southern Jutland where several foreign pimps had assigned their women numbers and ranked them by earnings, that is, how much they brought in per hour and how much per day. The information was useful when they later sold the women—maybe that was why they kept such a close watch on these women, Louise thought. They needed a way to estimate productivity and keep track of each woman's value. Someone at the Nest had explained how harsh the punishment was if the women didn't live up to what was expected of them. God, it must cause tremendous stress to have their pimps' eyes on them all the time like that, she thought.

"I saw Pavlína," Louise said, after her partner set food and drinks on the table in front of them. "She was walking with the girl she and Miloš picked up at the airport, but I didn't have a chance to ask if that was her sister."

Mikkelsen reported that he'd stopped in at the basement grocery and chatted with his other informants.

"People are worried," he said, explaining he'd heard from a number of sources that there were more new girls. "They've been reorganized a little, and the fee they have to pay to use the street has gone up."

"How the hell can they raise the price?" Louise exclaimed, accepting the cup of coffee Lars handed her.

"It happens any time there are suddenly a lot of women walking the street. Someone will offer to keep the sidewalk 'clean' for the prostitutes who pay. Then the neighborhood gets divided up into sort of zones where some areas are more attractive than others."

"I don't get why the women go along with this," Lars objected, looking at Mikkelsen.

"Yeah, I know," Mikkelsen agreed. "But if you think about the long lines of women standing along the old rural highways out by the border between the Czech Republic and Austria, and then they find out that they could be earning a lot more if they just went to Copenhagen, well then maybe it's not so strange. I mean, don't forget, quite a few of the women are here of their own free will, because they can make a lot more money here than where they come from. They're not just here because greedy men have forced them up here with violence," he added. "The percentage of prostitutes who are victims of human trafficking is surprisingly quite small."

Louise nodded but argued that human trafficking would increase if the police didn't start coming down harder on the traffickers.

"True enough," Mikkelsen said. "But as long as we have a minister of justice with no compassion for these women, it'll be damn hard to prevent. If she ever mentions the police stepping up their efforts against trafficking in women and pandering, I suspect it will have more to do with political strategy than because she really wants to fix the problem."

Mikkelsen smiled sarcastically. "If she can go to the press and say that she's increasing the sentences for violent crimes, that will do her some real good. That's the kind of thing that gets you votes," he continued, snapping Louise out of her reverie. "Not prostitutes."

"Well, we certainly can't praise our own higher-ups for being particularly committed to the cause, either," Louise pointed out. Lars immediately backed her up on that.

"Until we put more resources into cleaning up the pimps and traffickers, they can pretty much continue to operate with impunity," Lars said.

"Except of course when they start murdering people," Louise added and finished off her coffee.

Mikkelsen nodded and stood up. "I'll meet you guys here in the morning and we can see what's going on." He yawned. "Should we say around nine?" he suggested, looking at Louise.

"It's a date," she said. Then she and Lars strolled down the length of the train station's main concourse out to the bus stop, while Mikkelsen headed off for the rear exit.

The next morning Lars called Louise's cell just before ten to report that Arian had just left his apartment. He hadn't taken the Audi and was instead walking toward the Valby train station.

"I'm at Central Station now," Louise said. She'd been standing in the bookstore but had stepped out when her phone rang.

"I'll call you again when we get close, so you'll be ready," Lars said.

"Sounds good."

Morning rush hour was over. The people in the station were more relaxed now, taking time to stop and study the departure screens before heading down to the various platforms. Mikkelsen had gone to get himself a cup of coffee and a croissant, and Louise was studying the bookstore's sale table, browsing through the books from one end to the other. Some caught her interest, others she rejected just for their covers. After Lars called back a little later to say Arian and he were on the light rail B line heading toward Holte, Louise found Mikkelsen and told him that Arian would arrive about 10:27.

That was three minutes away, and Mikkelsen nodded toward a woman with short, blond hair.

"I think she's the first one," he said softly. "It looks like she's hanging around, waiting, and I don't think it's for a train."

The woman sat down on the very edge of the bench in front of the Danish National Railways' fast food window. She looked at her watch and clutched her little purse tightly under her arm.

Arian came up from the platform below with his hands in his pockets. His hair was slicked back, and he had an ambling gait. As he passed the woman, she got up and quickly slipped him something. The next second she was gone. They didn't exchange a word.

Lars was still over by the escalators, while Mikkelsen had pulled back in case Arian recognized him. Although they'd never had anything to do with each other, people talked, and a lot of people in the prostitution world knew the folks from the local police station. Louise walked over and sat down on the bench. She set her purse in her lap and slowly opened a newspaper in front of her.

She watched the Albanian buy a cup of coffee and a roll. After that he sat down at the table Mikkelsen had just left, and started flipping through one of the free newspapers Mikkelsen had left behind.

They came, one at a time. Handing over their money and leaving. They looked like friends happening to bump into each other; a short greeting and then the women moved on. Arian only took a couple of bites of his food, and Louise had the sense he was dragging it out, killing time like every other person who was waiting for the next train.

A young woman approached him hesitantly, her eyes trained on the floor. Intermittently, she raised her face and glanced at him fleetingly, while everything about her body language suggested she did not want to walk over to him.

Louise instinctively knew that Arian had seen the woman, even though his eyes were still focused on his newspaper. When she finally made it up to his café table, Louise watched her lips forming the words while she gestured in despair with her arms. Louise also saw how quickly Arian was up out of his chair and how aggressively he pulled the woman to him so they were standing face-to-face. He leaned in threateningly as he chewed her out.

Several people walking by saw the incident but quickly looked away, opting to hurry on toward their destinations.

Just then someone came running toward Arian and the woman. Louise saw Mikkelsen step forward as Lars approached from the escalators.

Hamdi brutally pushed the woman away and pulled Arian aside as he angrily and nervously delivered a message. Whatever he had said drove the men to leave, running toward the station's rear exit and then down the stairs toward Reventlowsgade.

Lars followed them, and Mikkelsen walked over to the young woman, who had sat down, shaken.

Louise guessed Mikkelsen asked her if she was all right, because the woman quickly nodded, brushed aside his expression of concern, and hurried off.

There were two options, and Louise wavered between keeping an eye on the young woman or following her partner. But when Mikkelsen started to head for the escalator, Louise decided to stay, watching the woman's nervous looks and the scared expression on her face.

It took a little while before Louise realized her cell phone was ringing in her purse, and by the time she noticed it she was afraid it was too late.

Willumsen's voice was clear and precise; he didn't waste any time on hellos. "A German tourist just pulled a young foreign woman out of Copenhagen Harbor, alive," he reported succinctly. "I want you to go down to National Hospital right away and talk to her."

"Do we know what happened?" Louise asked.

"The tourist spotted her while he was pulled over, figuring out where he was on his map. She was lying in the water with both hands tied behind her back. A pouch hanging under her shirt against her stomach contained a Czech passport listing her name as Hana Simrová, born in 1990. There was also some cash. We're trying to get the female interpreter in right now, the one we used with Pavlína. We'll send her straight to the hospital when we get hold of her. Toft and Stig are on their way down to the harbor; their tracker shows that the Audi A4 left the Albanian's Valby address at 10:13 a.m. and, strangely enough, was at Kalvebod Wharf on Copenhagen Harbor only half an hour ago," Willumsen said.

"Wow, that's quite brazen, throwing her into the water

in broad daylight," Louise commented once he'd finished. "I'm sure you won't be surprised that the Audi showed up at Central Station less than ten minutes ago. At least—Hamdi came running in and got Arian."

Louise leaped to her feet and asked if he'd reserved patrol cars for the detectives so she could head straight to the motor pool, or if she had to go upstairs and sign a car out first.

"Just go straight there. I'll make sure there's a car waiting for you."

From the sidewalk out front she called Lars to update him on Willumsen's information.

"I'm on my way to National Hospital now, but I'd really like to know what the wiretap picks up for the next couple hours," Louise said as she crossed Bernstorffsgade and continued past Tivoli toward the police parking garage.

21

A young woman, pale and wrapped in a large bathrobe, was sitting on a chair in the examining room. She had a towel around her hair, so her face was exposed only from eyes to chin, to which she had pulled up the bathrobe like a collar. She was holding a plastic mug of hot chocolate, and her eyes wandered a little as Louise held out her hand and introduced herself.

The interpreter wasn't there yet, so Louise tried English and asked if the woman understood.

"A little," she replied, eyeing Louise uncertainly before confirming that her name was Hana Simrová.

The door opened and a nurse peeked in. She told Louise that she had been the first one to see the woman when she arrived in the ambulance.

"At first glance it doesn't appear that she's suffered any serious harm, but she is suffering from exposure and is of course in shock," she said. "I'll send the doctor in as soon as she's done with the patient in the next room."

Louise nodded and turned back to the young woman, but she didn't have a chance to say anything before the interpreter opened the door.

The interpreter smiled at Louise and walked over to the chair and said hello to Hana.

The girl crept further into the bathrobe every time a new person stepped into the hospital room, but when the interpreter started speaking Czech, Hana's shoulders seemed to relax a little.

"Have you spoken with Pavlína since that day?" the interpreter asked Louise as she took off her jacket and laid it over the back of the chair.

"Pavlína!" Hana exclaimed, and she seemed desperate as she spoke a long stream of Czech words directly to the interpreter.

Louise leaned forward in her chair and listened, even though she didn't understand the slightest bit of what was being said. To her, it sounded like chains of words being pulled through the room, rising and falling in strength. Hana gesticulated madly, and the interpreter's face turned serious. She pulled her chair all the way over to Hana while Louise stayed back. Finally, the flood of words ebbed, and the woman started shaking, and now Louise stepped over to the crying woman and introduced herself. The doctor slipped in quietly.

"I'm Karen," the doctor said quickly. "Would you mind waiting outside while I examine her?" She looked at Louise through small, gold-rimmed glasses. "But I'm sure I'll be needing your help," she said to the interpreter.

It took fifteen minutes before the door opened again. Louise asked if she could come in.

The towel around Hana's head had come loose, and her long blond hair hung like a fraying rope down her back.

"It turns out that Hana here knows a Pavlína, and I think

it must be the same Pavlína we talked to because she also mentioned a Miloš," the interpreter explained.

Louise raised an eyebrow and looked at the young Czech woman. Her head was bent as she studied her own hands, folded in her lap. It wasn't until Hana raised her face, holding out her empty cup to the nurse who came in to offer her more hot chocolate, that Louise recognized Hana from the airport and their brief encounter on the street.

"Ask her if she's Pavlína's sister," Louise said.

The Czech woman shook her head, and the interpreter explained that they were just friends. "She lost her cell phone in the water, so she can't call Miloš Vituk and tell him what happened. She wants to know if we can call them so they'll come get her. She doesn't know where they live."

"Of course," Louise said. "But let's go down to Police Headquarters first so we can take her statement. That's where Miloš's phone number is, anyway. If you didn't bring your own car, you can ride with us. You'll have to come so I can ask her about what really happened out by the harbor."

At HQ, they ran into Toft in the hallway. He had just returned from the harbor and was on his way into the small room where they were monitoring the wiretap.

He greeted Hana politely and told Louise that several witnesses had seen the Audi at the wharf, but no one had seen the woman being thrown into the water.

Louise nodded toward the office where Igli was sitting, listening in on the wiretap. "Has there been anything?" Louise asked.

"Surprisingly little," Toft admitted.

"I'm on my way in to call Miloš Vituk and tell him what happened. Then he or Pavlína can bring Hana some dry clothes. I'll come see you after I've taken her statement," Louise said, disappearing into her office and shutting her door behind her.

22

It didn't take long. Hana Simrová was eighteen and from Ústí nad Labem in the Czech Republic, just like Pavlína. She had come to Denmark to visit Pavlína and was staying with her at Miloš Vituk's apartment. That morning, just as she and Pavlína had reached the front hallway of the building on their way outside, a car suddenly pulled up to the curb in front of them.

"When did this happen?" Louise asked, watching her.

Hana didn't know. Maybe ten o'clock or a little after.

"It all happened so quickly," the interpreter explained. "She thinks they must have been watching them. Two big, muscular guys jumped out of the back seat and grabbed hold of her. Pavlína screamed, but they hit her so hard she fell down. And then they drove away, leaving Pavlína behind. Hana doesn't remember anything else."

Louise asked about the plastic ties Hana's wrists were bound with.

"They twisted her arms behind her back before she had a chance to fight. They put them on in the car, and it hurt. But she was so scared that she just closed her eyes, because she didn't know what was going to happen or what they were going to do with her."

"What did they look like?"

Hana shook her head and sniffled a little as she apologized for not paying closer attention. She was just so scared.

"What about the guy driving the car? Was he big and muscular, too?" Louise asked, focusing intently on the Czech woman.

Hana shook her head and said that only the other two men were. "The third guy just sat behind the wheel."

Hamdi, Louise thought.

"She never really noticed him; she saw him only from behind, but his hair was short and straight, and he drove really fast the whole way."

The car had driven down to C. But even there the woman didn't understand what was happening until she was in the water and the car was speeding off, its tires screeching.

"Tell us what happened after they drove away," Louise asked. "How long did it take before the German man rescued you?"

Hana closed her eyes for a second, as if she were trying to run through the whole scenario for details, but then she faintly shrugged her skinny shoulders and shook her head.

"Not that long," the interpreter said. "She says she kept her mouth closed and focused on trying to stay afloat. But she has no idea how long it was before she heard someone jump into the water and felt herself being pulled in toward the wharf."

Louise accepted that Hana couldn't provide any more information. The young woman still seemed quite shaken and was pale and weak from exposure.

"How long will she be in Denmark?" Louise asked,

looking back and forth between the interpreter and Hana as the question was translated. Again now, the woman shrugged, her skinny shoulders moving up to her ears.

"That hadn't been nailed down yet. They invited her in the first place because Pavlína was missing her girlfriends from home, and Hana was thrilled to get the invitation and the airplane ticket they sent. This trip was her first step away from a life on the streets, and once here she could see how well things had gone for her friend."

Louise watched Hana, wondering how much the woman knew about Pavlína's ordeal before she met Miloš.

"Ask her if she's here just on vacation," Louise instructed the interpreter.

Hana nodded and looked at her a little uncertainly.

Louise smiled apologetically at her. Just then the front desk called and announced she had a visitor. Louise got up to go meet them so Hana could get her clothes.

Miloš Vituk was alone as he approached with a white plastic bag in one hand. His mouth narrowed, and Louise could see that he was angry about the assault on Pavlína, even though he was mostly preoccupied with Hana right now.

"What happened?" he asked after greeting Louise. "Is Hana hurt?"

Louise shook her head and said she was mostly in shock. "Why do you think this happened?" Louise asked, looking at him for a long time.

It took him quite a while to respond.

"Could it be anyone other than the Albanians?" he finally said. "I don't really have any enemies in Denmark, but I'm guessing those two have it in for me because I'm taking such good care of Pavlína."

"Have they asked you for more money?" Louise wanted to know.

He shook his head, his shoulders drooping.

Louise refrained from pointing out that the Albanians probably thought he was a long-term source of money now, since they'd already pressured him into paying far more than their original demand. Now they were setting the limits, not Miloš.

"They don't have anything to do with Hana, but still they hurt her," he said. "Pavlína is really upset and scared."

Hana stayed in her seat when they came into Louise's office, but Hana smiled cautiously at him, pulling her bathrobe even tighter around her, as if she suddenly realized that all her wet clothes were in a bag.

Miloš walked over and kissed her head, where her hair was now mostly dry. He held out the dry clothes, and the interpreter offered to accompany her to the bathroom, where she could get dressed.

Louise studied Miloš when they were alone.

He had taken a seat and looked miles away. His thoughts were obviously elsewhere. "They're not going to leave us alone," he finally said, looking at her despondently. "This will continue as long as Pavlína and I stay in Copenhagen. But I won't stand for it. They have all the control, and they're violent with the girls. Pavlína was badly hurt today—I think they broke her nose. I'm going to take her to the doctor after we're through here."

When Hana returned, she was wearing a light dress that revealed her skinny body, which could have belonged to a child. There were no breasts or hips evident under the material.

Miloš offered her his sweater when he noticed her shivering again. His sweater was almost longer than her dress, a little bit of yellow peeking out from beneath the bottom of the sweater. Miloš took Hana's arm, and they walked close together as Louise followed them out.

"We'll put tails on the Albanians," Willumsen began once the whole group was present. He nodded at Toft and Stig, then moved his eyes onto Louise and her partner before he continued:

"You two keep an eye on Miloš Vituk and the girls. We don't want to risk anything else happening to them, and it doesn't seem like these guys are going to leave them alone until they're sure they can't get any more money out of Miloš. Mikkelsen's got his people on the street, and our interpreter Igli is monitoring the wiretap."

He nodded to the room behind him.

"And then I think it's time we drag those two Albanians in here for questioning. It's about fucking time we find out where they were when those two murders took place and confront them with the fact that they were seen at the wharf, right?" continued Willumsen, raising his voice as he spoke and looking at each of his detectives in turn.

"The car was there, but we don't know for sure who was in it," Toft corrected. He pointed out that no one had seen Arian or Hamdi, just the two gorillas who'd roughed the girls up so badly. "Until we have some evidence that they're somehow involved in prostitution, it's just going to hurt the investigation if we start talking to them now about their connection with those two killings."

Willumsen was about to say something, but Toft beat him to it.

"We can't bring them in for questioning until we have enough evidence," he said. "If we strike too soon, they'll close up shop. And right now, we don't have enough."

Willumsen grumbled a little as he contemplated the situation.

"Fine. But I want to see photo documentation of them receiving money from the girls. Pictures of conversations on the street and of the girls heading off with their johns, whether to cars or down into the booths at Club Intim. And they'd better be fucking close-ups."

The next day, they were standing in a doorway on Valdemarsgade, each with a to-go coffee and a sandwich. They'd been waiting a long time when Miloš finally came down the stairs in the early afternoon. He opened the door and stood with his back to the street, waiting. Pavlína emerged shortly thereafter. She was walking slowly, her head bent. Out on the sidewalk he took her under the arm and started walking so fast that she was having a hard time keeping up. Her eyes were trained to the ground, but Louise saw bruises on her face.

"I'll follow them. You stay here and keep an eye on Hana," Lars offered, crumpling up his sandwich wrapper, having taken his last bite.

Louise stepped out into the street a couple of times and looked up at the apartment's windows. One had been opened a crack before Miloš and Pavlína came down, but otherwise there were no signs of life to be seen behind the dark panes. She assumed Hana was still up there, and she figured they would be back soon so their young guest wouldn't be left on her own for too long following her experiences that morning.

Louise ate the rest of her sandwich leaning against the wall, and smiled at a woman who walked her bicycle up to the building with a baby in the seat on the back. Several people gave her curious looks as they came and went, but no one asked what she was doing. People were starting to come home from work, so there was a little more life on Valdemarsgade than earlier in the day, when it had been practically deserted.

Louise was lost in her own thoughts, still waiting, when she noticed a young couple who had stopped at the front door to Miloš's building. The man was carrying a couple of cloth shopping bags, and the woman was looking for something in her big shoulder bag, finally pulling out a key ring. They had just gotten the door open and the bags inside when a man in a dark, neat crew cut walked out. He was wearing a light gray suit. Louise watched them nod politely to each other before the man stopped abruptly on the sidewalk and looked at her. She thought he was going to come over, but then he started walking toward Vesterbrogade. Backing deeper into the doorway where she was standing, she typed a text message into her phone, wanting to find out where her partner was.

"Western Union," he texted back.

They must have gone to send some money abroad. People often did it that way: money transfers outside the banking system.

"On my way back," the next text said.

She strolled down the street a while until the man with the crew cut returned. He stopped at the front door to the building and rang the buzzer. As Louise waited, the man turned around; this time, she didn't have a chance to look away before their eyes met. Someone buzzed him in a second later.

Instead of returning to her doorway, Louise crossed the street and leaned against the front wall of Miloš's building to assure she wasn't visible from the windows above.

"It was nothing. They went and took care of their money matters and then went home again. No one contacted them along the way and they didn't seem particularly distracted."

Lars had come back shortly after Miloš and Pavlína.

"I'll just give Miloš a call and ask him how Hana's doing. Then I can also ask him if he's heard from the Albanians," Louise decided.

Miloš answered right away, as if he had been waiting for a call, and he sounded pleased that she was showing an interest. He assured her that Hana was doing better. He said she'd slept most of the day. And, no, no one had been in touch with him.

Louise could hear the TV and a quiet conversation in the background.

"I just ordered pizza," Miloš said, "and then we'll probably all go to bed early."

Louise said that sounded like a good idea, and he promised to call if anything happened.

"Well, have a good night," Louise said, jogging off to catch up with Lars, who was already walking down Valdemarsgade.

23

The funeral home was on Falkoner Allé, and when Camilla called to ask Louise if she would come, Louise assured her that it would be no problem.

"We spent the whole day yesterday keeping an eye on the building, and today Lars and I have been standing out here again since nine thirty this morning. Nothing has actually happened, so I'm sure he won't mind handling the surveillance on his own for a couple of hours," she said.

Camilla had found out earlier in the day that the police were ready to release Kaj Antonsen's body. No distant relatives had come forward yet. His ex-wife hadn't been in touch, either, and since she had declined to have any further involvement, Camilla was given permission to handle the practical details. She put in an obituary for tomorrow's paper saying the funeral would be at Stenhøj Church on Saturday.

"No, I don't have the deceased's birth certificate or baptismal records," she repeated patiently to the funeral director after she'd handed him the paperwork she'd gotten when the police released the body to her. "No, I don't have his spouse's birth certificate or their marriage certificate. But they've been divorced for years now."

Even though she'd already told him everything over the phone, the funeral director had wanted to run through the standard questions with her again in person.

Camilla gave Louise a pleading look. Camilla's smile was a little stiff, but she was trying to stay calm, and she just nodded briefly when the funeral director decided they would just have to do without the separation papers.

But when the funeral director repeated his question about a birth certificate, Camilla had finally had enough.

"Look, I assume you're aware that the deceased was the victim of a spectacular and extremely violent murder. The police are hard at work right now trying to locate his murderer, which is why they have not yet had the opportunity to provide me with all of his personal papers. But, of course, we could ask the police to switch around their priorities a little so they have time to get the paperwork in place before we plan the rest," Camilla said angelically.

Louise stayed back, pretending to study a framed poster listing most of the routine questions the funeral director would likely ask.

"And your relationship to the deceased?" the funeral director asked, looking up from his form. He had obviously decided to ignore Camilla's sarcastic outburst. "Ah, yes. You're the reporter who wrote the story in *Morgenavisen*, right?"

Camilla made do with a nod.

"Good," the funeral director finally said. "So, I'm going to assume you don't have a burial permit or a deed to a burial plot?"

"Correct," Camilla said tersely. "I don't think he was prepared to have someone slit his neck just then."

Louise turned and gave her a look.

The man behind the desk let her remark slide once again

and instead walked over to the wall where the urns were displayed. "Have you had a chance to think about which urn you're interested in?"

Camilla took a step back to look at the selection. "It doesn't need to be anything special," she said. "A standard one, if that's a thing."

The funeral director raised his eyebrow for a second and looked at Camilla. "That's not 'a thing.' But you can certainly get one without too many frills." He pointed up at a black vessel with a flat lid. The tag underneath said, "Simple." Next to that there was a "Simple Exclusive," and then the rest of them became progressively more ornate.

Camilla pointed to the no-frills urn and asked if everything could be arranged in time for the funeral on Saturday.

"We have the pastor scheduled for one p.m.," she said.

The funeral director nodded; he was obviously interested in wrapping up his business with Camilla Lind as quickly and efficiently as possible.

24

The afternoon sun shone from a spring sky practically devoid of clouds. They were lucky that Dells Bar had a free table out on the square in front of Frederiksberg Town Hall.

Louise ordered two beers in the hopes they'd help to shake off the funereal mood a little. Taking her first sip, she realized she didn't feel the least bit guilty about letting her partner hold the fort alone down on Valdemarsgade. At the morning briefing, Willumsen had made it clear he didn't think there was any reason to keep an eye on Miloš Vituk and the Czech girls anymore, but Suhr hadn't agreed. So they had decided to continue the surveillance at least for the rest of the day.

The only thing they'd noted so far was that Pavlína had brought a guest home with her—a young woman about the same age who had with her a bouquet of flowers that Louise figured were for Hana.

Louise watched Camilla sip at the thick foam at the top of her beer. She was worried about her friend, but not as much as she had been the first couple of days after the murder.

Camilla's chat with the crisis psychologist had apparently allowed her to acknowledge that some things were out of her control, even if she might have helped trigger them. Camilla was still weighed down in self-recrimination and guilt, but right now at least she was planning on using her leave of absence to reevaluate her goals in life and the steps she needed to achieve them.

"Right now, I don't have the slightest desire to go back to the paper," Camilla admitted when Louise asked what she was thinking.

"What do you want to do then?" Louise asked, holding her beer in her hands and tilting her head back, enjoying the sunlight.

"I don't know," Camilla said after a pause. "I might start writing books."

Louise smiled. What journalist wouldn't want to do that?

"Well, I recommend you write a murder mystery and become world-famous—then you'll be rolling in money," she said with her eyes closed, the warmth spreading from her face to the rest of her body. "Plus, it'll get you away from *Morgenavisen.*"

She heard Camilla scoot her chair slightly, but Camilla didn't say anything for quite a while.

"Maybe. But first I want to have a baby."

This news was so abrupt that Louise opened her eyes and gaped at her friend, who was watching a young woman pushing a stroller down the sidewalk in front of them.

Louise leaned forward over the table and set down her beer.

"You have a child," she reminded Camilla, who was watching the stroller with a serious expression, which confused Louise.

"I've always dreamed of having a whole bunch of kids, actually. And ever since I had Markus, I've known that I wanted one or two more, but nothing ever came of it. So, I've decided to do something about that dream so I won't have to look back and regret not even having tried."

"For Christ's sake, Camilla. You have plenty of time— you're only thirty-eight! You make it sound like you're closer to fifty. But you're also going to have to find the guy you want to have these kids with. Children are still something people dream about having together, usually."

Louise hadn't intended to sound quite so nagging, but Camilla picked up on it right away. "Why do you always get so uptight whenever kids come up?" she asked, irritated. "You're so down on kids."

"Oh, come on. That's ridiculous. But you already have Markus, after all, and he's the best. Besides, I guess I think people sound spoiled when they say their 'whole life' is a failure just because they haven't had the number of children they wanted, or something."

Camilla took a swig of beer and looked at Louise, who vaguely suspected the abandoned baby from the church had put this notion in her friend's head.

"I don't understand how you can be so negative when you don't even know what you're missing," Camilla said. "It's not like you haven't had a chance to have kids, either. If it'd been up to Peter, you'd have five by now. I think you're running the risk, yourself, of waking up one day and realizing it's too late."

Louise felt the emotion before it showed in her eyes. She went completely cold inside.

Here she'd been thinking they would spend a couple of pleasant hours together, Camilla would be able to get things off her chest, and maybe that would help her relax about all her inner turmoil. Instead the conversation had wound up here—where there was no comfortable way out.

She sat up straight and tried to sound more upbeat, holding in the cutting remarks that were on the tip of her tongue.

"I came to terms a long time ago with the fact that I don't think having kids is a right," she said. "Some people have kids, some don't. It's not something you can expect. Or an indicator of your life's success. You know I don't go around wishing my life were different than it is, and it's just turned out that my life doesn't include kids. But that doesn't make it a bad life."

Louise leaned back, realizing her voice was sounding defensive in spite of her best efforts.

"I don't mean to annoy you," Camilla said, trying to calm Louise down. "But it's different for me. I'm not sure I have time to wait for the right person to come along, so I'm considering artificial insemination."

Louise was speechless but then she shook her head. "As long as you don't make the government pay for it, well, good luck. I'll take care of Markus when you're breastfeeding."

Louise got up to pay. She was disappointed that the mood had been ruined. What bugged her the most, though, was that children had become a criterion for a successful life; who cared whether they were born out of love as long as you had them? If that were it, she'd rather be free. She remembered an old case where she had visited a fortune-teller, who in all seriousness told her that a child's soul chose the mother it wanted before it was born. Personally, Louise was just fine with the fact that no child's soul had picked her.

Camilla and Louise walked across the square to Falkoner Allé in silence.

"I can tell you've already made up your mind," Louise said.

Camilla nodded. "You know how I feel about people who talk up a storm about all the things they want but never step up and make it reality. If I'm going to criticize other people for all their empty talk, well then, I'd better fucking step up and do something about my own life. Otherwise I ought to just shut up," she said.

Louise smiled. "Well, I know you well enough to be fairly sure this shutting-up phase won't last long." She gave Camilla a quick good-bye kiss on the cheek and hurried across the street when the light turned green.

On the other side, she stopped and watched as Camilla's back disappeared toward Falkoner Center.

25

"This is going to take fucking months," Willumsen said, irritably, brushing cake crumbs off the papers on the table in front of him. The team was meeting around the conference table Friday afternoon before heading home for the weekend, and Willumsen was glaring at Stig, who had just said they still didn't have enough on the Albanians to take action.

"Obviously, we can haul them in for questioning and check their alibis, but that would make it pretty obvious that we've been watching them and we still don't have enough to hold them on," Stig continued. "We're going to have to wait until we have more. We just haven't gotten much out of the last couple of days of surveillance. We don't have any witnesses to the two murders, and after what happened to Kaj Antonsen, we shouldn't expect people to suddenly feel like talking to us, either. Instead, let's keep watching and gathering info. It's really not enough that they drive a car that's identical to the one that was seen on Skelbækgade the same evening that prostitute's throat was slit, or at the harbor, for that matter. And we have nothing at all to tie the Albanians to the location where Antonsen was killed."

"Yeah, which is exactly why we need to find out where

they were when all that happened," Willumsen growled loudly, staring at Stig until he eventually looked away. "You've been following them. What have we gotten out of that?"

Toft set a stack of pictures on the table. They were all taken in the last couple of days and showed the Eastern European women on and around Istedgade. There were pictures of the prostitutes standing on the sidewalk with different men, walking into Club Intim with their johns, and leaning over to talk into rolled-down car windows.

"Things really pick up around closing time," commented Stig, who had accompanied the photographer. "And then there's another rush after dinner and kind of steady traffic until a good while past midnight, depending on the weather."

"Did you see any Roma women, or girls?" Toft asked, pulling a menthol cartridge for his plastic cigarette out of the shirt pocket under his sweater. "Some of the girls on the street aren't much more than thirteen or fourteen, and I've heard their families are the ones who send them to Denmark in the first place."

Louise realized Toft's own granddaughter, Ida, was just that age.

"The group on the streets right now apparently arrived a few months ago. They have to earn money for the grand houses their fathers are building. According to one of the girls down at the Nest, the girls were sent to Italy first but couldn't earn enough there, so they were sent up here, and now they're hanging out down at Halmtorvet in front of the convention center."

Louise had also recalled the Roma girls as she absentmindedly reached for the plastic mug in front of her. If someone didn't know any better, they'd have no idea the girls were actually for sale. They looked like any other teenagers in their loose, white, low-waisted pants and tight tops. Grinning and goofing around, they stood in a little cluster waiting for the next customer to stop and flash his lights. One of them had been wearing a headband and was nothing more than a child.

Louise tried to focus and put the Roma girls out of her mind.

"What do we know about the girls you saw the Albanians collecting money from?" Willumsen asked.

Toft, who was visibly moved by the sad fates of these girls, said they were being put up in a number of cheap hotels.

"They can get a room for 5,000 kroner a month, and then of course there's no telling how many people they cram into one room."

"We need to get these girls to talk," Willumsen decided, poking a couple of the pictures with his finger.

Mikkelsen was still for a moment before he finally nodded. "We could certainly arrest them," he began. "But prostitution isn't illegal per se, so we can really nab them only for working without a valid work permit and smack a 500-kroner fine on them. And in cases like this you need to have all your evidence spic and span, otherwise the courts won't have it. You can be sure if we ask the women if they were being forced to prostitute themselves that they will most definitely say no—not because they don't want us to help them, but because they dare not say otherwise. They don't get a simple scolding if they don't do what their pimps say, after all; the pimps break them down psychologically with threats of retaliation against their families back home. They'll kill their parents, burn down their houses, rape and sell their sisters. That kind of thing creates such a deep-seated fear that the girls choose to keep quiet and just obey the pimps, no matter what. And if we go to the pimps, they'll just claim they don't know a thing about extortion or human trafficking. They'll say the women are turning tricks because they want to. So I agree we need a little more," he finally concluded with an eye on the throbbing blood vessel on Willumsen's temple.

"We could also drag things out so long that they have time to really ramp up their business," Willumsen said testily. "Then they'll have a chance to abuse even more of their girls because no one is intervening."

Toft pulled the plastic cigarette out of his mouth and rolled it back and forth between his fingers but stayed out of Willumsen's vortex. Experience had taught him that he would do best by dropping the subject now and waiting to bring it up again later when Willumsen's blood vessels weren't throbbing quite so obviously.

"When we investigate human-trafficking and prostitution cases like this, the outcome always depends on how patient we can be," Mikkelsen said, leaning forward, ignoring Willumsen's tone. "I think we'd be wise to spend some time developing an overview and tying all the pieces of the case together before making our move."

Mikkelsen spoke calmly and rationally, and Louise watched Willumsen's blood vessels continue throbbing. Willumsen's active vocabulary really lacked words like *patience* or *overview*. And yet, he seemed like he was buying it this time. At any rate, his face grew less gruff; he nodded a couple of times, and for the time being at least he stopped interrupting with comments. Instead, he changed the topic by pulling a couple of photos out of the stack and sliding them out into the middle of the table.

"Overview," he repeated, dwelling on the feel of the

word in his mouth, as he pointed to one of the pictures. "That's what we'll do then. But take a look at this, will you, and tell me what our friends are up to."

The pictures showed a small group of men, standing around a bench on Strøget, the famous pedestrian shopping street in the heart of Copenhagen. They were concentrating on something, but it was hard to see what. Arian was standing behind them. There were also pictures of money changing hands. Hamdi was in only a couple of the photos.

"The matchstick game," Stig said, and then Mikkelsen explained:

"It's a 'dexterity game' fairly common among Albanians—and it's not for small potatoes. They might make up to 4 or 5,000 kroner a day."

Willumsen nodded as Mikkelsen explained the police went after these games regularly.

"They are damn good with their hands. You have to guess which box the matchstick is under. Usually what happens is that the group gathers in a little crowd. One of them runs the game, a couple of them keep an eye out for police, and then there's one or two who pretend they're lucky winners. Then when some random person passing by stops to try his or her luck, the fraud begins. It's all sleight of hand and there's basically no chance of winning." Mikkelsen added that the downtown precinct regularly charged people with disturbing the peace or gathering without a permit. After a couple of those, they were usually banned from hanging out on Strøget at all. "But I don't know how much that impedes them, really, and it's certainly possible that they also use the distraction of the game to pick some pockets."

"I suppose Arian and Hamdi organize it and then give

the guys who run the games a little cut for doing the work," Louise guessed, pointing out that both of the Albanians were welfare recipients. "Arian came to Denmark in 1997 when he was granted asylum and then a residence permit. He's thirty-one and lives alone in his apartment out in Valby. It's subsidized public housing. In addition to that, he receives 1,800 kroner a month in welfare benefits."

"Well, he must be doing quite well then since he can afford to buy an Audi A4!" Stig exclaimed with poorly concealed jealousy.

"Exactly," Louise said, noting that a few con games couldn't be financing his lifestyle. "Hamdi arrived in Denmark the following year. He's twenty-six and also has a permanent residence permit. He lives in a fairly large one-bedroom apartment on Vesterbrogade and gets the same benefit check each month."

Willumsen nodded, with his hands folded under his chin contemplatively. The room suddenly turned quiet, as everyone in the room pictured the possible scenarios and tried to figure out what their next move should be.

"Is anyone out on Valdemarsgade watching Miloš and the girls right now?" Willumsen finally asked, breaking the silence.

Lars sat up a little straighter.

"The girls went out with a female friend in the late afternoon," he reported. "The friend picked them up at Miloš's apartment. He didn't leave the apartment until later in the evening when he met a male friend at a bar on Victoriagade."

"But he was already back home an hour after that, and I talked to him on the phone for a bit," said Louise, who had been watching the building from the doorway across the street. "It sounds like the girls have calmed back down again, and there haven't been any signs of commotion since the episode with Hana. No one has contacted them, and they said they didn't feel watched. Now their plan is for Hana to move to the friend's place tomorrow—the friend who came to visit. She apparently has a guest room. I understood from Miloš that the apartment was feeling a little too crowded, given Hana's long-term stay."

"How long?" Willumsen asked.

"Well, he says she's going to stay for the full three months she's allowed to stay in Denmark on her tourist visa."

Willumsen nodded. "All right. Let's call off the stakeout on Valdemarsgade," he decided, his eyes on Louise and Lars. "Make sure you give Miloš, Pavlína, and Hana your cell numbers so all three of them can get in touch with you if any problems should arise. And let's focus our efforts on the Albanians. We still need a list of the women working for them, and you're going to need to get photo documentation of money changing hands. If there's a demonstrable pattern, we'll be able to use that in court. Do we have anything else from Central Station?"

Mikkelsen nodded and said that Arian had shown up at the same location that morning and had accepted payments from the same girls as on Tuesday.

"We have pictures, but unfortunately they made me. Arian was really paying attention today, as if he knew he was being watched. Hamdi sat down on the bench so that he could see everyone who was anywhere nearby when the money changed hands. I expect they've already set a new location to accept payments in the future."

"Right. Get to work," Willumsen urged. "It's up to you guys to make sure we have enough to bring them in so we can find out if they have alibis for the evening of the

Skelbækgade murder and the Kaj Antonsen murder Friday night. We'll find out next week if CSI got any useful DNA from the murder locations. Meanwhile, keep focusing on collecting evidence on the two Albanians."

Louise looked over at Stig to see if he had noticed that the boss had backed down and agreed to wait. Their eyes met and she smiled at him. They would never say it aloud, but it was kind of amazing to know that even Willumsen could be moved if you kept at it long enough.

26

There were no cars outside the church when Camilla arrived Saturday morning. Louise was supposed to meet her, and she knew that the sexton would arrive at any moment, as well. She opened the back hatch of her car where she had the flowers for Kaj Antonsen's funeral service, and the wreath was in the front seat. When the woman at the flower shop had asked her if she wanted to order a sash and what it should read, Camilla drew a blank at first until she settled on a basic "Rest in Peace," which was printed in gold. At the time she thought that would be better than "Forever in Our Hearts" or any of the other standard phrases, but walking out of the flower shop she had had second thoughts and regretted not just leaving the sash blank.

Now all the self-recrimination came rushing back. If only she hadn't sat down on that damn bench with a bag of beer and had for once just left a good story alone. Looking at the flowers in her car, she was overcome by tears, even though she hadn't thought she had any left.

Camilla sniffled and checked her watch, noting that there were still ten minutes until her appointment with the sexton, so she pulled the bucket of small bouquets for the front pew out of the trunk, and after she set it on the ground, she carefully picked up the large bouquet for the altar. With the bouquet under her arm and the bucket of flowers in her hand, she started walking up to the church, the gravel of the drive crunching below her high heels.

The sun was shining down on the white church with its red-tiled roof, and fluffy banks of white clouds slid lazily across the blue sky, but the cheerful spring weather didn't do anything to raise her spirits. She could sense the deep abyss just below the surface that had been threatening to swallow her up for the last week. Camilla knew that the only things holding it at bay right now were the careful makeup she'd applied that morning and the dark suit, which was very tight. They gave her the sense that she could hold herself together no matter what happened.

She set the bucket down and grabbed the door's iron handle. The pastor had prepared her, warning her that she would need to push with her shoulder if she had trouble pressing the handle down. But the door opened without any trouble, and she walked over to the bench just inside the entrance to set down the altar bouquet. It wasn't until she turned around to go back and get the bucket that she stumbled over something.

It felt solid and yet soft under the sole of her shoe. She jumped back reflexively and felt her pulse speed up, her heart pounding.

The towel was dark blue, exactly like before, but that wasn't why she stood frozen, her eyes fixed on the bundle on the stone floor.

She was staring because it was totally silent. No movement, no sound. She still knew what was in the towel, but she couldn't make herself bend down and check, and it wasn't until it flickered through her mind as she ran for the pastor's kitchen door that it hit her that it could also be a dead animal. Maybe a cat, she thought, bounding up the five steps to the door and furiously banging the knocker hoping the pastor was home.

A cat, she thought again, hitting even harder as she yelled for Henrik.

And then everything started spinning as she admitted to herself that it wasn't a cat or some other animal, and that what was wrapped in that towel was no longer alive. She felt something fragile inside herself shatter as images of babies, dead and alive, flitted through her head along with Kaj, lying there alone in that courtyard in all his brutalized wretchedness. Everything got all mixed up, ultimately exploding in her mind like a sea of light.

"Help! Help me!" she sobbed, failing to support herself on the broad door, sliding down to the stoop, her façade cracking completely as the abyss engulfed her.

She didn't hear the footsteps running across the gravel courtyard, and didn't see the person who leaned over her and put a hand on her shoulder. Nor did she register the taste of blood that spread through her mouth from the wound in her cheek, from her own teeth.

Nothing reached her where she was.

In a swirling roar, she was pulled down into a black darkness that shut out the lights and sounds of reality.

27

Louise propped her bike up against the outside wall of the church. Swinging her bag over her shoulder, she unbuckled her helmet and strode toward Camilla's silver-gray VW Polo, its hatchback door wide open and the driver-side door ajar. She figured Camilla must be bringing things in, and she decided to help out by carrying something when she walked over to the church.

The back was empty, so she shut the door and checked the back seat before carefully removing the wreath from the passenger-side door and pushing the driver-side door shut with her elbow.

The flag wasn't at half-mast yet, but there was still a little over an hour until the funeral. Louise knew that Mikkelsen was planning to come. He still seemed genuinely shaken up as though he'd lost a family member, Louise thought, but he hadn't chastised Camilla for her article even once. To the contrary, he said that he ought to have talked to Kaj right away, that maybe he could have prevented the tragedy that way. And he had reminded Willumsen again that you couldn't blame people who weren't familiar with the world of prostitution if they broke some of the unwritten rules that people lived by in this part of town.

The scent of flowers filled Louise's nose as she made her way across the gravel courtyard. Louise saw the open door to the church and when she spotted the bucket filled with small bouquets outside, she assumed Camilla was already hard at work.

It took a second before she reacted to the voice and looked over toward the pastor's residence, where a heavy silhouette was squatting down over something that was lying on the stoop in front of the pastor's kitchen door. Louise recognized the blond hair right away and dropped the wreath and started running.

The man stood up and seemed a little confused as he pointed down at Camilla and explained, practically tripping over his words, that his name was Otto Birch and he was the sexton.

"She was lying here like this when we arrived a couple of minutes ago," he said. "She's crying and mumbling something about 'dead,' but she won't really respond," he said.

"Did something happen to her?" Louise thought of the brutality involved in Kaj Antonsen's death. "Is she bleeding? Does it look like someone hit her?"

Louise leaned over her friend and brushed her hair out of her face, which was frozen in an expression of stubborn denial, like you might see in a toddler throwing a tantrum.

Camilla's sobs were throaty and sounded more like a constant moan interrupted by muddled speech, from which Louise could only pick out a few words like "dead," "funeral," "baby," and "church."

Louise took hold of her friend and tried to get her to sit up. She studied Camilla's face and ran a hand through her blond hair to check and see if there were any signs of physical trauma.

"She's in shock," Otto said, trying to light a cigar.

The pastor was walking over from the parking lot, and when he spotted them he sped up. Jonas was just behind him, but he hadn't noticed the commotion yet, because his eyes were glued to the Game Boy he was holding in his hands.

"What happened?" Henrik Holm yelled, breaking into a run.

"Baby, church, dead..." The words were unclear and running in a continuous loop.

Henrik gave Louise a puzzled look. Louise had managed to get Camilla up into a sitting position, her back leaning against the kitchen door.

Even though she didn't think it would matter, she still stepped out of range of Camilla's hearing before admitting that she'd been afraid of a mental breakdown ever since Kaj Antonsen's murder.

"But maybe it's not so strange that it didn't happen until now," Louise said, explaining that she'd tried to talk Camilla out of assuming responsibility for the funeral several times. Then Louise went back and sat down on the steps with an arm around her friend.

"The baby is dead," Camilla mumbled into her shoulder.

Now Louise felt her own tears coming. She knew there wasn't much she could do to alleviate her friend's incapacitating pain. She could try only to comfort her as best she could.

"What is she saying?" Henrik asked, moving in a little closer. "It's just a bunch of unconnected words."

Louise shook her head a little, and then looked over to Jonas and noticed how he lit up when he spotted her. But an instant later he stiffened when he spotted Camilla on the steps.

She turned back to Camilla, thinking that she was going to have to call Jakobsen, even though the crisis psychologist had the weekend off.

"Let me hear what she's saying," Henrik urged. He quickly glanced at the church and asked if the sexton had been over and finished getting things ready.

Otto shook his head and explained that he'd spotted Camilla before he'd ever made it over to the church.

Henrik got up abruptly and started running toward the church door. When the shout came, Louise was already on her legs.

The shape and size matched a tiny newborn, so Louise was prepared when she carefully loosened the towel after having pulled the bundle farther out onto the floor in the triangle of light the sun was making through the door opening.

The infant was dead, just as she had guessed. It was a little boy, she confirmed, as she slowly let her eyes move down over his body covered with dried blood and vernix caseosa, which had a faint greenish tinge.

Louise took a deep breath and looked up at Pastor Holm, who was watching from the open door. The stone floor of the church was cold and there was a draft along the floor. The little baby's eyes were closed, his face looked like a dried mask that had never had a chance to be shaped by movement and expressions. Neither his joints nor his muscles were stiff anymore, the way they would be right after death, and he had a rancid smell, not the pleasant baby smell you associated with a newborn. The greenish tinge could come from an amniotic fluid infection, Louise thought, clearing her throat before she said anything.

"He might have died right after the birth," she guessed and straightened up partway. Henrik had a deep furrow in his brow. Then he went and sat down on the bench next to

Camilla's altar bouquet. At Louise's request, he dialed 114 and was connected directly to the local police station that served the neighborhood.

"Ask for the officer who was here when you found the little girl," Louise said, standing up. She heard Henrik ask for Officer Rasmus Hem, and heard him briefly explaining that they had found the body of an infant wrapped up in the church in the same location where they had found Baby Girl.

"I don't understand what's happening," he said, shaking his head as he spoke to the officer. He explained that Camilla Lind had apparently found the baby when she walked into the church bringing flowers for today's funeral; he and Jonas had been in downtown Frederiksberg doing some shopping

"We left a little after ten, but I didn't go into the church before we left, and we went out the other way, so I didn't notice anything."

Louise looked at her watch. It was a little past twelve. She nodded as Henrik stuck his cell phone back in his pocket and said the police would be right there.

"Then we ought to go out and keep the door locked until they arrive," she said, taking one last glance at the bundle in the blue towel.

"That's just completely absurd to have two such similar events one right after the other," he said, heading for the door. "Officer Hem thought it was related to all the media coverage following the discovery of the abandoned baby here, that maybe that was the reason someone decided to copy that."

"That is also quite possible," Louise admitted. "Copy-cats aren't all that uncommon. My immediate guess is that the child has been dead for twenty-four hours and that it might have been stillborn to begin with. It doesn't look like the birth took place in a hospital. If it had he would have been cleaned up and his umbilical cord clamped."

"No, it looks more like a birth that happened without any professional assistance," the priest agreed, pulling the door to the church closed. Then he nodded a couple of times as if he were trying to convince himself of something.

When Louise emerged from the church, Camilla was still sitting on the steps with her eyes closed and her back against the kitchen door. Jonas was sitting cross-legged on the gravel in the courtyard with his Game Boy on the ground next to him.

Henrik walked over and helped him up, then picked up his Game Boy and they started slowly moving toward the residence.

"We'll go in the other way," he said. Then he stopped and turned to the sexton, who was sitting on the stairs as if he weren't really sure what he should do.

"There's a baby in the church," the pastor said to Otto. "I called the police. We're going to keep the door closed until they arrive."

"What about the funeral?" Otto asked, standing up with difficulty.

"It will have to be postponed."

A confused expression passed over the elderly sexton's face as his schedule for the whole day was instantly canceled, but then he nodded and glanced up at the church clock, which now said a quarter past twelve.

Louise watched Jonas as he disappeared with his father. Poor little guy, she thought, wondering if he shouldn't be offered a chance to talk to Jakobsen, too. That was twice in fourteen days that something so devastating had happened right outside his front door. Then Louise walked over to Camilla and leaned down over her.

"You're going to have to get up. The police will be here soon, and they're definitely going to want to talk to you."

Her friend was just staring into space. Then her eyelids shuddered a little, and she turned to look at Louise.

"I don't know if I'm up to that," she said so softly that Louise had to lean forward to hear. "It feels like somebody drained out everything that's usually inside me. Suddenly I'm the figure with the scythe who appears in people's back seats right before a traffic accident happens."

Camilla was as pale as a corpse, and her words emerged through lips that hardly moved, as if her face had grown stiff along with the rest of her body.

A dove had hopped up to the second step of the stairs and had its back to them, poking at something on the step. Louise watched it before taking a deep breath and psyching herself up to tell Camilla what they'd found in the church.

"You were right. The baby was dead. But it was probably a stillbirth, so it wouldn't have made any difference if you had gotten there sooner."

Louise was silent for a bit before finally taking her eyes off the dove and then adding, "If that's even the kind of thing you're thinking about?"

The dove flew away when Louise stood up. She held out a hand to Camilla and pulled her up.

There were cups out on the table and the kettle was on. It was warm in the kitchen, a little stuffy. The sun had been shining in the big windows over the long kitchen table.

Louise settled Camilla on the bench and took a seat while Henrik remained standing, a little hesitant.

"I have an op-ed column I need to finish writing, but I

don't suppose there's any point starting on that before the police have been here," he said, setting milk and sugar out on the table.

His words hung in the air as silence took over the room, because no one was really sure how to respond.

Louise finished making the coffee and poured some into Camilla's cup before filling her own. She was familiar with Henrik Holm's columns in the paper. He was one of the people the media turned to when they needed a religious point of view—a "media priest," as he was sarcastically called by some of the slightly harsh satirists. For her part, Louise had always found him to be a good, plain-talking writer, and she enjoyed reading his weekly column.

"Why here?" Camilla asked, finally breaking the wordless vacuum.

"Basically, it just makes sense," Henrik said, explaining that in Germany there were still churches that had little trapdoors to leave newborns in. "It's really not such a ludicrous idea to choose a church if you're in that situation." He added that he would much rather the unhappy mothers choose his church than toss the baby into a river.

"But who decides to give birth outside the system, without a doctor or a midwife or anything?" Camilla wondered out loud to herself.

They were interrupted by the sharp ring of the doorbell, and the pastor stood up to let the police in and accompany them over to the church.

Exactly. Who does decide to give birth completely alone? Louise thought. She hadn't heard anyone coming up the kitchen steps, so she jumped a little when there was a hard knock on the door.

It was the sexton, who stuck his gray-haired head in while the rest of him stayed out on the stoop.

"Someone is here for the funeral and insists on knowing why it's been postponed," he announced. "He says he's from the police, but he doesn't have his badge."

Louise got up and went out to fill Mikkelsen in on what had happened. Two police cars had just pulled up in the courtyard next to the church, almost as if they felt at home there. Louise heard one officer yell to another that the techs would be there within five minutes.

Mikkelsen was wearing dark trousers and a dark suit jacket, which was a little tight around the gut. She could tell he wasn't comfortable, not in the clothes and not with the situation, and his eyebrows shot up like two seagull wings when he spotted her.

"Oh, right, your friend," he said when Louise reached him.

Louise nodded and explained that the funeral had been canceled, because Camilla had found a dead baby when she arrived to decorate the church. Every time she finished a sentence, he nodded as if she were filing a report. Something about his posture told Louise that it had been a struggle for him just to show up. A lot of people had trouble with funerals, but in his case, it probably had more to do with how involved he was with the Istedgade neighborhood beat. It was rare for a death to happen in such a brutal fashion as the former chef's, and Mikkelsen wasn't hiding the fact that he feared this was something they were going to be seeing more of. No other funeral guests had arrived, not that Louise had been expecting any.

They stepped back a little out of the way as the crime scene investigators arrived and pulled their car in. Louise nodded at Frandsen, as he and his people started taking out their equipment.

Mikkelsen, who was from the downtown precinct and so

wouldn't be involved in this particular investigation, looked at his watch.

"I suppose I might as well head home and have a little breakfast," he said. Louise walked him out to the parking lot, but stopped when Rasmus Hem from the Bellahøj precinct walked over and introduced himself before asking to see Camilla.

"She's in the kitchen," Louise replied, and then said good-bye to Mikkelsen so she could accompany Rasmus in.

Camilla was still sitting right where Louise had left her, and she just nodded when Rasmus greeted her.

"So you're the one who found him," Rasmus stated, and Camilla nodded again. When he didn't ask anything else and just sat down across from her, she started to explain on her own.

"I went into the church with some flowers for the funeral, and when I was on my way out again, I stumbled," she said in a voice that sounded mechanical.

"Did you see what had caused you to fall?" Officer Hem wanted to know. Then he asked if she had done anything else just inside the entrance of the church there besides set down the flowers.

Camilla shook her head and said no to both.

"I'm probably the only one who touched anything," Louise interjected, showing how she had moved the bundle before taking hold of the corners to unwrap the towel. "Besides Camilla, the only people who have been in the church since the baby was found were the pastor and myself."

Behind her, Louise heard Henrik coming down the stairs from the second floor. He'd brought Jonas a soda and a bowl of popcorn.

"He's reading *Harry Potter*," Henrik said when Louise

asked how he was doing. "But it would be nice if we could avoid any more dramatic events," he said in a forced, upbeat tone, "People are going to end up being afraid to go to church for fear of finding an abandoned baby on the floor."

Officer Hem smiled at him and agreed that things couldn't continue like this.

"Would it be all right if I just sat off on the side and did a little work on my computer?" Henrik said, asking Officer Hem for permission. "I have a piece I need to finish writing for tomorrow, and I haven't quite decided yet how I'm going to approach it."

Hem nodded and said that would be fine. He was just going to write down what Camilla had told him.

It didn't look like anyone other than Louise had noticed that Jonas had come downstairs while they were talking. He was standing over next to his father, looking at the policeman, whom he obviously recognized from the last time.

Henrik absentmindedly stroked his son's hair before going into the living room, but he shook his head when Jonas whispered something to him. It was obvious that he was already thinking about how to word the introduction to his op-ed column.

Jonas stood there for a second, hesitantly, as if he couldn't quite decide if he should go back up to his room as his father had told him.

That made Louise stand up and go put her arm around him. They walked up to his room together.

Camilla watched them as they disappeared up the stairs. She wished she could go with them and avoid having to relive what happened in the church. Instead she dutifully responded to the questions, which were being asked in chronological order. When had she arrived at the church? Had she seen anyone as she walked across the courtyard? Was the door shut all the way when she entered the church?

Camilla thought about the last time they had been sitting in the pastor's kitchen and how the boys had said the door had been open.

"It was shut all the way," she assured the officer, pushing her cup of now-cold coffee away a little and putting her elbows on the table to rest her head in her hands.

After they'd run through the brief explanation, Camilla felt as though everyone was staring at her, and she noticed she was breathing heavily. Finally, he added one last thing.

"Could we agree that you'll hold off on writing anything about this until tomorrow?" he began. "I'd really like to have a chance to find out what's going on before we go to the press with this."

Camilla made a little face, which silenced him. "You don't need to worry about that." She let her hands drop down onto the table and shook her head slightly. "I'm not working right now."

Officer Hem raised one eyebrow.

"I'm on a leave of absence," Camilla explained briefly, adding wanly that he didn't need to worry that she would inform her editor, either.

"I would actually prefer not to have any contact with the paper at all while I'm on leave." She looked down at the table. "But of course, I can't guarantee that they won't find out about this on their own," she added after a brief pause. "*Morgenavisen* does have quite a track record of doing stuff like that."

Officer Hem nodded, and Camilla got the sense that he wanted to say something else, but he was interrupted by Louise coming back down the stairs.

Louise walked into the living room where Henrik was bent over his computer. She waited for a moment before she interrupted his writing.

"What would you say to Jonas coming with Camilla and me when we leave?" she asked. "I think it might be nice for him to get out of here for a little bit, while the crime-scene investigators are here working in the church. Then you can also finish writing your piece."

He ran his hand through his hair, and Louise could see that he found the offer tempting, but at the same time he didn't want to be any trouble.

"He's very welcome," Louise reassured him. "And he can stay until tomorrow, when Markus will be home from his dad's place."

"I really want to go," they heard Jonas say from the stairs, and Louise could see that that settled the matter.

"But remember your toothbrush," the pastor called and smiled at his son as he turned and ran back upstairs to pack.

"Thank you," he said. "If you don't have any family, you don't get many chances when a situation suddenly comes up and you need a little break." He looked at his computer screen. "Then I could use my evening cleaning up my sermon for tomorrow. Today certainly turned out a little different than I'd planned." He looked at his watch, as if he had been reminded yet again that a good portion of the afternoon was already gone.

"If they're even going to let me use the church tomorrow, that is," he added, giving Louise a questioning look. "There's a baptism tomorrow."

"We'll just have to see what Frandsen says, but I would

gine the investigators can get enough done today that they'll be gone before tomorrow."

"Although if the parents for the baptism hear that it happened again, they may decide not to come." He ran his hand through his thick blond hair again.

"Well, but that doesn't have anything to do with the church or you," Louise said, trying to allay his concerns.

The pastor nodded and got up to give his son a hug before he left.

Officer Hem had gone, and it looked like Camilla had pulled herself together enough that she was ready to get going.

Louise told her they would be having an extra overnight guest and bent down to pick up her friend's bag, which had slid down onto the floor.

"Did you remember your cell phone?" Henrik asked Jonas, after one more hug good-bye.

"Yes, and the charger," Jonas said, sounding impatient to get going.

Camilla was pale as she waved to Henrik but said that she would call him so they could set a new time for the funeral.

"I just don't know if I'm up to planning the whole thing another time," she admitted, as they crossed the courtyard away from the police cars. A couple of curious bystanders had taken up position by the wall of the cemetery, and Jonas shuddered faintly as they walked over to Camilla's car.

"Maybe we ought to drop the ceremony and have a beer and play a Johnny Cash number in his honor instead," Camilla mused.

Louise smiled at her and asked if she wanted to bring any of the flowers she had brought into the church home.

Camilla made a face. "What do you think? Do you have enough vases for them? Oh, how fun to be surrounded by them for the rest of the weekend!"

Louise left her bike there. She shut the passenger-side door after Camilla and Jonas got in Camilla's car. Feeling like she was responsible for two convalescents that she had to have on the mend before the weekend was over, she climbed in behind the wheel and started the car.

28

It took Willumsen less than a minute to yank Louise back to reality after he started the briefing Monday morning; he announced that the group researching the two murders had just been cut in half.

He was standing there holding his coffee cup in his hand, staring at each of them—Toft, Stig, Lars, and finally Louise, who was leaning back complacently in her chair, looking forward to a calm start to the week after a Sunday that had turned out to be quite pleasant.

Saturday afternoon, everything had been forced and tedious. Camilla lay down in Louise's guest room with some magazines, and Jonas had alternated between sitting in front of the PlayStation that was hooked up to the TV in her bedroom or being engrossed in his Harry Potter book.

It was funny that in a lot of ways he was the diametrical opposite of Markus. Camilla's son had short blond hair, and Jonas's was dark and hung way down over his eyes. Jonas was very focused and liked to concentrate on the things he did. He had played guitar since he was seven without losing interest, which left Louise pretty impressed.

Markus was more impulsive and got all excited about

new things, but he still hadn't managed to find anything that really, truly, held his attention. The last thing had been break dancing. Louise wished that at least a little of Jonas's love of reading would rub off on Markus—and even though the pastor's son seemed a little introverted and shy, she couldn't help but notice that Markus really admired him.

Louise had spent her time in the kitchen with a news-paper until she offered to go pick up some pizzas around seven. After that they'd watched a 1970s Danish con-men movie about the Olsen Gang and turned in early.

Mik Rasmussen had called in the middle of the movie and asked if she wanted to come out to Holbæk on Sunday. He tempted her with sea kayaking, sex, barbecue—if the weather held—and maybe a single Irish coffee. She had been a little too curt when she turned him down, and she could tell right away that she'd hurt his feelings. She hadn't meant to do that, but she knew that what they had together was part of a totally different world right now. She spent most of the evening worrying that Jonas was regretting hav-ing accepted her invitation to spend the night. They hardly knew each other, so she'd told him several times that he should just let her know if he'd rather go home, but each time he said he wanted to stay.

They had all slept in on Sunday, and it wasn't until around eleven that they headed down to Belis Bar for brunch. Camilla was still a little quiet and withdrawn, but when Markus came back from his dad's place in the early afternoon, they had managed to convince her to go to the pool with them. In the beginning, she just sat there wrapped in a big bathrobe watching the boys as they jumped off the diving boards, but then they managed to lure her into go-ing down the slide, which curved down into the pool from ceiling height, going in and out of the wall of the building. The two boys almost threw up from laughing so hard as Louise and Camilla thundered down into the water shrieking at the tops of their lungs.

When Louise took Jonas home that evening, she suddenly felt like she was part of a real family. Not that that was something she craved, but just then she had to admit it felt nice.

Her mission had also been a success. The convalescents seemed to be doing better.

"We have a new case, so we're splitting up our resources," Willumsen announced, his eyes on Louise as if he'd noticed that her thoughts were still elsewhere.

Louise straightened up and pulled her chair all the way in to the table.

"We'll have to make do with just two people continuing to work with Mikkelsen and his people on solving the Vesterbro case, while the other two move on to the new case."

Stig was about to protest but was stopped by Willumsen's hand.

"It's too early to move people off this," Toft said over the raised hand. "If we pull back, they get free rein again. You know there's no way we'll be able to get to the bottom of what they're up to and keep an eye on things without more people."

"Of course you can, and I'm going to need to see some progress soon. We're not getting anywhere and nothing's happening," he grumbled, staring grimly at them before straightening up and changing his tone. "This Saturday a dead infant was found out in Stenhøj Church in Frederiksberg, and this is something you're aware of, Rick."

It wasn't a question, and he wasn't expecting Louise to respond, because he continued himself.

"Our colleagues from the Bellahøj station were out there

for a similar case a couple of weeks ago. In that case, the infant was found alive."

He pulled the top sheet of paper out of the case file he had on the table in front of him.

"They did an autopsy on the infant yesterday afternoon, and I have the provisional findings here. Flemming Larsen writes..."

He pulled his reading glasses out of his chest pocket. Louise felt the anxiety moving from her stomach toward her solar plexus. To anyone who knew anything about Willumsen, the sign was obvious. Something was wrong. They must have found something in the autopsy that changed the case from a family tragedy to a particular type of crime, otherwise the case wouldn't be assigned to them. The Bellahøj precinct was perfectly well equipped to handle most things on their own.

Louise considered Willumsen's face as he read the text, paraphrasing it in his own words. He ran through it quickly at first.

"The infant was wrapped, a newborn boy, no more than a couple of days old. The body had a faint greenish tinge as you might find with chorioamnionitis, or amniotic fluid infection, and it was still covered with dried blood and vernix caseosa."

Here, he slowed down slightly.

"Beyond that Flemming writes that the umbilical cord had been crudely severed from the mother and the skin had peeled off in several locations."

The door suddenly opened and Suhr came in and sat down with a face that made it clear he wanted to cause as little disruption as possible so they should just continue. The look was wasted on Willumsen, who didn't respond to the homicide chief's arrival at all.

"The peeling is a type called maceration and may indicate that the infant died prior to the birth. But the reason this case has landed on our desks now is..."

Finally, he looked up to make sure he had their attention.

"...that the infant is missing its pinky toe. And we're not talking about a birth defect. It was chopped off or cut off after the birth. The surface of the wound is smooth and even, so it was amputated with a sharp instrument. Flemming is sure the toe was removed after the boy's death, otherwise there would have been a reaction in the form of bleeding, and that is why he concludes with great certainty that we're talking about a stillbirth."

Now Willumsen looked directly at Lars and Louise.

"This is your case now. Bellahøj will continue to investigate the abandoned baby that was taken to Skodsborg Orphanage a week ago. At the moment, there is no reason to think that the two cases are connected, but obviously you should consider that. For the time being we'll run the two investigations separately and think of them as two separate cases. It's far more likely that the church was chosen because of all the media attention. The injury the infant boy incurred doesn't have anything to do with Baby Girl. She was in good condition when she was abandoned. This will definitely involve a ton of routine work, and I want you two to personally get in touch with all the mothers who were scheduled to give birth within the last two weeks, and the ones whose due dates are within the next fourteen days."

Suhr's forehead had contracted into deep wrinkles, but he remained silent.

"You'll have to go check out the maternity wards, and if there are cases that seem interesting, compare the DNA. If that doesn't give us anything, we'll have to broaden our search by asking the public for help and appealing to people to get in touch with us if they know a pregnant woman whose baby bump has disappeared but who doesn't have a baby in her arms."

Lars started shaking his head.

"Who are you going to assign to assist them?" Suhr asked, looking at his lead detective. Willumsen's eyebrows shot up as if he had no idea what Suhr was talking about.

"To begin with we'll handle this ourselves. We're going to have to be able to keep several balls in the air," Willumsen pronounced, once he finally detected the heavy silence that had settled over the room. "Working on one case at a time is a luxury we just don't have."

Louise nodded. This wasn't the first time and certainly wouldn't be the last when she wouldn't have a chance to follow a case through to its conclusion. She took the thin case folder Willumsen handed her and got up to follow Lars back to their office.

29

"What does it say in the report we got from the pathology lab?" Lars asked, waiting patiently while Louise plugged in the electric kettle on the shelf and got a glass with a tea bag ready.

He opened the window and a mild spring breeze blew in, freshening up their dark office a little.

By the time the water was finally boiling, he had the phone to his ear and was waiting to talk to the court. They were going to need a warrant to obtain the patient lists from the various maternity wards.

Louise set down her glass of tea and opened the case file, which so far contained only two pieces of paper. She started reading but was interrupted when her partner hung up, having obtained the warrant.

"Read it aloud," he asked, unscrewing the cap to a bottle of mineral water and pulling his chair back so he had some support for his back when he put his legs up on the edge of the desk.

"Saturday, April 26, at approximately 10:55 a.m., a woman entered the front door of Stenhøj Church.

"That was Camilla," Louise interjected before continuing.

"There was a bundle wrapped in a towel lying on the

floor immediately inside the door. The woman ran out of the church without touching anything. Approximately ten minutes later, Assistant Detective Louise Rick, Copenhagen PD, arrived; she was at the church on private business. The detective and Pastor Henrik Holm of Stenhøj Church examined the bundle together, which turned out to contain a naked newborn male infant who was dead at the time he was found.

"This doesn't really say that much," she said and skimmed the rest of the text before she continued.

"The area was cordoned off, and scent dogs were brought in to try and pick up a trail. They didn't find anything. Preliminary questioning: Negative.

"Nada," she commented and read on.

"A postmortem was conducted at the scene and an autopsy the following day. The male infant's weight was 3,750 grams and length was fifty centimeters."

"Well, that's completely normal, so the mother must have been to term," said Lars. He was the more knowledgeable of the two of them about babies, even though his own twins had been adopted from Bolivia when they were about six months old. They were seven now and had left a little of the craziness behind them. They used to be terrors, though, and on several occasions when their father brought them to work they had taken great satisfaction in scattering case files all over the office.

"The umbilical cord appeared to have been severed by biting or tearing and was not tied off," she continued, brushing the twins out of her mind. "It was seventeen centimeters long. The time of birth was estimated as one to two days prior to the discovery of the body. The child's race is Caucasian."

Louise glanced up from the report. "Well, that pretty

much just means he's not black or Asian, but it doesn't narrow it down that much. Caucasian is still a pretty broad
spectrum!"

Her partner nodded and asked if there was any more, but
she shook her head and pushed the piece of paper away.

"Nothing aside from the fact that he had thick, dark
brown hair."

They were interrupted when Suhr, after a quick knock,
opened the door and sat down on the low bookcase just inside the doorway.

"I talked to Sillebrandt from out at the Bellahøj precinct.
He's still got four people on the case and is offering to expand the search for witnesses so that they're looking for
people who might have seen something around the church
from Friday night until Saturday morning. That's the time
frame during which we assume the boy was left. They've
found two witnesses who said independently that they saw
an older-model light green car by the cemetery around six
a.m. Saturday morning. One of the witnesses, an elderly
man who was out for his morning walk with his Labrador
retriever, was very sure that it was a Fiat Regata from the
mid-1980s. He had a similar model himself, just in red. The
other witness, a young guy, was on his way home to sleep
off a night on the town, and all he remembered was that
there was an old light green 'bucket of bolts,' which he peed
on. And that description certainly fits pretty well if we're
talking about a car that's over twenty years old."

The homicide chief smiled, probably because he never
let his own Volvo get more than two or three years old before he swapped it out for a new one.

"Based on the witnesses' statements, our colleagues
have been searching for a Fiat Regata in that color. They
found seven registered in Sjælland, and they're looking at

the owners. But otherwise they don't have anything," he continued, scratching his chin, which was thoroughly shaved every morning and slathered with expensive after-shave. "I recommend that we accept their offer to expand their search for witnesses."

Louise and Lars nodded. So she had been right when she'd thought she could tell what he was thinking in Willumsen's office. Obviously he was aware that the group leader couldn't leave this entire case to just two people, but since the homicide chief was a polite man he hadn't challenged his subordinate on this point in front of everyone else. He had bitten his tongue instead.

"Let's start by going after the most obvious. Concentrate on checking the hospital lists of women who are supposed to give birth soon or have just done so."

He looked at them to confirm that they agreed.

"Take the metro Copenhagen region," he continued after they both nodded in confirmation. "In other words, Hvidovre, Herlev, Glostrup, National Hospital, Frederiksberg, and Gentofte, and let's see what we get from that."

"We already requested a warrant, so we can get the hospitals to hand over the basic information on the women of interest," Lars said, receiving a satisfied nod.

"I'll send a press release to the Ritzau news service in a bit, and I've already arranged for us to meet a TV Avisen reporter at the church for the six thirty p.m. broadcast. In addition to that, I'm planning on appearing on the TV2 News at seven p.m. We're going to have to go public with this, and I don't understand why Bellahøj hasn't already been more aggressive. Sillebrandt hasn't really been very proactive."

Louise scrupulously avoided looking over at Lars. There wasn't that much gossip about the homicide chief, but people did joke about his frequent appearances on TV whenever they got the chance. Louise didn't actually think he overdid it. To the contrary, she was glad to have a boss who was respected by the general population, and no one could deny that when they hit a dead end with a case this approach was usually what brought them new leads.

"While we wait for the lists from the hospitals, I want to drive out and see Henrik Holm and run through the whole thing with him one more time," Louise said. "Maybe there's something he just hasn't thought of, and I also just want to mention the light green Fiat to him."

"Bellahøj already talked to him," Suhr said, as Louise was collecting her purse from the floor and stuffing her cell phone into her pocket.

"Yeah," she replied, "but now the case has been assigned to us, so we'll talk to him."

The homicide chief nodded and smiled at her. "Of course."

"We also need to tell him about the pathologist's report, before the whole story is splashed all over the media," she added. "But you're not planning to mention the toe when you talk to the press, are you?"

He seemed to consider this briefly, and then he shook his head.

"Not to begin with. As long as we don't know if that has any significance, we might as well spare people that detail. But mention it to the pastor. How the hell should I know—maybe there's some sort of religious significance to it that our limited insight into biblical history is causing us to miss."

"Well, that's a possibility," she conceded, and then told him that Pastor Holm was a little worried that the two tragic events would harm his church.

"You certainly can't blame him for that. I read his column yesterday," Suhr said as Louise was on her way out. "It was about the 'maternal instinct,' which doesn't always kick in right away, and he wrote about the scientific explanation, which is that the production of female sex hormones drops off dramatically after giving birth, and that can affect both a woman's attitude and her maternal instinct. His own theory was more that the infant's soul just needed time to settle into place before it was ready to bind itself to its mother and awaken those strong feelings in her. Some just took longer to move in than others, as he put it. It was very interesting, but the piece was obviously inspired by Baby Girl's mother, so he must have written it before the boy's body was found."

"Why did it happen two times, so close together?" Louise asked, her mind back on the stillborn little boy. "Years can go by without there being an abandoned baby."

"Every once in a while we have cases of abandoned stillborn infants just months apart, and in rare cases even just weeks. Unfortunately, it's not all that uncommon," Suhr corrected. He was interrupted by Stig, who had stopped to listen from the open doorway, as he unscrewed the cap from a half-liter bottle of cola.

"I'd hazard a guess that you won't be finding the mother in the upper echelon of society," he said with the same conviction in his voice as when he'd informed Louise that you could always tell by looking at a whore if she came from Eastern Europe. "It's only in the lowest classes that children aren't viewed as status symbols. Quite the contrary, they're sometimes perceived of as trash if you're unlucky enough to get pregnant, and then it's easier to get rid of the kid than struggle with some government caseworker about institutions and forcible removal."

Stig paused for effect and took a swig of his soda.

"After all, it's easier to dump a kid than take responsibility," he continued. "And the people we're talking about here certainly aren't the sharpest tools in the shed, so it's not really a surprise that they use the same place as a dump. That way they don't have to have a single original thought."

Louise had a hard time stomaching his tirade and thought about just walking out and leaving him to the others, but hung back when Stig continued.

"Do they know if the stillborn baby's mother was a drug user?" Stig looked from Louise to Lars.

Lars shrugged and looked over at the provisional report, which was in front of Louise.

She shook her head.

"We don't know yet," Suhr said and got up off the book-case.

"The baby's autopsy was yesterday," Louise reminded Stig. "The results from the blood tests won't be back until this afternoon or tomorrow."

"If this were my case, I'd be asking the crackheads and hookers some questions, before I spent too much time on the mothers who've been dutifully going to their prenatal appointments and eagerly awaiting the birth of their babies. Those other women, though, you can certainly imagine that there might be some of them who aren't particularly eager to go through official channels with their pregnancies. Especially not if they already knew from the beginning that they were going to get rid of the kid," he concluded before disappearing off to his office.

Suhr stood there in the doorway, watching him go. "Actually, he might have a point," he said, resting an arm on the doorframe as a thoughtful expression came over his face. "Have a chat with the folks at the Nest and find out if they know anyone who had started to show but never turned up with a baby."

Louise sat there with her elbows on her desk and her head resting heavily in her hands. There was always someone who was good at putting other people to work. He could have offered to ask around himself, since he was out there anyway working on those two murder cases, but that would have been too much to expect.

Before Louise heard the sound, she felt the phone in her pocket vibrating. Anonymous caller, the caller ID said. She excused herself, assuming it must be a personal call, maybe her mother, who she had never called back over the weekend.

"Hi, it's Jakobsen," the crisis psychologist said, and Louise instinctively glanced at her watch. Camilla had had an appointment at nine fifteen that morning. It was eleven now. For a second she was afraid, thinking maybe he'd decided to admit her friend or drug her so heavily that he felt he ought to inform Louise.

"She never showed up," he said tersely, sounding irritated. He was already overbooked before they'd managed to convince him to squeeze Camilla in, so he was justified. "She didn't even call to cancel."

Louise stared out the window. Camilla had still been asleep when she left a little before eight, and she had assumed her friend would wake up on her own and make sure she got off on time.

"I tried calling your place, too, because I understood she had spent the weekend there, but no one's answering, and she doesn't answer the cell phone number I had for her, either."

"I don't get it," was all Louise could think to say. "I'll stop by home and get her. I'm really sorry. She must have overslept." She apologized and added that Camilla had been very tired since her experience out at the church. "I should have made sure she got up myself."

"Call me when you get a hold of her. We'll have to set up a new appointment." Jakobsen still sounded pissed.

Lars and Suhr were looking at her as she put her phone back in her pocket.

"Camilla just blew Jakobsen off," she explained. "I have to drive home and find out if she's OK."

Lars nodded, but she could tell that Suhr was about to lose it, given all the work they had ahead of them.

"It won't take long," Louise promised, pulling on her jacket. "And it's on the way to Stenhøj Church anyway."

30

At first, she couldn't find the alarm clock on the night-stand, so she propped herself up on her elbow and then spotted it down on the floor. Still half asleep, she reached for it and determined that it was almost ten.

Camilla had been up most of the night, but she must have eventually fallen asleep just before dawn. She hadn't heard Louise or Markus get up. He had slept on a mattress on the floor right next to her bed, and the whole time she was lying there awake, staring into the darkness, she had listened to his relaxed breathing.

She set down the alarm clock and after rubbing her eyes, spotted the note on the nightstand.

I LOVE YOU, MOM. MARKUS.

She read the sentence again and suddenly felt afraid and let the affectionate note flutter down onto the comforter as she lay back down on the pillow. It occurred to her that she didn't feel anything. The warmth she usually felt in her heart when she read one of his little declarations of love did not come, nor the smile that always appeared without her even being aware of it, nor did she picture his face. And she didn't try to imagine him sitting in the kitchen writing it for her.

Again, it struck her that everything that was usually inside her was gone, and what scared her was the thought that it might be gone forever if even one of Markus's little notes couldn't make her happy. When she thought about it she realized mostly what she felt was apathetic.

She closed her eyes and lay there for a long time without moving. Kaj had kept appearing in her thoughts overnight. She thought about his life, which she didn't know shit about aside from the few details he'd shared with her, and at one point overnight she had cried because it was so unfair that she'd had to postpone his funeral. She realized she'd been looking forward to the funeral, to taking care of it, doing a little something for him, decorating with flowers and playing Johnny Cash for him.

She pulled the blanket up over her head and lay like that for a long time. She heard the phone ringing in the living room, but pulled the blanket in closer around her face and lay like that until it stopped. She'd turned off her cell phone the previous evening. It was on the nightstand, and she couldn't be bothered to turn it on. She was sure there would be at least one message from Høyer.

Suddenly she remembered Jakobsen and her appointment with him at National Hospital. She couldn't remember what time it was for—it was on a slip of paper in the kitchen—but she knew she was already too late.

She swung her legs out over the edge of the bed and wriggled a little on the mattress to reach the sweatpants she'd tossed on the floor the previous night. She kept on the T-shirt she'd slept in and went to the bathroom.

The phone rang again, but she closed the door behind herself and sat down on the toilet. She wasn't hungry and didn't need coffee, didn't have any needs. The only thing she could feel was an all-encompassing melancholy. All the same, she decided to go out and get a little air.

The sun was shining, and down on the street below people were walking around in shirtsleeves or lightweight jackets. She stuck her bare feet into a pair of Adidas sneakers Louise had sitting in her hallway and pulled a white sweater on over her head. She pulled her blond hair into a loose ponytail. Her Mulberry brand purse was the only thing that revealed that she was normally much more put together.

She walked all the way down Gammel Kongevej to Central Station. She wanted to go to the Plaza, where Kaj had reigned in the kitchen in his day, and she thought she might settle for a cup of coffee in the bar. The sun hurt her eyes. She'd forgotten her sunglasses, so she walked with her eyes squinted shut a little, heading into the bright daylight. It wasn't until she passed the Planetarium that it occurred to her that the Plaza had been sold many times since the legendary hotel magnate had owned it and turned it into something special. Several international hotel chains had owned it since, so there probably wasn't much of Kaj's spirit left. She decided to get her coffee from somewhere inside Central Station instead. There was also something appealing about the idea of sitting in there and being an anonymous face in the crowd. Blending in with all the other strangers who were just passing through.

She took a free paper from the holder on her way in and walked down through the high-ceilinged railroad station concourse with its shops and newsstands along one side and the stairways down to the train tracks on the other. There weren't very many people in the DSB café, so she tossed

her papers on an empty table and went up to the window to
get a coffee.

The Meat Baron. She didn't know what he looked like, had
only seen his silhouette behind the steering wheel of the
dark green Jaguar, and then she'd heard his story. But if
she went down to the Meatpacking District surely someone
would know who he was. She wanted to hear more about
Kaj's time as a chef when everything had been different.

There were more people in the café; some of them
knew each other and chatted briefly before they hurried on,
Danish mixed with foreign languages. She watched lazily as
people came and went.

After half an hour, she folded up her newspapers and
drank the last of her cold coffee before getting up to go.

She walked down past the convention center along
Kvægtorvsgade and past Rysensteen High School toward
Halmtorvet. She had her eyes on the ground and didn't see
the Audi or have a chance to react when a guy with dark
hair said her name and grabbed her arm.

31

Louise ran up the stairs to her fourth-floor apartment. Putting her key in the lock, she thought about how she'd run up the stairs and was a little surprised she could do so without getting winded, especially since she hadn't gotten out to run much lately.

"Hello?" she yelled as she entered.

The guest room door was open, and both beds were unmade and empty. Louise went to the kitchen to see if there was a note and knocked on the bathroom door.

It didn't take her half a minute to determine that Camilla wasn't in the apartment. She saw Camilla's jacket still hanging on the hook but noticed that her purse was gone. She tried calling her again. A female voice had only just started to tell her that the number she'd called was not in service when she spotted Camilla's Sony Ericsson on the nightstand next to the bed, turned off.

She leaned against the doorframe for a second, wondering if she ought to start looking for Camilla. She decided it would be almost impossible to know where her friend had gone. The only obvious place was if she'd gone home to her own apartment for some clean clothes.

Louise tried Camilla's home number, but no one answered. Louise felt the touch of concern that had flitted through her mind now take a firmer hold on her. A glance at the clock showed that it was eleven thirty. She was going to have to drive if she were going to have time to stop and see Pastor Holm and be back to Police Headquarters by one o'clock as she'd promised.

She locked her apartment door behind her and found Flemming Larsen's direct number at the pathology lab. Even though he was probably down in the autopsy rooms working, she needed to try to get hold of him and ask about the blood tests. Visiting all the new mothers the hospitals had records of would be a waste of time if it turned out that the baby had been born to a drug addict. Or it would rule out a large percentage of the potential suspects. Stig had had a good point.

"They're not back yet," the secretary told her after checking for the blood test results. Then the woman explained that she didn't expect Larsen to be done until sometime between two and three that afternoon. "They've got a busy schedule after the weekend."

Louise thanked her and said that she'd call back later.

The trip out to Stenhøj Church took her ten minutes. Louise had called to let Henrik Holm know that she would be stopping by, and he didn't sound that curious, so she decided to wait and explain when she got out there.

He greeted her with a smile and thanked her again and again for having watched Jonas. "He had a great time and thinks it's the coolest thing ever that you're a police officer," he said after they'd taken a seat in the kitchen.

"Ah yes. Well, that's actually why I'm here," she said, seizing the opportunity. "In my official capacity as a police officer, that is."

Henrik raised an eyebrow and cocked his head at her.

"The case of the deceased baby we found Saturday was officially assigned to us this morning," she said, adding that it had wound up on her desk specifically. Then she explained that they'd done the autopsy on the baby on Sunday. "The pathologist says he was stillborn. His lungs, heart, and other internal organs were fully developed, so the baby was viable. The cause of death was the chorioamnionitis, or a bacterial infection of the amniotic fluid."

Henrik's eyebrow was still raised.

"In the worst cases, it can kill both the mother and the baby."

He nodded, and his eyebrow finally returned to its normal position.

"Something else was discovered during the autopsy which is actually the reason the case was transferred to the homicide division. After the birth, one of the baby's pinky toes was removed. The pathologist is convinced that this was not a birth defect."

She decided to spare him the details and avoided telling him that Flemming had noted that this had been done with a knife, scissors, or pincers.

She saw the look in his eyes change. Henrik leaned back on the bench and looked at her, as if he didn't quite understand. An uncertain shadow flitted over his face.

"Is it possible that the child had a defect in the toe, so the parents removed it before they placed him in the church?" he suggested.

"In principle, yes," Louise consented, "but the fact that someone harmed the dead infant makes the act a criminal matter. As opposed to before, when we considered it a deeply tragic and sorrowful event, which is what it is when someone decides to abandon a stillborn baby."

"Some babies are stillborn," the pastor said absentmindedly. He looked through the living room, out at the tops of the trees in the yard. "As far as I can remember there were about 320 stillbirths in 2005."

He didn't say anything else, and they sat there for a bit before Louise explained that the Bellahøj precinct still had officers on the case, but she and her partner were now officially in charge.

"We have a couple of witnesses who saw a light green Fiat Regata parked here outside the cemetery early Saturday morning. Does that mean anything to you?" Louise asked. She was surprised when he nodded and made a face.

He ran his fingers through his wiry blond hair as if he needed to pull himself together before he got sidetracked. This left his hair somewhat tousled.

"If it's the people I'm thinking of, Otto Birch, my sexton, has had problems with them before," he said and then smiled a crooked smile. "It's a middle-aged couple, I'm guessing they're in their late forties or early fifties. We've caught them having sex in the cemetery several times. That's a bizarre thing to be turned on by, and Otto has thrown them out several times and forbidden them from coming here, but I've never heard yet of a person getting a restraining order against coming to a cemetery."

He laughed wryly.

"Now they've started coming at times when they don't think we'll catch them. It used to be mostly in the evening, as if this were part of their evening stroll."

He shook his head and stood up.

Louise had the sense he wanted to go back to what he'd been doing before she arrived, and she asked if he knew the couple's names.

"No, unfortunately I can't help you there. Otto just tried to scare them away. He threatened to report them to the police, but he never made a big enough deal out of it to ask their names."

Louise set her card on the table and said that he should just call if he had any questions or wanted to find out how the investigation was coming. She was almost out the door when she turned around and added that unfortunately there was no getting out of having the church in the spotlight again because of this.

"If my boss hasn't already called, I'm sure he will," she said and explained that Suhr wanted to appeal to the public in the hopes of finding witnesses.

Henrik nodded absentmindedly. Despite his previous concerns, it didn't appear to bother him that both of the big news broadcasts wanted to use his church in their broadcasts. At the last minute, it occurred to Louise that she probably should have said that the baby's pinky toe was something they wanted to keep confidential.

"We would prefer not to have that made public."

"Of course," he said.

32

Camilla Lind."

He repeated her name twice before she turned to look at him. The glasses' metal frames were reflecting the sunlight, and her arm hurt. She tried to yank it back. She ought to have been feeling nervous but instead she felt a rage that only grew when he continued to hold her in a tight grip, like a vise being tightened around her bone.

"Let me go," she hissed, trying to break free again as he pushed her up against the wall of the building and held her with both hands. A bicyclist rode past, but looked away when she tried to make eye contact with him.

"We know you were the one who wrote the article about that wino, who saw a car like mine down on Skelbækgade. And we'd like to have a little chat with you," he said, receiving help from a second guy she hadn't noticed until he started pulling her over to the car, which was stopped with the motor idling out in the lane of traffic.

"I don't have anything to talk to you about," she said, but felt her rage withdrawing, making room for the fear that suddenly rushed through her with such force that her throat tightened.

Why hadn't it occurred to her that they might come after

her the way they'd gone after Kaj? Finally, she felt something move inside her body, but they shoved her into the back seat so hard they knocked the wind out of her and then slammed the door shut.

A second later one of them got in behind the wheel and the other climbed into the back seat with her with a hand on her shoulder, which tightened its grip any time she made the slightest movement. The Audi started moving, she heard the automatic door locks engage and stared out the windshield as they drove across Halmtorvet.

What had she called it? A Balkan necktie, brutal payback for those who snitch on the perpetrators. She was breathing in such short jerky gasps that her chest was hardly moving.

The car continued down Sønder Boulevard and turned onto Enghavevej, past Enghave Square, and back to Istedgade.

"We didn't kill him," the guy sitting next to Camilla said. The driver kept his eyes on the road and seemed to be concentrating fully on his driving. "And we didn't kill the woman in the courtyard, either, even if that's what the police think."

Camilla closed her eyes as he spoke, didn't want to look at him or participate in what was going on around her right now.

The pain stabbed through her shoulder as he shook her. "Listen!" he shouted into her ear.

The driver was still staring straight ahead, but Camilla nodded.

"Go to the club," he ordered and the driver nodded and drove a little farther down Istedgade before turning onto Saxogade. She could tell they had Eastern European accents, but she couldn't narrow it down any more than that.

They passed Estlandsgade past Litauen Square and parked at the corner of Letlandsgade and Saxogade. She hurried to get out when the door on her side was opened.

Three steps led down to the front door, where a little sign said that they were entering an Albanian club. The basement space was larger than she had expected. The color of the walls was tired and sad and showed signs of the thick cigarette smoke, which hung densely in the space. There were a bunch of tables, each with four or five chairs around it. Men were sitting at four of the tables playing cards; each man had either a glass or a mug in front of him. It took Camilla a second to look around and determine that there was a single woman in the room. Along one wall there was a bar which appeared to be tended by an elderly man, who was changing the filter in a coffee-maker.

She was pushed through the room to a door at the back left.

"We're going in here," the man in the glasses told the bartender and received a nod back. No one reacted to the way they were holding her. Several of the men didn't even look up when they came in.

The room in back must have been some kind of combination office and storeroom, she thought. There was an old desk with a calculator and a couple of three-ring binders, and beer and soda crates were stacked along the wall.

"Sit down."

He gestured toward a worn-out armchair and then walked over and took a seat at the desk. The driver stayed by the door, and for a second Camilla wondered what would happen if she didn't obey but asked if she could leave instead. Would they hit her?

She went and sat down.

"We read what you wrote," he said and nodded at the guy by the door to make it clear that they'd both seen the article.

"That old fool didn't see shit," he continued angrily. "And if he did, then he was wrong."

He took a deep breath and she could tell that he was trying to curb his temper so the rage didn't subsume him.

"Or someone made him believe that story," the guy by the door said. That was the first time the driver had said a word.

The man with the steel glasses and the smooth hair nodded. "There is, of course, a third possibility. That someone paid you." He leaned over toward her menacingly. "Is that it? Did someone pay you to write all that crap?"

She shuddered when a little glob of spit hit her cheek. "No one paid me or asked me to write anything they didn't think was true," she said, deciding not to wipe her face, continuing to look him in the eye as she spoke.

He folded his hands behind his head and tipped his head back. He sat like that for a bit looking at the ceiling before he dropped his hands again and looked at her.

"We didn't do it," he repeated. "But someone really wants the police to think we were behind it." Now his tone was more subdued.

The man by the door was doing something with his phone, like he wasn't really involved with whatever was going on with Camilla.

"It's true that we were on Skelbækgade that night. I was also in the courtyard, but she was already lying on the ground when I got there with the blood pouring out of her."

He glanced over at the door before he continued. "I actually knew the girl, so I ran out to the car. Hamdi"—he nodded toward the door again, and the guy reacted when his name was mentioned, but then looked away again quickly—"and I drove down to Halmtorvet to look for the person who did it, but the police came quickly, so we pulled back."

Camilla gathered up her courage before she interrupted him, her voice steady and clear. "Why am I getting mixed up in all this? I don't want anything to do with this," she said, maintaining eye contact. Which was how she saw his rage return.

"I want you to go to the police and tell them it wasn't us. They need to lay off our asses and start looking at the people who did it. You got it?" His eyes were hard and they bore into her as he spoke.

Camilla took a deep breath and nodded. Even here, with her ability to think rationally paralyzed by fear, she knew her only option right now was to humor them. The fact that they wanted her to go to the police meant that at least they weren't planning to kill her.

"The police listen to you, and you're going to tell them to leave us alone and go after the right killer."

"I knew Kaj—not that well, but I knew him, and I know what happened to him in that courtyard."

Camilla was interrupted by Hamdi, who came over from the door to stand next to the desk.

"We weren't in that courtyard and we didn't touch him. Instead why don't you ask the police if they know why Ilana wasn't on the flight from Prague that day we went to the airport to get her. We know they were there, too, and if they haven't already talked to their Czech counterparts, then I suggest that they do."

The guy with the glasses nodded.

"Then they'll find out that she couldn't have taken that flight because she was found that same day in the apartment where she rented a room, her throat slit. They can also ask what the police have on that Serb we heard was seen in the building in Prague the day Ilana was murdered, because he was also in Copenhagen when the two murders took place."

"If he was seen, then I'm sure the police are already searching for him," Camilla said, watching him.

"No point in searching for him," he said, a smile rippling across his lips. "He's not the type who gets caught."

Again, she had that feeling in her throat. She didn't know how long she'd been in this back room, but she had no desire to know all the stuff she'd just been told. Mostly she wanted to go home to bed, so she could pull the covers up over her head and shut everything out.

"I don't know anything about a flight from Prague or some Ilana who didn't show up. I suggest you tell the police about this yourself, just the way you told me, if you think they know what's going on."

The arms were around her shoulders before she saw them coming and she was lifted up off the chair.

"We'll drive you over to the police now and then you will tell them what I just told you. And tell them they should leave us alone."

She was yanked toward the door. They quickly exited the premises, and Camilla felt like someone was holding the doors for her, so she flew through until she was sitting in the back seat of the car and listening to the motor start.

"If I'm going to talk to the police, you need to drive me

to Police Headquarters. I know someone there, someone I can make listen to me."

Something had relaxed within her; the fear didn't seem quite as paralyzing to her thoughts anymore. On the other hand, she was fully aware that they would come after her again if she didn't do exactly as they said.

33

There was a printout of names waiting on Louise's desk when she returned from the pastor's residence. She exhaled slowly as she skimmed through the pages and counted about fifty women who had been due to deliver their babies during the period of time they were working on. There'll be even more once we track down the women who were past their due dates, Louise thought and glanced over at her partner.

"Should we just divvy the list up and work our way through?" she asked Lars.

He nodded and noted drily that of course calling the women wouldn't do any good.

"You're right about that." She undid her ponytail and shook out her hair before gathering it into a bun and wrapping the elastic around it. "The only way is the hard way," she said, mimicking Willumsen's brusque tone as she spread out the pages, "and if we're lucky, we'll be done by August."

"I suppose you're most interested in your local area, so why don't you take Herlev, Hvidovre, and Glostrup? Then I can do National Hospital, Gentofte, and Frederiksberg." She was interrupted by the phone on her desk ringing. It was the front desk informing her that a Camilla Lind was downstairs and wanted to talk to her. Would Louise come down and escort her in, or should they send her away?

"I'll be down," she said quickly. Lars gave her a questioning look.

"It's Camilla. Of course, she wasn't there when I went home. I have no idea what she's been off doing or why she blew Jakobsen off this morning. I was starting to get a little worried about her," Louise said and darted out the door.

Down in the courtyard, Louise stopped short when she spotted Camilla in the waiting area. The only sign of life on her was the red access badge she had clipped to the waistband of her loose gray sweatpants. Her face was pale and without any makeup at all, and her hair was flat. But what stopped Louise in her tracks most was something in Camilla's face, a tenseness that made Louise break into a jog for the last few steps before putting her arms around her friend.

They stood there for a moment, both stunned. Then Louise loosened her grasp and said that she was assuming Camilla wanted to come up to her office. Camilla nodded mutely and Louise saw that she'd begun to cry. She put her arm around Camilla again and then led her across the courtyard.

While she'd been down there, Lars had organized his list of names by addresses and had already planned the order of his visits. He'd turned off his computer and was standing up, his denim jacket over his arm, clearly about to leave.

Camilla had stopped crying and dried her eyes on her sweater sleeves, but they still looked red. When they were still out in the hallway, she had started telling Louise about what the two Albanians had done to her. Now, in the office, she assured them both that she was only crying out of relief, that they hadn't actually harmed her.

"Have a seat," Louise ordered, pointing to the visitor's chair.

Lars tossed his denim jacket aside and offered to make a pot of coffee. Louise nodded to him, found a 10-kroner coin in her pocket, and asked him to stop by the vending machine in the lunchroom on his way and buy a bag of gummy candies.

"They didn't do it," Camilla said once the door had closed behind him.

Louise took a seat and studied Camilla before she even tried to understand what Camilla was talking about. Had she been drinking? Or what was wrong? She wasn't making any sense.

"They didn't do what?" she asked.

"Kill Kaj. Or that prostitute in the Meatpacking District. They admit that they were on Skelbækgade, but she was already dead when he went into the courtyard."

Camilla's words swirled past her and Louise asked her to hold on.

"You blew Jakobsen off this morning even though he moved around his whole schedule and canceled on another patient to make room for you," Louise said, trying to slow the pace down a little. "Did you do that so you could go play private detective?"

Camilla shook her head.

"I overslept." She apologized and promised to call Jakobsen and set up a new appointment if he was still willing to see her.

Lars pushed the door open with his foot and walked in with a thermal carafe, three cups, a bag of Eldorado, and a roll of chocolate cookies. Louise smiled at him and got up to close the door as he set everything down on the desk.

"Were they watching you out on the streets?" Louise

asked after Camilla told her about her morning and her visit to Central Station.

"Yeah, I was on my way to Halmtorvet to see if I could find one of Kaj's old friends and I didn't hear the car stop," she explained and then blew on her coffee before taking a sip.

"What did the guys look like?" Lars asked to get the details squared away.

"The one who grabbed me had kind of smooth, shoulder-length hair and glasses."

Louise and Lars exchanged looks.

"So, it was Arian and Hamdi," Louise said, and Lars agreed. Camilla nodded when she heard the name Hamdi.

"God damn it!" Lars pushed his chair back against the wall, put his legs up, and rested his mug on his knee. "Well, then they've figured out that we're tailing them."

"Yeah, I'd say so," Camilla said with a sarcastic little smile. The first one Louise had seen since she spotted her downstairs. "But I was supposed to tell you something— aside from the fact that they claim that they didn't kill those two people. The guy you say is named Arian knew her and says that he's sorry she's dead and that he sped off to get the killer. That's where he was going when he came back out of the building."

"And what did they say that's supposed to convince us it wasn't them?" Louise urged, trying to get Camilla back on track.

"Something about how they were out at the airport waiting for a girl who never showed up. Evidently, you guys were there, too," she said, watching them until they both nodded in confirmation. "That girl was found dead in her room the day she was supposed to come. Her throat had been slit, and he recommended that you guys call your counterparts in Prague and ask about the Serb who was seen in the girl's building at the time of her murder. According to them he was in Copenhagen when the two murders here were committed."

Louise suspected that Lars thought this was a story they just came up with, as if the two Albanians were trying to hamstring him, and she had to admit she was leaning that way herself.

"We'll bust them for unlawful imprisonment," Lars said once Camilla was done. "How long did they hold you at the Club?"

"No, no. Please, don't bother," Camilla responded quickly. "But you're going to have to investigate if there's any basis to what they said, because otherwise they're going to come after me again."

"It's not our case anymore," Louise explained, watching a look of confusion come over Camilla's face. "But I can either pass this on, or you can talk to Toft and Stig yourself. It's their case now."

"What does that mean? You mean only two people are working on it?" Camilla stiffened, looking at them in disbelief.

"Well, and Mikkelsen," Louise added.

"Two people were violently slain and there's only three men on the case? What the fuck's up with that?"

Louise wasn't sure why Camilla suddenly sounded so agitated. Camilla set down her cup and looked like she was getting ready for battle.

"Some folks from the downtown precinct will back them up when they need it," Louise said in an attempt to tone things down a little.

"Well, what the fuck are you two doing then, sitting around the office drinking coffee and eating chocolate cookies?" Camilla burst out, nodding toward the open roll of cookies on the desk. "The two people you suspect of flaying open two human beings just pushed me into their car and hauled me down to some basement room on Saxogade. What the fuck! You have to do whatever you can to catch these people!" she shouted frantically. "If what they said is right, that someone else did it, you're going to have to go find out who it was."

Camilla took a deep breath, down into her abdomen, and sank back in the chair. "I'm sorry," she said, rubbing her face to wipe the anger away. "It was just a huge shock to be detained like that. And in a way, I think they were telling the truth when they said it wasn't them. Why else would they have let me go?"

Since no one seemed to have an immediate response to her question, she now asked why they'd been taken off the case.

"We're investigating the stillborn baby you found in the church," Louise said, quickly trying to assess whether it was a good idea to tell Camilla what Flemming had discovered, but before she was able to decide, Lars was already doing it.

"It turned out the little baby was assaulted after birth, and we got the case because the injury occurred after death."

Camilla's face stiffened into an incredulous grimace. "Someone hurt him?" she asked, looking from Lars to Louise. Louise nodded.

"His pinky toe was amputated," she elaborated by way of explanation.

She watched the vacant look in Camilla's eyes, which suddenly seemed to focus on a point just to the left of the window. Camilla stared at that spot for a second, trying to reason her way through this labyrinth of new information.

Then Camilla seemed to snap out of it and she asked, "From which foot?"

"The right."

Camilla's farewell was rapid and happened before Louise even had a chance to stand up. But Camilla turned around in the doorway and looked at her.

"Make sure you check your information," Camilla urged before disappearing.

For a second Louise just sat there staring at the empty doorway, before she turned to her partner and shook her head a little despondently.

"Do you think it was wise to let her just leave after what happened to her?" Lars asked, concerned.

Louise shrugged and rolled her chair up to her desk. "I don't know. I mean, we can't put a man on her, and she's also not the kind of person who would accept a bodyguard, even after a frightening experience like that."

"But I guess it would be worth checking on whether the woman they were waiting for really was murdered," Lars said.

Louise nodded.

"What was her name again? Ilana... but what was her last name?" Lars asked, flipping through the stack of papers in front of him. "Procházková. We'd better tell Willumsen what happened."

"Let's go tell Toft instead. Then he can contact Interpol or e-mail the police in Prague directly," Louise suggested, getting up. "Willumsen will just chew us out for not being done with the lists of all the mothers-to-be."

She quickly walked over to Toft and Stig's office first, which was two doors down from her own.

"A Serb? Well, there's quite a few of those," Toft exclaimed, scratching the thick, full beard he had grown over the winter, but which he already seemed to be rethinking now that the weather was warming up again.

"But, of course, it ought to be checked."

He crossed his arms in front of his chest and glanced over at the row of certificates and trophies he and Michael Stig had brought home from all their bowling tournaments, both in Denmark and abroad, as he contemplated.

"If I can find the Serb's name, I have a good relationship with the criminal investigations unit in Prague. She's won a bunch of bowling tournaments and for a while she played professionally, but went back to police work after a couple of years. She said she missed it."

Louise smiled.

"What do we know about this Serb?" Toft asked, pulling out a sheet of paper, but they had to disappoint him then.

"Nothing aside from that he was seen in the woman's building. We don't have a description, but the police down there apparently know who the Albanians were referring to. Or at least they told Camilla that asking for 'the Serb' would be enough."

Toft nodded and stuck his plastic cigarette in his pocket.

"Maybe we should go pick up those two Albanians and haul them in here and find out if they have any more to tell us instead of letting them steer this show!"

Stig had appeared in the doorway with two sodas and a piece of fruit in his hands, and Lars made room for him so he could enter.

"Yeah," Toft said. "There might be something to that, but let's just check if they're leading us off on a wild-goose chase or if what they're saying is true."

He was already looking through his address list to find the Czech criminal investigations unit.

"Well, at least we don't have to sneak around after them

anymore, since they already know we're breathing down their necks," Stig said, using one cola bottle to pop the lid off the other.

"Here she is!" Toft exclaimed, pointing at his screen. "I'll write to her."

"Well, we'd better be off," Louise said, nudging her partner in the side.

34

There was no answer from the first doorbell Louise rang, but the next address on the list was only two blocks away.

"Copenhagen Police. I'm Assistant Detective Louise Rick. May I come in and talk to you for a second?" she asked over the intercom after the woman answered.

When she got to the second floor, there was a woman standing in the hallway with a belly so enormous it looked ready to burst.

Louise hurriedly smiled to allay the fear on her face, which people typically had when receiving a visit from the police. Then she apologized for bothering her and quickly explained why she was there. After the woman confirmed that her name was Gitte Larsen, Louise crossed her off the list and left.

Eight of the nineteen on her list lived in the four bridge districts—the dense residential neighborhoods of Nørrebro, Amagerbro, Østerbro, or Vesterbro, which had once been linked to central Copenhagen by gates through the old city walls—so she decided to cover them by bike. After that she would go back to Police Headquarters and check a squad car out of the garage.

It was almost eight p.m., and there were three women left on her list when she rang the doorbell at Maja Lang's place. She lived in a little row house in Gentofte, and a dog barked noisily as the doorbell elicited a melody in a scale of shrill tones.

This woman had neither a bulging stomach nor an expectant glow. To the contrary, her skin was so pale it almost seemed translucent or blue, and the veins in her temples were visible, making her face seem sensitive and exposed.

Louise explained why she was there and felt a pang when she saw how the woman pulled back as if she'd struck her.

"It's been almost three months since I lost her," she said, slumping a little.

Pictures of autumn trees in warm golden colors hung on the wall behind her, and in the living room there was a lap blanket on the sofa, as if she'd just gotten up. The candles were lit, and there was a quiet that suddenly seemed striking given that the row house was right off the heavily trafficked Lyngbyvej.

Maja Lang nodded toward a room that opened off the living room.

"We had everything all ready, but one morning suddenly I just couldn't feel her, and then I knew something was wrong. Really wrong."

She pulled back, sat down on the edge of the sofa, and pushed the blanket aside a little apologetically.

"Four days after that they induced the delivery, and we buried her the last Saturday in January."

She started crying and pointed to the armchair on the other side of the coffee table.

Louise quickly decided not to sit down and apologized profusely for having bothered her. On her way out, she swore to herself that Gentofte hadn't struck Maja Lang off their list of women who were due. Now she'd ripped open the woman's grief completely unnecessarily.

35

When Louise and Lars gave their status reports the next afternoon, they had to acknowledge that none of the women on the maternity ward lists seemed to have given birth outside the official health-care system. In the previous twenty-four hours, they'd been in touch with everyone who had been due during the right time period in Region H, or Greater Copenhagen.

Louise hadn't gotten home to her empty apartment until almost ten thirty the previous evening. Camilla had left a message on her kitchen table that she and Markus were spending the night at their own place, because he needed to get some of his schoolbooks and his gym clothes there anyway. Louise had briefly considered calling to make sure her friend had calmed down after her dramatic afternoon, but she didn't want to risk waking them.

At eight o'clock in the morning she was back at it, starting with a couple in their early thirties who were busy timing contractions.

Two women had been admitted that same day with preeclampsia and were going to be kept under observation until their labors started; four were having contractions, including the couple Louise had visited that morning. Everything had been the way it was supposed to with all the rest. They had opened their doors with their big bellies jutting out in front of them and had immediately been crossed off the list and given an apology for the disturbance.

Maja Lang and a very young girl that Lars had spoken to out in Glostrup were the only ones for whom things had not gone the way they should. The young woman had had an acute abortion as the result of a serious traffic accident she had been involved in a month earlier. When Lars visited her, she had just returned home from the hospital and assumed that was why the maternity clinic still hadn't been informed of what had happened.

Louise glanced over at the door in irritation when someone knocked three times, hard, and was about to ask whoever it was to go away and let her work when Toft came in and said he'd just received an e-mail from Jana Romanová.

"She's a detective at Bartolomějská Street, which is Prague's 'hard' police precinct," he explained, closing the door behind him. "She confirmed that last week Monday they found Ilana Procházková in an apartment just behind Václavská Street, where a lot of the city's prostitution takes place."

Louise reached for the half-empty roll of chocolate cookies and offered Toft one. Then she helped herself to one and pushed them across the desk to Lars.

"OK," she said, feeling the little hairs on her arm stand up.

"True enough, her throat had been slit. Jana's going to have the most important details from the pathology report and the crime-scene investigation results translated into English and promised to e-mail them ASAP."

Louise rested her head in her hands. This was starting to feel like a Sudoku in which someone had switched all the numbers around.

"Did you ask what she knew about the Serb?" Lars asked out of curiosity, taking a bite of his cookie.

Toft got a deep wrinkle in his forehead and nodded pensively.

"Yeaaah. She's guessing they might be referring to this guy named Bosko. They know him from the prostitution scene, but she hadn't heard that he had allegedly been seen in the area. They did have a couple of witness statements that said that a man with short hair and a leather jacket had been seen in the building, but he hadn't been identified yet."

"What else was she able to tell you about him?" Louise asked, taking another cookie. "I mean, it certainly sounds like she knows who he is."

"Nothing else. She seemed a little reticent about him, but maybe that's because she wants to look into him first and see if there's a connection. They're working on looking for a match for the fingerprints they found in the apartment and in the stairwell right now. The results aren't back yet. And she said there was a lot of blood around the body, which means that the jugular was severed and sprayed, and the murderer must have had a fair amount of blood on him when he left the site. And that doesn't match the description of the man witnesses saw leaving the building around the time of the murder."

"Well then, I guess you're going to have to get a hold of Arian and Hamdi and get them to tell you some more," Louise said. "If they think there's a connection, and if they want to get out from under the cloud of suspicion that's hanging over them."

"They're being picked up right now." Toft nodded and added that Mikkelsen and Stig were going to question the two Albanians. He would stay in touch with Jana so they could compare the technical findings from Prague with what they'd found at the murder locations in Copenhagen to help determine if the cases were connected.

"That's good, because that will let them know that Camilla held up her end of the agreement," Louise said to Lars after Toft had shut the door behind him.

Willumsen had asked them to turn in a report to him once they had finished going through the list. He nodded toward the conference table when they knocked and quickly gathered up the papers that were spread out in a little heap in front of him.

"Was there anything suspicious?" He stood up and came over to sit down across from them.

"Unfortunately not," Lars said. "But I suppose that would have been awfully lucky if it had been so easy."

The lead detective nodded and rubbed his chin as he thought about it. "Let's just compare with what Bellahøj found in their search for Baby Girl's mother." He added that it would surely take a couple more days, or maybe a week, before the boy's DNA came back.

"So I guess there's no way around it. We're going to have to appeal to the public and ask people to come forward if they noticed a woman walking around with a big belly but without a baby carriage since losing the weight. Obviously, we run the risk of offending someone by assuming that she might have been pregnant if she turns out to have only gotten a little fat, but that's a risk we'll just have to take," he said, looking as if it wouldn't bother him in the least to hurl an insult like that.

The lead detective got up and walked over to the stack of papers, which he hadn't had a chance to look at yet.

"Do the techs have anything on the towel he was wrapped in?" she asked, looking at Willumsen.

He shook his head absentmindedly as he flipped through the pages.

"Yes, here!" he exclaimed when he was almost through. "But all it says is that they can tell from the brand that it was made for the Føtex chain."

"That's the same type of towel Baby Girl was left in," Louise said with a start. "And the same color," she added with a level of enthusiasm that made Willumsen look at her eagerly.

"Are you sure?"

"A hundred percent! A dark blue terry cloth towel from Føtex. That's pretty damn interesting, wouldn't you say? There's no way that's just a coincidence."

Willumsen didn't say anything, but she could tell he was inclined to agree with her. "We'll have the two towels compared for prints and DNA," he decided, then walked back over to his desk and picked up his phone. "Oh, and Bellahøj picked up those two lovebirds with the green Fiat. Sure enough, they were in the cemetery from about four a.m. until about six or six thirty, but they didn't see or hear anything. People get turned on by the weirdest things these days," he said, then started dialing Frandsen's number.

36

It was just past six when Camilla and Markus ran across the courtyard in front of the pastor's residence. Markus was carrying the wine and the big bottle of soda, and Camilla was carrying the two bags from Meyers Deli. They were supposed to be there at six, but they'd had to wait in line to get the takeout, so the time had gotten away from them.

She stopped in surprise when she spotted the black women's bicycle with a basket on the handlebars parked at the base of the kitchen stairs. The kitchen door was slightly ajar.

"Just a sec," she called to Markus, who was already on the first step. "Maybe we ought to go to the front door if he has guests."

Markus looked from his mother to the bicycle, not understanding what she meant. "That's just the girl's," he said. "Jonas said she was going to do some cleaning and stuff."

Camilla looked at him in astonishment. "How do you know that?"

"He told me at school. She started yesterday."

They walked up and used the knocker.

"Come in." Henrik Holm took the bags and put them on the kitchen table.

Markus instantly disappeared upstairs, even though Camilla called after him that they were about to eat.

"How are you doing?" the pastor asked, looking at her with concern.

He really didn't need to ask, because it was perfectly obvious to anyone who looked that things were falling apart. She had finally worked up the energy to take a bath before Markus came home from school, and she'd also found some clean clothes in the very back of her closet, but she hadn't done much else. All the same, she appreciated his concern.

Someone ought to be showing some for him, too. It occurred to her that his cheeks looked hollower and his skin more ashen than when she'd last seen him, but she certainly hadn't been paying that much attention on Saturday that she would have noticed if the changes had already started by then.

She accepted the glass of wine he handed her.

"Markus says you have a housekeeper," she said, nodding toward the open kitchen door, where the bike was parked.

He seemed embarrassed and turned around to take the food out of the bags.

"Yeah," he said with his back to her. "After everything that's happened in the last few weeks, I suddenly felt like it would be nice to have a little help on that front."

Camilla walked over and started to get out the plates. "I can certainly understand that," she said, then walked over to get the salad Henrik had made. "I could use a little help myself to make it through the day, you know, just from first thing in the morning until it's time for me to go to bed again."

Henrik smiled at her and refilled their wineglasses, without her really having noticed that she'd emptied hers.

"How often is she coming? Once or twice a week?" Camilla asked, trying to concentrate on tasting the wine instead of just chugging it down.

"I've taken her in as an au pair, so she's living here. Three months to start with. I'll just see if I can get used to that, and hopefully by then things will have settled down again in our lives. Right now, I'm being bombarded with messages from the parish council and parishioners who want to know what's going on."

Camilla nodded and put the plates out on the table.

"Plus, maybe this way I'll be able to spend a little more quality time with Jonas," he added with a little smile, as if he felt like he needed to find excuses to justify finally having accepted a little help.

Camilla nodded and abruptly turned toward the door to the living room, from where she'd suddenly heard the sound of a woman's voice. A tall, young woman walked into the room with her cell phone to her ear and her eyes on the floor, as if she were concentrating on the phone call and hadn't noticed that they were looking at her.

Camilla recognized the dark pageboy hair and the dark eye makeup right away. "Well, but then it looks like it ended up working out very nicely," Camilla said and greeted the woman, who smiled at them uncertainly before leaving the room again.

Henrik nodded and said that some things worked out on their own. He stopped Camilla when she offered to set another place, and explained that Tereza didn't eat with them.

"There's a little mother-in-law apartment in the attic," he explained, pointing toward the staircase. "It has its own bathroom and a little kitchenette, so she prefers to eat on her own."

I suppose that makes sense, Camilla thought. It probably

suited Henrik best, too, that he and Jonas could continue to do things the way they usually did without having to involve a stranger.

"Boys!" Camilla yelled up the stairs, hoping that would be enough to get their attention.

"Would you rather have coffee or tea?" Henrik asked once they'd cleared the table. "I've given up drinking coffee in the evenings lately. It's no good to have it interfering with everyone's sleep."

There was still more wine in the bottle, so Camilla said she would stick to that.

"Have you had any thoughts about what you think we ought to do in terms of the funeral?" Henrik asked after sitting down across from her with a cup of tea in front of him. "I have it tentatively scheduled for Saturday."

If she were thinking about it, that would probably have been her choice. She set her hands on the table and looked at him.

"I'm going to have to back out of it and leave it to you, or you can leave it to other people. I can't do it anymore. It eats away at me night and day and I'm going crazy, so I've decided that I'll have to wait to say my good-byes to him, until after he's in the ground in whatever pauper's grave somewhere. Someday when the sun is out, like it was today, I'll go there with a bag full of beer bottles and a ghetto blaster and play 'I Walk the Line' for him. That'll be my way of doing it."

Henrik's tired eyes twinkled at her. "That's a good plan," he conceded and said he'd be sure to show her where the urn was interred.

Camilla took a deep breath and then changed the topic. "Did you hear that the case from last Saturday has been turned over to the Homicide Division?" she asked after she'd poured the last of the wine into her glass.

He nodded and said that Louise had stopped by.

"Do you think there could be a connection between the two cases after all, even though the police are investigating them separately?" she asked, swirling her wine around in the glass.

He shrugged, but then shook his head. "Obviously, I've been thinking about it a lot, but I don't see what they could have to do with each other," he said.

"But it is sick, isn't it, to abandon a stillborn baby."

She studied his face to find a reaction and then looked away when he looked up from his teacup and nodded with a deep furrow in his brow.

"That's one of the things that depresses me the most," he admitted. "Most people have no idea how many mentally ill people are left to their own devices. People who are lonely and unhappy cry out for help, but only a tiny number are ever actually heard. Only in the most glaring circumstances, when it turns into a shootout with the police or something, where the mentally ill person is doomed to lose from the beginning."

"Maybe abandoning the baby last Saturday was an attempt to get you to listen," Camilla said, after a couple moments of silence. She could hear the boys playing *World of Warcraft* up in Jonas's room, and based on the cheers she was guessing one of them had just made it to a new level. "I'm thinking about the thing with the toe," she added. She waited for his reaction, but when it didn't come, she continued, "Markus told me that Jonas is also missing a pinky toe."

She knew she was overstepping her bounds, trespassing on his privacy, and she watched him to see if he was taking it the wrong way. At first, he looked at her in surprise, as if he were surprised that she knew about that detail, but then he looked over toward the breadbasket, which was still sitting on the table, and looked lost in thought, in a way that made her not want to bother him.

"Obviously, I've thought about that," he said after a while. "But I don't see how those two things could be connected. My son has a congenital defect on his foot, which anyone who has seen him barefoot knows about, but otherwise it's not really something anyone would notice. If someone is trying to tell me something, I really hope they'll come forward so I can help them."

There was a look of resignation in his face, which Camilla interpreted as tiredness. It was a little after nine; she had to be getting home so that Markus wouldn't be too much of a basket case when he had to get up for school the next morning.

She smiled when he thanked her for bringing the food, and while he yelled up to the boys that Markus should come down, she got their jackets.

37

On the way down from the cafeteria, Louise spotted the interpreter. Igli was on his way to the monitoring room. She overtook a couple of the office girls, who were taking up most of the stairwell, chatting as they walked, and received a snide comment as she squeezed by.

She jogged to catch up to Igli and asked him if he had time for a cup of coffee. She knew that he'd worked for the police in Belgrade for years before moving to Denmark during the war in the former Yugoslavia.

He smiled at her in surprise and said that he thought she and Lars had been reassigned and weren't following the wiretaps that he was working on anymore.

"True enough," she hurried to say, as they started heading back up to the cafeteria together.

"Do you take milk or sugar?" Louise asked as the cashier rang them up.

"Sugar," he requested and added that he wouldn't mind a pastry to go with the coffee.

Louise pointed to the two last chocolate chip rolls on the plate and paid before carrying the tray over to the table in the back corner of the room.

"So, what is it you want?" Igli asked. He then apologized for having to leave his cell phone on while they talked, because his son was going to call when he left school. "He's just started taking the bus home by himself."

"That's fine," Louise said, passing him one of the rolls and mopping up the coffee that had sloshed over onto the saucer. "I want to find out if you know anything about a Serb named Bosko."

Igli's teaspoon stopped stirring for a minute as he watched her attentively. "That's really a very common Serbian name," he said and then kept stirring.

She nodded and thought, I suppose it is. "I'm talking about a person who is known to both the Czech police and the two Albanians whose phone calls you've been monitoring, and I imagine that might be the same guy they're talking about. Does that tell you anything?"

A gloomy look slipped over his face and a deep wrinkle formed on his forehead. "Well, then I have an idea who you're thinking of. Why do you ask about him?" Igli asked, as though she'd asked him to pull out a shadow from the past.

"Because his name has come up in connection with the Meatpacking District case. We don't know if there's anything to it, but I'd like to find out who he is."

She explained what had happened to Camilla and told Igli about the tip Arian had given them, which had turned out to be true.

"But when Toft tried to get information from his source with the police in Prague, she just wormed her way out of it and said that they hadn't heard he was in town. So he was obviously someone they were familiar with."

Igli nodded and leaned his head over his full coffee cup before admitting that Bosko was someone who was known throughout most of the Balkans.

"Personally, it's been my opinion that it's best to know as little about him as possible, but if you think you need to know, I'll be happy to tell you what kind of person he is."

Igli pushed the plate with the untouched chocolate chip roll away and leaned in over the table.

"I ran into him the first time when he was in his midtwenties. That was more than twenty years ago. He's from Belgrade and started his criminal career as a soccer fan of the Belgrade Red Star, the professional Serbian club, which recently received a big fine for violent riots during a league game. A policeman was attacked and seriously injured. Several of the club employees are suspected of having started the riots, so things haven't changed much over the years."

Soccer and league games were not something Louise knew much about, and she had to admit that she'd never heard of the Belgrade Red Star.

"He became the lead fan," Igli went on. "Then in 1992 he joined up with Arkan's Tigers; that was right after the election when Bosnia became independent, and he was behind some of the nastiest ethnic cleansing by the paramilitary unit, which caused thousands upon thousands of Muslim citizens to flee."

Igli gave her a very somber look.

Suddenly Michael Stig was standing at their table without Louise having noticed him walk up. He said, "You guys shooting the breeze?"

"I guess you could say that," Louise said, irritated, as Stig got ready to join them. "Igli was just telling me about Bosko." She asked Stig if they had gotten any more out of Arian or Hamdi during the questioning sessions the previous day. They'd still been going when Louise had left.

Stig shook his head and eyed Igli with curiosity, as if it

hadn't occurred to him that Igli might know anything about the Serb. "They're not saying a word. Just keep repeating that we should check where Bosko was when the two murders took place. But then when we ask them to tell us any more about the Serb, they completely clam up, even when we try to explain to them that that makes it a little hard for us to get anywhere if they don't want to say anything."

Igli nodded as Stig spoke. "No one's going to talk if Bosko is involved. But is there any reason to think he's been in Copenhagen?" he asked.

Louise could see the anxiety in Igli's brown eyes.

"Just what those two say," Stig responded with a shrug of his shoulders. "And no one here seems to have heard of him before, not even Mikkelsen, who otherwise is familiar with most of the rumors going around in the neighborhood."

The interpreter shook his head again. "I haven't heard anything about Bosko starting to be active in Denmark," he confessed. "And I hope he doesn't decide to turn up, either."

"I interrupted you in the middle of something," Stig said, opening his soda bottle against the edge of the table. Louise nodded and asked Igli to continue what he had been saying.

The interpreter sighed and took a deep breath, as if he would have preferred not to finish what he was saying. He glanced at his cell phone on the table, which hadn't rung yet.

"He got his own military unit, weapons and trained people from the ultranationalist parties, who were interested in cleaning out the Muslims and claiming land for the Serbs. But that's not how I ran into him again."

Louise could tell that Stig didn't find Igli's old wartime memories particularly interesting and that he was hoping their chat would be more closely related to the case they were working on.

"Two years after the war broke out and was at its peak, Bosko realized how much money could be made if he used the situation to his own advantage. That was during the siege of Sarajevo, when Serbian forces created a blockade around the city and stopped all supplies from entering. Residents were short on food, and emergency supply convoys were having a hard time making it in. That's when Bosko started building up his smuggling business."

The look in Igli's eyes made it clear that the memories were painful.

"The Bosnian-Serb forces were shelling the city daily with mortars, and snipers were killing people in the streets, and they weren't distinguishing between civilian and military targets. It was in the middle of all that chaos, while the city was in a state of emergency, when Bosko made his first millions."

The plate of chocolate chip rolls remained untouched, and the coffee in Igli's cup had grown cold.

"We think he brought in the first war tourists in April 1994, but he may have started even earlier than that. The route ran from Moscow to Budapest or Sofia, and then from there they were brought to Belgrade by car and on to Zvornik, which is the border between Serbia and the Serbian part of Bosnia, which is now called the Republika Srpska," Igli explained. "From Zvornik, a team leader brought them to Pale, the little town up in the mountains, which has since become the capital of the Serbian territory. The town is about twenty kilometers from Sarajevo."

The cafeteria was empty by now, and the employees were sitting at the other end of the room having a cup of coffee. They didn't seem bothered that the last of the customers hadn't left yet.

"The war tourists were housed in some of the luxury

hotels, which had been built for the Winter Olympics in 1984. We thought it was mostly the newly minted millionaires from Russia and Ukraine he was bringing in when he arranged what we started calling his human safaris. They were the ones who could afford to pay the big money for an adrenaline rush that they could hold on to long after they'd returned home again."

Louise was staring at Igli in disbelief but didn't interrupt, and Stig no longer looked like Igli's story was boring him.

"You bought a basic package, which covered the trip to Serbia, your room and board, and after that you could say the price depended on the level of danger or the size of the adrenaline rush you wanted.

"The trips were broken up like this:

"Tour Number One was the economy trip. Participants were allowed to fire mortars out over Sarajevo without a chance to see what they'd hit, or whether anyone was killed.

"Tour Number Two was more like coach. A guide would take you down into the city so you could follow the fighting and see where the mortars you launched had hit and how many people you'd killed.

"Tour Number Three was the exclusive one. Here, a personal guide and a bodyguard would take you down into the city with a sniper rifle so that you could shoot right at people."

Igli paused for a bit.

"Rumor had it that if you hit anyone, you got a discount on the price of the tour. But we never managed to confirm that, and the police only managed to figure all this out after the fact. We were just never anywhere near catching Bosko, even though he never hid the fact that he was the man behind the tours. People like Bosko are rarely caught, because men of that caliber are known by Serbs and Muslims, and there will always be someone willing to cover up for them."

For a second, Louise thought what she saw in Igli's eyes was respect, but then she realized that it was profound fear.

"I hope for your sakes and everyone else's that he hasn't come to Denmark. Bosko goes wherever there's a lot of money to be made, and he uses unscrupulous people to increase his fortune. Now I've heard that in the last few years of the war, he was trading in children, that he was trading in women and smuggling people over borders for big sums of money. But the truth is I want to hear as little news about him as possible."

The cell phone on the table rang, and Igli quickly looked at his watch before answering it and arranging with his son that the boy would call again once he was home. Then Igli excused himself and said that he was going to go down to the monitoring room and see what was on the computer so they could keep on top of it.

Louise and Stig sat there for a bit without saying anything before Louise cleared the table and then took the full tray over to the garbage area.

"It's not going to do any good for us to check the airlines' passenger manifests around the times of the killings," Stig said, once they were on their way back downstairs. "He can cross national boundaries freely by car, if he turns out to be the one who was here."

Once they got down to the second floor, where the Homicide Division offices were, Louise proceeded down the hall and cautiously knocked on the door to the monitoring room.

"Excuse me," she hurried to say, as Igli pulled his headphones off. "Do you think your old colleagues might have a picture of Bosko that they could e-mail us?"

Igli thought about that for a moment, but was interrupted by his cell phone ringing.

His son must have made it home and the father's shoulders noticeably relaxed. Igli folded his hands over his stomach and gave Louise a somber look. "I would really like to ask you to keep me out of this. I told you about Bosko because you sounded like you might need to know. But I'd rather not have any further involvement," he said, an urgent look in his eyes.

"Of course," she said quickly, taking a reflexive step back, surprised by the intensity in his voice.

"Don't misunderstand me. It's not that I subscribe to the idea that some people should be allowed to demand to be left in peace, but I swore to myself that I would never have anything to do with Bosko or his people ever again. Both of my brothers worked for the police. They were the ones, along with a couple of other people, who figured out the war tourism thing. When Bosko learned that they'd detected his smuggling business, he went looking for the four men who'd been working on the case, he went to their homes, and gunned them down in front of their wives and children."

The pain was evident in his face as he gave a quick nod, as if to emphasize that that's what happened when you went up against a man like Bosko. Then he turned back around to face his computer and reached for his headphones without reacting to Louise's good-bye.

38

Louise stopped abruptly in the doorway to her office when she saw Camilla sitting there waiting for her with a mug of steaming tea in her hands.

Lars had already been out to a private birthing clinic in Østerbro before lunch to pick up a list of the names of pregnant women who were due to give birth or whose due dates had just passed. The manager there had not been favorably disposed toward handing over the list even though Lars had a court order, but it did seem to mollify her when he offered to come pick it up in person so there was no risk it would fall into the wrong hands.

"Hello," Louise said, noting that her voice sounded a little lackluster. She was still mulling over Igli's story and especially his own personal involvement in it. She took the electric water heater that had just boiled and got out a packet of green tea before she sat down to find out why Camilla had stopped by.

"Markus and I had dinner with Pastor Holm and Jonas last night," Camilla began slowly.

Louise tossed her tea bag into the trash, leaving a line of wet drips on the floor, before she swung around in her chair and told Camilla that of course it was nice of her to stop by, but that she and Lars were in the middle of a monumental assignment, since Willumsen had left it up to them to find the mother of the stillborn baby. She didn't have much time for tea parties.

"Did you know that Jonas is missing the pinky toe on his right foot?" Camilla asked, without paying any heed to Louise's attempt to send her on her way.

There was a pause, as they each held their mug of tea and looked at each other while their thoughts took over.

"No," Louise said, shaking her head. "I didn't know that."

"Henrik is totally convinced that the toe wasn't amputated, that it just happened to be like that, but I don't believe in that kind of coincidence. I just can't tell if he has noticed the similarity, or if he's really as clueless as he's acting."

Louise set down her mug. "What do you mean by that?" she asked, eyeing Camilla expectantly, hoping she would fill her in on whatever idea had occurred to her. Without question, it seemed too absurd for someone to cut the toe off a newborn baby just because they knew the pastor's son was missing a pinky toe, but Louise did agree that it didn't sound like a coincidence. Especially since it was the same toe.

"Maybe someone feels like he's let them down, or that it's his fault their child didn't survive," Camilla suggested, shrugging her shoulders at the lack of an obvious explanation.

"But if that's the case then, whoever left the baby in the church must be someone who knows that Jonas has that defect," Louise said, picking up her phone and dialing Willumsen's extension.

"Yeah?" Willumsen said tersely.

Louise realized how tired she felt as she asked if he had time to stop by her office. "I thought you had enough work to keep you busy," he said sarcastically when he spotted Camilla in there, drinking tea.

Louise didn't even have the energy to explain, just motioned toward Lars's chair and asked Willumsen to take a seat.

Camilla smoothed back a tuft of hair, which had come out of her ponytail, and repeated what she'd just told Louise.

Willumsen grunted slightly, while the two women watched him to see what his assessment was.

"What does the pastor have to say about it?" was the first thing Willumsen asked, eyeing Louise. She had to shrug because she hadn't spoken with Henrik Holm about it yet. "If this isn't a coincidence, then it does kind of look like someone has decided to go after him. That there's a personal motive, at least behind that last event."

Camilla nodded. "But he's not saying anything," she said, watching Louise's boss.

Willumsen got up and paced back and forth a bit. Then he pointed to Louise. "You need to go talk to him. If it was someone trying to tell him something, then we're going to have to start a completely different kind of investigation."

Louise agreed. She contemplated calling the pastor's residence first, before she left, but decided to just hope he was home.

"I brought my car," Camilla said and offered her a ride out to the church. "It's not far out of my way, after all." They walked down toward Otto Mønsteds Gade. "But I'm not going in with you," she hurriedly added before they climbed into the car. "It's bad enough that I've been blabbing to you about his kid's toes."

39

Louise climbed the steps to the pastor's kitchen door and banged a couple of times with the doorknocker. She smiled shyly at the tall, dark-haired woman who opened the door a second later. Camilla had told her about the housekeeper on their way out there, but now she realized she was interrupting them in the middle of a conversation. There were three girls sitting around the table talking softly in a language Louise didn't understand. Now their conversation stopped, and they all looked down at the table a little uncertainly and avoided looking her in the eye.

"Could I come in to speak to Henrik Holm?" Louise asked in English.

The housekeeper pointed over to the church without saying anything, but her meaning was clear enough, so Louise smiled and thanked her before turning to walk back across the courtyard, where the sexton had just come into view.

"He's in the middle of a wedding rehearsal with a couple who's going to get married here this weekend," the sexton said, squinting slightly at the sun as he turned and looked at the clock on the church tower. "I think they'll be done soon."

"Oh, that's fine. Then I'll wait for him," Louise said and walked over to sit down on a bench in the sun. It was positioned such that she had her back to the whitewashed church wall and had a wonderful view of the cemetery, where the beech tree buds were just about to open.

It still didn't make any sense to her that someone would remove the infant's toe to harass or provoke Henrik Holm, but sometimes it didn't take much to make people act based on emotion. Often it seemed like a trivial matter to other people, but to the person who felt like they'd been wronged, a relatively simple occurrence could cause their world to fall apart.

A couple in their midthirties walked out of the church with the pastor. Louise watched them say good-bye and didn't get up until Pastor Holm started walking toward the residence.

"Hi," she called after him and apologized for coming by unannounced. "There was just one thing I wanted to discuss with you."

He turned around, surprised, and smiled when he saw her. "No problem," he assured her. "Let's have a seat," he suggested and they walked back over to the bench.

Instead of getting right to the point, Louise said she'd just met his new housekeeper. "What does Jonas think about her?"

"He hasn't said much," the pastor admitted. "But I think that's a good sign. Tereza told me yesterday that for the last month she's been the leader of a network that tries to help Eastern European women who've been forced to come to Denmark and work as prostitutes against their will. The network tries to help them get back home safely."

Louise listened with interest and thought about Pavlína. A network like that would be great for her.

"There are already a number of people involved, and I got the sense that there would be even more. So, I gave them permission to meet out here, where they can talk in peace and quiet," he said.

Louise sensed a new dedication in his voice and was sure it hadn't been there during her last visit. But his eyes seemed tired and kept darting around the courtyard anxiously and over toward the parking lot, as if he were having a hard time concentrating.

"If they're not already familiar with the Nest and Stop Trafficking in Women, they might like to talk to them," Louise suggested. "They also have some resources that can be used to help victims get back home, even with a little money in their pockets, so they can get by for a while and not be susceptible to being rounded up again right away." She could tell that this was all news to him, but that he was clearly interested.

Louise took a breath, which ended up being a little deeper than she'd been planning, and then turned to face him and changed the topic. "You should have told us that Jonas is missing his right pinky toe," she said, watching him to see what his reaction would be. When there was none, she continued: "It's certainly possible that that isn't significant, but that is a piece of information we're going to need to include in our considerations as we investigate the case."

Finally, he nodded and leaned forward so that his forearms were resting on his knees with his fingers interlaced. He nodded again but remained silent.

"It makes us think there might be a personal motive behind the event," Louise explained, watching his wiry hair flutter a little in the wind as he shook his head.

"I can't imagine there is one," he said, focusing intently on his fingers, which were moving in and out of each other.

"I wouldn't have even given it a thought myself if Camilla hadn't mentioned it yesterday." Louise could almost physically feel his reluctance to talk any more about it.

Now she was forced to ask, "Are there many people who know about his little defect?"

The pastor slowly shook his head.

"Whether there's any connection or not, I'd like to ask you to make a list of the names of the pregnant women you have had any recent contact with for any reason," she requested. "And also, a list of names of anyone who has already scheduled a baptism or who had at least discussed possibly wanting to baptize a child in your church."

She hazarded a guess that having a pastor who was familiar from his media appearances might make people more interested in him.

"Maybe we should also consider whether you might have written something recently that might have triggered this action," she finally suggested.

He turned to her then, and to her surprise, she saw a look of profound irritation in his eyes, and she jumped slightly when he suddenly got up from the bench.

"I'm going to need to ask you to respect that as a pastor I'm bound to keep certain things confidential. But having said that, I don't need to even think about it to know that there haven't been any episodes here in the church that could have triggered what you're thinking of."

Louise was about to tone things down a little, but she didn't have a chance to say anything before Henrik continued:

"If someone wanted to come after me because of the things I write, then I can pretty much promise you it would've happened a long time ago. But you're welcome to go through everything if you think it might have some significance. All my columns and commentaries are on my home page."

She hadn't meant to make him mad, and she was so surprised at his violent response that she just sat there staring at him as he walked back toward his kitchen door. Then she closed her eyes and turned her face to the sun and composed herself for a second with the back of her head resting against the wall.

She decided to cut through the cemetery and walked along, lost in her own thoughts, her eyes trained on the gravel, which was why it wasn't until she'd passed the young girl on the path that it occurred to her there was something familiar about her. Louise turned around, but then she wasn't sure it had been Hana. From behind it was only the long blond hair that confirmed her guess.

At the end of the graves, she exited through the gate and crossed the street before continuing on into Frederiksberg Park. When she reached the lake, she stopped abruptly and enjoyed the view of the white swans and coots walking along the shore. The mild spring weather reminded her that summer was on its way. Suddenly she felt an almost overwhelming urge to get out of town, to head for the fields and woods and water. She sat down on the bench closest to the ice cream stand, which wasn't open for the season yet, and pulled out her phone.

A quick glance at her watch told her that it was just past four when she sent Mik a text message inviting herself to go kayaking with him on the Holbæk Fjord. "If you have the kayaks ready in an hour, I'll pay for dinner at the harbor when we get back to shore," she wrote and smiled as she pressed Send.

The response came before she'd even had time to get up off the bench. "Great. See you soon."

40

Mik Rasmussen and Louise overslept. She'd planned to leave at about seven; now it was almost eight thirty. Of course, they'd ended up having Irish coffees when they got back to his traditional thatch-roofed farmhouse after they'd eaten soup, monkfish cheeks, and a "sumptuous symphony of chocolate," as the chef had elegantly dubbed the four different chocolate desserts that had been dusted with powdered sugar and served together in one square glass dish.

They hadn't gotten much sleep, but her body felt great and she was humming, "Wake up, it's a wonderful morning," as she backed out of the courtyard and blew him a kiss through the driver-side window.

Once she was on the highway she turned on the radio and sang along to "Billie Jean," glad that P4 still played Michael Jackson.

She stopped in Frederiksberg to park her car and biked the rest of the way in to Police Headquarters. She was still humming as she biked along Gammel Kongevej with her sunglasses on and the wind in her long, dark curls. Out in front of Police Square she spotted Mikkelsen walking down the sidewalk.

"Hey!" she called, waving to him before swinging her leg over the saddle of her black mountain bike. "You want to walk up with me?"

He nodded, breathing a little heavily.

"Too many cigarettes and not enough exercise," he admitted honestly.

Louise was about to add "And too much barbecue" but managed to bite her tongue. It really wasn't any of her business.

"Are you guys meeting?" she asked Mikkelsen and nodded at the guy at the front desk as she showed her ID.

"Yeah," Mikkelsen grunted, still not quite having caught his breath. "We really want to find out where the Albanians are meeting with the girls now when they make their payments. They're not going to Central Station anymore."

"Could they have put their business on hold for a bit?" Louise suggested, but Mikkelsen shook his head, smiling.

"No, no way," he said. "That's the last thing they'd do, even though they know we're watching them."

She gave him a blank look.

"You have to keep in mind that even if they get caught and charged with pandering or in a worst-case scenario, trafficking in women, the penalty isn't that high. Considering what they make in a single day, it's not enough to scare them. It's no skin off their backs if they wind up in the slammer for a year or two, because they're raking in so much money when things are going well."

Louise listened with interest as he continued.

"Right now, human trafficking is the most lucrative crime. That's where they get the money to buy weapons and drugs!"

That last bit was a little dig, justifying why they still

ought to take down the people behind the scenes, even if it was only for a year or two.

Louise stopped outside her office and watched Mikkelsen as he continued two doors farther down the hallway and knocked on Toft and Stig's door.

It was five to ten when she said good morning to Lars, who was facing his screen, but watched her as she took off her jacket and turned on her computer.

"Good morning," he teased, implying that he'd been working for several hours already and that he no longer really considered it morning.

"Yeah," she said apologetically. "I overslept. I should've called you when I woke up, but I didn't think about it."

He shook his head. "You didn't need to," he said quickly.

Suddenly she noticed something in his expression that she hadn't seen before. Louise sat down and looked at him. "Were you afraid something had happened to me?" she said.

His eyes were back on his computer, but after a second he nodded and admitted that the thought had crossed his mind.

She smiled. "You were worried about me," she said, and he looked embarrassed.

He mumbled something about given what had happened to Camilla it didn't hurt to pay a little extra attention...

"You shouldn't be apologizing. I'm just glad you care," she exclaimed, but was interrupted by a knock at the door. Toft stuck his head in and she saw Suhr standing behind him.

"Could we come in?" Toft asked.

She nodded, casting a quick glance at Suhr to see if he'd noticed that she'd come in late. If he had, she would have to apologize. If he hadn't, she didn't see the point in drawing his attention to it.

"We succeeded in getting a picture of that Serbian man, Bosko," Toft said.

Louise could tell right away that Suhr did not deserve any of the credit for this accomplishment. Toft, in his terrier-like style, had doggedly pursued and obtained the photo. "We sent the picture around to all the precincts last night, but so far no one has responded to it," Suhr reported. "But at least they have him up on their radar now, and the patrols have been informed."

Suhr stepped all the way into the office while Toft remained in the doorway, leaning against the frame.

"We would really like your assistance for the rest of the day," Suhr said. When he saw Louise's expression, he added that Willumsen had suggested it himself, that they put everything they could into confirming or disproving whether the Serb had been seen in or around Skelbækgade and Sønder Boulevard around the times of the two murders.

"We're going to make the rounds on Istedgade and the rest of the neighborhood with this picture," he continued. "If it turns out that there aren't any witnesses who saw him moving around in the area, then we'll drag the two Albanians in and charge them with the killings and hope that that's enough to make them talk."

"We have had them in here for questioning for the last two days," Toft added, as if to justify this harsh-sounding decision. "They're not saying anything. Nothing at all. Except that they keep claiming it wasn't them. They also clam up completely when we ask them to tell us what they know about Bosko. They just shake their heads and repeat that we should find out where he was when the two murders took place."

"So that's what we're going to spend the rest of the day on," Suhr concluded. Then he corrected himself. "Of course, we'll also find out if anyone saw him during the interim between the two killings."

Louise was still happy it was spring, but some of the effervescence was gone, replaced by an expectant restlessness. It suited her just fine to go back to Istedgade, even though she was kind of hoping they didn't find him. Hard to tell what the consequences would be if an international criminal with a background like that set up shop in Copenhagen. She also knew that the reason she was looking forward to taking a little break from her own case so much was the way her conversation with Henrik Holm had ended the day before.

"We'll split the area up between you," Suhr said, adding that Mikkelsen was providing four people from the downtown precinct. "Willumsen will go with you, so there'll be five of us from here." He dropped the pictures on the table.

Louise pushed one over to Lars and took the other one herself. She didn't know what she'd imagined a man with so many human lives on his conscience would look like, but she was sure she'd seen him before, and she knew where, too.

41

Camilla had brought her comforter in to use on the sofa, and now she turned on the morning shows as soon as Markus left for school. She hadn't slept well at all. She shouldn't have told the police about Jonas's toe. The thoughts kept swirling around in her head, but she'd seen the pastor's reaction when she mentioned that she thought there might be a connection. It had been there, but then it was gone again. At three a.m., she'd gotten up and shaken six sleep-inducing valerian pills out into her hand, but they hadn't helped. The last time she looked at the clock it was a little past five. By that point there were just under two hours until she had to get up to see Markus off. Now she ought to do some laundry. Markus had been forced to wear a pair of sweats and a long-sleeved T-shirt whose arms were too short when she was forced to confirm that there was nothing else clean.

But instead of getting up and gathering the laundry, she took her thoughts back to that evening, when she'd been sitting in the pastor's kitchen. And suddenly a new thought struck her. What if the stillborn baby in the church wasn't related to the pastor, but to the son's mother? Then maybe that would explain why Henrik so categorically rejected that the two things had anything to do with each other.

That was a possibility that hadn't occurred to her before now, surely because she'd never known the boy's mother. She'd seen only one picture of her, a photo of the three of them at a dilapidated farm in Sweden where Markus had once spent Easter with them. Once in Laholm she had almost not been able to figure out the last bit of the way to the farm when it was time to go pick him up. Alice Holm smiled from the photograph on the bookshelf, and she guessed it was taken when Jonas was about three—one year before she died.

Camilla tried to remember what Henrik had said about his wife and their time in Bosnia. Camilla didn't know where they'd been stationed in the country as aid workers, just that the camp had been in a small town, which had been subjected to several brutal massacres in short succession.

Camilla tossed the comforter aside and went into the bedroom to get her laptop. It was Srebrenica, where the bodies from the brutal ethnic cleansings had been carted off to a huge mass grave outside of town.

She also searched Infomedia to see if the pastor had written anything about his experiences in the Balkans. She determined that he had. There were six articles. Camilla felt a little flutter in her stomach where she hadn't been feeling much of anything lately, but there turned out to be nothing to go on. They were all objective descriptions of the area, of the mood that weighed on the city like an overcast sky. He wrote that no one ever produced a concrete number of how many people had died in the brutal cleansing, but that it had affected all portions of the civilian population: men, women, children, the elderly. No one escaped. Maybe five, or eight, or ten thousand dead. Who knew? he wrote, and his point was that the correct number didn't mean that much to the residents who were left anyway. "The people are broken and humiliated. There couldn't be more sorrow, even if the tally went up."

He wrote well, Camilla observed, after she'd read all the way through. Gripping and clear. Even though the events were from fourteen years before, they got under her skin and gave her the sense of being a snotty-nosed, overprivileged dolt like the rest of the Danish population. No one here had experienced anything that came anywhere close to what the Muslims in the Balkans had suffered, and despite that many Danes still felt an inflated sense of arrogance toward the people who had been affected and had since come to Denmark to make a fresh start.

She suddenly sat up, alert, concentrating as if she were listening to something. She didn't move, trying to be sure, but then she realized she had no doubt that it had been there. Her cheeks pulled up and for a second she smiled, a smile no one saw, as to her great relief she noted that everything in her wasn't dead after all.

She felt indignation, rage at how ridiculously smug and egocentric people were. She was struck by it, and it made her want to write. Maybe it was a little late to be scolding people for the cold shoulder so many asylum seekers from the former Yugoslavia had been met with, but she yearned to do it. Over the last couple of weeks she'd totally written off ever feeling this way again. Apparently, she just needed to be prodded hard enough.

Camilla got up and went in to print out the six articles. Then she read them again, but aside from eliciting her compassion, there was nothing in what Henrik had written that seemed in any way related to his private life.

She did manage to figure out that they'd been sent by the Red Cross and that one of the people they'd shared their barracks with was Elsa Lynge. Camilla had run across her in connection with one of the big emergency-aid collection drives, so she knew Elsa was still somehow affiliated with the organization.

After a quick shower and reinvigorated, she sat down on the sofa and called the Danish Red Cross. She had to talk to only two people before she had Elsa Lynge on the line.

"I'm calling you about a personal matter," Camilla admitted right off the bat and asked if she should call back at another time.

"No, no, now's as good as any," Elsa responded. "But could I ask you to call me back on my cell in three minutes? Then I can just duck out and have a smoke."

Camilla smiled and jotted down Elsa's cell number on the back of one of the pages she'd just printed out.

"Henrik and Alice Holm," Elsa repeated after Camilla had her back on the line. "Yeah, I know him, although now of course it's mostly from the media, but I don't think I can remember her."

Camilla sank back in the sofa a little. "Can you think of anyone else I could try calling? Someone that you think might remember her?"

"I'm going to need longer than a smoking break to think about that one," Elsa admitted after a moment's contemplation, during which Camilla could hear her puffing away heartily on her cigarette. "It was so long ago, and I've done so much traveling, but if you tell me what you need to know, then maybe that would make it a little easier for me to think of who you should talk to."

Very briefly and without going into too many details, Camilla explained that she had been the one who found the stillborn infant out in Henrik Holm's church and that she had reason to believe that there might be some connection between the baby in the church and the baby the Holms had while they were living in the refugee camp.

Camilla heard Elsa's lighter clicking and a hoarse cough as Elsa lit the next cigarette. "I can tell you one thing for sure," Elsa said once she finished coughing. "Which is that in the two and a half years I was there none of the aid workers in our camp had a baby. The conditions just weren't suitable for babies." Elsa cleared her throat when her voice became gravelly. "Of course, there were tons of kids and babies who had survived with their mothers, or who were left behind after the rest of the family had been wiped out." Again, she paused to take a drag off her cigarette.

Camilla thought for a moment before she asked her next question. "And when exactly were you there?"

"From the middle of '96 until the end of '99," Elsa said without stopping to think. "I had just come home when we celebrated the new millennium. But there was something about his wife getting sick, and as far as I can remember they left early."

Camilla could hear that Elsa had started walking. "And you're sure we're talking about the same pastor?" she asked, even though she knew the question was unnecessary.

"Yeah, there weren't any others," Elsa confirmed. "And then there was his wife's death. A few years after that and so tragic, to die at such a young age. I don't know where you got the idea that they supposedly had a child while they were there."

Camilla sat holding her phone in her hand long after the call was over. Maybe she wasn't finding her way back to her old self after all. On the contrary, maybe she was really losing it.

42

At Police Headquarters, Suhr had summoned Willumsen's investigative team to his office. Mikkelsen was just pulling the blinds to keep the sharp May sun out of their eyes, but he was listening attentively as Louise told them where she'd run into Bosko.

"He was coming out of the building on Valdemarsgade, the one that Miloš Vituk's apartment is in," Louise said. She was able to tell them that without a doubt it had happened on the Wednesday after Kaj Antonsen was murdered, because she'd looked up her report from her stakeout, and she now had it lying on the table in front of her.

She explained that the Serb had come out the front door while she was standing in the doorway across the street. "There was something about his eyes and the way he looked at me that gave me the sense that maybe we knew each other. But we didn't, and now I'm sure he was just being vigilant. He noticed that I saw him."

"Is this something you're totally sure of, or is there a chance you're confusing him with someone else?" Willumsen asked her, looking tense.

Louise smiled at him stiffly and noted how a few hairs on the back of her neck were standing up. Because she was completely sure that the man in the picture and the man she'd seen on Valdemarsgade were identical.

She just said, "I'm sure," and was struck by the tense silence that had come over the room. She looked at her partner and saw the anxiety in his eyes, the worry that made the blue in his eyes a shade darker.

"We made eye contact twice," she said. "Both when he left the property, and when he returned again a little later."

Suhr was sitting behind his desk with his hands folded, his thumbs circling each other, and Toft had taken out his plastic cigarette while his partner, Stig, was tipping his chair back perilously.

Louise caught Stig's eye; the chair's front legs hit the floor as he tipped back down, forward, and she asked him to help her explain what Igli had told them about Bosko.

They listened in silence, but Louise noticed with growing concern the looks that Suhr and Willumsen were exchanging as she and Stig talked, because it hit her that right now they were both trying to decide, on their own, whether Bosko was of such a caliber that they were about to hand the case over to the PET, the Security and Intelligence Service, Denmark's equivalent of the CIA. She noted how Willumsen moved to speak the instant they were done.

"We'll get a court order so we can start a wiretap on Miloš Vituk as soon as possible," he decided, not even looking over at Suhr as he spoke.

Something inside Louise fell into place. Clearly, he didn't want to hand over a case that might be of international importance, and she respected him for that.

"Bring those two Albanians in for questioning again." Suhr looked at Mikkelsen. "This time don't let them leave until they've told us exactly what the fuck they know about Bosko. How did they find out what happened in Prague?

Who saw Bosko? And where was he seen?" He slapped his desk with the palms of his hand, making a loud bang, and looked at them.

"What about the pregnant women?" Lars asked.

Willumsen looked at him, as if he'd just farted audibly. "To hell with the pregnant women right now. The baby was dead, so it's not like that case is going anywhere."

Louise and Lars looked at each other and Louise subtly shook her head. That hadn't really been his attitude when Willumsen put them on the case.

Suhr cleared his throat and waited until he had everyone's attention. "Two things," he began, hesitating a little.

Louise could tell that he didn't completely agree with Willumsen that they should race headlong after the clues the two Albanians had given them.

"First of all, we only have the two Albanian men's tip that we should be interested in this Serb, Bosko. OK, so far, they've been right, but I'm sure we can agree that this could still be an attempt to clear their own names. Their car was actually seen at the one crime scene and at the harbor."

"We don't have squat on those two boys," Willumsen interrupted, slicing through the air with both hands. "And you know that. Otherwise they'd have been in jail ages ago. Since when can we arrest someone because a stinking drunk alcoholic thought he saw an identical car? I'm just asking! And besides that, do you understand how many dark blue Audi A4s there are driving around in this country? We'll burst the prison if we stuff all the car owners in there!"

It was clear that Willumsen was in top form, so he must have believed they were close to a breakthrough.

"Second of all," Suhr continued impassively, "we don't know anything about why Bosko suddenly showed up in

Copenhagen. We don't know if it's a coincidence that he came out of the building Miloš Vituk lives in."

Michael Stig made a face.

"And we don't know why he would be interested in murdering a prostitute," the homicide chief finally said.

"I can answer that last one for you," Mikkelsen said and took a step forward from his spot by the window. "If Bosko has set his sights on Vesterbro, then it's because he sees money to be made and is getting into the Danish prostitution market. Which would make several pieces start to fit together in my mind."

He hit himself on the temple to make the point.

"So far Arian and Hamdi have been doing pretty good business, and there's definitely no doubt that they've pretty much cornered the trade on the Czech girls. Iveta's murder out in the Meatpacking District took out one of their girls; the murdered girl in Prague was on her way here to work for them. The way I see it, the signs are extremely clear—if you want to clear the playing field and send a signal to the competition about what's coming."

"And Kaj?" Louise asked.

Mikkelsen shrugged apologetically. "Kaj was punished for talking to the press, but it was probably mostly a sign for everyone else that that kind of thing just isn't done. When you're dealing with a person who's taken war tourists into a besieged city and been well remunerated for bringing them close enough that they could kill people just for the fun and excitement of it, well that shows you very clearly that human life doesn't mean much to him," Stig interjected and Louise was inclined to agree with him.

"Wait a second, though," Louise suddenly blurted out so loudly that everyone turned to look at her.

She grabbed her head. "God, Miloš Vituk—that bastard

coming here with his sob story about the Albanians extorting him during his noble attempt to buy Pavlína's freedom from them! I'm sorry, but there isn't any other fucking thing to say if the Danish police get a reputation among shepherds for being the easiest to fool in Europe."

"Shepherds?" Toft repeated, cocking his head and raising his eyebrow at her.

"People who traffic in women," she explained succinctly. "He was obviously using that story about Pavlína to push those two Albanians into our search lights, to make room for himself."

Louise shook her head despondently; she was irritated that she hadn't seen it herself. They'd just bought his story and tried to help without checking into him. And when the theory had briefly been mentioned, they'd brushed it aside because Pavlína had been so convincing in telling her story.

"Couldn't you just spell this out for those of us who are a little dim?" Toft asked, clearly confused by her excited outburst.

But Louise could tell Mikkelsen was with her. "Miloš Vituk works for Bosko," Louise said. "And I'm betting he was the one Miloš borrowed money from when he wanted to buy Pavlína's freedom the first time. Which was how Bosko got his claws into him, and since then he's been part of Bosko's network. When Miloš went to borrow money from him, Bosko took advantage of the situation to make his debut in the Danish marketplace. The money he paid to free Pavlína was chump change compared to what he could earn on the women."

Louise paused for a second, trying to put all the pieces together.

"I'm sure that's right, that it was a coincidence that Pavlína specifically was their way into the Danish market.

I believe her story, but he took advantage of her when she asked for help, and by buying her freedom he simultaneously bought her loyalty and tied her to him."

"And then maybe Arian and Hamdi tried to respond by sending young Hana on a little tour of the harbor?" Willumsen suggested, looking like he was starting to understand how it all fit together.

"But those two guys are surely just a couple of loogies. If Bosko decided to take over the market, then they were done," Stig said thoughtfully after a little pause. "And without question, they knew that. That's why they ratted him out to us."

"But if they didn't do the two murders, then they could have just come in and told us what they knew. They didn't have to send Camilla Lind in," the homicide chief said hesitantly, as if he still couldn't get everything to fit together.

Mikkelsen nodded, and a smile brought out the laugh lines around his eyes. "Of course they sent her. They would never dare to blab directly to us. If it turns out that this is all how it fits together, then that's also why they're not saying anything when we have them in here. I'd bet that we won't get them to talk, either. No one wants to wind up wearing a Balkan tie," he added, and now his smile was gone.

"Well, then I guess we're going to have to find out if it was Miloš or Bosko holding the knife at the two crime scenes," Suhr said after contemplating the unexpected turn the case had taken.

"I'd be really surprised if Arian and Hamdi realized who they were up against in the beginning," Mikkelsen said, as everyone started getting up. "They probably thought that Miloš was on his own, but at some point they realized that he has one of the Balkans' most notorious criminals behind him, and then they start shrinking back into their shells. And that fits quite well with Bosko coming to Denmark again after the episode down at the harbor."

Louise nodded and explained what had happened to Igli's brothers when they started figuring out how Bosko's business in Sarajevo worked. "They were gunned down in front of their families," she said. "He obviously doesn't like it when people get all up in his business."

"I want a tail on Miloš Vituk," Willumsen rumbled, unnecessarily loudly, and then looked at Michael Stig. "The wiretap should be up and running today, and if there are any problems getting a warrant so quickly, have that idiot at the preliminary hearing come see me."

He was looking at Mikkelsen now. "Find out if Pavlína and Hana are working for them," he said without waiting for Stig to respond. "We need to find out how many girls they have working for them. There must be a pattern, right? Like with the Albanians?"

"That's not how it works if they have the girls work in a brothel," Mikkelsen objected, explaining that that was a possibility since they hadn't seen Pavlína or Hana on the street.

"Well, but you haven't been looking for them, have you?" Willumsen asked him irritably.

"No," Mikkelsen admitted. "But now you are."

Willumsen looked at Louise and Lars. "Find those two girls and keep an eye on them." Finally, he looked over at Toft. "And you bring in those two Albanians, and don't let them leave until they've told us what they know. And take whatever time you need at it."

Toft nodded calmly.

Now Willumsen looked around the room, from one person to the next. "Ladies and gentlemen," he said with hard-won calm, "I'm sorry, but this means we're going to be working over the weekend. You need to be able to account for every step Miloš Vituk makes. Find out who saw Bosko while he was in town. We're going to get him this time, that jerk. Who does he think he is, pushing us around as it suits him?"

Willumsen's face was coppery-red as he stood up and adjourned the meeting.

43

Camilla had been to Føtex to stock up her fridge. The cupboards had been bare, and she threw out what little was left based on the looks of it. She had the washing machine going out in the bathroom, and she'd also pulled herself together enough to change her sheets and air out the apartment a little.

Now she was back on the sofa, sitting cross-legged and with an open-faced sandwich on rye bread in one hand. Her thoughts raced through her mind, jockeying for attention.

It had been ten years, she thought. Elsa Lynge might be remembering wrong, but if you spent a long time with a person who later became a well-known media personality, as was the case with Henrik Holm, then you'd remember the time you had spent with him.

On the other hand, she had no doubt that you would remember it if someone had a baby while you were living in a primitive barracks with them. There was something about crying babies and lost sleep overnight that people just didn't forget. As long as she was willing to trust Elsa Lynge's memory. But maybe the timing was just a little off, she thought, brushing off the crumbs that had landed on her blouse.

If she now imagined Alice Holm getting sick because

of her blood disease, then maybe she was in a hospital for treatment. After that they might have been moved to a new camp to continue their work, and maybe Elsa didn't necessarily even know about that.

She didn't know, and she thought she probably shouldn't get mixed up in it, since Henrik didn't seem to want anyone stirring up the past.

Nonetheless Camilla reached for her phone, which was on the coffee table. She pulled her laptop over to her and went to www.cpr.dk, the site of Denmark's Central Office of Civil Registration, to look up the number. She called, then waited patiently until a woman's nasally voice said, "Ministry of Social Affairs," and put her on hold for the switchboard.

"Office of Civil Registration, please," Camilla said to the switchboard operator, then waited again. Her call was eventually transferred to their legal staff.

Camilla explained that she was a reporter working on a story about a Danish citizen, and she wanted to learn a little more about the procedure for a Danish couple who had a child abroad. What happened when they came home again? How did the child acquire Danish citizenship and get assigned a social security number?

"We mostly just need a birth certificate that documents that both parents are Danish citizens," the helpful woman told her. She read a list of criteria that had to be met before the child could be issued a social security number. "This is all described in the Danish Civil Registration Act, which you can find on our home page. It's in Annex 1 of Act No. 1134."

"And the documents you need from the hospital where the child was born—do you need to have a physical copy, or is it enough for someone to write the information down and send it to you?" Camilla asked.

"No, we need all the relevant paperwork and copies of the parents' birth certificates before the child can be registered," she replied. "But in the case you mention, we would also go in and record that the parents returned to Denmark. You see, the Danish government keeps track whenever a Danish citizen is employed or stationed abroad, and it is recorded in someone's file when they've left the country—and then, of course, that needs to be changed if they come back again with a baby."

"OK," Camilla said. She asked if it were possible to find out if the couple in question had had a baby abroad and brought it back to Denmark with them after having been outside the country for a couple of years.

It didn't surprise her to learn that this was considered confidential personal information. After all, she had been a journalist for some time, but she had been one long enough to know that you could sometimes get someone to tell you how you could obtain the information even if they wouldn't actually give it to you.

"Under Paragraph 42 of the act, the standard information for regular citizens is accessible to anyone," the friendly woman said. Camilla had been lucky to wind up talking to her. "If you can identify the person you want information on, either by name and address or name and social security number, then you can certainly get the basic details confirmed—although that won't really get you very far. We wouldn't be able to tell you if they had a child or where or when it was born, for instance."

"I understand," Camilla hurried to say, but she confirmed that someone would be able to see the child's birth date and the date the couple returned to Denmark if someone had access to the Civil Registration database.

"Yes, all the information is in there," said the woman.

Camilla was betting the woman was about her age; she had used herself as an example, saying that someone could easily tell she had had a son in 1998 as well as in what city. "But that is considered family information, and we can't give you that."

Camilla thanked her profusely for being so helpful. Before she hung up, she asked if the police had access to all the information.

"Yes, they have full authorization," the woman confirmed. When Camilla thanked her again, she replied, "You're welcome."

44

"Pull over!" Louise cried immediately after they turned the corner from Absalonsgade onto Sønder Boulevard.

It was almost seven p.m., and they'd spent the day driving through the neighborhood at random looking for the girls. They were in Louise's old Saab 9000 to avoid drawing attention to themselves by using one of the police's unmarked cars. Oddly enough, people always seemed to recognize those even though they really were totally unmarked.

Lars braked, causing the empty soda bottles on the floor of the car to slide forward.

"Drive up to Skelbækgade and turn around, so we can get closer," Louise ordered. She pointed across the planting strip with bicycle parking in the middle of the street over to the big Borch building, which was on the corner across the street.

Two girls were standing on the corner talking. One was skinny with dark hair and the other had long blond hair. Louise had straightened up and was now leaning forward a little. They hadn't seen hide nor hair of them until now, but she was sure it was Pavlína and Hana.

Her partner turned the Saab sharply to the right and just

then Louise saw a silver-gray Citroën hatchback pull over to the curb at the corner across from them. Both girls walked over to the car and leaned up to the passenger-side window, but the dark-haired one quickly jumped in next to the driver, and the one Louise was pretty sure must be Hana moved back and leaned against the wall with her hands in the pockets of her short jacket, which stopped just above her waist, right over her tight jeans.

They drove up to Skelbækgade, turned around, and drove back just in time to see the girl's long hair disappearing into a little black Peugeot. She pulled the passenger-side door shut, and the car pulled away at high speed.

"There are obviously plenty of customers," Louise noted drily. She nodded as Lars pointed across the street where a parking spot had just opened up.

"We can wait there, then we can see them if they come back here," he suggested.

Louise nodded, thinking they would certainly come back. It wasn't that late, it was a lovely, warm spring evening, and there was no soccer game on TV that night.

Lars parked and they settled in to wait. They were both prepared for it to be a long wait, until the girls' workday was over, but they were determined to find out where Hana went after work.

"They did a study that showed that the younger a man is the first time he has sex with a prostitute, the greater the chances that he'll be a lifelong customer," Louise said, breaking the silence.

Her partner nodded and said that he'd looked into it and found out there were about seven hundred brothels in Denmark, 120 of which were in Copenhagen.

"Well, I suppose there's your proof that quite a few young men must have picked up the habit," Louise remarked, looking across the street, where the girls had returned and a new car had just stopped. She noticed the little pat Pavlína gave Hana's shoulder before she climbed into the car.

"Prostitutes can buy in at a brothel for somewhere between 800 and 1,800 kroner a day, depending on how nice the place is," Lars continued, his eyes following Pavlína. "For that price, they get ads in the print and online editions of *Ekstra Bladet* as well as condoms and maybe phone privileges—and then of course it covers their rent, electricity, and heat."

Louise looked at him, surprised.

"I called the Nest," he hurried to explain.

"How much do they get per trick?" Louise wanted to know.

"Between 500 and 1,500 kroner, again depending on how exclusive the place is and what the johns want," Lars guessed. "But out here on the street the girls sell themselves for between 100 and 300 kroner. These are the foreign women and the drug addicts, who would go down on a dog. The latter just need enough for a fix, and once they've made their 1,000 kroner, they stop. But the women with pimps are on the street until they've made whatever their pimps demand. If they go down to South Harbor with the tricks, then they can only turn one an hour, but if they take them down to Club Intim, they can do three. Down at the Nest several people have overheard witnesses in Copenhagen's Municipal Court testify that some of the young foreign women supposedly service twenty-five to thirty men a day—seven days a week—before their pimps leave them alone so they can get a little food and be allowed to sleep."

Just then the car came back and dropped Pavlína off.

"I was under the impression that it's mostly addicts, foreigners, and the mentally ill who turn tricks down here," he continued. "The rest stick to the brothels and clubs, and many are single mothers who can't make ends meet."

Louise eyed him skeptically. "Isn't that an old wives' tale, invented by the men?"

Lars shook his head. "Picture a single mother with two kids and a job as a cashier, or maybe she's getting unemployment. How's she supposed to get the finances to work out if she has to pay rent, utilities, and day care or after-school care, and if she also wants to give her kids a new cell phone or some cool clothes so they don't get teased at school?"

Louise shrugged.

"If you don't have that much else, it gives you status, so you can easily imagine that the material things suddenly become important, and maybe she even wants to take her kids on vacation?"

Louise was going to object, but she knew that there were quite a few people living on what was basically the poverty line if they were sole providers on welfare.

Her eyes wandered back over to the girls on the street corner. Hana was back now, too, and Louise saw how she was laughing as she pulled her cigarettes out of her pocket. Based on her arm gestures, she guessed Pavlína was telling some story that had gotten Hana laughing even harder.

There was something about her feigned laid-back attitude that made Louise think about survival. They had to keep the tone cheerful to get through it, because Louise didn't believe the myth of the "happy whore." That came exclusively from the way men wanted to see it. The same men that drained the household budget and pretended they were doing a good turn by spending a 500-kroner note on a whore, so she received some of the family's wealth, too.

In principle, Louise didn't have anything against men visiting prostitutes, if the girls were acting of their own free will and there was no pimp waiting in the shadows to cash in on the day's earnings.

"It's just so bizarre that the men who come here are the same ones who dutifully donate to the Red Cross and the SPCA, when they have fund-raisers," she said. "They kiss their wife and pet the dog when they leave for work, but they turn a blind eye when they pick up a woman who's the victim of sex trafficking or a young Roma girl who's been forced onto the street by her family. It's enough to make you puke."

Seven hours later they were still parked there. It was two a.m., and the girls had averaged about one or two johns an hour. Louise was trying to read their body language, but there was nothing that gave away how they were doing. In between johns they stood around, relaxed and chatting, but they paid a lot of attention to the cars that drove by, and they reacted right away when a big four-wheel-drive vehicle with white plates already started blinking its lights from a distance. They both moved over to the curb and were ready when the car pulled over a second later.

Louise couldn't see over the car's roof, but when it drove away again, both of the girls were gone.

"Two thirty in the morning and there are still customers," she noted a little later, starting to feel the need to sleep. She yawned out loud and jumped at the offer when Lars suggested that she go home and go to bed. He would stay in the car and follow Hana when the girls decided to go home.

"We have to find out where she moved," he said.

"If you follow her when she leaves here, you can text me the address. Then I'll go out there tomorrow morning and keep an eye on it, see if she goes to meet anyone to pay up. But with the hours they work, they must stay in bed until sometime after noon, otherwise they wouldn't be able to keep this up," Louise added, as yet another yawn overcame her, and her own night without much sleep caught up to her.

45

The apartment was out behind Enghave Square. The text message was waiting for her on her cell when she got up.

Heavy winds were blowing through the streets, and even though the sky was still clear, it wasn't hard to spot the dark clouds that were gathering out past the Valby Hills and rapidly approaching.

Maybe a raincoat would have been a good idea, Louise thought, warming her hands on the grande drip she'd gotten to go on her way out here. She looked up at the windows in the building Hana had gone into, not knowing which one was for the apartment where Hana was sleeping.

Lars had texted that the girls had gone home around four, almost immediately after Louise herself had left. He'd followed them down past the apartment on Valdemarsgade, where Pavlína went, while Hana had unlocked a bike and ridden it the last portion to the outskirts of Vesterbro.

It wasn't even ten in the morning yet, but Louise didn't want to risk Hana having a chance to leave the apartment before she arrived. She should have brought an extra jacket along, it occurred to her, because the temperature had dropped a few degrees.

She shivered slightly, finished the coffee, and was looking around for a trash can when the front door suddenly opened and Hana walked out and leaned over to unlock a bicycle. Her hair was in a tight braid that had been wrapped up into a bun. She was wearing the short-waisted jacket but with loose-fitting, casual pants.

Louise deposited her empty coffee cup in a stranger's bike basket before turning her bike around and following Hana down Enghavevej and out toward Vesterbrogade. She kept a good distance as they approached Pile Allé, and she dropped back even farther when she guessed where Hana was going.

She let Hana park her bike by the gate and walk all the way past the graves before following.

Her pulse was racing as she sat down on the bench, where she couldn't be seen from the kitchen window, and after a deep breath, she slowly exhaled again to calm her heart rate down again. It had come as a shock, but she shouldn't have been so surprised that the network met early in the day, before anyone was interested in what the girls were up to. Later in the morning it was probably harder to slip out without being discovered.

It had been good to sleep. The worst of the fatigue had left her body, and the unexpectedly quick departure from Enghave Square had removed the last of the sluggishness that remained.

Louise quickly hid behind the wall of the church when Hana came back a little later, moving toward her bicycle. Hana walked past with her eyes on the ground, pale and tired. Louise thought she looked younger than eighteen. She still was just a big kid, even though there wasn't much that was childish about the life she was living.

Louise waited until Hana was almost to the gate before she started walking down the neatly tended gravel paths, and she caught a glimpse of the girl's hair over the church wall as Hana got onto her bike and headed back toward Enghave Plads.

"She's still in the apartment," Louise confirmed when Willumsen called at five p.m. A couple hours earlier, Lars had stopped by with a sandwich, and they'd swapped so that she had the car, and he had taken her bike over to Valdemarsgade to keep an eye on Miloš Vituk and Pavlína. It had been nice to come in and sit, even though something in the heating system had broken, so it either blew maximally hot or ice-cold air into the cabin. There was no longer anything in between.

"I did a little digging into young Hana," Willumsen said with more dedication than Louise had heard in him for a long time. "Would you believe, it turns out she's actually registered as a prostitute. The same goes for the twenty-two-year-old Pavlína Branková."

"You're kidding!" Louise exclaimed, thinking that was smart of Miloš, because then the police didn't have anything to get them on. But it didn't make her look any less forward to the questioning session they were planning to drag him and the girls in for after the weekend was over. Hopefully they would have a pattern to present him with.

Her thoughts slid back to that day at Police Headquarters and all his rubbish about how Pavlína had become his girlfriend. Maybe she was, but she was certainly back out on the street all the same.

"What about the questioning session?" Louise asked, turning off the car's engine once the heat had finally become too much.

"We're tapping the numbers Miloš gave you, both the cell phone and the landline, but there hasn't been much so far; only three calls. Either nothing is happening, or he has another phone that we don't know about."

That sounded most likely, Louise thought, fascinatedly watching a young guy with a bandana wrapped around his head that was so dirty it was almost black. He was staggering his way toward the front door of a building with his key out in front of him, as if he were on horseback, jousting and holding a lance in his hand. A big black dog with an equally dirty bandana around its neck was trotting along behind him.

"Mikkelsen and his people rounded up a bunch of the women who work for Arian and Hamdi last night. They caught them with their pants down, literally, and none of them had their prostitution paperwork in order, so they were slapped with the 500-kroner fine and, as Mikkelsen put it, the admonition not to let it happen again. Oddly enough, not one of them knew anything about the two Albanians. But Mikkelsen is making plans to wake them all up early tomorrow and drag them to the downtown station. Then they'll put them through their paces again and hope that something comes of it."

Louise heard a quick laugh before Willumsen rounded off the conversation by saying that their colleagues from Halmtorvet had also learned that the Albanians were now meeting their girls at a pizza place on Istedgade to collect their money.

"You'll be relieved by someone from the downtown precinct around eight, then you'll be on again tomorrow."

Louise nodded toward the windshield, where the bandana-wearing pair had finally managed to make it in the door.

46

The foam was thick and dense on the top of the Czech pilsner that had just been set on the table in front of Camilla. Svejk just wasn't the same since the ban on indoor smoking had gone into effect for all pubs over forty square meters. It was certainly easier to breathe inside, but a little bit of the pub atmosphere that she so enjoyed had been lost. Two musicians were setting up their instruments, but otherwise there was only one other couple in the bar aside from herself. She looked at her watch: it was only just after eight, so there were two hours until the music started.

She'd spent most of her day lying on her sofa, staring up into space. Her boss had called and left a couple of messages, but she'd just listened as he asked how she was doing. She couldn't even muster up the wherewithal to pick up the receiver and get the conversation over with, but she was prepared for the fact that he would try again.

The psychologist from National Hospital had also called and left a message that he'd had a cancellation for Monday, which he would hold open for her. If he didn't hear otherwise, he would plan to see her at 10:15. She'd written it down on a slip of paper and stuck it on the refrigerator door, but at the moment Monday felt so far in the future, because she still had her hands full getting by one day at a time.

Markus was at Jonas's place, and she didn't need to pick him up until tomorrow morning, so Camilla had called and asked Louise if she wanted to get a beer when she got off work.

Camilla looked up as Louise walked in the door and greeted the owner, who was manning the bar, before she headed for the table in the back of the room where Camilla was sitting. It would be the quietest corner once people started arriving. On the other hand, there was a permeating odor from the urinal cakes in the men's bathroom.

Camilla asked for another beer when Louise ordered and ignored the look aimed at her half-empty glass.

"Light or dark?" the waiter asked.

"A tall light," Louise said.

"Henrik and Alice didn't have a child while they were at the camp," Camilla began without any sort of lead-in once the beers arrived at their table. She didn't elaborate until she saw the confused look on Louise's face. Then she explained that she'd called and talked to a woman at the Red Cross who'd lived with them at the refugee camp in Bosnia.

"She was totally sure that Alice Holm was not pregnant and did not have a newborn during that period," Camilla emphasized. She added that the woman had even lived in the same barracks with them. But the woman had thought there was something about Alice getting sick at one point.

Camilla was a little irritated that Louise wasn't really paying attention. She knew the police had new clues in their quest for the culprit behind the two murders, but she was just so preoccupied with the news Elsa Lynge had provided. She was feeling more and more certain that there was a connection between that dead baby in the church and the pastor's own son.

"There's something wrong," Camilla said. "Something he doesn't want to say."

Louise raised one eyebrow, and Camilla was distracted for a second by a group of people who had just walked in and sat down at a table close to the bar. They looked like they were in their forties and could easily have been co-workers closing out their week with a night on the town.

Camilla turned back to Louise and looked at her earnestly, raising her voice a little to make herself heard over the music. "They didn't have a child. Not one on the way, not one in their arms, during the period when he claims his wife gave birth to Jonas. They left the camp at the end of the summer in 1998, and according to him his son was almost one when they returned home in August."

Camilla pushed her beer aside a little and leaned in over the table.

"I called the Office of Civil Registration," Camilla said. "But, of course, they can't pass on confidential personal information to unauthorized civilians."

Louise shook her head, but Camilla could tell that she finally had Louise's full attention.

"What was that about Alice Holm getting sick and them leaving the camp?"

Camilla shrugged. "That was obviously the excuse they gave when they cut their stay in the camp short. But Henrik hasn't mentioned that his wife got sick and they had to go home early."

"Maybe they just switched camps. That's possible, right? Maybe your source just got something mixed up?" Louise suggested.

"No. I read some of the articles Henrik wrote while they

were there, and they clearly state that he was in Srebrenica the whole time. But I haven't asked him directly. He just talked about their great joy when they discovered that his wife was pregnant, even though they had started to think they might never get pregnant. I mean, that didn't exactly make me start to have doubts about the case."

"Of course not," Louise said.

"But it's not true, and I have a theory about how it all might fit together."

"*Out!*" they suddenly heard someone shout from the bar. It was the owner, yelling so loudly the glasses were clinking. "*That's it! You're out of here!*"

Camilla and Louise smiled at each other and turned to look at a dark-haired, heavyset woman from a big group of people, who were standing by the bar. The woman had a frightened expression and was trying to appease the owner.

"'Shooby Dooby Doo-Wop,'" Camilla suggested, and Louise nodded.

Anyone who knew the least thing about Svejk knew that you would be kicked out immediately if you were dumb enough to request "Shooby Dooby Doo-Wop." If the woman had wanted to hear something by Herbert Grönemeyer, by contrast, she would have received an appreciative nod, but there was no way she could have known that. Now it appeared that she was mercifully being allowed to stay if she behaved properly.

Suddenly Camilla laughed and shook her head at the bartender's quirks. That was exactly what she loved about this place. The place was so liberatingly chic, and the owner did what he felt like.

"You should go in and see what the civil registry says," Camilla said once the patrons had settled down again.

Louise appeared to be thinking, but she didn't protest as Camilla had feared she would.

"My guess is," Camilla said, leaning even farther forward, "that they adopted Jonas right after they returned home from Bosnia, and for some reason or other they didn't want to admit that they're not his biological parents, and therefore they put together this story that he was born while they were away."

"But why?" asked Louise, her eyes fixed on Camilla. "Why would the pastor and his wife come up with a story like that?"

Camilla shrugged. She looked around the room, which had really filled up. "I don't know," she admitted, feeling the wind slowly starting to go out of her sails. She wanted to go home and go to bed.

"I'll check him in the registry," Louise promised when they were standing out on the sidewalk unlocking their bikes. "But don't let it go to your head if I let you read over my shoulder, because it's still confidential personal information, but obviously, I'll let you take a peek..."

"Say no more," Camilla stopped her tiredly.

Whenever they got involved in each other's professional lives, they always had some iteration of this conversation. It would never end.

"As long as you find out if this has some connection to Jonas. I'm afraid for him. I couldn't bear it if something happened to him. Or Henrik Holm, for that matter," Camilla added, and she flipped on the headlight she had strapped to her handlebars.

47

Camilla found the boys at the big dining table in the kitchen when she arrived at the pastor's home the next morning. They were sitting across from each other in total silence, each with a plate in front of him and a cup containing cocoa that had once been hot.

The breadbasket was full of fresh morning rolls, but it looked like they'd hardly touched it. Suddenly she noticed how quiet it was in the house. There were no voices, no footsteps, and she could tell from looking at the boys that they'd been sitting at the table for a long time in this oppressive silence.

Earlier that morning Louise had called and woken her. She was calling from Police Headquarters, where she was going to assist Toft in questioning Arian and Hamdi, but she had just looked Henrik Holm up in the civilian registration database. When she sank back into her bed after their conversation, Camilla had a hard time deciding whether she was filled by relief or disappointment.

According to the information in the database, Alice Holm had given birth to a son at the hospital in Sarajevo on June 14, 1997, while the couple was stationed in Bosnia. There was a birth certificate from the hospital to document it. It also said that they returned to Denmark in August of that same year, just as the pastor had said. Shortly thereafter, once all the documents had been approved, the Danish civil registration database recognized Jonas Holm as a Danish citizen and issued him a social security number.

It took Camilla rather a long time to make it out of bed after that call, because once the information sank in, she realized that it was mostly for her own sake that she had been hoping the explanation lay somewhere in the past.

However egocentric it was, it really just came down to the fact that she needed an explanation in order to move on. An explanation that gave some sense to everything that had happened, even though it was far from clear that she had the mental capacity to understand it.

While she'd been lying in bed with her arms under her head staring at the ceiling, she'd felt profoundly grateful that she hadn't voiced her suspicions to the pastor. She could easily have had doubts and started opening up old wounds pertaining to his dearly departed wife. As soon as she'd had her chat with Elsa Lynge, she'd wanted to confront him with what his former colleague had said, and she hadn't been concerned with whether Elsa might have been wrong or not.

"Did you guys have an argument?" Camilla exclaimed, helping herself to a poppy seed bun out of the basket. "What did you do to your dad and the housekeeper?"

She was watching Jonas and when he slowly looked up, she immediately dropped the chipper tone and set down the bun before leaning over and putting her hand on his arm.

"What happened?" she asked, worried, casting a quick glance at her son, who she had an easier time reading.

"Where's your dad?" she repeated.

"Over in the church," Jonas finally said, turning his face toward her.

She suddenly felt afraid and wasn't able to hide it so the boys wouldn't notice. "And Tereza. Did something happen?" Her voice was higher pitched now and sharper than it should have been, and Jonas pulled his arm back.

"They had an argument," Jonas said so softly that she almost couldn't hear him. "Dad got really mad."

"And then he threw her out," Markus continued, "and then he got all her things and threw them out after her—"

Markus stopped abruptly when his friend very quietly started sniffling.

"Why were they arguing?" Camilla asked, not really knowing if she ought to put her arm around Jonas or if he would rather be left alone.

Both boys shrugged, but neither of them said anything.

"Is he still over there?" Camilla asked and then got up, heading for the kitchen door.

They both nodded.

"Well, then I think I'm just going to go over there and talk to him. Meanwhile, you guys just go back up and play," she suggested.

They both got up right away and disappeared up the stairs.

48

At first, she couldn't see him, but she heard the quiet sobs and when she walked up toward the altar, she spotted him in the front pew, where he was sitting with his face hidden in his hands. His shoulders were moving softly in time to the rhythm of his sobs.

She quietly walked over and sat down next to him. She started out not saying anything, just sitting there in the silent church listening to his breaths, as he tried to get himself under control. She knew he could tell she was there, but he hadn't looked up.

Five, maybe ten minutes passed before he wiped his face and straightened up. He didn't turn to face her, but looked like he was about to say something, and she hurriedly beat him to it.

"I really owe you an apology," she began and was met by his confused stare, as he hurriedly turned his head to her.

She heard him swallow, and she cringed a little when she saw that his face was filled with despair and something she interpreted as fear, but which could also have been anger.

"What on earth for?" he asked hoarsely and cleared his throat, trying to ward off whatever crying was left in his body.

She said that she'd called Elsa Lynge and explained how she'd doubted him when she couldn't get things to add up. Without looking at him, she admitted that she'd passed the information on to Louise and had asked her to check whether he and his wife had brought Jonas home with them when they came back from Bosnia.

She looked down at the wide grooves between the stones in the church floor. "Please forgive me for being so nosy. I was confused and thought you were keeping something to yourself, something that might give the rest of us some kind of explanation for what happened out there." She nodded in the direction of where she'd found the stillborn baby. "But obviously, you weren't, it was just me . . ."

When she tried to recall the sound later, she had a hard time saying whether it was a dull laugh or a dry sob that spontaneously emerged from Henrik's chest. But the expression in his eyes was unmistakable as he slowly turned and looked her in the eye.

Camilla collapsed onto the pew when she realized she was sitting next to a man who'd lost everything.

He reached for her hand and gave it a squeeze, and she saw that he was trying to pull it together so that he would be able to say something.

"You're certainly entitled to try to find out what happened," he began. "I would never hold that against you, especially not since you and Markus were so involved, and I'm so sorry that I've only just now really put together how the events all fit together."

He pulled his hand back and rubbed his forehead hard, as if he were trying to gather up his strength to keep going. Then he took a deep breath and leaned back in the pew.

Camilla could almost see his thoughts slipping back through time.

"Alice and I started dating when we were eighteen. We were married two years later, and we started trying to have a baby from day one. I had just started my theology program and she was going to nursing school. We dreamt of having a big family and a parsonage in Jutland."

The little laugh Henrik emitted now was unmistakable, but it was for the memories and seemed very remote from the present moment.

"Five years later we were still dreaming. There was still no sign of any kind of expansion to our family, and we started to concede that the doctors were right when they blamed it on the blood disease Alice had been treated for since she was very little. So, we decided we would adopt our children instead. We went to visit an adoption agency and started the process of getting preapproved as potential adoptive parents. But we didn't even make it through the first phase because of Alice's disease—even though her doctor at National Hospital wrote to the agency that it was extremely likely she would live with the disease until she died of old age. But back then people didn't take any chances. Since then they've eased up on the requirements some. Nowadays single people can be approved, so maybe they would also accept that a father could handle a child on his own in the unfortunate event that his wife up and died on him."

He cleared his throat and took another deep breath, while Camilla sat very still so as not to interrupt.

"For a while, right after they rejected us, Alice really took it hard. It was the first time her illness had really impacted her life. Up to that point it really hadn't limited what she could do; it had only lurked in the wings like a dark shadow she was forced to live with. Now it was preventing her from becoming a mother, and for a long time we were really depressed about it—Alice more than me. But one night after dinner, she asked if I wanted to come with her if we got permission to work in a refugee camp. She had made up her mind that she really wanted to go and do something to help the people who had lost everything. That was right after the Dayton Agreement was signed in Paris, the peace agreement that was supposed to put an end to the war—but far from that, the war went on from one day to the next."

He stopped for a moment and looked at Camilla, as though he were looking right through her. Then he slumped a little and sighed heavily.

"Clearly, it was escapist of us, a way of getting away from the life we'd fantasized about but would never have. But I guess we were also hoping that by going someplace where people had suffered real loss, it would help us see that the loss we were suffering really wasn't so bad in comparison."

Camilla nodded, shifting slightly on the hard bench, and feeling like she understood.

"As I told you before, it was both a wonderful and a painful time. Never have I seen people in such torment, and never have I seen people fight so hard for their right to live, even though everything around them should have broken them down. Of course, there were many people who couldn't handle it, and some of them went over to the darkest sides of the human mind, where evil takes over and overshadows everything else.

"A year, almost a year and a half," he corrected himself, doing the math quickly, "went by with the camp as our world, and we no longer dreamt of the life we had hoped to have. We lived in the barracks with the youngest of the children, the ones whose parents had been killed in the war or who had been forced to abandon them for other reasons. So our desire to be around little kids was really fulfilled. Every once in a while, a stranger would come and knock on our door with a baby in their arms who had been left alone in one of the surrounding villages. When they brought us little ones like that, it was always done in the cover of darkness, and it was never something anyone discussed. We took them in without asking too many questions. Srebrenica was predominantly a Muslim area, but the villages around it were mixed, and no one wanted to have anything to do with a Muslim baby in a Serbian area. A baby like that had no chance of survival if it wasn't brought to us."

"But how could anyone tell the baby was Muslim?" Camilla couldn't help but ask.

For a second the pastor seemed to snap out of it, but he flew back in time again before he answered.

"The same man came to us many times with toddlers or infants who he'd saved from Serbian areas, and eventually we got to know him and he became our friend. Bosko was a Serb; he moved around in the villages and told us about the Muslim families who had been victims of the ethnic cleansing his fellow countrymen had been subjected to. After the peace agreement, many of the Muslim families came back to reclaim their houses and possessions. But they didn't get anything back. Instead they were gunned down and left lying in the streets."

Henrik sighed, and Camilla saw that he had to pull himself together before he could continue.

"One night he brought a bottle of slivovitz with him, and I guess all three of us had had a little too much by the time we started talking about the little kids who were sleeping in the big room next to ours. Some were just infants, others toddlers, but none of the ones living in our barracks were older than three.

"We told him why we were working in the camp, about Alice's disease, and about our dream of becoming parents and how the adoption agency had rejected us. At some point in the conversation he leaned in over the table a little and asked if we hadn't considered taking one or more of the children who didn't have any future in Bosnia anyway back to Denmark with us and giving them a proper life far from the aftermath of the war.

"'You could give them a life of love and security and a good education,' he said, and he reminded us that there was nothing for them where they were now. No one wanted them, and they were going to grow up and live their daily lives in an orphanage if they ever made it out of the camp.

"'That's not a real life. If you really want to help these children, then help make sure they get out of here and help them find a good home with parents like you, who dream of having a child but aren't able to themselves.' That's how he said it," Henrik remembered.

"And at that point it sounded totally right. We saw the little children every day, we sat with them, fed them, and comforted them, but everyone knew that one day they would be on their own. It was unbearable, and the only way you could deal with that was to try not to think about it. Luckily, it also happened fairly regularly that a mother or father would come to the camp looking for their child, and sometimes they found each other. But the very littlest ones...no one ever came looking for them. They were there because their parents were no longer alive."

He swallowed one time before continuing.

"The next night he brought Jonas. We guessed he must have been about a year old, based on the number of teeth he had. But he was small for his age, and he was totally silent, just lay there in a big blanket and watched us with his brown eyes, and he had a big bandage around his right foot.

"Bosko told us that he was the son of a young married couple from outside Srebrenica who had found their home burned to the ground with everything they owned inside it. All they had left was the garage, and when the man went to pull the car out, they were attacked and shot at close range. The mother was holding Jonas in her arms when she was shot, and the bullet had sliced his pinky toe right off."

Henrik emitted a grunt, which was a mixture of laughter and a statement of fact, before he proceeded.

"I knew it was already too late when he set the boy in Alice's lap. Still, I tried to explain that we couldn't just take the child home to Denmark with us illegally. At that point, my wife was ready to stay in Bosnia if it meant she could keep him."

Henrik ruffled his hair so it was sticking up in the air, while he reported the agreement they entered into on that night; that first time they met their son.

"Back then you could pay to get any kind of paperwork or document made. We never heard about that side of things here in Denmark. There was a big problem with driver's licenses being issued to people from the former Yugoslavia even though they'd never had so much as one hour's worth of driving lessons. When they came to Denmark, they would just send a picture and some number of German deutschmarks home to a contact person, and one month later they received their Yugoslavian driver's license with whatever issue date they wanted, and they could just walk in to the department of motor vehicles and swap it for a Danish one. Easy-peasy. The same for birth certificates. We paid Bosko ten thousand marks to get a certificate that said Alice gave birth to Jonas on June fourteenth the previous year at a hospital in Sarajevo."

The tears overwhelmed him before he managed to choke them back, and he sat for a moment with his eyes closed until he appeared in control of them again, and slowly shook his head.

"It's not so much that we paid and broke the rules. I could certainly live with that. The only thing in the world we wanted was to have the little baby, and the alternatives for him weren't even worth thinking about. But I can't forgive myself for not realizing that it wouldn't end there. I was so naïve in my joy at our wish for a child finally becoming a reality. And I believed Bosko was helping us for the sake of the child. I try and justify that with the fact that we were just so over the moon with our own happiness, when we made the agreement with him, that we would help other infertile couples and orphaned children find new homes in Denmark."

He took a deep breath.

"A couple of months earlier, I had received a message that I could start my post as pastor of Stenhøj Church in September of that same year. By that point, I had almost forgotten that I'd applied for it, but that fit just fine with the agreement we made with Bosko. There was no exchange of money between us, aside from what we paid him for the forged birth certificate. I suppose that was also one of the reasons we still believed that he was doing it for humanitarian reasons, that he wanted to help the children have better lives. If we'd known he was planning to do it to earn money, a lot of money, we wouldn't have agreed to it.

"According to the agreement we were not supposed to

be involved in bringing the children illegally into Denmark or finding families who wanted them. Our only obligation was to be a way station when they arrived in the country, and it always transpired like that, that they would be left in the church early in the morning. We didn't know who brought them, and didn't want to know, either, and later that same day the new family would come pick up the baby. They handled the paperwork themselves; we weren't involved with that. It seemed so innocent to see the same joy in other childless couples that we had experienced ourselves.

"The agreement was that we would help find new homes for three babies. But it kept going. Every time we made a new agreement, he broke it, and we couldn't stop it. If we hadn't accepted the falsified birth certificate, we could have severed our ties to him whenever we wanted. But the way it was, he had something over us. If we didn't do what he said, we would lose Jonas."

"Yes, and you would probably also have lost the reputation you had built up in the media if the story about an illegal baby came out."

"Oh, whatever, I wouldn't have cared about that!" Henrik exclaimed. "But we were not going to risk having Jonas taken away from us and sent back to Bosnia. We had gotten trapped in Bosko's web and we were stuck, no matter how hard we wriggled. Things went on like that for several years, and then suddenly we stopped hearing from him. You can probably imagine what an incredible relief that was when we realized it was over."

He watched Camilla, who didn't have time to nod before he continued. "But then everything with Alice happened, and suddenly there was only me and Jonas left. At that point I obviously should have told him how everything fit together. Alice and I talked about that many times, why we'd done what we'd done, but then when she died I just couldn't get myself to do it. His mother's death was just so hard on him, that wasn't the right time to tell him that she and I weren't his biological parents. Then he was missing her so much, it still wasn't the right time. And now it almost feels like it's too late. I know I should have done it, but it just never felt like it was the right time."

Henrik shook his head and ran his fingers through his hair despondently.

"And if I'm being honest, it's not something I've really given much thought to since. In my heart he's my son, and it doesn't make any difference to me if we gave birth to him. But I know that it might mean something to him, that he doesn't know about his heritage. In the last few days I've also become horribly aware that I'm risking his turning against me, because I haven't told him the truth. The question is if it will even be enough anymore to explain how much we loved him from the first moment we saw him and how right it felt to make him our child."

"Do you need to tell him that now?" Camilla asked after a bit. She had to clear her own throat to get her voice to work properly.

Henrik nodded. "This is never going to end. I don't want to keep going anymore, and I don't want to lie anymore. I haven't heard from Bosko in so many years, and I refused to believe there was a connection when the boys found that little girl in the church. It wasn't until you found the little dead one who was missing a toe that I started to suspect what was coming."

He smiled sadly. "I also didn't get that he was the one who had sent Tereza the first time she rang the bell and asked for work. Even though that happened the same evening. I turned her away the second time she came, too, even though she brought a letter with her. It just didn't occur to me that he might send me a housekeeper."

Camilla was concentrating, but it was hard for her to get everything to fit together so that all the events made sense.

"After I turned her away again, still without understanding what it was all about, he cut the toe off that little boy, and then there was no longer any mistaking his message."

"But how does Tereza fit into the picture?" Camilla asked, confused.

"I didn't figure it out until now, either. He needs to stash her somewhere where the police won't be watching her."

Camilla raised one eyebrow, still not understanding.

"I was supposed to employ her in my home. In the beginning, I didn't like the idea, but when she told me about the network I was glad to help. Then it dawned on me that it wasn't really a question of my generosity, but rather that the girls should have free access to my home. It wasn't until this morning, when I overheard a conversation, that the chips fell into place. I had just gotten back from the bakery and was about to put breakfast on the table for the boys, and Tereza obviously hadn't heard me come in."

Henrik looked at Camilla, as if he were ashamed of himself.

"They're prostitutes," he said, slowly and clearly. "And Tereza is some kind of madam. Every day the girls meet to hand over the money they made the previous night. One of the girls is only fourteen. And you can call the police and tell them that they don't need to look for Baby Girl's mother anymore. It's Tereza's baby. Bosko's people took it from her the second it was born. She never got to see her and only knows her daughter from the pictures on TV."

Camilla's mouth hung open as she pictured the little

baby in her mind. A deep desperation hit her when she realized that the circumstances that had separated the mother
from her infant were far more unbearable than what she had
imagined.

"And quite right, that little boy was stillborn. His mother
is from Romania, but she works as a prostitute in Malmö.
Bosko trafficked her, too."

"How do you know all this?" Camilla whispered.

"I asked Tereza to pack up her things and get out of here
when I realized what she did and what she was using the
pastor's residence for. Initially, she was all tough and threatened me, because she knew the whole story on Jonas. But I
decided that I wasn't going to let myself be threatened anymore. I yelled that she could go right ahead and tell Bosko
that it was done, and that I wanted her out of here right
away. When she realized I meant it, she completely broke
down and told me about her baby, which he'd taken from
her. In exchange for that she no longer had to turn tricks
herself and just collected the money from the other girls instead. She was more than willing to pay that price."

Camilla slumped, suddenly noticing the cold had crept
in under her skin while the pastor was talking.

"She was afraid and she swore that Bosko would come
after me when he heard that I'd kicked her out."

"Will he?" Camilla asked, and Henrik nodded.

"I have no doubt. I see now that I'll never be free of him
if I don't stand by what's happened."

"What about Jonas, then? Isn't there a risk that you'll
lose him if the truth comes out?"

The pastor nodded with a sad smile. "Yeah, and that's
why he and I need to leave. This will never end so long as
I remain in Denmark. Bosko will always be able to find me.
We're going to have to start all over again, establish our-

selves somewhere else under new names. I have no doubt that that business with the toe was his way of saying that if I don't do what he says, then it will be Jonas next time. Our only chance for escape is to run away."

Camilla nodded, feeling the tears running down along her nose, because she knew he was right.

"I've decided to tell the police everything I know about Bosko and his business undertakings in this country, but once they get my version of events, I will have already left."

"Where are you going?"

He shrugged and seemed to be avoiding looking her in the eyes. She could tell he'd made a decision, and he wasn't going to tell her what it was

49

Arian ran his fingers through his shoulder-length black hair and looked at Louise over his steel-rimmed glasses.

She couldn't read anything from his expression, but knew that he was lying to their faces when he repeated that, yes, he did know a few of the girls from the Istedgade neighborhood, but that he didn't have the foggiest idea what they did for a living.

He shrugged his shoulders exaggeratedly.

"I don't know anything about their working as prostitutes. That kind of thing goes against my religion," he repeated, holding out his hands as if it were an affront that they might even consider his being involved in such a thing.

Toft had been through the same thing all morning. Louise had joined him after lunch, after she finished waiting for Hana outside the apartment by Enghave Square. She hadn't gone anywhere else, which was what Louise had expected. On the other hand, Tereza had suddenly gotten out of a cab with two big bags, clearly nervous that someone would see her. She'd looked around several times before quickly walking over and ringing the bell as she again surveyed the street and waited to be buzzed in. Pavlína came by a little before eleven and rang the bell several times. She had seemed angry or upset, Louise thought as she watched Pavlína walk out into the street and look up at the windows before walking back to the door and ringing the bell some more. She spent fifteen minutes doing that before she gave up and left again.

Toft had started with Hamdi, but as he explained to Louise, Hamdi had pretty much not even opened his mouth. He sat in complete silence, shaking his head in response to every question.

When she biked back to her office and was on her way down the back side of Central Station, her thoughts kept circling around Miloš Vituk, Bosko, and the Czech girls. She agreed that they were only going to have one shot at it when they decided to haul Miloš in, and if they struck too soon he'd pack up his whole business, he and Bosko would be long gone, and the case in the Meatpacking District and Kaj Antonsen's murder would end up in the unsolved-cases file.

But when would they have enough?

Her train of thought was interrupted as the cell phone in her jacket pocket started ringing. She thought she'd explained herself clearly when she declined Camilla's dinner invitation by saying she was probably going to have to work late. But Camilla had just said that she'd have the food ready at six. She added that it was important that Louise come, because there was something Camilla had to tell her about the pastor and all the business out at the church.

Louise had shaken her head as she waited for a red light, then set the phone down in her purse, which was in her bike basket.

Up in the division, she went to the kitchenette and got two pieces of crisp bread, which she quickly scarfed down as Toft filled her in on what they had gotten out of the questioning sessions so far.

"It's not like we've really gotten very far," Toft admitted, before they walked into his office, where Arian had been asked to wait.

The Albanian had been politeness itself and obligingly answered all their questions as long as they didn't have anything to do with the business they suspected him of being behind. Arian willingly admitted that for a while he had been going to Central Station every morning.

"I drink a cup of coffee and read the free papers," he explained.

"Who are the girls who walk up to you?" Louise wanted to know.

Once again, Arian's shoulders took up a defensive posture, but after a little contemplation he ended up admitting that he knew a couple of them.

"But you haven't received money from any of them?"

He shook his head apologetically, as if he were sorry he couldn't be of more help to her.

Toft had remained silent after Louise took over the questioning session, but now she saw him take out the surveillance pictures of Arian meeting with the girls. Toft pushed them across the desk one at a time.

"Then just explain to us what's going on here." Toft added that to his eye it looked like the girls met him daily to pay him. "You can see the dates in the corner of the pictures. These were taken over the last few weeks."

Arian took the pictures and it looked as if something suddenly occurred to him. "Now I remember!" he exclaimed, flipping through the photographs without really looking at them. "I loaned a bunch of those girls money and they came by to return it."

"What did you loan them money for?" Toft asked.

"Food, or clothes if they were short. Back where I come from we help each other. If I talk to the girls it's to make sure they're doing all right. It's friendliness. I'm just looking out for them."

Toft gave Louise a look and changed the topic. He pulled out the lists with the phone calls, and with a nod Arian confirmed that it was for his cell phone.

"We have a number of calls made on that phone," Toft began. Arian gazed at him with his accommodating look and nodded interestedly, as if it didn't really have anything to do with him.

"A lot of the calls go to the phones of the six girls named, whom we've identified as the girls you met with at Central Station. At the moment, all six of them are down at the Halmtorvet police station telling our colleagues how they're connected to you and Hamdi."

Suddenly, his hands flew up into a defensive position, and an expression came over his face that said that they were subjecting him to a great injustice. "Well, if they really are prostitutes, as you say they are, then they'll just tell you what their pimps force them to say. But it's not true, I don't have anything to do with their work."

His hands fell back down to rest on the edge of the desk, and Louise saw the little curl around his mouth that was supposed to show that he didn't have anything to hide even if someone claimed otherwise. But she also saw the flutter in his eye.

Toft ignored his vehement outburst and kept on calmly. His plastic cigarette was lying next to his pad of paper. Now he picked it up and sucked it a couple of times, before carefully stuffing it in his pocket, as if he had all the time in the world, as if Arian could just take all the time he needed to answer the next question.

"It is also still your contention that you don't know any of the girls, even though you're in daily telephone contact with them, multiple times per day?"

Toft popped a menthol in his mouth and watched the Albanian, who didn't show any sign of response with his face but did sit for a long time, contemplating.

"As you know I go to the Albanian club on Saxogade every single day," he began, looking from Toft to Louise. "We don't have a phone down there, and when I'm there, my cell phone is almost always plugged in, recharging, and while it is there are a lot of people who could use it."

"We've listened to calls in which you threatened the girls that you'll send the police after them if they don't pay. We hear you say that you're cooperating with the police so the girls have to do what you say, what you command, and that the money they pay goes to the police so the girls will be left alone."

Louise felt a sharp sting of irritation at the way he was trying to shirk any and all responsibility and not even trying to hide it. She asked him how he would explain that.

"I've never said anything like that. Someone borrowed my phone," he replied curtly.

"Well, then give us some names," Toft asked patiently while Louise tried to keep her irritation from turning into rage because he thought it was so easy.

The Albanian shrugged yet again. "I don't keep track of who, but anyone could use it and I don't know who they call."

Louise sighed: it was money they'd borrowed, the girls were paying it back, the cell phone could have been used by anyone. It was inconceivable that he could even get himself to say all this shit without their detecting the least bit of un-certainty in his eyes.

They gave up on getting anywhere with the cell phone right now and confronted Arian instead with the fact that they knew where and when his car had been driven. He shrugged again, as if he didn't feel like that was something he needed to answer for.

"Anyone in the club can use the car. When I'm there, my keys are on the desk. I don't know who takes it out for a drive or where they go."

Louise took a deep breath, but then let it slowly seep back out again. It was no use getting all worked up; that wouldn't make him talk.

"That's a pretty nice car you drive. It doesn't worry you that you don't know who's using it?" Toft asked, receiving only a shrug in response.

"Your Audi is less than a year old and cost about 400,000 kroner," Louise said, taking over again. "I'm a little curious to know how you can afford such an expensive car since you're on public assistance."

"I borrowed money from my uncle," he replied without blinking.

The phone in front of Louise rang, and Mikkelsen said briefly that all six of the girls they had brought in for questioning had confirmed, to a one, that they made their livings as prostitutes, but they all claimed that they did it of their own free will and that they didn't give anyone money.

"One of them was dumb enough to say that she didn't pay anyone except for the money she gave the police to leave her alone," Mikkelsen said with a dry laugh.

There was a long silence after Louise hung up. They had agreed in advance that they would draw the questioning session out until they heard from Mikkelsen and knew whether the girls had said anything they could use. They hadn't been expecting them to talk, but they wanted to be sure before they changed tacks.

Toft got up and asked if Louise or Arian wanted him to bring them a cup of coffee.

Louise nodded and looked at Arian. He had very obviously been expecting that he would be allowed to leave once they'd run through their questions. Now for the first time he looked slightly uncertain, but nodded and asked for milk and sugar.

When Toft returned, setting a little brown wooden tray on the desk, they started again. It was obvious that Arian still felt like he was getting off scot-free and wasn't prepared for the change in tactics that arrived along with the coffee.

"We've heard that you received rather a lot of money from Miloš Vituk to let him buy one of your girls, one by the name of Pavlína."

Louise didn't phrase it as a question, just as a statement. She ignored him as he began to make objections and told him instead how Miloš had come to them and told them his story.

"He was the one who suggested that we start keeping an eye on you and your partner. He also helped by pointing out where you were meeting the girls for them to pay up."

The Albanian leaped up out of his chair and leaned over the desk to make her stop, but Toft quickly got him back in his seat again.

"The police have no doubts that you and Hamdi are earning a great deal of money off several of the Czech girls who work as prostitutes around Skelbækgade. Your car has been seen down there daily, as either you or Hamdi drive around keeping an eye on the girls. But it surprises us that you have not chosen to do it as professionally as Miloš

Vituk. He, for example, has made sure that his girls' paper-work is in order so we have to let them go again if we stop them. And he also covers his tracks, so it's very hard for us to prove what he's up to."

Louise saw the provocation hit home, but Arian took his time before he said anything.

Instead, he clenched his teeth together so hard that his jaws jutted out like two rock formations. And when Toft took over and turned the topic to Arian's knowledge of Bosko and the police's suspicions—that Miloš Vituk was working for the notorious Serb, and that Miloš and Bosko were working on pushing Arian and his business out of the market—Arian seemed to shut down completely, his eyes hard.

Toft was starting to maneuver in his patient fashion, and even though Louise was betting they had a one in a million chance of getting this pimp to talk, she watched with interest as the game played out between the two men. When she felt her cell phone vibrating in her pocket, she quietly walked over to the window to answer the call without disturbing what Toft was up to.

"I'd bet 1,000 kroner that Bosko just picked up Miloš Vituk out here on Valdemarsgade," Michael Stig yelled into her ear to drown out a truck that was driving past him right then.

"Did you see him?"

"Just from the side, through the car window, but I'm almost positive. He was driving a big Volvo with Swedish plates. Unfortunately, I didn't get the license number, because it didn't occur to me that it might be him until Miloš hopped into the front seat."

Louise bent over and picked up her purse.

"Hurry up and pack your makeup bag and get out here so you can confirm it's the Serb if they come back."

She didn't bother scolding him for the way he was ordering her around, since she was the only one who'd seen Bosko and could say for sure he was the one with Miloš.

"I'm off," she told Toft, noticing Arian following her with his eyes as she got up. He was on the edge of his chair, and it was obvious that he was dying to know what was going on.

She gave him a quick nod before disappearing out the door. Then she took the stairs down to Otto Mønsteds Gade, where her bike was parked.

50

Michael Stig pulled a piece of chocolate out of his backpack and offered it to her once she'd parked her bike. Even though the sun was shining, it was cool in the doorway, where big graffiti tags overlapped each other, leaving hardly ten centimeters of contiguous, untagged concrete wall between all the faded colors.

She quickly glanced up at the window on the second floor, but the curtains were closed, so there was no indication of whether anyone was in the apartment. Stig thought that Pavlína must still be up there; at least he hadn't seen her leave after she came back from Enghave Square.

Louise let the chocolate melt in her mouth while Stig told her about how the big Volvo XC90 had pulled over to the curb and then left again immediately thereafter.

"He honked the horn one time, and two seconds later Miloš came out the door. It was obvious that they must have arranged for him to be ready."

"Any sign of calls on Miloš's phones?"

Stig shook his head and smiled. "No, so that means he has a number we don't know about."

"What about Pavlína?"

"Nope, her either. Aside from the calls she made to

Hana's number a little after ten, but they weren't answered, so they couldn't have set up the meeting that way."

It didn't surprise Louise that Miloš was using a cell phone they didn't know about.

There had been surprisingly little activity on his phones, so of course he was using a prepaid cell phone for calls he didn't want to risk the police being able to trace.

"Well, then I guess there isn't anything else for us to do but wait," she said and leaned back against the doorway. "What does Willumsen have to say?"

"He asked Mikkelsen to keep some guys ready in case we need to tail them by car if they show up again. My car is parked down here." Stig indicated a silver station wagon with a tip of his head. "I'll follow him when he leaves here, but it definitely seems like a good idea to have a succession of people ready to help out with tailing him so we're not too obvious."

Louise nodded and looked over at her bike. Maybe she should have brought one of the police vehicles, but it was often quicker to get through town by bike, so she hadn't even thought about it when Stig called.

"The downtown precinct people are also on standby in case Miloš and Bosko make a move on foot. At some point or other Pavlína and the other girls will probably go to work, too."

"I'm supposed to relieve Lars Jørgensen at Enghave Square around five or six tonight," Louise said, looking at her watch.

Stig gave a wry laugh.

"I'm pretty sure your partner is going to have to bail on Saturday night dinner with the wife and twins, because I'm not so sure you'll be getting out of here in time to relieve him."

Sometimes it was clear that Michael Stig lived alone, and that he had only scorn for anyone who was tied down by family life and its obligations, but sometimes Louise also suspected that there might be a touch of envy or longing. She'd never called him out on it, and she bit her tongue now, too, thinking that given the trouble Lars was having at home these days Stig really couldn't be more wrong. Lars would probably be just as glad to have to work late.

"Don't worry your pretty little head about Lars," Louise replied snidely and added that her partner was never the kind of person who went home early because he had to stir the sauce or watch a soccer game.

That last comment was a little dig at Stig, because at least once a month he was so busy with his bowling tournaments that he was forced to trade shifts with someone.

But then all the comments on dinner obligations made Louise realize she'd better call Camilla, who was surely not going to be happy to be stood up.

"It's just not going to work out for us to have dinner tonight," Louise began the second Camilla answered. Before Camilla had a chance to get a word in, she continued, "We believe the Serb we suspect of being behind the murders of Iveta and Kaj is in town. Michael Stig thinks it was Bosko who came and picked Miloš Vituk up an hour ago, so now we're waiting for them to come back. We're going to have to have our talk another day."

"Bosko," Camilla repeated softly. And for a second Louise could hear Camilla breathing. Then she hung up on Louise.

Louise figured Camilla was either pissed off or disappointed or both, and sighed, but she pulled herself together when she realized that Michael Stig was watching her. She took a breath to defend herself, because he knew perfectly well that Camilla wasn't working right now, so he didn't need to worry about scolding her for telling a journalist about Bosko.

Camilla was very involved in the case and besides, the homicide chief trusted her, damn it. "How's she doing?" Stig asked in an unexpectedly friendly tone, causing Louise to instantly forget her anger.

She studied him for a second. His gray-blue eyes, which usually made people keep a certain distance, looked concerned and intense. Louise nodded slowly and realized that even though she'd been working closely with Stig for several years, she still couldn't quite figure him out. This wasn't the first time he'd surprised her with one of his infrequent expressions of concern. The last time had been for her after a case that had ended rather dramatically down in Roskilde, and now it made her wonder if he had a hidden nurturing side, which he didn't reveal unless he was really concerned that the person he was talking about might be losing it.

"She's doing better," Louise said, half-expecting the arrogant look to return to Stig's eyes.

But Stig just nodded and turned back to survey the street and then look up at the apartment.

51

For a second, Camilla felt paralyzed. She'd turned off her phone but was still holding it in her hands, all the thoughts in her head having come to a standstill. It hadn't been more than two hours since she and Markus had come home from the pastor's residence, and Henrik seemed to expect Bosko to react quickly. But not that he'd be in Copenhagen already.

She wanted to call and warn Henrik. Her fingers felt stiff, as she found the number for the pastor's residence in the phone's memory, and anxiety coursed through her body with her blood as the phone rang and rang and eventually started beeping in her ear. She let it ring out one more time before she got up and went to the front hall to find her wallet.

Markus asked her several times if there was something wrong. He watched her, not understanding that she had no mental capacity left for anything besides the thoughts Henrik Holm's story had left in her mind. But she hadn't been able to bring herself to tell him that his best friend had to leave and was never coming back.

Now he was standing in front of her again with a frightened look, watching her as she feverishly rooted around in the outermost pocket of her wallet where she stuffed all her old receipts.

"Please go to your room," she said.

She found the little torn-off scrap of paper on which Henrik had written his cell number, ran into the living room, and grabbed the phone. For a second she felt a wave of panic as the cell phone went straight to voice mail, and she could tell the phone was turned off. She ran back to the entry, snatched her jacket from the hook, and checked to see that her car keys were in her pocket.

"I have to run out," she yelled to Markus, who was lying on his bed with his face to the wall.

For a second she stood there, looking at the rejection of his skinny back, before she turned around.

"I'll be back soon," she promised as she turned the lock.

If the police had stopped her, they would have confiscated her license on the spot, but she carefully avoided looking at the speedometer as she darted down Nordre Fasanvej.

From the second she got home from the pastor's residence, part of her had really been pushing for her to go down to Police Headquarters and tell them what the pastor had confided in her so they could head out there and protect him. At the same time, another part of her forced her to keep her promise and give him the head start he was going to need in order to get himself and Jonas to safety.

His car was gone, she noted with a little sigh of relief as she pulled into the parking lot and turned off her engine. There weren't any other cars, either. The only thing she could see was the sexton's bicycle, which was propped against the wall of the church. There wasn't a person in sight.

She inhaled all the way down to her diaphragm and let it

out again slowly before walking across the courtyard, then stopped to listen for a second. No movement, no voices, nothing.

Even in the car she'd decided to hightail it out of there if there were the slightest indication the Serb was out there. Then she'd have to call the police and let them take over, but mostly she just wanted to make sure that Henrik and Jonas had managed to get away, then she would tell Louise afterward why Henrik had fled.

Now she was feeling rather sure that Henrik had already left, and if this was where Bosko and Miloš Vituk had been coming, they must have already left again.

The sun was reflected in the kitchen window as she walked up and let the door knocker fall. For a second she stood there waiting, then leaned to the right and peered in the window. The basket of morning rolls was still sitting on the table. Things looked pretty much as they had when she and Markus had left.

Camilla walked down the stairs and around the building before continuing out into the yard. Over by the patio door she put both hands up against the window and peered into the living room. It was hard to see if he'd packed anything, but she did note that the laptop wasn't sitting on the desk anymore.

Again, a sense of relief caused some of her tension to dissolve.

She scanned the road leading to the cemetery for the sexton to find out if he knew when they'd left. She walked down and around the shed, by where the wheelbarrow and watering can were, and where she'd occasionally seen the sexton enjoying a cheroot when the weather permitted it.

Finally, she walked up toward the church and hesitated slightly before walking in. But the floor was bare; there weren't any more newborns there. On the other hand, there was an open box of white candles on the bench next to a yellow plastic watering can.

She walked over and opened the door from the entryway into the main body of the church, calling to him to avoid startling him in the event that he was in there finishing something up.

The blood was the first thing she saw. The light from above, from the broad windows in the roof of the church, cast reflections down, making it shine on the dark stone floor.

The door slammed shut behind her as she ran forward without giving even a thought to the fact that maybe she should have been running out instead of in.

52

His eyes were closed. He was lying on his side with his torso half up on the kneeling pillows in front of the altar, and the blood had dyed his light summer jeans and shirt dark red, where it had spread through the material in big splotches. It spread across his chest all the way out over the shoulder and left arm, which was resting on the floor, and there were colored areas on both knees, like two oval patches with frayed edges.

Camilla instinctively stepped back and sank down into a squat. She inhaled deeply a couple of times to keep herself from hyperventilating before she eventually got up to put a finger on the sexton's wrist. If there was any beat at all, the pulse was so weak that her inexperienced fingers couldn't find it.

She managed to tell the dispatcher clearly and precisely what she'd found once she'd gotten through to emergency services, but she couldn't answer the question of whether or not he was still alive.

"I think he was shot. He's bleeding from both knees and his chest."

As she was talking she got up and in uncertain steps started backing away through the church, her eyes trained on the sexton's powerful body. She should stay with him until the ambulance arrived, she thought, but she didn't dare. She knew that if Otto Birch were still alive, he might need her, but her fear that Bosko would return trumped that thought. She was almost out the door when she suddenly stopped.

"Is he still breathing?" the dispatcher's voice calmly asked into her ear.

"I don't know," she answered hoarsely, and cleared her throat before repeating herself a little louder.

The thought *It's too late to be a coward* flashed through her head. The only thing that made her consider trying to run away was the image of Markus, lying in bed at home with his back to her. But that wasn't enough given that there was a man lying on the floor in front of her, a man who was dying if he hadn't already.

"Feel his throat and see if he has a pulse," the man's voice urged. He added that the ambulance was on its way.

Camilla ran back up to the altar and dropped down onto the floor next to the seemingly lifeless body.

"Take two fingers and hold them gently against his throat. Don't press," he instructed her.

"I think there's a pulse," Camilla whispered, closing her eyes to concentrate.

"Find something that you can press against the wound on his torso and hold it there until the ambulance arrives."

There was no acceptable way to tell the dispatcher that she didn't know if she would be sticking around that long, and as she tossed her jacket aside and pulled off her cardigan, she felt a strange sense of calm belaying the fear that a moment earlier had been on the verge of making her flee the scene.

She unbuttoned his shirt and determined that the gunshot wound was in his chest, and she put some muscle into it as she leaned over him and pressed her cardigan against the bloody opening.

In a relatively calm voice she started talking to the wounded man. If he could hear her, it might help him to know the ambulance was on its way. If he couldn't hear anything, repeating those same words made her feel calmer, and she promised that she would stay until the EMTs got there and took him to the hospital.

The words sounded like pebbles, but she understood the last part and straightened up a little.

"I told where the house is," he whispered, still with his eyes closed, and she had a hard time telling if he was still conscious.

With her free hand, she pulled her cell phone out of her jacket, which she'd tossed on the floor when she took her cardigan off.

Louise's number appeared after three quick taps.

"Just shut up for a second," Camilla hissed into the phone, turning her head away from the injured man, as Louise started to object. "I'm sitting out in Stenhøj Church. The sexton is lying on the floor next to me. He's been shot at least three times. The ambulance is on its way. I'm trying to keep the blood from gushing out of him until they get here."

At last, Louise was starting to listen, and Camilla told her how she'd arrived at the church and found Otto Birch on the floor.

"While you've been standing around waiting, Bosko has been out here assaulting this poor, elderly man, and I know why, too. He's looking for Henrik Holm and Jonas, and we have to get to them before Bosko finds them."

"What do you know about Bosko?" Louise asked, astonished.

Camilla felt like she could almost see inside Louise's head, where the pieces were not all quite fitting together.

"Just get out here now; then you can find out," Camilla implored, concentrating the whole time on pressing her cardigan against the wound. "It goes back to when the pastor and his wife were in Bosnia."

53

The ambulance and the EMTs pulled up in front of the church just as Michael Stig drove into the courtyard and parked.

Camilla came running out of the church toward them and pulled open the back door of the police car.

"We're going to Sweden," she yelled with her jacket over her arm, getting in. "I think Henrik Holm might have driven up to his house there and I'm afraid Bosko is right on his heels."

Louise hadn't been able to tell Stig much as they had stood in the doorway and Louise suddenly ordered him to scrap the stakeout and drive out to the church, aside from that there was a seriously wounded man, and that it sounded like that might be where Bosko and Miloš Vituk had gone.

On the way to her colleague's car, Louise had called Willumsen, who had just been notified of the shooting victim by the central duty desk, but it was news to him that Camilla Lind was at the church. Louise told him Bosko was after the pastor. He did not want to obey Camilla's request, though, and wanted to bring Lars and Toft out to the church instead of Louise and Stig.

"Are you sure it was Bosko and Miloš?" Stig asked,

looking at Camilla in the rearview mirror as she slammed the car door shut.

She nodded.

He watched her face in the mirror and listened as she started her story—in hectic snippets—which was news to the two policemen.

Camilla desperately brushed a couple of long strands of hair out of her face before she continued.

"This morning he told me the whole thing. He said he had to disappear, and the man in the church, Otto Birch, said that he'd told him where the house is. So, I'm guessing that he went up to the summerhouse to start with, to gain a little time. He had no way of knowing that Bosko would react so fast."

The gravel flew around the tires as Michael Stig put the car in gear and backed up to where he could turn around; it flew up and hit the underside of the car as he accelerated and navigated his way out of the narrow driveway into the courtyard.

Louise looked at him in surprise. It was one thing that Louise knew Camilla well enough to know that her friend was serious about this, but Louise was taken aback that Stig didn't ask any more questions before he started obeying Camilla's orders.

Camilla sat there breathing deeply for a bit as they sped down Stenhøj Allé. Then she leaned forward between the front seats and started to tell them, in more or less coherent sentences, why Henrik Holm had been forced to flee.

Louise listened intently while trying to figure out who they ought to contact with the Swedish police to request assistance, so they could have a patrol sent out to the pastor's summer home and also get permission to drive into Sweden.

"Afraid I can't help," Camilla said, resigned, when Louise interrupted her to get the address and then recommended that Stig get it from central dispatch. "I don't know the address. It's a numbered road, a little forest service road, and they use some idiotic system that doesn't make any sense to people like us who are used to roads with names and houses with numbers. But I was there over Easter and could certainly recognize the place. We just head up toward Helsingborg to start with and then on toward Laholm."

"We'll take the Øresund Bridge over to Malmö in Sweden; that way we won't have to wait for the ferry," Stig decided, pulling onto the highway heading toward the airport.

Eventually Camilla's breathing settled down some, and she told them about the forged birth certificate that ended up being the lifelong shackle Bosko had on the pastor, and how that had forced Henrik Holm into his decision earlier that day.

"They forced Otto Birch to tell them where the pastor and Jonas had gone. And, fuck," she exclaimed vehemently and said that she hadn't been able to get a hold of Henrik even though she'd tried many times. "His cell phone is off."

A desperate note had snuck into her voice, but she tried to tone it down.

"Well, we don't know how much Otto told them," Louise said, turning to look at Camilla.

"No, but he told them where the house is, and that's enough," Camilla responded, closing her eyes.

Louise received a text from Lars in which he wrote that he was just getting in touch with Otto's next of kin and that he would go to National Hospital later and try to talk to him if he was conscious. Right now, he was on the operating table.

Camilla shook her head and sank into the back seat as they zipped past Kastrup Airport, where a large KLM plane was slowly taxiing out to the runway. They continued on over the bridge that linked Denmark to Sweden.

With a sudden jolt, Camilla sat up and slapped her hands to her face. "Markus!" she cried so loudly that Michael Stig slowed down for a second. "He's all alone at home, waiting for me. I told him I'd be right back."

Choking up, she took out her phone but ended up passing it to Louise and asking her to call Tobias and ask if he could go over and stay with their son until Camilla came home.

Louise found his number and explained as little as possible, but added extra emphasis when she said that it was a life-or-death matter and that she was the one who forced Camilla to come. Actually, that was a little unfair, because Tobias didn't usually put up a fuss over getting a little extra time with his son, but every now and then he did accuse Camilla of being too disorganized. Once that was all arranged, Louise passed the phone back over the headrest.

"But you've pretty much got to assume that an elderly man says what he knows if a couple of guys show up and shoot his kneecaps to smithereens," Stig said, getting back to Louise's conclusion as they drove through the Øresund tunnel. "I'm guessing they shot before they asked their questions to show that they were serious and then he told them what he knew."

"But he did have the last word," Camilla admitted, as they had water on both sides of them.

Michael Stig nodded.

"Bosko doesn't leave witnesses."

Louise sighed and thought it was no wonder that Mikkelsen had been so concerned about the violent trend he'd seen beginning to show up on the scene a few weeks earlier. The kind of brutality they'd seen recently was unheard of—beyond even the knifings that got citizens and politicians so upset, even though they were standard fare in Copenhagen.

As they approached the tollbooth, Louise spotted the Swedish police cars. She'd been notified that an APB had gone out in Sweden; Bosko was heavily armed and considered extremely dangerous, but if he'd made it over the sound more than forty-five minutes ago, then he'd have gotten away before they had started watching the border. That would have been true of the crossing from Helsingør also, where officers had been stationed at both ends of the Scandlines ferry route to Helsingborg.

Willumsen had ordered two men from the Nordsjælland police department to go to Helsingør and review the surveillance tapes from the ferry terminal; two of Mikkelsen's guys were doing the same thing at the bridge's control center, but Willumsen had reached out to Louise to let her know that it would take a couple of hours before they knew if a man matching the picture of Bosko the police had circulated had crossed the border.

As they pulled away from the tollbooth on the Malmö side, Stig pulled over and quickly jumped out to greet their Swedish counterparts, who were ready to follow them the rest of the way. Once he was back behind the wheel a second later, he announced that while the Swedish police had been there, two Volvos of the model they were interested in had gone by, but neither of them with a driver of the nationality they were looking for.

"One was a woman, and she was Danish. I don't know, I might consider moving to Sweden if I could afford to buy a car like that over here," Stig said getting back onto the highway.

As they drove toward Landskrona, Camilla again started telling them how the pastor had discovered early that same morning that the network he thought his housekeeper was working with didn't have anything to do with helping women from Eastern Europe.

"To the contrary," she said indignantly. "The reason for the lively traffic in young women at his house was that they had to go out there to deliver their earnings. And Henrik wasn't going to put up with that. There was no way he was going to let himself or his church be pressured into helping exploit young women like that."

Suddenly things added up for Louise. Now everything fit, but she wasn't sure if she would have been able to put it all together, even though she'd been studying the pattern closely for several days and would have continued to do so.

Louise thought about Hana and the other young women, who had passed her with their eyes on the ground, and of her conversation on the bench with Henrik Holm, whose eyes had kept flitting to the door whenever someone approached. But it hadn't occurred to her that he had been under so much pressure, and she didn't doubt that at that point he still believed in the network's and Tereza's good intentions. Otherwise he wouldn't have spoken to Louise so passionately about it.

Michael Stig kept up the rapid pace and the light greens of Skåne County in the springtime flew past. Louise glanced at the speedometer and saw he was doing about 150 kilometers an hour—but even so she had a niggling knot in her stomach that told her it was too slow. The tense silence made her reach over and flip on the radio, but after two verses she shut it off again and sighed, then leaned back and closed her eyes.

"He's not coming back," Camilla finally said, breaking the silence. "Not even if you succeed in catching Bosko."

Louise thought about Jonas, who sometimes seemed both shy and a little withdrawn.

Still, he had opened up that weekend he'd stayed with her.

She was assuming he knew the truth by now. Henrik would have a hard time explaining that they weren't going back to the pastor's residence without telling him why.

Who even knew how much Jonas would understand? Louise thought, feeling a pang in her heart that everything the boy had considered part of his secure, everyday life was gone, just like that. But he was a great kid, and she was sure that with time he would adjust to the situation his parents had gotten him into.

They were driving the last little way up E6 toward Laholm when Willumsen called and said that a Volvo XC90 with Swedish plates had been spotted at the harbor in Helsingør.

"The car was rented from Avis in Malmö by a man named Hendrich Müller with an address in Hamburg, but there's no trace of anyone by that name, so now I'm sending some techs up so they can look at the car."

"So he's still on board as a pedestrian, or someone picked him up at the ferry terminal, or he had another car waiting," Louise said, looking over at Michael Stig, who nodded to show that he'd understood the latest development.

"Miloš Vituk returned to his apartment half an hour ago," Willumsen continued. "He came sauntering down from Vesterbrogade but was dumb enough to have a Smith & Wesson .38-caliber in his inside pocket. What an idiot. He's being questioned by Toft as we speak."

He gave a little, satisfied chuckle. "Where are you guys?" he wanted to know.

"We'll be there in about fifteen minutes," Louise said, glancing back at Camilla, who nodded in affirmation. "Ten minutes," Louise corrected herself as she noted her colleague had sped up, even though they'd left the main road.

54

The woods closed in around them, and the roads got smaller. Stig had been forced to ease up a little on the speed and was now working to avoid the worst of the potholes in the poorly maintained asphalt.

"We turn right up by that big farm," Camilla ordered, pointing toward a forest road, which was almost hidden behind a high pile of logs.

The pavement turned into gravel, and the speedometer was down to twenty as Stig coaxed the car along the uneven road.

None of them said anything, and aside from Camilla's brief instructions to turn or go straight, there was an oppressive silence that became more and more intense the thicker the trees got around them and the closer they got to the pastor's house in the woods.

Their Swedish colleague was still right behind them, and the agreement was that they would stop a couple hundred meters away from the house.

"We're going to go down around that little lake, and then there's an old, dilapidated tractor where we turn off to his house."

The sun had dipped behind the tall treetops, and an early

twilight sent a light bluish gray through the narrow openings between the trees and onto the forest road.

"The house is in there," Camilla said, pointing toward a thick copse with yet another high pile of cut logs. Only a little white mailbox revealed that someone lived behind the densely growing trees.

Stig signaled and then slowed down.

Camilla stayed in the back seat while Louise and Stig got out of the car to talk to their Swedish colleagues before they approached the house. She had rolled down her window, and aside from the police voices, it was completely quiet. Not a sound made it in here, no car engines, no noise. The only sound came from the birds flying low between the branches.

Most of all, she wanted to run to the house and get the pastor and Jonas so they could get out of there, but she had been ordered to remain in her seat until they told her they were ready to go in. The two Swedish officers were armed, unlike Louise and Stig, and would approach the house first.

As they started walking, Camilla got out of the car and immediately noticed the scent of freshly chopped pine. A little farther in, the forest road ended and turned into a narrow path that led into a jungle of toppled trees—a relic from the powerful storms that had claimed large portions of the forest several years earlier.

Her fear impeded her movements, but when they waved to her from the driveway, she slowly started following the others. At first a little hesitantly, but then her footsteps became more confident and finally she was jogging. Even from a distance she spotted Henrik's black car, which was parked in front of the red-and-white wood house, and she saw the light in the kitchen window and the smoke curling up from the chimney from the wood-stove in the living room.

The two Swedish officers came around from the back of the house and nodded, as Louise signaled that they were going to enter.

"There's no one visible in there," one of the Swedes said, glancing up at the house's second floor, where a window was ajar. "There's no sign of a confrontation. Everything looks peaceful."

After a quick knock on the front door, Louise waited for a second before pressing the door handle down and pushing the door open. She stood in the doorway listening before she took the first step into the front entryway.

Camilla stood in the driveway watching her. She was still afraid and her muscles were stiff, her heart pounding, and her hands clenched, her fingernails cutting into her palms. At the same time, she felt like they'd made it in time. She filled her lungs with fresh forest air and slowly exhaled, feeling slightly dizzy.

Through the window, she watched Louise walking into the kitchen. The others had gone upstairs. Camilla watched Louise walk toward the living room, which they knew was empty. Camilla's shoulders relaxed since the Swedish officers had already peeked in all the windows on the whole ground floor.

The wind pulled at her hair, blowing it over her face as she turned around and started walking around behind the house and over the large lawn, which had been left wild and natural. She sat down at the table by the fire pit and for a second enjoyed the silence and the scent of the thick carpet of pine needles that formed a natural carpet under the tall trees.

Louise was puzzled by a sound from the room at the back of the house and slowly walked forward through the living room, past the woodstove. She spotted Camilla out in the yard by the long, wide picnic table, which was made of a split tree trunk resting on two stumps.

Camilla had described the layout of the house. On the ground floor, along with the kitchen, bathroom, and living room, there were two guest bedrooms, which were mostly used for storage. Upstairs there was a second bathroom, three bedrooms, and a little attic room.

There was the sound again. Louise stood still and listened until she realized it was the ceiling creaking as her colleagues walked around upstairs.

She put a hand on the dining table and stood there for a second to let her heart calm down. She didn't know what she'd expected, and she decided that most of all she was trying to avoid expecting anything.

She heard the others coming down the stairs, and Stig came over and opened the door of the woodstove, which was burning briskly. A big log was still going strong even though it had obviously been in the stove for a while.

"Well, there's just no telling," Stig said after he shut it again. "They could be absolutely anywhere, but it must be somewhere they can get to on foot. What about neighbors? Are there any?"

Camilla had told them about the Jønssons, who had a farm on the other side of the band of pines, which ran through this stretch of woods like a belt.

"About a kilometer away, through the woods," Louise said, but she didn't know if Camilla knew the way. She walked over to open the lock on the patio door and call to Camilla when she saw Camilla suddenly jump up and start running toward the woods bordering on the backyard.

The lock jammed and wouldn't budge despite Louise hitting it. She watched Camilla disappear into the edge of the woods. Louise ran through the kitchen and had just gotten to the corner of the house and around into the backyard when the screams ripped through the silent forest.

Louise ran through the tall grass past the table, past the fire pit, but stopped suddenly when Camilla came staggering back from the edge of the woods with her hands clenched together over her head in helplessness, as she ran, tears streaming, shrieking. Then Camilla collapsed, her violent sobs filling Louise with fear.

Stig and their Swedish colleagues were right behind Louise as she went farther into the woods where a small, narrow path wound its way between the pine trees.

Henrik Holm was lying on his stomach with one arm over his head and the other out to the side. Killed from behind by one shot in the back of the head and two more in his back.

Louise gasped for air and doubled over, as though she suddenly had a terrible stitch in her side. The others kept going past her and kneeled next to the body.

Louise didn't need to go all the way to know that the pastor was dead. Liquidated. She was also experienced enough to know that he had been shot at close range. He hadn't had a chance to get away and was still lying in the place where he had been shot.

Camilla's sobs sliced through her bones. It went black before her eyes, and she didn't have enough air to stand back up and walk back to her. Instead, she sank even more and let herself fall onto the forest floor, where she sat with her back against a tree and ignored the sharp pine needles that pierced her knit sweater.

They felt for a pulse, looked at his face. The bullet exited where his mouth had been.

Louise looked away, into the darkness between the tree trunks, as she heard the Swedish officers on their cell phones, both calling for backup.

55

It was his eyes she noticed first. They found her through the dense branches. There were several rows of trees between them. Still, she could see his face quite clearly.

Stig had stayed on the footpath, while the other two ran back to the house.

Louise was slowly crawling her way forward on her knees, squeezing her way between the trunks. When she got there, Jonas's face was hidden in his hands and he was sitting perfectly still. Louise put an arm around him and pulled him to her. Squeezed him and felt his face against her shoulder. He wasn't crying. He wasn't making a sound. She could hardly feel him breathing.

Tears streamed down her cheeks and landed on his hair, but otherwise she felt nothing. The sound of Camilla's deep sobs didn't penetrate this far into the woods, nor did the piercing tones of the first sirens. Not even Stig's gentle voice, talking to her right before he grasped her elbow and started helping her out, while she was still holding the boy in her lap.

Jonas kept his head buried in against her shoulder, until they were out on the path. Then Stig lifted him up into his arms and carried him to the house, with Louise walking right next to him.

As they reached Camilla in the grass, she slowly got up onto her knees and took the hand Louise held out to her. Together they walked up to the house, where the first responders' flashing lights made the place feel too crowded. The ambulance and police cars were parked in a long line down by the driveway. None of them had driven all the way up to the house, since the driveway had already been cordoned off.

Louise followed Stig into the living room and let Camilla collapse into the room's only armchair, in front of the woodstove, which no longer showed a glow behind the soot-covered glass door. Louise sat down on the sofa, as Stig let Jonas slowly slip down next to her.

"Do you think it would be better if we put him to bed until we leave here?" her colleague asked, searching her face to see what she thought.

"Just let him lie here," Louise said and swallowed a couple of times in quick succession when she saw how the boy curled up into a fetal position and hid his face in a cushion.

A weak shiver ran through him as she carefully placed a hand on his shoulder and then quickly pulled it back again; she couldn't even fathom the misfortune this eleven-year-old boy had suffered in just one day, and now he may have just witnessed his father being gunned down, as well.

The silence in the living room was oppressive.

Jonas was still curled up into a tight ball, breathing so quietly that occasionally Louise feared he'd stopped.

Camilla sat in the armchair staring straight ahead. She was pale and staring off into space. Every so often, she reacted as an almost invisible shiver ran through her, and she mindlessly clasped her hands together hard, as if a sharp pain were jabbing through her.

Stig had gone out front and was talking to Willumsen

by phone. From what she could hear, Louise was going to take Jonas and Camilla back to Denmark in the car after the Swedish police questioned them, knowing full well that the boy was definitely too deep in shock to be able to tell them anything. Jakobsen would be waiting at National Hospital to receive them so Jonas could get emergency crisis counseling.

Darkness had fallen outside, and Louise counted about six or eight CSI techs from the Swedish crime lab working both in front of and behind the house. Three were leaning over the tire imprints in the driveway and preparing to take plaster molds.

Louise held Jonas's hand as they walked out to the car. As expected, the boy hadn't been able to tell the police anything about what happened, so they decided to wait and have him try to talk to them when their own expert crisis psychologist could be present.

Louise noticed Stig standing and watching them as she carefully turned his car around on the narrow forest road and slowly started driving back through the darkness, avoiding the biggest of the potholes.

56

The murder of the popular pastor Henrik Holm filled all the newspapers' front pages on Monday morning. Only a little bit of the story had leaked to the public, but it was enough to leave people in shock about the brutality of his killing.

The investigative team was gathered in Willumsen's office. No one had slept more than a couple of hours since Louise had arrived at National Hospital late Saturday night with Jonas and Camilla, who were both admitted to be treated for shock. Louise had sat with them until Sunday morning, going directly from the hospital to Police HQ.

"Miloš Vituk pleaded guilty to the four killings," Willumsen began, eyeing them with tired eyes, his face unshaven.

"Four?" Louise and Stig exclaimed simultaneously.

"Otto Birch died overnight," Willumsen informed them sadly. After a moment of silence as that news sank in, he returned to the topic of Miloš Vituk. "We searched the cell phone we found on him when we arrested him and, sure enough, it had a different number from the ones we knew about. Igli is just compiling all the numbers. He'll bring a list as soon as he's done."

He signaled he was changing subjects by taking a gulp of his coffee. "Late last night Lars spoke briefly with Otto Birch."

Willumsen nodded to Louise's partner to have him take over.

"He was very confused about what had happened. He went into the church and was swapping out the candles in the candleholders when two men came in. They asked for the pastor and an instant later his legs exploded in pain, and he collapsed onto the floor. One man walked right up to him and held a big revolver to his forehead, demanding to know where they went. So, Otto told him about the house in Sweden and gave them the address. Then that man disappeared—we're assuming this was Bosko—while the other one, who had stayed in the background, stepped forward and aimed at him."

"Is there any evidence that Bosko was there?" Louise wanted to know. She had asked that same question many times since Sunday morning, but Willumsen had shaken his head each time.

"Miloš Vituk was brought before a judge yesterday at two o'clock, and after confessing was sentenced to jail for four weeks."

"But he wasn't the one behind the murders," Toft said, without removing the plastic cigarette from his mouth. He'd been sitting with the Serb ever since his arrest Saturday afternoon right up until they had escorted him down to see the judge for his preliminary hearing.

Willumsen shook his head. "That's not what we're trying to prove here. Frandsen has had his CSI techs working all night, and he called twenty minutes ago to say that he was on his way over from Slotsherrensvej. But obviously, he has to make it through morning rush hour traffic before he'll be here." Willumsen pulled the printout of an e-mail out of the stack he had in front of him on the table.

"We received a report from the DNA lab. They confirm that the same DNA was found on the girl murdered in the Meatpacking District and Kaj Antonsen. And," he said, drawing it out a little, "the murdered prostitute in Prague. They sent the results to the international database, and we have a match with Bosko. He's been charged multiple times for violent assaults, but they've had to let him go each time because of a lack of evidence. We don't have anything on Miloš Vituk. We ran the fingerprints the techs found in the big Volvo in Helsingør through our own automated finger-print ID system, but we didn't get any hits.

"However, Interpol did find a match when they ran it through their system. Helsingør also sent us prints from the surveillance footage from when the ferry disembarked in Helsingborg."

He pushed two pictures out onto the table. "Bosko!"

The Serb was walking purposefully down the hallway, making no attempt to hide his face. To the contrary, he was looking right up into the camera in one of the pictures. In the corner, the time stamp read 3:07 p.m.

"He had a car waiting on the other side, and we were standing on Valdemarsgade at that time," Louise calculated. She looked over at Stig, who was clicking the pen he was holding in his hand. There was a half-empty cola on the ta-ble in front of him, even though it wasn't nine a.m. yet. He might have slept even less than she had. He had stayed be-hind in Sweden so that he would be available to the Swedish police during the first few hectic days of the investigation. They had found the pastor's computer and the letter he'd written to them but had not had a chance to send.

Everything matched what Camilla had repeated to

their Swedish counterparts and then again at National Hospital. It had also been confirmed that Baby Girl was Tereza's daughter. The baby was still at Skodsborg Orphanage, and Toft had brought the mother out there that same afternoon so that she could sign the necessary paperwork now that they had the mother's permission for the baby to be put up for adoption.

"What about the father?" Louise asked, her eyes drifting over toward her partner.

"Bosko," he said. "The first time she met him, he raped her in a little apartment in Malmö. After that he forced her to work until a week before she gave birth. He sent her to Denmark the day before the birth, and she stayed in the apartment out at Enghave Square. Miloš Vituk was with her when she gave birth, and he was also the one who immediately took the baby and left it in the church."

Louise sighed, then took a deep breath when Toft added that the little stillborn baby boy had been born in Malmö and the mother didn't know what had happened to it after Bosko's men had taken it.

Frandsen didn't knock before he walked in and quickly greeted everyone around the table. "Bosko was in the church," he began without any introductions. "We also have evidence that he was at the crime scenes in the Meatpacking District and in the courtyard off Sønder Boulevard, but there are no traces of Miloš Vituk in any of these locations."

Frandsen looked over at Willumsen, who just nodded.

"The three bullets that hit the sexton were not fired from the same weapon. The two bullets in his knees were fired from a pistol and match the casings from a Glock

SARA BLAEDEL

9mm that our people found in the church, while the shot in the chest was fired from a revolver, which in all likelihood was identical to the Smith & Wesson you confiscated from Miloš Vituk when he was arrested. And," he continued, glancing around, "the pistol is the same as the one that shot and killed Henrik Holm up in Sweden, which occurred while Miloš Vituk was in custody being questioned by you guys."

He tossed his report onto the table in front of Willumsen and looked over toward the door as Igli knocked and stepped in.

The interpreter apologized and asked if he were interrupting. Willumsen shook his head and waved him into the office.

"Miloš Vituk still insists that he was responsible for all three shots even though he can't explain what happened to the other weapon," Toft confirmed.

Igli stood against the wall, ready to distribute the copies he'd printed out of the numbers from Miloš's "secret" phone. Once everyone had a copy, he cleared his throat.

"You're not going to get Bosko," he said softly and sounded sure. "Miloš Vituk will continue to claim that he was responsible for the whole thing and doesn't know anything about Bosko. In return he will be well looked after for the rest of his life. That's how it usually goes. I'm guessing that Bosko has already been back in Serbia for ages by now, and a man like him won't be caught there."

Louise was lost in her own thoughts when Lars tapped her on the shoulder and pointed to the door. Suhr had stuck his head in and waved for her to come out. She spotted Jakobsen behind him with his silver-gray hair, appearing all business yet with a concerned look in his eyes.

Out in the hallway, Suhr took her by the elbow and led

her down to his office. The somber look in his eyes kept her from saying anything as he asked her to take a seat and pointed to a chair for the psychologist, who must have come straight over from National Hospital.

"We're going to have to talk about Jonas," Suhr began once he'd taken his own seat behind the desk. "There's no reason to doubt the information the pastor gave us. According to the civilian registration database, there is no next of kin either in the pastor's family or that of his deceased wife."

Louise nodded. That matched what Camilla had said Henrik had told her about his wife's death.

"That leaves Jonas Holm all alone. Without a family or any next of kin, and we're going to have to concede that it will be darn near impossible for us to try to track down any potential biological family members in Bosnia, since no one knows his parents' identities."

"I've talked a bit with the boy." Jakobsen took over now, watching Louise with his clear, penetrating gaze. "Jonas is still in a state of deep shock, but he did say that he was walking around at the edge of the woods gathering some kindling for the fire, when his dad suddenly ran out of the house. Almost at the same time he heard a car door slam and the stranger came running along behind his dad. He crouched down and hid only a few meters from where his father was gunned down."

Louise's throat constricted.

"I sat with him a long time last night," Jakobsen continued. "This is a tough period he's going to have to make it through, and this trauma will be with him for a very long time. I tried to talk to him a little about the fact that—along with his input, of course—we're going to have to find him a new family that he can move in with and live with."

"How is that going to happen?" Louise asked, leaning forward.

Jakobsen looked at her, a serious expression on his face. "Normally the social welfare authorities would find a foster family for him or maybe even a family that wants to adopt him. In his case, of course, they will have to keep in mind that it might be best if they live nearby so Jonas can keep going to the same school and stay in touch with his friends."

"Normally," Louise repeated, watching Jakobsen. "What do you mean by normally?"

Jakobsen folded his hands together in his lap and leaned back a little in the chair. "In some cases, the child expresses a desire to live somewhere in particular." He added slowly, "And Jonas Holm would very much like to live with you."

Louise stood up and turned away as Suhr took over.

"Do you even know this boy?" her boss asked.

Her eyes wandered to the window, watching a bird fly past before heading farther up into the sky, where there was no limit to how far it could go. Then she nodded.

"It's a very big responsibility and no one expects you to—"

He hadn't finished when Louise spun around and walked out of the office.

Once out the front door, she started walking down the street, heading away from HQ. Her thoughts were racing. Sitting down on a concrete wall, she looked over at the main library and Iceland's Quay across the water. She watched the bicycles zoom past and a few boats sail by. She concentrated, recalling that fortune-teller who had once very convincingly told her that when a woman had a child, it was because the child had chosen her to be its mother. Now Louise's number seemed to have come up—she'd been chosen by a big, eleven-year-old boy.

Life sure is weird and unexpected, she thought as she jumped down and started walking again.

THE NIGHT WOMEN
ACKNOWLEDGMENTS

From my very first publication and onward, I've been a stickler for thorough research, which is essential if the goal is storytelling that is believable, authentic, and realistic. I've had enormous help along the way. Special thanks go to my now old friends at Copenhagen's Police Headquarters, without whose help the framework around Louise Rick wouldn't hold. A big, fat, massive thank-you to Tom Christensen, Flying Squad, who has been with me all along the way, and has generously contributed with talk and details as the book developed. Deep gratitude for your time and compassion.

Heartfelt thanks go, as always, to my brilliant friend, forensic expert Steen Holger Hansen, who is there to help out when a plot needs to be spun together. Without you there would be no books.

Great thanks to my talented Danish editor, Lisbeth Møller Madsen, and to my publisher, People's Press. It's a pleasure to work with you.

A billion thanks to my wonderful, super-smart American editor, Lindsey Rose, and to the spectacular, endlessly committed team at Grand Central. It is a thrill, an honor, and an enormous joy to work with you all. I appreciate every single effort you've made on my behalf. So happy to be here.

Thank you so very much to my fabulous and savvy American agent, the unparalleled Victoria Sanders, who works magic for me, and to your incredibly wonderful associates, the lovely and talented Bernadette Baker-Baughman and Jessica Spivey, whose great work, all around the world, leaves me filled with gratitude and aware of just how fortunate I am.

Thank you to the clever and tireless Benee Knauer, who knows what I am thinking and what I mean, and how to capture it perfectly. It means so much to know you are there, to have you beside me.

I want to express my heartfelt appreciation of the American crime-writing community, and to my dear American readers. I cannot sufficiently convey how much your warm welcome has meant to me; you have made my dream come true. I love this country so much and am delighted to call it my second home.

My warmest thanks must go to my son, Adam, whom I love with all my heart, and who has traveled every step of the way with me on this indescribable journey.

ABOUT THE AUTHOR

Sara Blaedel's suspense novels have enjoyed incredible success around the world: fantastic acclaim, multiple awards, and runaway #1 bestselling success internationally. In her native Denmark, Sara was voted most popular novelist for the fourth time in 2014. She is also a recipient of the Golden Laurel, Denmark's most prestigious literary award. Her books are published in thirty-eight countries. Her series featuring police detective Louise Rick is adored the world over, and Sara has just launched her new Family Secrets suspense series to fantastic acclaim.

Sara Blaedel's interest in story, writing, and especially crime fiction was nurtured from a young age. The daughter of a renowned Danish journalist and an actress whose career included roles in theater, radio, TV, and movies, Sara grew up surrounded by a constant flow of professional writers and performers visiting the Blaedel home. Despite a struggle with dyslexia, books gave Sara a world in which to escape when her introverted nature demanded an exit from the hustle and bustle of life.

Sara tried a number of careers, from a restaurant apprenticeship to graphic design, before she started a publishing company called Sara B, where she published Danish translations of American crime fiction.

Publishing ultimately led Sara to journalism, and she covered a wide range of stories, from criminal trials to the premiere of *Star Wars: Episode I*. It was during this time—and while skiing in Norway—that Sara started brewing the ideas for her first novel. In 2004 Louise and Camilla were introduced in *Grønt Støv* ("Green Dust"), and Sara won the Danish Academy for Crime Fiction's debut prize.

Originally from Denmark, Sara has lived in New York, but now spends most of her time in Copenhagen. When she isn't busy committing brutal murders on the page, she is an ambassador with Save the Children and serves on the jury of a documentary film competition.

If you loved THE DAUGHTER,
don't miss the sequel!

Turn the page for a preview of

Available now.

If she'd known what was about to happen, she probably would have just leaned back and enjoyed the show. Instead, Ilka stared anxiously over at the house, steeling herself to walk up and knock on the door. The coffee in the paper cup was cold, but she drank it anyway, hoping it would help. She clutched the five letters in her lap. It was hard to see the most recent one as anything other than a threat.

"You have a week to pay, otherwise, the truth will come out. Maggie."

It had been lying on the reception desk yesterday, inside an envelope at the bottom of a stack of mail. Immediately Ilka had recognized the feminine handwriting. Several days after arriving in Racine she'd discovered the first four letters in an upstairs room at her father's funeral home, bound together by a brittle rubber band, all from 1997–98, with Maggie's signature on them. The envelopes had no stamps or return addresses. Nothing in the letters hinted at what her father could have been trying to conceal. But honestly,

Ilka had plenty on her plate without having to deal with this mystery. She'd recently inherited his Wisconsin funeral home, despite the fact that she and her mother hadn't heard from him, not a single peep, since he'd abandoned them thirty-three years ago.

The first letter was dated June 1997.

Dear Paul,

Your wife is having an affair with my husband.

Maggie

Ilka read the short message again. Her fingers were frozen, and the car's windows were fogged up, further blurring the hazy residential street. The sun was trying to peek through, but the gray morning mist still covered Racine.

She had no idea who this Maggie was, but if anyone were being blackmailed, surely it must be the two people accused in the letter. After a few cups of morning coffee, she'd driven her father's silver-gray Chevrolet over to give the letters to his second wife, Mary Ann. On the way, though, she'd begun to consider her motives. To throw some light on her father's life since he left Denmark? That's what she wanted to think. But more likely it was to pay Mary Ann back for how she'd treated Ilka when they first met.

She glanced up at the house again. Mary Ann and her daughters had practically thrown her off their porch. All she'd done was bring them some drawings her two half sisters had made when they were kids. Ilka had found the drawings while cleaning her father's room, along with a clay figure and some photos she'd also taken along. They'd given her an excuse to meet the family her father had started after leaving Denmark. And to be shunned, as it turned out. Later that evening, when she'd returned to the funeral home, the younger sister had been waiting for her in the dark in her father's room.

"Don't come by the house again," Amber had said. "It's not good for Mom. It's not good for anything."

Amber's mother had been in a car accident years ago and was confined to a wheelchair, but Ilka couldn't understand why getting to know her half sisters could harm Mary Ann.

She turned back to the letters. The next one was from March 1998.

Dear Paul,

I came home this morning and found your wife and my husband in our bedroom! He says he wants to leave me. You have to make them end it.

Maggie

And two months later:

Dear Paul,

Finally! My husband is heartbroken, but I'm sure we can find what we once had together.

Maggie

These first letters had troubled Ilka when she found them, but the fourth, from June 1998, was the one most difficult for her to give Mary Ann.

Dear Paul,

I hear your wife is paralyzed from the waist down. And that it's a miracle you walked away from the accident without a scratch.

Maggie

Ilka emptied the paper cup. As she was about to crush it down in the cup holder, her phone pinged—she had a match on Tinder. Shortly after arriving in Racine, she'd created a profile, to have something that could distract her from the funeral home, which already had become her responsibility. She grabbed the phone. The photo of the smiling blond man interested in her showed him holding hands with two young children. Ilka deleted him at once and looked up. Two black four-wheel-drive vehicles were parked in front of the house—how could she have missed them driving up?

She laid down her phone and watched six men in dark suits climb out and gather on the sidewalk. Moments later a monster of a moving van drove in and blocked the driveway. The quiet street where her father had lived was suddenly a traffic jam.

She leaned forward to get a better look at the man approaching the front door. He knocked and rang the door-bell several times, but no one answered, though Ilka noticed a curtain moving to the left of the door. He knocked one last time and waited before rejoining the others.

The door finally opened when the rear cargo door of the moving van began folding down. It took Ilka a while to spot Mary Ann's wheelchair behind a long wicker sofa on the porch. Her blond hair was pinned up, and a thin shawl covered her bare shoulders. Then Ilka shot up in her seat: The woman was holding a rifle on her blanket-covered lap. Slowly she rolled toward the steps, picked up the rifle, pointed it at the dark-suited men, and yelled something at them. Ilka nearly jumped out of her skin when the woman pointed the rifle in the air and pulled the trigger. All six men immediately pulled out handguns, which startled her even more.

Mary Ann's older daughter, Leslie, hurried out onto the porch. She wore a short-sleeved flowered dress, and her hair was wet. Insignificant details, given the situation, yet they caught Ilka's eye before the next shot rang out. This time a bullet smacked into the side of the moving van.

Mary Ann planted her elbow on her wheelchair's armrest and kept the rifle aimed at the van, where the men had taken cover, though they still held their guns. Ilka opened the car door and froze; she was scared, but she couldn't just sit there and do nothing either. A deep voice ordered Mary Ann to put the rifle down.

The sun had briefly broken through the clouds, and its rays in the side mirror blinded Ilka when she finally worked up the courage to get out. Mary Ann concentrated on reloading as Leslie dragged her back to the door, and when she started shooting again Ilka hit the asphalt behind the car. The sight of the small, frail woman handling a lethal weapon was simply too surreal; it made no sense at all. None of this did.

Mary Ann managed to fire one more shot before disappearing inside the door. Immediately the six men started shooting back, then they spread out and surrounded the large wooden house. One of them ran up on the porch and pointed his gun at the front door, yelling for Mary Ann and Leslie to come out with their hands up. The others ducked around back.

Desperate now, Ilka peered over the low hedges of the neighbors' houses, but she saw no sign of anyone calling the police or doing anything to help the two women.

The door opened slowly, and Leslie walked out with one hand over her head, the other pushing the wheelchair. Mary Ann held her thin arms straight in the air. The man ordered them over to the far end of the porch, then signaled to the moving van. Ilka stared in bewilderment as a small army of broad-shouldered, muscular men poured out of the van and entered the house. A few moments later they began carrying furniture out. While they quickly filled the van, another man changed the front door lock, then picked up his tools and walked around back.

A car turned onto the street, and the driver honked in irritation at the blockade of vehicles in front of the house. Before he could get out, one of the black-suited men trotted over to him. Ilka was back in her car and out of earshot, but she got the drift of the conversation. A moment later the driver whipped his car around and drove off.

The whole episode seemed utterly insane to Ilka. For a split second she wondered if it was some sort of hidden camera show, or a scene in an action film. Then she noticed her half sister covering her mouth with both hands, fighting to hold back her tears.

Suddenly it was over. They shut and locked the front door, and the furniture movers climbed into the van. When it began backing up, the two black SUVs made U-turns on the street, and before she knew it they were gone. Once again, the street was quiet and deserted. Neighbors cautiously ventured out on their porches, though none of them dared walk over to Mary Ann's house. Ilka sat for a moment, wondering how long it had lasted, but she'd lost all sense of time.

Leslie stepped down off the porch, as if she were thinking of chasing the men who had taken everything from them. She was crying now, her head bowed as she wiped the tears from her cheeks. Then she noticed Ilka. Or maybe it was her father's car she recognized, because she looked startled when she met Ilka's eyes. She rushed back up the steps to her mother.

Ilka had just turned forty, and she guessed that Leslie was about ten years younger. Maybe in her late twenties. It was hard to tell. Her cardigan sweater and wavy blond permanent made her look like a middle-aged woman in an ad for a floor cleaner, but earlier Ilka had noticed her smooth, silky skin. It was hard to imagine her half sister had ever been young. After nursing school, she'd taken over the care of her mother.

Ilka sat for a few moments before getting out of the car and walking to the house. She left the letters from Maggie on the front seat.

She stopped at the front steps. "What on earth happened? I hope neither of you were hurt?" She tried to sound calm, though she wasn't. At all.

Leslie didn't react when Ilka stepped onto the porch, but Mary Ann abruptly turned to her. "What do you want?" she snarled. It began raining; heavy drops pounded the porch roof. "Leave us alone."

"But somebody just emptied your house! And it doesn't exactly look like you hired them to. You both could have been killed, have you called the police?" She gestured toward the neighbors. "Surely somebody has!"

"We don't want the police out here, and anyway it's all over."

Mary Ann's thin shawl was already soaked from the rain, and Ilka started to pull her farther under the roof, but the woman waved her away and rolled her wheelchair back herself.

Leslie didn't budge an inch.

Ilka had to lean in close to hear Mary Ann. "Leave us alone. This is none of your business, keep out of it."

Ilka seldom cried, but now she could barely hold back the tears. She'd been about to offer them her phone to call for help or suggest they all go to the funeral home and talk about what to do.

Without a word she turned and walked to the car.

She was still quivering with rage when she stopped at a filling station for ten dollars of gas. She slammed the car door shut, counted the coins in her small coin purse, and decided to buy a pack of cigarettes. She longed to fill her lungs with smoke, hold it in until she felt dizzy. Something was stirring in her chest, a vague emotion, an uneasiness she couldn't put her finger on, though she was certain it had nothing to do with the humiliating rejection her father's second family had put her through again.

You never really know someone you live with before you're seven, she thought. *You're not old enough to see him as he really is. You're just with him, and you feel safe. Until one day he suddenly disappears, and you're panic-stricken when you understand you've been abandoned.*

She still remembered that feeling of being around her father, how much she loved him, counted on him. But she didn't know him. And why should she suddenly spend time getting to know his idiotic second family? They meant nothing to her.

Ilka glanced around when she realized she was talking

to herself. Her pack of cigarettes was open, and she was about to light one when she noticed the gas pump close by. It reminded her of something embarrassing back when she'd just gotten her driver's license. She'd been smoking a cigarette while filling up. An older man yelled at her, but several days passed before it came to her why. Luckily nothing had happened, but that was the moment she gave up cigarettes. At least until now, after moving to Racine had interrupted her stable Copenhagen life.

She stuffed the cigarettes into her pocket and got in the car.

It had stopped raining, and now patches of blue sky began peeping out from behind white clouds. A glossy sheen covered the asphalt. Ilka let a pickup pass before pulling out and heading for the main drag. She drove by several empty stores on the way back to the funeral home; few businesses were left in West Racine, where her father had lived. Many of the neglected façades looked as if they'd been closed for years. She stopped for a red light at one five-way intersection and noticed firewood and bottled gas stacked up outside a convenience store on one corner.

When the light turned green she took off, but in the middle of the intersection she flashed on what had been nagging at her earlier. An image of herself popped up: a little girl with much-too-long front bangs, standing in the living room in her pajamas. She must have been three or four years old. The doorbell had rung, and several people stood outside. A bailiff, a policeman, a locksmith, and a woman from their district, her mother had explained to her later.

Ilka hit the emergency lights and managed to pull over to the corner, where she scraped against the high curb. She'd forgotten the incident, but now the memories of the small apartment overwhelmed her. The sweet aromas from the bakery; her bed by the living room window. The black-and-white checkerboard linoleum in the kitchen. They'd had to take the back stairs down to pee.

The memories were only flashes, fragments from deep in her subconscious, repressed but now brought up to the surface by what she had witnessed earlier. It *had* happened. She remembered being thrown out, losing all their possessions. Ilka had hidden behind the sofa, but the woman from the district had grabbed her and dragged her away.

Now she saw herself as a little girl crying down in the courtyard, alone with the woman holding a few bags filled with Ilka's clothes. But none of her toys. After they left the apartment, her father argued with the strange men.

When her mother finally came down and joined them in the courtyard, she was crying too, though in a different way. And later her father left. Back then Ilka thought he was gone for a long, long time, but now she wasn't so sure. She'd been so young and had missed him so much.

She lit a cigarette, and slowly the car filled up with smoke. How could the memory of something so dramatic vanish, only to pop up again so many years later? And where had they lived after that? She couldn't remember. Up until now, her only memories had been from the house in Brønshøj she'd thought of as her childhood home.

She rolled the window down to get rid of the smoke, and after crushing out her third cigarette in the tiny ashtray she felt clearheaded enough to drive again. She wanted to call her mother, but instead she slowly pulled away from the curb.

She turned into the parking lot behind the funeral home and parked beside Artie's black pickup. He sat on the back steps with a cup in his hand and a cigarette hanging from his mouth, watching her. His weird longish hair was knotted up in a bun, and he wore a Hawaiian shirt. All in all he looked a bit quirky, yet for a moment she was tempted to sit down and cuddle up to him, hold him, let him cheer her up. Though not just because of all the forgotten childhood memories suddenly returning; as she began loosening up after the wild episode at her father's house, a sort of delayed shock set in.

Artie Sorvino had worked for her father for eighteen years. He was the closest thing she had in Racine to a friend she could confide in, though that wasn't saying much, because she still couldn't figure him out. Most of the time he backed her up, but occasionally he acted like he wanted nothing to do with her. At least their relationship at work hadn't suffered after the night she'd seduced him; he seemed to be okay with it as just a one-night stand.

Without a word she sat beside him and fished out her pack of cigarettes. He watched her reach for the lighter lying on the steps.

Finally she said, "She could have mowed them all down." She took a drag and blew the smoke out. "Okay, she shot above their heads first, but then she aimed right at them. It's a miracle nobody was hit."

"Who are we talking about here?" He turned to her and leaned closer to the doorway.

"Mary Ann, that's who! She and Leslie were thrown out of their house, I was there when it happened. A bunch of men came and emptied the place. They took everything away in a big moving van. But before that she shot at them with a rifle. The woman's crazy!"

"Sounds like she was trying to defend her property," Artie said.

"But they hadn't done anything to her! She rolls out onto the porch with a gun on her lap, nobody says a word, and she starts shooting. It was absolutely insane! She shot right out into the street! Somebody could have been walking by! Then one of the men started shooting back, and nobody did anything to help, not even call the police. What's wrong with everybody?"

"Maybe you should just be happy you Danes don't have to defend yourselves that way over there. People don't buy guns here just for fun. In Wisconsin, nobody needs a special license to keep a gun in their home, as long as it's for defending yourself, for hunting, or for anything else legal."

He ticked that off as if it was something every single person in the state knew by heart.

"Listen," she said. "The men weren't even close to the house when she started shooting. You can't say you're defending yourself before someone threatens you or does something."

"They were on her property. I understand it's different in Denmark. You're so busy having fun, or whatever that *hygge* of yours means, that no one has time to shoot at people. Your father told me about the Danish police, all the time they spend helping mother ducks and their little ducklings across the street. Well, guess what, the cops over here have other things to do. We're prepared to defend ourselves. We have to be."

She ignored his attempt at humor. "That's not true. It's just that in Denmark it's not legal to have a gun on the table beside your bed."

He shook his head at her, but he added that there must have been a reason why Mary Ann felt threatened. "I mean, we don't just start shooting at people who happen to stop by."

She stared at him for a moment, then he shook his head again and smiled. "No, I don't own a gun. But I do have a fishing knife, if it came down to that. Why don't I get you a cup of coffee, then you can tell me exactly what happened out there."

Before he could stand up, Ilka said, "No thanks, I've already had three cups. Another thing, in Denmark the person who takes over someone's property doesn't show up carrying a gun."

He looked at her in surprise. "The bailiff?"

"If that's what he's called, yes. Six men in fact, plus the ones who emptied the house. Mary Ann and Leslie didn't hire them, that's for sure."

"It couldn't have been the bailiff."

"Well, they were put out on the street, anyway. I saw the man changing the locks."

"That sounds strange." Artie swung his legs to the side so Sister Eileen could get out the door. Her gray habit grazed Ilka's shoulder. She was associated with a parish outside town, and for the past twelve years she had worked as an unpaid volunteer for Ilka's father, though she did accept donations for her church. Yet she was often the first to show up for work in the mornings, and she knew the most about managing the funeral home. Her small apartment was next to the coffin storage room, and it seemed that Ilka had inherited her along with the business.

She stepped past them and turned around. "Who's been put out on the street?"

"Mary Ann and Leslie were thrown out of their house," Artie said. "But the law didn't do it, I'm sure of that. It's got to be somebody else."

"It was so humiliating for them, standing out on the porch, watching them drive away with everything they owned," Ilka said. "They didn't even get to keep their coats and bags."

"You don't need to feel sorry for them," Sister Eileen said without blinking an eye. "They probably went right out to Mary Ann's father. He lives very comfortably, and his daughter and granddaughters will too."

Ilka raised her eyebrows.

"Raymond Fletcher is one of the richest men in Wisconsin," Artie said. "And one of the most powerful. He owns a stable and breeds these insanely expensive trotters on his ranch."

Ilka's heart skipped a beat when he mentioned trotters. And a stable. Now it made more sense why her father's financial situation had collapsed, why he'd left everything in a big mess. Not that it changed anything. She hadn't forgiven him for dragging her into it. Just thinking about it made her angry, and suddenly she felt no sympathy at all for the two women. Apparently, they had no money worries, yet obviously they weren't going to help her, even though legally they were Paul Jensen's nearest family.

She pulled Maggie's letters out of her bag and handed them to the nun. "Do you know anything about these? The reason I drove over to Mary Ann's house was to give them to her. Honestly, I don't care anymore about anything that comes out."

The nun skimmed the five letters, then folded them up again and handed them back.

"Who's Maggie?" Ilka said. She looked at Sister Eileen, then at Artie, who stood up and shrugged. He held out his hand when Ilka started to rise. "The name doesn't ring any bells." He dumped the rest of his coffee on the ground.

Sister Eileen shook her head and turned to go to her

apartment, but Ilka stopped her and asked them to come into the office to discuss the future of the funeral home.

"I've been going over the books," she began after they sat down around her father's desk. "We have an agreed overdraft in our bank account of almost two hundred thousand dollars. Besides that, we haven't paid several suppliers; that adds up to over forty thousand of debt. The two hundred thousand comes from withdrawals this spring. If I close the funeral home and go home now, I'll be paying off this debt the rest of my life. So I have to talk to my bank before I make any decision."

Ilka had thought about how to say this so it didn't sound as if she was abandoning them, yet that's what it came down to. Her father had been broke, and when he died he left the business deeply in debt. The past several days she'd gone through all the books for the past five years. She had no choice: She had to shut down.

"If they even let you leave the States with a debt like this," Artie said. She knew he might be right. Her mother had warned her about that before Ilka flew over to Wisconsin. Her ears began ringing.

"Right now we don't have the money for the funeral tomorrow. It's not prepaid; we'll have to wait for the family to pay the bill. Luckily, it's not one of the more expensive funerals. We just have to deliver the body to the church. But we're still responsible for the flowers and decorations."

"I'll take care of the flowers," Artie said.

Ilka knew he had stolen flowers from the common grave for an earlier funeral, but decided not to say anything. She saw no alternative. "What about embalming supplies?"

"I think we have enough for five or six more jobs."

"The biggest problem is the coffins," Sister Eileen said. "The suppliers have shut us down because of what we owe them. There's only one white coffin left, and then there's the light-blue used one out back, waiting to be hauled away."

"When we need more coffins, I'll order them online from Costco. We'll just have to say we can't trust our regular suppliers. I don't feel bad at all for blaming them, it's their fault for not giving me a chance to get the business back on its feet."

Artie and Sister Eileen stared at her.

"Really, though, we don't need to tell anybody where the coffins come from," she added.

Most people wouldn't even notice if the white coffin in the catalog was different from the one they got, she thought.

Sister Eileen spoke sharply. "But will you charge them the catalog prices?"

"We'll see." Ilka asked if they'd eaten lunch, if she should bring them something when she went out to shop.

Artie offered to make her a sandwich from what he had in the refrigerator, but Ilka politely declined. Her father's partner had already sunk a great deal of money into the bottomless pit of the funeral home's debt by paying back taxes that would have shut them down. At the time they'd believed they could sell the business to another undertaker in town, and Artie's dream was to start up an embalming business and freelance for other funeral home directors in the region. That way he could avoid all the pickups, conferences with families, and services themselves. Unfortunately, it didn't happen. Golden Slumbers Funeral Home had been bought out by a large chain, American Funeral Group, which almost certainly wouldn't make use of Artie's special talents. The chain had also been interested in Ilka's business, but she'd played her cards all wrong. At best Artie would be left with the funeral home building, and his dream of freelancing would probably remain just that—a dream.

Abruptly she stood up. "I have to go out anyway, there's something I have to take care of." She grabbed her coat and umbrella and started down to Oh Dennis!, a local pub that also served as a hangout for people in Racine who had run into hard times. A week earlier she'd been standing in front of a one-armed bandit in back, unable to stop pouring coins in it. She was hoping he was working today—the young bartender who had finally refused to break more bills for her. She wanted to thank him.

He was off work. A younger woman with colorful tattoos on her brawny forearms stood behind the bar. Ilka scanned the menu prices and ordered the cheapest lunch without even looking at what it was. She felt dirt-poor, down and out. She remembered back when she was a kid, on Children's Aid Day at the Triangle in Copenhagen with her friends. A small carnival had been set up, and Ilka had emptied her piggy bank and coaxed a little extra out of her mother. She'd spent most of the money on a one-armed bandit, the rest on a scratch ticket at the hot dog stand while her friends ordered hot dogs and chocolate milk.

Ilka paid for the lunch and was about to sit down when she noticed Larry out on the sidewalk. Less than a week earlier, she'd met him in a bar and screwed him behind a shed down by the canal, and a few days later he stopped by the funeral home and invited her out. She explained she wasn't looking for any sort of relationship, that it had only been a physical thing, and though she'd tried to put it nicely, she felt she'd made it clear she wasn't interested in seeing him again.

She turned quickly, but it was too late; he'd spotted her. He was on his way to the door, and to avoid him she hurried to the back of the pub, where the only other person in the place sat at a table against the wall. A small man in a light-blue windbreaker. He'd been sitting at the same table the evening she'd lost it. She didn't know him, but she pulled a chair out and asked if she could sit down. "Would you do me a favor and pretend you're talking to me?"

"Who are we hiding from?" He was old, and from his rusty voice she guessed it wasn't often people sat down wanting his company.

Suddenly Larry was standing at their table. Ilka smiled politely up at him.

"Hi!" Larry unzipped his jacket and told her he'd been trying to get in touch with her. Ilka glanced at the elderly man out of the corner of her eye and nodded as Larry rambled on about a visiting delegation from a European architectural school they were going to show around their headquarters.

Ilka had no idea what he was talking about, and before she could react he pulled a chair out and sat down beside her. Then she remembered he worked for Johnson Wax, which was in Racine.

"It's a historical building," he continued, as if Ilka had begged him to describe Racine's architectural wonders. "In fact, the administration building and the research tower were designed by Frank Lloyd Wright."

He scooted over so his leg grazed against hers. Ilka moved her leg away; forcing this spectacle onto a stranger enjoying his afternoon coffee was embarrassing. Her food arrived, but before the waitress could ask if Larry was ready to order, the man leaned over the table.

"Excuse me, I hope you don't mind, but I've been look-ing forward to this lunch with the daughter of my deceased friend from Denmark."

Ilka and Larry were both surprised. Larry because he likely couldn't imagine her having lunch with an old bum, and Ilka because the man knew who she was. And apparently had known her father.

Larry regrouped and stood up slowly. He held Ilka's eye, as if to give her a final chance to reconsider.

She watched him walk off. He was in good shape, and he did have a nice ass, but she turned and instantly forgot about him.

"Your father and I were colleagues," the man said. He explained that he'd been a funeral home director in town before her father had arrived. "But that was years ago. I had to give up my business. He was a fine man. It's hard knowing he's not around anymore."

Suddenly the memories seemed to overwhelm him, and he fell silent. Ilka ate her chicken wings. After she'd gnawed the last bone clean, she tore open a tiny plastic sack, pulled out a damp napkin, and wiped off her fingers. "Did you see much of each other? You and my father?"

"We did a betting game, a weekly lottery where you paid to keep the same numbers year after year, and for a long time we went together to the track, harness racing, but the track went bankrupt. And it wouldn't be the same without him anyway."

Ilka pushed her plate away. Of course her father had kept betting over here. She was about to mention that weakness in her father's character when the man nodded, as if he were reading her mind. "It wasn't always easy for Paul to control his gambling—it was in his blood—but he tried. And there were long stretches when he stayed away from the track. In the end he wasn't out there at all. He paid the price for his habit, we knew that. His friends. By the way, did you know he bought a horse for you, not long after he came here?"

Ilka nodded slowly. She'd read it in one of the letters she found in his desk. A packet of letters he never sent. But it touched her that he'd told his friend about her.

"The pony died just a few years ago. At a ripe old age, very ripe. Toward the end it didn't even want to leave its stall. But it had a good life, and the kids loved it."

Ilka stared down at the table. When she was a kid she would have given her right arm—both arms—to have a horse. It was strange to think she'd actually had one waiting for her over here.

"Another friend of your father's, Frank Conaway, boarded it at his family's stable. Occasionally Paul drove out and checked on it. Sometimes I rode along. It's a nice drive, and we'd known Frank for many years. When the pony wasn't out in the pasture, your father walked it in the woods behind the stables. Like he was walking a dog."

He looked away while the tattooed waitress picked up Ilka's plate and asked if they wanted coffee. Ilka shook her head, but he held up his cup.

"I haven't heard about Frank Conaway," she said. "I'm sorry, but what's your name?"

"Gregg." He put his cup down and held his hand out. "Gregg Turner, and your name is Ilka Nichols. Your father told me. Back then I had no idea I'd ever meet you. But word gets around when strangers come to town."

"Please excuse me if I'm being nosy, but are you the one who sold your funeral home to the American Funeral Group?"

Artie had told her about a funeral director who made a deal with the large chain, and as soon as he signed, things went downhill. And not only for the man Artie described as a shadow of himself: The funeral home was abandoned. Now it was boarded up, the Old Glory out front in tatters.

No one had been inside since the sale. American Funeral Group had only been interested in wiping out one more competitor, which sent a message to all nearby funeral homes.

His smile disappeared as he nodded. "The past is dead and gone, you can't change it. I was naïve. I thought they'd keep their word, but they just wanted to crush me. It was my uncle's old business, and I figured they'd keep me on. I was out of work before the ink on the contract dried."

They sat for a moment in silence.

"Is Frank Conaway one of his friends from the race-track?" Ilka asked. She imagined her father had hung out with others interested in horses, just as he had in Denmark. Several times she'd gone along to the stables, where he visited the sulky drivers he knew. While the grown-ups talked, or while he watched the horses being trained, she was allowed to run around in the stables. Once in a while she'd even ridden in a sulky.

He nodded. "They had a long friendship. They met back when Paul first came over. Frank was young, he was a groom in the stable your father worked for. Over the years they grew close—it's like he was almost a son to Paul. And Paul was the godfather of Frank's older daughter. Later on, when Frank had his own stable, your father boarded the pony with him."

Ilka was overwhelmed at learning he'd taken on responsibility for someone else's child as a godfather, had considered this Frank to be his son. She felt split: She wanted to know more, yet it scared her. It was all too much.

But a moment later, without considering the consequences, she pushed on. "Where does he live? Do you think it would be okay for me to go out there? It would be fun to hear about the pony."

He didn't hesitate. "I'm absolutely sure Karen would be very happy if you stopped by. She's his wife. It's not far away, an hour's drive, maybe a little over."

Ilka wrote the name down and waited while Gregg brought out a notepad from his inside coat pocket and gave her a phone number. "If you look the number up, I'm sure you'll find the address. I'm so glad I got to meet you."

His rusty voice had livened up during their conversation, and when Ilka scooted her chair back to leave, he smiled. "Anytime you need to be rescued from some other young man, just let me know."

She smiled back and turned to go, but then thought of something. "Do you happen to know if my father knew a woman called Maggie?"

After a few moments he shook his head. "Don't believe so. Not that I recall."

Ilka had borrowed twenty dollars from Artie for gas. She'd also asked him what he knew about his father's friend, but Artie had only met Frank Conaway a few times, and he made no secret of his fear of horses. He wouldn't dream of setting foot in a stable.

She punched in the address on the GPS and turned on the radio as she left Racine. The highway ran straight as a string, all the way to the horizon, and she gripped the wheel to fend off the occasional gusts of wind. It didn't take long to see this stretch wasn't going to be a nice little Sunday drive. At least she wouldn't get lost.

As she neared the Conaways', she and the car behind her had the highway to themselves. Farmhouses were spread out, some close to the highway and others set back, hidden by windbreaks. Fenced-in pastures and hay barns were frequent reminders that she was in horse country now. She noticed several training tracks beside pastures, horse trailers parked by driveways.

Two gigantic round hay bales were stacked up beside the gravel drive leading to the Conaway family's farm; a hand-painted sign with their address stood in front. Ilka slowed down and double-checked the address before heading up the driveway. She spotted the woods behind the buildings, then the trail leading from the broad barn. She didn't at all consider herself sentimental, but the thought of her father leading the pony down that trail moved her.

"Stop it!" she snapped at herself. As if him taking care of a horse was some great thing, when he hadn't so much as sent her a single birthday card.

Gravel crunched under the tires, and a small black-and-white dachshund raced around the house and started yapping. Before Ilka shut the motor off, the farmhouse door opened and a middle-aged woman stepped out. A little girl clinging to her from behind stared wide-eyed at the stranger.

Earlier Ilka had called to ask if she could stop by. "But Frank's not here!" Karen Conaway had said. Ilka suggested she could come later that week if it was more convenient, but that it didn't matter if Frank was there or not. She just thought it would be nice to see where the pony had lived.

"Of course, I understand, sure," Conaway's wife had said. "And I know my daughter would love to show you our stable. You're more than welcome to come. I'd love to meet Paul's Danish daughter too. We've heard the stories about you charming the pants off everyone at the track, after your father said you were named after a Derby winner."

Ilka had offered to bring along some kringles from Racine, even though the pastry wasn't at all like what she was used to at home. But Karen told her it wasn't necessary, that she'd baked some Danish cookies and she'd like Ilka to taste them.

They greeted each other at the door before going inside. The dog hid under a kitchen chair while Karen handed Ilka the coffee cups. Her young daughter was shy, but she followed them into the kitchen and sat down at the far end of the table. Soon she was absorbed in coloring in a page in a coloring book, though every so often she glanced up at Ilka in obvious curiosity.

Karen poured coffee. "My husband knew your dad most of his adult life. In fact, Frank was the one they sent to pick Paul up at the airport, when he flew in from Denmark."

Ilka sat down at the plank table. Karen placed in front of her an old-fashioned cookie tin covered with elves and gold hearts, similar to the ones Ilka's grandmother had.

"Your father bought this at the museum. Have you seen it yet? They have tons of Danish things, and occasionally they hold a bazaar."

She offered Ilka a vanilla cookie. It was a bit odd for Ilka to see what to her was a Christmas cookie in late September. She laid it on her saucer and waited for Karen to serve her daughter juice and a cookie and sit down herself.

"Paul gave me the recipe. I also make the flat brown cookies. But Lily and I like these the best."

"I didn't know my father could bake Christmas cookies."

"They're not Christmas cookies to us," Karen said. "They're just Danish cookies. Or like your dad said, Danish *smo-kay-ger*, right?"

Ilka smiled. "*Smah-kay-uh.*"

"I don't think he baked either. He just handed me the recipe and said if I got bored, he'd be happy to taste them. He was a charmer, that dad of yours! He gave me the cookie tin too."

"How long did my father and your husband work together before he went into the funeral home business?"

"It was before I met Frank, so I don't really know. At first I got the feeling something had happened that kept Paul away from the stable. I thought it was weird Frank was friends with an undertaker! I got used to it, though."

She smiled sheepishly. "When Paul married Mary Ann, Frank and I were invited to the wedding. After that, he started showing up at the stable here and there."

Ilka hadn't touched her coffee or the cookie. "What happened?"

Immediately she regretted asking; Karen looked uneasy, as if she wanted to ignore the question, but then she straightened up and focused on what to say. "Well, I don't know all the details. It wasn't something people talked about. But when someone struggles with an addiction, they can lose control, the devil gets the upper hand. That's what happened with your dad."

"He gambled?" Ilka said, to help her along.

Karen nodded. "Frank said that when he came over, the plan was that he'd make a big investment in the stable he'd been hired to manage. Several other investors were involved too. And private people also put up some of the money. They aimed to establish one of the most successful trotter stables in North America. And the way I understood it, your dad's job was to hire the best sulky drivers and get on the good side of the best breeders, so the stable would get first dibs on the new foals. That's how he met Mary Ann. Her dad owned the stable."

She paused and gazed out the window.

"But he couldn't stop himself. The bets were small at first, but he also gambled when he traveled around visiting racetracks, scouting the sulky drivers and horses. My husband thinks it got serious when he tried to cover losses by upping his bets. It ended up with him losing it all."

Karen peered at Ilka for a moment. Checking to see if

she could handle the rest, Ilka thought. Lily had stopped drawing and was staring at them.

"So besides losing all the money he'd brought with him, nearly two hundred thousand dollars, he also gambled away the investors' money. Frank called it a fever Paul couldn't shake. He was deep in debt, and it was a disaster for everyone involved. Frank can give you more details. I remember once they talked about Paul leaving it all behind, going back to Denmark. But he knew he couldn't just run, it would catch up to him. Things didn't settle down until he got married."

"But what about all the money he owed?" Ilka asked.

"His father-in-law covered the debt. Mary Ann was expecting their first child, so I'm guessing Raymond Fletcher wanted the scandal to go away."

"When did my father meet Mary Ann?"

"They were married a year or two after he came. It all happened pretty fast."

"I guess so," Ilka mumbled. Lucky that she and her mother hadn't known, she thought. "And that's when he started the funeral home?"

Karen nodded. "He needed a job to support his family. More coffee?"

"No thanks." Her stomach ached from what Karen had told her. She pushed the half-full cup away.

They listened to the girl's crayons scratching in the silence that followed.

"I'm looking forward to meeting your husband." Ilka didn't know what else to say. And she needed to get up, move around. She kept jiggling her cup, until the teaspoon inside hopped out and clattered on the table.

"Things are a bit difficult at the moment." Karen looked away. "But I'll have him call you."

"It wouldn't have to take long," Ilka hurried to say. "I just want to talk to the people close to my father in the years after he left. There's so much I don't know. Maybe all I really want to know is how he felt, if he was happy. And if your husband doesn't have time to meet with me, a phone conversation is okay."

"I understand, and of course Frank will talk to you. How long are you staying in Racine?"

"I don't know yet."

Karen stood up, and Ilka carried her cup over to the sink.

"Don't bother with that, just leave it," Karen said. She asked her daughter if she wanted to show Ilka Benjamin's old stall.

"Yay!" The girl jumped up.

Ilka slipped her jacket on out in the hallway and peeked into the living room at the high ceiling, heavy furniture, empty walls. Several rows of shiny trophies stood on shelves of dark wood.

"Frank isn't a sulky driver, of course, but sometimes trophies are handed out to an entire team when a driver wins a race. And it means a lot to my husband to be appreciated that way. If it was up to me, I might decide they don't all have to be here in the living room."

She smiled, then walked over and opened the door. The mood was lighter now, and the little girl was already headed to the stable. Ilka asked Karen if she'd heard her father mention a woman named Maggie. She frowned in thought, then shook her head.

"Is it someone he met at the racetrack?"

Ilka shrugged. Of course, that was a possibility. "It's just that she wrote a letter to him, and I'm trying to track her down."

"Sorry I can't help."

Ilka held out her hand and thanked the woman for letting her come on such short notice. Suddenly the situation felt awkward: A handshake seemed too little, a hug too much. Ilka smiled at her and walked over to the girl waiting at the stable door. She took a deep breath and closed her eyes a moment before stepping inside.